TORN BETWEEN LOVE AND FRIENDSHIP

"Miyuki, I have no proof," Cotton said.

"Yes, but even if you just told the embassy you suspected Kiyoshi of being a spy, they'd follow him at least, wouldn't they?"

"I guess, yes."

"And then the Americans wouldn't even have to send Kiyoshi back to Japan, because he wouldn't be of any value anymore, and so *we* would bring him home . . . wouldn't we?"

"Well, yeah, I guess." He shrugged.

"So either way," Miyuki said, "if you tell, either way Kiyoshi would come back home . . ." And she waited, and Cotton saw at last where all this was going; but even then she added: " . . . back home to me."

Cotton took a few deep breaths. At last he said: "Please, don't make this any harder for us. We're never to talk about this again."

"All right," Miyuki sighed, but she also stepped toward him. "All right. All right . . . my darling . . . but just this one time," and she held up her arms, her elbows pointing toward him, and then she touched her right elbow with her left hand and smiled. "Just this one time, you have to let me have my elbows."

Cotton was terrified, but he smiled at her, and then she stepped up to him and looked into his eyes, wrapping her arms around him, waiting for him to do the same. And he did. They held each other for a long time, and then they kissed and kissed in the moonlight, scared to stop because they both knew that the moment their lips parted, they could never touch again.

LOVE AND INFAMY

Frank Deford

PINNACLE BOOKS
KENSINGTON PUBLISHING CORP.

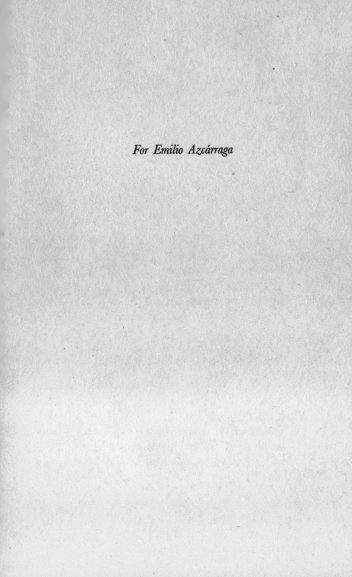

For Emilio Azcárraga

1943

Mizuno to Hitsuji

THE YEAR
of the
WATER SHEEP

Miyuki didn't hear about Admiral Yamamoto's death till weeks after it happened, when the word finally reached the Japanese garrison. She was washing her baby's diapers when the news came over the radio. The whole camp was stunned. Some of the soldiers seemed near to tears. Immediately, then, Miyuki picked up the baby and started over to Major Tanaka's quarters. She knew she had better go to him at a time like this.

The way Yamamoto died was that his plane was coming in for a landing at Bougainville after a flight from Raboul. Officially, he was on an inspection trip; but really, he was just hoping that his appearance would lift the spirits of the Japanese troops. The Americans knew all about Yamamoto's plan, though; they had broken some Japanese naval and diplomatic codes years before. Perhaps that was the single most amazing thing about Pearl Harbor: that Yamamoto pulled it off beyond his wildest dreams even though the American gentlemen had been reading his government's mail all that time. All the things he worried about—the great distance of ocean the fleet had to cover in secret, the subarctic weather, the refueling at sea, the extraordinary timing and logistics required, the magnitude of it all, the blessings of the gods—all that was risk enough. Just arguing the case had nearly ripped the admiralty apart, and Yamamoto had to threaten to quit the navy before his Pearl Harbor plan, Operation Z, was finally approved. And even by then—for months, since September of 1940—

the Americans had deciphered the code. They knew what the Japanese diplomats were saying to one another. Not only that, but Cotton Drake, the one loyal American who learned about Pearl, couldn't get anybody to listen to him. It was amazing that Yamamoto's fleet got within two thousand miles of Hawaii without being blown out of the Pacific.

Miyuki cut across to Major Tanaka's quarters, carrying her baby. He'd be a year old soon. She'd named him Kiyokuni, which means Pure Country, the way she wrote it. She chose that because she wanted her child to have some of both Kiroyshi and Cotton.

Miyuki hurried along. She needed to stay with Major Tanaka—and on his good side—as much as possible. At the beginning of the war, when the troops first landed and marched in, she had no one to count on; and no one could understand what she was doing there, a Japanese woman alone. They were suspicious of her; worse, sometimes they raped her. But Miyuki, even pregnant, dirty, and in rags, was much too pretty for the officers to leave on the free market. Miyuki was a spoil of war, even if she was a spoil of her own countrymen. But they were all away from Japan, posted out in the steaming jungle, and so the rules were forfeit. She might just as well have been what the army called a "comfort woman," shanghaied and shipped to the soldiers from some conquered place like Korea—not unlike the "comfort bags" of canned food, soap, magazines, and whatnot that were mailed to the troops.

In fact, it began to get better for Miyuki only when Major Tanaka learned who her brother was. Everybody in the military knew of Miyuki's brother, of course; but Tanaka had actually been present, a young sublieutenant in the Gem Division, when Captain Takeo Serikawa had helped lead the mutiny. Tanaka had *known* Miyuki's famous brother. Indeed, Tanaka had followed him, gone out in the snow with him that night to kill the enemies of the emperor. So now, he considered it an honor that he could watch after Serikawa's sister . . . allowing her to care for him and satisfy his needs. Miyuki was like his own contract geisha. He didn't even pressure her anymore to tell him how a Japanese woman had gotten to the air base in the jungle with a baby in her belly.

Tanaka and the other officers were in his quarters when Miyuki walked in with her baby. They were talking about Yamamoto, although nobody knew many of the details. The government had made it sound as if the great admiral had died in heroic combat; in fact, he had merely died in a clever ambush—what amounted, in its way, to a Pearl Harbor in miniature, only this time perpetrated by the Americans. U.S. Squadron 339—P-38s, sixteen of them, fashioned with special long-range fuel tanks—had flown more than four hundred miles from Guadalcanal in total radio silence, their wings barely above the waves, so close the pilots could make out a pod of whales and spot the larger sharks; Lieutenant Doug Canning even spotted a giant manta ray. Canning was also the one who first saw the enemy planes just as they approached Bougainville. "Bogeys, eleven o'clock high," he said crisply, breaking the radio silence at last.

And sure enough, there they were, right on schedule, right out of the coded message: Yamamoto in his Mitsubishi bomber, number 323; his chief of staff in a companion Mitsubishi; and six escort Zeros. It was a trim, blue Pacific morning, and none of the Japanese suspected that the enemy was near—even less that the Americans might sneak up from below.

Squadron 339 jettisoned its long-range tanks and soared into the sky. The Japanese never even saw the P-38s until they'd closed within a mile of Yamamoto's Mitsubishi. Finally then the Zeros turned for action, while the two bombers dove down, frantically trying to escape, seeking to blend their camouflage into the island greenery.

The Zeros scrambled to drive back the American fighters; but when one of the Yanks, a fellow by the name of Tom Lanphier, downed a Zero, that gave his wing, Rex Barber, clear access to Yamamoto. Number 323 was coming in at two hundred feet, not much above the tops of the palms, when Barber scored on the right engine first, then on the other side. Lanphier peeled around and finished it off. Number 323 thudded into the jungle, bounced once, and exploded. Two bodies were thrown clear, though, and one of them was Yamamoto. The admiral was in his formal dark green uniform, with his medals and ribbons aligned upon his left breast. He wore a white glove on his right hand and clutched his dress sword in the glove. One bullet had entered his left shoulder blade, and another had pierced his lower left jaw, emerging with his life at his right temple.

Yamamoto's body was retrieved, and his ashes were put in a simple wooden box lined with papaya leaves. Papaya was his favorite fruit. A small Shinto shrine was erected there, by the tail of number 323, and a state funeral was ordered. Yamamoto was only the twelfth commoner so honored. The only other admiral in Japan ever to receive such a distinction was Heihachiro Togo, the hero of the Battle of Tsushima Straits, where the Japanese destroyed the Russian fleet, defeating the West the first time they ever had a go at the bigger men who ruled the globe. Yamamoto was also at Tsushima, in his first action as an ensign; and now he would rest forever beside Togo in Tokyo, in Tamabochi cemetery. Posthumously, Yamamoto was given the Grand Order of the Chrysanthemum, first class, and made admiral of the fleet.

"I met Admiral Yamamoto once," Miyuki said. The other officers had gone, and she was washing Major Tanaka's back, as he sat in his little tub. He whirled around in amusement, even splashing a bit of the water. Only if Miyuki had said that she had met the Emperor himself could Tanaka have been more impressed. In fact, Miyuki had met the emperor once; she had almost slept with him—long ago, when she was a virgin. But that was another story, and it took place before the war, and she barely pondered such things past anymore.

"You met the admiral?" Tanaka gushed.

"Oh, yes. It was a party in Tokyo, and he was there with Kikuji."

"I know, I know," Tanak said, and rather sharply. "Everybody knows of Kikuji." She had been one of the most famous geishas in the land even before Yamamoto fell in love with

her and made her his mistress. Her name meant Chrysanthemum Path.

"Well, they were there together. It was '41, still the summer, I guess." Tanaka eyed her in some wonderment. He
could have pressed her on these matters—he could have
made her tell him *anything*—but sometimes he let her have her
past so he could have her mystery. Miyuki smiled; she saw it
all vividly now. She was with Kiyoshi, and she met the admiral because he needed to talk to Kiyoshi about Hawaii. "He
was such a short man. Broad." Miyuki lifted her hands off
Tanaka's back and gestured, forming the impression of wide
shoulders. "Very broad. But exceptionally short. I was much
taller than Yamamoto-san."

"You're tall for a Japanese girl."

"And his hand—he lost two fingers—"

"At Tsushima."

"Yes." Miyuki studied her own hands. "I was trying to
think. Yes, the left." She held that one up. "He lost these
two."

Tanaka swiveled back to her. He probably sensed that she
was through with rubbing his back, and she was. She rose up
off her knees. "But he was so gentle. So very thoughtful. My
father was a warrior, and my brother too. And Admiral
Yamamoto wasn't like them at all. And yet he was the one
who gave us Pearl Harbor."

She scooped up Kiyokuni. Somehow, she had done a
pretty good job of putting Pearl out of her mind, but now
Yamamoto's death had brought it back again. She hoped that
Tanaka wouldn't want her to sleep with him tonight. She
couldn't bear that sort of thing right now. When she was feeling sorry for herself, Miyuki sometimes thought of herself as
the first casualty of Pearl Harbor.

Tanaka watched her go. He let her go. He had enough
sense to understand that something of Yamamoto, something
of Pearl, had touched a nerve in her. "Good night, Miyuki"
was all he said, but she didn't even reply, just held Kiyokuni
close and walked off into the tropical dark. After a while, to
herself, she sighed, *"Noren ni udeoshi."*

A *noren* is a short type of curtain that hangs in the entrance, say, to a little restaurant or a teahouse. *Udeoshi* means pushing with the arm, but since a *noren* isn't a whole curtain but, rather, one split into strips, when you push a *noren* in order to enter, your arm goes through, and you go through, and then the curtain quickly falls back to its original place, and it's as if you were never there, although, of course, you've gone through and are now safely on the other side. *Noren ni udeoshi.*

Pearl Harbor ni udeoshi, Miyuki thought.

1936
Hino E Ne
THE YEAR
of the
FIRE RAT

1

In February of 2596, the eleventh year of Showa—Enlightened Peace—in the reign of the Emperor Hirohito—Broad-minded Benevolence—who was one hundred and twenty-fourth in a direct line from the first emperor, Jimmu (himself the great-grandson of the Sun Goddess), it began to snow.

It snowed now and again in Tokyo, and February was the one cold month in any year; but this great snow blanketed the city, silencing the cacophony of vendors and streetcars, of the bells and the clogs and the cries, burying the city deeper than it had been in all this century, even deeper than any snow since the Emperor Meiji had decreed, more than a half-century ago, that Japan would hereafter be grown-up.

After the first day, when the storm temporarily lapsed, the people stranded here and there (some even spent the night together in theaters) tried to get home. Only those who absolutely had to be out—to clean the streets, restore the telephone lines, bring Tokyo back into this century—were visible. The others were content to stay by their hibachis, enjoying tea or sake, telling tall tales of the great storms of their youth or perhaps of that terrible earthquake that struck thirteen years ago.

Miyuki herself listened to her mother, Setsuko, remind her of the winter of her birth. That was in the Year of the Christian Lord 1917, up in the mountains of the Nagano prefecture, where snow was common. Her father, Colonel Serikawa

Shinji, of the Japanese Imperial Army, was stationed there that winter, and when his daughter was born in the midst of a howling blizzard, he named her Miyuki—Beautiful Snow. She had heard the story of her birth so many times, but her mother never tired of the telling.

Suddenly, to their surprise, the two Serikawa women heard someone in the snow, and then a pounding on the *amado*, the outside door that afforded at least some protection. Before they could get to the door, Takeo managed to slide it back into the drift enough to force an entrance for himself, and he almost fell into the house, into the arms of his happy mother and sister. He was in his olive drab coat, crusted with snow, but the red band on his cap told the world that he too, like his father before him, was an officer in His Majesty the Emperor's army. Any red attire was rare. Children wore red, and then they put the color aside until they were at the other end of their lives. In between, red was in evidence only as a hint—a braid, a chevron, a sash. It was so unusual that the young women who assisted passengers on the streetcars were known, officially, as the red-collar girls. Policemen shone with red stripes down the sides of their trousers. And above all, the army wore the red band on their caps; only the rising sun was redder and higher.

Takeo moved over to warm himself by the hibachi, and the heat there, such as it was, fogged up his spectacles, so that he had to remove them. "Oh, how handsome you are!" Mrs. Serikawa cooed, fawning over him the way Japanese mothers do too much with their sons—especially the oldest. Japanese mothers kept breast-feeding their boys right up till they walked. The best thing to be in Japan then was an eldest son. The worst thing was a daughter-in-law.

Takeo himself had not yet brought a wife home. Perhaps that wouldn't have disturbed Mrs. Serikawa so much, but here Miyuki was, facing down twenty, and she wasn't married either. In fact, Mrs. Serikawa was especially glad that Takeo had come to visit, because it would give her a chance to corner him and see if he couldn't light some sort of a fire under his old friend Okuno Kiyoshi—or, even better, under

Kiyoshi's parents. After all, Miyuki and Kiyoshi seemed like such an obvious pairing; the two of them had grown up together, and their families had known each other through the years. Why, it was conceivable that Kiyoshi and Miyuki might even enjoy each other's company a little bit.

On the other hand, Mrs. Serikawa had decided that if the Okunos weren't going to make any sort of matrimonial move, then it was time for her to bring in a matchmaker who could find some suitable mate for Miyuki. At the very least now, she wanted Takeo to write Kiyoshi and invite him to Tokyo. Mrs. Serikawa was aware of several trial marriages that had tilted potential pairings into the real thing. There was more than one way to skin a cat.

But now she could see that Takeo looked very serious. Miyuki brought her brother a cup of sake and waited for him to speak. "I have only come to be with my father," Takeo declared after a time, and he nodded across toward the corner, toward a small, simple "god shelf" that served as the Shinto shrine of the house.

Shinto was so primitive and naive that when Buddhism came from China several centuries ago, it almost casually subsumed the people's everyday religion. Recently, though, the government had molded Shinto to become more of a cult—even, really, a populist political movement, more allegiance to be sworn than creed believed, with some resonances of Nazism in Germany. Shinto was, more than ever, *our* religion, with *our* gods, and above all, *our* Emperor.

Once a day, as was the case all over the land, Miyuki and her mother moved to the god shelf and genuflected toward the imperial palace a few miles away. Takeo joined the women in paying that obeisance now.

"The evil ones about the throne must be taken care of," Takeo announced to them.

Mrs. Serikawa sighed at how ominously that thudded; she knew it meant revolt, and maybe death. But Miyuki was excited. "When?" was all she asked.

"Wednesday, near dawn. If there's no more snow."

"It's so very deep," Mrs. Serikawa said—pleading, really.

Takeo waved his mother off. "Aw, a lot of it should melt," he said. The short winter in Tokyo made it difficult for the ground to freeze, and anyway, spring was drawing near; the sun was up longer every day. It was Monday afternoon now; if there was no more snow Tuesday, men could act the next dawn. Then they could try and kill whomever they had to.

"Yes, but why must you be the Namazu?" Mrs. Serikawa asked. Namazu was the great catfish who was responsible for all the Japanese earthquakes in antiquity, for he was supposed to reside on the floor of the Pacific, and when he happened to stir, he disturbed Honshu and the other smaller islands of the archipelago that he bore upon his scaly back.

Takeo frowned at his mother's concern. "It is my honor," he declared.

"It is his honor, Mother," Miyuki repeated, even more emphatically, and with a measure of patronization, too.

"The election results have shown that our people are being led astray by rich capitalists, who would steer the Emperor away from the purity of the Japanese cause," Takeo proclaimed. Sometimes now, on occasions such as this, when he spoke conversationally, even to his mother, it was as if he were reading from a pamphlet, or writing one.

Miyuki translated that to the marrow: "Father would want it, Mother." She grasped her brother's strong arm in both her hands and held tight to him. "I only wish *I* could go with you."

Takeo beamed. "Oh, Father would be so proud of his girl."

Colonel Serikawa had lived the most stalwart Japanese life and died a Japanese hero's death. He had been killed five years before, in the very first Japanese action abroad in these times, in the controversial campaign that bound Manchuria— Manchukuo, the Japanese called it—to the empire.

Takeo was at the academy then, and he was raised to captain of the honor guard almost as soon as the word came that he was so lucky as to have a father who had given up his life for the Emperor in Manchukuo. There were not that many Japanese who had died there, which made Colonel Serikawa all the more a hero. It also made Miyuki even more valuable a virgin should the Emperor choose to take her and thrust his seed in her so that Japan would at last have a son and heir.

Takeo took the box off the prayer shelf, where his mother still kept a sample of her husband's hair and nails that he had left her when he went off to Manchukuo in 1931. His ashes had come back and had been buried, but Setsuko had kept these tokens. "I would like to have this with me, Mother," Takeo said, and she bowed and nodded.

"Father would approve," Miyuki assured her. She remembered how proud she had been when she learned her father had been killed. Why, not a single friend of hers even had a father in Manchukuo, let alone one who had given his life for the Emperor. The interweaving of sorrow and glory was almost too much for a girl of fourteen to manage. Miyuki had planned, then, to be a geisha, and her training as an apprentice, a *maiko*, had been just about ready to start. But she did not want to leave her mother right after her father's death, and so she gave up that idea, and the two women came to Tokyo, with a hero's pension.

"There is one other thing of Father's I want," Takeo said, and he walked over to the *tokonoma*, a special alcove where his father's old samurai sword was kept. He took it and stood, legs apart, like a warrior of old, flashing the sword. Miyuki clapped gaily "Banzai!" Takeo cried.

"Let me have it now and bring it to you when it is time to act," Miyuki said.

"Oh, you could have been a warrior, too!" Takeo said, hugging her. "But I can't get a girl into the barracks."

Mrs. Serikawa did her best to join her children in their exultation, but it was difficult. In fact, she wanted to cry. She knew she must not, though. Japanese women were not even allowed to cry in labor, for that would be a loss of face and a terrible reflection upon the poor husband. She only retreated away from her children. Takeo called for a toast to his father and to what he was about to do to serve the Emperor. He let Miyuki take the sword, and she brandished it boldly with both hands, like a samurai of old, or like her father, or like her brother in these glorious times of insurrection.

2

It was not easy to get to Hawaii in 1936, which is why it could still be accepted as a paradise then. In a luxury liner, it was about a week either way, to Yokohama going west or to San Francisco (open your Golden Gate), going east. Oh, that was an occasion whenever the cruise ship came into Honolulu: Boat Day! There at the dock at the foot of Nuuanu Avenue, the band would play, and people would throw confetti and streamers, and the brown-skinned kids would dive for tourist coins, and the pretty, tawny girls would hula and install leis around the necks of the wide-eyed visitors. Nobody had jet lag, and everybody had arrived in another world.

Pan American had started flying its clippers across the Pacific only three months before, belly-flopping from San Francisco to Honolulu, Wake, Guam, Manila, and Hong Kong, but even then it was only the rich people who could vacation in Hawaii. Because more rich people tended to be tasteful in those days—or more tasteful people got rich—it was a precious place to holiday.

In Waikiki, which had been salvaged out of swampland, there were only three hotels, the Noana and the Halekulani and, of course, between them but beyond them, the Pink Palace—the Royal Hawaiian!—where thrilled middle-aged men and women sipped exotic drinks and swam and danced and enjoyed licit sex more than they had in years. It was heavenly; and thereafter whenever anybody who had been there remembered the best things in life, they thought of the time they had sailed to Hawaii on the *Lurline* and made love at the Royal Hawaiian. It would never be the same again, because after that there was always a war in between the memories.

On this night, when the snow lay deep in Tokyo, and the stardust fell on Diamond Head with more glisten than it did

on any other place in the world, Liz Hundley and Cotton
Drake made the sweetest of love in room 336 of the Royal
Hawaiian, and then threw something decorous on and stood
on the balcony and looked out over the palms and the white
sands and the shining Pacific toward whatever it was that lay
out there for three thousand miles under the stars above.
Then, for all that, they stared at one another and were over-
come with that sight.

"I love you, Cotton," Liz said.

"I love you too. Only I love you more."

She was so fair. Cotton had been in Hawaii for two months
now, and he was not used to this. Even the haoles who lived
here, come west to the islands, were tanned, objects *du* sun.
But Liz was white all over, blond and pale, except, as in so
many songs, for the blue of her eyes and the red of her lips.
She was almost as tall as he, so their eyes met (as in a lot of
other songs), and then they started attacking each other
again, standing up in the stardust, stumbling back to the bed,
where they made love with all the joy and passion they had,
and then they fell asleep in one another's arms.

Cotton gave Liz everything she could want, so she didn't
even wonder what more there was, or even if there might be
anything more. Never is ignorance bliss more than when it in-
volves bliss. Besides, Liz loved Cotton genuinely, generously,
desperately, and most times he felt sure that he loved her that
same way, too.

Liz had never slept with another man. The others she had
loved had been boys, and that she would let one of them
sweet-talk her into sin had never been even a serious possibility. She had held out for a Cotton Drake, and she had cashed
the bet. Cotton was fair and handsome, strong and muscled,
with the stocky body of a third baseman, which is what he
had always been, for every coach ("And Drake—Drake, you
play third").

Cotton might as well have been a virgin the first time he
slept with Liz, because she was his first real girl. The others
before were all whores, and one punchboard townie he always seemed to end up with whenever he got drunk at Yale.

Takeo and Kiyoshi had gotten Cotton his first whore on his sixteenth birthday. He was shy and self-conscious, but he was also layered over with the absolute panic that someone might find out, because he was the only son of missionaries, the Reverend and Mrs. Bennett Drake, and had always been a pretty good boy, and if either one of them ever heard that their dear child was out screwing the local whores . . .

Cotton need not have worried. Nobody cared much about that sort of thing in Japan, not even the fervent new Christian souls. In Aimoto, the little town down between Kyoto and Osaka where the Drakes were stationed then, seeking out putative Anglican communicants, there was no proper brothel; the bar, though, doubled as a part-time whorehouse. Nobody blinked. If the Bennetts and their missionary colleagues did their job well, they might succeed in bringing guilt to Japan; but in the meantime, everybody was occupied enough with face—putting it on, saving it, and so forth. Overall, face probably causes just as many emotional problems as guilt, but, in the specific, sex tends to create more guilt trauma than it does face trauma. So, all things considered, Japan was a good place for a missionary's son to get laid.

Kiyoshi was his contemporary and best pal. Takeo was senior by three years and something of an idol; he was a figurative older brother to Cotton and Kiyoshi as much as he truly was for Miyuki. Takeo and the two younger boys were bigger than almost all the other Japanese kids, too, and they were good athletes. Takeo was by far the best, though. Cotton, who was good enough to start at third base at Yale and bat .310, gauged that Takeo might even have had enough talent to make the majors in America. Takeo even played right field, after Babe Ruth; and while the other little boys in Japan bunted and poked it the other way, as was the custom there, Takeo always swung from the heels and for the fences.

In an odd way, Cotton felt that Takeo was the most American Japanese boy he knew; but paradoxically, with each year Takeo grew more Japanese—except when he was standing there tall at the plate with a bat in his hands.

In any event, on this particular occasion, Cotton's sweet

sixteen, Takeo was back home in Aimoto for a few weeks of
summer vacation from military academy. The whore he lined
up for Cotton was barely semipro, hardly more experienced
than the boy whose tender loins she introduced to the ways
of the world. Her name was Eiko, and she came off the farm.
The farmers were really starting to struggle in Japan then,
and so they would send their daughters into town or even
into a big city to see if they had any special talent for whoring. It was the only living they could make, and there was no
shame in it. A lot of them who weren't that pretty or who
didn't have much aptitude for the life would go back home
after a while and just marry the boy next door.

Takeo cared the most about what forced this sort of prostitution. He'd go down to the bar and buy one of the farm
whores when he had a little yen in his pocket, but before he
screwed her, he would chat with her about the conditions on
the farms and explain how the Western-style *zaibatsu* capitalists were all to blame. Sometimes he would go out into the
sticks and talk to the farmers themselves. Cotton and Kiyoshi
even went along with him once. Takeo wanted them to see
for themselves what he had been telling them, about how the
weak, greedy, immoral men around the Emperor were destroying the pure Japan, twenty-six centuries' worth.

Cotton remembered how Takeo had found a farmer names
Kitamura whom he knew and had said to him, "Kitamura-
san, I was with your daughter, Kiku, back in town the other
day, and . . ." And Mr. Kitamura had understood exactly
what Takeo meant and he asked how she was doing at her
job, what precisely she could learn to be better at fucking
men, and so forth and so on. It was a very strange conversation. Cotton had, till then, lived almost all his life in Japan,
but every time he thought he had the place figured out, a little something like this would come up. It must be far easier,
he thought, to take ignorant black heathen, Hottentots and
the like, and just mumbo-jumbo them into Christianity,
rather than trying to *convert* Japanese. The longer he stayed in
Japan, the more Cotton admired what his parents were trying
to do.

He could never put that aside, the church. The problem was, he liked it. Cotton never understood other church people talking about that thing they referred to as "a calling." He only saw how happy his parents were with the gospel, and that was the prime emotion he remembered and understood: the pleasure of it. But it sounded goofy to tell anybody else that missionary work seemed joyful.

"Joy? You mean like fun? Being a missionary is like *fun?*" Liz said once when he tried to explain that to her. "Fun? Like what?"

He knew right away his instincts were correct; he shouldn't have tried to get into this. "That doesn't mean it isn't serious, too," Cotton began. "I mean, some people are very serious about baseball sometimes, and *it's* fun. So yeah, being a missionary is a lot of fun if you're built that way."

Liz only shook her head, and Cotton dropped the subject, never to bring it up again, even when he started to think about it more and more, even when he knew he had to discuss it with her.

The problem was further complicated by the fact that the other thing Cotton could never sufficiently explain to Liz was Japan, and why it meant so much him.

"Sometimes you seem more Japanese than American," she said once.

"But you don't know Japan."

"I know," Liz said. "But there's a part of you I don't understand, and I don't understand Japan, so I figure that's your Japanese part."

"That makes sense," Cotton said. And it really did, in a Gracie Allen sort of way.

Of course, one Japanese experience he did never share with Liz was the loss of his virginity to Eiko. It had gone well enough, and of course he *liked* it just fine—although it somewhat disconcerted Cotton that he was as much a novelty to her as she was to him. Eiko had barely seen a Westerner up close before, let alone shared any intimacies with one, and she couldn't get over Cotton's hairiness. Actually, he wasn't particularly hairy, but Japanese were fascinated by the hair on Western men's bodies. It especially beguiled Eiko.

So Cotton got through his initiation to manhood, and the three friends went off to the Shinto festival which had come to town. It was like a country fair back in America, and they hung out and did the equivalent of kicking tires, Cotton and Kiyoshi and Takeo.

They saw Miyuki and Mrs. Serikawa across the way, fishing in the carp tank. The colonel was away in Okinawa then. There was always a carp tank at the little Shinto fairs, but the carp never bit. It was sort of like the claw machines in penny arcades in the United States, where you kept putting coins in and trying to pick up a prize, even though you knew you surely never could. Carp are generally braver than they are intelligent, but even a dumb carp could figure out not to bite in a tank. Little Miyuki—she was eleven at the time—was yanking on her line and cooing and coaxing the carp, but without any luck. When her brother came over with Kiyoshi and Cotton, she just turned and chirped: "Did you like your first sex, Cotton?"

He was mortified. He threw his hands over his face and turned around and scurried away. Mrs. Serikawa and Miyuki and the boys all looked after him, laughing and shaking their heads. Westerners were such a screwed-up bunch; no wonder they weren't gods.

Cotton woke early the next morning at the Royal Hawaiian. He and Liz had hurried so to get back to bed from the balcony that they hadn't closed the curtains, and now the first light streamed in. Liz was lying on her stomach next to him, her golden hair spilling over the bed, her back bared by a sheet that just covered here rear. Cotton just lay there and stared at her back. It was so glorious. It had never occurred to him before that a woman's back could be so magnificent, so provocative, so alluring, so . . . frontlike.

This was their second night together in room 336. Cotton was standing in for Emily, Liz's friend and traveling companion. In 1936, respectable girls certainly did not travel alone to the next town, let alone several time zones to a tropical island. So Emily had been enlisted as a confederate, to accompany Liz from Philadelphia, across North America and on to Hawaii. Then, as a true friend, she promptly had gotten lost as soon as the *Lurline* docked, heading off to the Big Island with Darlene Ushijima, the daughter of Sammy Ushijima, Cotton's business associate in Honolulu. Everybody was a willing confederate to help the lovers, and if Liz still felt a little immoral, transporting herself across state lines for carnal purposes, the visit was really only the certified final prelude to holy matrimony. The last thing her father said to her, before her train pulled out of Thirtieth Street, was "Don't come back without that ring."

And her mother had said, "Oh, Lawrence."

And Liz had laughed. "Oh, don't worry, Mother, it's a done deal."

Now she felt Cotton slipping out of bed. "Where are you going, darling?" she asked, and he was surprised because he didn't know that the sun had awakened Liz, too.

"You know, I told you—I had to meet with Kiyoshi and Sammy this morning."

"You said we were going to have breakfast in bed together this morning," Liz pouted.

"No, no, honey—that's tomorrow. Today was the one day I—"

"You told me there wouldn't be any business the whole week."

"No, I'm sorry, I said just this one time I *had* to meet with Key and Sammy." That was an outright lie, but Liz was too much in love even to suspect that. Besides:

"Well, you can't go meet them like that, silly boy."

"Like what?" He bit. Liz pointed at him. Cotton had a considerable erection. "No," he said.

She had turned over on her side to talk to him, and her hair fell down to her breasts, like Rapunzel up in the tower. It was a glorious sight—it put her back in perspective—and Cotton rolled over and kissed her.

Cotton and Liz hadn't spent enough nights together for him to remember that even though she might be the most gorgeous, Rapunzel-like girl in the world, still, even Liz Hundley had bad breath in the morning—and so did Cotton Drake. He was kissing her open-mouthed before he remembered that, and then he was terribly embarrassed, and he didn't know quite what to do until Liz just laughed and put him inside her, and they held each other tightly and laughed some more and cooed and loved and loved and loved, and only when they were finally through did Cotton fall off beside her and stare at the ceiling and begin to wonder again how crazy he must be that he could even consider giving up this magnificent woman whom he seemed to love with all his heart and soul.

But that was the way it was.

3

Miyuki and Mrs. Serikawa prevailed upon Takeo not to go back to his barracks but to stay the night at home. Mrs. Serikawa was convinced that things would not go well; she had given a husband to the Empire, and now she would surely donate a son, too. She was positive of that, so she fed Takeo better than ever and hugged him longingly and sent him on his way with tears behind her eyes, that Tuesday morning, February 25. If the weather held clear and their resolve held strong, Takeo and the other conspirators would go into action early the next morning, 2/26: *ni/ni-roku.*

Miyuki walked down to the streetcar line with Takeo. She was so proud of him in his striking army uniform, carrying his father's samurai sword. She squeezed his hand and gave him a kiss, and he clambered onto the open-air platform at the back of the car next to one of the red-collar girls and waved to Miyuki as the streetcar pulled away toward his barracks, downtown, near the Palace grounds.

It was still bitter cold, but the battalions of workers had been out, and the streets were almost free of snow; and suddenly, before Miyuki really knew what she was doing, she reversed her field, and instead of going straightaway back home, she walked over to the telegraph office a few blocks away, at the Asakusa railroad station, and sent a wire to Kiyoshi at his export company office in Honolulu. Laboring to put it into English so that it would go through quickly (and impress Kiyoshi), she wrote (almost correctly): DO NOT SURPRISE STOP TAKEO AND SOME FRIENDS PLANNING WONDERFUL MOMENT STOP GO TO SHRINE AS HIM AND TELL COTTON ALSO TALK TO JESUS PLEASE MIYUKI.

Then she went back home and consoled her mother and tried to work some more on her English. Takeo had agreed with Miyuki and Mrs. Serikawa that if Kiyoshi and his parents were ever to be serious about Miyuki as a daughter-in-law, she would have to better understand the English language and other Western ways. But Takeo was not sure that he would permit such a union for his sister: he found Kiyoshi increasingly more liberal and international and therefore very possibly corrupted. "He sees Japan through blue eyes," Takeo said—a terrible insult to another Japanese. To say that a Japanese viewed his own land through blue eyes meant that a countryman was turning *gaijin*.

Still, Takeo reserved some judgment about Kiyoshi, because he had known him—looked out for him—since they were kids. "Always," he told Miyuki, "there must be some Japanese working outside of Japan, and they'll all be tempted by Western ways. Maybe it's better to have Kiyoshi out there, because he's known the West all his life. Probably we can trust someone like him better."

"Yes."

"What do you think of having a trial marriage with Kiyoshi when he returns to Tokyo?"

"Mother thinks that's a good idea," Miyuki replied, patently avoiding the question.

"I know," Takeo said, smiling at her shyness. "Well, let me

think about it. Who knows, maybe Kiyoshi has an American girlfriend."

Miyuki stiffened a little bit at that, but she wouldn't take the bait. "Well, Cotton does. Kiyoshi says Cotton's going to get married."

"Is that so? What's she like?"

"Kiyoshi says she's very, very pretty. Blond. And very big." She cupped her hands by her own smaller chest.

"Ah so," Takeo said. "Good for Cotton. And we'll talk about Kiyoshi and you after this is all over."

Kiyoshi had grown up differently from all the other Japanese boys. His father was a businessman, and the family had spent two years in San Francisco and another two in Singapore. He had learned to speak English, when he was very small, and when he came back to Japan and met Cotton, he loved to go over to the mission and speak English. Sometimes Mrs. Drake would hold little English-speaking sessions, trying to teach the neighborhood kids, and Kiyoshi would even fill in as a teacher's aide.

That was where Miyuki started to learn a little English—with Cotton's mother at the mission. She kept it up in school; and now, of course, she was concentrating all the more. Mrs. Serikawa, however, was doubtful at first. "Why do you have to learn this other language?" she asked. "If Mr. and Mrs. Okuno want Kiyoshi to marry you, so what? Kiyoshi will still speak Japanese at home with you."

"It is different in America, Mother. You know, there are no geishas there, and when the men go out, the wives come along."

"On business?"

"On business."

Mrs. Serikawa shook her head at such a frightful revelation. "You mean the wives entertain the businessmen like geishas?"

"No, no, no, Mother. You just accompany your husband, eat and drink, maybe do a Western dance with your husband."

Mrs. Serikawa frowned, cocking her head. "Are you turning into a moga?"

Miyuki laughed. "Oh, Mother!" "Moga" was a stylish term in Tokyo. It came directly from the English: modern girl. Moga. (There were also mobos, the indecently westernized boys who led the mogas astray.) "It's good for Japanese to know another language, Mother. It's especially good to know English. And German. Takeo thinks that someday Germany will rule Europe, the United States will rule America, and we will rule Asia, so we must be prepared for when the world is divided that way."

Mrs. Serikawa nodded, but grudgingly. She still wasn't altogether convinced that this wasn't all a lot of mumbo-jumbo cooked up on Miyuki's part just to conceal the fact that she was turning into a moga right before her eyes.

A few miles away, just beyond the Imperial Palace, stood the magnificent American embassy, and today, inside, beyond the handsome wrought-iron gates and the official-size, snow-covered croquet field, the place was all atwitter. Alice Grew, the ambassador's wife, bustled about, directing the staff, switching fluidly from English to Japanese and back. Mrs. Grew was no less than Commodore Perry's granddaughter, and she had been raised in Japan. She passed on the word: the weather report was out that there would be no more snow today, and so the party was on for tonight.

It was a very special, almost sweet evening that was planned, one that went well beyond the usual diplomatic niceties. The guest of honor, Viscount Admiral Makoto Saito, was an old personal friend of the Grews; and as a surprise for him and the viscountess, after dinner, in the salon, all would assemble for a private showing of *Naughty Marietta*, starring Jeanette MacDonald and Nelson Eddy. The viscount was nearly eighty by now, almost doddering, everybody's favorite ancient uncle, and never in his long life had he ever seen a newfangled sound film. The Grews settled on *Naughty Marietta* because it was so undeniably dulcet, free of the vulgar intrusions of the real world.

There was a sparkling guest list of thirty-six for the party, Western and Japanese alike. Admiral Kantaro Suzuki, the grand chamberlain of the imperial government, would be there, with Mrs. Suzuki; and at the last minute Mrs. Grew was thrilled to receive the acceptance of Admiral and Mrs. Yamamoto. The admiral had led the Japanese naval mission to London the year before, successfully championing every Japanese demand, returning as the hero of the nation. He was the prize catch for any hostess.

Unfortunately, this happy turn of events left Mrs. Grew in a quandry. With three such distinguished visitors and their wives, whom would she place next to her husband and herself? Someone would have to be left out of the places of honor.

She explained the dilemma to her husband. Joseph Grew was a Boston Brahmin who had been trained all his life to treat such diplomatic issues (even if he hadn't happened to become a professional diplomat), and he considered the matter, twirling his mustache. "Well, dear, let's see," he said at last. "Who would you say is the most beautiful and charming woman at the dinner—present company excepted, of course?"

Alice Grew pondered. "Felicia," she said in time.

"Of course. And the most charming gentleman?"

"Desmond," she replied straightaway.

"No doubt—although I wish you hadn't answered so quickly, my dear."

"As you said yourself, Joseph: present company excepted."

"Of course," he chuckled. "In any event, Felicia and Desmond shall make perfect consolation prizes. You will place Viscount Saito on your right, and I the viscountess on my right. I will place Mrs. Yamamoto on my left."

"And you'll be very solicitous to her, dear. The whole of Tokyo knows that her husband is in love with his geisha."

"That's just Japanese."

"I don't care how Japanese she is, Joseph, there must also be some pain."

"As a wife."

"As a woman."

"What?" The ambassador was a little hard of hearing, which wasn't normally a problem, except perhaps on those few occasions when he had an audience with the emperor and ended up speaking too loudly, which was unintentional but terribly inappropriate, inasmuch as no one was supposed to raise his voice to His Majesty.

"As a *woman*, dear."

"Oh yes."

"And who goes on my left?" Alice Grew asked her husband.

"Admiral Suzuki. And then, you see, we'll place Desmond on Mrs. Suzuki's right, and she'll be instantly charmed and forget that she's not dining with the ambassador. Likewise—"

"Yes, I see. Felicia goes on Admiral Yamamoto's right."

"Exactly," said the Ambassador.

"You're a regular Solomon, my dear."

"Yes indeed—and after we're through in Tokyo, maybe Frank'll make me the head of protocol." Even though Ambassador Grew had been appointed by Herbert Hoover, he came from the same social background as the incumbent President, well above the salt, and so he still casually called him Frank—and Mr. President smiled and answered him when he did that, too.

"We seem all right on the snow, too," Mrs. Grew said. "There may be more on the way later, but it seems we'll get through the evening."

"Good. Thank you, darling." She started to leave, and was at the door when the ambassador called to her. He was twirling his mustache again, and his heavy eyebrows were more knitted. "Alice, can I assume we have a couple extra men?"

"Twenty gentlemen, sixteen ladies."

"All right, then, put Bowersox on Admiral Yamamoto's left."

"Oh, darling, you can't mean that. Punish the admiral?"

"No, I'd like to have Bowersox see for himself what a brilliant, civilized gentleman a Japanese military officer can be."

She wrinkled her nose. "Well, I suppose we have to inflict Bowersox on someone."

"Just as Washington inflicted him on us." And the ambassador piped his wife out of the office, whistling a little Victor Herbert.

It was just about then that Takeo stepped off the streetcar and walked the little bit back to the barracks, when he met with the other rebel leaders. For the last time, they went over their assignments. Captain Ando rose. He and Captain Koda were senior. "I assume for myself the honor of assassinating the grand chamberlain," he said. Admiral Suzuki.

Koda rose next, but he beckoned to Takeo. "I defer to the son of the noble hero Serikawa."

Takeo stood and bowed to Koda. "Thank you, Captain. Then it is my humble honor to kill Viscount Saito," he declared. And thus did the privilege of slaughtering Ambassador Grew's esteemed guest of honor fall to Takeo Serikawa.

4

The Honolulu office of the American Orient Export-Import Company was located by the harbor on Alakea Street. It was only a branch, but a most important one, nearly coequal with the dual home offices in San Francisco and Tokyo. Isamu Ushijima, who was Sammy now to most of the people he dealt with, ran the Hawaiian operation. Sammy was Issei, first generation, come off the farm from Okayama prefecture, in the southern part of Honshu, thirty years ago. He had learned to speak good English and had adapted haole ways faster than most of the other Issei, which is why he had long since moved off of the sugar cane plantations and into town and, at last, into a position of some importance: manager, Honolulu office, the American Orient Export-Import Company.

Sammy had no sons himself, only two daughters, and he took Kiyoshi and Cotton on as much as his boys as his associates. He was positively thrilled when they joined the company after college. They had gone about it very systematically, applying to a number of the best trans-Pacific companies as a team: one Japanese, educated at Harvard; one Yale American, reared in Japan; both perfectly bilingual—a double-or-nothing package deal. It was the depth of the Depression when they came on the market, the summer of '34. There were no jobs anywhere, absolutely none at all in this business. Even so, Cotton and Kiyoshi bore such outstanding credentials that they received firm prime offers from five of the best import-export companies in the Pacific before settling on American Orient.

At first, both were posted to San Francisco for a few months; then they were sent to Tokyo for the balance of '35; and now they were serving a tour of Hawaii together. Soon, one would go east, one west—although, perhaps surprisingly, the current thinking in the executive suite was that with the increasing strain in Japanese-American relations, the company might be better served with the young American going to Tokyo and the young Japanese to San Francisco. The company was not afraid to flaunt the fact that it owned the brightest two rising stars in the business. Drake and Okuno, Okuno and Drake—the Pep Boys of the Pacific.

After Cotton left Liz at the Royal Hawaiian, he borrowed Sammy's car and found Kiyoshi down at the docks, where he was just finishing up off-loading a freighter in from Seattle. "Hey, I didn't expect to see you here, rover boy," Kiyoshi said, purposely mispronouncing his "L," the way Japanese so often do.

"I just need a couple minutes to talk to you, Key."

"She's wearing you out, huh?"

Cotton gave a weary smile to that and pointed toward Sammy's ear. "Come on, we'll take a little drive."

"The house dicks give you any trouble?"

"Aw no, I can outslick those guys."

"Well, you know our deal," Kiyoshi said. "Any problem, I'll move in with Sammy, and you can bring Liz over to our place."

Cotton shot him a thumbs-up. They'd rented a little house together in Waikiki, within walking distance of the beach and the Royal Hawaiian, a bungalow tucked under some sheltering palms, brightened with the kind of glorious flowers that seemed to cover every house in Honolulu in those precious times.

They climbed into Sammy's car. It was a green DeSoto convertible—Sammy really was moving up in the world. Cotton started driving down King Street, west, away from Diamond Head, out toward Pearl Harbor. He didn't say anything for a long while, and Kiyoshi allowed him not to say anything; he pretended to look out the window and even whistled to emphasize how nonchalant he was. In fact, Kiyoshi was pretty damn excited, because he was sure his old buddy was going to tell him that he had proposed and that Liz had accepted and that he was getting married.

But when Cotton finally did talk, that wasn't what he said. Instead: "I started to tell Lizzie something last night, and I couldn't."

"That you love her?"

"Hell no—I can tell her *that*. I'm not Japanese. I've been telling her I love her since Yale."

"That you wanna marry her?" Cotton answered that only by staring ahead, studying the road much too intently. Kiyoshi laughed. "See, I keep telling you—that's the trouble with you Westerners. You try to put love and lust together in the same dame, and it only messes you all up."

"Oh, stop it. You damn Orientals aren't always as slick as you think you are. Somebody like Miyuki, a good-looking skirt like that—you've always been friends, and the way you were flirting with her the last time we were back in Tokyo—"

"Hey, knock it off—she's like my kid sister!" Kiyoshi snorted, and now he was the one who turned away, looking out the window, pretending to study the hideously famous Dole landmark as they drove by it: a huge water tank painted to resemble a pineapple.

"Kid sister my ass," Cotton said, rubbing it in. "She sure doesn't *look* like anybody's kid sister anymore," and he took his right hand off the steering wheel and waggled it in a form of lecherous approval.

Kiyoshi turned back, regrouped. "You know what all the wise elders say: 'Those who come together in passion stay together in tears.' "

Cotton shook his head woefully. "I thought we made a deal a long time ago," he said. "You wouldn't give me any of that 'Confucius say' bullshit, and I wouldn't give you any *Poor Richard's Almanack.*"

Kiyoshi nodded, trumped again, and they laughed together, as Cotton drove on, moving into the Kamahameha Highway, out of the city, up into some cane fields. Finally, Kiyoshi said: "So, you wanna marry her, but can't tell her that?"

"No, I can't," Cotton said. Only he said it in Japanese: *"Tie, dekimasen."*

"Oh, we're talking Japanese now?"

Cotton didn't answer. He just pulled the car off into a little clearing and popped out. They were in the Aiea Heights, and Cotton walked away, looking down on Pearl Harbor and then *makai,* out to sea. After a while, he called back to Kiyoshi. "Know what they are?" he asked, pointing down to the ships at anchor. There were only a handful of them, the "Hawaiian detachment." The bulk of the United States Pacific fleet was moored a couple thousand miles east, in California.

Kiyoshi accepted the invitation and came over. "I don't know," he said. "I can tell you merchant vessels, but the navy ships all look the same to me, just some big and some little."

"Except the carriers."

"Yeah, right—they're the ones with airplanes on them."

"You have to get up early in the morning to put one over on Okuno and Drake," Cotton said, chuckling. Then he put his hands on his hips and shook his head. "God, Key, when was the last time we did this?"

"A long time. Kids," Kiyoshi said. When Cotton had started speaking Japanese a few minutes ago, Kiyoshi had stayed in English. They hardly recognized, consciously, what they were doing, for it was a game they had played with themselves when they were growing up, each trying to learn the other's language. When they were together, the foreigner would speak in English, the *gaijin* in Japanese. It drove other people, even bilingual people, crazy. It bound them together. And now they laughed together, remembering, and Cotton sighed, and Kiyoshi knew he was ready to talk about it, whatever it was.

Well, almost ready. First Cotton picked up a stone and threw it down the hill with all his might. Then: "I've decided to go into the ministry," he said. "Missionary—just like Dad."

Kiyoshi took a deep breath. Otherwise, there wasn't a sound. "And leave the business?" he said at last.

"And leave the business."

"Shit!"

"I'm sorry," Cotton said, returning to English.

"Damn it, Cot, you never told me this! The whole time we were talking about working together, you never even mentioned this. Not a word. Not one goddamn word! And you lay that 'mysterious East' crap on *me*."

"I didn't know then, Key. I promise you that. I just began to understand it."

"Well, what did Liz say?" Cotton dropped his eyes. "Hey, you told her, didn't you? Cotton?"

Only very softly: "No. Not yet."

"Are you nuts? You gotta tell the girl."

"I know. I'm just scared, Key."

"She won't marry a missionary?"

"No, it's the other way around. I'm not sure she *should* marry a missionary."

"She's a good girl, Liz. She's a real good girl."

"She's a great girl. But I'll tell you, it's one thing to marry a guy in the shipping business, making real good bucks, living in San Francisco, and it's another thing marrying a guy without a pot to piss in, trying to save souls out in the rice paddies."

Kiyoshi shook his head, looking sour. He was disgusted with Cotton. "Well, she's right about that. She would be crazy to marry that jerk in the rice paddies."

"I know." He hurled another rock.

This did not divert Kiyoshi. "You are crazy, Cotton. You are one crazy goddamn blue eyes."

"Key, I know I am. I love that girl. I love you. I love what we're doing. I could do this the rest of my life, till you and me are—are . . . till we're running the whole damn Pacific Ocean together! But . . . " He sighed. "It just started nagging at me."

"When?"

"I don't know. Who cares when? Maybe it was always there. Every other preacher's son I ever met in my life was all one way or the other—either a carbon copy of the old man, all sweetness and light, or a hell-raiser who denied everything his father believed. But me—me, I never fit in one way or the other. I never figured me out. All I know is, every time I'd try to get away from the church, even just a little bit—every time, it'd bring me back."

"What?"

"What?"

"*What* would? What would bring you back?"

"Who knows exactly *what?* Just *it.* Jesus. Jesus Christ would pull me back. And I'd be happier. I don't know. Maybe it *is* my calling. Goddammit." He paused. "I'm sorry," he said, looking up to God for taking his name in vain. "Forgive me," he said to Kiyoshi for going back on his promise to him.

Kiyoshi put his hands on Cotton's shoulders. "Well, I never could figure out that God of yours. It's the one Western thing I could never buy."

"Yeah." Cotton gave his cheek a little tap with his fist.

"Maybe that's why I'm so determined to keep on trying with you little bastards."

Sammy handed the telegram to Kiyoshi as soon as he and Cotton walked into the office. Kiyoshi's expression hardened. "Mutiny," was all he said. "The damn fool."

Cotton read the wire; then Sammy took it back. "What's this mean?" he asked. " 'GO TO SHRINE AS HIM'? "

"It just means Miyuki was trying to send it in English and didn't get it quite right," Kiyoshi said, his voice growing in bitterness. "It means *for* him.' Pray *for* Takeo, because the dumb sonofabitch needs it."

"She's even asking the Christian boy to get his licks in," Cotton said.

Sammy said, "Well, as the haoles say, 'Any port in a storm.' "

Liz tugged at Cotton, almost whispering: "Please, what's this all about?" As soon as the telegram had been delivered to the office, Sammy had called her room, trying to track down Cotton and Kiyoshi. Of course, Liz didn't know where they were, but the urgency in Sammy's voice alerted her, and she came right over.

"I'll fill you in," Cotton said, almost brushing her off. A few minutes ago and all he'd been thinking about was her . . . and his life, his future life, her life, her future. But ever since he'd returned to the office, ever since he'd seen the telegram from Tokyo, he'd barely acknowledged Liz's presence.

Kiyoshi was even more upset. He was rude to everyone in the office, he was so angry at Takeo. "What it means is, Liz, there are damned fools in every country, even if they might be your friends—even if they might be your oldest friends." And with that he shot a glance over at Cotton. "Tell her, Cotton—tell her all about the Land of the Rising Sun. Tell her all about what us *Japs* do. Excuse me, I gotta go outside." And he did, slamming the screen door behind him.

Sammy shrugged with embarrassment and followed Kiyoshi out into the street.

Cotton started and stopped a couple of times. Then he took Liz's Coke, and after a healthy swig he drew the cold bottle across his forehead. "Okay, okay. First, you've got to understand that Key loves Takeo. Well, so do I. And Key's in love with Takeo's sister, too. I think, anyway. In some kind of Japanese fashion."

"She's the one who sent the telegram?"

"Yeah. Miyuki. So it's all very emotional, and Key's a helluva lot closer than I am with Takeo just because he's Japanese."

"You're almost Japanese."

Cotton grinned and shook his head. "No. I told you, maybe it seems that way to you, but to them—especially to someone like Takeo, who's a purist—I might as well be a muskrat. I'm *gaijin*—the outside, forever."

"Oh, I see."

"No you don't." Liz looked hurt at the patronizing way Cotton said that. "Oh, don't take that personally, honey. I don't catch on to a lot of it either, and I've *lived* there most of my life." Cotton gestured over to the door. "You talk to Sammy any when you came over here before we did?"

"Mr. Ushijima?"

"That's right. Ushijima-san. Isamu Ushijima. Sammy. He's got a wife at home two miles from here wearing a kimono who can barely speak English. You met Darlene, the one daughter, who took Emily to the Big Island. She was a cheerleader at McKinley High. She surfs, and she imagines she's Myrna Loy. The older daughter went to Oregon State and lives in Portland. She's in a bowling league. And by now both of them practically need their father to translate what their mother is saying to them. And Sammy wears aloha shirts and clock socks, he drives a DeSoto, roots for the St. Louis Cardinals—and he's also got a Shinto shrine in his pantry. You get it? Sammy Ushijima doesn't know who the hell he is. And in a way, neither does Japan."

"Sometimes I just don't understand how you ever stood it, living over there."

Cotton looked at her, but he let it pass. "Well, you gotta understand I grew up there" was all he said.

"So, what's-his-name, Ta . . ."

"Takeo?"

"Yeah. I can't keep all those names straight. What's he so worked up about?"

"Well, Kiyoshi could probably explain that better than I could. But Takeo and his guys don't like what's changing. They're samurai—warriors—and they want to go back to that simple world where you just went around cutting the bad guys' heads off."

Liz made a shivering action. "Oh, it just sounds perfectly awful. The whole place."

Cotton let that pass, too. "Well, it's tricky. It's not like just voting the President out, or even overthrowing a dictator. Takeo and his buddies, they can't blame the Emperor. Hirohito's God, you know. He's divine. He's the father of the whole Japanese family. So the smart guys, the ones like Takeo, say, hey, it's the people *around* Hirohito. They're the evil ones. There's this new thing—*Western* thing—called democracy, and there's a depression—ergo, get rid of democracy."

"That doesn't make any sense at all."

"You tell Takeo Serikawa and his buddies that. It's a fake syllogism, which I believe I learned in Philosophy 101 back in New Haven."

"So what will happen? Will they really mutiny?"

"I guess. But you gotta understand, honey, it's not like Captain Bligh–style mutiny. It's not like *our* mutinies. I know this is crazy, but Japan is very hierarchical, and yet in some odd ways the military is the most democratic organization in the whole society."

"That doesn't make any sense either."

Cotton chuckled. "What'd I tell you? It's really very meritorious, the army. That's where the American dream lives in Japan. The army's full of all these kids off the farms. A guy like Admiral Yamamoto, who's the big military hero over there, he came from the west country, the other side of the mountains. Like some hillbilly. Dirt poor. So they feel pretty good about themselves in the military. Especially when all the smart guys are going broke. Still, everybody back on the farm is starving, and their sisters and girlfriends had to go to Yokohama to be whores."

"Oh," Liz said.

"It's winter now. The farmers are hungry. I guess mutiny's a little easier when Mom writes that she's starving."

"What'll they do?"

"Oh, if Takeo and his boys follow form, they'll assassinate some people and try to take something or other over."

"Assassinate?"

"Yeah."

"My God, Cotton—you know this guy?"

"The whole family—real well. They're wonderful people."

Liz just shook her head. "You see, darling, I'm sorry, but I just never understood how you could even think about going back and living there."

"Look, I know you're not a mean person. I know how you can feel that way, but—"

"Really, Cotton, I think any normal, sensible person would think that way. They're just not like *our* . . . people."

"But, Liz," Cotton said, groping. He gestured outside. "Key, Liz. You think the world of him."

"Oh, come on, Cotton. Key's different, and you know it. He's spent a lot of time abroad. He went to Harvard. He really doesn't even look as yellow as the rest of them anymore." Liz chuckled at that observation.

Cotton grabbed the Coke bottle back. There wasn't anything left in it, so he just rolled it across his forehead again. She was making him sweat. But the worst of it was, Liz didn't even recognize that anything she had said had bothered him—hurt him. That was the hardest part. Her feelings were ingrained in her, unquestioned. There wasn't any point in arguing with her.

"Let me tell you, though, honey, it's not that easy. Not even with Key. You know, the Japanese have a word—*minzoku*. We translate it as 'race,' because we think in those terms. But what it really means is our word 'tribe.' They're a tribe, the Japanese. They're themselves, since way back before Christ. They're not all mixed up with English blood and Irish blood and Jewish blood and colored blood and—"

"Could Key—could *he* assassinate someone?"

Cotton wasn't ready for that, and he didn't answer right away. He walked over to the door and looked at Kiyoshi, sitting there with Sammy.

"He could?" Liz asked. Persisted.

Cotton turned to her. "No, wait. I'm just trying to phrase this. All right, yes—Key could . . . I guess. If it had to be."

"Jesus."

"All right, but what about me?"

"What's that mean?"

"There was a draft, you know, just twenty years ago. Suppose that happens again? They drafted Sergeant York, and he said he couldn't possibly shoot anybody, and then when he had to, he killed all kinds of Germans."

"War's different. Battles."

"I don't know, Liz. Assassination is different to the Japanese. But it's all killing, and 'Thou shalt not kill.' Who's to say that the other tribe's murder is worse than yours?"

Liz was rattled, but she held her ground. "Assassination is cold blood."

"I guess, yes. But it is pretty accepted over there. I know this sounds crazy to you, but the Japanese sort of have more sympathy for the assassin."

"You mean, more than for the victim?"

"Yeah. Often enough. They'll figure, well, a fellow must have a real good grievance for doing that sort of thing."

"That's absolutely insane. They're simply not human. You can't—"

"We lynch Negroes, and nobody ever gets arrested." Liz had to nod, ruefully. "The last time there was a popular assassination in Tokyo, they kept the killers in jail, and other young men from all over Japan started cutting off their little fingers and mailing them in. Sympathy."

Liz held her head. She turned away from Cotton, and

when she turned back, Cotton could see that now, where there'd been disgust, there was confusion. She pushed her golden hair away from her American face, and she appeared terribly vulnerable. Because, after all, and above all, she was very much in love. "The company—" and her arms swept through the office—"they won't send you back to Japan, will they? I mean, they'll send Kiyoshi, won't they?"

"I don't know, honey," Cotton said. "It's very possible."

She stepped up and took his hands in hers. "If they do, please, go back to San Francisco and work for somebody else. Please."

"Liz, let's not talk about this now," Cotton replied. "Let's not talk about me . . . about us." He paused; she didn't know the half of it. "It's enough to think about Takeo now. Okay?" She kept looking at him. "Okay?"

She dropped his hands. "Okay? I'll be a big girl." She sighed. "So, what will happen to him?"

"Well, the odds certainly aren't with them," Cotton said. "I suppose that's why Kiyoshi's so upset. They're prepared to die, that's for sure. But death is honorable in Japan. I don't quite know what death is in the States, but it's very honorable there." Liz nodded, taking this all in. Cotton could sense, though, that she was going to plead with him again about not going back to Japan to work, so he denied her the opportunity. "Come on," he said, wrapping an arm around her. "Miyuki asked us to pray for Takeo, and so we will."

Outside, Kiyoshi and Sammy were just sitting on the curb. People were walking by, and the cars in the street, but they were just sitting there. Cotton rested a hand on Kiyoshi's shoulder. "Where's the nearest Buddhist temple?" he asked.

There were a lot of those in Honolulu; it was the largest Japanese city in the world away from Nippon itself. Even the haloes, in good humor, called McKinley High School "Mikado High." Sammy gestured behind. "Up in the valley," he said. "And there's a Shinto shrine, Izumo Taisha, even closer, just on the other side of Nuuanu."

Kiyoshi rose, like an old man, stooped and resigned. "Well,

we'll touch all the bases," he sighed, "so we might as well start with Jesus."

"Right here?" Sammy asked.

"It's as good as anywhere," Cotton said.

"Go on," said Kiyoshi, "you're the preacher."

"Well, my father was." Something flickered between Cotton and Kiyoshi, but nothing in the exchange registered with Liz. "Bow your heads," he said. He took Kiyoshi's hand, then reached to his left and took Liz's and nodded at her; she took Sammy's hand, and the four of them stood there on the busy sidewalk, holding hands, heads bowed in prayer.

"Dear God," Cotton began, "we ask you and your blessed son, Jesus, to watch after our great friend Takeo Serikawa. Help him to better understand those that he might not agree with in these difficult times in Japan, and help him to find peace with all his neighbors there. Guide him and teach him and help him to learn, for, as Jesus said, 'blessed are the peacemakers, for they shall be the children of God' . . . wherever on God's earth they may be."

Silence. A horn honked. Cotton kept his head down, and the others followed his lead. And then Cotton prayed some more. "And God," he said, "if you cannot save Takeo, then welcome him into your arms for all eternity . . . In Jesus' name . . . Amen."

They all said "Amen." And they kept standing there, holding hands, until Liz finally looked up and said, "That was beautiful, Cotton."

"We'll walk over to the shrine on Kikui Street," Sammy said.

"No, no—wait, everybody," Kiyoshi said. "Would you pray for Miyuki, too, Cotton?"

"Of course," he said, and he bowed his head, and without even realizing it, Cotton began to pray for Miyuki in Japanese. "Amen," he said in English. Then he looked over at Kiyoshi until his friend raised his eyes. "Miyuki?" was all Cotton said, softly, just smiling.

"Amen," Kiyoshi replied.

5

Colonel Carey Crane, the military attaché, handled the introductions. "Viscount and Viscountess Ishii Saburo . . ." In deference to the guests from the host country, he cited their names in Japanese style—last names first, first name last. " . . . Mr. and Mrs. Roscoe Phelps . . ."

"Evelyn, how do you do?"

"I want to hear all about your flight on the Clipper."

". . . His Excellency the ambassador from Belgium, the baron de Bassompierre, and the baroness . . ."

They shook hands with the Grews, a kiss on her cheek perhaps, or upon the hand. Most everybody felt obliged to mention the snow; there was talk now that there would be more arriving before morning.

". . . The Lord Keeper of the Privy Seal, Viscount Admiral Saito Makoto, and the Viscountess Saito," Colonel Crane boomed out.

The old man, a former prime minister among the many duties he had performed for the empire, managed to enter on his own, but it helped that he could lean a bit on the viscountess's arm as he escorted her. He was seventy-seven, but it was a full three score and seventeen. Born to poverty, he had worked his way up through the navy into politics, escaping one assassination and making few concessions to life, charging through all the days. In a nation where almost all the men drank long and hard and often not very well—there were so many cheap drunks in Japan that it was generally postulated that there must be some genetic failing when it came to alcohol—the viscount was known, with respect, as Mr. Morning. This was because once he accepted a drink in the afternoon or evening, it was his intent to drink through the night. Nearly everybody liked old Saito-san, and now, as the Grews greeted the guests of honor, the ladies and gentlemen who had already arrived applauded heartily.

And so the ambassador bowed, and the viscount bowed, and then they shook hands. Saito responded as best he could. No matter how long he and other Japanese had been in Western company, practicing Western customs, few of them ever quite got the handshake down. It was almost like properly pronouncing r's and l's—constitutionally impossible. Awkwardly, the viscount sort of let his right hand drift out, almost as if to see what Ambassador Grew might do with it. The handshake was one of the things even the most sophisticated and sensitive Westerners always laughed at when they cited all the civilized things that these funny little yellow people in their thick spectacles and crumpled suits always got wrong. Why, they couldn't even shake hands properly, the silly little devils.

". . . His Excellency the vice-consul general of Australia, the Honorable George Tremaine, and Mrs. Tremaine . . ."

"Now, Felicia," Alice Grew said, slipping her a quick kiss, whispering, "you'll be with Admiral Yamamoto tonight. I know it'll be easy for you, but be at your most charming."

"Ohhh, I already hear so much about his geisha. Kikuji."

"Not a word, not a word! Best behavior."

"Hello, Joseph dear."

"Ah, Felicia, the belle of every ball!"

". . . His Excellency the ambassador from Great Britain, Sir Robert Craigle, and Mrs. Craigle . . . His Excellency the vice-minister of the Imperial Navy, Admiral Yamamoto Isoroku, and Mrs. Yamamoto . . ."

The Grews glanced up immediately, curiosity showing on faces that had been scrupulously trained not to reveal that sort of thing. The ambassador had never met Yamamoto before, although he had filed so much background on him to Washington that he felt he must know the man. In the previous year, Yamamoto had led the Japanese naval mission to London, meeting there with a United States delegation as well, and he had returned to Tokyo without yielding a ship to the Western powers. The British and the Americans had sought to keep the same old formula of power, allowing the Japanese the right to construct three ships for every five that both the United States and England could build.

"Ah," said Admiral Yamamoto one night at dinner at Chequers, "I am not so tall as you, but would you tell me to only eat three-fifths what you do?"

He returned to Tokyo a hero, and even the crazies who wanted to assassinate almost anyone couldn't lay a hand on Yamamoto—at least for the present. The admiral had no illusions, though. His politics were too liberal; soon, he knew, the bodyguards the army had so sweetly assigned to protect him would become the men who would execute him.

Commanding as Yamamoto was, he stood small before Grew. The ambassador reckoned that he couldn't be any more than five foot three, but he appeared all the shorter, perhaps, because Reiko Yamamoto towered over her husband in her heels. She, like all the Japanese women at the party, wore a Western evening gown.

Yamamoto clicked his heels and bowed to Mrs. Grew. "Admiral," she said, "it is our distinct honor and pleasure to have you and Mrs. Yamamoto with us this evening." Yamamoto took her hand and kissed it with as much grace as aplomb. Still, a flicker of surprised admiration crossed his face. He had been advised that the ambassador's wife had grown up in Japan and spoke the language; but, like all Japanese, he was nonetheless momentarily discombobulated when the words tripped so easily from her lips. When it came to Occidentals speaking Japanese, the Japanese were reminded of Samuel Johnson's remark after he had seen a dog standing on its hind legs—that although it was not done well, he was impressed enough that it was done at all. And Alice Grew even did it well.

Ambassador Grew bowed and extended his hand, but the admiral had mastered that trick; he took it and shook it as casually and correctly, as firmly, as if he had been a guy in Evansville, Indiana, running for public office. "Thank you for coming to help us honor Viscount Saito," Grew said. "And

I'm sorry I cannot welcome you in your language. My wife is the only Grew who speaks Japanese capably."

"That's all right, sir. A Harvard education can't provide you with everything."

Grew was taken aback for an instant, and then saw the sly grin on Yamamoto's face and remembered that he'd studied in Cambridge for two years himself. "Yes," he said, recovering, "it's always nice to meet another Harvard man far from home."

"Someday, perhaps, I can also meet our fellow John Harvard in the White House."

"When next you're in America, please advise me, and I'll guarantee that Mr. Roosevelt will spend some time with you." Grew said that with assurance.

"Thank you. I will take you up on that, Mr. Ambassador."

Grew turned to include his wife in the conversation. "I had forgotten that the admiral studied at Harvard," he said.

"Oh? And what did you study there, Admiral Yamamoto?"

"I concentrated on your . . . oil industry."

"Oh," said Mrs. Grew. There was no more sensitive issue in Japanese-American relations than oil. She had assumed he was going to say something benign like "politics" or "economics."

"Don't worry," Yamamoto said, the essence of diplomacy. "This is not an evening to talk about such dreary matters. Besides"—the Grews smiled with some relief—"as much as I learned about petroleum, what Harvard taught me best was poker. I took more of a degree in poker out of Harvard."

"I've always heard how well you understand America, Admiral," Grew said.

"And respect it, too, sir. Any country that gives the world both poker and baseball is a land that I'll always appreciate and revere."

". . . The grand chamberlain to the Emperor," Colonel Crane bellowed, "Admiral Suzuki Kantaro, and Mrs. Suzuki . . ."

"Perhaps we'll have a chance to chat again," Grew said.

"At your pleasure, Mr. Ambassador," Yamamoto replied,

and he and Mrs. Yamamoto bowed to the Grews and went off to pay their respects to Viscount Saito. Old Mr. Morning had already waved off the silver champagne tray and was enjoying an old-fashioned.

6

That same evening in Hawaii—or, anyway, at about that same moment in time, but almost a day earlier—Cotton and Kiyoshi and friends all assembled for a luau on the beach in Waikiki. This was Monday night, the twenty-fourth of February. Relative to Tokyo, Hawaii was then four and a half hours late, yesterday. For example, if you were of a mind to attack Pearl Harbor at eight o'clock one Sunday morning, it would be 3:30 A.M. Monday in Tokyo when the bombs hit.

Sammy and the American Orient Export-Import Company, Hawaii branch, threw the luau in honor of Liz and Emily, who was back from her tour of the Big Island. It also provided an excuse for American Orient to invite some of its best customers, and there were hula dancers and ukelele players and caterers to provide genuine Hawaiian food, like poi, and other sorts of foods that everybody actually ate. A roast pig was the centerpiece. Both Liz and Emily got a little tiddly drinking strange, sweet pastel beverages, and they started doing the hula and saying "aloha" to each and everybody. Neither one of them could do the hula worth a damn, but all the men told them they could and encouraged them to do it some more, because they both had such great asses.

Emily was having a whale of a time because of Lieutenant Howard R. Wylie, an officer she'd met coming over on the *Lurline*. Liz thought Emily could be possibly falling in love with Lieutenant Wylie, which was a relatively easy thing to do on a beach at Waikiki, with hibiscus and banyans and ukeleles and strange, sweet pastel beverages.

Howie had a friend with him. Cotton didn't get his name;

all he understood was that he was Howie's classmate at "the Point." He was a rangy, good-looking guy, who clearly fancied himself a ladies' man, probably because he was. At the beginning of the party, he had swarmed all around Liz. An hour or so later, when she had started to hula, he spotted Cotton sitting all alone and came over. "Mind if I sit down a second?" Howie's classmate said, and Cotton nodded and introduced himself.

The guy plunked himself down. "Win Tolliver," he said.

Cotton shook his hand. "I knew a guy at Yale named Tolliver," he said, "but he spelled it funny. Let's see. T-A-L-I-A-F-E-R-R-O. Spelled like 'Tal-ee-ah-fer-roh.' "

"Yeah. Me too. It's the Taliaferro family affectation. We Anglicized the pronunciation but left the spelling.

"Oh." They watched Liz and Emily hula some more. One of the customers, a chubby Japanese, got up and tried too. The ukelele people played "My Little Grass Shack."

"Listen, can I ask you a question?" Taliaferro said.

"Sure."

"I have the feeling there's been sort of a misunderstanding here, and I'd—"

"Misunderstanding?"

"Oh no, not on your part. But see, my friend Howie, he got kinda sweet on Emily on the *Lurline* over, and he told me she had a real knockout for a girlfriend, and I oughta come by tonight and meet her."

Cotton chuckled. "Yeah, I think you can say there's been a misunderstanding."

Taliaferro got the picture. "Well," he said, "Howie got one thing right. She is a knockout."

"I know." Cotton said.

Taliaferro got up and stuck out his hand. "Okay, I think I'll get outta here."

"Hey, stick around. It's a good party. You hula?"

"No thanks. I'm shipping back to the States the end of the week, and I think I've had enough of hulas and luaus."

Before he got away, though, Liz all of a sudden got tired of dancing and stopped in mid-swivel and dashed over and plopped herself in Cotton's lap. "That can wear out your fanny," she said, and kind of nuzzled with him. She really had had a little too much to drink. "Oh, hi, Win. Have you two met?" They nodded and mumbled. "Win and Howie fly airplanes."

This obliged Cotton to feign some interest and make some conversation. "Where you stationed?"

Taliaferro wanted to clear the hell out. "Wheeler," he said, itching to go.

"Where's that?" Cotton asked, pretending an interest.

"Inland, about five miles up from Pearl."

"Oh, I'm sorry, I didn't know." Win shrugged. The ukeleles launched into "The Song of the Islands." "I never even heard of Pearl till I got out here."

"I know," Win said, and he pretended to look at his watch. "Well, I'm sorry, I gotta go."

"Are you sure?" Liz asked. "I wish we could find a girl for you."

Taliaferro said he appreciated the thought, and then they all said "see you's" and as soon as he left, Liz started nibbling on Cotton's ear.

"Hey, come on," he said, pushing her away a little.

"But I love you, darling."

"Yeah, but there's people," and he shoved her a little more, and so Liz looked up pouty and hurt, which bothered Cotton, because he knew what he had to tell her about himself, about them, about all their lives, and if a little thing like this could upset her, what would his news do to her?

She crossed her arms but stayed put in his lap. "You're still upset because of that stuff in Japan, aren't you?"

"Yes, I am. That has nothing to do with this. But . . . yes, I am."

"All right, then," Liz said, and she popped up, dusting some sand off her rear. "Aloha," she added, and she left Cotton there, punished, and went over to Emily and Howie. Cotton ducked his head, and then slowly, as the ukeleles started in to "Across the Sea," he raised it back up and snuck a look around just to make sure that nobody could possibly have been watching that awkward little scene.

Of course, someone had. Kiyoshi was leaning against a palm tree, smoking a cigarette and sipping a drink, smirking. He strolled over. "A little—what do you call that?—a snit?"

"I think that fits the definition adequately enough," Cotton replied.

Kiyoshi waited for him to say something else, even to smile or groan or spit or something, but he didn't. So Kiyoshi was a good guy and changed the subject. "I booked passage back on the *Tatsuta Maru* tomorrow."

Cotton's head jerked up. "Has something happened?"

"No, I haven't heard anything. I just sent the telegram to Miyuki. I told her to tell Takeo that I was coming home."

"Any guesses?"

Kiyoshi doodled in the sand with his bare feet. "I don't think anything will happen tonight. But . . . dawn, first light. I'd worry about that."

"Yeah, that's very—"

"Very Japanese," Kiyoshi said. "You're right. Anyway, I'm not going to wait, and the *Tatsu's* here. Sail tomorrow, we dock in Yokohama next Tuesday."

"I'm glad you're going."

"Yeah." A pause. "Now, also, listen—I'm heading over to our place in a little while to pack, and Sammy's going to put me up at his house tonight."

"No, no—don't do that, Key."

"Whatdya mean? Emily's back now. You can't take Liz back to their room at the Royal Hawaiian."

Cotton paused for a moment; the ukeleles strummed. "Pearly Shells" with special vigor. Finally: "I can't take her anywhere anymore. I've made up my mind. I'm not going to marry her."

"You're sure?"

"It won't work, Key, I know that now. Not in Japan."

Kiyoshi took a drag, pondering that. "Well, what the hell— take the house tonight, and tell her tomorrow."

"Oh, come on. You know I couldn't do that to her."

"Nothing wrong with *sleeping* on a big decision," he said with a huge grin.

"Oh, please," Cotton said, holding out his hand so that Kiyoshi could yank him up. "I'll just assume that was an attempt at a very bad joke," he said, but smiling.

"The trouble with you guys . . ." Kiyoshi replied, but smiling.

"Yeah?"

"The trouble with you guys is you're entirely too hung up on right and wrong."

" 'You guys' meaning the end product of the entire Judeo-Christian tradition?"

"Uh-huh." He took another drag. "You know what we see, blue eyes? *Yasahii and kibishii*. Gentle and rough."

Cotton waggled a finger at him, but smiling—sort of. "Naw, that's too easy, Key—gentle and rough, bitter and sweet, yin and yang. Come on: sometimes, Okuno-san, sometimes somebody has to stand up and say. 'No, that's just not *right*. You weren't just a little bit rough. You were . . . *wrong.*' Otherwise . . ." Cotton reached back down for his drink and listened again to the ukeleles for a moment.

"Otherwise what?" Kiyoshi said.

"I remember one of the first times I came into Tokyo when I was a little boy, and my father took me out to Asakusa—"

"To Sensoji?"

"Yeah, the temple, and we came in through that big gate, and there are all these stalls, all the good food, everybody buying things and having a ball, and I said: "This is a *church*, Dad?' And he laughed. And he showed me how to buy an *Omikuji* stick for good luck and breathe in the *yakuyoke* incense smoke for good health, and we bought stuff to eat and *ramune* to drink and some souvenirs, and then he showed me the shrine, people chucking a few yen in, clapping, praying. And I said: 'That's it, Dad? That's church? And he said yeah, sure is, and I knew then, I knew he was going to have one helluva time bringing any of this bunch to Christ."

"Too good a time in our church."

"Oh yeah. We were sitting there—I remember this so well,

Key. We were sitting there drinking *ramune*, and my father started reciting this poem to me. By William Blake. The Englishman."

"Hey, I went to Harvard. I know William Blake's English."

"Yeah, well, it goes like this:

" 'If at church they would give us some ale,
    And a pleasant fire our souls to regale,
    We'd sing and we'd pray all the lifelong day,
    Not ever once wish from the church to stray.' "

Kiyoshi just nodded and smiled—sort of. He thought Cotton was absolutely full of crap, but he let it go. One of the best things about their friendship was that neither one of them felt compelled to always try and get the last word in—otherwise, that's all they'd ever do. He just clapped him on the back and said: "Well, you'll make a helluva missionary, Cot. Just like your old man."

Cotton didn't say anything for a moment. He was looking past Kiyoshi to Liz. The ukeleles had started in on "Lovely Hula Hands." Finally, he just said, "Godspeed, Key," and put out his hand, and they shook American and then they bowed Japanese. But when Kiyoshi was a few steps away, Cotton called to him, and when he turned around, Cotton said softly, "Whatever happens, tell Takeo how much I love him."

7

"Admiral Yamamoto, I am E. St. George Bowersox, political attaché here." He shook the admiral's good right hand fiercely.

Yamamoto turned to his other side and introduced Bowersox to Felicia Tremaine, then helped her into her seat. After some chitchat with her, and, when the opportunity arose, a discreet peek down her magnificent bosom,

Yamamoto turned back to Bowersox. "Well," he said cheerily, "I imagine the teams are already on their way to spring training."

Bowersox looked back at him vacantly.

"Think the Tigers can repeat?" asked the admiral.

Bowersox smiled weakly.

"Baseball, Mr. Bowersox," Yamamoto finally said. "Baseball. *Your* national pastime."

"Oh," Bowersox said. "I'm afraid I'm not much of a baseball follower." It took a lot to remove the bluster from St. George Bowersox, but Yamamoto had accomplished that effortlessly, right off the mark.

"I see," said the admiral. He had completely lost interest in this fellow; he didn't hold much brief for American men who didn't follow baseball. Unfortunately, however, Admiral Yamamoto's polite overtures to Bowersox had allowed the gentleman on Felicia Tremaine's right to start boring her with a dissertation on the internal politics at the Yokohama Country and Athletic Club, so Yamamoto was stuck with Bowersox. "We're starting our own professional league this spring. Were you aware of that?"

"No, sir, I can't say that I was."

"Well, we are." He reached for a roll and noticed Bowersox glance at his two missing fingers. "I finally found an advantage to this," Yamamoto said quickly.

"To what?" Bowersox replied, off his stride again already.

"To this." He held up his left hand.

"Oh, I didn't notice that."

"Really? Everybody else does."

"Well, what is the advantage, sir?"

"Manicures," said Yamamoto. "I like to get them at the geishas'." Bowersox nodded. "If you don't care for baseball, Mr. Bowersox, I do hope you enjoy—"

"Oh yes."

"Well, I found out something that I wasn't supposed to. It costs a yen to get a manicure at the geishas', and I heard the little bitches were calling me 'Old Eighty Sen' behind my back. Get it? Ten fingers for a yen, eighty sen for eight."

Bowersox smiled weakly, trying to figure out if he was to smile at all. "So the last time I was in there, some new, young geisha—hardly more than a *maiko*—gave me the manicure, and afterwards I only gave her eighty sen and said, 'I understand I get a special price here,' and she was so mortified she had to leave the room." Yamamoto chuckled some more at the memory.

Bowersox started to jump in then, to change the topic of discussion, but he missed the opening. "Well, perhaps you've heard that we are building a new stadium in Korakuen," the admiral said.

"Yes," Bowersox fibbed. "I had heard about that."

"It's for the 1940 Olympics, but it'll also be our Yankee Stadium for baseball. Or maybe I should say our Polo Grounds. The best team we have is the Yomiuri Giants, you see. In fact, they're over in California now, playing some of your minor league teams."

"Oh," said Bowersox. He was swamped and he knew it. He'd boned up to impress the famous admiral, but the tough little sonofabitch had pulled the rug right out from under him by talking about baseball, his own national pastime, which he didn't know a damn thing about. It was as if Yamamoto hadn't known anything about tea or rice. It made Bowersox feel terribly foolish, the one emotion he most preferred to see others succumb to.

Bowersox was a smug sort, but he took the quality in himself for dash and brains. Certainly, he knew he was the smartest American serving Uncle Sam in Japan. Bowersox had been posted to the embassy only months before, late in '35; and if Ambassador Grew found any consolation in his presence it was that Bowersox was transparent—he was so obviously an in-house spy. Both Mr. and Mrs. Grew (as well as the ambassador's embassy counselor, Eugene Dooman) were generally considered in Washington to be too inclined toward giving Japan the benefit of the doubt or even to be well-meaning dupes. So Bowersox had been dispatched to keep an eye on them, to try and keep the policy more balanced, and to report back personally to Stanley Hornbeck, who, since

1928, had been the head of what everyone in Washington just called the FE: the Division of Far Eastern Affairs.

Hornbeck had been raised in the States, in the Midwest, but after college he had studied in China and then in Manchuria. Hornbeck considered the Japanese to be constitutionally duplicitous. This made U.S. policy rather simple: if the Japanese did something wrong, well, it was in keeping; if they did something right, it was clearly only to fool America in the double-dealing that lay ahead—especially in all matters that related to China. Those who could not embrace this view soon departed the FE, leaving behind a proper, monolithic policy.

In a city that even then was swamped by memoranda, nobody was a match for Stanley Hornbeck. From both his office and his bachelor apartment, he flooded the State Department—right on up to the secretary, Cordell Hull—with his confident, unyielding assessments of Japan. Any underling who disputed Hornbeck on any point was the subject of Saturday-morning harangues, delivered to the disloyal minion before the entire, cowed staff. It was a miniature J. Edgar Hooverville, and Hornbeck's ideas became more and more fixed, in a government that increasingly devoted its foreign focus to Hitler and Mussolini and the Anglo-Saxon brethren. In Washington Presidents came and went; even the parties in power changed; prosperity turned to Depression. But Stanley Hornbeck remained as the chief of the Division of Far Eastern Affairs, his view the vision of the American government when it came to Far Eastern affairs.

So it was that when Hornbeck at last became resigned that he couldn't get the amiable and distinguished Joseph Grew replaced in Tokyo, he conspired to convince Secretary Hull to dispatch at least one correct thinker to those environs—and on the first Pan American Clipper flight over the Pacific, late in '35, Emerson St. George Bowersox was returning to Asia.

Till now, too, till this dinner party, everything had gone quite smoothly for Bowersox. But Yamamoto wouldn't let up. "So, who's your favorite team?" he demanded to know. "At least you must have a favorite team."

"Uh . . . the Yankees," Bowersox replied in desperation, at last summoning up the only team he could think of under pressure.

"I hate the Yankees," Yamamoto said, flat out. "I always rooted against them when I was in America. I liked the Cardinals. They play the game more like we do. We're not as big as you Westerners, Mr. Bowersox. How big are you?"

"I'm six feet."

"And?"

"And?"

"How much do you weigh?"

"Two hundred."

"A home-run hitter's build. Too bad you never played the game. But look at me. I'm only five foot three."

"But you're a very solid man," Felicia suddenly interjected, turning to enter the conversation anew.

"Yes, of course. But we're talking baseball here. Do you know baseball, Mrs. Tremaine?"

"Not really. We play cricket in Australia."

"Well, the only good thing about being five foot three in baseball is you have a small strike zone."

"And what is that?"

Yamamoto explained a strike zone to Mrs. Tremaine. And then, on again: "Nah, I couldn't hit for much power even before I lost these." Quickly, he waved his left hand, where the two fingers had been left behind at Tsushima. "But neither can most of us Japanese. So we bunt, hit and run, work the pitcher."

"I had no idea you cared so much for baseball, Admiral," she said.

"Well, I'm hardly alone. And that's interesting. Logically, it's not a game that we Japanese should take to."

"Why's that?" Bowersox asked.

"Because of all the team sports, baseball is the most individualistic. You look at soccer, at your football or basketball, hockey—all those games depend on working together, becoming a team, depending on one another, being an integral part of the group—"

"All the things Japanese value."

"Exactly, Mr. Bowersox. But all of the team sports, baseball alone obliges each member of the team to stand alone, one by one. Take your bat and swing. Your turn. My turn. We all must stand up by ourselves and face the pitcher."

"And so why did the Japanese embrace baseball?" Mrs. Tremaine inquired.

"I suppose because it's an escape hatch. It's a game, and as such, it allows us just once to safely step outside our skin—to be like you. But it's still a team sport, and so, if you fail, if you don't get a hit, if you let the team down, you still have the team to comfort you. So really, it's a perfect game for us, and I thank you for inventing it."

"I shall have to study baseball more," Bowersox said.

The admiral turned to face him more squarely, even at the risk of being rude to Mrs. Tremaine. "And, if I could ask, Mr. Bowersox," he said, "where are you from?"

"My family is from Ohio."

"Your family? Did you grow up there?"

"No sir, I grew up in China. My father and mother were missionaries."

"Oh yes. Of course. And tell me. China is every Western-er's favorite Oriental land. Americans love looking after China. Did China ever take up playing baseball?" Bowersox had to shake his head. "Or the Phillipines, your colony now for forty years?"

"Now, now, Admiral—not our colony."

"Yes—I'm sorry. I forget sometimes. To America, only ev-erybody else's colonies are colonies. Just as only America can have a Monroe Doctrine. There are different doctrines for North America."

Felicia Tremaine just sat back and listened. She was enjoy-ing this.

"But—" Bowersox said.

Yamamoto held up his good hand. "No, no, not now. Just tell me: did they ever start playing baseball in the Philip-pines?" Bowersox had to shake his head again. "No, we Jap-anese are the only ones in Asia fond or *your* national pastime."

"What am I to make of that?"

"Well, perhaps our two countries share much more in common than anyone might have imagined—especially, perhaps, your Mr. Hornbeck." Bowersox kept a wan smile pasted on his face. "And also, perhaps I'd let us into your World Series, Mr. Bowersox. In altogether too many things, America plays by itself and imagines that's the whole world."

Bowersox replied: "And if we did *play* each other, how would you beat us?"

"Played *baseball* against each other?" Yamamoto said, smiling. He was having a great fun with this. "How would Japan *beat* the United States—" long, long, pause, then quickly—"in baseball?"

Bowersox smiled back, at last finding his chance to be mischievous.

"You're very mysterious, Mr. Bowersox, very coy, very . . . inscrutable," the admiral went on, still grinning. "Almost Oriental, wouldn't you say, Mrs. Tremaine?"

"Well," Bowersox snapped back, "your critics here say that *you* are too Americanized, Admiral."

"Ah, touché. And I'll grant you, yes, there is a certain xenophobia here. But there's also a lot of us who think it's valuable that some Japanese—like myself—have gained an insight of America. It takes time. I'm afraid a lot of us simply have no concept of your country."

"A lot of the army?"

"Oh, let's not be too harsh on my army friends. They're farm boys. But they'll learn in time how big the world is, how big you are."

"Will they, Admiral?"

"You know, unfortunately, I was on my way to London the autumn before last when Babe Ruth and his all-stars came to play here. He slugged home runs right and left, and many of my friends—even some of my colleagues in the army—wrote me saying they had no idea how powerful Babe Ruth would be, how awesome. No idea. They were overwhelmed. And I wrote them back." Yamamoto paused for effect.

"What did you write?" Felicia asked, taking her cue for the straight line.

"I simply wrote: 'You see? Now you see.' Only a fool would want to play baseball against Babe Ruth."

"So, all right, how do you win, Admiral?" Bowersox asked, pressing Yamamoto with relish. "If you want us to let Japan into the World Series, then how do you beat us?"

Yamamoto paused for a moment and lit Felicia's cigarette. "I think what I would do, Mr. Bowersox, is that I would contrive something very dramatic so as to convince Babe Ruth that there's really no need for him to play against us, that it would profit both of us for him to take his big bat and go hit home runs somewhere else."

8

"Hey," Cotton said, "let's take a walk down the beach." The luau was finishing up, and Liz, who was pleasantly, harmlessly high, had her arms draped around his neck, making terrible plays on the word "lei." He tried to disentangle her; there were still a few folks around. "Come on, we'll head up Waikiki."

"Do we have to?" she pouted. "I'm your lei." He didn't smile. "Don't you get it?"

He just frowned, so she winked at him and skipped in the little waves, laughing gaily, making it all the worse for him.

"Come on, Liz."

"Oh, come on yourself." She was right and he knew it. "All right, Mr. Party Pooper, come on and let's go skinny-dipping," she cooed, and she came back to him and reached out for a button on his shirt.

"Hey, Liz—now cut that out." She was surprised how harshly he threw her hand off him. If she hadn't been a little bit drunk, she would have realized how terribly wrong Cotton was reacting to everything. But she was, and so she couldn't.

So she just pretty-pouted. "I'm sorry, darling. I never went skinny-dipping before . . . with a *boy*. But then, I never even made love before you."

"Hey, come on, Liz."

Suddenly, with that, she stopped being silly. "No—hey, come on, Cotton. *You* come on." He turned away from her. "Cotton," she called softly after him. "Come on."

He knew exactly what she meant: that he propose to her—sweetly, formally. He knew, too, that he could not avoid the subject anymore. And so he looked out over the ocean and took his breath in, and then he turned back, and he told her that she was the only girl he had ever loved and that he loved her with all his heart. "And," Cotton said, "Liz, I can't marry you."

She tilted her head when he said that. In fact, she reminded him of a dog he had once that cocked his head that way when he was confused. "I'm going to be a minister. A priest. I'm going to the seminary this fall."

"I didn't know." It seemed to him that she might cry, but she was still to mixed up. She was utterly in shock.

"I didn't really know myself."

"You what?"

"I said, I really didn't know myself."

She put her hands on her hips. "You didn't know? What the hell does that mean?! You didn't know?" After that first blow, when she'd been knocked out on her feet, Liz's head was clearing, and now she started to cry. She turned away, and when Cotton approached her to console her, she elbowed him away and put another step between them for emphasis. Only then did she wipe at her eyes and turn back. "You knew all along, didn't you?"

He tried to shake his head. "No. No, Liz, I—"

"Yeah, you just put this off till you could bring me out here and fuck me awhile."

Cotton swallowed at that. Ladies didn't say "fuck" then. Even gentlemen didn't say "fuck" in polite company. This was long before "fucking" as an all-purpose, quotidian adjective, replaced "damn" in nice people's conversation.

"Liz!"

"Don't play holy with me, Cotton. You're worse than one of those guys Jesus was always arguing with. The . . . whatdya call 'em?"

"Pharisees?"

"Yeah. That's you, Cotton."

"Liz, I swear, this has been going on in my mind for months . . ." He made the mistake of trying to approach her again, and Liz backed up, and when she found that she was in the water, she purposely drew one leg back and kicked as much water as she could on him. It wasn't that much. So she backed up a step, where the water was a little bit deeper, and she kicked again, and again, splashing Cotton lightly, but all over. He just stood there, wet, the water hitting him here and there, and running down.

"I am sorry, Liz," he finally said, his voice breaking low. "I am so sorry."

"You could have asked, Cotton." She stopped kicking.

"Asked what?"

"What?" She kicked again. "You could have asked me. 'Hey, I'm thinking about leaving business and being a preacher. If you love me, you wanna be a preacher's wife?' You could have asked that. I'm confirmed, you know. I'm a Christian, too."

"I thought about it."

"Yeah, sure. But you were afraid I'd say no thanks and then you wouldn't get to fuck me for a week in Hawaii."

Cotton reached out and grabbed her by the shoulders. "Dammit, Liz, cut that out. That's not true."

"So what? So you decided to become a preacher because I didn't fuck *good* enough?" Liz was like a little child now, saying the dirty word for effect just to irk him.

"That's not true, and you know it." He paused. "As a matter of fact, you're the best fuck I ever had." Then he took his hands off her shoulders. "There, how you like those apples?" Liz began to sniffle a little again, but he made a half-turn away, looking up toward where the moon shone on Diamond Head. "Listen, I thought about it. I'd tell myself, sure, Liz could be a preacher's wife, and it'd be terrific, and we'd have a nice little church in the best part of town with a whole bunch of Episcopalians from Yale and Philadelphia and Cape May, just like us, and they'd let us in the country club and let our children in the right schools, and everybody's think we were so terrific because I'd be working for God. Probably even God would think I was terrific, too ... you know, if I just played my cards right."

He was being strictly facetious; unfortunately, she saw a glimmer of hope. "Well, Cot, is that so bad?"

He shook his head. "No, I guess not. Only what I finally understood was that wasn't what it was all about." He paused. "It was about Japan."

Liz scrunched up her nose. "You mean be a missionary? Like your parents? In *Japan?*"

He nodded. "Yeah. And I wouldn't ask any girl who hadn't grown up with it to do that with me."

"Oh, I see. So you'll marry some biddy who plays the organ, with her hair up in a bun."

Even Cotton had to smile at that, but he covered his mouth quickly to make sure she couldn't see that she might be getting to him. Then, back on track: "It's just too different for you, Japan. I kept telling myself that you could be happy there, but then, finally, this morning—"

"What about this morning?"

"You know, when we heard about Takeo and—"

"So what about it?" She was so angry, so confused, she was almost screaming.

"I could tell, Liz. You could never like them. Never. You could never live that life in some little Japanese town out in the middle of—"

"What are you talking about, Cotton? We were talking about some goddamn nuts going around assassinating people and cutting off their fingers and—" Liz was so frustrated at that that she reached out like a little girl and banged her fists on his chest.

"Stop it, Liz!" It was the first time he'd even raised his voice, and it wasn't by much, but she did stop. "It wasn't all nuts we were talking about, honey. We were talking about the Japanese."

And this time she just shook her head at him. "I don't get it, Cotton. I don't understand. You and those little, ugly people. You can't do anything for them. If they're going to go around killing each other, it's too late for the Ten Commandments."

"Lizzie, listen—I grew up with the Japanese, and I love them, and if I don't reach out to them with Christ, we're going to end up fighting each other."

"How 'bout loving me?" she asked. *"Did* you? Just tell me that truth. Did you ever, really, love me?"

"Oh, Lizzie, I love you now. Still. I probably always will."

"Then you're just an ass, Cotton Drake. What are you, some martyr? Are you showing off for Jesus?" For the moment, the moon broke out from behind a cloud and fell across her face. Even with the tears and the red eyes, she'd never looked so pretty to him.

"You wouldn't be happy there. And I can't make someone I love so unhappy," he said softly.

"Try me. Is that so wrong?" She stepped up close to him and looked into his eyes. He reached out and touched her cheek, and just then the moon went back in. It wasn't dark; the stars were still all over the sky. That's the way this should be, Cotton thought. The moon and the rising sun belong to Japan. It's right we only have the stars here now.

"Sometimes it isn't a matter of right and wrong—it's just a matter of gentle and rough," he said. "It would be too rough."

She could feel the tears forming in the back of her eyes again, and she didn't want to let him see her cry again. Quickly, then, Liz reached out and kissed him on the lips, and before he even knew it she had pulled away. "Goodbye, you fool" was all she said, and then she was running away, stumbling down the beach, weaving in and out of the little waves. Cotton thought about running after her, but he stopped himself, because when he caught up with her, what could he do? He couldn't kiss her, because that would lead her on, and he couldn't argue with her, because he wasn't at all sure that he wouldn't end up taking her side.

There were eight comfortable chairs arrayed before the movie screen in the salon, and, after the toasts, Ambassador Grew escorted Viscount Saito to the softest chair of all. The Lord Keeper of the Privy Seal plopped down in it, the viscountess to his one side and Admiral Yamamoto to his other. Mrs. Yamamoto, the Suzukis, and the Grews took the other seats of honor; and as the other guests settled in their chairs, *Naughty Marietta* began, words and music and noises all.

Grew kept sneaking peeks over at Saito, for the Japanese as a rule were early to bed, and he was fearful that old Mr. Morning might nod off at any moment. The ambassador needn't have worried, though, for even as the movie rolled past Viscount Saito's bedtime, he remained enthralled, glowing like a kid, poking Yamamoto on his one side and his missus on the other, exulting in the wonders of Jeanette MacDonald and Nelson Eddy singing right before his very ears.

Grew shook his head and, with respect, stared at the old fellow. It was difficult, even for a world citizen as sophisticated and mature as the ambassador, to contemplate, in its full range and metamorphosis, the incredible span of life of any Japanese of Saito-san's age. Why, he had been born hardly after Commodore Perry had forced the veil to be lifted around the islands, and he had grown up at a time when samurai still walked the land, their hands poised on the hilts of their huge swords, serving feudal masters in a quaint confederation that lacked a constitution and any pretense of the seventeenth century, let alone the nineteenth. Grew looked back down at Saito and Suzuki and Yamamoto, and then he chuckled to himself and touched his mustache: it was as if Thomas Jefferson, Benjamin Franklin, and Paul Revere were sitting here, watching sound movies with him.

And yet, by the time Saito had begun approaching middle age, Japan was already advanced enough to whip the vast

Chinese dragon; just another decade and it had routed the huge Russian bear and sent it skulking back to the West. Now, still in his lifetime, Japan demanded equal footing about the face of the earth with the British Empire and the United States of America—and it seemed quite prepared to do whatever was necessary to obtain that purchase. But why not? In the blink of history, only since Saito was a young man, the Japanese had taken to wearing strange new clothes and going to school; they had learned to read and write, to build factories and railroads; from scratch, they had constructed great ships that carried their new products, however invariably shoddy they were, to every corner of the blue-eyed globe. Made in Japan!

Indisputably, no other cohort anywhere on earth at any time had lived their years such as Viscount Saito and his island colleagues—moving pell-mell, rumbling forward in one short lifetime through centuries past. And it was made all the more ironic since now, for all they had accomplished, barely a mile away from where Saito-san sat, younger Japanese were planning his murder. But in Japan then, whatever the changes, death remained cheap and murder particularly articulate.

Jeanette MacDonald held a note, and Grew peeked back down the first row to Saito and Suzuki and Yamamoto. They were so damned impressive, medals and braid and faces of steel, obviously ready to take on the world (or settle for a good part of it); but at the same time, their uniforms—and their wives' gowns—fitted over such short little bodies that they looked like children playing dress-up. The great Yamamoto's feet barely reached the floor from his big chair, and so many of them had bent, barrel legs that the Japanese themselves thought that their women took after radishes. Clothes wrinkled naturally on them. Their faces were hard for *gaijin* to accept. Japanese teeth protruded; smiles were jack-o'-lantern; too many of them had bad eyes, and all of them seemed to be the wrong dull shade. They came naturally to doing most things backwards from what Westerners did, and they talked funny and walked funny and sat funny, too, on their haunches, seldom employing the rear end that God had provided for that specific purpose. Altogether, they had been stuck alone on their little islands for so long that they didn't even come up to the same temperature as other human beings; "normal" for Japanese was 96.8, not 98.6.

They are still a work in progress, Grew thought. But, of course, the ambassador (as Stanley Hornbeck at FE kept telling Secretary Hull and President Roosevelt) was generous. The Japanese were certainly different, though. Everybody is different, Grew thought, but right now the Japanese are more different than anybody that matters in the world ever would be again.

When the movie ended, the viscount was still so wide awake that he stayed for the light supper afterwards, and it was eleven-thirty before he and the other guests began to leave.

"I enjoyed our discussion," Bowersox said, reaching Yamamoto at the door, "and I would love to continue it some other time."

"Of course. But on one condition, Mr. Bowersox—that we resume our conversation at a baseball game. I'm used to Americans instructing me about Asia. I would welcome the occasion to teach an American about baseball."

Bowersox forced a smile. Yamamoto turned and bowed to the Grews and the Suzukis; then he took Viscount Saito's arm and helped him to the door, bidding his wife offer the same assistance to the viscountess. The temperature was below freezing again, the snow crusted, the path slick. "Ah, it's like Kushigun Sonshomura," Yamamoto said as they came into the night. That was the little hamlet he grew up in, the raw and desolate west country, on the wrong side of the Japanese Alps, where the winds blew down from Siberia and kept the winter on ice for months. "I was so poor, Saito-san," Yamamoto said, "that in the winter, when we moved about through ice tunnels, I only had kimono and sandals to wear— nothing else. I can remember my fingers freezing up as I tried to learn to write my ideographs."

"So much has changed," Saito said. "So much for one people. Don't these boys in the army who cry out about wiping out poverty and telling the rest of the world what to do—don't they understand anything?"

"Come now, it's time for us all to go home, Saito-san."

"Me, anyhow, Admiral. There is still more for you to do. You must not let the army run wild." Suddenly, as they reached the viscount's limousine, the snow began to fall again, the flakes large, graceful as they tumbled upon Tokyo. "Look," the old man said, chuckling. "They almost look like cherry blossom petals. For a moment, I thought the spring was here already."

9

In Japan, elementary school children kept the same teacher year after year, and when Cotton returned to the mission at Aimoto and went into the fourth grade after his parents had taken a year's sabbatical in the States, the teacher he'd had since first grade, old Saburo-sensei, asked him to enlighten his classmates on the differences between Japan and the United States. The schools were still rather open-minded then, not yet indoctrinated by military nationalism.

But Cotton was no fool. His parents had carefully impressed on him how unusual it was for a *gaijin* to be allowed into any Japanese school. It was only because the town was so small that the people all knew the Drakes as good friends, unusually understanding of Japan and its ways. So Cotton's list of American-Japanese differences was predictable, and presented blandly, without prejudice. He cited silverware instead of chopsticks, suits instead of kimonos, chairs instead of tatamis, driving on the right instead of the left, and so forth. Saburo-sensei smiled at this benign recitation.

But then another little classmate pipe up and asked: "What does Kiyoshi say? Kiyoshi has lived in the United States, too."

"Ah, yes," said the teacher, giving the floor to Kiyoshi, who rose.

"All that my friend Cotton tells you is true," he said. "But for children, I think, the biggest difference between our countries is the stories grown-ups tell you, the books, the movies you see."

The old teacher nodded. This was quite a sophisticated response for a ten-year old, but Kiyoshi was both the brightest and the most mature child in the class, so he was not altogether surprised. "Can you give us an example, Kiyoshi?"

"Yes, Teacher. In America, everybody tells stories about the cowboy."

"The cow . . . boy?"

"Yes. He is in the West, and he is all by himself, fighting Indians and bad men. Alone on his horse."

"Is this true, Cotton?"

"Oh, yes, Teacher. The cowboy's brave. He always wins."

"If I was an American, I would want to be a cowboy," Kiyoshi said, and he pulled out two imaginary six-shooters and pointed them around, making shooting noises. All the boys laughed and all the girls snickered. "But in Japan, we don't have any cowboys. Our stories are about *ronin*, and the *ronin* are not as good as cowboys. They cannot—"

"Okuno Kiyoshi—silence!" the old teacher thundered.

Kiyoshi bowed his head. So did Cotton. So did every student in the classroom. Never, in all their four years in school, had they ever heard such a bold, independent statement; never, either, had they seen Saburo-sensei so beside himself. *"Ronin* are among the most gallant of Japanese. Many fought to restore the glory of our imperial Japan. Do you understand that, Kiyoshi? Did any of your cow-boys ever do so noble a thing?"

"But the *ronin* all die. Who wants that? The cowboys in America go wherever they want, and they win. Don't they, Cotton?"

Cotton looked over. He didn't want to get involved here; and, luckily, he was saved by Mr. Saburo, who held up his hand to the little American boy and said: "Please, no more.

Clearly, I must help you all understand by telling the wonderful story of the forty-seven *ronin* better. Sit down, Kiyoshi." He did, sneaking a sideways glance at Cotton. "Now, how many of you have heard of the forty-seven *ronin?*"

Naturally, every hand shot up, for every mother's child in Japan had been told the tale. Poems were written about the forty-seven *ronin,* songs sung to them, Kabuki acted, and plays, and doll theater, then movies. It was like George Washington and the cherry tree, the Boston Tea Party, the Alamo, and Ben Franklin flying his kite all rolled into one and raised to another power. There was even a special memorial holiday, December 14, Gishi-sai, celebrated still in honor of the forty-seven, dead all before Franklin and Washington were born. "But perhaps some of you—perhaps you, Kiyoshi—do not altogether understand the glorious story. Is that possible, Kiyoshi?"

"Perhaps, Saburo-sensei."

"So listen carefully now. In March of 1701, a minor lord named Asano was insulted by Kira, who was the chief minister of the shogun. A very pompous fellow, Kira; and, regrettably, he made Asano so angry that he drew his sword on Kira. It was a great insult to the chief minister. And so, what was Asano called upon to do?"

The hands shot up all over the room, and Saburo called upon a big boy to the side. "Commit seppuku," he called out.

The old teacher nodded solemnly. "But then what happened? Who entered the picture?" The hands went up again. "Yes, yes, say it—all of you."

"The *ronin,*" came back the voices.

"How many?"

"Forty-seven."

"Yes, yes. Indeed. Oishi was first. Loyal, brave Oishi. He was a samurai who had served Asano. Oishi was heartbroken at his master's death, but also distressed for himself. For now, children, without a master, he was no longer a samurai. He was only a *ronin.* So what did Oishi do?"

This time, not all the hands shot up. The story was getting more complicated. But Cotton was one who had raised his hand, and it was he Saburo called on. "So, does our *gaijin* know the story of the forty-seven *ronin* better than some Japanese children?"

Cotton frowned; he didn't want to show any of his friends up. But still: in for a penny, in for a pound. He spoke up directly. "Oishi pretended, Saburo-sensei."

"Ah? How so?"

"He pretended to be a drunk and maybe a little crazy, too."

"Oh? Why?"

"Oishi wanted to mislead Kira. All the time he was going around acting drunk, he was really rounding up Asano's other samurai."

"Yes, yes," Saburo went on, enjoying the story as much as the kids. "And sure enough, at last Oishi and the other forty-six *ronin* were ready to strike back. So, on December 14, 1702, they swept down on Kira's castle, caught him by surprise, and cut off his head . . . And where did they take it? Kiyoshi?"

"The forty-seven *ronin* took Kira's head to the temple of Sengaku-ji."

"Yes. Why? Why there, Kiyoshi?"

"Because, Saburo-sensei, it was there at Sengaku-ji that their master's ashes had been buried by a plum tree."

"Ah yes. So you do know the story, Kiyoshi. And perhaps someday, perhaps when you are in Tokyo, you may visit Sengaku-ji."

"I would hope so, sir."

"Because, of course, soon all of the forty-seven would lie there with their lord Asano." Old Saburo was growing ever more emotional and theatrical, marching about, throwing his arms out, his voice rising. "As much as the devoted example of allegiance to their master charmed the great shogun, of course, he simply could not tolerate this sort of disobedience to the order of Japanese society, and so he decreed that all forty-seven *ronin* must be executed." He shook his head. But then, quickly, a bright smile, and: "But the *ronin* were granted one wonderful concession, weren't they?"

Everybody murmured a yes, and Saburo barreled ahead. No more questions. He was saving the climax of the story strictly for himself: "Yes. In honor of their gallant fealty to their master, the forty-seven *ronin* were permitted to commit seppuku. Wasn't this a grand honor?"

Saburo looked around the room, all the students dutifully nodding—except over in the corner, where, when the teacher turned away, Kiyoshi turned to Cotton and screwed up his face. "An honor? To kill yourself?" he whispered. Cotton suppressed a little smile.

"So, you see, the gracious shogun allowed the forty-seven *ronin* to die like the samurai they had been. And most happily, then, they all assembled at Sengaku-ji, and one by one, Oishi first, they shed their last life's blood before the grave of their beloved lord Asano."

Saburo sighed, then smiled beatifically down on his class. How he loved telling his students the saga of the forty-seven *ronin!* After all, it was perhaps the quintessential Japanese story—no lone wolves here, no cowboys, and culminating in self-slaughter, that uniquely Japanese badge. Suicide in the West was no good business for brave men; and over and above the canons of Christianity, it marked a man as a quitter, an escapist—it was "the coward's way out." But in Japan, the way one died could validate a whole life; and *isagi-yosa*, dying without any regrets, was something men planned for their whole adult lives.

"Any warrior must be prepared to die on the job, Kiyoshi," the teacher concluded. "You see now?"

"Yes, Teacher," Kiyoshi said, as he was supposed to.

"You all see what noble Japanese the *ronin* were?"

"Yes, Teacher," they all said, Cotton the loudest.

"Good. Now we will do our sums."

When Kiyoshi and Cotton were walking home that day, though, Kiyoshi said: "I had to show Saburo-sensei respect and agree with him, but I can tell you, I'd rather be a cowboy than a *ronin*."

"But you can't . . ."

"Why can't I?"

"Because there aren't any Japanese cowboys, that's why. The Japanese are *ronin*."

"That's not fair," Kiyoshi said.

"Come on," said Cotton. "Let's play baseball. We can both be baseball players."

And so it was hardly surprising that years later, on the afternoon of February 25, 1936, Captain Takeo Serikawa found time to depart the barracks and go to the temple at Sengaku-ji, where the forty-seven *ronin* were buried. It was a long trip, requiring a streetcar transfer, but he made it before the winter's night fell, and he trudged up the hill in the snow and paid homage to them all, bowing at Oishi's grave.

A few hours later, the day had turned, and it was two o'clock in the morning of Wednesday, February 26, 1936—what would become known simply as *ni/ni-roku:* 2/26. At the First and Third Regiment barracks, a few blocks from the Imperial Palace, reveille sounded. The young soldiers staggered out of bed and assembled in formation, surprised to discover that it was still the middle of the night. Most of them concluded that some sort of special maneuvers must be in the offing, and in a way this was true.

It was a bizarre gathering, for whereas everything was being conducted in the open, and rumors of some sort of impending incident had been flying about the army for days, no one over the rank of captain appeared on the premises. Takeo and the other young bloody ideologues had taken over, and so the senior officers prudently stayed abed, playing possum.

Major Tanaka was there, a callow sublieutenant then, and he told Miyuki all about it seven years later, one afternoon when he had her over to his quarters to scrub his back. There'd been some guerilla action a few miles away, and the major was particularly tired and wet, the dust and the jungle bags pasted to him. "Your brother was wonderful," Tanaka told her. "It's still so vivid."

The young leaders had started screaming at the troops as soon as they formed ranks. Takeo's friend, Captain Koda, was the first speaker, the firebrand. "You are samurai, and I invite you to die for the Emperor!" he hollered. "Die with me! Die with Serikawa!"

The soldiers shifted on their feet, quite happy to die for Hirohito, of course, but not altogether sure why. It wasn't quite like "Take this hill!"

Koda started enumerating all the evil that surrounded them. There was corruption and greed in the government but poverty and hunger in the land. The Western world laughed at Japan, placing unfair limitations on its naval power. The Americans wanted the Pacific for themselves. They hated Asians and wrote special laws to keep them out. The honor of the Sun-Begot Land was tarnished, the national essence—*kokutai*—besmirched. Who but those here could save the nation, save the Emperor? "Join me—join me!" Koda bellowed.

"I was so confused," Tanaka told Miyuki, as she kept on scrubbing his back. "And young as I was, I was an officer. I came from a big city. Most of the troops had no idea."

"And so what did you do, Major?" Miyuki asked, moving to wash his legs.

"Nothing. I was scared to move. I hated Koda. I wanted to hear from your brother. I admired him."

"You're just saying that."

Immediately, Tanaka cuffed Miyuki—not only enough to make the point but almost enough to knock her off balance. "*Oi*, don't dispute me, woman! Everyone admired Serikawa Takeo."

"Yes, I know, Major. I apologize." She rubbed her cheek where he'd struck her.

"And so I waited, looking over to my friends."

The farm-boy soldiers searched about even more helplessly for guidance. Rootless and disenfranchised, most of them were probably less afraid of death than they were of the wrath of the hideously cruel sergeants who controlled their unexamined lives. "Join us!" Koda cried. "Join the Emperor! Save our Japan!"

The movement forward began then. The hotheads first; that was easy. Next across the line came others not so sure—

one or two, perhaps a sergeant followed by his cowed squad, some more here, some over there. The ranks were filling, but still not with nearly as many as were needed. There were a lot of assassinations planned, a lot of evil *genro* to be murdered; and the clock was running: the bloody deeds were all to be accomplished, simultaneously, by dawn.

"Captain Koda got angrier and angrier," Tanaka went on. "His voice was growing shrill. It even seemed to me that the mutiny was dying out, and I was ready to turn and leave."

"But you didn't."

"No, because that's when I saw your brother step up from behind Koda. And I waited. I could see what Takeo was doing, looking for an opening, and when he found it, he moved ahead of Koda, and he took his long sword out of its scabbard—"

"It was my father's sword."

"Yes. And all he did was hold it high. Not a word. And suddenly, the whole place was dead silent." Even the dimmest rubes from the hick prefectures knew that Takeo's father, Colonel Serikawa, had been the highest-ranking Japanese killed in Manchuria—in fact, the ranking soldier lost in the Emperor's duty since the Russian War in 1904.

"Do not let my father's death go in vain," Takeo began, and the troops nodded reverently. "He took Manchukuo for us, and now we must take Japan back for him. Russia and China, England ... the United States are within a hair's breadth of ensnaring our land of the gods and destroying our culture, our bequest from our ancestors. Can't you see this? Isn't this clear? Isn't there light in the fire?"

The troops up front, the ones who had already committed themselves to the coup, began to cheer; but Takeo held up his sword and stilled them. "This is no time to cheer. It is a time to act. We must show the nation that we—we young men— can preserve our land. We must do it. I'm sorry, Captain Koda, we are not samurai. We have no masters. We are *ronin!*" There was a murmur, and Takeo screamed it out this time: "We are *ronin!*"

Takeo swung his father's sword once more, wielding it in

the proper fashion—both hands on the long hilt, which was purposely fashioned that way, so that the samurai could swing it all out, completely on the attack, without any ability to be safe, to defend. Around and around he waved the great sword. "And *I* am the forty-eighth *ronin!*" he cried, and the men roared back at him.

There was not a man or boy among them who did not know that the forty-seven lay at Sengaku-ji, only three miles away. And they all knew, too, that that night two hundred and thirty-four years ago when the forty-seven *ronin* took off Kira's head and brought it to Asano's grave was a night when it snowed heavily in Tokyo, when the city was blanketed in white. The omen was clear on this snowy night, all the more so for what white means in Japan. Brides wear white, but not for purity: no, white stands for death in Japan. And for rebirth.

"And on this night of snow, you too are the forty-eighth *ronin,*" Takeo shouted, pointing at a sergeant who had already pledged his service. Louder roars. "And *you* are the forty-eighth *ronin!* And you —and you—and you!" The cheers rose with each citation, then fell back, then louder still, louder again, louder, louder. Takeo waved his father's sword one more time, and then he held out his hand to the soldiers in the back, the ones who had stood their ground. And this time he spoke softly, so that they had to lean forward to hear him. They were almost falling toward Takeo. "And any one of you—you, or you, or you there—any·one of you who join us is the forty eighth *ronin.*"

It was electric, and more and more of the soldiers pressed forward then, some of them screaming "Banzai! May you live ten thousand years—may Japan!" or calling Takeo's name, surging, screaming.

"And you, Major!" Miyuki asked, washing his feet now.

"I started forward. When Takeo called, I followed his voice. But"—Tanaka sat up in the bath, growing more animated—"then I stopped. You know, I really didn't believe what he believed."

"So you stayed behind?"

Tanaka smiled. "No, I went. It was all so emotional. It was scary. Even the ones who didn't go along—no one blew the whistle. We were all so young, so confused. That's why, finally, I went along. Because even if I couldn't believe what your brother said, I could believe in him." Miyuki smiled. "Oh, he was magnificent that night. Quite a man, your brother."

"Yes."

"And so we went out. I was even assigned to your brother's group—the ones going to Viscount Saito's."

"You were right with Takeo?"

"Well, yes and no. It was a big contingent—a couple hundred men or more. Even some of the Imperial Guards signed up—the Emperor's own guard. It was for the Emperor, you know. We were doing it all for him. For Japan."

"Yes, I remember," Miyuki said.

"So I hung back. I guess I still wasn't sure. But I remember Takeo. I remember especially how he reminded us all that we must be courteous and not upset anybody if we could possibly help it."

"You mean . . ." She paused. "When you were killing them?"

"Well, yes. After all, Takeo reminded us how polite the forty-seven *ronin* had been to the family and the servants and everybody when they cut off Kira's head."

"Of course."

And indeed, all the rebels were most courteous. After Captain Ando fired three bullets flush into Admiral Suzuki, he had his men kneel by their fellow warrior and present arms to him. "I am particularly sorry about this," the captain told Mrs. Suzuki.

At the house of the finance minister, Korekiyo Takahashi, after the rebels shot him and lopped off his right arm and disemboweled him, the lieutenant in charge, Nakahashi, apologized to Mrs. Takahashi for the mess. "Excuse me for the annoyance I have caused," he said.

Tanaka went on. "It was a little tricky at Saito's. Did your brother tell you about it?" She shook her head. "You've read about it, then?"

"No. Afterwards, I could never bring myself to."

"I understand."

"No, but Tanaka-san, please, tell me now. I would like to hear," Miyuki said, pouring water over the major's head.

"I didn't see it all, of course," he began, "because I wasn't up close. But I heard from the others that night. The trouble began after they pumped the bullets into Saito. After he raised up on his futon and your brother nodded, and they shot." He paused, checking his memory. "Three times, I think. Two, three, four. But then the viscountess threw her body over her husband's. 'Kill me instead.' she said."

"Oh my."

"Yes. Your brother said, 'Be careful of the viscountess.' So they had to work around her, you know."

"Shooting him some more?"

"Oh, a lot more. I could hear where I was, by the front door. Thirty, forty, maybe fifty bullets." Miyuki swallowed. "And then one sergeant stepped up with his revolver. Mean guy—can't remember his name, but from Nagoya. I remember that. And he started to shoot the old man in the temple. And the old lady, you know what she did?" Miyuki shook her head. "She just put her hand over the gun. Right over the mouth of the gun."

"So he didn't shoot?"

"No, no. Tough sonofabitch, the sergeant from Nagoya. Shot her hand—the old lady's hand. But she kept it right there on her husband's head."

"But he's already dead?"

"Oh yeah. Fifty bullets?" Tanaka shrugged. "So another sergeant stepped forward with a knife to cut his throat—"

"But he was already dead."

"Can't be too sure, I guess. Anyway, Mrs. Saito managed to inch forward so that she could lie across her husband's neck. The sergeant tried to budge her. Gingerly at first. Couldn't move her."

"Where was Takeo?"

"Right there. In charge."

"Oh. Of course."

"Then the sergeant yanked at her, and this time he got her off the neck. But that old lady—damn if she didn't flop herself back on his neck! And the sergeant started to grab her again, and that was when your brother stepped forward and held the sergeant's arm and said: 'It's okay, Yuzuru.' I remember—that was the sergeant's name, Yuzuru. I still can't remember the one from Nagoya. But Captain Serikawa took his arm and said, 'It's okay, Yuzuru. Let it be.' "

"And then you left?"

"Well, first your brother had everyone light candles. In respect for the viscount. He'd had us bring candles. And then at the door to the room—I could hear this from where I was at the front door—he said, to the viscountess, he said: I'm sorry, madam. I'm sorry, but I'm sure you understand.' "

"And what did she say?" Miyuki said.

"I don't think she said anything. I'm not sure Takeo expected her to. Right then, after that, at the front door, where I was, Takeo had us shout three banzais. In celebration. And then, after we left the house, Takeo had us go to a shrine and give thanks."

"I see," said Miyuki. "I appreciate your telling me, Tanaka-san." She made sure to stay behind him then, working vigorously on soaping his hair, so that he wouldn't know she was crying.

The next day, after the murders, from his suite at the Sanno Hotel downtown, which the rebels had commandeered as their headquarters, Takeo called his mother and sister at their home up in the Asakusa section of the city. He assured them that he was well and that the gods appeared to have favored their noble efforts. Besides killing a good number of their targets, the mutineers had taken over the prime minister's residence and police headquarters and a few newspapers, too. The banners of rebellion flew above the captured buildings, standing out brazenly against the slate-gray sky. In Tokyo it was said, "The day after a snowfall is the poor man's washing day," but this time the sun knew better, and it stayed away, the weather still grim and raw and dark and ominous.

But surely now, Takeo told Miyuki, it must be as clear to the Emperor how he had been deceived by the traitors around him, and only saved in the nick of time by the men of *ni/ni-roku*. Miyuki concurred. It certainly was obvious enough to her, she said.

She passed on some messages to her brother from well-wishers, including a radio telegram that had come from Kiyoshi at sea: TATSUTA DOCKING TUESDAY STOP TELL TAKEO WILL COME IMMEDIATELY TO SEE HIM STOP COTTON SENDS PRAYERS TOO.

"That's all?" Takeo asked.

"Yes."

"He doesn't send his support in the cable?"

"It's very expensive, telegrams from a ship," Miyuki replied.

"I'd rather have Kiyoshi's support as a Japanese than Cotton's prayers from his Jesus."

Miyuki did not tell her brother that she had originally solicited Cotton's help from the Christian deity. "Kiyoshi's support is obviously behind any words he might cable," she said. "He's coming to you himself. He had no plans to return to Japan for now. He only booked passage when he heard."

"All right," Takeo said, backing down a little. But it was hard for him to concede any gray in the world now. There were the rebels, the true believers, and then there were all the others. The only one who could be allowed in the middle was the Emperor.

"Have you heard what Tenno Heika is thinking?" Takeo asked. "Tenno Heika" was the specific term the Japanese used to refer to their emperor, as opposed to any garden-variety Western emperor, who was called *kotei*. Just as the Japanese had to bow and avert their eyes when their emperor passed by, so also could they not utter his name. They could not say "Hirohito," which was personal. They had to say

"Tenno Heika," which meant Celestial Emperor Whom One Regards from Below the Steps of the Throne.

"No, I haven't heard anything," Miyuki said. But she was lying to her brother. Two newspapers lay before her, papers her brother's troops had not taken over, and both dailies said the same thing, that Tenno Heika was not pleased, that he held no sympathy whatsoever for those presumptuous young mutineers who dared to act so brutally in his name. She could not even bring herself to show these accounts to her mother, for Miyuki knew they would only confound her. Mrs. Serikawa, like her daughter, recognized Takeo as only one thing: *aikokusha*, a patriot—a patriot of the first water, like the colonel his father, like all the Serikawas back through the ages.

"Now, don't you believe anything that some of the papers are writing," Takeo said. "It's only third-page stuff." Page three was where the Tokyo newspapers jammed all the juicy, scandalous gossip.

"Yes, I know," Miyuki replied, but she thought to herself that it could not be like page three, for she could not imagine any newspaper in the empire printing what Tenno Heika thought unless the editor had been told very explicitly that this *was* what Tenno Heika was thinking. Miyuki was her father's daughter and her brother's sister, and it frightened her that for the first time in her life, she had let even a fleeting doubt of what her men told her creep into her head. She made herself put away such dreadful apostate thoughts.

But, of course, the doubts kept coming back. And, of course, she was right.

10

No, Hirohito was not at all pleased. Tenno Heika was not, perhaps, as withdrawn and bashful a man as he was often portrayed in the West, the myopic milquetoast longing only to be left alone with his beloved specimens of marine biology. (After all, nobody took President Roosevelt for a wimp just because he loved to escape into his stamps.) Hirohito had never been under any illusions; he always understood that he was a god who must someday rule a nation of eighty million gods.

True, he was not a prepossessing man. He was round-shouldered, short by any standard in the world, even among his own little people. Besides the very thick spectacles, he had a weak chin, a very unfortunate mustache, and a timid face full of ugly moles. And, much like the absent-minded professor, Tenno Heika would regularly forget the most ordinary human things, like buttoning his fly. In other ways, though, he was merely disarming, shuffling about the Palace in shabby clothes. *"A so desu ka?"* he would say unassumingly, genuinely interested, quite charming subjects who were meeting him for the first time. "Is that so?"

Most unfortunately for Tenno Heika, he was obliged to speak in a stilted, archaic court language, which sounded garbled to all but the most learned of his subjects. It was, for virtually everyone else, like suddenly encountering a Shake-spearean figure from one of his lesser plays, *Timon of Athens,* say, or *Titus Andronicus,* where you didn't even know the plot well enough to allow you an educated guess at the dialogue.

But above all, Hirohito was unique because he was a god on earth. (Everybody in Japan would become a god at death, the Shinto *kami;* so Westerners had to understand that Japa-nese divinity was blurred: though even in Japan you couldn't be a little bit pregnant, you *could* be a little bit godly.) Hirohito, though, was also more powerful a god than many of his ancestors. Ironically, as Western royalty was becoming more ceremonial, the Japanese line counted for more. In feu-dal times, the average citizen gave allegiance first to his local lord, the daimyo, then to the most powerful military boss, the shogun, while the emperor existed as some sort of a shadow creature, a cross between a stained-glass saint and Miss America. But when Japan abandoned its antediluvian ways in the 1870s and opened itself up unto the undivine world, the emperor was elevated, the better to hold the people together as the nation went through the process of jumping several centuries in a day. The new constitution of 1889 boldly declared the Emperor "sacred and inviolable," and the story of his direct descent from the Sun Goddess had to be taught in school as a matter of historical record.

In fact, the only time that Kiyoshi and Cotton ever really fought as children was one day when Cotton was innocently telling his Japanese friend about Jesus, about Him being the only son of God, and Kiyoshi, said, whoa, hold on, you've got it all wrong, pal, because in school we learned . . . and soon they were rolling around in the dirt, pummeling each other in the name of religion, just like adults do.

They were in the schoolyard at recess, all the other kids enjoying the show. Takeo, standing with his older classmates, heard the commotion and came over and broke it up. Cotton was getting the best of it, but not by much.

Takeo made a point to walk home with Kiyoshi that day to hear him out. He listened carefully, and then assured Kiyoshi that he was absolutely right, of course, but *gaijin* weren't themselves divine, and so you had to tolerate their bizarre idiosyncrasies. After all, they were also hairy and blue-eyed and *bata kusai*, which the Japanese always said behind the Westerners' backs—meaning they smelled like butter.

"Wait a minute," Kiyoshi said. "Cotton doesn't smell like butter." If Kiyoshi was going to fight his buddy and call him names, that was one thing, but he wasn't going to abide anybody else doing it. "He smells just like us and he speaks Japanese just like us."

"But he is not us," Takeo said. "He is just copying us so he can live with us. But don't let that fool you."

And so, as Kiyoshi had explained to Cotton with his fists, the Emperor reigned as lord god. All of the people of Japan are saddled with *on*, obligations they have inherited—from their parents who gave them birth and nurtured them, from their teachers and employers and so many others. But above

all, of course, everybody possessed *ko on*, which was received
from Tenno Heika.

Most of his subjects also accepted the Chrysanthemum ta-
boo, which meant they wouldn't even speak of him—
especially in times of stress (which was fast becoming most of
the time). If a school anywhere in Japan was lucky enough to
obtain an official portrait of the Emperor, the photograph
had to be placed in a fireproof safe when it was not on display, so that in the event of a conflagration, even if the school
and all the children and all the teachers in it burned to a
crisp, the photograph would be saved. Anyone approaching
the Imperial Palace would have to stop and bow deeply; and
in front of the Sakuradamon, the most magnificent gate into
the palace grounds, even the streetcars going by would slow
down, and the passengers would genuflect toward the
grounds across the moat. It played some hell with the traffic,
but what mattered was to acknowledge that Hirohito was a
god, Japan a land of gods in a mundane world.

And Tenno Heika was growing angrier at Takeo and the
other mutineers with each hour. He sent one unmistakable
signal to those around him, removing his Western suit and
putting on his uniform as general of the army. Perhaps at last
Hirohito understood that events were in command now, that
he could only hope to ride them out astride his handsome
white stallion. Not one day thereafter for another decade
would he appear in mufti. The next time Hirohito would be
seen in public without his uniform, the war would be over
and he would be going out to pay homage to MacArthur, the
first conquering general of the land of the gods.

Now, Friday the twenty-eighth, Tenno Heika was presiding
in the Imperial Palace, sitting on his throne atop a high dais
draped in gold brocade. "I want this rebellion ended," he said
firmly, "and I want to see its instigators punished. Now go to
it."

The ministers backed out. Already, most of the fleet was
steaming up the coast toward Tokyo Bay, and loyal army
units were poised. But the Emperor was determined not to allow any indication that the rebels had enjoyed even a modest

success. The city's and the country's business went on much as it did before; the only evident manifestation of revolution was that service on the one existing subway, the Ginza Line, was suspended, inasmuch as it rolled directly into the downtown area controlled by the rebels.

Ambassador Grew took the precaution of having sandbags placed about the American compound, and Mrs. Grew decided that she would sleep in another room, just in case; but Americans and other *gaijin* mostly only marveled at how strange it all was: a rebellion in the middle of the nation's capital, two thousand armed regulars in revolt, murders most foul—and business as usual.

In the Sanno Hotel, Takeo waited the day, secretly growing more unsure and nervous, although he barely admitted these emotions even to himself. And then, on Saturday morning, someone called to him, and he ran to his window, and he saw a balloon outside, with a trailer that read, "Imperial Order Issued—Don't Resist the Army Flag," and Takeo's heart sank. Was this genuinely a message from the Emperor? Right then Takeo heard, over the main radio station, JOAK, the most familiar announcer's voice in the land declare: "His Majesty, the Son of Heaven, orders you to return to your units. If you continue to resist you will be traitors," and Takeo knew that Tenno Heika had somehow not understood the true message that he and the others were delivering with their sacred action. The unscrupulous men around His Majesty had blinded him even more than he had ever imagined.

So, at last, Takeo called Koda and the other leaders together and told them that there was only one thing left for them to do, and that he was the one to do it. He went back to his room, put on his dress uniform, strapped on his samurai sword, and then called his mother and sister on the telephone. He told them to meet him back at the Sanno later that day.

Takeo chose to walk from the Sanno, sucking in the bracing winter air; he needed it for his courage. Snow was in the air again. He had been advised to go to the northern end of the Palace, Chidori-gafuchi, where the Imperial Guards were barracked, and so he skirted the road by the moat, the steep, gray walls almost blending into the dull sky, the white watchtowers here and there seeming almost like hinges, connecting the Emperor's walls to the Emperor's heavens. Briskly, Takeo walked past Sakuradamon, seeing the two armored vehicles that had been placed there, where the big bridge passed over the moat, and he stepped along past where the moat widened into a pond, where the concubines and other members of the court were rowed about in the summer. Just beyond, at the farthest extremity of the grounds, the moat broke for a few yards and there was a small gate. Takeo's contact was there, and hardly without a word he was passed through. A whole company of the Imperial Guards, the Emperor's own men, had gone along with the rebellion, and others were waiting to see how the coup broke. And so, without difficulty, without even much effort at stealth, Takeo was passed inside the grounds, escorted south past the army barracks and toward the inner palace.

Perhaps because Takeo had been inside here once before it did not seem so forbidding. Then, three years ago, it was a soft summer day, and he had been invited to bring Miyuki, his young virgin sister, to see if she passed muster sufficiently to qualify for the Emperor's bed. Miyuki was in her shiniest kimono, and all the other court ladies were scurrying about in theirs, amidst the birds and the butterflies and the bees; the Sun Goddess herself might well have been there that halcyon day.

But now, nothing moved upon the snow, and Takeo wouldn't have realized that he was walking down a fairway of Hirohito's own nine-hole golf course if one of the guards hadn't idly mentioned it. Everything lay still under the snow; even the besieged city beyond the great walls and the moat seemed silent. All that Takeo heard were the crows, cawing, cawing. Down a knoll he and the guards came, into the Fukiage Gardens. Takeo remembered the Calabash Pond there, near the Concubines Pavilion; but the guards led him another way now, down a path, up and around, until Takeo suddenly found himself at the Emperor's library.

It happened so quickly. It was all understood. There was saluting and bowing, the sentinels backed away for a moment; and as Takeo's escorts faded away, the door was opened, and he was guided inside and directed to a Western-style door down the hall. Reflexively, he proceeded down the corridor. At the door, he smartly executed a right turn, and, without hesitating lest he lose nerve, he grasped the handle and threw open the door.

And there, before Takeo, alone at his desk, in his general's uniform, but with his collar loosened, sat the Celestial Emperor Whom One Regards from Below the Steps of the Throne.

Takeo crumpled to his knees, forgetting, in his anxiety, to follow proper protocol, to first untie his father's samurai sword. When he remembered that and fumbled to loosed the sword on his knees, the sword made a great clatter. Takeo appeared very foolish.

"Don't bother," Takeo heard the Emperor say, "unless you plan on killing me with it."

He had an alarm buzzer under his desktop, and his hand moved toward it, but he held it back and relaxed. He stayed his other hand from the revolver in his desk. Hirohito was really quite comfortable. Had Takeo been taken to him across the gardens in the ceremonial palace, Hirohito would have been a god; but here, in the library, he was officially only a man.

Takeo, however, was still too flustered to consider any of this protocol, his head spinning all the more because Hirohito, man or god, had addressed him in his unfamiliar, antique court Japanese. "It is my honor, Tenno Heika," Takeo did manage to say.

Hirohito said: "You're one of the rebels, aren't you?" He saw Takeo sifting the archaic words through his mind, and so, thoughtfully, Hirohito gave up the formalities and repeated the remark in modern Japanese.

Takeo tried not to show any expression. He didn't like "rebel"; he regarded himself as *aikokusha*, a patriot. But he certainly did not consider engaging His Majesty, the Son of Heaven, in any debate. He only said: "I am Captain Serikawa Takeo."

"Oh yes."

"My father was Colonel Serikawa Shinji, who was killed fighting for the empire in Manchukuo."

"I am well aware of your father, for he was a hero to us all."

Takeo beamed at that encomium for his beloved father from Tenno Heika himself. He sucked in some breath. "And my sister is Serikawa Miyuki, who was prepared to be the mother of your son, who would succeed you to the imperial throne."

"That was never my idea," the Emperor said, almost without expression. "Your sister is most beautiful, but it was not my idea to take her. And Manchukuo is no longer an issue. The only way you can honor your father is to give up this insane effort and tell your men to put down their arms and return to their units."

"But—"

"Your efforts are murderous. They insult Japan before the eyes of the critical world—"

"But—"

And here Hirohito leaned forward and spoke carefully: "And ... they ... demonstrate ... no ... respect ... for ... me." Takeo could hardly breathe. "Your efforts have disgraced Japan."

Takeo tried to catch his breath, but had he managed to, he still would have had no idea what to say. Hirohito waved him away. "Please, now, I'm busy. Leave."

Takeo looked about, distraught. Not only had the Emperor rejected all he had to say, but he had insulted Takeo and all his colleagues. Finally, he struggled to his feet and tried to say something.

"What?" snapped Hirohito.

"We wanted to be the forty-eighth *ronin*."

"You what?"

"We sought to be the forty-eighth *ronin*."

The Emperor shook his head in wonder. He took off his

eyeglasses and looked at Takeo straight on. "You dishonor the forty-seven" was all he said, and he looked back down again at his work. Takeo staggered backward, his big sword clattering as he grabbed for the door handle.

Hirohito glanced up. He had not planned to. For best dramatic effect, he had figured on just staying head down; but perhaps because this place was, after all, where he was a man, a streak of humanity came to him, and he lifted his head. "Captain Serikawa," he said, and, tentatively, Takeo turned back, eyes down. "Somebody will be the forth-eighth someday. That part I accept. But none of you. All that is misguided."

Takeo nodded, humbly. It was a crumb, at least, and he backed out of the room and headed down the hall, so shattered he forgot to close the door after him.

Hirohito clicked on an intercom. "He's leaving now," he said. "It was a good idea." He paused. "Let him go. His father was Colonel Serikawa, and he understands."

Then he went back to his fungi.

11

Miyuki and Mrs. Serikawa were waiting in the lobby of the Sanno, their anxiety heightening with each minute, when Takeo finally entered, his drawn face tinted pink by the cold. He had run all the way, run, run and gasped, staggered for air. He bowed to his mother and invited her up to his suite, and right away she knew that it wasn't good at all. Miyuki started to follow, but Takeo bade her to wait.

Mrs. Serikawa handed him the kimono that he had asked her to bring. Then, in the room, he carefully took off his uniform and presented it to her, neat and folded. He didn't have to tell her that she was to put it with his father's uniform.

She didn't ask him about the details of his visit to the Palace, and he didn't volunteer any. It was sufficient that Takeo presented her with his uniform and put on his kimono. He then embraced her and thanked her for the gift of life. He told her to send Miyuki up, and then Takeo bowed to his mother and said, *"Korede owakare."* Good-bye forever.

She bowed and left the room. The Japanese have never been much for big goodbyes, for embraces and kisses and carryings-on. And, of course, Mrs. Serikawa didn't cry. She was a Japanese woman, and she could not let the selfish devotion to her son stain this honorable death he was about to give himself.

Takeo was kneeling serenely when Miyuki entered the room. He knew she would be proud of him, and she was. She bowed to her brother and went into the bathroom, where she washed her hands so that they would be clean for what she was to do, and then she slipped out of her Western dress and put on a kimono, carefully tying all the ribbons, then wrapping the obi around her waist, binding herself tightly. Ready now, she came out and kneeled across from her brother. "I can get tea."

"No, thank you," Takeo said. "I'm already at peace. Is Mother all right?"

"She understands. She's been the wife of a warrior."

"She must appreciate that . . ." He had to suck in more breath before he could go on. ". . . that I've greatly offended His Majesty, the Son of Heaven."

Miyuki rocked forward, nearly pitching onto the tatami. She had to close her eyes as tightly as possible to keep the tears from pouring out. This was the worst she could have imagined: insulting Tenno Heika, His Majesty, the Son of Heaven. Takeo had no choice but what he must do now.

"He is so angry for what we have done," Takeo went on. "I've already phoned the others and told them they must give up, and perhaps then Tenno Heika will forgive them."

"But you cannot be forgiven."

"Oh no, I'm without excuse," Takeo said, nearly dispassionately. "I can only save all my ancestors from shame this way."

"Yes," Miyuki told her brother. The long sword was on his one side and a dagger on his other. He handed her the sword, for her part, but she said, "No." Takeo looked at her curiously. "No, I cannot be forgiven either, for although I'm a woman and couldn't go with you on your mission, I wanted to go. I wanted to be with you, because I believed in what you said. In my heart, I share it all." Miyuki shrugged. "I have to come with you."

Takeo pondered that. He couldn't help breaking a little smile, and that made Miyuki smile too. "That is so noble," he said at last. "I know Father is proud of his daughter."

"First, I have to tell Mother," Miyuki said, and she went over to the phone and called down to the corporal at the front desk and asked him to send Mrs. Serikawa up to the room. Then she opened the door and took her position again, kneeling across from her brother. She and Takeo stared at each other, serenity on their faces, for they were content, sure of what they must do to themselves to make amends for what they had done to the Emperor of Japan and their land of the gods.

Mrs. Serikawa entered, her face carefully arranged to accept the sight of her only son dead before her. Surely, that was why Miyuki had called her up. But there he sat, still. "Takeo," she gasped. But then, there sat her daughter, across from him, in the same pose, which could only signal the same intent. "Miyuki?" she said, fearfully tentatively.

"I'm sorry, Mother, but I'm at fault, too, for I really wanted to be with Takeo today," Miyuki said.

Mrs. Serikawa gulped. She could not plead with Miyuki, for that would be unseemly, dishonorable of her. But neither could she calmly accept her daughter's suicide too. "But you are only a woman. You are only Takeo's sister. It would be different if you were a wife, following a husband."

"But I have offended Tenno Heika as much as Takeo, because in my heart I agreed with him. I was with him."

Mrs. Serikawa was stunned at that revelation. She turned to her son. "You offended Tenno Heika?"

"Yes, Mother," Takeo replied, ducking his head.

"Oh."

"And my spirit was with Takeo when he went to the palace," Miyuki said. "And so it is only right that, as a Japanese woman, my spirit go with Takeo now."

"You really want this, Miyuki?" Mrs. Serikawa had to at least *ask*.

"Yes, Mother. Father's spirit will be so proud of me. I hoped I could honor Father by having Tenno Heika's son, but now I can please him this way."

"But it was not your fault that you could not bear Japan a son."

"No, but it still must have disappointed Father greatly."

Takeo broke in then, and with an edge to his voice. "Please, Mother, Miyuki is as honorable as any man, and we must be proud of her."

Mrs. Serikawa bowed. "Yes, of course, I am," she said, and Miyuki rose and granted her a brief embrace. No hard feelings. Takeo held his place. Miyuki walked her mother to the door, and they bowed to each other across the threshold and across death, and then Mrs. Serikawa took the elevator downstairs to allow her only two children the graceful opportunity to kill themselves. She felt a bit ashamed of herself for questioning her daughter.

Miyuki knelt back down again, stopping only to kiss her brother gently on the top of his head before she took her place. *"Korede owakare,* brother."

"Korede owakare, sister. I will see you with Father in a few moments."

Takeo took his dagger back up. He would have the more painful task, to cut open his belly so that his entrails spilled out.

"I will perform *kaishaku,"* Miyuki said. That meant she would rise with the long sword and cut off his head.

"No, that is not for a woman."

"Please, Takeo, please. I'm strong enough. Father would—"

"All right, Miyuki. I'll grant you that. But then you must die like a woman."

She smiled. "Of course." That meant, for herself, that after she beheaded Takeo, she would kneel back down, take the dirk, cut the carotid artery in her neck and bleed softly, sweetly to death. A woman was not supposed to rip open her belly first. Miyuki sorely wanted that privilege, but she understood that men and women were not equal, and she could not expect such an honor. Performing *kaishaku* was enough. She tried hard not to be envious of her brother, so that such an ugly emotion wouldn't intrude on a sacred moment like this.

Takeo examined the knife before him. He was happy, for if he did a good job, he would clear his name and reinstate himself to fond memory. He took the dagger and steered it over to his left side, above his waist. The Japanese had always believed that whatever the heart, whatever the mind, the abdomen harbors a man's sincerity; and so now, if he could properly open himself up and empty out his entrails he would be displaying his sincerity for all to see. It was honorable and purposeful, more so even than what he might have done with his silly living.

Takeo bowed his head to his sister, and, for more power, he reached over with his right hand and placed it above his left on the hilt. He could feel the prick of the point, and Miyuki could see her brother quiver, as he prepared to jam the dagger into his bowels. She tingled that her own dear death was drawing so near.

On the dock, Cotton was jammed in with all the others saying good-bye. Lieutenant Wylie was only a few steps away, waving frantically at Emily. They were lovers by now, and he was going to come visit her in Philadelphia and meet her parents, and possibly then, if all went well and the romantic memories of Hawaii didn't pale with time, ask for her hand in marriage.

The whistle of the *Matsonia* blew. All ashore who's going ashore. Emily was crying. Win Taliaferro was there, shipping back to California for his new assignment, and he put a brotherly arm around her. Down below, in the harbor, the natives rushed about in their outrigger canoes. They were part of the pageant; they followed the ships leaving Hawaii all the way out to the mouth of the harbor. The band from the Royal Hawaiian played "Aloha Oe," the anthem Queen Liliuokalani had written herself.

The *Matsonia* began to back off, and here and there the passengers began to take off their leis and sling then into the water. If you did this, legend had it, you would return to Hawaii.

Emily took off her lei and lifted it into the air, watching it spin away and hit the water and drift back to shore. Almost everybody else threw their leis, too, although not nearly as adroitly as Emily.

The liner began to hold the engines on one side, spinning around, to point in the right direction, out to sea. The outriggers darted about here and there in its wake like baby ducks.

Liz had a place at the rail, too; but she also was the last person there who still had her lei around her neck. She gave one last look at Cotton and blew him a kiss. It was a kiss she blew; she raised her fingers to her lips and tossed her hand away, toward him. But it didn't have the spirit of a kiss. It was, in fact, more like a military salute.

Then Liz turned and started to head down to her cabin. She didn't want to see Honolulu anymore. She didn't want to see the Aloha Tower. She didn't want to see the Dole Pineapple tank. She didn't want to see Waikiki. She didn't want to see Diamond Head. She didn't figure on coming back here again.

She slipped by Win Taliaferro on her way down. "Don't you know?" he said. "If you throw your lei, you'll—"

"I know."

"You don't want to come back?"

"Not particularly," Liz said. "Aloha." And she swished her tail in the general direction of the island.

Cotton left the dock without a word or a sign. He had noticed that Liz had not thrown her lei, and he was glad, somehow, that she didn't want to come back to Hawaii. Neither did he, because nothing would ever be like this with him and a girl again. He was angry at Japan and Jesus that they had cost him this, and he was scared to death that it was all a terrible mistake.

Miyuki waited, ready to snatch up the long sword, to rise and bring it down upon her brother's neck. Takeo put more pressure upon the knife, ready to drive it home.

But then, suddenly, unexpectedly, he relaxed his grip. "No," he said, shaking his head.

Miyuki gasped, shocked that Takeo was unable to be a man of honor. She could not believe that he would avoid doing what he must do. She wanted to cry for her father, for the shame his spirit must be filled with now. She wanted to cry for herself. Instead, she leaned forward, trying to grab the knife from Takeo, forcing him to pull it away from his stomach and hold it out of her reach.

"I'm sorry," he said. "I apologize for not thinking this through. I know you must feel great shame, too, but you cannot be so fortunate as to join me in death."

Miyuki caught herself as she realized what Takeo was saying. He wasn't running from his own seppuku; he was denying her hers.

"But I want to," Miyuki said, and she held out her hand, begging for the knife.

Takeo only shook his head and smiled avuncularly at her. "No, Miyuki. You must stay on this earth and bear a child so that the Serikawa line doesn't end. If there's any chance at all, the Serikawa family must endure."

Miyuki took another tack. "Who'll want to marry a woman who lacks honor?" she asked.

"No, no. My action will clear the whole family honor," he said, and this time he took one of his hands off the knife and reached out for Miyuki's hand. "Swear to me."

"If I must."

"You must. For me, for Mother, for Father's spirit, for *you* . . . for the Serikawas. You must give us a child." Miyuki clutched his hand harder and bowed her head. "Kiyoshi," Takeo said.

"What?" Miyuki asked softly, raising her chin up.

"You would like to have Kiyoshi's child? You would settle for Kiyoshi, wouldn't you?"

"I don't know if he'd want the match."

"He owes it to me. I am his *on* man, going back to school days. You remind him that no matter how much time he spends in the West, he can't forget the debt he owes me." Takeo beckoned across the room, where there was a Western desk. "Get me the paper."

Miyuki rose and fetched it, but she said: "Look, I don't want Kiyoshi to marry me just because he wears an *on* from you. Then he'll hate me."

Takeo nodded. He took the stationery from her and began to write his letter to Kiyoshi. "All right. He owes me a trial marriage when he comes. If it doesn't work, I'll tell him the *on* is repaid, and he is free."

"All right," Miyuki said softly.

"You tell Mother to have him in the house." She took the envelope.

"He would have to become our *yoshi*, wouldn't he?" Miyuki asked.

"Of course he would." A *yoshi* was a man who upon marrying a woman enters her family, rather than taking her into his. Admiral Yamamoto, for example, was a *yoshi*, born a Takano, adopted into the Yamamotos when he married Reiko at the age of thirty-two. Takeo said: "Kiyoshi's older brother already has two sons. And he'd be proud to be a Serikawa, wouldn't he?"

"I think."

"Never mind his *on*," Takeo said, chuckling a little, rolling over in his hands the weapon that would kill him. "I am the father in this family now." He shrugged. "At least for another moment or two. So, you remind my friend Kiyoshi: *Jishin, karminari, kaji, oyaji.*'" Miyuki smiled. The words were the punch line to an old saying: What are the four things to fear the most? Earthquake, thunder, fire, and father.

"Yes, Father, I'll tell him," Miyuki said, brightening. She

laid the envelope aside, and when her brother beckoned her, she took her place again, across from him.

"It's much better this way," Takeo said.

"Perhaps."

"You will have the child, the Serikawa child. You will carry the flame for the family and the empire." Miyuki bowed. "Good" was all else Takeo said, for then, with dispatch, he took his hands and placed them both back on the dagger, placed the point back on the left side of his stomach, gritted his teeth, and forced the short sword into his body. He couldn't keep his face free of pain, but Miyuki remained utterly without expression, for it would be dishonorable of her to shade the ceremony in any way. She did not show her anguish for Takeo, and neither did she display her envy of him, and that was even greater.

Slowly now, purposefully, Takeo brought the blade across his stomach, carving it, then he yanked up, opening his abdomen full, placing its contents on proper display. His energy was spilling out too, though, with the blood and the guts; and there was no more he could do himself. With his eyes he signaled that to Miyuki, so she rose and took the long sword and, with all her might, brought it down upon her brother's neck.

Unfortunately, it wasn't successful. Miyuki wasn't quite as strong as she thought. It took two more good blows to cut through Takeo's neck. His body had slumped forward, and at last the head tumbled off and lay there, on its side.

Miyuki could have imagined all this. It was the blood that surprised her. She had no idea how much there could be. It was even scattered all over the walls, from where it flew a long distance off the long sword.

She took her bloody kimono off and, naked but for the red undershirt she wore underneath, moved carefully about the room, cleaning it up. It would not do for the room to be messy when others came. It required all the towels.

Then she took her kimono and folded it as neatly as she could; gently she placed Takeo's head upon it, next to his body. She put his long sword next to his head and tucked the short sword into the belt of his kimono.

Finally, she knelt beside him. "I'm sorry I can't be with you and Father, but I'll try to do what's best for us all." She bowed as she knelt, and then she got up and put on the Western dress that she had worn to the hotel, and her warm coat on top of it. She picked up the letter to Kiyoshi, which was spattered with blood, placed it in her purse, and went out to the elevator.

Naturally, Mrs. Serikawa was very surprised to see Miyuki enter the lobby.

"I apologize, Mother, but Takeo asked me to stay and have the children he couldn't have."

Mrs. Serikawa hugged her and told Miyuki that she was sorry for her that she hadn't been allowed to commit seppuku; but, of course, deep inside she was happy that she still had a daughter, even if she knew how much Miyuki ached at having been left behind.

Miyuki waited there in the lobby while her mother went up to pay her respects to her son. Miyuki hoped that she had made the room sufficiently clean. When Mrs. Serikawa came back downstairs, she looked pleased, and she was very composed when they spoke with the officer in charge about the details of Takeo's cremation. Then, that done, Miyuki helped Mrs. Serikawa on with her coat and they went outside. There were a few flakes in the air, but, in fact, it really wasn't going to snow anymore, and tomorrow would be the first day of March.

The two women hurried out of the Sanno, around the corner and down the block, where they could wait for their streetcar home. Soon it came, and they found seats. When the streetcar passed by the Sakuradamon, the driver slowed almost to a stop, and Miyuki and her mother and the other passengers all turned in the direction toward the Emperor in his palace across the moat.

If they could have seen inside, over the walls, Tenno Heika, His Majesty, the Son of Heaven, was still in his office, where he was just a man, monkeying with fungi at his desk, exactly as he had been doing when Takeo had barged in, two or three hours before.

The two Serikawa ladies bowed with the others and then the streetcar started up again for Asakusa, taking them home for dinner.

12

It was finished. All the rebels had surrendered long before the *Tatsuta Maru* docked at Yokohama. Kiyoshi made it up the bay to Tokyo just in time for the funeral. The incense rose thick before the alter where Takeo's bones rested, as the shaven-headed monks recited Chinese sutra. *"Isagi-yosa,"* Miyuki assured Kiyoshi afterwards; Takeo had died without any regrets. And, of course, it is the journey that matters, not the coming and going, the now and then.

She handed him Takeo's letter. "It was the last thing he wrote," she explained, so Kiyoshi understood then what the dried blood speckled on the hotel envelope meant. He started to open it, but Miyuki blushed and bowed, then scurried away in her kimono, scuffling across the floor.

Kiyoshi waited until he was back in his room at the Imperial to read the letter. He was thrilled and touched by what Takeo wrote, inviting him to enter the Serikawa family, but for a long time Kiyoshi mostly cried, reading Takeo's hand, thinking of him, thinking of what he had done moments after he wrote this. He ran his fingers over the blood, and then he got up and paced, all but banging into the walls. Frank Lloyd Wright had designed the hotel, but it was also very Japanese in scale, with corridors you could hardly squeeze through, tiny rooms, low basins. It made Kiyoshi feel even more confined, more unsure.

Here he was being invited to take Miyuki, beautiful Miyuki—she was his for the plucking, compliments of her family. And if he didn't care for her, for whatever reason, he could say thank you very much anyway and walk away. What a setup! But Kiyoshi didn't want it. What he wanted was to take her out, to "date" her, the way Americans did. Even, Kiyoshi wanted to love her.

"Takeo," he said out loud, "sometimes we don't get it all right. Even if we are gods. Even if we've been around almost twenty-six hundred years. Sometimes there just are better ways." He shook his head and then, softly: "Please, don't get angry at me, old friend, but I wish just once or twice you could have seen us through blue eyes."

And, to himself, Kiyoshi thought in English: "And then, surely, you wouldn't be dead now."

He wished Cotton was here; the best person in the world he could have talked to now was his best friend. But when at last he reached for the phone, it was to call his parents in Kobe. He asked his father for permission to have a trial marriage with Miyuki Serikawa, and Mr. Okuno immediately understood that if it worked, Kiyoshi would become a *yoshi*, someone else's son, an Okuno no more.

Mr. Okuno expressed his condolences on Takeo's death, but quickly he went on: "The Serikawas are an honorable Japanese family, and it's a match I can approve of." It was all in keeping; when Mr. Okuno had been betrothed to Mrs. Okuno, he had never even laid eyes on her.

"Thank you, Father," Kiyoshi said, and he walked over to the Ginza, to the subway, which was working again, took it up to Asakusa, and walked to the Serikawas' house. Miyuki greeted him in surprise and invited him in, but Kiyoshi said no, he wanted her to put on her shoes and take a walk. That was a moga-type thing for a young woman to do, but Mrs. Serikawa approved.

Miyuki and Kiyoshi walked aimlessly, bashfully, small talk or no talk at all, picking their way through the snow that melted and ran through the streets; the sun was finally back. They came to a little Shinto shrine, tucked in a few blocks away. It had just been renovated with government money, sparkling, a picture-postcard gem, glistening under the snow that melted off its roof.

Kiyoshi left Miyuki. He strode forward, threw some sen coins into the alms box, clapped his hands, and prayed. Miyuki peeked over at him, but was uncertain of what was expected of her, so she ducked her head, and when Kiyoshi turned back to her and pulled Takeo's letter from his pocket, she didn't know what he meant when he said: "Do you agree with this? Do you?" She looked up then and saw him waving the letter. "Do *you* want what Takeo wants?" She was scared and shy; she didn't know what to say. "Miyuki, do you want this trial marriage?"

"Takeo wanted it."

"I know *that*. But I don't want it if you don't. I have an *on* from Takeo, I know. I'm much in debt to him for all he did for me when I was young. But I will wear that *on* for the rest of my life if I have to . . . if *you* don't want this."

Miyuki's eyes darted about. She was confused; Kiyoshi wasn't supposed to ask this sort of question.

"If you don't want to . . . try me," he said, personalizing it—westernizing it—all the more.

She couldn't look at him. Instead, eyes down, she brushed by Kiyoshi and went up to the altar and prayed there. When she turned back, Kiyoshi was still standing there, holding the letter. "Yes, I want this," Miyuki said, the words coming slowly, as if they were being squeezed out of a tube. "I want to try . . . I want us to try."

Kiyoshi broke into a big smile that made Miyuki duck her head again. "Good. Tell your mother that I'll check out of the Imperial and be at your house tomorrow evening." Then he bowed, and when Miyuki saw that out of the tops of her eyes, she bowed back. Only when Kiyoshi turned to go to the subway did she smile. "I really must be a moga," she thought to herself. It was very mischievous, being a moga.

Miyuki didn't tell her mother that, though, when she got home. Now she was nervous for a different reason. "What do I do to make him pleased?" she asked.

"Oh, that doesn't much matter," Mrs. Serikawa said. "Soon enough, especially a wealthy man like Kiyoshi, he will go to someplace like Yoshiwara." That was the brothel district. "Why, as successful and powerful as Kiyoshi is going to be, he'll probably bring a geisha home. Or maybe even he'll have a second wife and family." Miyuki wrinkled her nose. "So, he'll be very rich, and you'll just be *oku-sama*, his first lady of the house. I wouldn't worry about keeping a husband happy, because geishas and prostitutes are trained to do it better, so why bother?"

"Yes, but the Western wives try to do what the professional girls do."

Mrs. Serikawa wrinkled her nose. "Moga," she muttered.

"Please, Mother—there must be something you know." Mrs. Serikawa threw up her hands and told Miyuki two little special tricks of pleasure that the colonel's contract geisha had used to please him when he had been posted for a time in Okinawa and that he had then told Mrs. Serikawa about one sake-steeped night.

Miyuki listened intently. She was still every bit a virgin, but she thought she got it. Then Mrs. Serikawa remembered something, and she went to the room upstairs and rooted around and came up with a "pillow book," a carefully illustrated guide that was traditionally given to young women as they embarked on a honeymoon or an at-home trial marriage. Takeo had bought it for Miyuki when he thought she might be given to the Emperor.

Miyuki lay on her futon that night before going to sleep and read the pillow book carefully; she had always been a good student. Mrs. Serikawa smiled at her daughter for being so diligent in preparing for the loss of her virginity. Purity had nothing to do with the very practical business of joining two families, of bringing in an adopted son to carry on the line. Miyuki lay down the book for a moment. "What're you thinking?" her mother asked.

"Takeo. I know how proud he was of his death, but still . . . I miss him, Mother." And she fell into her mother's arms.

"Me too, dear. I miss both my men. Kiyoshi will be a fine son for me, though."

Miyuki drew back, smiling. "I always liked Kiyoshi. He was always nice. Takeo was so much older than I, and so his friends were like uncles, but when Kiyoshi and Cotton would come over, they were friends. They were special. I think maybe I always dreamed that Kiyoshi would accept me as his wife."

"He's going to be very successful, and it's a fine family, the Okunos," Mrs. Serikawa said staunchly. She simply did not approve of premarital affection. It was bad business— certainly immodest and unbecoming, and verging on the immoral.

The next evening, after dinner, when Mrs. Serikawa bid her daughter and probable new son goodnight and took her futon to the little four-and-a-half-mat room upstairs, Miyuki did the best she could. Of course, she was nervous and unsure, and after Kiyoshi kissed her, she was all fumble-fingers unfastening her obi and not much better taking off her kimono, although by then it wasn't altogether her fault, because Kiyoshi was kissing her and caressing her and sprawling all over her. And she kept worrying about her *tabi*. She wanted so much to do this right, and she remembered that in all the drawings in the book, the woman had her *tabi*, her socks, off when she was making love, and here she was with her *tabi* on. She was sure that's all Kiyoshi was thinking: What a disappointment this girl is, making love to me and still in her *tabi*.

It was all so new and it proceeded so haphazardly (not at all like turning the pages in the pillow book) that she forgot almost everything she had gleaned from her reading. Then she remembered—too late. All of a sudden Kiyoshi was fully on top of her, and saying things, and he was going inside of her, and it hurt a little, but it was more the newness of it than the unfamiliar pain . . . and then Miyuki realized that it was over. She was Kiyoshi's woman now—and she still had her damn *tabi* on.

Well, she thought, there goes that. There goes the shortest trial marriage in the history of the Japanese Empire.

But all she would have to do was look at Kiyoshi to see the glow on his face. Takeo's kid sister had grown up, and she was gorgeous and rapturous; her legs were long and Western, and her breasts were all a man from anywhere in the world could want to touch and kiss. She warmed him even where she didn't touch him. And Kiyoshi realized all the more that it wasn't just about having sex and thinking about marriage. No, Cotton had seen it in him even before he understood it. This wasn't just love; it was "in love." *In* love. There really was such a thing, and it didn't belong only to the blue-eyed.

Miyuki rose up and made a big thing out of taking off her *tabi*. At least she wanted to show him: better late than never. And that was when she dared study the expression on his face, and even though there wasn't an expression like that in the pillow book, she knew she had seen it somewhere, and she remembered it was in the American movies, after the moga and mobo had kissed on the screen. So she breathed out happily—that sigh that turns into a smile at the end. She threw her kimono around her shoulders and got up and moved across the room to Takeo's altar. His ashes were still there, next to three photographs of him, and there were some small bowls, with a few grains of rice, some sake, and an orange. Miyuki could feel Kiyoshi's eyes looking at her, but she could feel more than that; she could feel all of Kiyoshi admiring her.

Miyuki was not, either, the least bit ashamed standing there all but naked before her brother's spirit or making love in his presence, because she already knew that Takeo approved of Kiyoshi for her, and now she also knew that Kiyoshi approved of her. She bowed and clapped her hands and prayed that if Kiyoshi should want her again tonight, this time she would remember to do the things she had studied.

Suddenly, Kiyoshi called out to her: "Miyuki, tell Takeo hello, and tell him that I'll marry you." Miyuki could only look over at him in ignorance, though, for Kiyoshi had said that, purposely, in English, and she really couldn't understand English unless it was spoken directly to her, carefully, word by word. "Tell him I'm in love with you," Kiyoshi added impishly. And then, more softly, just to Miyuki: "I love you."

Kiyoshi wasn't just being coy, though, saying that in English. There are words in Japanese for a man to say "I love you" flat out to a woman he loves, but they're never really used. The sentiment is too unspoken, too threatening, because it all but forces the other party to say "I love you too." Besides, it's so personal, "I love you"; it punctures the group. And worst of all, for a man, it's such an effeminate expression. Kiyoshi could hardly believe what he had said. It was all he could do not to sniff himself to see if he reeked of butter. Instead, he just laughed, happily.

"What did you say?" Miyuki asked.

"It's my secret. You have to learn English better."

Miyuki came back over and kneeled before him on the futon. "I'm trying to learn. I know I have to speak English if we're to make a marriage." That was bold of her, to say the word.

"Look, there's something I must tell you," and he sat up and pulled her kimono together across her breasts.

"Don't you like them?"

"Very much. That's the problem. They're distracting. And I have to tell you something."

Fear flushed over Miyuki again. "You don't want to marry me."

"No, silly," and he laughed. "I want to marry you. I even said that, in English. But we can't get married now." And he told her about Cotton leaving on business, and about how he probably would be assigned to San Francisco for a while, and that wouldn't be fair to her, to start off a marriage in a new land. "But it'll be soon, as soon as I come back to Tokyo."

"Boo-hoo, I'll be a Christmas cake," Miyuki said, feigning a pout and crocodile tears. A Christmas cake was an old maid of twenty-five years.

"No," Kiyoshi said, "you'll be my wife soon." And he reached up, then, to her hair. "No more *shimada*." As a child, a girl wore her hair in a large chignon, signifying a bud about to bloom. Then, when she was twelve or thirteen, the chignon was changed into more of a heart-shaped knot, suggesting the divided loyalties of a young woman about to leave her family for a husband's. When she was betrothed or married, she changed her hair back to the style of the earlier chignon; the bud had bloomed. "You'll wear *maru-maje* for me now, for all to see."

Smiling then—beaming—Miyuki reached up and helped Kiyoshi undo her *shimada*. As she shook the tresses down, he reached out and parted her kimono. "You're a flower—my flower," Kiyoshi said, and he looked at her, then brought Miyuki to him and kissed her, and they fell into each other's arms, and he said "I love you" again.

"What is that? You said those words before."

"No one says it in Japanese."

"Is it nice?"

"Oh, it's very nice."

"Then say it to me again."

"I . . . love . . . you."

"I rove you," Miyuki repeated. He laughed for happiness. It was the most wonderful thing he had ever heard. He kissed her again and again, and this time Miyuki managed to remember to do some of the things she had read about in the pillow book and one of the things her mother had told her, and when they made love she enjoyed every moment, and it crossed her mind that this was the best fun she had ever had with a friend.

"O rove you!" Miyuki cried out, not getting it quite right (but in the right spirit), and they fell asleep, smiling, in each other's arms, hardly stirring again until the fire watchman came by hours later, clapping his two sticks together.

Kiyoshi rose and put more coals on the hibachi, and when he came back to Miyuki she was crying, because she was so ashamed that she was so glad that she had not committed seppuku over the weekend.

1940

KANO E TATSU
THE YEAR
of the
METAL DRAGON

13

The Reverend Mr. Shelby Carruthers told the congregation: "We welcome to the pulpit today an old friend of many of you who has ascended from the pews. [*Chuckles.*] *Escaped* from the pews? [*More chuckles.*] Whatever, those of us up here are glad to have him with us. Cotton Drake was an active member of this parish four or five years ago when he was a businessman—a successful businessman—here in Hawaii, and now he returns to our midst, ordained, the Reverend Mr. Drake."

Cotton beamed and rose to the pulpit. "It's so nice to see so many familiar faces," he began, "and I trust it's not too difficult for you to greet me in these unfamiliar garments—well, unfamiliar on me, anyway. [*Chuckles.*] I'm sorry, too, that I can't stay with you for long, but I'm leaving tomorrow on the *Asama Maru* to assume a new ministry, in the Missionary District of Tokyo, in a town a couple hours north of the capital, named Tochigi."

Baffled faces stared back at this statement: why would anybody in his right mind go *to* Japan now? "It won't be easy, I know," Cotton said. "God knows it would be easier to stay here with you, in this loveliest of places, this paradise you are so blessed to enjoy. Some of the happiest times of my life were spent here, and perhaps it was because I was so happy in Hawaii, and because it is so easy on this gorgeous island to see the grandeur and the beauty of God—perhaps that is also why it is no coincidence that it was here on Oahu that I made my decision to change my life and enter into the ministry of our Lord Jesus Christ.

"But nothing is ever so simple. The joy of that time I spent here and the comfort of that decision that I made for myself four years ago was balanced by my awareness that I could not leave here and enter the seminary without making the most painful sacrifice of any man's life. You see, that decision meant that I had to give up ... the woman I loved. [*Uncomfortable seat shifting.*] And so, as I embark from here now in the joy of this task that God has given me, I know too that this may well be the most difficult period that I will ever endure. I go to a land where I was raised, to a nation that I adore [*a few coughs*], but to a land that feels such enmity toward my country—toward *our* country. But I leave with the knowledge that just as the great purpose of my life was measured by the most agonizing sacrifice, so too will this next trial that I face in Japan be tinted by some special gift from God. [*Sighs, more seat shifting.*]"

Cotton himself paused and took a sip of water; his eyes swept the congregation. He recognized a lot of his old friends from the parish, but a lot of strangers, too. Honolulu was a boomtown these days, with many newcomers arriving from the mainland. It was still the Depression, but there were good wages to be made here in the burgeoning defense industry. Good grief, Cotton had even seen haoles doing hard manual labor these last few days, and he'd surely never witnessed that before in Hawaii. Looking out from the pulpit, he also noticed a lot of old friends who were not members of the congregation but who had come to hear Cotton Drake preach. There'd been a notice in the *Advertiser*, and anyway, the fleet was usually docked Sundays. It was a full house.

Sammy Ushijima, his wife, and his younger daughter were way in the back. Cotton was staying with them while he was in Honolulu. He'd assigned a vestryman to sit with the Ushijimas, to let them know when to get up and kneel and so forth, so they could be comfortable in a Christian church. Cotton looked at the Ushijimas now, but he was distracted, for a few rows before them there was a young man Cotton recognized, but he couldn't figure out who he was, and it bugged him so that he finally had to look away, to the other side of the church, before he could resume his sermon.

"Enmity," he said. "I used that word a few moments ago, to describe the way Japan feels toward us. But we also heard that word one other time today." Cotton held up a Bible. "Here, from our second reading today, from St. Paul's Letter to the Ephesians, which he wrote when he . . . was . . . in . . . jail. For although Paul felt enmity every day from the Romans who held him captive, still he could write: 'But now in Christ Jesus, ye who sometimes were far off are made nigh by the blood of Christ. For Christ is . . . our . . . peace . . . Having abolished in his flesh the enmity.'

"And that's why I go to Japan now. Far off. Yes. So far off. But I have faith in our leaders who seek to find peace, and I have faith in the military"—and Cotton purposely swept his arm out over the pews—"who seek to keep the peace between us."

He found that he had set his eyes again upon the handsome young man in the rear, and it appeared to Cotton that the young man was listening intently. "And so, old friends—and new—I go happily to Japan, to, with Jesus, help abolish the enmity of these troubled times. Amen."

Cotton came down from the pulpit feeling good. He had given some sermons back in the States, filling in, so he'd developed a pretty good sense of when one of his sermons went over. This time he felt he had neatly melded the words from the Bible with the mean reality of the day, and he could tell that the people had been listening. And they meant it afterwards when he greeted them at the door and they said, "I enjoyed your sermon."

That was when Cotton saw the good-looking young man again. He was holding back, letting all the others greet the Reverend Mr. Drake first. And that was when it finally came to Cotton who the man was, so that when at last he got in line and stepped up and put out his hand, Cotton could easily say: "Hi, Win."

"Hello, Cotton," Captain Taliaferro said. "I read in the paper that you were the visiting preacher."

"So, you're stationed back here?"

"No, I wish, but I'm just passing through from the States. I'm reassigned to the Twenty-seventh Bombardment Group at Clark Field."

"The Philippines?"

Taliaferro nodded. "Flying B-17s. I think we're going to be able to reach Tokyo with those babies soon, so if your brand of peace doesn't work, maybe the Japs will be a little bit more fearful of the sermon I can deliver."

Cotton winced a little. Perhaps Taliaferro hadn't been listening as attentively to Paul's intercessionary words as it had seemed. "I hope we're not down to those options quite yet," he said, and he put a hand on Taliaferro's forearm. "Wait just a second," he added. Outside, on the church lawn, lemonade and cookies were being served, along with the opportunity to greet the Reverend Mr. Drake, so Cotton waved to the rector and the Ushijimas and his other friends. "I'll be right there," he said, and then he pulled Taliaferro away from the door, inside the empty church. "Listen, Win, I never would have said what I said in the sermon about Liz if I'd known you were here."

Taliaferro shrugged, smiling. "You mean the Duke of Windsor stuff—'the woman I love'?"

"Well, yeah. I never would have said anything that personal from the pulpit if I'd known you were—"

"Cotton, it's been four years since all that happened. Hell, it's almost two years Liz and I've been married."

"Well, I know, but you're never sure there's a statute of limitations on this sort of thing."

"Look, to tell you the truth, I can't wait to write Liz."

"Oh, come on, Win."

"No. No." He lowered his voice, remembering his wife. "As much as she loved you, she was never sure whether you really and truly loved her. Or whether you just used the missionary thing as an excuse."

"Are you serious?" Cotton asked.

"Dead."

"Damn." Cotton turned away a little, staring at the stained-glass window they were standing by. It was of St. Andrew, doing some of his own missionary work on the Sea of Galilee. For the moment, though, Cotton was thinking more of Andrew's less stalwart colleague Thomas. It piqued Cotton that Liz had doubted him. He turned back to Taliaferro. "I sure told her I loved her enough times."

"But you broke her heart, Reverend. You know, they always say you can get a dame easy on the rebound. But not Liz. Not after you. I fell for her right away. I think I was in love with her the minute I saw her at that luau here. But it took her forever to believe me when I told her I loved her, because you'd told her that, and she believed you, and then you walked away."

"That had nothing to do with not loving her."

"Okay. But now I can tell her that you stood up before a whole church and you confessed before God that she was the love of your life."

"Thank God," Cotton said.

Taliaferro tilted his head, not quite sure how to take that. Cotton just smiled. "What?"

"We always go around—especially us in the business—and tell everybody to thank God. Well, Win, you're one guy who can thank God personally, because if God hadn't taken me into this"—and swept his hands around the church—"then there wasn't anybody else that would've taken me away from Liz Hundley. If you'll excuse me, God"—and this time Cotton glanced up to the top of the church—"for saying this here, but you are one lucky sonofabitch, Win."

"I know," Taliaferro said. "But it's not all God's doing now, Reverend."

"How's that?"

"Liz is having a baby."

"Hey!" Cotton cried out. "That's great!" And he clapped Taliaferro on the back.

"Yeah, we just made it. I didn't find out till Liz called me in San Francisco. She's not even three months yet."

"Tell Liz to send me a picture of the baby," Cotton said, but he felt guilty saying that, because, as soon as he did, he knew that he was hoping that whenever the picture came it would be of the child *and* the mother, both.

14

Kazuko Ushijima started to cry—not because Cotton was leaving, but because she was standing on the deck of the *Asama Maru* and she wasn't going anywhere. Sammy had always promised her that they'd return to Japan for another visit, but it had already been a decade since their only trip back. Kazuko was all the more upset because everybody all around her was so excited; they would all be in Tokyo in time to celebrate Kigen, Japan's twenty-six hundredth anniversary, on November the tenth.

The festive air on the *Asama* was palpable. The joy bubbled for everyone so lucky to be going back to the Sun-Begot Land. There were some Issei, who had been born in Japan, and some of their children, the Nisei, born in Hawaii, but forever citizens of the land of their blood, even if they never set foot there in all their lives. Everybody was going home for Kigen, so that for all that Cotton could see, he might well have been the only Westerner on the whole ocean liner.

Sammy put his arm around Kazuko when the whistle blew, and kissed her. He promised her the family would go with him the next time American Orient sent him to Japan on business. Kazuko turned away. "I've heard that before," she said.

So Cotton laughed and hugged her and invited her to come visit him, stay at the rectory in Tochigi anytime. "Can I go back down home to Hiroshima, too?" she asked, playing along, and Cotton said sure, laughing and teasing Sammy some more.

Like a lot of the Issei on Hawaii, Kazuko came from the

farmland around Hiroshima. The times had been desperately
poor in that part of Japan then, 1915, and many who could
left. The government wouldn't let just anybody go, of course.
It screened the applicants and held back those who didn't appear to be top drawer; it wouldn't be honorable for Japan to
pass out bad samples of what had been produced in Nippon
for going on twenty-six centuries.

Kazuko had never know Isamu Ushijima, but she saw a
photograph of him that his cousin had. At that time, Isamu
had been in Hawaii for several years, but there weren't many
Japanese women there, so he just worked hard and learned
English and satisfied his needs the best he could, paying for
the Filipino whores Saturday nights. Probably this was a
blessing in disguise; probably if he'd had a wife and family to
support, he'd never have gotten beyond the arduous field
work on the pineapple plantations, and he'd still be there, laboring in the tropic sun.

Kazuko, back in Hiroshima prefecture, liked Isamu in his
photograph and asked the cousin if he would send her own
picture to Hawaii, so that Isamu might accept her in a *shashin
kekkon*, a photo marriage. Isamu was delighted with what he
saw, and in fact Kazuko was one of the prettiest of the picture
brides in the whole shipment that docked in Honolulu a few
months later.

So Isamu took Kazuko's hand, shyly, and they stood together on the dock with all the other picture brides and their
grooms, going through a mass Christian ceremony, inasmuch
as the haoles didn't concede the sanctity of Japanese proxy
marriages. Kazuko didn't have the foggiest idea what was going on, but she was anxious to begin her new life with Isamu
in his little place in Chinatown. Mostly, what were called
AJAs—Americans of Japanese ancestry—populated Chinatown, but Caucasians tended to call all Oriental enclaves
Chinatowns, notwithstanding what particular slant-eyed,
yellow-skinned aliens inhabited them.

Soon Sammy—leaving the name Isamu back in Chinatown—began to take his good English into the Western white-
collar community. Kazuko started to urge Sammy to take

them back to Japan on a visit so that they could show off their two daughters to their families, but Sammy didn't want to go. He accepted it that the law forbade him, an Oriental, ever to become an American citizen, but his two daughters had earned that privilege at birth on American soil, and that was good enough for Sammy.

The daughters themselves grew up caring nothing about Japan or things Japanese. Josephine even moved to Oregon, and Darlene would have left for California, but she found a good job in Honolulu and stayed for the time being. Laborers in Hawaii could make eighty cents an hour, and the semi-skilled as much as a buck and a half. That kind of money just wasn't available on the mainland. But then, on the mainland, nobody much had yet heard of "defense spending."

Sammy walked along with Cotton to the gangplank. "Hey," he said, "what're ya doin' to me? I don't wanna take Kazuko back there."

"Aw, it'd be good for you to go home again," Cotton said.

Sammy stopped and gestured, his arm sweeping over Oahu from Diamond Head. "This is my home, Cotton."

"Yeah, I know, Sammy. A bad choice of words."

"But I'm glad you're going over there. You've lived over there, and you can tell those guys——"

"What guys?"

"The guys running the damn country," Sammy said. "The army guys. You tell 'em not to cause any trouble. Not to *my* country . . . here."

Cotton gave him the thumbs-up, and then he embraced Sammy, and Kazuko after him, and waved at them as they went down the gangplank. When he turned back, right away he could feel it: all the Japanese on board staring at him. Obviously, they'd all thought Cotton was on the *Asama* to say goodbye to Sammy and Kazuko, and not the other way round. Now they examined him like a specimen.

All his years in Japan, Cotton had grown used to people staring at him. Sometimes, out in the sticks, the rubes would even come up and touch him, especially to feel his beard or stroke the hair on his arms—and then giggle. He grew up with it, so he understood it, and it never bothered him. But this time on the *Asama*, one of the jewels of Japan's proud NYK Line—this time it felt altogether different. It wasn't even just that he was *gaijin*, a mere alien; rather, for the first time, Cotton felt that he was perceived as a threat, an intruder.

On board was a naval officer, a young lieutenant, a *taii*, returning from attaché duty in Mexico City. He was in his summer whites when they departed Hawaii, and every time he passed by Cotton he would put on a sour face and give him wide berth. The evening of the third day out, the *Asama* lifted out of the tropics into more temperate waters, and the officer switched to his winter dress blues. It seemed to color him in other ways, too; he was home now, bolder . . . and ruder still.

When Cotton took an open place at the other end of the man's table at dinner, the officer rose as if to leave. Hurriedly, Cotton bowed, backing away himself and looking for a seat elsewhere. In its abject submissiveness, the move trumped the officer; but he quickly recovered and smirked, folding his arms akimbo like some kind of conqueror. The other Japanese seemed terribly pleased, and no one ventured conversation with Cotton during the meal.

After that, Cotton gave up trying to mingle with the other passengers. He came in for meals, but otherwise withdrew to his cabin. He always carried a book with him, so that there would be less opportunity for any sort of conversation. Cotton had never been in a situation like this, where his very presence offended others, and he did his best to avoid confrontation. He knew the Japanese well enough to understand that the group had fallen in behind the lieutenant, and that there was no social mechanism to review or correct that.

The last morning at sea, November 9, Cotton woke early and went up on deck to pray, just as the sun was coming up. He didn't see the young officer nearby, meditating, and so Cotton was at the rail, looking out over the Pacific when he was surprised to feel someone standing close by, at his elbow. "Harroo," said the officer derisively, mocking Cotton.

"Good Morning," Cotton replied, in his politest Japanese.

"You do not think I can speak English?"

"No, you speak it very well indeed," Cotton answered in Japanese. "But you were courteous enough to address me in my language, so I replied in kind."

The officer nodded, all the more surly because he didn't know how to counter that in any language. Cotton's insufferable humility was out-Japanesing the Japanese. "So, why are you here?" he asked at last.

"Just to pray."

"I don't meant that. I mean: why are you going to Japan?"

"I'm a priest. I have a church there."

"We don't need Christians. Shinto is our national religion now."

"Oh, there're a lot of Japanese Christians, Lieutenant. Probably half a million. We're legally accepted, you know— since 1912—before you were born."

"That was a bad decision."

"Oh, come on, Lieutenant," Cotton said, and he beckoned to the sun, rising in the Pacific sky. The sun shines on us all, whoever we pray to. No one's ever wrong in prayer."

"The *asahi* starts in Japan." Cotton didn't say anything. "You don't think so? You think it starts in Washington?"

"No, I don't, Lieutenant. I don't think the *asahi* starts anywhere. There's always a dawn somewhere on the globe, some moment of the day."

The lieutenant only eyed Cotton and shook his head. Cotton could tell he was looking for a fight, but be would not indulge him. He was determined to turn the other cheek, and if that was not enough, turn the other cheek. Stymied, at last the officer reached out, without a word, toward Cotton's Bible. He examined it then, turning the pages, pausing to look at the few pictures: Jesus as a boy in the temple, Jesus healing someone, Jesus on the mount. "You believe Jesus is divine, right?" he snapped.

"Oh yes," Cotton said.

"What about Tenno Heika?"

"Well, you believe *he* is divine," Cotton said.

The lieutenant mulled over his response. "Tell me, Reverend," he said after a while, "if you saw Jesus and Tenno Heika both coming toward you, who would you bow to first?"

"Oh, Tenno Heika."

The lieutenant was surprised. "Why?"

"Lieutenant," Cotton said, "I'm sure Jesus would understand."

The young officer stared back at Cotton, and then he simply handed the Bible back and walked away.

When Cotton returned to his cabin, there was a note pushed under the door. It was a telegram, and he opened it and read: IF YOU HAVE TIME IN TOKYO APPRECIATE VISIT STOP PLEASE CALL UPON ARRIVAL. It was signed by someone Cotton had never heard of, E. St. George Bowersox, but underneath his name it said, "Political Attaché, United States Embassy."

Especially now, at this moment, it was comforting for Cotton to be reminded that there were at least some Americans still left waiting for him in the Sun-Begot Land.

15

Cotton found a certain relief as soon as the *Asama* started up Tokyo Bay for port. Surely, he told himself, it would all change, *they* would all change, once the passengers were all let loose from the confines of a ship, and they found themselves celebrating Kigen on the beloved earth that was Japan.

The captain had gone all out from Honolulu to make sure the *Asama* arrived in time for the anniversary, and they were almost half a day early as they glided up the bay toward a night's berth in Yokohama. It was evening, already dark, but Cotton could make out the spectral forms of all sorts of ships, scattered at anchor throughout the harbor, standing out against the lights of the city.

Still, nothing prepared him for the next morning. The passengers were going to disembark first thing, so that all who wanted to—and most all did—could travel up to Tokyo for the midday celebration. Cotton was up and packed before first light, then out on the deck just before dawn—the hour of the hare, the Japanese call it.

And here came the *asahi,* peeking above Chiba, lighting up Yokohama across the bay. With just the first rays a panorama was revealed that took Cotton's breath away. Sampans and pleasure craft were spotted here and there, and with them, one after another, warship upon warship, arrayed, all riding silently on the tide, all as clean as whistles, throwing up sparkles as the dawn's rays touched them for the first time. Still, though, the seamen scurried about, shining and polishing one more time, checking the cannon to make sure that nothing could possibly go wrong when the signal for the twenty-one-gun salute came at eleven-thirty: it was the most amazing armada, military and civilian together—like the newsreels Cotton had seen recently, some sort of serene Dunkirk. It made the view of what Cotton had seen just a few days before, looking down at the fleet in Pearl Harbor, seem puny.

Then the disembarkation began, and he hurried back to his cabin and fetched his valise. When he came back out on deck again, the *asahi* was in all its splendor, the autumn-orange ball firing down through a hole in the clouds upon this great cavalcade of ships, all of them flying *asahi* flags themselves.

Cotton pushed toward the gangplank, and in the crush, there was the young naval lieutenant almost next to him. The sullenness was all gone, and Cotton even thought the smirk had changed into a proper, friendly smile. Anyway, he waved one arm toward the heavens, bringing it down in an arc toward all the ships that lay softly in the velvet water. "Now, Reverend," he said (with just a little bite), "now, how can you say anything but that the day begins here?"

"Okay," Cotton hollered back, "this day the dawn starts here in Japan!" The lieutenant nodded, and Cotton shouted again, for good measure, "Today there's no dawn anywhere else in the world!" and the lieutenant roared at that and reached out his hand, and Cotton stretched his own hand above the heads of all the others, and the two young men touched, and then the happy crush pulled them apart and carried them along the rest of the way.

Cotton's foot hit the dock then, and instantly he felt buoyant. Whatever his heritage, whatever his parentage, Japan was where he came from. Sometimes he forgot that when he was away. Around him, too, everybody was smiling and cheering. It's going to be all right, after all, Cotton thought. It's going to be just fine.

The whole way up to Tokyo on the train, nobody looked at him crossly at all; nobody even seemed to notice that he was a blue-eyed butter-eater with a collar on backwards. And for his part, if Cotton noticed that the people wore clothes a little more ragged, that their faces were a little more drawn, their shoulders a little more hunched than the last time he'd been here, before the war with China started, well, he was polite enough not to pay much attention. Not today. Not on the twenty-six hundredth anniversary of the birth of the Sun-Begot Land.

Cotton looked out at the beauty of the maple trees, afire, as the train rolled along. Everybody raves about the cherry blossoms of the Japanese spring; but when he was away, it was always the maples of the fall that Cotton remembered most. "Yes indeed," said an old Japanese to whom Cotton casually mentioned that once, "you do know our islands, don't you?"

That was quite a compliment, the best he could ever hope for as a *gaijin*. It wasn't just that the Japanese considered themselves gods. So what? All sorts of would-be cultures were forever tracing their royalty back to gods. In one way or another, Cotton had to admit, that's what the whole Bible was up to. No, what really set Japan apart was that the place itself was hallowed, for, as everybody knew, when Izanagi, the senior male god, sitting up there on the Bridge of High Heaven with Izanami, his bride goddess, dipped his spear into the waters that covered all the earth, some of the drops of moisture on the end of the spear congealed as a divine mist, and, as everybody knew, when they fell back toward the waters, they plunked down and started Nippon. Everybody knew that. It was the vanity of the land, more so even than the people, which distinguished Japan so. Cotton knew that.

In the West, the Garden of Eden was always idolized; it was also always somewhere else. Nobody even had much of an idea where it was supposed to have been. And anyway, it didn't matter, because everybody had gotten thrown *out* of there, and then spent all their time looking for a new Promised Land somewhere else. In Japan, though, the Garden of Eden *was* Japan, and the idea, pretty much, was for the Japanese to throw everybody else out. That was the big difference. It casts everything in a different light when you are a whole nation full of Adams, and everybody else in the world is an Eve or a serpent, living in the lower-rent districts.

And then the train pulled into Tokyo. It was Cotton's intention to take the elevated line and transfer to a streetcar up to Asakusa, drop his bag off at the Serikawas' house, and come back downtown; but only a few steps off the train and he knew if he tried that, he'd spend the whole day in transit. The throngs were incredible. It was as if all of Japan were arrayed before him. Everyone, all ages, was turned out in their most magnificent kimono, packed together along the sidewalks, while out in the streets children marched by carrying portable shrines, and kendo athletes staged exhibitions of the ancient martial sport. Above, everywhere, banners and pennants and lanterns rippled in the breeze. Nothing was left undecorated, not even the streetcars, which were adorned with flowers, or the mounted police, in special green trousers ordered just for the occasion. As Cotton quickly noticed too, the happiness that reigned was not just on account of patriotism; the rules of austerity had been waived today and daytime drinking was permitted, a largess most of the men took full advantage of.

Cotton fought his way on foot toward Hibiya Park, trying to get close to the grounds of the Imperial Palace, where the ceremonies were being held; but it was hard going, and his valise slowed him on all the more. He moved gingerly; the last thing he wanted to be in Japan on Kigen was a rude *gaijin.* Cotton was not a tall man, but he was too tall ever to go unnoticed among the Japanese; he could never fade in.

Suddenly then, as he moved onto the Hibiya-dori, in front of the palace gardens, the crowds began to hush, and Cotton strained to hear. Sure enough, he could make out the sounds of bugles, far away, wafting softly, dimly over the treetops.

The heraldry stopped, and the people roared. Cotton turned to the old man next to him. "What was that?" The old fellow only gasped and covered his ears. "I'm sorry," Cotton said, "but I've been away and just returned. What was that?"

The old man shook his head and almost shrieked: *"Ah, kimochi ga waruii!"* Ah, it gives me the creeps! He turned and nudged his wife beside him, then turned back to Cotton. "Talk again, please, please."

Cotton laughed. How many times had he heard someone say those very words to him? *Ah, kimochi ga waruii!* Japanese simply could not accept that some Westerners could speak such perfect, idiomatic, inflected Japanese.

Hmmm, Cotton thought, pleased with himself: five years away and I haven't dropped a stitch. He bowed and said: "It is my distinct honor to be back in the land of my birth on this most glorious of anniversaries."

"Ah, kimochi ga waruii!" shrieked the old woman.

"Ah, kimochi ga waruii!" hollered the old man again, and all around him other folks cried out: *"Ah, kimochi . . . !"*

"But please, what were the bugles for?" Cotton pleaded, and finally one man marshaled his composure sufficiently to tell him that it meant that it was exactly forty-eight minutes past ten o'clock, the time appointed for Tenno Heika and the Empress to be summoned from the Palace.

And the excitement grew. Someone passed Cotton some sake, and it warmed him, and from somewhere, softly, drifted the singing of the "Kimigayo," the national anthem, and it swept down to them, and they all joined in, Cotton included.

He looked over the multitude and saw the people as far as he could see, except—now he noticed, how strange!—of course there were no people in the upper stories, nobody on the roofs, for no one was allowed to look down on the Celestial Emperor Whom One Regards from Below the Steps of the Throne. How odd that appears, Cotton thought. It made him think of a child's drawing, where there is the ground, and people and buildings on the ground, and the sky is just a blue band across the top of the paper, and there is nothing at all in between.

Quite nearby, Kiyoshi and Miyuki and Mrs. Serikawa were behaving much more decorously. A huge pavilion had been constructed inside the palace grounds, and fifty-five thousand Japanese had been carefully chosen to attend the ceremonies. The Serikawas were invited—and, of course, Kiyoshi was a Serikawa himself now—in grateful tribute to Colonel Serikawa, the hero of Manchukuo. They might not have had the best seats in the pecking order, but they were indeed within the pavilion, and they were three of only fifty-five thousand human beings in all the world who saw Tenno Heika come out in his white robes and approach the altar.

It was a religious ceremony above all, and the sacred hush that calls up to heaven fell on the crowd. It was precisely twenty-five minutes after eleven o'clock in the morning of November 10, 1940, the fifteenth year of Showa, and outside the Palace and all over Japan, all over Manchukuo and Korea and the China she ruled, all over the burgeoning Empire of the Rising Sun, everything stopped still. Everything. The streetcars and the trains and the moving pictures. Kiyoshi took Miyuki's hand and clasped it in his, and they both cried. And then everyone who possible could, rose and shouted three banzais: May you live ten thousand years!

Only softly, to himself, Cotton prayed: "May we live ten thousand years together—Japan and the United States."

Down off Yokohama, from all the great ships, the cannon fired twenty-one times, and in the pavilion, Kiyoshi could feel the tears tumbling down his cheeks. He turned to the two ladies and said: "Forgive me for crying, but I am so proud to be a Japanese, and I am so honored to be a Serikawa." He did not add that the ceremonies were making him feel guilty, too, because he was Western-tainted and torn sometimes that Japan was not acting wisely in the world. But Kiyoshi never

admitted that, and certainly not now. Instead, he only bowed
tearfully to his mother-in-law, and then he whispered to
Miyuki: "And now I know why we haven't been able to have
a baby yet."

"Why?" she whispered back.

"Because the gods want him to be conceived tonight, a
child of Kigen 2600."

Miyuki winked at Kiyoshi and whispered banzais three
more times.

16

What a party they had at the Serikawas that night! There
were *unagidomburi*—eels over rice—and *mochi*—rice cakes that
were usually served on New Year's Day; but this was a special
day, too, wasn't it, a new epoch's day? And there were even
sembi—seaweed biscuits that were traditionally served for new
neighbors. "You are our neighbor again, Cotton," Miyuki
said as she laid them out, and she leaned down and kissed
him again, on the cheek. "Our neighbor in Japan."

"Arigato." Thank you. Cotton took her hand and held on to
it for a few seconds. "You're a very luck man," he told
Kiyoshi.

"Ah, she can cook rice," he said, but with the measure of
a facetious smile they all understood. The ability to cook rice
was the simple old Japanese standard of gauging a wife. Otherwise . . . what good was a wife for? It was the same as at the
end of a life: if an old Japanese couldn't do enough work in
the paddies to account for his own rice quota, then it was
time for him to go up into the mountains and move on peace-
fully, dying of exposure.

"Is that all?" Miyuki said, playfully snatching Kiyoshi's
plate away. "Then no *sembei* for you."

"Aw, let 'im have one," Cotton said.

"A moga wife—right, Mother?" Kiyoshi said, and Cotton

and Miyuki laughed with him. Not Mrs. Serikawa. She was perfectly appalled at Miyuki, not only sitting there with her husband and her husband's friend but enjoying a joke with them. Mrs. Serikawa wouldn't even have dinner with the younger people, notwithstanding all their entreaties. Instead, in the old Japanese fashion, she had already eaten. That was the way it should be: first the wife serves the parents, then her husband (and the children, should he invite them to join him). As for the wife herself, she usually grabbed what she could, standing up in the kitchen.

But then, Mrs. Serikawa was generally dismayed at the appalling lack of respect Miyuki showed her husband when they were together in their house—and it didn't matter that Miyuki remained properly obsequious in public. Her poor father and brother would be appalled. It wasn't just a matter of impropriety, either; Miyuki was on shaky ground as long as she failed to give Kiyoshi a child—let alone a son. Oh, to be sure, there had been the one miscarriage, but she hadn't even managed to get pregnant since then. Any time soon, Mrs. Serikawa was sure, Miyuki was going to pay for this performance and find another woman in the house, an *omekakesan,* someone fecund and grateful. Kiyoshi had the money to afford a second wife, that was for sure. And money isn't everything, either. Mrs. Serikawa knew that even on a military salary, the colonel damn well wouldn't have put up with a barren wife this long.

If the situation even perturbed Miyuki, though, she didn't let on. The doctor assured her that nothing was wrong; and besides, what could she do if American Orient had sent Kiyoshi back to San Francisco for several months and the damn government hadn't given her permission to go along?

"Hush!" Mrs. Serikawa said when Miyuki complained about that—out loud—one time. "I will not have you talk that way about the Emperor's government."

"They send enough men to fight in China," Miyuki replied. "They could allow one woman to go to San Francisco."

Mrs. Serikawa swooned and walked away. It was bad enough that Miyuki really had become a moga. That's just

social misdirection, and curable if caught in time, presumably
with a baby at the breast. But the sort of disrespectful political
remarks—even *wisecracks*—that Miyuki and some of her new
friends in Tokyo were not above delivering these days went
beyond the pale. She was simply too flip—and Kiyoshi tolerated it, just like some foolish Western man. Really, Mrs.
Serikawa thought sometimes, Miyuki hadn't been the same
since that long honeymoon in Hawaii, when she saw the way
the *gaijin* women carried on. It was a wise government indeed
that wouldn't permit her to go off to San Francisco when
American Orient assigned Kiyoshi there.

Miyuki usually figured out whenever she'd overstepped her
bounds though; and this time she apologized and chased after
her mother. "Oh, come on, Mother, Kiyoshi's back now, and
he'll be around for a while. You watch, you'll have a grand-
child before the Year of the Snake is over." That would be
1941.

Mrs. Serikawa melted quickly. "Hmmm. And that would
still be metal, too," she mused. "Like Takeo. Your brother
was a metal baby."

Miyuki nodded, even if she had long since forgotten. There
were two calendars, running concurrently: one celebrating a
dozen creatures, the other the five elements—and Mrs.
Serikawa had decided that 1941, the Year of the Metal
Snake, boded quite well. Every day since Miyuki had promised her mother that she would give birth in that twelve-
month, Mrs. Serikawa would go to a little shrine near the
house and pray for a grandson. Once, on the day when
Kiyoshi was returning from San Francisco, she kind of tricked
Miyuki and took her over to the Sensoji, the great shrine of
Asakusa, and bought every possible goodluck charm,
breathed in the *yakuyoke* smoke for yet more good fortune, and
then tried to rub Miyuki's belly. That was where Miyuki drew
the line—having her belly rubbed in public. "Mother, come
on! Kiyoshi and I will handle this ourselves."

Well, maybe; Miyuki got her period two weeks later, and it
required all Mrs. Serikawa's diplomacy to keep silent. No
matter how tired she was at night, she could never fall off to

sleep in her little room upstairs until she could hear her daughter and her *yoshi* making love below. Or not making love.

Only then, in joyful anticipation or befuddled despair, could she close her eyes.

Now, after dinner, Miyuki brought out some brandy for Cotton and Kiyoshi; she'd picked up the custom in Honolulu on her honeymoon. Then she went across the room to help her mother tidy up.

"So how long before you go up to Tochigi?" Kiyoshi asked Cotton.

"Hey!" Miyuki called out. "Speak English. I've got to work on my English again, and if we've got Cotton here—"

"Cotton Dlake," Cotton said.

"Yeah, Cotton Dlake-san," Miyuki echoed, laughing. She was standing across the room, in a brocaded baby-blue kimono. They all were still wearing kimonos for Kigen, and Cotton couldn't help saying out loud what he'd been thinking all through dinner: "Gosh, you look pretty, Miyuki."

"You always thought I was just another little Japanese girl with daikon legs."

"Yeah, but I did too," Kiyoshi sniped, "and I'm not even *gaijin*."

"Well, I've seen the light," Cotton said, raising his brandy glass. "May all your children take after you."

Kiyoshi lifted his glass too. "We will conceive on Kigen!" he cried out, quite dramatically.

Mrs. Serikawa, suddenly beaming, bowed to everyone and departed upstairs.

"I'll just be here for a couple of days," Cotton said then, embarrassed, returning the conversation to a more prosaic subject. "Some guy at the American embassy wants to see me. And I just want to look around the city. You know, I haven't been back here since '35."

"It's not as nice," Miyuki called from across the room, but Kiyoshi shot her a knock-it-off look and said:

"Gotta see the bishop?"

"Naw, he's long gone. They forced him out."

"Oh yeah," Kiyoshi mumbled, ducking his head. "I'm sorry."

"Don't apologize, Key. Maybe it's to the good." The Japanese, in their nationalistic fervor, had come down on the Christian churches a few weeks before, demanding that they hand over control to the indigenous priests. "We had to give up authority eventually, and probably, if we'd been smart, we'd have made that decision ourselves."

"Come on, you two, let's not talk politics," Miyuki said, bringing her own drink over and joining them on the tatami.

"Oh no, this isn't politics," Cotton said. "We're just talking about me. I'm very lucky to be here, you know. The U.S. stopped allowing citizens in last month, and I'm not so sure they'd have let me come if everything hadn't already been in place. The paperwork. Most missionaries are getting out."

"I can't blame them," Miyuki said.

Kiyoshi glared. *"Oi!"* was all he said, sharply—hey, you! It was the classic traditional address, the boss husband to the subservient wife.

Miyuki got the message, but if she backed down, she didn't yield completely. She bowed to her husband. She bowed to Cotton. "I'm sorry," she said, "but it is a different land now, Cotton. You're our friend, and we can say that." She put her hand on his.

Kiyoshi was seething, but he resumed appearances, Western-style, and addressed Cotton, Japanese-style, as if Miyuki were not there. "Miyuki does not understand sometimes. It's war. It's hard. The world is not just *onna daigaku*—woman's way."

Miyuki smiled foolishly and bowed; she'd gone far enough. Cotton was embarrassed for them all and tried again to change the subject. "Well, what about you, Key? Can you keep on working for American Orient?"

"We're worried about the draft," Miyuki said, and Kiyoshi shot her a look, and Cotton realized she was probably a little tipsy.

"Actually," Kiyoshi said evenly, "Admiral Yamamoto wants to see me."

"Yamamoto? Himself?"

"Well, you know, my father got pretty friendly with him years ago when we were both in the States. I've known the admiral since I was a little boy, so it's no big deal."

"But see you?"

"I'm guessing he wants to take me into the navy. And if it's a choice I have to make, fine. The navy's a helluva lot more civilized than the army."

Miyuki picked up the brandy bottle and offered it to Cotton. He put his hand over his glass. "No thanks, I think we've all had enough," he said, and out of the corner of his eye he saw Kiyoshi nod some kind of thanks. If Cotton had taken one more, Miyuki would have wanted one too, and Kiyoshi would have told her no, and it would have been unpleasant.

"So, anyway, I'm seeing the admiral day after tomorrow."

"I guess that's the end of you and American Orient, then."

Kiyoshi shrugged. "Yeah, the end of *us* and American Orient."

"What do they want to see you about at the embassy?" Miyuki asked Cotton.

"I don't know. I didn't recognize the man's name."

"Do they want to use you?" she said.

"Miyuki!" Kiyoshi snapped.

Cotton held up his hand to Kiyoshi. "Please," he said. And to Miyuki: "Listen, nobody is going to use me. I'm only here to spread the word of Jesus Christ. And that's all."

"I'm sorry, Cotton," Miyuki said, and she bowed to him.

Cotton bowed back. "It's okay."

"Things are just getting so much more difficult."

"I know. But this is Kigen, and it's time for bed now." Cotton leaned over and kissed Miyuki and slapped Kiyoshi on the shoulders and headed upstairs. He didn't dare look back; he could hear Kiyoshi whispering angrily to her, and he could all but feel the glare. He could hear Miyuki mumbling too, and *"oi"* and *"oi"* again after that.

Cotton stepped around Mrs. Serikawa. He thought—he hoped—she was asleep, but then she said, "Hello, Cotton."

"Oh, hello, Mrs. Serikawa. I'm sorry if I woke you."

"No, that's okay. I'm just waiting to hear them make love."

"Oh, yes," Cotton said, getting down on his futon.

"Listen. A good time to make love, on Kigen."

"A very good time," Cotton replied, not quite sure how much of a lead he should take in this conversation. Never before had he chatted with a mother about her daughter getting screwed downstairs. He wasn't sure of the etiquette.

"It's about time they have a baby," Mrs. Serikawa went on. "Maybe Kigen will do the trick."

"Maybe."

"Shhhh," Mrs. Serikawa said, listening carefully. "Probably not much foreplay tonight. A long day. Both very tired."

"Yeah," Cotton said, and he listened closely himself. He was kind of getting into the swing of things. "This is sort of like listening to a radio program, Mrs. Serikawa."

She laughed. She liked that. A little rustling came from downstairs then; a little grunting. Cotton didn't hear a peep out of Miyuki. This must have occurred to Mrs. Serikawa, too. "Miyuki's very quiet tonight," she explained. "Usually, she makes a lot more noise."

"Well, you know, she's had a lot to drink."

"That's a good point, Cotton." And then there was a little holler out of Kiyoshi, and no more noise at all. "Pretty quick tonight," Mrs. Serikawa observed.

"I guess," Cotton said.

"Never heard Miyuki so quiet."

"Oh, I see."

"Doesn't matter, Cotton. The colonel always told me that the whores make a lot of noise." Cotton didn't respond. "Isn't that so?"

"Well, it's been a while since I've been with one, Mrs. Serikawa."

"Oh. Don't have to make a lot of noise when you're a wife, though. It's not necessary."

"No ma'am."

"It's not necessary for babies, Cotton. Either when you start them or have them. Noise just isn't necessary for a good Japanese wife."

"Well, you know, I've never had a baby."

"Okay. Just keep it in mind. Goodnight, Cotton."

"Goodnight, Mrs. Serikawa."

17

The next morning, the Serikawas got all dressed up again in their fanciest kimonos and went back to the Palace. They had the same seats, only today's was a more secular celebration. Even *gaijin* were included, and Ambassador Grew, as the senior diplomat in Tokyo, had been invited to make the address to Japan on behalf of the lesser rest of the world. He was effusive, and the day was sunny and every bit as festive too.

Alone, Cotton struggled with his hangover, puttering around, reading the newspapers. He had enough of the crowds. Finally he went out strolling, renewing his memories of Tokyo. After a while, almost on a whim, he hitched a streetcar ride, then took a transfer, moving aimlessly, but skirting the great throngs in the Palace area. He ended up, by chance, near the American embassy on Reinazaka Hill, and so he got off and walked the rest of the way there.

Cotton remembered the embassy well. "Hoover's Folly" it had been called almost from the moment it had been constructed—a big, white, heavy building, earthquake-proof, some sort of strange combination of the Moorish and the colonial. When Cotton ambled down the driveway—flanked by the big bushes overlooking the croquet lawn—the one thing that occurred to him was that the place had not grown on him one bit.

As he had anticipated, the embassy was deathly still today. The guard at the wrought-iron gates just waved him on, and the receptionist inside, who was reading a trashy novel, was irritated that she had to look up. Cotton was only the second visitor of the day.

"I don't suppose anyone's here." he explained, but he was in the neighborhood, etc.

"It's Kigen," she said, as if this had not occurred to him. She had a Southern accent, which seemed downright bizarre in Japan.

"Well, yeah, but ... uh ... Mr., uh, Bowerschmidt?"

"Mr. Who-all?"

Cotton fumbled the telegram out of his pocket. "Uh, let's see ... Bowersox."

"Oh, Mr. Bowersox."

"Yes, he cabled me the other day that he'd like to see me when I got in. Can I just leave a number where he can call me?"

"He's in."

"Mr. Bowersox is in now?"

"Yeah, he's the only one."

"Well, could you let him know I'm here?"

"Mr. Bowersox's not expectin' any visitors today."

"Well, I wasn't expecting Mr. Bowersox today either."

The receptionist mulled that over. "Well, can y'all give me your name?"

"Cotton Drake. The Reverend Mr. Drake."

She considered that. "I wouldn't have taken you for a preacher," she assayed. "If y'all don't mind my sayin'."

"Don't worry. Sometimes I feel that way, too."

So she called Bowersox, and pretty soon he appeared and escorted Cotton back down the hall to his office. "Well, Padre, this is a surprise," he declared, lighting up a Lucky Strike. If there was one thing Cotton despised, it was people who called him "Padre." He got one about every three or four months. It made no sense to call him "Padre" then to walk around Nebraska calling people "Monsieur" or "Fräulein."

Cotton explained that he hadn't thought Bowersox would be in, but he happened to be in the neighborhood, etc. Bowersox replied: "One day of all this Kigen crap was enough for me. Even in a normal year, these people got more holidays than Carter has little pills. And frankly, Padre, I

couldn't give a hoot about the last twenty-six hundred years.
I'm only interested what these little SOBs are going to be
doing in the next twenty-six weeks—or twenty-six days, for
that matter."

"You don't sound very optimistic about things."

"They want war, and we'll let them have it, thank you very
much."

Cotton didn't respond to that, so Bowersox took another
puff and appeared thoughtful. "I hate to be that blunt before
reverend clergy, but that's the bald truth . . . and that's why
I'd advise you to take the next stage out of town."

"I grew up here, you know."

"Yeah, I'm aware of that." He slapped a folder on his desk
to let Cotton know that he was up on him. "But we're not as
different as you might imagine, you and me. My parents were
missionaries, too."

"Oh?"

"Methodist. I was raised mostly in Changsa."

"China."

"Hunan province. Different country, same experience. And
we're still the same kettle of fish, pretty much. You chose the
church, I the government. Two bureaucracies, same low pay.
I've lived in them both. More similarities than differences."
Cotton granted him a smile. "But the fact of the matter is
that there isn't much the government can do now about
Japan—and not a damn thing *you* can do." He ground out his
Lucky when he said that, even though it had a couple puffs
left in it. Bowersox had an actor in him that Cotton rather
enjoyed. Unfortunately, he wasn't sure he was all that keen on
the real article.

"That's your opinion, Mr. Bowersox."

"Saint. Call me Saint. My mother named me St. George,
she always said, so the family would always be assured to
have one saint in it. Actually, I'm afraid that was a large dose
of false humility. Both of them, Mother and Father, were convinced each personally was a saint and the other one was bor-
derline. But it sounded good in the missionary community."

Cotton laughed. "Yeah, I think my parents named me for Cotton Mather, but they'd never admit it to me."

Bowersox nodded, took out another Lucky Strike, lit it, looked out the window, came back to the desk, and did some other calculated bits of business before he got back to looking directly at Cotton. "Look, I know how it goes. Most folks pussyfoot, they gild the lily when they deal with a man of God. But excuse me, I can be honest." Cotton nodded. "You see, I grew up with the church, and I know. I know preachers make love and drink whiskey and fart and maybe even lie a little and cheat a little and are just as human as the rest of us mortals."

"No argument," Cotton said, when the opportunity presented itself.

"Right. So listen to me. How long since you were here last?" He went over to his desk and flipped open Cotton's folder.

" 'Thirty-five," said Cotton.

"August of 'thirty-five," Bowersox said, rapping the folder for emphasis. "Well let me tell you—'thirty-five. This is a different place in 'forty, Padre."

"Not 'Padre,' please."

"Oh, excuse me," Bowersox said, missing the point as he careened by at top speed. "Excuse me, you're not High Church."

Cotton didn't bother. " 'Mister' is fine. 'Cotton' is fine," is all he said.

"Well, all right, Cotton, things were just starting to come alive in 'thirty-five. It was before the Panay incident, before we finally started to get a little prickly ourselves. FDR started to see that Stanley Hornbeck over at FE had the goods on these fellows. Savvy? But never mind the politics. Never mind what I'm saying. *They* just don't want *you* here."

"Who's 'they'?"

"The Japs. All of 'em. They just don't want anybody here walking around saying you should worship this guy who's divine, but he's not Hirohito. Savvy? You are a . . . sore . . . point."

"It was never easy here."

"Look, I know that. I'm not being antichurch. I lived that life. And I also know damn well what missionaries *can* do. Even if you didn't save a single soul, you could do good. Because, if nothing else, you were American. Hey, you might have been carrying the cross, but you were showing the flag in the bargain. That rubbed off. So missionaries were good for us, for the whole country. But listen to me."

"Okay."

"You're just not gonna be able to do that anymore here. They're gonna constantly be on your ass. Ooops, pardon my French, Padre."

"Cotton."

"Cotton. They're going to make it very tough for you. And the idea in your profession is to save souls . . . is it not?"

Cotton held out his hands. "Well . . ." he began.

"In a nutshell—right?"

"All right. In a nutshell: save souls."

"Nutshell, right. I'm not getting theological here. I'm just saying, saving souls is the general idea. That's why you're here—to spread the gospel and to bring people to Christ. Or anyway, to the Protestant Episcopal Church." Cotton winced a little. It wasn't the substance of the remark but just the tackiness of it. Bowersox took another long puff. "I'm sorry, I couldn't resist that. The Methodist in me."

"I'm not offended."

"Well, you are simply not going to be able to do that anymore here, Reverend Drake."

"I—"

"Please understand. This is no reflection on you. I'm not saying that you're not a good missionary. For all I know, you're a *whale* of a good missionary. But you can't save souls here, because the little yellow buggers who run the government will simply not allow it. Or, to give the devil his due, the law of diminishing returns will be so great that even if you scare up one or two, it's just not going to be worth your while. Savvy?"

"Every single soul matters, Saint."

"Absolutely. And you can do a damn sight better totaling up souls somewhere else. If you're gonna be a fisher of men, you better go where the fish are biting. That's all I'm saying."

Cotton started slowly. "I know you're right," he said, and Bowersox nodded confirmation of the obvious. "I know that. I appreciate your frankness."

"Good."

Now Cotton rose. "But I grew up here, and forgive me, sir, but they're not 'little yellow buggers' to me."

"I'm sorry. That was the hyperbole of the moment."

"I'm sorry. It was more than that."

Bowersox bowed his head. "I apologize."

"Thank you. You see, I always loved these people, and I think I can do some good here. I think I can introduce some of them to Christ. And if I can't—and maybe your right— well, I have to find that out for myself."

"I understand," Bowersox said, and he really did sound contrite. "I understand, because my father felt the same way."

"Listen, I do appreciate your warning me."

"And I hope you prove me wrong. I hope before you're done you put up a cathedral in . . . where you going exactly?"

"Tochigi."

"Oh yeah. A cathedral in Tochigi." That pushed a button with Bowersox. He went back over to his desk, pulled out a drawer, and started through some files. "Tochigi, Tochigi . . . let's see." He yanked a folder out. "Yeah. Here. There used to be a geta factory up there, just outside of town. Know it?"

Cotton shook his head. "Never been there before. When I was growing up here, we were mostly down near Osaka and Kyoto."

"Yeah, well, there's a lot of timber up there, and silk's nearby, so there was this geta factory."

"Makes sense." Getas were the clogs Japanese wore, the big toe and the one next to it separated from the other three toes by a strap made of silk. In the old days, and even now, still, away from the cities, men and women alike wore getas instead of shoes. People speculated that walking on them might have been one of the reasons why the Japanese stayed so small, because getas bowed the legs.

"Well, yeah, it was a natural place for a geta factory. Only they're not making getas there anymore. The factory was kind of built under a bunch of pine trees, so they took advantage of the natural camouflage and switched over and started making Zero parts."

"I'm sorry. What are zero parts?"

"Airplane parts. For Zeros."

"For what?"

"Zeros. The new fighter planes. The round suns on either wing—they look like zeros. So they named them Zeros, in honor of Kigen—two-six-zero-zero."

"Oh."

"So maybe if you could just keep an eye on the old geta factory . . ."

Cotton had caught the drift that this might be coming. Still, when it did, he was astonished. He put his hands on his hips and shook his head. "You want me to spy?"

"I want you to keep an eye on the factory."

" 'Keeping an eye on' is damn well spying."

"As you wish, Mr. Drake. As you wish. But understand one thing. These dear old friends of yours are going to go to war with us. And probably sooner than you think. You don't want to leave, fine. You want to stay here and bring new lambs to Christ—fine, I honor you. Frankly, I think you fail to appreciate the difficulty and . . . the danger. But, as you say, see for yourself. But I also suggest to you: render unto Caesar. And right now, you're in my church, and I'm telling you that we are about to explode, and maybe, Reverend, maybe if we do, and you have kept an eye on the old geta factory, then just maybe you can save some lives as well as some souls. Savvy?"

Cotton took it in. It bordered on a tirade, but it also made sense. "You're very persuasive, Saint."

"I listened to my father's sermons."

"But you also have me at a disadvantage. I've been away. I can't speak with authority. Let me go to Tochigi. Let me see the people. If I agree with your assessment then, I promise you, I'll get my ass out of Japan. Pronto."

"Good" was all Bowersox said. He was terribly pleased with himself. He had not expected the young missionary to be such a tough nut, and so then to have extracted even this provisional promise was a signal success.

"And," Cotton went on, "if I find the opposite, if I find that these are still good people who're just intimidated by a bunch of the army thugs—will you help me work for peace then?"

"Hell, I'm working for peace now."

"Funny way you're going about it."

"Don't forget," Bowersox said, "if you really know the Japanese that well—they always get up early, they shoot first and give answers later."

18

Cotton didn't bring up to Kiyoshi his conversation with Bowersox, and when Kiyoshi inquired casually, Cotton was vague and artful. "Quite a coincidence," he said. "This fellow Bowersox, his parents were Methodist missionaries, and, uh, apparently, they knew my folks. Very nice of him to ask me by. We had a nice chat about the church." Well, didn't we chat about the church? he thought. Some . . .

It wasn't till then that Cotton realized he'd also purposely avoided telling Kiyoshi about his trip on the *Asama*, about the nasty lieutenant and the ugly treatment he'd received from most of the passengers. That bothered him when he thought about it, for there had never been anything he had not shared with Kiyoshi. Now, here he was protecting Kiyoshi from bad news . . . or was he protecting himself?

Or couldn't he trust Kiyoshi anymore? No, please. Of course he trusted him.

Well, Kiyoshi wasn't interested in Bowersox, anyway. Instead he said: "Hey, look, I got an idea."

"Shoot," said Cotton, relieved.

"First thing tomorrow, I'm going down to Yokohama—"

"To see Yamamoto?"

"Yeah, for lunch. But I'm not coming right back. I have to go on to Kobe on business, and possibly even over to Nagasaki. The earliest I'll be back is Wednesday night. Maybe not till the weekend. So—"

"What?"

"Why doesn't Miyuki go with you tomorrow up to Tochigi and help you get settled in?"

Cotton said: "Hey, that'd be great."

"You know: a little woman's touch. Tidy the rectory up, that sort of thing."

"Terrific. What'd she say?"

"I haven't asked her."

"You haven't?"

"But she'd love to," Kiyoshi said.

"*Oi*, huh?"

"Don't be a wise guy, Cotton. Listen to me: if you show up there with this Japanese woman, and they find out she's the wife of your good Japanese friend, that'll help you."

"You think that's important?"

Kiyoshi just said, "I think it'll help." He lit a cigarette.

"You know, Key," Cotton finally said, "I wasn't—I mean, I didn't tell you . . . that guy at the embassy. He wasn't very optimistic. In fact, he was pretty depressing."

"Oh?"

"He's sure there'll be war between us. Soon. You think so?"

"Look, okay, it's obviously not very good," Kiyoshi said. "But things will get better."

"You're sure?"

"No. But everybody's not a hothead. We've still got people like Admiral Yamamoto. We can iron things out."

* * *

Everything about the Japanese was always so confounding to *gaijin*, so contradictory. That made it all the more difficult for Westerners that the Japanese were totally in agreement: Of course there are contradictions. What's your problem, butter eaters? The whole point of man, the essence of us all, is contradictions.

Nothing exemplified these paradoxical antitheses more than the way the Japanese named their warships. Westerners christened their gunboats by saluting earlier warriors and battles or by playing the politics of democracy and celebrating places. But Kiyoshi had to chuckle to himself as he rode on the tender out to Yamamoto's flagship. For there, off Yokohama, lay the rest of the armada, including the *Kasumi*, the *Shiranuhi*, the *Tanikaze*, the *Shokaku*, the *Zuikaku*, the *Akagi*, the *Soryu*, the *Hiryu*, and the *Kaga*, which were: Mist of Flowers, Phosphorescent Foam, Valley Wind, Soaring Crane, Happy Crane, Red Castle, Green Dragon, Flying Dragon, and Increased Joy. It did not strike the Japanese as at all odd that vehicles of death and carnage should have such poetic names. On the contrary, this was the way of logic, of the whole. "No wonder we have such a hard time understanding one another," Kiyoshi thought, smiling, as he climbed aboard the flagship, the *Akagi*.

The admiral hurried out of his cabin to greet Kiyoshi, and they bowed, and then he showed his young friend around the great carrier before they joined his staff for lunch. Kiyoshi was impressed at the company; these struck him as men of some style, even intelligence and wit. Many of them had been posted abroad—the older ones, generally, to the United States and England, the younger to Germany—and they all showed, he thought, at least an appreciation of the West. Kiyoshi, in fact, could not avoid mentioning this impression as soon as the lunch was concluded, when Yamamoto had escorted him to his private quarters.

"Unsaid, I gather," the admiral replied, "is the presumption that most of our military is boorish and uncouth."

"I suppose, Yamamoto Shirei Chokan," Kiyoshi said, using the most formal title, bowing his head. "Forgive me for any condescension, but the army does sometimes give off that impression, and I beg to apologize to the spirits of my father, Colonel Serikawa, and my brother, Takeo Serikawa, for those opinions."

Yamamoto just threw up a hand. "Ah, you're probably right." Kiyoshi sighed. "The problem with the damn army is that too many of the soldiers are from the rural prefectures. Then they keep too much to themselves, and they reinforce themselves—even at the highest levels." Yamamoto paused. "We understand ourselves?"

"Yes sir."

"The army is too much like some religious order—damn near like monks. Unfortunately, there's no military class anymore in this country. The samurai are gone. There's no German junkers here. But it is a fact that we—the navy—tend to be more open and worldly. And the army resents that."

"Yes sir."

Yamamoto suddenly shifted to English. "Just us chickens," he said.

"Sir?"

"Ever hear that in the States?"

"Sure," Kiyoshi said. "Just between us chickens."

"A fellow I used to play bridge with in Washington—from their Department of the Navy—used it. I liked the expression, although he never could explain to me why it was 'just us chickens' and not 'just us ducks.' Or 'rabbits.' Or 'pigs.' But anyway, this is all just between us chickens."

"Yes sir."

"All of it."

Kiyoshi nodded. Whatever, this must be important. Yamamoto was speaking in such an unusual manner—at once more intense and more familiar than would be expected from a dignitary of such high rank. "You have my word, Yamamoto Shirei Chosan," Kiyoshi replied.

"Good. The trouble with the army is not the army. The trouble with the army is the constitution: that damn provision that permits the army to report directly to Tenno Heika without bothering with the prime minister."

"Doesn't the navy have the same option?"

"Absolutely. Only we play ball. We would never exercise it."

"But, tacitly, the army has a veto power?"

Yamamoto nodded solemnly. "You understand. And ultimately, it's a war power. And that's where we stand."

Kiyoshi gulped. This was extraordinarily blunt language coming from an admiral of the Japanese Imperial Navy. But then again, what Yamamoto was saying did not in itself surprise Kiyoshi, for the words were consistent with the sort of thoughts Yamamoto was supposed to bear.

"Whatever," the admiral went on, "we cannot be naive now. And we cannot be weak. And . . . I'm afraid we may have to be expedient rather than principled." He paused for a moment, then stood up, bowed, and resumed speaking in Japanese: "Serikawa Kiyoshi, I would invite you to join us on a vital mission as an officer in the Imperial Navy."

Yamamoto stepped to the bar then, while Kiyoshi took another deep breath. The admiral proffered a bottle of sake. Kiyoshi shook his head. "Don't feel you shouldn't take a drink now just because I don't ever," Yamamoto said.

"No, I—"

"Well, I have some Scotch, some gin. Boodles"—he held up the bottle. "I hear that's the best. I even have some bourbon—sippin' whiskey." Yamamoto said those last words not only in English but with a fairly passable southern accent.

"No, thank you, sir. I had some sake before lunch. I'd best keep my head clear here."

"Good. Fine." Yamamoto pointed back to his desk. "Those are your army draft orders. I had them pulled . . . temporarily. Now understand, you go in the army, they're not going to strap a bayonet on you and send you into China. I'm sure they'll employ your considerable English-language talents. If I were a general—if—and if—*when*—the war is ever expanded, I would think of all the places where English is spoken. Singapore, surely."

"I even lived there for a couple of years when I was a kid."

"Yes. And the Philippines. Burma. Possibly even Australia." Kiyoshi swallowed at that. "You'll be an intelligence officer with some responsibility for these places. Quite likely you'll never leave Tokyo. Not bad."

"And if I serve in the navy?"

Yamamoto paced. The overhead fan whirred, but they had been together for a long time in the cabin, and the admiral threw open a porthole to catch the harbor breezes. Then he turned back. "What do you think of the United States?"

"That's not hard to answer," Kiyoshi said straightaway. "I like the place. I like the people. America's had a great effect on me."

"Me too. But then, I'm sure you've heard my critics quote me to that effect with more bite. We can learn so much from America. So much. They can learn from us, too, of course, but they can teach us more. And I suppose we've both got a great deal of learning ahead of us, because—" He stopped and let it hang there. Finally, Kiyoshi took the cue.

"Because?" he said.

"Because we're going to war with each other. You learn so much, killing one another. The Chinese know us much better now."

"You think war can't be avoided, sir?"

"Well, the army thinks it can't. So it can't. You see, my young friend, we've never lost a war. That makes you very brave. And the only time we were even threatened with defeat was seven hundred years ago, and, well, you know—"

"The kamikaze. The divine winds came up and blew the evil enemy away."

"Yes indeed. So we feel very secure. We even have the kamikaze on our side." He chuckled. "Match that, America." He patted Kiyoshi on the shoulder. "I'm sorry. I was being facetious. I'm sure many of your good friends are American."

"Hell, my best friend is."

Yamamoto twisted his neck back to eye Kiyoshi. "Oh? Who's that?"

"Cotton Drake. He's a missionary, going up to Tochigi."

"Oh yes, of course," Yamamoto said, gesturing back to his desk, indicating that there was some reference to him in

Kiyoshi's file there. "I remember now. You worked with him at American Orient."

"Long before that. I've known Cotton all my life. He grew up here."

"You mustn't tell him any of this."

Kiyoshi got his back up. "Admiral, I don't plan to tell anybody any of this. I gave you my word."

"Of course," Yamamoto said.

Kiyoshi bowed. He also realized he was being somewhat disingenuous. After all, he had already told Cotton that he was meeting with the admiral. Still, he didn't volunteer that. Or that the missionary was staying at his house right now. Instead, as dispassionately as he could remain: "So, you really believe we'll go to war with the United States?"

"Well, I still pray that we can avoid it. But oil, Serikawa. Oil. Oil is the flint that will fire the guns. And America is already starting to squeeze our oil supply. Then, there's always China. America has come to see itself as China's protector, its kindly uncle. Very odd—doesn't have these sorts of feelings about any other country. And, of course, in that little morality play, we're the predators, the big bad wolf. You know the little fairy tale of theirs?"

"Yes sir."

"Your American friend, the missionary. What's his name again?"

"Cotton Drake."

"And why did he grow up in Japan?"

"His parents were missionaries too."

Yamamoto threw up his hands. "No reflection on Mr. Drake, but sometimes I feel like I'd rather deal with the American army instead of the American missionaries. Especially the ones who served in China. The whole China lobby is missionary-driven. Pearl Buck—*The Good Earth*—missionary parents in China. Henry Luce—*Time* magazine—missionary parents in China. One of the top guys in the embassy in Tokyo, a fellow named Bowersox: missionary parents in China. You know, when I served in Washington, I was appalled at how little they really know about Asia. There's a fellow named Hornbeck, Stanley Hornbeck, who's been in charge of their Far East desk for years now, back to the twenties—"

"Missionary parents?" Kiyoshi asked.

"Not quite. Wishes they were. His father was a minister in the States; then Hornbeck went to China to study. Hornbeck has basically driven U.S. policy over here for years. And the man is on record as saying that America is a 'missionary race.' Can you imagine if someone like our 'American expert' said that about Japanese—'We're a missionary race'? God, they'd accuse us of trying to take over the world."

"Well, I can't speak for missionaries in general, sir, but my friend, Cotton, loves this country. He loves us."

"Nice to have one of the do-good bastards on our side," Yamamoto said. "And please understand. Just because America is so irrational and sweet about China doesn't mean that our army can't be just as obstinate. Let's face it, they'll never pull out of China."

"So it's inevitable?"

Yamamoto just shrugged. "The trouble is, the army has no idea how powerful—how huge the United States is. These stupid bumpkins think an overnight train ride to Nagasaki is a distance. And since they won't listen when I try to educate them, I've given up making the effort. Instead, now . . ." He paused.

"Yes sir?"

"Now, all I want to do is make damn sure that if—when— war does come, I'm not tossed along in that current, but *I* have some control of the situation." And with that, Yamamoto beckoned Kiyoshi over—the younger man was glad just to have a chance to get on his feet—and flipped over his wall maps, going from one of Tokyo Bay to another of the whole Pacific. "Now understand, I'm not telling you anything here that isn't common knowledge—war game stuff for the last five years."

"Yes sir."

"Everybody's favorite hypothesis is that if the generals start to get expansive, if they move on from China and move south

after the oil—and the rubber, and the land, all of it—
eventually the U.S. will get worked up, and Roosevelt will
send a fleet after us. And they'll steam down here"—he indicated broadly, the South Pacific—"and I'll cleverly lie in wait
for them, engage them on my terms, best the pants off the
white devils, and send them limping back to Hawaii."

"And I take it from your tone, sir, that you don't think this
will happen."

"Not . . . on . . . your . . . life. They'll build enough ships
and draft enough sailors that—"

"How many?"

"Enough. But let's suppose the best. Let's suppose we take
their measure in this first action; still, it couldn't be devastating enough. Not with their resources. They'll be back. And if
we beat them again, they'll be back again. And again, and
again. Because they simply have too much—of everything." A
shrug. "And our great ally, that imbecile Hitler, will also find
that out, too. In time."

"So?"

"I have always believed, that, as a military man, if you
want a tiger's cubs, you must go into the tiger's lair. Now, unfortunately, there is no assurance that any maneuver will succeed just because it is bold and romantic. Yet that is all we
have here." He swept his arm toward the map on the wall
again and put on the best smile he could. "I have an idea."
He looked deeply into Kiyoshi's face. "And this is where I
seek your special service. You possess the very attributes we
need to make it work. This is your fate, Serikawa."

"Can I ask, sir: what is the plan?"

"No. Not until you choose to join me. I can only tell you
that it will be exceptionally dangerous, but that you will be incredibly vital to the enterprise." Yamamoto paused; then,
more simply, more personally, almost poignantly: "I need
you."

"I will do it, sir. For you and for Tenno Heika."

"Thank you," Yamamoto said, and be bowed before the
young man. "You honor your father of your birth, my dear
friend Okuno Osami, and you honor the spirit of your new

father, the noble hero Colonel Serikawa Shinji. You honor all your ancestors. You are only the fourth person to know of this, and you must be prepared to leave soon."

Kiyoshi bowed. "Yes sir. Where do I go?"

Yamamoto flicked his hand back toward the map. "Hawaii."

Kiyoshi swallowed. "I see. And what will my duty be?"

"Oh, you will be a spy," the admiral replied evenly. "The kind they shoot at dawn."

"I see," Kiyoshi said. And then: "I think I'll have a drink now. Scotch, sir. Two fingers. Neat."

19

In Tochigi, Miyuki followed Cotton at a respectable distance out of the train station. She hated that Kiyoshi made her come up with Cotton—and never mind how much she liked Cotton. It was just that she felt so uncomfortable. She wasn't this man's wife; she wasn't even a Christian. Yet here she was, obliged to escort the new missionary into his new house in a town she'd never visited before in her life. And here Cotton was, obliged to accept his friend's offer of his wife's service.

It really didn't bother Miyuki that, as a female, she didn't possess any civil rights. She had no problem accepting her place, because that was the nature of things once and always in Japan. What was so irksome to Miyuki—what seemed so unnecessary—was simply how thoughtless and discourteous men were to women, especially to their own wives. But, of course, Miyuki didn't talk about that to Cotton on the train; and instead, for two hours, they chatted about safe, inconsequential subjects, like how much Cotton was looking forward to Tochigi.

It was a beautiful little city, too, cut down its spine by a river, the Uzuma, that flowed out of the handsome mountains looming to the west. The familiar matsu trees were all around, persimmon trees, cherry, even a few palms. There were also an abundance of shrines and temples, the Episcopal mission, and five movie theaters, although there certainly wasn't much worth seeing these days after the censors got through. War films without any kissing were the ideal.

Cotton asked an old man where he could find the church, and the old man explained that it was up off the main thoroughfare. Of course, the road didn't have any name. Cotton always wondered why the Japanese, as precise and efficient as they were, usually didn't put names on their streets like everyone else in the world. The church was just down the Street That Goes Along the River, the old man explained; anyway, it's across from the baseball field and the town hall.

Cotton ambled, passing a *kingyo-ya*, a goldfish vendor, his wares splashing in tubs that he carried on shoulder poles. He slowed down to chat with the fellow. Behind him a few steps, Miyuki slowed down. A block or so later, a man selling *furin*, wind chimes, came round the corner, his tinny clinking preceding him. Cotton stopped and bought one; Miyuki stopped. For the length of the transactions, she held back, pretending to examine the laundry that hung along the houses. Finally, Cotton just reversed himself and went back to her. "Oh, come on, Miyuki," he said. "We've been walking together since we were seven years old. Walk with me. What difference does it make? Everybody's watching us anyhow."

"It would not show the proper respect to my husband."

"It was your husband who had the idea for you to come with me. He wants you to walk with me."

"Please, Cotton, it is too confusing." She couldn't even look at him, but played with the *furoshiki*, the big handkerchief that held her belongings like an overnight bag.

"Okay." He dropped it. Nothing was worse to a Japanese—particularly a Japanese woman—than something being socially confusing. So Cotton just eased along, making his own pace, acknowledging the bolder citizens who came out of their shops and houses to take a closer look at the white stranger. Christopher Evans, the missionary who was departing, was the only other *gaijin* left in Tochigi.

Past the park, where the river widened, then up by the public bath; then Cotton spotted his church. It was white clapboard with a somewhat truncated steeple. But it was high enough, and the cross on top was visible over all the town. Cotton paused one more time at the ball field, where the young men and boys on the town team were practicing. One of them got into a pitch pretty good and gave it a rip, and the ball rocketed between the left and center fielders. "Wow! Yeah, Kensuke!" the players screamed at the slugger. Since it was just practice, neither of the fielders made much effort, so Cotton dropped his bag, vaulted the fence, retrieved the ball, and heaved it on a line toward home plate. It popped into the catcher's mit on a second, lean bounce. The batter, the powerful Kensuke, had just loped around the bases and didn't even know a throw was on the way. He was a dead duck. "Yer out!" Cotton screamed in English, jerking up his thumb, and the boys all whooped and laughed at the surprised Kensuke when the catcher put the tag on him.

Cotton quickly popped back over the fence. He was afraid they might ask him to stay, and he hadn't made a throw like that in six years, since Yale. At least.

Impressed, the players watched him practically till he got to the church. The Reverend Mr. Evans, who had come out to meet him, was impressed, too. Cotton bowed first, before he shook hands. Then he introduced Miyuki, when she caught up the few steps. Evans cocked an eye. "Will Mrs. Serikawa be staying?"

And Miyuki cocked an eye, the way Evans said that. "Just a couple of days to help me get settled," Cotton replied quickly. "Her husband's an old friend, and he's traveling right now."

Evans led them into the rectory, which was across the small lawn from the church itself. The rectory afforded much more room than Evans required for himself, and so he used the large eight-mat room downstairs as a meeting hall, or, most regularly, for kindergarten, which was in session now. There were eight little children seated on the floor, with pictures of Jesus pinned up around the walls. The selection inclined toward pictures of Christ before he grew up—as a baby, working with his father, learning the carpentry trade, lecturing the elders in the temple. But at this moment, the curriculum was altogether secular. The boys and girls were inspecting maps of Africa and drawing elephants and giraffes, just as in any kindergarten, anywhere.

"I'm afraid this will occupy quite a bit of your time," Evans said. "My associate, Miss Sweet, handled the Christian education, and her departure left quite a void."

When'd she leave?"

"Right after the Japanese issued the decree." That had been August 27, when the government ordered all Western churchmen to vacate their executive positions in Japan. "It was really quite upsetting. This was Miss Sweet's first post, and she'd grown increasingly disturbed by all the sniping from the authorities. She told me she was afraid she wasn't cut out for mission work, and it was all I could do to convince her that this was an unusual political situation. Finally, though . . ." Evans shrugged. "I just got my first letter from her last week, though, and she seems to be really happy now."

"Where is she?"

"Zamboanga, in the Philippines. It's a good mission situation there, and, of course, she's darn happy to be free of the Japanese."

A little girl who had gotten her lions and tigers mixed up, had come over to Evans for help, but as he was talking to Cotton, Miyuki had interceded, and leaned over and explained to her which one had the stripes, and how that one didn't have the big mane. Miyuki caught Evans's eye, kind of nodded in the little girl's direction, and Evans nodded back.

"Come on, we'll take advantage," Evans said, and he led Cotton into the rest of the rectory. There was a toilet, a small kitchen, and two other rooms—a three-tatami and a four-and-a-half-tatami—with hibachis in the middle to provide some heat. Evans steered Cotton over to a corner and lowered his voice. "Unfortunately in that letter Miss Sweet made some references to the situations she had just left here that I wish she hadn't."

Cotton cocked his head quizzically. "Whatd'ya mean?"

"I'm sure they're reading all our mail now, listening in on the phone. Suddenly, after Miss Sweet's letter, it's gotten kind of prickly with the authorities. They can make life very unpleasant. How long since you've been here last?"

" 'Thirty-five."

"Well, you'll see the differences. You just have to pick your way through. Even now, I don't get the sense that they're against Christians. You know, there's never been as much religious strife here as in our own neck of the woods."

"They're a helluva lot more civilized than we are on that score," Cotton said.

"Yes indeed. But everything is just so darn nationalistic these last couple of years."

"And the Christian church is the opposite."

"The church is one foundation is Jesus Christ, her Lord," Evans said, giving just a lilt to the words of the old hymn.

Cotton forced a smile. He wouldn't admit it even to himself, but Cotton was probably prejudiced against ministers. Having been the son of one, and now being one himself, he had met too many bores and goody-goodies in the profession. "Well, you know," he said to Evans, "my father used to tell me that when he was first sent here they called Japan the Land of Happy Atheists."

Yeah. Let me make a little suggestion."

"Shoot."

"On some Shinto holiday, go by the shrine. Make an appearance."

"Worship?"

"Throw a few sen in."

Cotton grimaced. "Gee, I don't know."

"Look, I'm just suggesting. That's really no different than going over to the Rotary Club luncheon during Interfaith Week when Rabbi Goldstein lights the menorah."

"I guess," Cotton allowed.

"What the heck? I like to sprinkle a little Shinto stuff into my sermons every now and then. After all, a lot of it is very jovial, feel-good stuff altogether consistent with the gospel. Don't forget: they're going to be all over you."

"Who?"

"Army. Police. It's all the same. They'll drive you crazy. Why are you doing this? Why did you say that? Et cetera. So I'm just saying: throw 'em a bone now and then."

"Well, gimme a for-instance."

"Okay, I did a thing this summer, where I talked about how Jesus would have subscribed to the eight forms of dust that Shinto says we should sweep under the rug."

"Hmmm. I'm not sure I remember that."

"Let's see now," Evans said. "There's holding a grudge. Evil desires. Impure attachments. Hatred." He was ticking them off on his fingers. "That's four. Enmity. Anger. Covetousness-just like in the Ten Commandments." He had seven fingers up now. "And, uh . . ."

"Arrogance," Cotton said.

"I thought you didn't remember."

"Well, it came back to me."

"Good—that's a dandy one to keep in mind. The one thing *we* can never be is arrogant. All their alarms go off then."

"Don't worry—I'm not looking to raise any hackles."

"I know your father was a missionary," Evans went on. "Probably a darn good one or you wouldn't have wanted to follow in his footsteps."

"Absolutely."

"But I'm also sure, like all good missionaries, it wasn't only the gospel that increased the flock."

"I know—there's a lot of rice Christians everywhere," Cotton agreed.

"Yes, there are. It isn't a perfect business. So I'm just telling you, tread lightly."

"Thanks."

"Of course, they'll still be on your heinie. Come on, I'll show you the church. Can Mrs. Serikawa watch the children for a few more minutes?"

"It looked to me like she'd love to," Cotton said, and he followed Evans down the stairs.

"Of course now, Cotton, I don't want to scare you. I never worried they were going to chop my head off or boil me in oil."

"Oh, I'm not worried. My father told me—the Japanese only did that sort of thing to the Japanese who converted. They'd crucify 'em upside down, then run water into a tank under their head and drown 'em."

"Well, at least that sort of stuff has gone out of style," Evans said, pausing at the bottom of the stairs to peek in on Miyuki. She'd gathered all the kids around her and was reading them Babar. She barely glanced up as the two men went out the door. "But don't push it, Cotton. Don't be a martyr. Leave the country if it gets any worse. St. Peter doesn't check passports, you know. And we don't raise up saints the way the Roman brethren do."

Evans held the church door, and they went in. It was a spare place of worship, but not without some cozy charm; it felt quite holy enough for Cotton. They moved together down the aisle, and Evans kicked a prayer cushion back in place. When they paused at the next pew he kicked another one, rather as you would a tire down at the gas station. "One thing you got going for you with the Japanese: they're used to getting down. Bingo—down on their knees." He chuckled, then turned a more serious face to Cotton, swinging his arm around. "Well, how do you like your first church, Parson Drake?"

"I like it. It's beautiful."

"Good, I'll leave you alone with it and go back and help Mrs. Serikawa," Evans said, and he bowed to the altar and departed.

Cotton couldn't help feeling somewhat proprietary. He'd been in a whole lot of churches, but he'd never been in one before that he shared with God as a partner. It was an altogether different sensation. Did any man feel this way when he stepped across the threshold of his first house? Did a young teacher feel this when he stood at the front of his first classroom? Did a doctor feel this way in a hospital? Did Win

Taliaferro feel this way when he settled into the cockpit of his B-17?

He decided not. Conveniently, Cotton decided that because this was the house he shared with Jesus, this was certainly a better, different feeling. He stepped up to the altar and laid his hands on it, and he looked up at the cross, and he said: "O Lord, bless this church, and please bless this poor fellow who's going to look after it in your behalf." And he bowed. "And Lord," he added, "please bless the Japanese people. Amen."

When he turned around, Miyuki was standing silently at the back of the church. She bowed—not a church bow but a Japanese bow. "Welcome to your new home, Cotton," she said.

On the *Akagi*, about that same time, Yamamoto took his seat in his cabin. He was so short, and used to being so short, that it didn't tax his ego to stand when he was talking to subordinates. First, he went over the procedures. Kiyoshi would hand in his resignation to American Orient, effective in a few weeks, to become a *taii*, a lieutenant in the Imperial Navy, but publicly reporting that he was accepting a promotion to join Nippon Yusen Kaisya—the NYK Line. His first posting would be to Honolulu.

"I don't think, the way things are, anybody would be surprised if any Japanese left an American company for a domestic corporation," the admiral said.

"Can I bring my wife to Hawaii?" Kiyoshi asked.

"No. I don't want you to have that distraction. And frankly, if you should be caught, it's no place for a woman. Besides, I don't want her to have any idea what you're up to."

"All right, sir."

"Please understand. I only emphasize the potential for danger because I don't want to misrepresent the situation to you." Yamamoto reached out on his desk and picked up a little notebook. "You know what this is, Serikawa?"

"No sir."

"I carry it with me, wherever I go. It holds the names of all the men whom I've lost under my command. So far, it's a small number. Training accidents for the most part. I fear, however, that too soon the numbers will grow so that this book will be insufficient." He handed it to Kiyoshi. "I don't want your name in there, and I promise you that I will do everything in my power to keep it out." Kiyoshi started to speak, to thank the admiral for his special thoughtfulness, but Yamamoto held up his hand. "And really, you shouldn't be caught. Most of our spies work out of our embassies, and at some point in this operation, normal intelligence will assign someone to Honolulu—probably out of the consulate. Fine. No one but me will even be aware of your existence there."

"No one?"

"Well, perhaps three or four others, as matters progress. We'll need a go-between, that sort of thing. But yes, essentially, you'll be working exclusively for me. Then no one can betray you—especially not any of the Japanese living in Hawaii." Yamamoto shrugged. "After all, they'd all think we were insane to attack America."

"Then, Admiral, if—"

"does that make you want another Scotch?"

Kiyoshi forced a smile. "No sir, it's just . . . if you think it's that hopeless, why are we doing this?"

"Because realistically, it's the *only* way we can construct any hope. If we win a big victory in Hawaii, it's conceivable that America will fall back. Of course, it's stupid to fight the United States, but we're controlled right now, you'll forgive me, by stupid men. And Tenno Heika cannot stop them. Therefore, if we must be stupid, what's the least stupid we can be?"

"Attack Hawaii."

"Go into the tiger's lair, yes. It must be done quickly. Any war of attrition, we lose. We have six months, a year at the outside. And even then I'm counting on the stupidity of racism."

Kiyoshi scratched his head. "Sir?"

"You've been to America—you know how they denigrate us. They'll let in any dummy from Europe and turn away the most brilliant Japanese. Fine."

" 'Fine' . . . sir?"

Yamamoto smiled broadly. "Don't you see? None of them will ever imagine that you're intelligent enough to be spying on them."

Kiyoshi said: "So I play the fool?"

Yamamoto laughed. "Just be yourself. That's good enough for the Americans to ignore you."

"Okay, that I can do. But one more thing."

"Yes?"

"If this works, sir—"

"If?"

"I'm sorry, Admiral. I didn't mean to say that."

"Oh hell, that's okay. It's what I say. This whole thing is like filling to an inside straight. 'If' is just fine."

"Well, *if* we make it work, why wouldn't the Americans be so furious that they'd do anything to get Hawaii back? I know Americans. Hawaii isn't a state, but it's like Okinawa with us. It's part of . . . of America. They'll never back off that."

"You're absolutely right," Yamamoto said.

"I am?"

"Completely. But I never said I wanted Hawaii. I don't want Moscow either. I don't want San Francisco. As far as I'm concerned, you, Serikawa Kiyoshi, are the only Japanese who is ever going to land on Hawaii in this war. The only."

"Am I missing something here, sir?"

"The fleet, Kiyoshi. To hell with Hawaii. To hell with the land. I don't want the goddamn tiger. I only want his cubs. His carriers and battleships, his cruisers—any bucket that floats with a gun on it. Destroy the American Pacific fleet, watch Hitler jump in on the other side, and hope that somebody over there in Washington will say: 'Really now, haven't we got our hands full enough with Adolf? Let's just let the little yellow chaps have a bit of China and some oil and rubber, and we'll worry about what really matters to us. White people. *Our* people.' "

"Can it work, sir?"

"Doesn't matter."

Kiyoshi's eyes widened. "It doesn't?"

"No, because it's the *only* conceivable strategy that can work. Proceed from the premise, and we simply do our best for the Emperor and accept the fate of the gods." He chuckled to himself and pointed at Kiyoshi, having some fun. "Hey, Serikawa-kun, fifty years from now, win or lose, when Japan and America run the world together, we can tell our grandchildren that you were the only samurai ever brave enough to fight on American soil."

20

Much of the congregation in Tochigi came by the next day to bid farewell to the Reverend Mr. Evans and to examine the Reverend Mr. Drake. The women brought food (a lot of *sembei* for the new neighbor), and there was much tea and plenty of sweets. It was a bit warmer, the sun was out, the air sheer; and Miyuki volunteered to take the kindergarten children out so that all the grown-ups could meet Cotton in peace. She led the kids down by the river where they could try and spot some carp.

It felt good for Miyuki to be back in the countryside. She was glad now that Kiyoshi had made her go with Cotton. Tokyo had grown so depressing—equal parts deprivation and conformity, it seemed. And if Tochigi wasn't very prosperous itself, and more and more of the wives were being dragooned into working in the airplane parts factory, and if three of the young men had come home from China just ashes and bones ... still, Tochigi was a much more pleasant place than was the capital. When Miyuki walked by the schoolyard with her kindergarten charges, one of the older boys recognized her from the day before and screamed out gaily, asking her where the *gaijin* with the great throwing arm was. She could sense it: there was still some fun to be had here.

At the rectory, Evans could see right away that the parishioners were treating Cotton differently than ever they'd treated him or Miss Sweet, or even Bishop McKim, on the Sunday he came up from Tokyo year before last. All the parishioners seemed impressed with Cotton, even a little frightened at how well—how absolutely perfectly—he spoke Japanese, and how beautifully he moved Japanese and stood Japanese and sat and bowed Japanese. *Ah, kimochi ga waruii.* "They're quite taken by you," Evans whispered to Cotton. "Also, I believe they think you're a spy."

"Good. If they're curious, maybe we'll get a few more back."

Evans had already advised Cotton that attendance was down. *Going* to worship regularly wasn't part of the everyday Japanese life, Buddhist or Shinto; and so Sabbath services had to be learned as a way of doing something new and Western. Now that the authorities were frowning on Christmas, the sunshine soldiers were dropping away, in Tochigi and everywhere else. "We'll just have to cast some wider nets," Cotton said.

That irked Evans a little, as he presumed Cotton was suggesting that he hadn't been doing a thorough enough job himself of net casting. He was a little put out, anyhow, because although he'd been Jesus' man, Anglican division, in Tochigi for three years now, all the to-do was being made over the new fellow. When Miyuki came back with the children, there was even more buzzing, and Evans felt obliged to introduce her. "This is Mrs. Serikawa, who is visiting from Tokyo."

Cotton stepped up while she was bowing. "Miyuki is an old, old childhood friend, and her husband is my closest friend." Miyuki blushed some and bowed again. "Her father was Colonel Shinji Serikawa, the hero of Manchukuo." Titters and gasps. "And her brother was Captain Takeo Serikawa, another patriot we're all familiar with."

This time, when Miyuki bowed again, there were more

gasps, and some sighs, and if Cotton still lacked any credentials from God, he had certainly established them with the empire. By the afternoon, there wasn't a soul in town who hadn't heard that the handsome new Christian priest not only could throw a baseball better than anyone around but could speak Japanese perfectly, and the beautiful woman traveling with him was the daughter and sister of the Serikawas. By the next morning, in Tokyo, the *tokko*, the special police, had received several reports on the new Westerner in Tochigi.

"Well, now," Evans said. "Any questions for Mr. Drake?"

There were perhaps a dozen parishioners present. Three were old men, and one a young soldier, Ichiro Kobayashi, who was winding up his furlough at home before getting shipped out to China. The rest were women, about evenly split between the young and the old. They all tittered now when the most ancient of the lot, Mrs. Watanabe, took Evans up on his invitation and posed the question everybody wanted to: "Is Drake-san married?"

"Ah, yes," Evans said. "It's the time for marriages." November in Japan, for weddings, was like June in America, only carried to another power.

"Not this November," Cotton cut in. "Is there any girl in Tochigi who's as pretty as Mrs. Serikawa?"

Miyuki had not been expecting that, and she ducked her head. The giggles continued, though. "Well," Miyuki finally said, "do any of you ladies have a daughter for Mr. Drake to marry?"

More titters. But someone did say: "Hanako."

"Hanako?" Cotton asked. He was flirting with them all a little now.

One of the women looked up—well, she was even sort of pushed forward. "Hanako is my daughter," she managed to say.

"And you are?"

"I am Mrs. Nakagawa—but," she added quickly, "Hanako is not in Tochigi. She's in Tokyo." There were some murmurs, the getas shuffling.

"Drop it," Evans said under his breath. "She's in Yoshiwara." Cotton nodded. Yoshiwara was the main brothel section.

"Hanako is not Christian either," Mrs. Nakagawa added.

Cotton purposely stepped toward Mrs. Nakagawa and smiled. "Well, you know, *oku-samu*, honorable housewife, we Christians are always looking to find new Christians."

Evans spoke up again. "Mr. and Mrs. Nakagawa have just started coming to our services. Right now, they plan to be baptized soon."

"I hope so," Cotton said, and he bowed deeply to Mrs. Nakagawa. "It would be my honor to perform my first baptism in Japan upon you and Mr. Nakagawa." She beamed, and Cotton gestured back over to Miyuki. "And now, since I see that the children like Mrs. Serikawa so much, why don't we let her stay with them a bit longer, and bless Mr. Evans's journey ahead, and give thanks for the job and grace he has brought to this town."

It was a wonderful touch, unexpected, and Evans greatly appreciated it. He sat in the pews with the parishioners, fully one of them at last, and heard Cotton conduct the whole service, taking the bread and wine from him, and listening to him deliver a little homily about the changing of Christ's guard.

Later, Miyuki and Cotton put Evans on the train to Tokyo. His belongings had already left, for he was catching the *President Coolidge* back to San Francisco on Friday. Then Cotton and Miyuki strolled back to the church. She walked side by side with Cotton this time, showing him the grocer she had found for him here, the tofu shop there, the hardware store, the barbershop—even a seamstress, because she knew he'd never manage that sort of thing himself. Back at the rectory, Miyuki helped Cotton put away all his clothes. His trunks had arrived that day. Cotton could tell they'd been searched, but he didn't say anything to Miyuki.

He took the room upstairs for his sleeping quarters, just as Evans had done, and used the three-tatami room downstairs for his study, putting his books and papers there. One folder held his sermons, and he pulled out the one he'd delivered in

Hawaii; he glanced through it and also through some notes he'd made on the *Asama Maru* about how he could adjust the sermon to his new audience in Japan. "Tell how essentially same sermon preached on American soil," he had jotted down. That, Cotton thought, would be a message by itself, as much as the message inherent in the sermon, for it would show the oneness of the world, and how the lessons of Christianity could be applied equally everywhere. Now, as he read over the part about St. Paul, and especially about enmity, he took out a pencil and started to write down:

"For, as we know, *all* the great religions of the world caution against enmity. Why, when I was growing up in Japan, many of my friends were Shinto, and I remember that enmity was one of the eight forms of dust which must be swept away. Right?" He nodded at his enthralled imaginary congregation and saw them nod back sagely. Good. Good idea. Then he proceeded to read the rest of the sermon to himself. Hmm: not bad. With a few changes here and there, it would make a terrific speech on Sunday. Another idea—he scribbled it in. Audience participation: "How many of you can recall the other seven forms of dust that must be swept away?" He looked at the wall in front of him, over the heads of the phantom parishioners. And suddenly, from behind him:

"Holding a grudge," said a voice. "Anger. Hatred."

Cotton turned back, and there was Miyuki, smiling at him. "Evil desires," she went on. "Impure attachments."

"Don't worry," Cotton told her. "I'm not talking to myself. I'm just practicing my sermon for Sunday." He paused. "It's too bad you have to go back tomorrow," he went on, "or you could hear me preach it."

"Couldn't I read it?"

"Of course. I'd love you to." Cotton began to gather up the papers for her.

"I'll read it after dinner. First we must go down and take a bath."

"Now?" is what Cotton said, which was clever, because " 'We'?" is what was in his mind.

"It's almost dark out."

"Oh yeah." Cotton swallowed a bit. He'd been surprised to find out that while the rectory had a toilet, it lacked a bath. To attend to that which is next to godliness and that which is particularly important to the Japanese, Cotton would have to go down to the public bath, which was located on the main drag—Fish Street, in the vernacular.

He'd grown up using the communal Japanese baths, but at a certain point his typical Western modesty genes had kicked in. Luckily, though, in the more cosmopolitan areas, the bath-houses had begun to be constructed more in the grown-up Western way, with the men and women separated. Cotton didn't know whether the Tochigi bath had yet entered the middle of the twentieth century. Even worse, he didn't know whether he hoped it had or it hadn't.

Which is the lesser of two evils? Cotton thought. Or, more simply: Am I having evil thoughts? In fact, what came into his mind was David and Bathsheba. "You go ahead," Cotton said quickly; then, "and I'll be down in a few minutes after I make a few changes."

Miyuki said "No"—and so emphatically it took Cotton aback somewhat. She put her arms akimbo. "I am not going to be a Japanese wife with you, Cotton. I am going to be an American woman, and I am telling you, we have had a long day, and we have had a lot to do, and now it is time for a re-laxing bath before dinner."

"But—"

Miyuki tugged at him. "You can work on that sermon all day tomorrow, after I go back to Tokyo."

So, sheepishly, Cotton got up and went with her to the bath on Fish Street. As they walked along, he remembered that not only did David lose complete and utter control of his senses af-ter he saw Bathsheba, but he also conspired to have her hus-band rubbed out. The king broke about half of the Ten Commandments and exhibited at least as many of the eight forms of dust that he should have swept under a rug.

But when Cotton and Miyuki reached the bathhouse, Cot-ton was relieved to see that Jehovah was not going to test him then and there. At the entrance was a sign indicating women to the left, men to the right. Tochigi had reached the big leagues. Phew. Only . . .

Only then, when Cotton got into the men's bath, he saw that this wasn't quite what it seemed. Yes, a partition had been thrown up, formally dividing the bath in half; but it was only a skimpy arrangement, and it didn't come close to blocking out the view to the other side. Even the purest and noblest of male creatures, seeking most earnestly to avert his eyes from the other side, couldn't help seeing something or other.

Not only that, but hardly had Cotton removed his clothes and dropped them in the little wicker basket, barely had he started soaping himself up, than the bath began to be overrun with the citizenry of Tochigi. It was as if everyone in town had decided all at once to take a bath. The men poured in on his side, and although God knows how he pointedly turned away, he could hear the women yakking and splashing on the other. Cotton finished soaping and rinsing himself off and got down into the bath, and although God also knew (because Cotton reminded Him) that he didn't mean to, there were so many women, he couldn't help seeing—well, God, *catching a passing glance at*—some of the naked ones climbing in and out.

Cotton tried to content himself with soaking. The pool kept filling up with men, and he had to be polite and nod to this one and that one—he certainly couldn't be arrogant, buck naked—so he couldn't enjoy the bath as much as he normally did. He even felt that he should nod when a couple of women came around the corner of the partition to advise their husbands that they were ready to go. The ladies did keep in place the little towels that were provided at the bath, but in fact this served curiosity more than concealment.

Fixing on her face the best he could, Cotton recognized one of the women to be Mrs. Nakagawa, from the church. "Why, hello Drake-san," she said, leaning in.

Cotton had never greeted a parishioner quite this way before, and he rose. Not all the way up, you understand: he rose to where the water was at waist level, and pretended that he had, of course, risen to his full height. Then he bowed. "How do you do, Mrs. Nakagawa. It's so nice to see you." Had he kept his wits, he would have seen Miyuki, just beyond, watching the whole scene and holding in a laugh.

The Nakagawas departed, so Cotton sank back into the steamy waters and relaxed ... but when he did, he happened to glance over, and there, around the partition, was Miyuki, climbing out of the bath. She was lovelier than he had imagined, faultlessly proportioned—and if all the Japanese men were so damned blasé about this sort of thing, then why were they staring too? Cotton couldn't imagine how Kiyoshi could ever bring her into a place like this.

Of course, Cotton ducked his head immediately, and even closed his eyes, neatly capturing the vision on the emulsifier of his memory. A caption came with the photograph too, and this is what it read: "And it came to pass in an eventide that David saw a woman washing herself; and the woman was very beautiful to look upon."

He still felt so guilty and so foolish when he met Miyuki outside a few minutes later that all he could say was: "Gee, I never saw so many people jammed into a bath before."

Miyuki shook her head in wonder at him. "Oh, silly," she said. "Couldn't you tell?"

"Tell what?"

"They all came to see you."

"They did?"

"Sure. As soon as they heard that the *gaijin* was on his way to the baths, everybody hurried over."

"Well," Cotton said, "I'll be."

"They were pretty impressed, too."

"They were?"

"Yeah," Miyuki said. "All the women told me that you had more than Mr. Evans."

Cotton gasped. "What?" Japanese women may be casual about these things, but still, coming from Miyuki ...

"Well," she said, "I don't think anyone was really surprised."

"They weren't?" Cotton didn't know whether he should be pleased or not; after all, he'd never seen Evans.

"No," Miyuki said. "They told me Evans-san didn't have any hair at all on his chest."

"Oh," Cotton said, tossing it off, pretending as if he'd thought she'd been talking about hair all along. What Miyuki said had reminded him: the Japanese men thought they had more hair than other Asians, but then they discovered that Westerners had so much more, and so the Japanese grew convinced that this drove women crazy with lust. "I've never been particularly hairy."

"I know," Miyuki said. "I was looking at you when you got out of the bath."

"You were?"

"Well, sure. Didn't you look at me?"

Cotton was already a bright pink from the hot bath, but now his cheeks went the color of rose. How easy it is to be a moga, Miyuki thought. "You're blushing, Cotton," she cooed, teasing him some more, which was even more fun because he didn't understand she was teasing him.

"Dammit, Miyuki, you forget sometimes that even though I grew up in Japan, I'm still American."

"And it's hard for you to go bathing with naked ladies if you're an American?"

"Aw, come on, Miyuki—it's hard to go bathing with a naked lady when the naked lady is your best friend's wife." They had turned off Fish Street, walking by the river up toward the church. "Did you ever hear of King David?" Miyuki shook her head. "In the bible?" She shook her head again. "Well, I was thinking about him, because one evening he was minding his own business, and he looked out and saw this beautiful woman named Bathsheba bathing—"

Cotton stopped there. Now he was sorry he'd brought it up. He looked away, to the river; the moon was glimmering off the Uzuma. "So?" Miyuki said. "So, what happened?"

"Oh, that's not important," Cotton said. He was *really* sorry he'd brought this up. "You know, it just occurred to me . . . because of, you know, the bathing . . . us. Bathing."

"But it's a story, in your Bible."

"Well, yeah."

"Don't you want me to hear about the Bible?"

"Of course I do, Miyuki." They'd resumed walking again, and now the moon glanced off the cross on the top of the little steeple. It caught Cotton for a moment, and it made him feel secure: the moon, which belonged so to Japan, and the cross, which belonged so to Jesus. "Well, eventually . . . eventually, it was a real happy ending, because King David and Bathsheba had a child named Solomon, and he turned out to be almost as great a king as David."

"That's all?" Miyuki asked. "That's the story?"

"Yeah, sure," Cotton said. "David and Bethsheba had Solomon." Of course, this was a somewhat bowdlerized version, leaving out, as it did, lust, adultery, jealousy, murder, retribution, and a number of other attitudes and atrocities.

"Well, all right," Miyuki said. "I guess that's always the way it is with kings." They'd reached the rectory and she chuckled to herself. She was remembering now, and starting to wonder whether she should say anything to Cotton. The only other person she ever told was Kiyoshi. Finally, she decided: why not? Well, she suddenly *wanted* to tell Cotton. "It's something like my story."

"Your story?"

"Yes, I was sort of like Bethsheba once," Miyuki said.

"What do you mean?"

"I was chosen to sleep with a king." Cotton just stared at her. "With Tenno Heika, at the Imperial Palace."

"What?"

"I was going to have his baby."

Cotton held up his hands. "Whoa. When did this happen?"

Miyuki laughed. "Sit down. I'll give you some sake and tell you."

"You have a drink too."

"Oh, I don't think so."

"Listen, I went bathing with you, like Japan. Now you have a drink with me, like America."

"I remember that when Kiyoshi and I were allowed to take our honeymoon in Hawaii."

"Good," Cotton said, and Miyuki poured two cups of sake and sat down on the tatami across from him. "This is the cocktail hour in Tochigi."

21

"It was 1933, the Year of the Rooster," Miyuki began. "I was sixteen. You were back in the States."

"I was in college then, and my parents were home on sabbatical, too."

"That was when I grew up, when I became a young woman. I'm really no bigger now than I was then." She put her hands to her breasts and shrugged. "Daddy had been killed two years before, and Takeo was in the army. The tension was building, everywhere, and more and more, everyone was looking to Tenno Heika."

Miyuki reminded Cotton: Hirohito needed a male heir. In times past, before the Meiji revolution late in the nineteenth century, if the Emperor couldn't sire a son, he could simply make an heir by adopting a *yoshi*, as the Serikawas had Kiyoshi. But the new constitution obliged him to father a blood son. It was not, however, picky about who bore this successor. If the Empress wasn't up to the task, then many other women of the realm could qualify. In fact, Hirohito's own father, the Emperor Taisho, had been born of one of his father's concubines.

Hirohito had selected Nagako to be Empress when she was but fourteen and married her in 1924 when she was still only seventeen. The Japanese people were terribly distressed that it was 1926 before Nagako managed to get pregnant—and she compounded her tardiness by delivering of a girl. When the child came out, the Empress, hanging on to a cord, gritted her teeth, making certain not to utter a cry lest she shame her husband and all the empire, saw her deficiency. All over the Sun-Begot Land, sirens blew. One blast meant a girl, two a boy; the people sighed when they realized there wouldn't be another blast.

The next year, the Empress, at least displaying more aptitude for fecundity, was pregnant once more. But again only one siren blew. Worse, this poor little girl was sick from the day she was born, finally dying, mercifully, when she was two; so when Nagako then produced yet another daughter, the nation was somewhat forgiving, for it understood that the Empress believed that the new daughter, Takanomiya, was a divine replacement for the dead child.

Still, patience in some quarters was beginning to wear thin. Some of the *genro*, the wise old men, like Prince Saionji and Count Tanaka, and Count Makino, the Keeper of the Privy Seal, had approached Hirohito and delicately suggested to him that it might be time for him to pay a visit to the Concubines pavilion. Despite the great temptations that paraded before his windows, however, the Emperor made it plain to the *genro* that times had changed and he wanted to remain faithful to his Empress. Sure enough, too, Nagako got pregnant again, for the fourth time, in 1931, and there was much hand-clapping at the Shinto shrines all over Japan.

And then Nagako delivered for a fourth time, and a fourth time the siren blew only once.

Now the pressure on Hirohito to place his seed in other vessels really began to build. His Majesty even acquiesced sufficiently to start paying social visits on the ladies-in-waiting, and, in their turn, the ladies of the court were encouraged by Prince Saionji to be more forward. Still, though, as 1932 wore on, empty, the Emperor held firm in his fidelity until, finally, Count Tanaka came up with an even more enticing scheme for Hirohito. He would find the likeliest young candidates from outside the court. The nominees would be unknown, virgins who possessed both beauty and family qualities that would please the emperor and his nation.

"And that would be you," Cotton said, leaning forward, fascinated.

"Yes. There had been pictures of our family in the newspapers at Daddy's funeral, and someone in Count Tanaka's office remembered, and they sent an emissary to see Takeo. I guess they were sending people all over Japan, checking on the girls."

"It sounds like Cinderella," Cotton said.

"What's that?" And he told Miyuki the story of the glass slipper, of the handsome prince's men scouring the country for the midnight belle. "Well, that's very interesting," Miyuki said. "First I am Bathsheba and then Cinderella. But never mind, I can assure you that it was not any foot that interested them. It was my, uh—"

"Your virginity," Cotton said. He leaned in closer and poured them both some more sake.

"Yes. And Takeo swore to that. And he also assured the emissary that nothing could be more honorable for the Serikawa family, for him, and for my mother, and especially for the spirit of my father—nothing could be more honorable than for his sister to have the opportunity to lie with Tenno Heika and bear his child."

"But no one bothered to ask you?"

"Why would they have to? Who could imagine any greater honor for any Japanese woman?"

"Well . . ."

"To give birth to an Emperor? To give birth to a god? You still worship your Mary two thousand years later for the same thing."

Cotton nodded ruefully, "And then what?"

"They came and took pictures of me, and they must have liked them very much, because then they brought Takeo back from Kanazawa, where he was stationed, and, together, we went to the Palace and met with count Tanaka."

"When was this now?"

"The spring of thirty-three—and everywhere people were saying, 'When is His Majesty going to stop fooling around and take another woman?' "

"You didn't meet the Emperor?"

"No, not then. Just the count. And he looked me over, and

they put me in a magnificent kimono, and we went outside, and they took pictures of me. Takeo was so proud. And then, finally, they brought me to the royal doctor and he examined me."

"To see if you were a virgin."

"Oh yes, of course, but also in every other way. If I was to produce an heir for Japan, they wanted to make sure that I was very healthy."

"And you were?"

"Oh yes. How do you say it? I passed with bright colors."

"Flying colors," Cotton said. "Like flags on parade. Flying colors."

"I see. And Takeo told me that then they handed my photographs around, to Prince Saionji and the Lord Keeper of the Privy Seal, maybe some others."

"The old farts," Cotton muttered in English.

"What?"

"Never mind. Go on."

"No one could really pressure His Majesty about a thing like this. It had to be very delicate. Only the wise old men could approach him about such matters." Miyuki smiled, and it occurred to Cotton how oddly disconnected she seemed. At once, it was as if she were recalling some silly teenage adventure she'd had, but then again, it was as if she was telling some old fable from long ago that she'd read in a book. "And they all thought I looked pretty good, I guess, and—"

"I'm sure."

She blushed a little. "So there'd been about five or six girls they were considering, and I was one of the three photographs that the count discreetly laid on Tenno Heika's desk."

"Do you know who the others were?"

"No, but Takeo told me they were all army girls. It was very political, you see. All of us had to have fathers in the army. It wasn't like your Cinderella. It wasn't that they were looking for the prettiest girl in all of Japan." Cotton thought that he would take issue with that assessment, but he kept that to himself. "They were only looking for a fairly pretty girl who came from the right family. And my father was still a most revered man. He was still a national hero."

"He still is," Cotton reminded her. "Your family was invited to the Kigen ceremonies because of your father."

Miyuki smiled. "Perhaps," she said.

"What does that mean?"

She raised her head and held the pose. "I've often thought that Tenno Heika remembered me. I tempted him, didn't I?"

"But only your photograph," Cotton said.

"Well, yes. Sitting there on Tenno Heika's desk. With the others. But after a few days, His Majesty called Count Tanaka in, and he said, 'This is the one I prefer.' "

"And that was you?" Miyuki nodded. "The Emperor chose you in all the land?"

"Well, I told you, Cotton . . . kind of."

"So then?"

"So they came to see me again, and this time they brought me a beautiful gold kimono, and a seamstress to make it just perfect on me. I still have it at home. I've never worn it again. And they fixed my hair and made me up. It had to be just right. They all kept fussing over me and saying: 'Count Tanaka says, for heaven's sake, don't make her look like a geisha. Make her fresh and sweet and pure.' And they did, I guess.

"And the next day . . . oh, what a glorious day it was. Cotton! The cherry blossoms were at their height, all over Tokyo. They gave me a parasol that matched the shade of the blossoms, and they took me to the Palace. To the grounds. It was so beautiful. The lawns, Cotton. Oh, I remember the lawns. The pine trees came out of them like lampposts. The grass went right up to the trunks. They must have been cut with nail scissors. And the crows cawing, and the swans, and the cherry blossoms in bloom. I always wonder when ever I will see that again."

"Go back to the Palace?"

"No, just have a moment like that again. Anywhere in Japan. That was my country, Cotton. You know?" He nodded. Miyuki took another sip of sake. In a way, it was almost as if he were not there, that she was just using him to relive this for herself. "They had me take a seat on the rainbow bridge that goes over the Calabash Pond. There was no one else around. Anywhere. I'm sure they planned it that way. I was all by myself. And after a while, maybe fifteen minutes or so, I saw Tenno Heika walking toward me down the path."

"Alone?"

"No, he was with Count Tanaka and Prince Saionji. And, of course, I bowed as low as I could, but Count Tanaka called to me, 'No, no, no, please keep standing, my child,' and His Majesty nodded, and so I mumbled my apologies and just lowered my head, and His Majesty said hello."

"That's all he said?"

"Yes. He only said. 'Hello.' And I dared to raise my head, and then he said: 'Your father was a great hero.' It was very strange. He was the one who could barely look at *me*. He was very shy. And I thanked him, and then they walked on, and I didn't know what to do, and so finally, I just sat back down on the little bench on the bridge."

"And?"

"I did hear His Majesty say, as he walked away: 'She's even prettier than her picture.' But that was all. And soon someone came to get me, and they took me home. Count Tanaka came to our house the next day, and he told me that His Majesty had been very taken with me, and that he would surely call for me next week. He asked me questions about, you know, my period. It was all arranged. I went to the shrine and prayed that the gods would let me bear Japan a boy."

"Were you scared?"

"I was most nervous, but only because, you know, whether it was Tenno Heika or anyone, I had never been with a man before. No one had even touched me. My brother bought me a pillow book, but it—" Miyuki stopped.

"What happened?"

"Count Tanaka had wanted His Majesty to take me to bed that very night, the same day he met me on the bridge. But His Majesty said no, he thought maybe the Empress was pregnant again, and they must wait and see. The count was miffed, but what could he do? And so he told me: next week. But the Empress was indeed pregnant, and so they came by and told me I wouldn't be needed just now."

"And that was the end of it?" Cotton asked.

"No, they would check in on me every now and then. Mostly, I think they just wanted to make sure I didn't get naughty with any boy. I did have a boyfriend, and I had kissed him once, but he would get very confused because I would tell him, 'No, you cannot touch my breast, because I must save that for the Emperor's hand."

Gee, Cotton thought, that's the greatest turn-down line a girl ever had.

Miyuki shrugged. "Finally, he gave up and went on to another girl. I didn't know what to think. I wanted to have the Emperor's baby, but I knew it would be best for Japan if the Empress gave him a boy right now."

"And she did."

"Yes. We heard the two blasts on December twenty-third. Prince Akihito was born, and I was happy for the Empress and for His Majesty. I was happy for Japan. And that was the end of it. Nobody ever called from the Palace again."

"Still," Cotton said, "you think the Emperor remembers you?"

"I know Takeo mentioned me to Tenno Heika the day he saw him just before he committed seppuku, and Takeo told me that His Majesty didn't want to talk about it. But he remembered then. I'm the girl he chose, Cotton. I would have been the one if the Empress hadn't gotten pregnant, and I would have still been the one if she hadn't given birth to Akihito. So I think about that sometimes, and I think that if I ever did see His majesty again, he would remember me. I know it was just a moment, but it was the only moment like that he ever had in all his life, and so I'm sure he would remember me. Don't you think so, Cotton?"

"No man would ever forget you, Miyuki. Not in a gold kimono and a cherry-blossom parasol."

She smiled. "I think Tenno Heika would say to me: 'What happened to you, Miyuki? What happened to you after Japan didn't need you? Who did you marry?' And then I think he would say: 'Did you bear him a son?' You see, now I must do that for Kiyoshi."

"I'll drink to that," Cotton said, and he poured more sake into both their cups, and they raised them and drained them together.

"And so the cocktail hour is over, and it is time for dinner," Miyuki said; and when she started to get up, Cotton helped her to her feet, like a good Western gentleman. "So you see, I am neither your Mary not your Bathsheba nor your Cinderella. I am only Serikawa Miyuki."

1941
KANO TO MI
THE YEAR
of the
METAL SNAKE
Oshogatsu, The New Year

22

Cotton awoke at six. Of course, everybody in Japan awoke then, because that was the unofficial order of the land. At six sharp, over the radio, the bugle blew. What few slugabeds there were still sleeping in the Sun-Begot Land opened their eyes.

Cotton could see that outside, down the Street That Goes Along the River, a lot of the townspeople had already come out of their houses and were bowing toward the flag. The town office, after all, was just across the Uzuma, and the police could be watching. If they didn't see you, how could you *prove* you were doing exercises indoors? Cotton staggered out into the chilly dawn himself. Back in November, when she had come up with Cotton, Miyuki had told him to go outside and set a visible example. And she had been right: the people were impressed, and the police gave him grudging credit, even if they never really let up on the Reverend Mr. Drake, keeping after him, making him answer to all sorts of nuisance charges.

It was especially freezing this morning, but before Cotton and the others could try and warm up with the mandatory exercises, the radio announcer portentously declared that he had some special messages for this particular day, Thursday, January 16, 1941, in the fifteenth year of Showa, Enlightened Peace, the twenty-six hundredth year of Japan:

First, as much as he hated to be the one to disclose this to the nation, the generals fighting in China were very upset, because the citizens on the home front were backsliding again and were simply not writing enough letters of support to the soldiers. Cotton's parish had two men in China—Ichiro, who had just shipped out, and Fujio, whom he'd never met—and Cotton made a mental note to himself to write them both again after kindergarten was over.

The announcer went on, then, on a happier note. He was delighted to have with him this morning a representative of the Dai Nippon Kokubo Fujinkai, the National Defense Women's Association. After a brief preamble, here was her message to the women of Japan: "Let us bear, let us increase, so that we will have more soldiers to serve the Emperor."

Cotton smiled. Well, he thought, Miyuki and Kiyoshi certainly are trying to be good Japanese.

Next. Loyal citizens would no doubt be delighted to hear that they would be helping the empire by reducing their use of *mokutan*, charcoal. Since even some automobiles had been converted to charcoal power because of the gasoline shortage, this was a more extreme rationing than it might have sounded.

Following was another period of martial music. Unfortunately, yet as Cotton's teeth clattered, there were more announcements. It seemed, said the voice on the radio, that any number of slothful Japanese had been seen chewing improperly. What did they think they were, "chewing-gum Americans"—Westerners who kept right on gobbling even after their stomachs were filled? At all times, the announcer cautioned, Japanese were to chew correctly and thoroughly, and only when swallowing. This was the patriotic way to eat.

Finally, the radio reminded everyone that as it was January 16, today was the traditional extra day that apprentices and servants were given off. He suggested, though, that any apprentice or servant who truly loved Tenno Heika would surely think twice before taking the holiday in difficult times such as these. Right? Right.

At last, then, the exhortations were concluded and exercises began. They started with jumping jacks and went from there, and at least so far as Cotton could see, everybody put out their best. It warmed you up. When the program was finished, the announcer wished everyone a good day, reminded everyone to work hard (and the women to increase as well), and then put on a recording of the "Kimigayo." The rising sun was hoisted to the top of its staff above the town office, and Cotton and all the others bowed again.

He went inside the church to pray then, and afterwards went back to grab a quick breakfast before the children showed up for kindergarten. That took so much of his time, all morning—and then he seemed to be struggling the rest of the day just to catch up.

This morning, too, the police chief, Hiranuma, and the highest-ranking army officer in the prefecture, Captain Kato, were waiting for Cotton at the door to the rectory. Although he wasn't surprised to see them together, still, this was the first time they'd ever come to see Cotton in tandem. He invited them in. They were all business and declined to wait till he made tea.

"You sent the children home before school was finished yesterday," Hiranuma started in.

"They were absolutely freezing," Cotton said.

"But it was ordered, Mr. Drake. The orders were approved by the Emperor," Captain Kato said. In effect, of course, every regulation in the empire, down to parking ordinances, was approved by the Emperor, but this never stopped any official from emphasizing the point when he wanted to be particularly overbearing.

Cotton was wise enough not to offer any debate. He only answered: "It was just so cold yesterday."

True as that was, yesterday had been ordained as a special day of sacrifice when schoolchildren throughout the land had been ordered not to wear overcoats to school, or shoes and socks—so that they might, by this example, show sympathy with the soldiers in China who were fighting the enemy and deprivation. There had been another such day in December, and Cotton had been appalled enough then, but at least that day had been fairly mild. Yesterday, though, had been especially cold, and the poor little five-year-olds had been frozen to the core from the start. After only half an hour, Cotton had bundled the whole lot of them in his clothes, and they all huddled together around the hibachi. When even that couldn't warm them all up sufficiently, he just called off school early and phoned those families he could to come pick up the children.

"No other schoolchildren in Tochigi—in all of Japan—were denied the opportunity to sacrifice yesterday," Hiranuma said.

"This is the way we toughen our children and make them appreciate what our brave soldiers are suffering in China," Kato added, then, gratuitously: "We do not enjoy the soft ways that you in the West do."

"I appreciate that," Cotton said, adding gratuitously himself: "I was educated here in Japan when I was a boy—"

"Not in Japanese schools," Kato interrupted.

"Oh yes, for several years." The policeman and the soldier glanced at each other in surprise. Everything they learned about Drake made him a more formidable *gaijin* than ever they could have imagined. Cotton went on: "I certainly do not dispute the policy . . . for older children. The boys and girls in high school could learn a great deal from a day of sacrifice. But it just seemed to me that the kindergarten children were too cold to understand."

"You will let us Japanese be the judge of what is best for our Japanese children," Hiranuma said, making it clear that there was no more room for discussion.

"Yes, I will," Cotton said.

To make up for the *gaijin*'s inappropriate decision, though, Hiranuma informed him that tomorrow his children would again be required to show up without outer clothes or footwear.

"Every day, too—the bath," Kato snapped. Each morning all the children were obliged to strip and endure a cold-water rub outdoors.

"Yes, every day."

Cotton cringed the next day, watching their little bodies shake. They came in from the outside, but barefoot, in their skimpy summer clothes. He couldn't teach them anything, for they were too cold to concentrate, and so quickly he gave up that ghost and had them play games—the more physical activity, the better.

Captain Kato came by to check things out when the children were playing an indoor version of Spud that Cotton had concocted, with bean bags instead of rubber balls. "Do these Christian children ever study, or do they just play?"

"It's recess now," Cotton said, and Kato left, grumbling. Soon he was replaced by Chief Hiranuma. By then, the room was a madhouse. Cotton had scouted around and come up with just enough chairs to make up a game of musical chairs. The kids were beside themselves with joy. They'd seen precious few chairs in their lives before, let alone played a game with them.

"Is this still recess?" the police chief asked.

"No, recess is over. But it is a day of sacrifice you ordered, so we sacrificed sitting and reading today." The children screamed as Cotton pulled out a chair and the biggest boy in the class fell down, right on his bottom. Hiranuma looked hard at Cotton; and though he didn't say anything, Cotton knew this meant another red mark in his file. He had pushed them to the limit.

Cotton had planned to pop down to Tokyo over New Year's and visit Miyuki and Kiyoshi, but he had been too busy to take off for the holiday. Finally, though, he found an excuse to get away. Since the American bishop had been stripped of his authority and sent back to the States, the Reverend Setsuo Kobayashi was filling in, and he invited Cotton to come down to Tokyo and report on how he was settling in. Cotton got some of the mothers to fill in for him running the kindergarten, and he took the train down after school one afternoon.

That first night, at the Serikawas', Kiyoshi told him he'd given his notice to American Orient and would be leaving to work for NYK Lines next week. Miyuki got up and left them to help her mother over at the kitchen counter as soon as Kiyoshi said that. "What happened with Yamamoto?" Cotton said. "You thought he might be putting you in the navy."

Kiyoshi shifted. He regretted it greatly that he'd ever mentioned to Cotton that he was going to see Yamamoto. "Actually, he was doing me a favor," Kiyoshi said. "He found out I was being drafted and he pulled my papers—but he told me that if I wanted to stay out of the military then I damn well better get a job with a Japanese company. So . . . NYK."

The way he spoke rang false to Cotton. Kiyoshi made too much of a pretense of being casual, when clearly the words were rehearsed. Only pretty good actors or very good liars could pull that off. Kiyoshi was neither.

But then, neither was Cotton. He couldn't remember ever being deceived before by Kiyoshi, and he wasn't any better at accepting a lie than Kiyoshi was at delivering it. Cotton looked away, but where his head turned, there was Miyuki, looking back at him. And their eyes both dropped, and quickly Cotton responded with the most innocuous remark he could that didn't abandon the subject. "So, NYK keeping you here in Tokyo?"

"Well, for now—though possibly we might have to move down to Yokohama," Kiyoshi said, and this time when he spoke, he made sure to fumble around for some matches. At the counter, Miyuki put some dishes down—too hard. Kiyoshi had already told her that he was being assigned to Hawaii, but he had to keep the news from everyone else until Yamamoto gave him the word to go.

But, then, Cotton didn't tell the truth, either. He didn't lie (he reminded himself); he just didn't tell the whole truth. He didn't tell Kiyoshi about how difficult life was in Tochigi and how much the authorities had begun to hound him. The world was coming between them, and it made Cotton sad . . . and scared. He thought: If Kiyoshi and I can't speak truthfully to each other, then what diplomats could? But he couldn't say that, and their conversation grew more circuitous and tentative, inane really, anything to keep them from lying to one another.

And then came the moment. Kiyoshi said: "Well, shall we go out somewhere tomorrow night?"

And Cotton said: "Oh, gosh, I've got a church dinner tomorrow."

Actually, he had made plans to go out with Bowersox. But that was how bad it was; somehow Cotton felt that he'd be betraying Kiyoshi and Miyuki if they knew he was meeting with another American—especially *that* one.

Kiyoshi looked away. Now they both knew they both were lying—and Miyuki's hands bumbled those damn dishes again.

Cotton grew even more depressed the next day. Had Tokyo deteriorated so much in only the couple of months since Kigen? Or had that just been the last day at playing dress-up? Maybe Cotton simply loved Tokyo so much he hadn't let himself see behind the facade. Whatever, it didn't matter anymore. Now, the city smelled; the air was grubby and asphyxiating from all the charcoal fumes. There wasn't a person he passed who wasn't wearing a *masuku,* a gauze mask; and though Cotton put one on too, the fumes crept down his throat. He was appalled at how much more ragged the people looked. Everything seemed patched. So many of the buildings were new, built after the great earthquake of '23; but the walls were dirty, the windows cracked. What few cars were left were mostly Chevys and Fords, but sometimes there would be whole blocks without any automobiles. Cotton hopped onto a street car. Once or twice, a taxi—one of the Datsun "baby cars"—would dash in front of the streetcar, and then the driver would get his tires grooved into the tracks and coast along as far as he could, saving every precious drop of fuel.

Happily, the meeting at church headquarters was brief and uneventful, and afterwards he borrowed a phone and called Bowersox. They were a good match. Bowersox was always curious to know what was happening in the sticks, and Cotton desperately needed to hear from an American.

"You probably want to know how much longer we've got till Armageddon, Japanese division," Bowersox said, as soon as Cotton called.

"The thought crosses my mind occasionally."

"Curiosity killed the cat."

"That's okay, Saint. Gives me eight more lives."

Bowersox chuckled: Drake was too damn quick to be a missionary. "All right. I got an even better deal for you than dinner with me."

"That's hard to believe," Cotton said.

"I know, but there's a big cocktail party tonight at the Dutch ambassador's, and I got you invited. Every Westerner in town—except the krauts and the dagos—will be there. Okay?" Cotton said it was fine with him. "And don't wear that damn collar or you'll ruin everybody's good time."

The terrible thing was (and Cotton knew it was a terrible thing), he listened to Bowersox and went looking for a shop to buy a shirt and tie. He still had money left over from his palmy days at American Orient, and anyway, there wasn't anything to spend money on in Tochigi. Besides, he needed to kill some time, and you could do plenty of that in a Japanese store. The pretty salesgirls wouldn't dare offend you by trying to *sell* you anything. Instead, they'd approach you only to *offer* you tea. Cotton wasted a lot of time before he finally purchased a snappy blue shirt and a handsome purple-and-green tie. He put them on, slid his clerical shirt and collar into his briefcase, slapped his *masuku* over his face, and began to negotiate the higgledy-piggledy streets to the party.

He had barely taken off his mask and handed his coat and case to the servant before the beautiful woman was upon him, her arms around him, kissing him and hugging him half to death. She probably would have bowled him over altogether, but he heard her scream "Cottonnnn!" just before she threw herself onto him. The last thing Cotton saw before she swallowed him up was Bowersox, holding a drink and a cigarette and staring at him in utter amazement.

Unperturbed, the ambassador's wife held out her hand. "I'm so happy you could join us, Mr. Drake—although I see you already have some acquaintance with our guests."

"We're old friends," Cotton said, gasping with embarrassment. It really was a terrific entrance—unless, perhaps, you're a priest.

"Cotton was the first boy I ever kissed!" the lady said. She was dark and guileless and spoke English with just a smidgen of an accent.

"You see, what did I tell you, Cotton?" Bowersox said, stepping up. "Take that collar off and the women throw themselves at you."

Cotton laughed and said: "St. George Bowersox, Marietta Santos."

"How do you do, Mr. Bowersox. I'm in the Peruvian embassy. I'm sorry, but I haven't seen the most attractive man in Japan in years, and now I'm taking him away from you both." Cotton sort of shrugged to the ambassador's wife and Bowersox and let Marietta tug him away by the sleeve. She hugged him again for good measure when she got him off in a corner.

"Oh, I heard you were back in Japan," Marietta began, and on and on she gushed from there, recapturing all the years since they'd first met at the Canadian Academy in Kobe, in junior high. Her father had been the consul there then. Cotton and Marietta had always been sweet on each other growing up, but what few Westerners there were in Japan were so tight with one another that it was all too much like being in the same family. It just didn't seem right once Cotton and Marietta got on the other side of French kissing. Too bad, he thought, because it would've been a good match—but they didn't have different enough pasts to come between them. Still, they always joked about what mighta/shoulda/coulda been. "The reason," Marietta said, "that it's particularly glorious to see you, dahling"—à Tallulah Bankhead "darling"—"is that I'm leaving Japan next week."

"Great. Just when I find you."

"Oh, don't give me that, Cotton Drake. I grew tired of waiting for you to come back to me." She paused, quite pleased with herself, for effect. "I'm going home to get married."

"Hey, that's wonderful, Marietta."

"Wonderful? *Wonderful?* Marietta raised a hand to her brow, feigning a swoon. "Isn't your heart breaking?"

"Well, it is, but I have to be a good sport—and it's wonderful for him." They both laughed.

"Fernando Pérez. He's a banker. I met him in Lima when I was on home leave last year. And I'm having a farewell party for all my best friends in Japan next Friday. You must come."

"I have to go back to Tochigi."

"I'm sure. And then you *will* return to my party. Jesus will allow you one day off." Cotton held up his hands in surrender. "Good," she said, but suddenly then the cast of her face changed, and she grabbed his sleeve again and pulled him even deeper into the corner of the room. "Listen to me, Cotton."

"What?"

Marietta took out a cigarette, and Cotton lit it for her. She blew the smoke and leaned closer. "Darling," she said—a real "darling" this time—"darling Cotton, you must get out of Japan. Now."

"Why are you telling me this?"

"Because there'll be war."

"Oh, Marietta, I've heard that. I've heard it for years."

"Yes, I know. But it's for real now. Believe me. And if there is war, they won't care if you're a priest."

Cotton studied her. "Mar, do you know something?"

"Yes, I do," she said directly. "I may not be the most important person in Tokyo, but I was in the right place."

"Oh."

"We've been hearing so much talk. There are so many Japanese that've immigrated to Peru, so we probably hear more. And then last week . . . It—it was the first definite thing." She paused.

"Well?"

Marietta lowered her voice even more, but she looked Cotton dead in the eyes. "They're planning to attack Hawaii."

Reflexively, Cotton tossed it off. "Oh, come on," he said.

"No, really, Cotton, it's true."

"Where did you hear this?"

"One of our cooks was telling the—"

"Oh, sure, that's a really reliable source, cooks."

She put a hand on his arm. "No, listen to me, darling. His brother is a cook in the navy. You don't get secrets revealed by the prime minister, you know. They don't call up from the War Ministry and hand out gossip. Believe me, this story was very precise. It had details. And there was one name . . ."

Cotton waited.

"Yamamoto," Marietta said.

"Honestly?"

"Yes."

"If that's so, it—when?"

"Oh, I don't think that's been set yet. Whenever they're ready. Whenever all the negotiations collapse. You still have time to clear out."

"Never mind that. Have you told anybody?"

"Well, when the story came to me, I immediately told the ambassador."

"Who's that?"

"Mr. Rivera-Schreiber. Ricardo."

"And what'd he do?"

"Nothing yet. This was only a couple of days ago. He wanted to see if he could find out anything else, and then, of course, he was going to tell Ambassador Grew. They know each other fairly well."

"God, I can't believe this," Cotton said.

"Yeah, I know."

"I don't wanna wait. I mean, a thing like this . . ." Suddenly, Cotton cocked his head toward Bowersox across the room. "That guy—the one you met when I came in."

"Uh-huh."

"He's the number-two or -three guy under Grew. I'd like to tell him now."

"Here, Cot? At a party?"

"I mean, we can find a quiet corner somewhere, Mar." She looked dubious. "Come on. A thing like this . . ."

"Well, okay."

Cotton cut through the crowd, snared a drink for himself as well, and signaled to Bowersox, who was closeted with a couple of English diplomats, instructing them in how Churchill should proceed. Cotton pointed toward Marietta, and Bowersox grinned and broke away from the others.

"Not fair, Cotton, monopolizing the prettiest girl at the party," he said.

"Too late—she's getting married. But she has something she wants to tell you."

"Oh?" They had reached Marietta now, and she and Bowersox exchanged nods again.

"This is pretty serious stuff," Cotton said. "Let's go outside for a couple minutes." He beckoned to the doors of a patio across the way and they stepped out into the brisk winter evening air.

"Is this too cold for you, señorita?" Bowersox asked, and he even moved to take off his jacket and hand it to her.

"It'll just take a minute, Saint," Cotton said. "Marietta has—listen, Saint—Marietta has heard a very convincing rumor that the Japanese are planning to attack Hawaii."

Bowersox chuckled a bit. "Really, that's too fantastic!" he said, and he took a long drag on his Lucky.

"I know," Marietta said. "But it comes from a very good source within our embassy. Low-level, but reliable. Mr. Rivera-Schreiber knows."

Bowersox perked up. "The ambassador knows? Himself? Really?"

"He's planning to tell Mr. Grew."

"Well, that won't be necessary any longer. Fill me in now, and I'll advise the ambassador." So Marietta laid out the same sketchy details as she'd given Cotton, adding a couple more points as the questions refreshed her memory.

"The cook?" Bowersox asked. "Where's he stationed with the army?"

"The navy. He's at Meguro, the war college."

"Any idea how long these plans are *supposed* to have been under way?"

"I don't know that. But it's not brand-new. It's been in the works a few weeks at least, I gather."

Cotton thought of Kiyoshi again and his connection with Yamamoto. Thank God Kiyoshi hadn't gone into the navy, that he was still a civilian.

Bowersox took out a small pad and made a couple of notes. "All right, Miss Santos," he said. "The United States of America thanks you very much indeed for this information. I will discuss it with the ambassador pronto, and I imagine he would want to cable Washington. Now, shall we go back inside again and enjoy the party?" He held the door for Marietta. "And really, Reverend Drake, the next time you get involved in international intrigue with a beautiful woman, make sure to choose one who isn't betrothed."

Cotton and Marietta both laughed. Cotton hated to admit it, but Bowersox owned a certain grudging charm. Besides, however surprised Cotton might have been himself, he was relieved to see that Bowersox, the professional, didn't seem particularly worried by Marietta's report. Why, for a moment there Cotton had been quite taken aback.

23

Cotton came back down to Tokyo the next Friday. He didn't want to, couldn't afford the time, but he'd taken Marietta out to dinner after the cocktail party, and he had too much to drink, and he didn't know how to say no to her party. The mothers filled in for him again at the kindergarten.

Miyuki was out for the day and Kiyoshi at work, so he hailed a baby car and went to the embassy, to see if Bowersox was there. The funny thing was, once Cotton had returned to Tochigi, once he had gotten out of Tokyo, he'd pretty much put Marietta's story out of his mind. It was all so outlandish. And besides, it was also taken care of now; Bowersox had the information and would know what to do with it.

Bowersox, though, only wanted to talk about Marietta, mostly in the language of double entendre—the lovely señorita having her first fling before marriage and motherhood with the innocent young parson. Cotton let Bowersox gurgle on until at last he had to break in. "So, what did Washington think of the rumor?"

"Haven't heard anything back yet."

"No?"

"Frankly, Cotton, I liked her tits a whole lot better than her information. Savvy?"

"It would just seem to me that they'd at least want to pursue such a story until—" Cotton stopped like that, in midsentence.

"Oh, excuse me, Bowersox, I didn't know you had anyone in here." The man at the door was obviously Ambassador Grew. There was no doubt in Cotton's mind: the patrician face, the magnificent mustache, the distinguished voice. If it was possible, Grew in person looked even more like the model of an ambassador than he did in his photographs. Cotton started to rise, and Grew waved him to stay in place. "Just drop by when you're free, Saint. No urgency. I only want to chat about this new business with Prince Konoe."

"Yes sir. Mr. Ambassador, this is the Reverend Mr. Drake."

"Oh yes," Grew said, considering Cotton before he took his hand. "I've heard about you, Mr. Drake. You were so determined to return to Japan. I hope things are going well."

"I'm accepted pretty well in Tochigi, sir."

"Episcopalian, aren't you?"

"Yes sir. And things are pretty quiet up there. The police watch me fairly carefully, but day to day they leave me alone. Of course, I was rather taken aback by that rumor Saint and I heard the other night."

The ambassador's heavy eyebrows arched up, but even more pronounced, Cotton saw out of the corner of his eye, Bowersox's mouth was set in a grim line even before Grew said: "And what rumor would that be, Mr. Drake?"

Cotton looked to Bowersox for guidance, but only a glare

came back. "I'm sorry, Saint, I thought you told the ambassador."

"I did not tell you that."

"Told me what?" Grew asked.

"Shut the door, Padre," Bowersox said—managed to say, it seemed, inasmuch as he never appeared to open his drawn mouth.

Grew closed the door before Cotton could reach it. Bowersox stood and lit a Lucky. "There was a little cocktail talk the other night," he said. "Right?" He stared at Cotton.

"Well, yes, we were *at* a cocktail party, but—"

"And a pretty girl the reverend knows passed on this rather incredible story about the Japs plotting to attack Hawaii. The source was a servant."

Cotton started: "Yes, but his brother—"

Bowersox whirled back. "I'm sorry, Mr. Ambassador, I've got it all written out here"—he slapped his desk—"but I just haven't gotten it to you yet. You see, Mr. Drake, rumors tossed about after a couple of cocktails are not an embassy priority."

"Now, now, Saint. I'm at something of a disadvantage here because I'm not privy to what you two are . . . yet. But any whisper, any gossip about the United States being attacked cannot be dismissed out of hand. Truth is stranger than fiction, you know. Lee lost Antietam because some fool enlisted man dropped the whole damn battle plan. Who'd believe that? For want of a shoe, and all that. So we can't be too blasé about what might seem to be inconsequential, can we now?" Bowersox didn't respond, assuming the question to be rhetorical, so Grew eliminated the assumption. "Can we, Saint?"

"No sir."

"What may seem farfetched to us, *by itself*, may suddenly take on paramount meaning if State heard the same sort of rumor in, say, Berlin. Or even Honolulu. Wherever. You can't expect the intelligence boys to add two and two and make four if we don't let them have one of the twos. Right, Mr. Drake?"

"Yes sir," Cotton replied, but barely. He could feel the anger emanating from Bowersox, and he wished Grew had left him out of it.

"Good. So Saint, bring me that report as soon as Mr. Drake and you are finished, and then I'm sure we'll get it right off to Washington. Certainly your friend Hornbeck will be delighted to hear more nasty things about the Japanese."

"Yes sir," Bowersox said. He was already moving around his desk as Grew shook Cotton's hand and departed.

Cotton was closing the door when Bowersox muttered: "Close the door."

Cotton whirled back. He knew what to expect, and he wasn't going to give Bowersox a clear shot. "You were the one told me you'd already sent the wire to Washington."

"I did not."

"You told me—"

"You asked me what sort of response we'd gotten from Washington, and I said none. And that's the truth."

"That's also very misleading."

"I'm sorry. We're not in your Father's house now, Padre, and in this house, in this business, that's how we have to operate sometimes." He jammed out his cigarette. "I would think that you would have been schooled enough in the niceties of ministering to the needs of others not to intrude into someone else's business—especially in front of their boss."

"And I apologize for that, Saint. I didn't mean to."

"I wouldn't pull a stunt like that on you with your bishop."

"Oh, come on, Saint. We're not talking about Emily Post here. If the Japanese are developing secret plans to attack Hawaii—"

"Listen to you! Listen to you! All of a sudden the pure fellow who couldn't dirty his hands in Tochigi is the boy spy, our dime-novel secret agent." Cotton had to chuckle a little; it helped the mood.

"Listen to me," Bowersox said, more gently.

"All right. I am."

"Okay, we'll cable this bullshit off to Washington, and all they'll say is: 'Why is Tokyo sending us this?' "

"You're sure?"

"Yes, I'm sure, because that's what I would've said if it hadn't been that good-looking dame of yours telling me this crap when I'm standing out there freezing my nuts off. You know what I heard last week at another party? Singapore."

"Singapore?"

"Right."

"Singapore what?"

"The Japs are going into Singapore, guaranteed. Or you want another rumor? The Philippines. They'll take Leyte. Or . . . wait—wait—wait. Never mind going south. Oh no, I can get it on the best authority at any geisha house in town that the southern talk is all a smokescreen, that the Japs are *really* going after the Russians. They'll hit Vladivostok. They'll go here. They'll go there. Different rumor every week."

"But maybe one of 'em is right. Isn't that worth the effort of checking them out?"

"Sure, if there was any sensible reason to pursue it. But where did this cock and bull come from? A cook in Meguro. Come on. Please." Bowersox had pretty much whipped Cotton, and so he let up a little. "You know, I'll tell you something else, too. The Japs aren't all that close-mouthed. They really aren't. It probably comes from being alone on these islands since the beginning of time. You'd be surprised the kind of secrets they let slip. They drink too much and then they babble in front of the whores and the geishas. They figure somebody hasn't got any balls, they must not have any ears, either. So I'm not unaware of this kinda bar talk. But if I reported to Hornbeck every time I heard a rumor about the Japs attacking, we couldn't do anything but run them down. Savvy?"

"Look, okay, I'm not that experienced in this stuff, but the thing about the Hawaii story that hit me was that it's just so incredible. You expect Singapore. Russia. This is so wild it just might be true."

"Jesus," Bowersox said in disgust. "If you followed that line of reasoning and you heard from some street sweeper that the

Japs were going to bomb Pittsburgh, we'd rush the whole Atlantic fleet down the Monongahela tomorrow."

"I can't win, can I?"

Bowersox lit another Lucky and blew a lot of smoke out of his nose. "Hell, you've already won. I'll have to send a report on this shit to Washington. Look, let me tell you: you think this Hawaii thing is original?" Cotton kind of nodded yes, although with the tone the question was phrased in, he knew the answer went the other way. "Yeah, sure, and Hitler never heard of Napoleon going into Russia." Bowersox chuckled; he was very pleased with himself over that. "This is like Buck Rogers and the Martians. People have written whole books about the Japs attacking Hawaii. It's studied in the military. Nine, ten years ago—'thirty-one, 'thirty-two, somethin' like that—we ran our whole Pacific maneuvers on that premise. It was the Red versus the White, but everybody knew the Japs were the Reds and we were the Whites."

"So isn't that all the more reason to think Yamamoto picked up the idea?"

Bowersox threw up his hands. "What are you, anyway? You're like a dog with a bone on this thing. Sure Yamamoto probably heard. He's probably heard about 'Hey-diddle-diddle, the cat and the fiddle, the cow jumped over the moon' too. That doesn't mean anybody can *do* it. Look at that. Look at it." He flung his arm toward the map on the wall. "That ain't the English Channel exactly, and Hitler can't even hop his ass over that. How the hell they gonna get there?" He pounded the wall approximately where Hawaii was.

"Well, they can get there a lot easier if every time we hear they're thinking about trying it, we don't do anything." Cotton couldn't resist that—but he also smiled to reassure Bowersox that he wasn't just being a wise guy. "I'll try not to be so naive and impressionable, Saint." And mocking himself, he placed his hands before him in prayer and lowered his head.

"Why, thank you, Cotton. And I'll try to be ever skeptical, the very soul of vigilance." And Bowersox laid his hand above his eyes and pantomimed intently scanning the horizon.

They laughed and shook hands.

Then, as soon as Cotton left, the first thing Bowersox did was to get on the phone and, in the best Japanese he could manage, ask to speak to General Yoichi Teshima.

24

"You're early," Marietta said. "I told you, Cotton, the party starts at—"

"No, I know. I'm here early on purpose. Can I close the door?" She nodded, and Cotton shut it.

"Great," Marietta said. "They'll all think, here I am leaving to get married, and I'm carrying on with another man behind closed doors."

"I wish." He leaned forward across her desk. "I want you to get the cook up here."

"The one . . . about Hawaii?" He nodded. "Cotton, I can't do that. He'll know he got his brother in trouble."

"I know. I know that. But I've got it all figured out. I'll tell him I'm with the American embassy, and we might be looking for a cook soon, and you recommended him, so while I was visiting here, et ceterera."

"Mr. Bowersox put you up to this, didn't he?"

"Well, sort of," Cotton acknowledged, sort of.

"What're ya gonna ask him?"

"Just roundabout stuff."

"No direct questions. No 'Did your brother?' "

"Promise. Marietta, you can stay."

"No, come on, I trust you, Cotton," Marietta said, and she called the kitchen and asked if Noboru could come up. She gave Cotton his personnel file to skim through, and introduced him when Noboru came in. Then she left.

"The reason I'm here, Noboru, is to go to Miss Santos's party, but I mentioned to her that we might be hiring another cook at the American embassy, and she praised you."

"I am very happy here," Noboru said. Cotton was sitting on the desk, but Noboru remained standing a distance away.

"Yes, I know. But this would be a promotion and a raise." Noboru looked up at that, and Cotton mentioned a perfectly outlandish figure. That caught Noboru's attention sufficiently for him to sit down when Cotton beckoned to the chair. Then he leaned back on Marietta's desk, picked up the file, and started going through it. "Where did you learn to cook?" What do you most like about cooking?" "Can you prepare Western dishes?" Noboru accommodated him with polite answers. Cotton glanced back at the file. "Let's see. You're twenty-eight years old—any chance you'll be drafted?"

"I don't think so, sir. I had an accident several years ago, and my leg is still not right." Cotton nodded, then went back to pretending to study the file.

"Oh, I see you have a brother in the navy, and he's a cook, too."

"Yes sir."

What a coincidence, Cotton went on, at his friendliest. What a coincidence that two brothers would both be cooks, and Noboru smiled broadly, and explained, with animation, how the family had lived next door to a restaurant in Yokohama, and so on and so forth, and Cotton teased him about who was the better cook, and they laughed, and Cotton said, "Let's see now, he's assigned to NCO quarters in Meguro."

"Oh no," Noboru said, sitting up in his chair, sticking out his chest. "Minoru had a big promotion."

Cotton could feel himself tingle. "Is that so? Where's he stationed now?"

"Oh, Minoru is one of the cooks in Admiral Yamamoto's own mess."

There it is, Cotton thought. There it is. Let Bowersox try and slough this news off. But "Really?" is all he said.

"Yes indeed," Noboru responded.

"Minoru doesn't actually get to *see* the admiral, does he?" Noboru's back stiffened. "Why, sometimes he comes right into the admiral's cabin when he prepares special meals for him and his staff. The admiral calls my brother by his name."

"Gee, I've heard Admiral Yamamoto is a wonderful gentleman."

"Oh yes. Minoru has told—" And there Noboru stopped. Maybe he remembered the things his brother had told him in confidence; maybe he remembered what nationality he was talking to here about a job; maybe he just decided that he was getting too chummy with a *gaijin*. Whatever, he suddenly stopped, and the Japanese mask came back on. Cotton understood immediately that the jig was up.

"Well," he said, "it sounds as if your brother has a fascinating job, and if this position opens up at the American embassy, I'll be sure to call you."

"Yes, *arigato*, thank you," Noboru said, rather stiffly, and he and Cotton bowed, and he left.

When Marietta returned and Cotton handed her back the file, she asked him if he'd learned anything. "No," Cotton said, trying to keep his own Japanese mask on. "I knew it was a long shot."

"Crazy, huh—Hawaii?"

"Probably," he said, and he pointed to the map on her wall. "So much blue. How would they get there?" And they both shrugged. Cotton thought that he would call Bowersox first chance he got in private. Let him put this in his pipe and smoke it.

It was late at night, well after dinner, when Cotton finally found his way to the Serikawas'. Most of the party had spilled out of the Peruvian embassy on to dinner at the Kaigan, which was the best Western restaurant in town, and the men in the group were starting to talk about going up to Yoshiwara when Cotton kissed Marietta goodbye and cut loose. Miyuki and Mrs. Serikawa were already asleep.

"I'm sorry," Cotton said to Kiyoshi. "I didn't know I'd be so late and miss the ladies. But I'll see you all again in a couple of weeks. I've got a diocesan meeting down here on the eighteenth."

"Well, you're always welcome, of course, but I'm afraid I won't be here then."

"Oh?"

Kiyoshi suddenly jumped up and moved away. "Hey, how 'bout a nightcap? I've got some good Scotch." In fact, he'd gotten it from Yamamoto.

Cotton held up his hands: what the hell? He'd already had too much to drink, and one more wouldn't matter. In fact, it wouldn't even matter if Mrs. Serikawa snored, which she did sometimes. "Where'reya gonna be, Key?"

Kiyoshi poured out the liquor. "Well, they've reassigned me ... NYK."

"You mean out of Tokyo?"

"Honolulu," Kiyoshi said, in the most offhand way he could manage, as he reached for the soda water.

The word shot through Cotton. He was glad he was a little high. He was sure it made his reaction seem more casual. "Honolulu," he finally said. "Gee, why?"

"Whatdya mean *why?*" Kiyoshi asked, sharply, still fussing with the drinks. Neither one of them was really looking at the other.

"Well, you know, uh, I thought they were going to keep you here."

"People change their minds. You know how big companies are."

"Sure. So you'll be in charge there?"

Another bad question.

"No, as a matter of fact," Kiyoshi said, "we've got a real good man in charge there. Hawaii's damn important to us." Quickly: "To NYK. We get two liners in there every week."

"I would've just thought that L.A. or San Francisco would be best for someone like you—you know, Key, with your experience."

Another bad observation.

"Maybe you would *think* that, Cotton. But NYK knows just a little bit about the shipping business, and they happen to think Hawaii is an important place." He handed Cotton his Scotch.

"Okay, sure, Key. That's great, I guess. How long will you be there?"

Even that was another bad question.

"I really don't know, Cotton. Does it matter? Do you know how long you're gonna be in Tochigi?"

"You're right. You're right. I was just curious. You know. And Miyuki loved Hawaii on your honeymoon."

At least when Kiyoshi frowned this time it wasn't so much at Cotton. "The bastards won't let me take her," he said.

"No?"

"Times are just too touchy."

"Yeah, yeah, that's true," Cotton said, and somehow this sort of cleared the air, and Kiyoshi plunked himself right down next to him on the tatami and clapped him on the shoulder.

"So, since this has come up, I got a favor to ask of you."

"Shoot."

"Mrs. Serikawa is very disappointed that I have to leave, and she's really not happy about living in Tokyo these days. She wants to go back down to Aimoto and live with her sister-in-law, but Miyuki is dead set against that. But she's also not keen on staying in Tokyo without me. And then she told me that when she was up with you in Tochigi, she helped you with the kindergarten, and she loved that, and she just started wondering . . ."

Cotton could hardly believe what Kiyoshi was saying. "Are you serious, Key?"

"Miyuki said you had plenty of room, and she could teach."

"You can't imagine how great this would be! The kindergarten was always intended just as a job for an assistant. It takes up so much of my time."

"And Miyuki said Mrs. Serikawa could help about the house."

"Miyuki *wants* this?" Cotton asked.

"It was her idea."

"Well, then, you are my *on* man forever. Never mind *can* they come! *When* can they come?"

"I'm sailing for Honolulu on the *Asama* Wednesday. Any time after that."

"Well, they're welcome for as long as they want. I hate to say this, pal, but I hope they never let you leave Hawaii."

"Okay. But one thing." And Kiyoshi put on a very serious mien and pointed his finger at Cotton.

"Well, what's that?"

"Absolutely . . . absolutely no more baths with my wife."

Cotton threw his face into his hands, and only slowly raised it at last, kind of peeking at Kiyoshi through his fingers. As easy as it was for Cotton to tell when Kiyoshi was lying, so could he tell when he was really joking. "Hey, it was *her* idea!"

Kiyoshi roared. "She couldn't believe you'd be so embarrassed. You know, Cot, I'm really glad you're back. You've been getting entirely too Western."

Cotton said: "That's funny, Key. I thought you've been getting too Japanese." But he was sorry he said that as soon as he did.

That night, Cotton didn't have to worry about Mrs. Serikawa's snoring. The two men decided to let Miyuki stay asleep upstairs with her mother; then they hauled out the two futons and Cotton slept on Miyuki's. "I haven't slept with you since we shared that house in Waikiki just before I went into the ministry," he said.

"I keep losing in this bargain," Kiyoshi said. "Waikiki, we were sleeping together and you throw me out for Liz. Tokyo, I'm sleeping with my wife and I throw her out for you."

"Go to sleep."

"Go to hell."

"Goodnight."

Kiyoshi didn't say goodnight. Instead, he said: "Remember when we were kids and we'd sleep together at your house or mine, and nobody ever wanted to be the one who didn't get the last word in, so we'd go one-two-three and then we'd both say—"

"One-two-three," Cotton said.

"Goodnight!" they both cried together.

Three more seconds. "Really goodnight," Kiyoshi said.

"Go to hell," Cotton said.

"Really one-two-three," Kiyoshi said.

"Goodnight," they both said together, laughing.

And then, as he lay there, Cotton decided it probably was foolish to call Bowersox. He was making entirely too much out of these silly coincidences. Instead, he started thinking about how wonderful it would be to have Miyuki back in Tochigi . . . helping him out. He didn't think about Mrs. Serikawa helping him out, not at all. He didn't think about her, and he didn't think about Hawaii. He was still thinking about Miyuki when he fell asleep.

25

General Teshima was already at the geisha house when Bowersox arrived. The general was a regular, accorded a fine room and the best women of the house. One of them, Sai, was playing her samisen and singing for Teshima when Bowersox was escorted in. The song was a favorite, a lament of the bar hostess (who was, of course, inferior to the cosmopolitan geisha), and Sai cooed to Teshima about the poor rouged night flower.

She bowed when she was finished. The general applauded her heartily, and bade the American to take a seat next to him. Quickly, Bowersox's sake cup was filled, and the two men raised their drinks. Teshima pivoted, to salute Sai. "You have nothing like these women anywhere in the West!" he crowed.

Bowersox merely raised his cup again to indicate it was empty, and immediately his geisha, Midori, kneeled by him and poured him another. It was the most spoiled of existences, to be with a geisha, a subject with which Teshima never got tired of boring Bowersox. "They sing for you, they dance for you, they arrange flowers, they pour your tea, serve your food. They entertain you. And they are wise. They possess intellect. What woman in the West can possibly do all this?"

"Wives," Bowersox said dryly, and even Teshima had to roar—and Sai and Midori with him. Bowersox had managed to pick up some fairly serviceable Japanese, and Teshima obliged him to speak it, when they were together, in such quintessentially Japanese places as a geisha house. Impressed, the geishas would ooh and ah every time the *gaijin* said so much as *"Sayonara"* or *"Arigato."*

"So why did you marry an Asian girl instead of an American?" Teshima asked.

"Chinese, Yoichi."

"I know, Chinese. You love everything Chinese."

"I loved her," Bowersox said, more sweetly than most anybody who knew Bowersox could have imagined.

"I know you did. I'm sorry." Bowersox's wife had died several years before, barely a bride, of tuberculosis, in Shanghai, where he was posted then. "So now we must find you a Japanese girl to marry. Anyone marries a Japanese girl soon loves all Japan. Then we get you a regular geisha, too. Right, ladies?" They tittered. "A man needs a geisha away from the house and family. It is too much to expect a woman to be all things to a man. It was never meant to be."

"Perhaps," Bowersox replied. "But even you all know that it's a dying art." Teshima grunted, but he couldn't deny what Bowersox said. Most of the younger Japanese men found geishas anachronistic. They'd rather go out with mogas, or dance with Western-style bar girls, instead of hearing geishas play the samisen melodies of old samurai times.

The two men raised their cups an inch off the floor, and instantly they were filled. They drained them again, and then Bowersox suggested a game of *yo yo ye,* the Japanese version of scissors-cuts-paper/paper-wraps-rock/rock-breaks-scissors. If a geisha wins, the man drinks a thimbleful of sake to her; he wins, she drinks. Soon, they all four were rocking with laughter, and Teshima called on the women for fan dances and more songs before dinner came.

A young geisha, Yuriko, helped bring in the food—fish and *tsukemono*, pickled cucumbers and turnips, and *kimpira*, fried burdock root mixed with carrots—the kind of feast you didn't see much more in Japan, even in geisha houses . . . unless, of course, it was a general being served. Yuriko could not have been much more than sixteen or seventeen, barely out of the *maiko*, the apprentice stage; but after she bowed to Bowersox, there was more of a shy smile for Teshima, a knowing nod of some sort. The other geishas smiled, too, and as soon as the young girl was gone, Sai turned to Teshima. *"Okāsan* was very pleased with the way the general handled Yuriko's *mizu-age."*

Teshima swelled up. "It was my pleasure. And any other *maiko*." Then suddenly a slap on Bowersox's back and bombast: "Or perhaps next time we get Bowersox-san for *mizu-age*. Can a *gaijin* perform *mizu-age?"*

Bowersox didn't know what the hell they were talking about, but it was clear from the geishas' expressions that, even in humor, General Teshima had committed some breach of good taste. They went back to making a big fuss of preparing the dinner. "And what is this *mizu* whatever?"

"You tell him, Midori!" Teshima thundered, raising his cup one more time.

"It is helping a young geisha enter womanhood."

"You mean deflowering her?"

"Aaaiieee!" Teshima cried. "Don't always be so blunt. It is so much more tender than the way you put it. In the old days, it would take a week or more if done properly. With little Yuriko, I took four evenings. It is not rape, my *gaijin* friend. It is not even your silly seduction. It is a beautiful initiation."

Bowersox screwed up his face. "You *tender*, Yoichi? You?"

Teshima shook his head, as much in disappointment as in scorn. It was a huge, bullet head, nearly shaven, wrapped with round, dark-rimmed eyeglasses. His body was blocky and unforgiving; even in the kimono he wore tonight, nothing quite flowed. "You never understand, Saint. You never understand the contradictions, *yasashii* and *kibishii*, the gentle and rough, in us all. You would be surprised how soft I could be, what a tender *mizu-age* I can perform."

This time, Bowersox only nodded, but really in contradiction: as if to say, yes, you're damn right I'd be surprised. Teshima owned the reputation as a butcher, a barbarian of a soldier. The atrocities that he and his men had committed at Nanking three years ago when he was a colonel in the Tenth Army would have merited summary execution in most armies; instead, it drew Teshima a promotion, shifting him to a high position in the third bureau, *jouhou kyoku*, intelligence. He not only spoke English well, having learned it abroad as a junior officer, but he had even picked up some German. Of course, Bowersox shouldn't have been surprised at some of the general's less obvious traits. After all, Teshima had been subtle and wily in attaining Bowersox's friendship; he was sufficiently clever to understand that this particular American was cynical enough to accept such a double-dealing association. Bowersox had even grabbed at the connection, for it gave both men a convenient window into the enemy's house.

It was a perfect relationship in its way, too, for as much as Bowersox and Teshima each hated all that the other man stood for, all his politics, all his ideology, they both recognized how much alike they were.

Yuriko returned to the room, and Teshima beckoned her to his side. "Tell the *gaijin*, was it a good *mizu-age?*"

She smiled broadly and bowed to the general. "It must be done just right, so the girls don't fear men thereafter," Teshima explained. "It is a great responsibility, an honor even, for a man to be selected for *mizu-age* by the *okāsan.*" All the geishas nodded. "Yuriko was put alone in a room—right, my dear?" She nodded. "And there she found four eggs that I had placed on her bed. An old man told me about this *mizu-age* many years ago. And then I came into the room, and I invited her to lie down, and then I cracked one of the eggs, and I ate the yolk myself, and then I took the white, and softly I rubbed it upon your thighs, didn't I?"

Yuriko nodded, and the other two geishas chorused a benediction. Teshima continued his account. The next evening he returned to the room with Yuriko. Now there were three eggs, and he repeated the maneuver, only this time when he addressed the thighs with the egg white, his fingers drew to the edge of the young girl's vagina, and then a bit inside. The following evening, when there were two eggs left, his fingers found their way within Yuriko, gently probing, sliding about. And then the fourth night, Teshima ate the last egg yolk, and with his slippery egg fingers he moved well inside Yuriko, and she seemed at ease, so following that, happily, naturally, came intercourse, the consummation.

Yuriko smiled proudly as Teshima completed their story. "This is how you make a woman, how you make a geisha," he said.

It was time for dinner then. It was impolite to chat over food; instead, the best form was to slurp and grunt approval, honoring the meal and those who made it. Teshima slobbered away, downing it all, and Bowersox did his best to keep up with him.

When they were finished, Bowersox asked Teshima if he was still sleeping with the girl whose virginity he had appropriated.

Teshima thundered back: "You never learn anything about Japan, you fool Westerner! The man so honored to commit *mizu-age* must never touch that geisha again. He has served her and is finished."

Bowersox shook his head and thought, You're right, I never do learn anything about you bastards. There was this odd, almost Victorian quality to Teshima. To him, geishas were raised to a companion pedestal with wives. When he tipped them at the end of the evening, he refused to think of the money as some sort of payment or gratuity; instead, he referred to it as "flower money" or "jewel money," as if it were different altogether from the sort of remuneration offered any others in the service industry. And even as Sai kept fussing and cooing over him—as Midori did with Bowersox— Teshima was already planning the balance of the evening with proper sex in Yoshiwara, the traditional old red-light district where foreigners, intellectuals, and roués still went slumming.

"I have found the most wonderful new prostitute," he said. "Sumiko. She works at a place called Shinyanagi, the New Willow." And here, as the two geishas listened every bit as attentively as Bowersox did, Teshima graphically detailed the specialties this whore delivered upon his body. As connoisseurs of pleasing men themselves, they approved of the woman's art. There was much nodding from the women, much approbation—not unlike they were hearing about the clothes of a new designer or the dishes of a new chef. "And," Teshima continued, "she's got a friend at the house, named Hanako, and my colleague Admiral Sakamaki—the only friend I have in the whole damn navy—came with me to Shinyanagi two nights ago, and he raved about Hanako. I have reserved her for you this evening, Saint-san."

Bowersox nodded his appreciation, while Sai beamed at his good fortune, and Midori not only clapped a little at this fine dessert but said: "Admiral Sakamaki says she is a very special whore. You will have excellent sex tonight."

"Good!" Teshima bellowed. "So let us go get laid now, Saint."

Bowersox, however, reached out and touched the sleeve of Teshima's kimono. "Wait, Yoichi-san. I told you we had something to discuss."

The general haughtily waved his hand. "So talk."

"Alone."

"No problem. You know geishas don't listen when they're not supposed to."

"I'd rather not test their abilities at pretense."

Teshima frowned, but he handed Sai some jewel money and waved her off. Bowersox did the same for Midori, and the geishas bowed and shuffled out in their getas. Teshima picked up his sake cup. "So, what is it?"

"I hear you've been very naughty," Bowersox said, and the general looked up, curious. "No, not you, my ugly friend. Maybe some of your colleagues in the War Ministry. Or Admiral Yamamoto, perhaps."

Teshima snapped: "I have nothing to do with that flower of a man."

"Well," Bowersox said flat out, leaning forward, "some of you bastards are planning to make war on us." He kept his eyes locked on Teshima. How the general looked would surely be much more revealing than anything he might say— and Teshima looked quite surprised, even confused.

"Not yet!" he roared. "And shall I tell you when, Saint-san? If it comes? Shall I send you an invitation?"

Bowersox shifted into specifics. "I heard there were plans to hit Hawaii."

Teshima looked genuinely shocked. He even laughed. "Hawaii? Where did you hear that?"

"It came to my attention.. Pretty reliably."

"Oh, Saint, Saint, Saint. How do we get there? And why? There's no oil there. And guess what? I don't even want you and the English . . . anywhere. I still want to go into Russia." Now the roles were switched, and Teshima studied Bowersox to see how he would respond to that. "That disappoints you, doesn't it, Saint-san? You want so much to have a war with us. Don't you? A lot of you do, don't you? Maybe even President Roosevelt himself, huh? Only it's not permissible, ever, for Americans to be for war until war comes." Bowersox smiled, as enigmatically as he could. "Ah, that's true, isn't it? I know Americans better than you think I do." He pulled playfully at Bowersox's kimono.

"Well, why *not* fight you? We would thrash you."

"And then you would have your precious China all to yourself." Bowersox dropped his eyes. He'd come to milk Teshima, but now it was his teats that were being pulled. "Don't kid me, Saint-san. I know you too well. We've drunk together, eaten together, fucked girls together. You'll do anything to fight us."

"You want war with the West just as much as I want it with you."

"Sure, I'm a soldier. And that's why you can forget this crap about Hawaii. That would be the navy's war—and why would we allow that?"

"I don't know. I just heard."

Teshima leaned forward. He enjoyed being mischievous. "Oh, you want that—don't you? You want to fight us so much."

"I hate what you sons of bitches did to China. So now, try us—we'll beat you and hang you up by the balls." And Bowersox laughed, almost gaily, it seemed.

Teshima only shook his head and laughed back at Bowersox. They were like two guys at the nineteenth hole kidding each other about bad putts. "China is ours, you stupid shit. China is yellow people, just like us. You whites have no business over here. But"—and here he roared and threw a jovial arm around his adversary's shoulders—"we're still at peace now, and we're still a couple of men, so let's go up to Yoshiwara and screw a couple of yellow girls together."

26

After Kiyoshi sailed for Honolulu, Miyuki and Mrs. Serikawa packed for Tochigi. It wasn't a hard task; they could come back and pick up summer things later, if it worked out and they stayed. They were going to take the train up Sunday, but that was February 23, and when Mrs. Serikawa thought about it, she demanded that they stay in Tokyo a few more days so they could visit Yasukuni on *ni/ni-roku*. Yasukuni is the most hallowed shrine in Tokyo, if not in all the land, for the spirits of all the soldiers who ever died for the empire are sequestered there, on eternal bivouac.

"It will be the fifth anniversary this year," Mrs. Serikawa said.

"I remember Takeo every day," Miyuki replied. "And my father, too. We can go to Yasukuni any day and pray for them. We can go today."

"I can't believe you, Miyuki. It is shameful enough that your own husband is not in the army. Your father and your brother surely cry that our *yoshi* is not serving the emperor when we are in the very midst of a war."

"Mother, there are many ways to serve Tenno Heika without being a soldier."

"Not for a Serikawa there isn't," she said, and Miyuki saw that it was useless. She phoned Cotton and told him they wouldn't be along till the twenty-seventh, and on *ni/ni-roku*, Miyushi and her mother went to Yasukuni.

Hardly had they arrived outside the great gate of the shrine, though, when Miyuki was all but attacked by a group of women, all wearing ugly outfits of some indistinct mustard color. "You are not properly dressed!" they screamed at Miyuki. "Your clothes are too luxurious! They shame the poor soldiers fighting bravely in our *seisen*—the sacred war against China!"

Miyuki tried just to smile and push through. For goodness sake, she only had on a plain gray dress and a modest overcoat (but it did have a fur collar). Mrs. Serikawa, though, was ashamed and obsequious. "My daughter offers much regret," she said to the protesters, who were members of the Dai Nippon Kokubo Fujinkai, the National Defense Women's Association.

"Come on, Mother," Miyuki said. "We are here to pray."

But the National Defense ladies wouldn't let up, and blocked the Serikawas' path. "The Empress is personally rolling bandages for our troops," the most strident one said. "Are *you?*"

Mrs. Serikawa quaked before her and mumbled apologies for their horrible deficiencies, and assured the patriots that she and her daughter both regularly helped make *senninbari*, the thousand-stitch belts that were sent to the soldiers at the front, where they were supposed to protect the wearer from bullets.

Miyuki was growing angry. She bowed to the National Defense ladies as politely as she could, and she accepted their pamphlets, but she yanked at her mother's coat. "Come along, Mother—we don't have to explain to anyone," she said.

"It is one thing to be a moga, another not to show patriotism," Mrs. Serikawa muttered; and inside, past the magnificent *torii*, Mrs. Serikawa devoted most of her prayers to her husband and her son, that their spirits might instill more of that old-time patriotism in Miyuki.

Miyuki prayed that Tenno Heika would find the best judgment in his decisions about war, and when Mrs. Serikawa heard that, she returned and prayed some more that her daughter would be forgiven for questioning Tenno Heika's thought processes.

Miyuki had a gin before dinner that night, and tried to read the English copy of *Gone with the Wind* that Cotton had given her. She refused even to glance at the flyers that the National Defense Women's Association had thrust upon her.

The unpleasantries between mother and daughter resumed the very first thing next morning, when Mrs. Serikawa stirred Miyuki and advised her that the six o'clock exercises were about to begin.

Miyuki just rolled back over. "I don't feel like doing them today," she said, as her mother turned on the radio.

The bugle blew. "Get up!" Mrs. Serikawa shouted at her.

Miyuki pulled the covers over her head. The radio announcer began to speak, welcoming all of the Sun-Begot Land to February 27, 1941, in the fifteenth year of Showa, Enlightened Peace, the twenty-six hundredth year of Japan. Mrs. Serikawa yanked at the covers. "Go away, Mother." She yanked at Miyuki. Miyuki buried herself deeper. "Go away."

"You cannot speak that way to Tenno Heika."

"I'm not speaking that way to Tenno Heika. I'm speaking that way to a damn radio announcer."

"It is important for all Japanese to begin each day in exercise, so—"

Miyuki didn't want to fight anymore with her mother. She didn't want to do the exercises, but she didn't want to fight, either. She reached out from under the covers and took her mother's hand. "Mother, really, I just don't feel like it. I'm tired, we've gotta go get a train, and my period just started."

With that, Mrs. Serikawa just dissolved, crumbling to the floor, starting to cry.

"Mother, really, missing one day of exercise is not that big a deal."

Mrs. Serikawa pushed Miyuki's hand away. "I'm not crying about that. I'm crying about your period. You are not pregnant."

"No, Mother, I am not pregnant. Again."

"Kiyoshi continues to bring dishonor to the Serikawa family that made him its son," Mrs. Serikawa declared.

That was too much for Miyuki. She rose up off her futon and went over to the radio and snapped off the announcer, just as he was beginning to announce the new dietary sacrifices. "Don't you ever say that about Kiyoshi again!" she yelled, and Mrs. Serikawa ducked her head.

Miyuki turned away and gritted her teeth. She could still hear her mother sniffling. At last she turned back to her and wrapped an arm around her. She really didn't want to upset her; she just wanted her to abandon the damn twin subjects of Kiyoshi's virility and Kiyoshi's employment. "Look, Mother, don't be so naive."

"And what does that mean?"

"It means I'm sure that Kiyoshi is working in some capacity for Admiral Yamamoto."

"He told you this?" Mrs. Serikawa raised her head; this gave her new life.

"Of course not, Mother. Did Father ever share such secrets with you?" Mrs. Serikawa shook her head. "But I'm sure it's true." She flipped the radio back on. "Now finish your exercising, if you want, and then we'll get some breakfast and go off to help Cotton . . . as my husband desires us to do."

One afternoon a few days before the Serikawas arrived in Tochigi, Mr. and Mrs. Nakagawa came in from their little farm to see Cotton. They were terribly shy, tiny people; their legs bowed; and they wore only getas on their feet, even though there'd been a snowstorm just two days ago. Already in Japan, the backwater types like the Nakagawas were appearing as a race apart from the cosmopolitan city folk. These country mice were shorter, stumpier, and dressed differently, as even the men remained in kimonos. Farmers like the Nakagawas still scratched out an existence on tiny garden plots in a life that remained remarkably simple and unchanged, yet feudal.

Indeed, Cotton was astonished that the Nakagawas would dare to consider Christianity—all the more so now that the government so inhibited any deviation from the norm. But, then, starting with the apostles, you never could tell quite who might join the flock.

"We are ready to be baptized for Jesus," Mr. Nakagawa whispered uneasily.

"Oh, that's wonderful news!" Cotton cried out. "What a glorious way to start Lent!" And he absolutely discombobulated poor Mrs. Nakagawa by reaching out and kissing her. "When shall we do it? This Sunday? Or perhaps the Saturday before Easter would—" The Nakagawas looked at each other, barely able to face Cotton. "What is it?" he asked.

"Our daughter," Mr. Nakagawa finally got out.

"Yes. Hanako?" They nodded. "She's in Tokyo."

"In . . . Yoshiwara, yes." But Mr. Nakagawa could go no further.

"Well, what about her?"

"We would like her to see us baptized."

"Of course . . . of course," Cotton said. "That would be wonderful."

Mr. Nakagawa looked back over at his wife. "But Hanako is a prostitute."

"That doesn't matter, Nakagawa-san. Jesus was very friendly with prostitutes. One anointed his feet. And what does it matter that Hanako is a prostitute? The profession is legal here. I'll bet she does a good job." The parents smiled broadly and nodded. "I've been to Yoshiwara. Before I was a priest. But I've been. I'm a man, you know."

Mrs. Nakagawa covered her mouth at such candor. The Reverend Mr. Evans was the only other Western man she'd

ever met, and she couldn't imagine him revealing that. Mr.
Nakagawa grew bolder. "Can you, Drake-san . . . can you—"

"Can I what?"

"Can you go see Hanako the next time you're in Tokyo
and personally invite her to our baptism?"

"Of course—I'd be delighted. I want to meet her."

They smiled and bowed. "Actually, I hear Hanako is a very
good prostitute," Mr. Nakagawa said.

"*Ichi-ban,*" Cotton said, winking, "number one." And this
time the Nakagawas positively beamed. Everybody everywhere always loves to hear compliments on their children,
whatever they're up to. So Cotton went on: "And do you
have any other children?"

The moment Cotton asked that, he knew he had ventured
onto some uncomfortable ground. He waited. The Nakagawas both lowered their eyes again. Finally, and only with difficulty, Mr. Nakagawa spoke. "We had a son. Keiichi. He
was, I'm afraid, killed in China two years ago."

And, so softly, hardly to be heard, Mrs. Nakagawa added:
"That is when we began to come to this church. Hanako
went to Yoshiwara then to make money, and we decided to
see about Jesus."

"I see," Cotton said, and he reached out and took her
hands. It was so Western a gesture, Mrs. Nakagawa really
didn't understand at first what he was doing. "I'm sorry. I'm
sorry about Keiichi. But he is with God now, and soon, we all
pray, these terrible times will be over in Japan, and then I'm
sure Hanako will come back to Tochigi. No doubt she'll find
a *yoshi* to carry on the Nakagawa family." Both of them
brightened considerably at that. "But first, first we will baptize you, and I'll make sure that Hanako is here that day to
be with us."

The Nakagawas paid for their faith, however—as all the
Christians in Tochigi did. The government kept dossiers on
all the families in the land. Many of the local officials, even
the schoolteachers, were moved from town to town, so that

they would remain more objective in their reports on the citizens. Hiranuma, the police chief in Tochigi, had been there only a couple of months, come from a prefecture far away, west of Tokyo. No one was going to cozy up to him.

Hiranuma even started attending services at Cotton's church, conspicuously taking notes, his very presence sufficient to intimidate the parishioners. The Christians all knew their names went down to Tokyo, too, where their spiritual affiliation with the *gaijin* Jesus was filed with the *tokko*, the secret police, the guardians of proper Japanese thinking.

Nothing yet had happened to any of the Christian faithful; but with Shintoism becoming more and more one with the government, one with Japan, Christians sensed they were an endangered species, and as Lent wore on, attendance began to lag some. Cotton started a women's bible study group, a youth fellowship, midweek prayer meetings, a "great religions of the world" class, and these efforts seemed to pay off; the congregation held pretty firm.

Miyuki had another idea why the little missionary parish remained so strong in the face of so many troubles and the government's hostility. "It is you, Cotton," she said.

"Well, yes, I'm God's instrument here," he said, blushing some.

"No, you're much more. They can feel you, Cotton—the people. They can feel how much you love them."

"The love comes from Jesus."

"Maybe. But we can feel it."

"You, too, Miyuki?" She ducked her head. "You can feel—?"

"Love. Jesus' love. Yes, I think," she said.

In fact, although it infuriated Mrs. Serikawa, Miyuki went to church every Sunday herself, listening, watching, and singing lustily, only leaving early on those Sundays when it was communion, nodding politely to Chief Hiranuma or one of his surrogates as she left.

Soon, though, Miyuki had her own problem with the authorities. The first Tuesday that she taught kindergarten was supposed to be, for schools all over Japan, a day in which the children were to reinforce their patriotism by eating Rising Sun lunches. This consisted, simply enough, of a ball of rice with a pickled plum in the middle, approximating the bright red circle in the middle of the white national flag. Somehow, although Miyuki heard the order when it was announced with morning exercises, she forgot it.

So on Wednesday Hiranuma showed up with Captain Kato. Both at their most officious, they marched in tandem into the kindergarten, right in the middle of a flower-arranging exhibition Miyuki was showing the kids. "You will come immediately with us, Mrs. Serikawa," Kato declared.

"But—but—"

"Come along now," Hiranuma snapped, and when he stepped up to Miyuki, even if he didn't touch her, he seemed so menacing that all of the children cowered, and a couple of them began to cry.

"But why?"

"We will discuss this across the way," Hiranuma said, while Kato stepped into the midst of the children, swinging out the back of his hand and shouting, "Shut up! You are Japanese. I will not stand for this!"

Miyuki ran over and took one little girl in her arms, but Kato separated them. "Enough of this!" And this time he yanked at Miyuki, and it frightened the children all the more. They didn't cry again, though; they were Japanese children. And they were scared.

"Please, Captain, I can't leave the children alone."

"We will stay in the building."

"Can't I call my mother down to watch—?"

"I am here, Miyuki," a voice said. They all looked up to where Mrs. Serikawa stood in the door, her eyes wide with fright. "I heard all the noise." She drew her hand to her face, and seemed ready to cry.

"It's just a technicality, Mother," Miyuki said, rushing to her, comforting her the best she could, even if she didn't have any idea what was going on herself. "We'll just be over in Cotton's office."

"Where is the *gaijin?*" Hiranuma asked.

"The *gaijin* is visiting a sick Japanese woman who is alone because her husband has been sent to the army. That's where the *gaijin* is."

That was enough for Kato. This time when he gripped Miyuki, he took hold of her roughly, and she stumbled as he pulled her. She could hear the children start to sniffle again as soon as the two men left the room with her and steered her across to Cotton's office.

"Sit down," Kato snapped. But when Miyuki started to settle in Cotton's chair, he grabbed her and forced her to the floor. "Sit down like a Japanese woman!"

Miyuki caught herself then. She still didn't have the foggiest idea what this was all about. And then they began to grill her, the one after the other, boring in on her, trading questions, accusations: Why didn't she have the Rising Sun lunch yesterday? Every other child in the whole empire did. Was she a traitor? Didn't she hear the order on the morning radio? Oh, don't you do morning exercises? The Emperor ordered everybody to do exercises—didn't you know that? Don't you think Japanese children should be patriotic? Didn't Mr. Drake remind you about the Rising Sun lunches? You mean he knew but he didn't tell you? We've had trouble with this missionary before, refusing to have Japanese children wear the proper clothes, etc., etc.

Miyuki tried to maintain her composure. "Really, it was just an oversight," Miyuki said, trying not to let them see how scared she was, how disgusted she was. They were taking down everything she said.

"So, how long have you been a Christian?" Hiranuma asked.

"I am not."

"You are not a Christian, but you teach at a Christian school?" he asked, raising his eyebrow toward Kato to show that he sure wasn't anybody's fool.

"That's right, yes sir."

"Do you believe Tenno Heika is divine?" Kato snapped.

"Of course I do."

"Is Jesus Christ?"

Miyuki pondered for a moment. "Probably" was all she said at last.

"Do you teach the children that?"

"Oh no, sir. I don't teach any religion. It's only a kinder-garten. I just teach the children to draw and color. I read to them. Mr. Drake comes in for prayers every morning he's here, and every now and then he reads a Bible story. They're good stories for children. That's all."

Both Hiranuma and Kato studied her dubiously, but Miyuki's answer was so preposterous they decided it had to be accepted. "So, where is your husband?" Chief Hiranuma asked.

"He's in Hawaii. He works for NYK Lines."

The army officer shook his head, disparaging such quotid-ian civilian labor.

"It's what the government wants him to do," Miyuki felt obliged to add. Kato snorted again. "Just as they want Chief Hiranuma to remain a police officer."

Hiranuma smiled thinly at that. "So, why are *you* here in Tochigi?" he said.

"Precisely because my husband must be overseas for the Emperor, and because it is very difficult to get by in Tokyo in hard times, and here I could help an old friend. Mr. Drake is my husband's closest friend."

"A *gaijin?*" Kato said, appalled.

"He grew up in Japan." They just looked at her. "You've met Mr. Drake. He loves Japan." Still from them: nothing. "He loves the Japanese." Neither man responded. Miyuki was growing more and more angry, raising her voice to hold back her fear. "Why are you doing this to him?" she asked. "Why are you doing this to his church? Cotton-san only wants to help."

Kato arose from Cotton's desk and pointed at Miyuki. "I would watch what you say, Mrs. Serikawa. We are at war, you know." "Yes, but we are only at war with China—not with Mr. Drake's country. Not with Mr. Drake's church, we're not, either."

The men looked at each other. Kato almost seemed to be

shaking at such impudence, and so Hiranuma finally laid a hand on his sleeve. "Tomorrow, Mrs. Serikawa," he said, "tomorrow you will devote the entire *Christian* school day to instructing the children how to write letters to our brave warriors at the front. Do you understand?"

"They can't write yet."

"Fine. Then they will draw pictures for the soldiers." Miyuki shrugged. "And on Friday, they will come to school without their shoes and socks and without any outer coats, so as to better appreciate the efforts of the brave Shinto men fighting there."

Miyuki did not let it go by. "There are brave Christian men fighting there for the Emperor too. Two from this mission."

Ignoring her, Kato only motioned to Hiranuma. "The chief will visit the school to make sure that Mr. Drake plays no tricks. Do you understand?" Miyuki made a to-do out of bowing this time, but she could feel the tears forming in her eyes. "And, that day, all of the children will be served Rising Sun lunches that you and your mother will make."

"Yes," Miyuki said, and she bowed again, but mostly so that neither of them would see the tears. When she looked up, Cotton was there, blurred.

He could see immediately that Miyuki was terribly frightened, but he stayed cool. "Is there something wrong, gentlemen?" he asked, altogether dispassionately.

Kato spoke up. "What is wrong is that you willfully continue to disregard the orders of His Majesty's government, and—"

"And if this goes on," Hiranuma concluded, "we will be forced to close down your Christian kindergarten."

"We've tried to live up to every requirement," Cotton said, prompting Kato and Hiranuma to unleash their best stage chortles.

Miyuki squeezed Cotton's hand. "I'll explain what Captain Kato and Chief Hiranuma have discussed with me."

"Yes, do that," the policeman said, and he and his colleague gathered up their notes, bowing stiffly to him.

They had barely left the room when Miyuki fell against Cotton and began to sob, deeply, catching her breath. He held her there, murmuring soothingly; but as she grew quiet, he stopped talking and just let her rest on his chest. At last she lifted her head a little and said: "Oh, Cotton, it's so horrible. This isn't what my father and my brother died for. This isn't our Japan anymore, is it?"

Quickly he took Miyuki by her shoulders. "Be quiet. You can't talk that way. You know that."

"I know," she said. "That just proves what I said." And she put her arms full around him now, so that it was all Cotton could do to hold his balance, poised there, on the balls of his feet. "I'm going to write Kiyoshi about this."

"Be careful, Miyuki. Please. They read all my mail. The *tokko* listen on the phone now too, I think."

She nodded, but she also started to cry some more, and for the first time Cotton understood that Miyuki wasn't on her government's side anymore. She was still Japanese, of course; she was still Kiyoshi's wife, but, no, she wasn't on his side. And things simply could not long work that way.

27

Not long afterwards, the sirens blew; Tochigi was having its first air-raid drill. Miyuki and her mother had lived through so many in Tokyo that they took it all in stride. Everybody else scurried about fretfully, chattering, while the Serikawa women helped Cotton shepherd the children down to the cellar. There, Miyuki took his arm—quite brazenly for a Japanese woman, really, and pulled him aside. "Who would bomb Tochigi?" she asked him, whispering.

"Oh, if someone was going to bomb the airplane parts factory, they'd probably end up hitting the town as well."

Miyuki sneered at him. "You don't really believe that, do you?"

Cotton shrugged. "I don't think we should talk about this."

Miyuki did anyway. "You know they're just having these drills to scare us and bring us all together. Then maybe we'll accept the food rationing and the ragged clothes better."

"Miyuki, please, be careful, dammit."

"Don't worry. I don't talk to anyone else this way. Just my *gaijin.*"

"Did you write your complaints about Kato and Hiranuma to Kiyoshi?"

Miyuki twinkled. "Did I? The day after. I hitched a ride on an ox cart over to Oyama and mailed it from there. I'm sure they aren't organized enough to look for our mail over there."

Cotton shook his head. "I just hope you're being careful."

"Oh, don't worry, Cotton-san. I only told Kiyoshi that the authorities were being unreasonable. I want him to know." The all-clear rang then, and all the kids sighed and started yakking away as soon as Miyuki popped up. It was terribly exciting . . . the first time.

They came up outside. Spring was here now. The cormorant fishermen took their birds out, and the lumberjacks started the logs down the Uzuma, headed for Tokyo. The swallows and baseball mitts appeared. And bicycles—but, as Miyuki pointed out to Cotton, there were fewer bicycles around this spring; the parts and the tires couldn't be found anywhere anymore. More food was rationed, too, even after everyone started digging up the daikons.

One day, after kindergarten, Miyuki heard that there were two lepers just outside of town. There were still a lot of lepers in Japan, and they would walk the land, from temple to temple, shunned, hoping to get a little food here and there. Miyuki put together some scraps for the men. She wanted Cotton to come with her, but he was away, with a parishioner, so she asked her mother to join her.

Mrs. Serikawa was instantly aghast. "Absolutely not."

"But Mother, they're sick. They need help."

"This sort of thing is not our affair."

"But of course it is. They're Japanese, we're Japanese."

"If the authorities believed that these people needed assistance, they would provide it."

"Well, the authorities are very busy," Miyuki replied carefully, trying to argue as gently as she could. "This way, I'm helping the government, too."

Mrs. Serikawa grumbled. "I cannot believe you, Miyuki. You grow more antinationalistic every day."

Miyuki threw up her hands. "I am not being antinationalistic, Mother. I am just being a little Christian, perhaps. Cotton preaches to the children that you must treat your neighbors as you would your own family."

Mrs. Serikawa threw up a hand, horrified. "But you are *not* a Christian."

"No, but I can be a Samaritan."

"What? What is that?"

"There are things to learn from others, from some *gaijin*."

"Please, Miyuki. Please do not talk this way to anyone else. It is not wise."

Miyuki found the lepers alone, by the side of the road, on the way from Oyama. Nobody had welcomed them there, either, so they had moved on. Miyuki couldn't tell how old the men were, for both of them had lost all their hair, even their eyebrows, and their faces were horribly swollen, filled with the most hideous black sores. One of them had gone blind and clung to the other. They were exhausted. Miyuki gave them what food she had scrounged up—leftovers from the children's lunch, mostly—and both the lepers cried. It had been almost two days since they'd been given anything. Charity wore thin in times like these. Miyuki also poured them some green tea, and they couldn't get enough of it.

They were so dirty, they stank. She pointed out where they could find a shallow spot in the Uzuma and told them to meet her there. She was going back to get some clothes for them. The two lepers cried some more at that.

Cotton still wasn't back at the mission when Miyuki returned. She was rooting around in his closet, looking for some of his old clothes, when Mrs. Serikawa burst into the room.

She looked terrified. "It is horrible!" she cried. "I am so frightened!"

"Please, Mother, please. Catch your breath. Now, what is it?"

"Captain Kato and Chief Hiranuma were both just here. They seemed very disturbed."

"About what?"

"They would not say. They only demanded that Cotton come with them both to the chief's office. They asked for you, too."

"For me?"

"Yes—hurry over, please. I told them I would send you over as soon as you returned home."

"No, thank you," Miyuki said. "I have something more important to do right now. For me. We all know that we must polish our souls sometimes to get the rust off our bodies."

"Please—please!" Mrs. Serikawa cried, but Miyuki just went back to going through Cotton's old clothes, leaving her mother to her tears.

In Chief Hiranuma's office, Cotton bowed to him and to Captain Kato, who stood there with the chief by his desk. The two officials kept looking back and forth to each other, uneasily. Cotton was sure he was going to be expelled and was ready for the boom to be lowered when Hiranuma handed Kato a letter. Even at a distance it looked very official.

But then, inexplicably, a secretary materialized with tea and rice cakes, and Hiranuma put on a phony smile and gestured grandly to a seat. "Captain Kato and I only hope everything is fine at the church."

"Oh yes," Cotton said, settling down, and taking a cake. "I believe things are going quite well."

Kato stepped forward, grinning to beat the band. "You will understand, Mr. Drake, that these are difficult times, and if we have ever—unintentionally—been rude to either you or Mrs. Serikawa, it certainly was not our, uh—uh—"

"Certainly," Cotton said. "We all must perform our jobs."

"Yes," both men said, in unison. They were terribly relieved.

Cotton couldn't figure out what the hell was going on.

"Anything that we can do to help your wonderful school, you please let us know," Kato said.

"Absolutely," Cotton said. "You're most kind."

"Good. Very good. And one moment please." Hiranuma bowed. "We have a request. If it is possible. If you will honor us to listen." Cotton shrugged. They both bowed again, lower still. Their newfound respect for Cotton was quickly degenerating into obsequiousness. Hiranuma all but pushed Kato toward the door, and as the captain backed out, the letter Hiranuma had been holding fell out of his grasp and fluttered to the floor. He rushed to retrieve it, but Cotton reached down naturally and picked it up.

In that flash, as he handed it back to Hiranuma, Cotton could not help seeing how impressive the stationery was. It was heavy, and there were stars on it. Generals, Cotton thought: generals have stars. Of course, he also thought, it would be difficult to explain why any general would be corresponding with the officialdom of some little nowhere river town about a Christian missionary. Hiranuma fumbled with the letter some more, trying to figure out how to make it disappear, when, luckily, Kato re-emerged, this time with two young students.

The boys were terribly nervous and bowed in unison. The one on the left, whose name was Sakao, had obviously been designated to speak. "Drake-san," he began, "we would be honored if you could find the time to coach the Tochigi baseball team this spring."

"Oh," said Cotton. So that's what this is all about. "Is it a good team?"

Sakao looked at his comrade, whose name was Tejiro, and they both appeared on the verge of tears. Even Kato and Hiranuma slipped down into some distress. It simply wasn't fair for Cotton to have asked such a direct question; Japanese

would just never do that to one another. Finally, Sakao began. "Drake-san, it is very difficult to—"

"Ah," Cotton broke in, "it is not a good team?"

"We lack many good players, and our coach has been
drafted."

"Hmmm. And if I'm the coach, will you listen to a *gaijin?*"

This also was too personal a question, but both the boys
did manage to nod. "Well, will you?" Cotton asked, giving no
quarter. "Will you pay attention to a *gaijin?*"

Finally, it was Tejiro who said "Yes" out loud.

"How 'bout you?" Cotton asked Sakao to his face. "Will
you do what a *gaijin* says? Will the other players?"

Everybody looked at poor Sakao. Kato and Hiranuma and
Tejiro finally almost pulled "Yes, Drake-san" from down out
of his throat.

"All right," Cotton said. "When's the next practice?"

"Tomorrow afternoon at three," Sakao said.

"All right, I'll be there—and you make damn sure every
player is there for the *gaijin.*"

"Oh, thank you, Drake-san," Sakao cooed, and the two
boys bowed out of the room.

Cotton then turned back to Kato and Hiranuma and wondered out loud why, only now, he was suddenly being asked
to coach the town team. "I've been here all along, and I
know the coach was drafted weeks ago."

The two officials blushed terribly, mumbling something
about how they simply had no idea why the boys had
dragged their feet for so long. Cotton kept his smile to himself, enjoying their distress, watching Chief Hiranuma grasp
the fancy letter even tighter as he replied. Of course no general would be writing to the officials of this backwater. Of
course . . . but an admiral would. Anyway, an admiral would
if a man who worked for him had a wife in Tochigi who
wrote her husband a letter of complaint. "That's quite an
honor," Cotton said, gesturing toward Hiranuma's hands.

The chief was altogether baffled. "What's that?"

"Why, receiving a letter from Admiral Yamamoto himself,"

Cotton said; and with a cheshire-cat grin plastered on his face, he picked up another rice cake and departed.

The sun was out and the wind down, but it was barely April, and so the air was still chilly most days and the water in the Ozuma-gawa cold. The lepers were just sitting there, on the riverbank, when Miyuki came back with Cotton. By now they had eaten all the scraps Miyuki had brought them.

Across the river, where the road into town came by, some of the townspeople who had heard that the lepers were there had assembled to watch. To Cotton, it looked almost like a posse, gathered to make sure the lepers didn't get any crazy ideas and come into their town.

"Undress," Miyuki said. She showed the leper who still had his sight the soap she had brought and assured them both that, cold as it might be, she had towels to warm them when they got out—and more hot tea, too. Cotton held up the clothes he had brought and let the blind man feel the Yale A.A.—Yale Athletic Association—sweatshirt. The blind man began to cry again, and Cotton helped him undress. "No one has been as kind to us as the lady," the other leper said.

"Yes," Cotton said, and he looked over at Miyuki.

The people congregated up on the little hill watched, and some of them also commented about how dumb the *gaijin* missionary was to touch the leper. The country people were sure that just the slightest touch could transmit the disease. Then Miyuki went over and helped the other leper take off his clothes, and the people didn't say anything more.

Cotton left her there with the lepers. Over the Uzuma, going back to town, there was a little bridge manned by an old toll keeper named Kadota. It cost twenty-sen passage, but the way it worked was, Kadota didn't charge the locals. Cotton held out his coin, but Kadota pushed it back. "You're okay, Drake-san." So Cotton thanked him and went on to where the townspeople were congregated. One of them was Mrs. Uesugi, who was a member of the church, and he asked her if possibly she could find a little food at home for the lepers.

"These are hard times," she said. "We barely have enough for our own family."

"I know how it is," Cotton said, and now he widened his remarks to include everybody: "Still, these men are even less fortunate than we are, and if we could all just contribute a tiny amount of food, it would help them more than we can imagine." He pulled out a handkerchief, laid it on the ground as a *furosiki,* and, without a word, put on it the one rice cake that he'd taken from Chief Hiranuma's office as he went out the door. He didn't say anything more, only went back across the river.

Miyuki had pushed the lepers into the water, and despite the cold she waded in herself to hold the blind man while his friend soaped him. Miyuki helped splash the men then, and then she cried "Okay!" and they dashed out of the river and grabbed the towels, shivering. Miyuki was cold, too, and when Cotton came back, he put his coat around her shoulders. For just an instant—did he even know?—he held his hands on her shoulders. She knew. The lepers began to put on Cotton's old clothes. The blind man got the Yale A.A. sweatshirt and the other one an old ski sweater.

And then an ugly voice from across the river called out: "Don't let their old clothes stay here in Tochigi!"

Miyuki wanted to yell back angrily, but Cotton put his hand on her arm. "Don't worry!" he hollered, but politely. "We'll burn all those."

A lot of the townspeople had left by now, but by the time the lepers had finished dressing, Cotton looked up and saw that the crowd was growing again. Mrs. Uesugi was one of the first ones back.

So Cotton said "Come on" to the lepers, took the blind one by the hand, and he and Miyuki led them across the bridge. Cotton said to Kadota, "I'll pay for them, but they're going right back," so the toll keeper nodded and let them all pass on the cuff. But when the man who had screamed about the lepers' clothes saw the lepers coming, he turned and hurried away. "I'm going to get Chief Hiranuma!" he called back. A few others left with him. Most of them only backed

away a little, though, and Mrs. Uesugi pointed at the *furosiki*
that Cotton had left on the ground. It was almost filled with
food—just little bits and pieces, all of it, but taken together it
would make a couple of good meals for both of them.

The leper who could see told the other one what was there;
then Miyuki tied up the *furosiki* and handed it to them. The
lepers wanted to embrace her and Cotton, but they knew
they couldn't do a thing such as that, and so they bowed, and
then Miyuki and Cotton bowed back, and soon all the townspeople were bowing, even the ones who had backed away
some.

Miyuki turned to Cotton and smiled. She was smiling for
all that had just happened, but when he smiled back it was
just for her. She was standing right next to him, but when she
spoke to him then, she purposely called out loud enough so
that everyone could hear. "This is the best I've felt about being Japanese in a long time!" is what Miyuki said.

This embarrassed some of the crowd, hearing such blas-
phemy from a Japanese woman before a *gaijin*, but nobody
protested or moved; maybe a few shuffled their getas a little.
Mrs. Uesugi was the one who changed the subject. She said:
"You know, Drake-san, it is like when Jesus fed the crowds on
the mountain."

Cotton smiled at that. "Yes, but this took the people to
share. *We* did this. Miyuki showed us what to do, but we did
it. Thank you all."

They began to disperse. Miyuki turned to Cotton, but this
time she spoke for only him to hear. "We're good people, the
Japanese."

Cotton said: "Yes, I know you are." And then, in a different voice, a different tone, he added: "And you're a really
wonderful person, Miyuki." He reached over and put an arm
around her shoulder. It was a natural gesture to make—but
what it meant was that he yearned to hold her in his arms.
He knew that now. He knew. Unmistakably, Cotton understood, at that moment, in the midst of the lepers and the
townspeople, what he couldn't deny to himself any longer;
that he had fallen altogether in love with his best friend's wife.

28

There must be, Kiyoshi thought, something wrong. It was so easy that before he sent a single report back to Yamamoto, he decided that he must have already been set up. Either somebody had snitched on him or the Americans had figured out on their own that he was a spy. Either way, obviously, they were just waiting to spring the trap and arrest him.

Probably, he assumed, they're holding off only because they think I can lead them to someone else. The Americans had concluded, Kiyoshi decided, that the Americans of Japanese ancestry in the islands—the AJA, everybody called them—must have a number of subversives in their midst and that Kiyoshi would be their contact with Tokyo. That's what I would figure, Kiyoshi thought, if I were an American. That's why they're giving me all this rope, and then they're tailing me, watching me, waiting to see where I lead them.

That must be it. It's so easy. I just go everywhere I want and check out everything I feel like most any time I feel like it.

And then one day the *Tatsuta Maru* docked in Honolulu again, and this time it brought the letter from Miyuki about the way the authorities were working her over in Tochigi. It made Kiyoshi furious, and it also gave him a benign opportunity to test his communications arrangement with Admiral Yamamoto. It was the essence of simplicity, what they had worked out. Kiyoshi would hand-deliver a letter to an officer on the NYK liner that docked in Honolulu, with the request that the man mail it when he arrived in Yokohama. The NYK officer didn't have any idea that he was being used as a courier; after all, Kiyoshi worked for the line. The letter was mailed in Yokohama to a third party with a bland local residential address, and it was that man who carried Kiyoshi's

letter to the admiral. There was nothing suspicious about any
of it.

The letter that Kiyoshi wrote to Yamamoto was almost all
about Miyuki and her difficulties in Tochigi; discreetly, might
something be done? He didn't report at all on Hawaii, except
to write that all was going extremely well and that a full, detailed accounting would follow shortly.

And then he went back to accumulating knowledge, day after easy day. There was no reason whatsoever to suspect that
the Americans were on to him except for the fact that Kiyoshi
couldn't conceive that it could be this much of a breeze unless
they were laying a trap.

Apart from these instinctive suspicions, only one thing truly
worried Kiyoshi, and that was Sammy Ushijima. Sammy was
just like Cotton; he couldn't understand why, if Kiyoshi had
been asked to leave American Orient to go to work for a Japanese company, he would be given a subsidiary position in a
mid-level post. "Any fool in the business knows Kiyoshi ought
to be running San Francisco or L.A., not backing up in Honolulu," Sammy mumbled to Kazuko one night. She agreed;
but then, she also didn't care.

At first when he arrived in Honolulu, Kiyoshi avoided
Sammy, but he knew he had to see him, and he had to be
able to pretend better than he thought he could—better than
he had when he had talked with Cotton. Sammy was a problem; Sammy was a threat.

Then, a few days later, when Kiyoshi drove his car up in
the Aiea Heights, he saw another Japanese up there, looking
down at Pearl from a parked taxi. The taxi pulled away almost as soon as Kiyoshi appeared. The very next evening at
the Shuncho-Ro, a Japanese tea-house that featured the finest
geishas east of Yokohama, Kiyoshi was sure he recognized
the same man again, and, discreetly, he asked the manager if
he happened to know who the newcomer was.

Certainly he knew him. Why, he had been brought to the
Shuncho-Ro only two nights earlier by Nagao Kita, the Japanese consul general himself. The new man's name was

Tadashi Morimura, and he was the latest addition to the consulate.

Damn, Kiyoshi thought. They've sent a spy to work out of the consulate, and it's so obvious even I've stumbled on it. Surely the Americans must know about him too; no one can be that blind. But, Kiyoshi thought, putting the best face on it, if nobody told me about another spy, then surely nobody told the other spy about me. Yamamoto had obviously kept his word.

So Kiyoshi went on about his work. Once he chartered a sightseeing plane and brought along a pretty young Nisei who worked at NYK. They flew all around, a couple of tourists. It was a weekday, and Kiyoshi saw only a few support ships docked at Pearl. While they were still up, though, a patrol flight came back toward Hickam, and it clicked with Kiyoshi that the planes were returning from the south. He tried to remember: had he ever noticed a patrol coming from the north? He couldn't remember; he'd have to keep an eye out.

When he and the secretary landed at Hickam, Kiyoshi drove her back to the NYK offices and then headed over to the nearest bookstore himself. The sightseeing flight had made him realize that he really couldn't identify most ships, and so he did the sensible thing and asked for a copy of *Jane's Fighting Ships*.

"Must be a run on those," the clerk said genially. "Another gentleman—young Japanese fellow, just like you—took a copy earlier today." He said he'd order another. This is insane, Kiyoshi thought—Morimura and I are stumbling all over each other.

So the next day he got the hell out of Honolulu, out of all Oahu, for that matter, and spent a week visiting the other island, looking for landing sites and defense installations. Sometimes in the past the Pacific Fleet had eschewed Pearl and instead had anchored off Maui, at Lahaina Roads, in the Auau Channel. Occasionally Kiyoshi would see patrol planes circling around there, or even further south, flying over the Big Island. When he got to Kauai, up north, though, he never saw or heard any American planes. He stayed an extra day: no planes. It was as if that part of the compass didn't exist for the American air corps; but of course Kiyoshi knew that couldn't possibly be the case, so he tried to figure out where he was missing out.

He couldn't put off calling Sammy any longer, though; and so a couple days after he returned from the other islands, Kiyoshi phoned and invited him to dinner. Sammy wouldn't hear about them going out; Kazuko would prepare a full-scale home-cooked Japanese meal.

As she cooked, Sammy and Kiyoshi talked. They talked about Miyuki, about her helping Cotton. They talked about Sammy's daughters, Josephine and Darlene. They talked about mutual friends. And business. They talked about Kazuko and Sammy going back for a visit to Japan in the summer. That is, in toto, they talked about nothing.

Finally, starting on another gin, Sammy ventured this much: "Hey, where ya been lately, Key?"

"Whatd'ya mean?" As soon as he said that, Kiyoshi knew he'd sounded too defensive.

"I mean, where—have—you—been? I've called the office several times, and you're always away."

"Oh. Last week." That was better. That was more offhand. "Well, yeah."

"Okay, if you won't tell my boss, I snuck off to the Big Island for a few days' vacation." Even better. A bit of humor, small secret-sharing.

"Oh? The girl said you were in Maui."

"That's right, Sammy. You got it. I haven't had a day off since Miyuki and I got a week in Atami last summer. I didn't even want my own office to know where the hell I was." Kiyoshi beamed, he was so pleased with himself. So glib. So cool. He really was cut out to be a spy.

And Sammy leaned closer, and his mouth turned down, and when he opened it, it was a whisper almost, and it was a new tone altogether, cold and intimidating, nearly threatening. "Listen, old friend, whatever you're doing, just don't do anything to my islands."

Kiyoshi smiled wanly, blasted out of his smugness. His

whole facade had crumpled so he snapped back: "And what the hell does that mean?"

Sammy just looked at him, contained and calm. If his expression changed at all, it was only to show some compassion. "If you understand what it means, Key, then listen to me," he said. "If you don't, just forget I said it."

He couldn't ignore Sammy any longer, and so in the next few days Kiyoshi made a point of calling him from the office every day, cozying up to him. They'd talk about friendly things, very American things, like the new pennant race, or whether Irish Billy Conn could possibly upset the Brown Bomber for the heavyweight championship. He had to win Sammy back. And thus did Kiyoshi learn the first law of spying; how easy it was intellectually, how different when the enemy had a familiar face. Well, Kiyoshi thought, better this, better mere deceit. I could never kill anyone, not even for Admiral Yamamoto. Spying is right for me—and what's a little treachery among friends? He called back Sammy again and took three to one on Conn.

Then Kiyoshi went back to writing out his notes and impressions, hiding them away in another office, in a musty log book he could tell hadn't been opened for years, detailing, as it did, the NYK arrivals and departures for the year 1923. The spring weather was pleasant, not too warm, and with the ceiling fan on and the windows wide open, he thought, he missed a lot; but still, all week, he never heard any coming from or going north. Maybe they fly at night, he decided. I'll have to take a few days off and stay up nights. Obviously, that must be why I never hear any planes from the north during the day, because the patrols fly north at night. Obviously.

The *Asama* would be docking again in a couple more days, and so Kiyoshi sat down and wrote another letter for delivery to Yamamoto. He began by advising the admiral what he'd learned so far, apologizing that he'd still been unable to pinpoint when and where exactly the patrol planes to the north operated. Then he switched gears, spending much more time artfully constructing a conversational tone: "I want you to know, too, *most important,* that I got three to one on Conn to beat Louis, because, of course, I obviously believe that a small overmatched fighter can whip a bigger, stronger opponent, if he's quicker and equipped with some surprise. Don't you, Admiral?"

And then, having segued into the more personal in this wonderfully clever, chatty way, Kiyoshi closed: "I think it's vital that I return in the next couple weeks or so, so that we might discuss the fight together. No, seriously, sir, I do believe it is time for me to come back and discuss matters here with you. There is so much I could advise you that is hard to put down on paper."

Kiyoshi labored to get that last part just right. Again and again he tore up a sheet, burned it, and started again. It was all so difficult because it was all a bunch of crap. There wasn't any valid reason to see the admiral in person. *Seriously, sir,* Kiyoshi simply missed Miyuki. He longed to be with his wife.

A letter had come from her the day before, brought in on the *President Coolidge,* and much of what she'd written upset Kiyoshi all the more. Oh, there was some good news:

"Your letter to the 'home office' paid off immediately," Miyuki wrote.

The Admiral wrote Chief Hiranuma and he and Captain Kato started quaking in their boots. They've let up on Cotton and me and the whole mission. They even drop by to see if we need anything! My, but it helps to have friends in high place (especially if those high places are military). Don't worry, sweetheart. I mail my letters in Oyama without return address so our dear friends in the thought police don't know and can't read my mail. (I'm afraid Cotton couldn't get away with that—all *gaijin* are watched so carefully now.) But Cotton says to thank you so much for what you did. Did you mention to Yamamoto that Cotton was good at baseball? [*Kiyoshi smiled.*] What a wonderful idea! The coach was drafted,

and they actually asked Cotton to take over the town
team. The boys adore him. Of course, so does everybody in Tochigi.

Kiyoshi smiled again, but then he grew sadder as Miyuki
went on explaining all the new shortages and sacrifices.
"What good is this war with China if we all must suffer so for
it? Can't we find a way to be friends with all our Asian brothers? Can't we find a way to love America like Cotton loves
us?"

Kiyoshi shook his head. He took out a cigarette, and after
he lit it, he tore off that part of the letter, put it in the ashtray,
and burned it. Was Miyuki talking this way to anyone else?

He missed her so. He missed Japan, too, in ways he never
had before when he'd been abroad. Maybe it was different if
you were working for your country. Surely Miyuki would understand, too, if only he could tell her what he was doing for
the Emperor.

"I wonder why you must be in Hawaii, darling, away from
me, away from our bed where we will conceive our Serikawa
son, and always I wonder how much longer you must stay
there," the letter went on; but Kiyoshi didn't read between
the lines, the way she hoped he would. All Kiyoshi read was
that she missed him, not that . . . well, not that she didn't altogether believe him.

And then Kiyoshi read on. There was more about Cotton,
and what a wonderful job he was doing, and about his team,
even about his sermons. Miyuki wrote about how she listened
to him practice his sermons. She wrote a lot of the letter
about Cotton, but she didn't realize that. Kiyoshi didn't think
it was odd, either. He missed her so much that he couldn't
tell that she didn't need to miss him anymore.

The next day was Saturday, and Kiyoshi finally had to get
away from the office. The streets downtown were jammed
with sailors. He'd never seen so many, not since . . . he tried
to remember. They were drinking a lot and whoring. He got
in his car and drove out of town, up to the Aiea Heights. He
had no intention of stopping there, but as he looked down at

Pearl, the sight was so impressive that he pulled over. What must have been the whole Pacific fleet was arrayed before him, at anchor.

He stared. That was when the tumblers in Kiyoshi's mind began to click. It was last Sunday when he saw so many sailors in town. And before that: the weekend before. And . . . No, it can't possibly be that simple. It can't just be that they take the fleet out during the week and bring it back in for the weekends. They can't be running the whole damn Pacific Fleet like it was an insurance office or a hardware store. It can't be that easy. If this were true, if the flag officers were keeping bankers' hours, coming back to play golf weekends, why then, half of Admiral Yamamoto's problems would be solved. He would know when to hit: on the weekend. Sunday, Kiyoshi thought. Their Lord's Day. He would suggest that to the admiral. Sunday.

Just then, though, just as Kiyoshi got back to his car, he saw another car down the hill, approaching. He looked again: a green DeSoto convertible. Kiyoshi slammed the door, turned on the ignition, rammed the gear into first, and scratched off, heading away from Honolulu, away from the green DeSoto convertible.

At the top of the hill, where Kiyoshi had stopped, the DeSoto pulled off the road, and when Sammy got out, first he looked down at the fleet in the harbor, and then he watched after Kiyoshi's car disappearing in the road that wound through the cane. "Oh, Key," he said softly to himself. "Oh, Key."

29

Because Cotton had asked to see him alone, the boy was petrified. He came to the rectory literally hat in hand, fingering it, eyes cast down, expecting the worst.

Cotton gestured for him to sit down, and when they

plopped onto the mats together, at least that made the boy feel more at home, much more than if he had been required to take a chair across from Cotton's Western desk. Mrs. Serikawa brought out some green tea and cakes, and the boy relaxed a bit more. His name was Kensuke Morishita, a strong, rangy kid who would have stood out in any land, in any culture. He was the slugger who had knocked the ball to the fence that day last November when Cotton first arrived in Tochigi. At six feet, Kensuke towered over the other boys in Tochigi, and Cotton had immediately penciled him into the lineup at cleanup and stationed him at first base.

Then, on the third day of practice, Cotton asked who the pitchers were, and Kensuke came forward, but shyly, uneasily. Immediately, then, he flabbergasted Cotton. Whatever he might have been as a hitter, the boy was a dramatically better thrower—with a whiplash arm, that God-given talent to catapult a ball rather than just throw it, the way mere human beings do. Not only that, but the balls Kensuke threw darted as they moved to the plate, as if thrown so powerfully they couldn't contain themselves.

Kensuke, though, was maddening to coach. Unless Cotton absolutely stood behind him and demanded that he fire the ball, the boy would throw junk. He was the quintessential Japanese player, all cuteness and tricks. Not only would he throw slow-breaking stuff most every pitch, but he would always chip away at the corners of the plate, tantalizing the hitters, drawing the confrontation on and on.

Of course, Kensuke had been instructed to play this way. Every pitcher Cotton had ever faced in Japan worked like that. Baseball in Japan wasn't a sport; it was more like some athletic Kabuki. No matter how Cotton pleaded with Kensuke, he could never get the kid to rear back and air it out, storming it right down the pipe with the great gift that God had given him. Kensuke was terrified to exhibit his skill for fear of seeming different. After all, the first thing Cotton had learned in Japanese grade school was: the nail that stands up will be hammered down.

Finally, one afternoon a week before their first game, Cot-

ton just lost his patience. He screamed at Kensuke in front of
the other players. Unfortunately, rather than stirring the boy
up, that only inhibited him more. His pitching grew more
tentative. So now, when Mrs. Serikawa brought out the tea,
Cotton carefully explained all this to Kensuke, outlined what
extraordinary talent he had, how far he could go with it.
Warily, Kensuke listened.

"Have you ever heard of Bobby Feller?" Cotton asked.

"Ferrer?" the boy asked, shaking his head.

"Well, a few years ago, when he was your age, he was a
farm boy just like you, in a place called Iowa, and he had an
arm like yours, and overnight he became a star in the major
leagues. That can be you, Kensuke." The boy's eyes grew big.
Cotton reached over and grabbed his right arm. "I don't
know where you got this. I don't know where you got your
size. But it's yours, and you must use it, or . . . or—"

"Or?"

"Or you are not serving your Emperor to the fullest."
Kensuke nodded solemnly; he could feel the burden.
"Kensuke," Cotton went on, leaning closer, "If you will just
let me teach you how to pitch, I swear, you can be playing
with the Yomiuri Giants in a couple years. Maybe next
spring."

The boy almost went into shock. If Cotton had told him he
would marry the crown princess a week from Tuesday he
couldn't have been more startled. "Do you have any idea
how good you are?" Kensuke shook his head, as much with
fear as in ignorance. "Well, you're great. And starting tomorrow afternoon, you're going to come here. Right here." Cotton pounded on the floor for emphasis. "And then you and
me are gonna go outside, and you're gonna pitch. You understand?"

"Where will the team be?"

"The team will be getting ready to practice, just like they
do now, and at three o'clock sharp, when practice does start
over at the field, we'll join them. But for a half hour, here,
first, you'll pitch to me."

Kensuke looked absolutely panicked. He wasn't just a Japanese boy; he wasn't even a Tochigi boy. His parents were poor farmers, working a garden plot barely a couple hundred *tsubo* large on the outskirts of town. Cotton wondered if Kensuke had ever had a piece of meat in his whole twenty years.

The boy shifted in his seat. He was terribly uncomfortable. At last he said: "Drake-san, I can't."

"Why?"

"It wouldn't be right. It would be . . . *kojinshugi.*"

Cotton sighed. *Kojinshugi* was the closest Japanese could even come to the concept of individualism, but it came off as almost a dirty word, with overtones of selfishness and anti-Japanese-ism.

"No, Kensuke, it is not *kojinshugi.* On the contrary, in this case it is the highest form of *wa* that I'm asking of you." Kensuke cocked his head; *wa* referred to group harmony—a very positive word. "You see, if you can become a good pitcher, you can help the whole group, and all of Tochigi. We only won two games last season, and we haven't beaten Oyama in five years. You are Tochigi's great chance to end this shame."

Nothing in Kensuke's upbringing, in his culture, prepared him for this sort of argument. But he didn't argue with Cotton. Maybe he was just too confused.

Cotton barged ahead. "When I took this job, I was promised by the captains, by Sakao and Tejiro, that the players would listen to the *gaijin.* They promised me, Kensuke. If you will not do this for me, then your team will lose its coach." Kensuke's eyes widened. "I will see you here at two-thirty tomorrow afternoon, ready to pitch, or your team will never see me again."

The spring was almost full upon Japan now. The cherry blossoms were ready to burst, and the daikons could be harvested soon. Everywhere, too, the land was prepared for rice. The trees and the *asahi* and the moon, the cherry blossoms in the spring and the maples in the fall, Fuji spreading above it all, the most beautiful bump in the world . . . but ultimately Cotton learned what was foremost: rice. Rice was the marrow of the nation.

He was walking along with Miyuki now. She had wanted very much to come with him. The young Christian soldier, Ichiro Kobayashi, had returned from China, and Miyuki had gone with Cotton to the train station to meet him and take him home to his family. Of course, it was only his ashes and bones in a small box that had come back, and that was what they were carrying to his house.

They were walking past the paddies, and Cotton said: "When I was a little boy, Kiyoshi and I had a wonderful teacher—an old man named Saburo. We were his last class." A Japanese grade school teacher took a class in first grade and stayed with that cohort of boys and girls all the way through elementary school. "It was very unusual for a *gaijin* to go to Japanese school, but you remember how respected my father was, and so they let me go for a couple of years. And then, around third grade, the idea was they were going to take me out and Mother was going to give me the Calvert School home instruction, like all the other missionary children got. But I didn't want to leave Kiyoshi, and I didn't want to leave Saburo, so they let me stay all the way through."

"Why are you telling me this?" Miyuki said. She was carrying the bone box now.

"The rice made me think of it. Saburo-sensei was the one who made me understand what rice meant to Japan."

"Still does," Miyuki said.

"Yeah. It's funny. I always have the feeling of exactly where I am here in the paddies that I don't get anywhere else in Japan."

But Miyuki really wasn't listening. "I don't see why the boy had to die," she said abruptly.

"We're not talking about that," Cotton said, and he took Ichiro's bone box away from her.

"Well, we should be."

"I'm going out here to try and console the Kobayashis and plan the funeral. This is not a time for why."

"It never is any longer, is it, Cotton? That's the trouble." He didn't respond, and they just kept walking along the road, their feet muddy from the spring muck.

Cotton said: "What Saburo told me one day—I remember, Kiyoshi was there, too—what he told me was that you ate rice with fish, and the rice really made the fish. The rice even made the water. If it wasn't for the rice, there really wouldn't even be a Japan."

"All right: why, wise Drake-san?" She smirked; he ignored her sarcasm.

"Because the water starts in the mountains." Cotton pointed to the ones in the distance. "All up and down the islands. The rain falls into the streams, and they flow into the rivers, and on into the sea. But the rice needs the water. And so the Japanese make paddies. And they hold the water, so the rice can grow. But they also enrich the waters, so when the water from the paddies goes on into the rivers and flows into the sea, it has all this living matter, organisms, insects, and then in the sea the fish feed on it, and then they're better fish for us to feed on. Old Saburo said: 'You see, we're the only people who really make the water. We make fish. We can make anything.' "

Miyuki smiled. "Thank you, Drake-san. I shouldn't have been so fresh. I never heard that before, not even from a Japanese."

"You see," Cotton said, and then he waved at some of the old women, who were dressed all in blue, standing in the ooze of the fields, looking back at the *gaijin* and the woman carrying the bone box. Miyuki gazed ahead, sweeping her eyes over the paddies and the kaki trees, out to the mountains before them. "You really love Japan, don't you, Cotton?"

"Yes, I do. You know that."

"Do you really love us, too? Do you love the Japanese?"

"Of course I do."

"Will you love us if we go to war with you?"

"Yes, I will. It'll be harder, but I will."

"I don't see how."

"That's what I've been taught all my life. That's what I teach."

"I don't mean that, Cotton. I'm not just talking about religion."

"What are you talking about?"

"Sometimes these days, *I* have trouble loving us," Miyuki said, and she picked up her step again. Then she stopped and handed Cotton back the bone box. "But I've learned why Kiyoshi has always loved you."

"I know why he loves you, too," Cotton said, and they both knew they weren't talking at all about what Kiyoshi loved, so they took their eyes off each other and kept striding ahead, very purposefully indeed.

Ichiro's funeral was late the next day, which meant that Cotton had to call off the team practice, but he was waiting for Kensuke at two-thirty, and the boy was there on the dot. He still looked pretty dubious, but once he started throwing there was nothing to hold him back. The ball pounded so hard into Cotton's catcher's mitt that he had to find a pretense to rush into the rectory, where he swiped a sponge from the kitchen. Miyuki and Mrs. Serikawa were there, preparing a few things for the funeral, and as Cotton dashed back out, he paused for a moment, then grabbed Miyuki by the sleeve of her kimono and snatched up a broom too.

Outside, Cotton handed Miyuki the broom and stationed her in front of him, to give Kensuke a batter to aim at. Cotton stood behind Miyuki, his arms conveniently around her, placing her hands on the broom handle, showing her how to hold it as a bat. Ostensibly. Then he stuffed the sponge into his mitt and resumed the catcher's position.

Miyuki giggled right up to the moment Kensuke let the pitch fly. Then she gasped and practically fell back into the river across the road. Cotton roared, and even Kensuke broke a smile—and the really funny thing, Cotton knew, was that the kid had pulled his punches. The ball wasn't three-quarters the speed at which he could deliver if he wanted to.

Miyuki was game, though; she screwed up her courage and stood back in as a batter, and Kensuke fired away, again and again. He did keep all the pitches safely outside. Cotton brought his mitt over near Miyuki, indicating he should bring the next pitch in closer, but the boy wouldn't do it. Finally Cotton got Kensuke to throw a curve ball, and when Miyuki saw the pitch heading right for her, she did what any sensible person would do and just collapsed to the ground in a heap . . . and then watched in utter amazement as the ball looped well away from her, fading over the outside corner of the plate.

They all laughed, and Kensuke dashed in to help pick Miyuki up, bowing and apologizing. Cotton already had her in his arms, lifting her off the ground. Miyuki turned away to Kensuke. She knew just the right thing to say: "Hey, you're really good!" The boy beamed.

"He can be a *great* pitcher," Cotton said. "Later on this spring, we're going to go down to Tokyo and see the Giants play at Korakuen." Kensuke's jaw flew open; he'd barely been out of greater Tochigi in all his life. Cotton handed him his jacket and told him to keep his arm warm.

"Thank you so much," he said. "And thank you, too, Mrs. Drake."

"Mrs. Serikawa," Cotton said softly, and the boy blushed.

"It's okay, Kensuke," Miyuki said, and she went back inside to help her mother in the kitchen.

Cotton began to prepare for the funeral. He knew the church would be filled, and it was. Many of the townspeople had never been in a Christian church before. Ichiro was the first Christian boy from Tochigi to die in the war. Cotton gently explained to the Japanese that they shouldn't worry about the process, about when to stand and kneel and sit. "None of that really matters. All that matters is Ichiro," he said.

Ichiro had been only a couple years older than most of the players on Cotton's team. In fact, he had played second base himself, so all the players came, too. One of Ichiro's oldest friends gave the homily. Cotton spoke next, and he admitted that he had barely met Ichiro, so he talked mostly about how sad it was whenever a young person died and how he hoped that Tochigi wouldn't have to lose any more of its young men.

His eyes happened to light on Captain Kato and Chief Hiranuma at that point, sitting together near the front of the church. Kato appeared to have a pencil and a piece of paper in his lap, poised, Cotton assumed, to make note of anything offensive or seditious that he might utter. And then he glanced further back, way to the rear, and spotted Miyuki, standing there with Kensuke and some of the other baseball players. For just a moment he stared at her, and their eyes locked, and before Cotton quite realized what he had done, he went on. He said:

"When there was the great earthquake of '23, and Tokyo was almost leveled, Bishop McKim, the head of our church in Japan, held a service, and he looked around at all the desolation, and he cried out: 'All is lost but faith in God.' As bad as things may get in these times, may we remember that? We must not lose our faith, because then we have lost all.

"And let us pray, too, that soon no nations of the world will have the need for wars to solve their differences, and so, then, our young men like Ichiro may serve their countries and their families and their god—whoever they worship—only in good and peaceful ways that will bring all mankind together, as one. Amen."

And he saw Miyuki nod her head to him in recognition and thanks, and he also saw Kato scribble furiously to get it on the record.

Cotton stood down from the pulpit and reached out and took Mrs. Kobayashi's hand, and when he did, spontaneously, her youngest child, Ichiro's little sister, stood up and threw her arms around his waist. Cotton let her hold on, and standing that way, in a loud, firm voice, Cotton called out: "Unto God's gracious mercy and protection we commit you, Ichiro. "The Lord bless and keep you. The Lord make His face to shine upon you and be gracious unto you. The Lord lift up

His countenance upon you and give you His peace, both now and evermore. Amen."

And he lifted one hand off the little girl and raised it in benediction; and throughout the church, the people, most of whom had never even heard the word before today, somehow understood that they were supposed to say it too, and many of them did. "Amen" echoed down the nave before the bone box went out.

Miyuki awoke in the middle of the night. She lay there, near her mother, for a long time, until finally she got up and went over to the stairs. It embarrassed her terribly; she'd done this twice before now. She'd just sit there on the stairs, looking down at Cotton where he lay sleeping, thinking about him. I can't do this, Miyuki thought. This is so foolish of me. This will be the last time. For sure.

Only Cotton wasn't on his futon. Miyuki panicked. He must be in the bathroom, she thought, and she turned around and dashed back up the stairs, tiptoeing around her mother to her place before he might spot her. She could see more easily now than when she left, because the moon had come out behind the clouds, and for some reason, just before she lay back down, she glanced out the window.

There, in the moonlight, Cotton stood by the Uzuma. He was just leaning on the rail by the river, peering into where the moon met the black river. Quietly Miyuki picked up her getas, slipped a shawl over her *dotera*, and made her way down the stairs and out the door.

Though she tried to walk softly, Cotton heard her coming, and when he waved at her, Miyuki's heart and her feet skipped, and she hurried to him.

"Couldn't sleep either?" he said, and she shook her head. "Something on your mind?"

"Maybe."

"Well?"

"I didn't want to say anything this evening, after the funeral. It was such a lovely service."

Cotton turned to her. "All right, tell me now."

"Captain Kato spoke to me afterwards."

"I was afraid of that. I knew better than to say anything about war being bad."

"Well, he didn't say anything directly about that. He just told me that I was supposed to take the whole class to see the new *Forty-Seven Ronin* movie." Yet another version had just opened in town. All the Japanese films now were very militaristic and fervently patriotic.

"What did you say?"

"I said I'd talk to you tonight."

"All right, we'll go see Kato tomorrow. I think seppuku is pretty heavy stuff for five-year-olds to sit through."

"He won't like that."

"No." He turned to Miyuki, but suddenly the moon passed behind a cloud, and there was hardly any light on her pretty face. "Maybe I better be a good boy this time and go along with what they want."

"Oh no you won't," she said stoutly—and it seemed even louder in the dark. Instinctively, Cotton put his fingers on her lips. Just as quickly, then, he pulled them away, but he kept his hand before her face and whispered, "Shhh."

More softly, but just as firmly, Miyuki replied: "No. Someone must speak up to them."

This time he took her shoulders. "Miyuki, you must be careful. Please. Don't say things like this to anyone else." The moon peeked out then and cast their faces in light, and they found their eyes were locked on each other. Simultaneously, they both turned away, and he let his hands drop from her shoulders.

"You're going down to Tokyo this week, aren't you?" Miyuki said. She already knew he was.

"Yeah. We play our first game Tuesday, and then afterwards I'm going doing to meet the Nakagawas' daughter."

"Are you dropping by the American embassy, too?"

"Gee, I don't know," Cotton said, stepping back, glancing away. Even in the dark he couldn't look at her, because he'd lied. And he really didn't even know why. Already, he'd written Bowersox and told him he was going to come by. He'd decided to tell him what else he'd learned about the fellow at the Peruvian embassy. He wanted to tell him he had his suspicions about a Japanese spying in Hawaii too. And he wanted to find out what Washington had said in response to the cable. He didn't have to let on to Miyuki about any of that. But sure, he could tell her he'd be dropping by. There wasn't anything wrong with that. What would be more natural, in fact, than an American in a foreign land going to the American embassy? But—

Miyuki could sense he'd lied too. She didn't press it, though; all she said was: "Well, if you should go there, find out how bad they think things are. It seems like things get worse all the time."

Cotton leaned back down on the railing. "It always seems worse when you have to bury a boy, like we did today."

Miyuki didn't respond. Finally, Cotton turned to look back at her, and only then did she say: "Why is Kiyoshi in Hawaii, Cotton? Tell me."

He stared at her. But not a word. And then, slowly, he leaned back over the rail and peered into the river. "Before you came . . ."

"Yes?"

"Before you came out, I saw one carp. In the moonlight. But I didn't see any more."

She got the message; she didn't ask about Kiyoshi again. Instead, she leaned over the rail next to him and pretended to look for carp, too. "I think maybe the Uzuma's too clean for carp," Miyuki said.

"Probably."

Miyuki didn't say anything else. They weren't touching, but Miyuki had come so close to him that she knew that if Cotton moved at all, he'd have to touch her. She could hear him breathing, and he could hear her breathing, and soon they were breathing together.

If he only knew: she thought she would explode if he didn't put his arms around her. If he only knew.

If she only knew: he wanted to hold her and kiss her for as long as she could bear it. If she only knew.

And they both knew.

How long did they stay like that, frozen, leaning side by side on the railing ... breathing together ... staring together into the bottom of the moonlight ... scared stiff: in love, together?

Finally, Cotton was the one who broke away. He had to. He pushed himself off the railing, so that he sprung back and only brushed her for an instant. "Well," he announced then, as formally as he could, "better try and get back to sleep."

But when he turned away, Miyuki could not contain herself anymore. She had to touch him—at least touch him once. She reached out and took his arm.

"Oh, Cotton," she said.

He swiveled back to face her, and there they were, looking into each other's eyes, as if they could find some neat little place inside where there were no complications and, particularly, no Kiyoshi. But they already had that place without Kiyoshi. The place was here. It was called Tochigi. It was called every day. And it was the worst.

"Yes?"

"I don't know," Miyuki said, sighing.

"Yeah," Cotton said. "Well, when I was in seminary, in Virginia, we were talking about what hell is. You know, all the devils with their pitchforks, fire and brimstone—whatever brimstone is." He permitted himself a little smile. "Hell," he said.

"Yes."

"So anyway, this one professor I had said: 'Gentlemen, here's the best definition of hell. It's all these people sitting around, and they're terribly hungry, and there's food all around. But their arms can't bend. The devil, old Beelzebub, has fixed it so they haven't got any elbows. Their arms can't bend, so they can't feed themselves.' " He pretended to put food in Miyuki's mouth. " 'You don't need elbows to help someone else. But this was hell, and these people didn't know how to do that. So they can't eat, and they starve.' "

"With the food all around them?"

"All around."

"Yeah, that's hell all right," Miyuki said. "That's so terrible, I think that's why we never had a hell in Japan."

Cotton shrugged. "Well, now you got your hell. And I got mine. We've got elbows, and we can't use them." He paused and stared into her eyes. "My darling." He barely whispered that, but he had to hear himself say it.

It made her step toward him, but he held up his hand and stopped her. "I told you, Miyuki. I told you. That's all. If you can't stand hell, then leave." She pulled back her shoulders. "Goodnight," Cotton said.

"No, wait."

"Yes?"

"Please. You must tell me about Kiyoshi."

He banged his hand on the rail. "That's not fair. I told you."

"You know something. That's not fair."

"Come on, Miyuki. He's your husband. You can't expect me to talk about your husband."

She leaned closer. "He's a spy, isn't he?"

"Miyuki, please."

"He is, isn't he?" Cotton dropped his eyes. Miyuki just went on. "Never mind. I know what you think." He pulled his head back up. "So, will you tell that man you know at the embassy? Will you tell him about Kiyoshi?"

"Miyuki, for God's sake! I can't talk about Kiyoshi with you, and you're being cruel to ask me to." He turned away, crossing his arms.

"So what do you think they would do if you told them you thought he was a spy?"

Cotton whirled back on her. "Dammit, Miyuki."

"They'd just send him home, wouldn't they?"

He paused. But she was breaking him down. "Miyuki, I have no proof," Cotton said.

"Yes, but even if you just told the embassy you suspected Kiyoshi, they'd follow him at least, wouldn't they?"

"I guess, yes."

"And then the Americans wouldn't even have to send Kiyoshi back to Japan, because he wouldn't be of any value anymore, and so *we* would bring him home . . . wouldn't we?"

"Well, yeah, I guess." He shrugged.

"So either way," Miyuki said, "if you tell, either way Kiyoshi would come back home . . ." And she waited, and Cotton saw at last where all this was going; but even then she added: ". . . back home to me."

Cotton took a few deep breaths. At last he said: "Please, don't make this any harder for us. We're never to talk about this again."

"All right," Miyuki sighed, but she also stepped toward him. "All right. All right . . . my darling . . . but just this one time," and she held up her arms, her elbows pointing toward him, and then she touched her right elbow with her left hand and smiled. "Just this one time, you have to let me have my elbows."

Cotton was terrified, but he smiled at her, and then she stepped up to him and looked into his eyes, wrapping her 'arms around him, waiting for him to do the same. And he did. They held each other for a long time, and then they kissed and kissed in the moonlight, scared to stop because they both knew that the moment their lips parted, they could never touch again.

1941
KANO TO MI
THE YEAR
of the
METAL SNAKE
Yayoi: The Cherry
Blossom Season

30

It was almost six months since he'd returned to Japan, and Cotton felt more Japanese all the time. He even wore kimono a lot now and had assimilated all the old Japanese ways of life: eating the whole herring, bones and all, drinking sake, squatting on his haunches. The most obscure idioms he'd long forgotten came back into his conversation, and he'd go to the public bath now, unashamed, curled up, soaking up to his chin, dreaming idly, as the steaming waters helped take the salt he'd eaten out of his body. He was even back to treating sleep like a Japanese does, cultivating it as a pleasure sometimes, pretty much ignoring it other nights when he had things to do. People didn't call him a *gaijin* anymore, but *gaikokujin*, a more polite term: a visitor, not an alien. Of course, winning also helps everywhere in the world. After Cotton's team opened the season with a resounding 8–4 victory over Isesaki on the road, the coach's stock soared all over town.

Miyuki was shopping in Tochigi the next day when she heard harsh voices emanating from the tofu shop. The manager there had referred to Cotton as a *gaijin*—and in rather disparaging tones—in front of Sakao, one of the team captains. "All right, perhaps Drakesan is a *gaijin* by blood," Sakao snapped, "but he is also a baseball daimyo." A daimyo was an ancient feudal lord. "He is our *gaijin* daimyo."

"You cannot have a *gaijin* daimyo any more than you can

have a man mother," the shopkeeper replied, furious at such sacrilege.

"If we keep winning games, you watch," Sakao said. Sakao was a very practical young man; he was the catcher.

Miyuki chuckled at this exchange and told Cotton about it when she got back to the rectory. cotton smiled, but he did wrinkle his forehead. "I don't know. That might offend a lot of people. I don't think I better try and be a daimyo. What I always tried to be was a *koken.*"

She screwed up her face. "What's a *koken?*"

"You're Japanese, and *you* don't know what a *koken* is?" Miyuki blushed. "When I was a little boy, my mother took me to see Kabuki. And whenever they needed a change of scenery, these fellows all dressed up in black would come out and move stuff around."

"Oh yes," Miyuki said.

"But nobody was supposed to see them—not the actors or the audience. Of course, everybody sees them, but we pretend the scenery is moving by magic. Or something."

"You call them *koken?*"

"Yes. And ever after, I wanted to be a *koken* in Japan. I know people see me, but if I do things absolutely right, they'll pretend I'm not really there. They'll accept me."

"Maybe you could be the *koken* daimyo," Miyuki said, and they laughed, and Cotton wanted to kiss her, and their eyes kissed, so he turned quickly away.

The next game, the home opener, against Ashikaga, wasn't until Thursday. After Oyama, Tochigi's top rival, Ashikaga was the best team in the league, and Cotton had held Kensuke out from pitching in the first game so that he could open the season at home against Ashikaga. Cotton couldn't miss that game, so he assured Miyuki he would only be gone overnight Monday to Tokyo, where he was going to meet the Nakagawas' daughter, Hanako, and invite her to the baptism.

It was barely a couple hours' ride into Tokyo, but Cotton usually sprang for a blue ticket—second class. This time, though, there was only third class on the train, so he bought a red ticket and jammed in. Every day now there was something else like this to contend with, something insignificant by itself, perhaps, but telling in the aggregate. In America, Cotton thought, people wouldn't put up with such hardship. And of course, that was precisely what the Japanese military thought about America, too. Maybe they're right, Cotton concluded. Anyway, Cotton didn't hear a single Japanese on the train complain.

He found his way to Hanako's apartment easily. It was near Yoshiwara, the brothel area, where she worked. She shared quarters with a colleague from the Shinyanagi house, Sumiko. And it was Sumiko, of course, who was General Teshima's favorite girl in all of Yoshiwara.

Hanako was waiting out on the street for Cotton. Her mother had written her that he'd be coming to speak with her this day, and certainly Cotton was no trick to spot: a white man with a priest's collar. No *koken* today in Tokyo. "Hey, Drake-san," the young woman called to him, and he went over to her and bowed, trying to mask the surprise on his face.

Hanako looked so unlike what he expected, so unlike what whores were supposed to look like. She was as short and dumpy as most Japanese women, with daikon legs and no significant breasts that he could make out under her blouse. Her face, to be kind, was plain—homely, really, with the protruding teeth common to so many Japanese. All Cotton could think was that she must be one helluva good lay if she could make a living looking like this.

"You're late," Hanako said. "My roommate's already left for work, and I gotta hustle."

"I'm sorry. I didn't know you went in this early."

"Usually get some guys on their way home from work. Good, fast money."

"Yeah."

She started walking. "You wanna talk about Mom and Pop, right?"

"It's very important to them."

"Well, I can't talk now. I gotta get the streetcar up here. How 'bout coming by Shinyanagi tonight? I'll give you a little extra time for the going price."

Cotton winced a little. "I'm not so sure this is a subject we should discuss, uh, in bed."

Hanako stopped. "Wait a minute now. You *can* screw, can't you?"

"Well, yeah . . . sure I can."

"I mean, you're *allowed* to?"

"Don't worry. I'm not Roman Catholic. I'm Episcopalian. We're not celibate."

"Good. That's a crazy way to run a religion, if you ask me."

"Me too," Cotton said.

"You ever been to Yoshiwara?"

"Yeah."

"Really?" Hanako cocked her head. "Come on."

"Yeah. Hey, Hanako, I haven't been a priest all my life."

"What's that mean? Whores are against the rules now that you got—" She pointed to his collar.

"Well, nobody ever told me that. I mean, it is legal here. But it's just that if I'm here to talk to you about something religious, I think we ought to keep it . . . you know." Hanako smiled. She was enjoying his discomfort. "I mean, like, if you were a . . . uh, red-collar girl, I wouldn't want to discuss this with you on the streetcar."

Hanako pondered this. "Well, how about my friend, then? Her name is Sumiko. I don't think she's as good in bed as I am. That's what everybody tells me. But she's real pretty. And I don't mean she's a *bad* fuck. Better than average." They'd arrived at the streetcar stop, and Hanako took out a cigarette. "Sumiko'd really like it, with you. We don't get many Westerners anymore." Cotton lit her smoke, and she looked him up and down. "Hey, how hairy are you, Drake-san?"

"Not very. In the middle, I guess."

"For a Westerner?"

"Yeah."

"Japanese men are so funny. They're always worried about

you guys impressing the girls 'cause you're hairy. And they treat women like shit. They're not like you Westerners. So I know they always wonder whether we'd give a damn for them if we weren't stuck here on these islands with them. Who the hell would think hair would mean anything to a girl? I'll tell you the truth, Drake-san, dicks don't always matter all that much." She winked.

"You're very refreshing, Hanako," Cotton said. "Very, uh, unique for a Japanese."

"Well, I've been around you foreign guys—and besides, Mom wrote that you were a special *gaijin*. You sure you don't want to come by Shinyanagi tonight? It's a class place—by far the best in Yoshiwara. And I can get you off real fast playing the flute"—Cotton blushed a little; that was the Japanese term for oral sex—"and then we'll have plenty of time to talk."

"Really, Hanako, I think it'd be best if we could chat without any, uh, distractions."

The streetcar was coming. Hanako shrugged. "Okay. Tomorrow?"

Cotton thought. He'd told Miyuki he'd be back by then, but the game wasn't until Thursday. "Okay," he said.

She pointed to a little restaurant across the way. "All right, meet me over there at that *sobaya* at noon tomorrow."

"I'll be there," Cotton said, helping her into the streetcar.

"Thanks," Hanako said. "You're a real gentleman, Drake-san. Not like these Japanese pricks."

"Look at you," Bowersox said. "That damn collar again! I tell you to wear a civilian shirt and bingo! you walk into the party and some beautiful señorita is all over you." He threw up his hands. "God, you'd think you'd learn."

Cotton smiled and settled into the seat at the Kaigan across the table from him. In the old days, Cotton remembered, the Japanese families would come here, or to the Pruniere Grill, up on the roof of the Imperial, for a special treat, an exotic Western meal, steak and potatoes. Now, though, as he glanced around, what few Japanese Cotton saw on the premises were all splendid in uniform. "What is this, Saint—the officers' mess?"

"There's just not many of 'em left that aren't in the army now." Cotton ordered a Scotch and a steak. "And the rumors, the rumors," Bowersox went on. "It's worse than it was the last time I saw you."

"And what exactly are the rumors these days?"

"Thailand's very hot now. Hong Kong. The usual minority whispers about going north against Russia. And you'll be happy to know, I even heard Hawaii mentioned a couple of times."

"You see?" Cotton said, laughing, going along.

Bowersox reached into his pocket and pulled out a copy of the cable he'd sent to Washington about Cotton's Peruvian rumor. "There, Reverend. Happy now?"

Cotton read it and handed it back. "So, what was Washington's response to this?"

"Zero. Nada. Goose egg. Not a single word."

"Oh, come on."

"I told you, there's no reason to place any more weight in this than fifty other cock-and-bull stories we hear around the world every day." Smugly, then, he lit up a Lucky.

"Oh, that's great thinking. We disregard what's likely because there's too many unlikely possibilities."

"You don't give up, do you?"

"All right, tell me, why is it so farfetched?"

"Look, anything's possible, Cotton. But you'd need a whole carrier fleet, attack planes, all sorts of transport ships, landing vessels. Move this whole armada thousands of miles and not get detected. Plus we've got the whole damn Pacific Fleet there to defend Hawaii." He sipped from his drink and grinned. "It does appeal to the Japanese penchant for surprise, though. Strategically it's insane, but it *is* perfectly in character."

Cotton leaned across the table. "All right, Saint, lemme tell *you* something. I did a little detective work—"

"Ah, you're getting to be quite the spy."

"I could say that I'm doing the embassy's work, but I won't."

"You know how Ambassador Grew doesn't approve of that sort of activity among gentlemen."

Cotton dropped his voice even more. "Remember how you didn't want to believe the story because it had come from a navy cook in Meguro?" Bowersox nodded. "Well, it turns out, he only *used* to be stationed out there. Since November, he's been—" Cotton stopped.

"All right, I give up."

"He's been none other than Admiral Yamamoto's own private cook."

Bowersox pursed his lips. "All right, that's interesting."

"And you know damn well how the Japanese can blab after a couple of drinks."

"Yamamoto doesn't drink."

"No, but you can be sure all the other officers do."

"I said, it's interesting. It doesn't prove anything, but okay, it does give your rumor a certain credence it lacked before. Is it all right to say 'I'll give the devil his due' in the presence of a man of the cloth?"

"Oh, thank you." Cotton nodded, sarcastically. "And one other thing."

"There's more?"

"Yes, there is. I feel very strongly that—" he paused—"that a Japanese guy I know has been sent to Hawaii to spy."

Bowersox perked up. "Who?"

Cotton thought about saying Kiyoshi's name. He hesitated. He didn't. "No, I can't tell you. Yet. It's all circumstantial. But I'll try and find out some more for you."

"Ah, now the good pastor is doubling as a master *international* spy."

"It all starts to add up, Saint."

"Except for one thing."

"What's that?"

"The why. Why make us mad? Why purposely bring the United States of America into a war?

"*Hisso,*" Cotton said without a moment's pause.

"What's that?"

"Certain victory for Japan. With all due respect, Saint, you don't have an inkling about them. You know the Chinese. You don't know the Japanese."

"Everything the Japanese learned, it came from the Chinese. Savvy?"

"Right, and everything we learned came from the Egyptians. So what? Who the hell cares about firecrackers and pyramids in 1941?"

Bowersox shrugged. "Then let them come."

"What?"

"Then let the bastards come to Hawaii. I'd like that."

"Come on, Saint, don't say that."

Bowersox raised his Scotch. "Hey, just joking," he said, lying through his teeth.

31

Hanako wasn't on time for lunch the next day, but at last Cotton saw her coming down the street with another young woman, taller and flashier than Hanako—stunning, really. He watched them pause on the corner, and then the other woman headed down the street and Hanako came into the *sobaya*.

"I'm sorry, Drake-san. My friend Sumiko, the one I think you ought to fuck, she had to go to the doctor's."

Cotton didn't let on that he'd seen her. So that was Sumiko, he thought. "I told her how handsome you were. If you change your mind . . ."

"Come on now," Cotton said. "I'm here on my business, not your business." But he was smiling. The waiter came over with tea, and they ordered miso soup and buckwheat noodles. There weren't many choices left on the menu at places like this anymore in Tokyo. Well, there weren't many choices left on any menus anymore, anywhere.

"We ought to go into business together," Hanako said. "You handling the souls, me the bodies."

"Like a department store—everything under one roof." Cotton went along with her, laughing. He was having more laughs with Hanako than with anybody else since he'd returned to Japan. Well, maybe he had as much fun with his baseball team. It figured, he thought: whores and athletes would be the two types most insulated from reality.

"All right, what's this thing Mom and Pop want?"

Cotton explained baptism. "Why?" Hanako interrupted. So he started to explain Christianity, and she interrupted again. "No, I mean, why my mother and father?"

"I don't really know. Maybe it had to do with your brother. Jesus didn't believe in fighting. He said, 'Love your neighbor.'"

"Is the United States Christian?"

"By and large," Cotton replied. He didn't go on. He could see what was coming. Hanako was no dummy.

"And you never have any wars?"

"We have wars, and we have fighting. We even fight each other sometimes. Someday, maybe, we'll be Christ's kingdom on earth. We're not yet—not by a long shot. But that doesn't mean we can't aspire. Christ lived two thousand years ago. The message must be a good one, because it lives on, and it attracts a lot of people everywhere. Like your parents." He paused then and looked into the soup, staring all the way to the bottom of the bowl. The soup was clear. An old teacher had told Cotton once that there was mostly just clear soup in Japan, because then you could see the beauty of the bowl even as you took the nourishment from it. Everything was always together; everything was bound so close.

Hanako stared at him for a while. Then quickly: "All right, Cotton-san, you tell my parents I'll be there for this baptism of theirs."

Cotton looked up and smiled, reaching out a hand to touch her. "Thank you, Hanako. *Arigato*. You're a wonderful daughter."

That embarrassed her some, but then the noodles came.

Hanako turned to the waiter, and for the first time Cotton noticed some sort of mark by her eye. "Hey, what'd you'd do to your face?" he asked. "I didn't see that yesterday."

Hanako shifted to profile to show him even better. Under her makeup there was some kind of a bruise and a bit of a scratch. "No, it wasn't there yesterday. Got the damn thing last night. That's why Sumiko had to go to the doctor. This asshole named Teshima comes to see her all the time. Big general." She lowered her voice and leaned forward. "All the army boys are assholes, if you ask me. Sumiko can't stand him either, but he's her best customer. And he usually brings a friend for me." She dug into the noodles. "Whores can't be choosy."

"Yeah," Cotton said. "Neither can priests. So what happened?"

"Well, last night he brings along this admiral, Sakamaki. They're both stupid drunk. Teshima's always drunk, always screaming. This admiral I'm with can't even get it up. I had to—"

"I'll use my imagination."

Hanako shook her head at Cotton. "No man ever wants to hear about another one who can't get it up."

"Okay—there but for the grace of God . . . But how'd this happen to your face?"

"Well, I told you, I'm good. I finally do the job on Sakamaki, and I go to wash up, and Teshima finishes up with Sumiko, and he comes over to have some sake with the captain, and they end up getting into a terrible argument, and Sumiko tries to break—"

"What're they fighting about?" Cotton posed the question idly, jamming noodles into his mouth, Japanese style.

"Some more army bullshit," Hanako said. "That's all they ever talk about. Who they're going to fight next. Samurai pricks all of them. So Sumiko steps in, and Teshima whacks her across the face to get her outta the way. Her face is all bruised. And she goes flying across the room and through the shoji and almost gets knocked out when she hits the floor in the next room." Hanako laughed.

"What's so funny?"

"Well, in the next room, there's Yuko screwing Mr. Sekimoto, and here comes Sumiko flying through the wall, almost right on top of them." She laughed some more. "You shoulda seen it, old Sekimoto-san."

Cotton dipped his chopsticks down for more noodles. "Musta been a helluva argument."

"That Teshima, he always argues.'"

"So what was this all about?"

"What do I care?" Hanako answered. "I rush in, and that's when I get scraped, too." She touched under her eye. "Teshima's still screaming at Sakamaki."

"Who?"

"The admiral. The navy shithead."

"Oh yeah."

"It's some shit about something they call Operation Z."

"What?"

"Operation Z. Some bullshit about the navy wanting to attack somewhere, and the army doesn't think that's right for them."

Attack. Cotton had looked up when she said the word "attack." But Hanako kept barreling on. "You know, I'm lucky I didn't get hurt more."

"Where?" Cotton asked in his most offhand manner, playing with his noodles, but thinking now: Z, Z—why Z? It meant something.

"Where?" He meant where would the attack come, of course, but Hanako wasn't thinking quite in those terms. "Right here! I *showed* you where. Right under my damn eye. He could've scratched my eye, and who the hell wants to fuck anybody with an eye all bandaged? You watch—Sumiko'll lose some business for a few days."

"Yeah. So, the army's mad at the navy, huh?" Cotton tried it one more time.

"I guess. The army always wants to run things. There's a challenge for your Jesus, Cotton-san. Baptize all the Teshimas."

"Yeah," Cotton said. But already his mind was even further

off. Z . . . Z. And suddenly—yes, that was it. It came to him. Z. Of course. Z was the signal Admiral Togo had used at Tsushima, when the Japanese whipped the Russians, and young Yamamoto lost two fingers.

Cotton could hear Togo's words. How many times had he been taught them in school? They were like "I regret that I only have one life . . ." or "Damn the torpedoes" or "Give me liberty or . . ." Togo's words came back now: "On this one battle rests the fate of our nation. Let every man do his utmost." And Z was the signal for that. Nothing had mattered more to Yamamoto, all his life. If it was to be dramatic, if it was to be extreme . . . if it was to be Hawaii . . . of course, the Admiral would pick Z, to honor Togo and the first great victory of the Sun-Begot Land over the West.

So Cotton didn't go back to Tochigi then. Instead, at eight o'clock he was coming through the main gate into Yoshiwara. He was wearing a pair of glasses he'd bought, a soft cap that looked more European than American (as if any Japanese really could tell), a Norfolk jacket, and a turtleneck.

He stood there at the gate a few minutes more, practicing speaking Japanese with a German accent (as if any Japanese really could tell). He hoped that the getup and the dialect were convincing enough—at least to someone he'd never met before. Then Cotton sighed and passed into Yoshiwara under the Mikaeri-Yanagi, the Looking-Back Willow—called that, he knew, because in olden times, once a young girl entered Yoshiwara, she would come through the great gate and stand by the Mikaeri-Yanagi and take one long look back at the world she was departing forever. In those days, a prostitute could leave Yoshiwara for only two reasons: to visit home when a parent died and, for one day each spring, to go over to Ueno Park and see the cherry blossoms at their height. He remembered that clearly now, for the blooms were just coming out in Tokyo.

A ways down the street from the gate there was a large teahouse, the Matsubaya, and Cotton went in there and had the

functionary at the desk call down to Shinyanagi and ask for
a date with Sumiko. That's the way it was done. Cotton gave
his name as Klaus von Kohorn—a good, solid German
name—and suggested an hour or so later, so that he could
have a couple of sakes to steel his nerve. The contact man
came right back from the phone, though, and said: "Sumiko
has had a small accident and is ready to go home for the evening, but when I told her you were a *gaijin*, she said that if
you'll come right away, she'll stay for you."

Shinyanagi was further along the main drag—the Oiran
Douchou, most called it, the Courtesan's Road—then off a
pretty side street with small cherry trees and apple-green wil-
lows on either side. One large willow rose above all the others, towering over the Shinyanagi, which had taken its name
from the tree: New Willow.

It appeared to be much the swankiest establishment in
Yoshiwara. The office was on the left, inside, behind a fancy
noren. "Sumiko," Cotton said, and the manager, Mr.
Okumura, bowed and took his money, rang a bell in her
room to herald her customer's arrival, and ushered the *gaijin*
down the corridor. Cotton tried to shield his face as he
ducked along, just on the chance that Hanako might come
out of her room and spot him. No one appeared, though, and
Okumura beckoned Cotton to pass through the *noren* into
Sumiko's room.

She awaited him, prettier even than the glance Cotton had
had earlier today—and never mind that the one side of her
face that she tried to keep from him was puffy and cut, obvious even under the makeup. Otherwise her skin was immac-
ulate, almost the color of old gold, much like Miyuki's. She
was slim . . . like Miyuki. She had, it seemed, Miyuki's legs,
and wore her hair in a permanent wave, with just a little bit
of a curl. Moga. Like Miyuki.

Sumiko bowed. "I must apologize for my condition, mister," she said, pointing to her face.

"I'm sorry," Cotton replied. "It's all right."

And Sumiko smiled and did the most amazing thing: she
curtsied. Some Westerner sometime had taught her to curtsy.

Cotton had never had a grown woman curtsy to him before. It was enchanting.

Only then, behind him, a gruff voice snapped: "Show him all, you whore." Cotton turned back. He'd been so caught up in Sumiko, he hadn't realized that the manager was still there.

Sumiko bowed to her boss and pulled one side of her kimono down, revealing a huge bruise on her shoulder.

"Show him, show him!" Okumura growled, and when Sumiko didn't respond quickly enough, he stepped in front of Cotton and all but yanked the kimono down to her waist, showing how her ribs were bandaged. "Maybe the gentleman doesn't want to pay for you like this."

Without expression, Sumiko pulled the kimono off her other shoulder and stood before Cotton naked from the waist up. "Turn around, turn around!" the manager shouted.

"No, no, that's fine. She's fine," Cotton said, and if either of the two Japanese had been paying attention, they'd have noticed that Cotton had spoken without an accent; he'd forgotten in the embarrassment of the moment. But neither picked up on it, and Cotton quickly stepped forward and helped Sumiko pull the kimono back up over her shoulders. "I'll accept her," Cotton said, over his shoulder, and Okumura shrugged and moved out through the *noren*.

Cotton turned back to Sumiko. "If you're not hurt," he said.

Sumiko shrugged. Men were always hurting her, and she needed this one other job to at least pay the rent for her room at the Shinyanagi tonight. It cost her a few yen down on top of the forty percent she had to give up on everything she brought in. "With all the trouble in the world, I don't see any Westerners much anymore."

"I'm German," Cotton said. "My name: Klaus."

"Kraus," she said, smiling, and right away he was sorry he hadn't taken the *r*'s and *l*'s into consideration. All the damn German names had *r*'s or *l*'s: Franz. Günther. Hermann. Christian. Damn. He should have picked Hans. Or Otto maybe. Otto was almost like Cotton. Why hadn't he thought of this before?

Quickly then: "My first name Otto. You call me Otto."

"Otto," said Sumiko.

"I'm sorry my Japanese is not quite right."

Sumiko shook her head. "Oh no, your Japanese is very good ... for a *gaijin.*"

He bowed a thank-you at the compliment, beckoned her to sit, and they plopped down together on the tatami.

Sumiko groaned a bit. "Don't worry, Otto-san. I went to the doctor today, and nothing's broken."

"How did you do this?"

"It was an accident."

"Oh, I'm sorry."

"It isn't for us to talk about. You have not paid to hear Sumiko's troubles."

Cotton took his hand and turned her head toward him, and she looked at him more sweetly than professionally, he thought. And he was probably right. Sumiko liked the German. She wished her face weren't banged up. She wanted him to see her at her prettiest, so he would come back. She was going to knock herself out for him when they got down to business. It thrilled her, then, when she heard him say: "I paid for Sumiko because I hear you are the most beautiful whore in Yoshiwara." She lowered her eyes until Cotton took her chin and held her face up so she had to look at him. "But they're wrong."

She blinked.

"No, you are the most beautiful in all the empire."

She beamed. *"Arigato gozaimashita."* He kept looking at her. "Who told you about me?"

"General Yoichi Teshima."

Sumiko tried to mask her surprise. It was not only the last name she'd expected to hear but, likewise, the last she wanted to hear. She drew back. "You're a friend of General Teshima?"

"No, no, not a friend. I only meet the general once. I am in shipping business. I meet the general at the German embassy some weeks past. He tells me, you return to Tokyo, Otto, go to Shinyanagi, for a girl named Sumiko."

"The general is most kind. You have been away?"

"I must often go to Kobe, Nagasaki, Shanghai on business. I leave for Nagasaki again in two days."

"Oh? Will you come back to Tokyo?"

Of course, she couldn't bring herself to ask him if he would come back to *her*, but then he answered: "Yes, I will come back Tokyo. And I will come back and see you," his hand resting on her cheek, holding her face toward him.

"I'm very glad you listened to General Teshima, Otto-san," Sumiko said, keeping her eyes on his, as his hand moved from her face to her shoulder and took her kimono and drew it down off her shoulder. Still she looked at him, even as he used her own hand to help him pull her kimono down. It fell to her waist.

Yet he kept looking into her eyes, transfixed on this beautiful gift of God that men of God were not supposed to monkey around with. Only when her eyes dropped did he let himself look at her breasts. Sumiko could feel him looking, and it seemed so odd, his just looking, so at last she raised her eyes again and watched him look at her.

It made her feel so pretty. Japanese took such pleasure in the beauty of things, the simplest esthetics of the sun and the moon, the flowers and the tea and the snow. And now at last her—her trim, curved little golden breasts. "Otto-san, it is strange: you are a *gaijin*, but you make me feel so Japanese," Sumiko said, and she reached out, smiling at Cotton, and took his hand and laid it on her far breast. She couldn't remember the last time she had had to take a man's hand, lead him. Tenderly, Cotton's hand stayed upon her one breast, holding it, moving so softly. Sumiko sighed. She didn't know that her breasts were the same size as Miyuki's. He'd only seen Miyuki's breasts across the way in a bath, of course. And Sumiko's nipples, too: the same type—the same as he'd dreamed about. He felt her breast, rising and falling. He felt her nipple in the palm of his hand. He so wanted this to be Miyuki. But this whore was the one with him now, with the breast and the nipple in his hand, and she was the one he smothered now when he could no longer hold himself back.

He didn't have much time to think, then, of Miyuki. It had been so long since he had had a woman—more than a year. Far too long.

Sumiko looked at him, a little surprised. She hadn't even had the time to slip out of her kimono, or Cotton out of all his clothes. He was awfully embarrassed, but he could only smile, foolishly. He couldn't tell her he was a priest who'd been away from this sort of thing and was out of practice. Finally, he just touched her face, gently, and said: "I want you once more, Sumiko. I'll be better this time." And he rolled over and tried to pull his money out of his trousers. He held out a bunch of bills; he couldn't remember how much it cost.

Sumiko pushed his hand away. "That's okay, Otto. That was so fast Mr. Okumura won't even know we went again."

However accurate the words, they were hardly calculated to make Cotton feel any better. He pushed the money at her again. "General Teshima was right about you. You're so beautiful. I want more time together with you. Please." She blushed. It had been a long time since Sumiko had blushed with a man, probably longer even than since Cotton had had a woman.

She snuggled up against him, stroking his face, and when she felt his hand moving up her thigh, she reached down and took it up to her mouth, kissing his fingers, before returning it to where it had been. Then they kissed, and some more, before he fell upon her, and she tingled that any man could want her so sweetly and so ardently alike. Why, it even surprised her that when she cried out, it was for her, it was for real, and not just to please a customer. Even though her ribs hurt, and her shoulder too, and her cheekbones ached, Sumiko longed not to let go of this strange, sweet *gaijin*. She could hardly wait to tell Hanako that although Hanako might have met the kind and handsome Western priest, she had found a Western customer who was even more special.

Cotton asked Sumiko, whispering, if she wouldn't meet him tomorrow, so they could go somewhere together and see the new cherry blossoms—so pleasing Sumiko that she went over to the little chest where General Teshima kept a bottle of Scotch, and she pulled it out, and she and Cotton drank a toast together.

Never before had she dared give any other man a drink from the general's Scotch. "I will show you the blossoms tomorrow, Otto-san," Sumiko said, raising her glass. "We'll go together to Ueno Park, where there are the most beautiful blossoms in Japan, in all the world."

"You are the prettiest blossom of all," Cotton replied, making her blush all the more, and blush for blushing.

32

The ships steamed out Pearl Harbor, through the stem that bloomed into the Pacific. It was an impressive sight—well, perhaps it was the first time you saw them cruise the stem. But this was the third Monday in a row that Kiyoshi had studied the exhibition, and by now there was an everyday quality to it, like watching some kind of traffic jam.

Here they all went, one after another, the *Maryland* and the *Nevada*, the *West Virginia* and the *Arizona*, the *California*, the *Oklahoma*, and the *Pennsylvania*, and the cruisers and destroyers, the *St. Louis* and the *Raleigh* and the *Helena*, the lot of them, on and on. The first Monday Kiyoshi had to scurry through his new *Jane's* to make sure of them all. Now, sometimes, he didn't even bother to lift his binoculars. He just nodded in the spring sun and wondered if there really was any need for him to dress up again like a farm hand and come back up here to Aiea Friday afternoon and hide in the cane and watch the fleet come in again. It was, after all, so obvious now, so cut and dried. The whole fleet: out Monday, back Friday for the weekend.

Who would ever believe such a thing of a navy on alert? But if what he concluded was so, then, clearly, the reason he could never find the planes to the north was because the planes never flew north. The Americans simply didn't bother. If Yamamoto demanded evidence of that, no, Kiyoshi couldn't prove a negative, but it was patently clear all the same. He chuckled to himself, idly doodling on his pad. The Americans, it turned out, were the ones who were as patterned and reliable as the Japanese were supposed to be.

The North was open. Kiyoshi was convinced of that. He'd been searching the records at NYK, and now it was time to study the routes of the other Pacific lines. But he remembered well enough how the American Orient ships crossed, and he was sure: at least come the fall and the bad weather, there were no ships that ever plied the trade routes north of Hawaii. And the Americans never even looked up there. Incredibly but surely, a whole quadrant of the compass lay open, unguarded.

He remembered something, and he took out his pencil and started to make a note that occurred to him—something that he knew would appeal to Yamamoto's sense of history and connection. "Yoshitsune," Kiyoshi wrote. And then the capital letter *M* and an *i* and—He heard the rustle behind him then, and when he started to swivel around, he heard the steely order: "Don't move except to put your hands up."

Kiyoshi obeyed. He heard the footsteps come closer.

"I ought to blow your brains out, Jap."

Cotton walked with Sumiko through Ueno Park, the whole place a soft tapestry of cherry blossoms. "They are each for our fallen warriors, Otto-san," she said. She picked up some of the blossoms that were already on the ground, held them up above her head and let them drift down again, colored wind.

Cotton watched her, and, self-consciously, Sumiko turned her face away from him. "I'm so sorry for this," she said, touching the bruise. "You're wonderful to be with a girl who looks so terrible."

"No, Sumiko, you're beautiful," Cotton said—and he

meant that, too—*that*. Deceitful as he was being, that was the truth. It wasn't as easy in the daylight, walking under the blossoms, to pretend that she was Miyuki. But she was so lovely, it was enough just now that she was Sumiko.

He had to force the issue, though. "How did this happen?" he asked, pointing to her face. He had to pressure her. He had to find out what Teshima and the captain had been arguing about.

"I don't want to talk about it," Sumiko replied, turning away. He let it go—for now. Instead, he hurried and caught up with her, and reached out, and she looked, and then, her heart racing, she let him take her hand. She probably would have been arrested, if anyone had just seen her displaying such wanton affection to a *gaijin* in public. But for Sumiko, it was worth the risk, for she had never held any man's hand in a park before. They wound down the cherry paths together, the whore positively glowing, for this was absolutely the most daring, *sexiest* thing she had ever done in her life.

Some places the blossoms had fallen so thick that they kicked at them, like sand on the beach. They laughed. "The blossoms never stay long," she said. They came with such reliability, and then they left straightaway, almost as soon as they had painted everybody's dreams again.

"I must leave in a little while," Cotton said. He'd given up all pretense of trying to put on a German accent, but Sumiko obviously had never noticed it anyhow.

"Will you be away long, Otto-san?"

"Oh no. Only Nagasaki for a few days."

"Good. The cherry blossoms will be gone when you come back, but then there'll be the wisteria and the peonies, the azaleas, the roses. I'll show them all to you."

"Morning glories?"

"You know our morning glories?" She squeezed his hand.

"I always liked them so much." And then suddenly he yanked her with him, and they dashed together across the way to where Cotton had spied an old candy artist. Cotton bought two. He kept the one shaped like a sampan for himself and gave the other, a rice rendition of Mount Fuji, to Sumiko.

She laughed. "I haven't had one of these since I became . . . since I started working. It's for children."

"We can all be children now and then." Cotton took a bite out of the little candy boat, but Sumiko only held hers up.

"Have you ever seen Fuji-san?"

"Oh yes." Quickly: "From the train." In fact, he'd climbed it when he was a boy, with his father and Kiyoshi.

"I have climbed it," Sumiko declared proudly.

"You?"

"I'm stronger than you think, Mr. German Man. Besides, it's an old Japanese expression that anyone who climbs Fuji will be wise."

"Oh?"

"Well, anyone who climbs Fuji *once* will be wise. Twice is a fool."

Cotton laughed, but suddenly she darted around him, and when Cotton turned around, Sumiko was playing with a little monkey on a string who belonged to a *saru-mawashi*, a sort of Japanese organ grinder. Cotton gave the old woman a few sen, and there was a great deal of bowing, most particularly by the monkey. Then, even better, the animal snatched a little drum away from his mistress and beat it for a while.

Sumiko took Cotton's hand back and guided him to a bench, and they flopped down and munched their rice candy together. "I think you must have been Japanese in another life," Sumiko announced.

"Oh?"

"You seem so at home here."

"I speak not quite right."

"Oh, good enough. My friend that I live with, she met this American, a priest, and he grew up here, and she said he was so Japanese it was eerie. She wanted me to have business with him."

"But you didn't?"

She shook her head. "My friend said he was very scared. Holy men shouldn't have whores, should they, Otto?"

"Probably not."

"That's what I told my friend. But then you called from the Matsubaya, and even though my side was hurting, there are not many Westerners anymore so I stayed for you. I'm glad I did."

"I'm glad too." But she had given him an opening again, and he pointed to her side. "You hurt still?"

"It's better. Tonight I can do all the business."

Cotton paused. He knew he had to get her to talk about Teshima. That was the point of all this; that was why he was here. He couldn't just go to Yoshiwara and then start taking whores to the park for rank carnal reasons. "It's some man hurt you, yes?"

"I don't want to talk about it."

"I don't like any man who hurts you, Sumiko."

She tightened. "He didn't mean to hurt me, Otto. He was fighting with another man, and I got in the middle of it. They do not want fights at the Shinyanagi. It's bad business."

Cotton took his breath in. "It's—Teshima hurt you, yes?"

She blanched. She didn't know how to react. Cotton hadn't played by proper Japanese rules. He had confronted her, left her no room to maneuver. Her eyes darted everywhere to escape his. She turned to her candy.

So he just went on. "Don't worry. I won't say anything. I heard that General Teshima was a bad man even before I met him."

"He would hurt me if he knew I had told anyone."

"I won't say." He paused and pushed on. "But you tell me: why was Teshima so furious? Why was he fighting?"

"Please, I cannot talk about this, Otto," Sumiko said, and Cotton realized he had to let it go for now. It was ironic, too, for he was sure that it wasn't what Teshima had said that made her so nervous, it was only the fear of Teshima finding out that she had disclosed his bad behavior. So Cotton would have to wait; he would have to deceive her more.

"Quick," he said. He pulled her up off the bench and behind some wisteria bushes that were full, ready to burst into bloom. He looked deeply into her eyes, into the perfect black *asahi* that were her pupils, then softly touched her cheek where Teshima had hurt her. "When I come back Tokyo—"

"Yes?" She couldn't wait.

"You go with me to my house and we will—" Her heart stopped now. *Aijin*, she wanted to hear: lovers. But that would be too much from the *gaijin*. "We will not be like a whore and her customer," Cotton said.

She sighed; that was good enough. And she parted her lips for him and he leaned down and kissed her full on them, holding her close, only remembering her bruises after a time and easing up. "Like an American movie," Sumiko said when their kiss ended, catching her breath. "I have sex with men every night, but I've never kissed like that before." It was not exactly the most romantic thing Cotton had ever heard, but he understood. "When you come back, Otto, I'll be all cured, all pretty for you, and we'll make love like a moga and a mobo."

"Yes," he said, and he kissed her again, not thinking of Miyuki, not thinking, either, of how he was betraying Sumiko. It was all for a noble cause, and betrayal has much to commend it when tucked into a noble cause. Especially when mixed with lust.

"All right, you can take your hands down and turn around." Slowly, carefully, Kiyoshi complied, swiveling in the grass, ready to look dead into the barrel of a gun.

But there was no gun—only Sammy Ushijima, unarmed, his eyes clouded with the film of tears. "Oh, Key," he sighed, holding out his hands, empty in despair.

Kiyoshi would have preferred a gun at him. "Look, Sammy, this isn't exactly what it appears" was all he managed, lamely.

"Oh, bullshit, Key. You're a spy. You're here spying on my country."

"No, Sammy, try and believe me. The only real enemy is the Japanese army. You know how they're misleading the—"

It was the most facile explanation. Kiyoshi could come up with, and it counted for nothing.

"Oh, fuck you, Key." Sammy's sadness turned to anger. "I've followed you, I saw you up here Friday when you watched the fleet come in. I tried to believe maybe that was some kind of coincidence, but . . ." His voice trailed off and he gestured to the pad. "What's that? Special delivery for the *jouhou kyoku?*"

Kiyoshi handed the pad up to Sammy. "You'll see. It's nothing. Doodles."

Sammy glanced at it, shaking his head. "Yoshitsune Mi," it said. "Jesus, what kind of an idiot you try and make me?" He slapped the pad. "Yoshitsune Minamoto. What Japanese doesn't know?" Sammy's hand shot up in the air then, a student from long ago answering teacher's question. "February 7, 1184, sir. Surprise attack from a completely unexpected angle. The great strategist. The greatest victory. The whole course of history is changed."

His hand came down, and now he was playing the teacher. "Thank you, Isamu. You are correct about the great Yoshitsune Minamoto." And Sammy ripped off that first sheet and fired the pad back down to Kiyoshi. It came so fast, he could barely get his hand up, and it bounced off his chest and tumbled into his lap. Sammy sneered. "Couldn't resist, could you? So where do they come from?"

Kiyoshi's mind was reeling. He tried again. "Look, you've just got to believe me when I say I can't tell you everything now. But I swear I'm working for someone who knows America and loves it. That's the truth."

Sammy paused—and Kiyoshi knew he had cracked the door. Sammy didn't have the foggiest idea what Kiyoshi could mean by that, but he desperately wanted to believe him, so the mystery and ambiguity of that remark at least slowed him down. Kiyoshi could see his wrath cut back to a simmer, maybe. Sammy turned and looked at the fleet, the last of the great ships just clearing the harbor. "You know, the funny thing is, of all you Japanese I know, I—"

"*You* Japanese, Isamu?"

He turned back to Kiyoshi, and there was more resignation now than anger. "Yeah. I really don't think I'm one anymore. Japan is only a place I come *from*." He turned away again but went on talking. "Of all *you* Japanese, I never would have figured you. Hell, sometimes when you and Cotton were together, he seemed more Japanese than you." Sammy even chuckled a little at that. "Here sometimes, when you were working for me, you didn't have any idea how native you went." Kiyoshi smiled; he was pleased. The more he could keep Sammy talking, philosophizing, the better.

"You're right. And that's what I'm trying to say. Things are so damn complicated now."

Sammy whirled back, livid again. "But goddamm it, that doesn't forgive you spy—"

Kiyoshi yelled back—the best defense, etc.—as if it were all Sammy's fault. "You think I like this? You think I like being here, away from Miyuki? You think I like what's happening back home?" He got to his feet then, finally, drawing more strength as he rose. "You think I give a shit about these boats?" It was all bluster, but it was effective, and Sammy even ducked his head, as if he was somehow now a bit unsure at what he'd seen with his own eyes. So Kiyoshi pressed his advantage, stepping up to him, touching him on the shoulder, dropping his voice. "You think I wouldn't give my right nut to be back with you at American Orient?"

Sammy nodded, but Kiyoshi feared the jig was up; he could only be buying a little time. The *Nitta Maru* arrived tomorrow from Yokohama, and maybe he'd better be on it, going back. No real damage had been done, for what could Sammy tell anyone—that he'd seen an old friend sitting in the sun, watching the ships pull in and out of Pearl? Hell, for three cents every day in the newspaper you could still find a lot of that sort of information. "Come on," Kiyoshi said. "Give me a chance to explain. We'll have a drink some night."

"Key, I can't have you hurt my country."

"*Your* country, Sammy? Your country? Come on, they won't let you be a part of their country. They only wanted you when they needed you to cut the cane, do the shit work. But citizens? You know. They made laws to keep Asians out, and just to make sure, they made special laws to keep Japanese out. So don't give me that crap, Sammy, 'cause we're only niggers to them."

Sammy pulled himself up straight. "Mr. Serikawa," he said, "Serikawa-san, both my daughters are citizens of the United States of America. Josephine voted in the last election. She voted for Mr. Roosevelt to be her President—and her father's President. You know goddamn good and well there's Koreans lived in Japan for centuries, and they still can't vote. The Burakumin have been on the islands forever, but they're not us, so we don't even count them as human beings, Don't tell me about somebody else's niggers, Key. We're the experts at niggers!"

The words carried out over the heights. Sammy was almost shouting.

Kiyoshi lowered his head. "I can't argue that. I've lived abroad. I know our faults better than anyone." He held out his hands. "But maybe we can start to make things better. Wednesday night, I'm free-lemme buy you a drink."

Sammy eyed Kiyoshi dubiously. "You think you can explain this?"

"Trust me, Sammy. I know it looks suspicious, but trust your old pal." He put both his hands on Sammy's upper arms, holding him there in that most manly embrace. "Next to Cotton, there's no man I ever loved more in the world than you." Sammy bit his lip. "You've been everything to me, and I could never lie to Sammy Ushijima."

Kiyoshi's heart was crying; it amazed him that he was capable of such deceit. And the worst part was, Sammy compounded his treachery by replying: "No, I know, Key. I know you couldn't lie to me. I'll buy the drinks Wednesday."

Kiyoshi stuck out his hand. *"Domo sumimasen,"* he said—I thank you so much for I feel like a heel. "I'm you're *on* man, Sammy."

Instead of taking his hand, Sammy waggled a finger. "Hey, don't give me that Jap shit." And they both laughed. Sammy threw an arm around Kiyoshi and they started trooping back down the road. "You know, Key, I never told you before, but I loved you so much, the one thing in the world I wanted was for you to marry my baby."

"Darlene?"

"Yeah, it broke my heart when you married Miyuki."

"Aw shit, Sammy, we never needed marriage to be a family," Kiyoshi said. "Not you and me."

As long as he lived, Kiyoshi would never get over those words. The world had made him into someone he'd never seen before.

That day, he couldn't go back to his office. Instead, he went to his apartment and drew the blinds and drank himself silly. The next-to-last thing he remembered thinking was: If preparing for war will twist men so, what will war itself to do them when it comes? What will it do to me?

And the last thing he thought about was Sammy, whom he did indeed love, save Cotton, more than any other man in his life. "That part was true, Sammy," he said. "That part was true."

33

Bowersox wanted Adair to come with him to the Shinyanagi. He promised him the best-looking whore in all of Japan—and not some cheap *shoufu*, but an *oiran*, a classy, gorgeous prostitute, a courtesan of these times. Adair's loins stirred as Bowersox described Sumiko, but he was scared. Like most people, even when he agreed with Bowersox, he still didn't trust him. Adair was a particularly nervous little fellow, a Princeton man, Quandrangle Club, number two in the Division of Far Eastern Affairs, and even though Stanley Hornbeck didn't control the department anymore, since he'd moved over to become Secretary of State Hull's Far Eastern adviser, Gil Adair was still scared to death of Hornbeck.

Adair was married. If Hornbeck merely heard that an official in his old department was consorting with harlots, it could scar his whole career. Bowersox read him perfectly. "Come on, Gilly, I won't tell Stanley."

"It's not that, Saint—"

"Hey, when in Rome, Gilly." And he made some familiar lewd just-us-boys motions with his hands.

"Really, Saint." Adair shifted in his chair. The Division of Far Eastern Affairs did not enjoy the sort of devilish behavior that formed the reputation of many other foreign departments. Hornbeck's mark was fixed upon it, and the men who stayed in FE tended to be mousy and prim. The brief time he'd been in FE, Bowersox couldn't stand the place.

Adair screwed up his courage. "I got it! How about geishas?"

Bowersox shrugged. "Jesus, talk about looking a gift horse in the mouth!" But he called out to his secretary to get him General Teshima on the phone, then closed the door, slapping Adair on the back as he walked by. "Well, if we can't get Gilly to take the best piece of ass this side of the dateline, at least we'll get him the best geisha."

"It's really better this way," Adair felt obliged to explain. "I mean, a man can get, uh, laid anywhere in the world, but only geishas are here in Japan."

"Yeah, uh-huh," Bowersox said, rolling his eyes, and he lit a Lucky and passed the pack to Adair. "So, Gilly, how long you be with us?"

"I'm booked out of Nagasaki for Shanghai Friday."

"Shanghai?"

Adair leaned closer. "This is what I gotta talk to you about, Saint. On the QT."

"My lips are sealed, pardner."

Adair's voice dropped near to a whisper. "I'm trying to get to Chungking to meet with Gimo—"

"Hey!"

"And Hornbeck wants you to accompany me."

"I'm your boy."

Adair took a letter out of his inside coat pocket. "This is the official request to Ambassador Grew."

"No problem." Bowersox lay back in his chair and chuckled. "Hell, Grew'd like to see my ass out of here permanently."

The buzzer on Bowersox's desk rang, and he picked up the phone. "I have General Teshima, sir," his secretary told him.

"Yoichi, *ohayo* . . . Listen, I've got a visiting fireman in from D.C., and I want to show him the best geishas in town. You've got clout. Can you see if Sai and Midori are free any time the next couple nights? . . . Thank you, my friend. We'll have to get together again soon. . . . Yeah, Shinyanagi. Absolutely. Bye." He hung up the phone. "Helluva contact, Gilly. General in intelligence—the *jouhou kyoku*. Yoichi Teshima."

Adair exhaled some. He blew it all wrong, in great bursts, then none at all; no matter how much he smoked, he always looked like he was just learning. "Teshima. Yoichi Teshima," he said, rolling the name over. "Wasn't he one of the bad guys in Nanking?"

"The real article." Bowersox sprang forward in his chair, leaning on his desk into Adair. "But Gilly, this here is not Washington. It is not that teddy bear's picnic you go to every day. We don't sit around and *talk* strategy here. We *do* shit. Savvy? And if we're ever going to get China back, we've got to really kick over a lot of rocks, with a lot of crap underneath them. Gimo can't do this by his lonesome."

Gimo was Chiang Kai-shek. All the loyal China adherents—even the ones, like Adair, who'd never laid eyes on the man—loved to refer to him by his nickname. It was almost a password, investing the noble Chinese quest with a clubby mystique. "I know, Saint. It's just that . . . damn, I get uncomfortable just being in Japan. These people." He shook his head. He blew some more smoke all wrong. It drove Bowersox nuts.

"Unfortunately, not enough of our people look over here to Asia, do they?" he said. "Even now?"

Adair nodded, drawing on his cigarette again. "You pick

up the paper every day, or the radio—it's all Europe, Germany, Hitler."

"Would we fight in Europe?"

"Well, Roosevelt gets us closer to that all the time. Lend-Lease—he's so tight with Churchill. But do the American people want war?"

"They never do," Bowersox answered the rhetorical.

"Still, eventually we can be steered into it. Wilson pulled it off. FDR's safe now that the election's behind him. And if Hitler gives him enough excuse . . ." He shrugged.

"Okay, so has anything changed the thinking about Asia? Would we ever go to war over here?"

Adair shook his head. "It's just too far away."

"Yeah, and they're not real people here. Little yellow things." Bowersox drummed his fingers. "But suppose the Japs went into Southeast Asia—say, uh, Singapore?"

"Look, Saint, if we don't go to war for England when England's under fire, why the hell would we go to war for one of their colonies?"

"All right, suppose it was the Phillippines?"

"That the Japs attacked?"

"Yeah."

"They wouldn't be that stupid. The Phillippines wants to be like some Switzerland of the pacific."

Bowersox lit another cigarette. "Well, maybe. But there are rumors. And Hawaii?"

"Attack Hawaii? Oh, come on. Be serious." Adair was not only incredulous, he was smug.

"But if they did?"

"Well, obviously, that's a whole different kettle of fish. Hawaii! There wouldn't be an isolationist left in the forty-eight."

"But no one expects that, do they? Hawaii?" Adair considered that, trying to sort things out. Bowersox went on, snidely: "Am I leading the witness?"

"No, it's just I never even heard that one before. That doesn't make any sense."

"Not to us. But Japanese sanity can't ever be measured by

American logic. Everybody in Washington looks for the same neat package with a big bad Hitler tying the ribbon around the people. That's always the way we see it, going back to King George and all the Indian chiefs. The Kaiser sank the *Lusitania,* didn't he? That makes sense to us. But the problem is, Gilly, there is no Hitler in Japan. No Mussolini. No Sitting Bull. Savvy? Here it's all consensus, and in that sense no one is in control. No simple one bad guy. If anything, the guys at the top are led by what's below. Savvy?"

Adair reached for another of Bowersox's Luckies. "Help yourself, Gilly."

Adair immediately pulled his hand back and grinned foolishly, but quickly he said: "Hornbeck believes the Japs won't use a sneak attack."

"Oh? Why?"

"Because they've been so belligerent all along. It doesn't make any sense to upset in advance someone you plan to surprise."

"My, that's good perverse Oriental thinking of Stanley."

"Besides, he thinks the army is too tired out from fighting in China to try anything crazy, and Yamamoto is the one officer so familiar with America that he'd never commit the navy to any foolish adventure."

"Perhaps. But they think *our* army is piss poor, and I'd never dismiss any surprises from Admiral Yamamoto.

"Let me ask you something, Gilly." Bowersox lay back in his chair and looked up at the ceiling fan, quiet on this pleasant spring day, collecting his thoughts before he flipped forward in the chair. "Now, you know we're not ready for war, and the American people don't want it. But if war comes, do you think we have the manpower and the willpower to fight in Europe *and* Asia? Two fronts. A *real* world war. Do we?"

"Sure," Adair said. "After we get cranked up, a breeze."

Bowersox rose from his chair. "So tell me, Gilly. Who's the patriot? Is it the ambassador down the hall, trying like all get-out to keep us from fighting a war we would win? Is that patriotism?"

Adair wasn't so cocksure this time. He didn't answer.

"Well?"

"Gee whiz, I don't know, Saint. That's tricky."

"Well, I don't think so. The Japs the ambassador likes are the ones that want peace. And I think that's all wrong. The Japs *I* like are the cocksuckers that wanna fight us. And I like them because I agree with you: we can kick their asses. Savvy? And take over the Pacific. Aren't I the patriotic one?"

Adair said, "Well, that's an interesting point."

"Don't be a pussy. When we get to Chungking and we see Gimo, you ask him that. We'll ask him who he thinks the real American patriots are. This time, Gilly, this time the patriots are the sons-of-bitches that want war."

34

Twice a year, in the spring and the fall, each and every town in Japan had one day designated for cleanup: *oosuiji*. Every house had to be made spotless, gutted of all junk that had accumulated in the last six months. Japan was too packed to abide excess rubbish, too meticulous to leave even housekeeping to chance. "Japan is the only place where cleanliness isn't next to godliness," Cotton's father had observed once. "It's just next to the police."

It was Cotton's good fortune that he had forgotten when *oosuiji* had been scheduled. By the time he arrived back from Tokyo that Wednesday evening, there was an official piece of white paper posted on the rectory door, where Miyuki stood on the threshold, tapping her foot, affecting a harridan with a rolling pin. He noticed the paper straightaway and realized it had been *oosuiji*. "Hey, we passed!" he crowed. They posted a red paper if a house failed.

"No thanks to you," Miyuki said, welcoming him inside with a mock flourish.

"I tried a couple times to call last night to tell you I had to stay over, but you know how hard it is to get long distance now." He felt bad, lying to her, but it was better than the truth.

"It's okay. Mom and I just figured you found a woman."

"Oh, come on, Miyuki," he said to her. Damn, he thought to himself, she can read me like a book.

"It's all right, Cotton. You're a man. You need a woman. I heard there was a terrific whore over in Oyama, and I was going to recommend her."

Cotton just let it go. He looked around the rectory. "Wow. Spic-and-span. What a job you did!" Mrs. Serikawa beamed. She was sitting on a tatami, helping mend clothes for the soldiers in China. More and more, that was how she spent her days.

"Your team helped," she said.

"Oh, you should have seen it," Miyuki said gaily. "Chief Hiranuma came over to inspect with his dress uniform on— the gold braids, even the ceremonial sword."

"Come on."

"I'm not kidding. I know why he came here himself. He wanted to post the red paper at the Christian house. I had to beg for more time."

She batted her eyes. "What's that English word you taught me?"

" 'Flirt.' "

"Yes, I frilt," Miyuki said, completely botching it. "I can't say that."

"But I bet you sure did a good job doing it."

"The boys were practicing their baseball, and as soon as Hiranuma left, I ran over and got them to come by and clean up. It was like magic. Hiranuma came back around four, and he was just furious. He couldn't believe how tidy everything was. He had to post the white paper."

They all laughed. "Thanks for taking care of things," Cotton said.

"Oh, the boys were so cute. They wouldn't even let Kensuke help, because he has to pitch tomorrow. Everybody is so excited about the game, aren't they, Mother?"

"The whole town has heard about the wonderful *gaijin* coach."

"It's perfect, too," Miyuki said. "The first game in Tochigi, and the cherry blossoms come out—the same day."

"For sure?"

"That's what everybody tells me. In Tochigi, the cherry blossoms bloom every April tenth." She pointed out the window, into the gloaming. "You see, they're ready to burst."

"It'll be a great day," Cotton said.

He headed into his study, and Miyuki followed him. "Can I get you something to eat?"

"Thanks, no. I had a *bento* box on the train." He looked back down at his desk, his notes and the mail. But Miyuki didn't leave, and in fact, when she spoke again, it was in English, so her mother wouldn't understand.

"I was joke you, Cotton."

He looked up. "I'm sorry?"

"About woman Tokyo. I know you no stay for woman."

Cotton put an indignant expression on his face. "Oh, maybe."

"You meet people Tokyo. You learn things. No?"

"I learn things, yes."

"Things go badder?"

Cotton mulled that over for a few moments before he finally nodded. "I think so, yes."

"Plan leave Japan now?"

"No, I'm still sticking it out. I don't cut 'n' run, kiddo."

She screwed up her nose at that, but she got the gist, and she went on. "You hear Kiyoshi name?"

"Kiyoshi?"

"Hawaii Kiyoshi."

The word rattled Cotton, and he knew it showed. She was wise enough, then, to leave him alone on the limb. At last he said: "All right, I can't lie to you."

"No."

"I could say no, I didn't hear anything, but I can't say that to you. I can only say: I learned things—not about Kiyoshi, now, but scary things. But I can't tell you them."

"Because I Japanese girl?"

"Yes, of course."

"Miyuki never Japanese girl with you before. Only Miyuki. Cotton never American boy with me before. Only Cotton. Now sudden I Japanese girl."

Cotton looked directly at her, which was hard for him. "Hey, I didn't do this, Miyuki. I don't want this, and I can't help this."

"So things, change much."

He nodded, grimly, "Very much, I think."

"Wrong time now?"

"For what?"

She didn't answer. She was playing with a piece of paper in her hand, and now she glanced at it. It was clear she didn't know quite what to do with it. So finally Cotton spoke up:

"Look, I'm sorry. I've gotta go see the Nakagawas and tell them Hanako will come up to their baptism." Miyuki smiled at that, but she kept turning the paper over. "Is that something for me?" Cotton asked.

"No, no. Is only mine."

He brushed by her out the door, but then he paused there and looked back at her. When he spoke, it was in Japanese. "Look, Miyuki, it's so hard. Sometimes I feel like I've been thrown in a river, and the water is rushing all around me, all over me, and I try to swim in it, and I can't, no matter how hard I try."

"This is so American of you," she replied, back in Japanese herself.

"Oh?"

"Yes. You must learn to stop trying to swim in the river, and just become part of the river."

"And you can do that? In these times? In this river?"

"I'm trying, yes," and she fiddled with the paper again, but even as he looked at it, she held it tighter. Only when he left did she hold it up again, for herself. It was a letter she had written:

My dear sweetest Cotton:

Ecuse, but I must write in English as say these things
to you. I am in love to you as American girl. Miyuki
not mad Kiyoshi, but now I am be with Cotton so my
heart is too with you finally. You must tell me you are
loving me to. I know is that. I see.

I want Kiyoshi give me divorce and we go from Japan together then. Bad time bring more war. Please. I
am read bible and hear you sermons. Do you see
Miyuki in back church? I want be Chrissten moga wife
for missionary anywhere in world with rev. Mr. Drake.

And she went all the way in English. She didn't sign it with
the Japanese characters that made "Miyuki," or even the let-
ters that formed that sound: M, I, etc. Instead, she signed it
"Beautiful Snow." or, altogether:
"Your
Beautiful Snow"

The steward escorted Kiyoshi down the passageway of the *Nitta
Maru.* It was NYK's newest cruise ship, and a beauty. Surely no
nation contemplating further hostilities would allot funds for the
construction of a grand leisure liner. The man who opened the
cabin door was a young Japanese dressed in sports clothes.
Without any acknowledgement to the steward, he nodded to
Kiyoshi, shut and locked the door, and then greeted the visitor
formally. "Lieutenant Serikawa, I am Lieutenant Commander
Tsujimura." He gestured around the small quarters. "I'm sorry,
but this is the only place we can talk safely." Then he pointed
at the briefcase Kiyoshi was carrying. "Didn't Mr. Wada advise
you not to bring anything?"

"It's only for show, Tsujimura Shousa," Kiyoshi replied,
flipping it open. "I just thought, for appearances' sake, that
an executive of the cruise line should be boarding one of his
ships with some material."

Grudgingly, Tsujimura nodded. He was unsmiling, the sort
who sees humor as a weakness. In fact, Tsujimura, was the

same lieutenant who had harassed Cotton on board ship last November, when they had sailed back together for Kigen. "You should know, Serikawa, that I am Admiral Yamamoto's personal emissary. You speak to me as if you are addressing him."

"My understanding with the admiral has been that I would deal in the mail, then communicate face-to-face with Yamamoto-san in Japan."

Without any expression, except perhaps for the glimmer of the inner glow that comes with setting a trap, Tsujimura then handed Kiyoshi an envelope. Opening it, Kiyoshi read a handwritten note from the admiral attesting exactly to the point Tsujimura had just made.

"The admiral suggested you would probably raise that point, and I was simply to advise you, on his behalf, that Z is moving ahead nicely—'quite expeditiously' were his exact words for you—and he wanted you to report directly to me so that matters may be rapidly advanced." Pause. "Anything else, Serikawa-kun?"

Kiyoshi tried to keep a blank face. The way Tsujimura expressed that—"Anything else?"—wasn't so much an invitation for Kiyoshi to speak up as it was a display of exasperation with him. "Yes, the admiral and I had an understanding that I could come home soon. I'd like to see my wife."

"Well, of course, there are a lot of Japanese serving His Majesty who must suffer such a conjugal separation now, but Admiral Yamamoto anticipated that request as well, and he advises me to inform you that if your reports are satisfactory, a trip home in July would be useful to us."

"July?" Kiyoshi had thought perhaps he could clear out by the end of this month, April.

"Well, July, August. You understand, these times are unsure."

Kiyoshi nodded, sort of. He'd never met such a disagreeable sonofabitch in his life. He took out a smoke.

"Please, Serikawa-kun, as you can see, it's very close in here." He pointed to the one porthole.

Kiyoshi put the pack away, and then, while Tsujimura made careful notes, he began to outline all that he had learned in Hawaii. Tsujimura barely had to prod Kiyoshi, so easy and complete was his memory. If Tsujimura asked Kiyoshi to dwell on anything, though, it was the fleet and the harbor.

"It's like clockwork," Kiyoshi reported. "I couldn't believe it. Out Mondays, back Fridays. Just tell Admiral Yamamoto, if he still plans to strike, any weekend will do just fine."

"Any weekend?"

"The fleet's lined up then. Target practice. Sunday'd be the best. A lot of 'em are hung over. A few go to church. Lot of the officers play golf. Hit 'em Sunday morning." Kiyoshi pointed to Tsujimura's notes for emphasis, making sure he wrote that down. Then he continued, reporting on American air reconnaissance—especially on the apparent absence of patrols north.

Tsujimura pressed him. "Let me understand this. You've never seen any planes searching in those skies north?"

"That's correct."

"So you assume there aren't any?"

"After a while, you're left with no other conclusion. I don't see them going north. I don't hear them going north. I've *been* north—Kauai—no planes. Nothing."

"Perhaps the Americans are being especially clever."

Kiyoshi shrugged. "I doubt it" was what he said.

"All right. I'll report now that you haven't found any planes flying north, but will redouble your efforts."

"I will redouble and retriple my efforts to find nothing, yes."

If the sarcasm touched Tsujimura, it was not apparent. He simply kept on with his notes until he was finished, then looked up. "Now, have your own efforts gone undetected?"

"The Americans seem completely unaware of my presence. I move about at will. I know there's another spy here, and he appears to be as loose as I am. I assume you're meeting with Morimura, too."

Tsujimura shifted in his seat. "How do you happen to be aware of Mr. Morimura?"

Kiyoshi chuckled and answered in English: "It takes one to know one."

"What does that mean?"

In Japanese: "Oh, let's just say we crossed each other's paths. I stay away from him now."

"All right," Tsujimura said, making more notes. "Is that all?"

"If you want my opinion, Tsujimura-shousa, which I don't think you do, you'd let me go home on this ship tomorrow."

"You've made it plain you want to go home."

"I'm trying to be objective," Kiyoshi replied, knowing he probably wasn't succeeding at all. Nevertheless: "It isn't the Americans who I'm concerned about. A lot of people knew me when I used to work here. They wonder why I'm here now."

"And so," Tsujimura said, "if you leave, they stop wondering."

"I think so."

"Anyone in particular?"

Kiyoshi paused, but then he went ahead. Sammy could be his ticket back to Miyuki. "A Japanese who worked with me at American Orient."

"Oh?"

"I'm having a drink with him tomorrow evening."

"And he suspects you?"

"No, let's just say he's *curious* about me." He'd lied to Sammy; he could lie *about* Sammy.

"I see. He's Japanese?"

"Well, Issei. He's been here almost thirty years. His two daughters are American citizens."

Tsujimura stared at Kiyoshi. "I thought you told me no Americans suspected."

"I did. Sammy is Japanese." His voice went up. He was sorry now he'd ever brought the damn thing up.

"Sammy?"

"Isamu Ushijima. He and his wife both still have families in Japan."

Tsujimura made a note of that, too. "When you meet with him tomorrow, it might be advisable to remind him of that." Kiyoshi nodded. Tsujimura went on: "And I would suggest that you might be more discriminating in your choice of friends."

"Sammy is—"

"I was primarily referring to the Reverend Mr. Drake."

Kiyoshi straightened up in his seat. "How do you know about—?"

"Curiously enough, I've met Drake. We rode back together on the *Asama* from here last November. But then I happened across his name in your file. You wrote a letter to the admiral a little while ago asking for some favors for him, for his mission in Tochigi."

"Yes, and proudly."

"I would just remind you, Serikawa-kun, that under the new National Defense Security Law, His Majesty has declared next week as Espionage Prevention Week. Be careful. Your friend here"—he checked his notes—"Mr. Ushijima of American Orient, clearly has American sympathies. Very dangerous. And your wife is staying in the same house with an American."

"I resent the innuendo."

"None was intended." His expression didn't flicker. "But I do resent your casual approach to security. It would take almost nothing to jeopardize Operation Z."

Kiyoshi soft-pedaled a little. "Then perhaps it would be wisest for me to leave Hawaii on board here tomorrow."

Tsujimura was unyielding. "You will see Mrs. Serikawa soon enough. And there is no assurance that your old colleague will put aside his suspicions of you simply because you depart. That may instead aggravate them."

Kiyoshi had to concede the argument was a fair one. "What should I say to Sammy tomorrow?"

"I would simply remind him of his relatives back home. And Mrs. Ushijima's relatives back home. And I would remind him that under the National Defense Security Law next week has been declared Espionage Prevention Week." Tsujimura smiled. "Should you see him, that should suffice."

35

The crowd swelled with each inning, the drab townspeople set off from the blaze of new cherry blossoms that danced down the shores of the Uzuma-gawa and ringed the green field. Mrs. Serikawa was there with her friends, knitting clothes for the boys in China. It was the first baseball game she'd seen since Takeo played. Even from the paddies they came, and Miyuki saw the Nakagawas and ran over to tell them how happy she was about Hanako coming up for the baptism. The time of *hanami* was always festive in Tochigi, but there was something even more special about the blossoms this spring, for the fear and deprivation had grown so, and there was little else even to hint of joy and hope.

Why, only the day before Chief Hiranuma had announced that, beginning immediately, Tochigi would be subject to the same rice rationing that had already been put in effect in the cities. That was bad enough, but on the same day, Mr. Uchida, the grocer, was forcibly removed from his store and detained overnight by Captain Kato. The poor man had been turned in by one of the more zealous members of the new *tonarigumi*, the neighborhood association that had been formed under the command of the House Ministry for the primary purpose of tattle-taling. Mr. Uchida had made the mistake of complaining about an army sergeant, assigned as security at the airplane parts factory, who had just come into the grocery store and swiped the only two oranges. Kato finally released Mr. Uchida, but with a black mark in his file. Soldiers did that sort of thing all the time. And everybody in town knew. And everybody in town knew that they couldn't trust each other anymore.

Maybe that was why the baseball game seemed so important. "You know," Miyuki said to Mrs. Nakagawa when the Tochigi team took the field for the first inning and everybody rose to cheer, "I'd forgotten how much I liked a boy in a baseball uniform." And Mrs. Nakagawa nodded slyly; she understood how Miyuki had emphasized the word "baseball" and not the word "uniform." The Tochigi boys wore baby-blue uniforms, and maybe they looked more benign what with all the soldiers strutting about in their more commanding, masculine colors.

Anyone could sense how much the team meant, how much the game meant. It wasn't just a cheer but a roar when Kensuke poured in the first strike, and after he got out the side on two easy pop-ups and a strikeout, the whole crowd came to its feet again. When Tejiro put Tochigi ahead in the second with a three-run homer, even Hiranuma and Kato began to strut about, as if they were responsible themselves.

Cotton had planned for Kensuke to go only five or six innings, not to rush him this early in the spring, but the boy was breezing so easily—Ashikaga managed only two cheap hits and one walk on a full count—that Cotton decided to let him pitch through the seventh, too. The fans were oohing and aahing every time Kensuke fired the ball; they'd never seen anything like this, ever. And he just kept pouring fast-balls in. After he struck out the lead-off man in the seventh, the Ashikaga manager even went out to complain, but, as the umpire patiently explained to him, Kensuke wasn't doing anything illegal. He couldn't call balls on pitches that were right over the plate.

"But this is *gaijin* baseball," the Ashikaga manager groused, nodding darkly toward where Cotton sat, arms crossed, eyebrows knitted, in his finest big-league managerial pose.

"But *gaijin* are the ones who invented baseball," the umpire replied, and when the manager still wouldn't leave, Chief Hiranuma stormed out onto the field and ordered the manager back to his bench. The fans cheered even more, and Hiranuma bowed grandly.

All the hullabaloo certainly didn't upset Kensuke, though.

He promptly struck out the next man and got two quick fast-balls over on the next batter, the last one he would face. Cotton yelled out to Sakao, behind the plate, and when the catcher glanced back at him, Cotton touched his ear and then drew his left hand across his chest. Sakao nodded, and when he got back into position, he signaled Kensuke: two fingers.

Cotton turned over to where Miyuki was sitting, gave her a stage wink, and called: "Watch out, here comes the famous Miyuki pitch."

And Kensuke took his biggest windup and delivered the pitch—and it was headed straight for the batter's head. But just like the time Miyuki had stood in against Kensuke with a broom for a bat, the pitch was a big old jug-handle curve ball, and just like when Miyuki had collapsed to the ground, so too did the batter. He let the bat fly from his grasp, threw his hands up to protect his head, and crumpled in an ignominious heap—just in time to see the pitch swerve right smack over the center of the plate. The umpire threw his right hand up and cried: "Strike three!"

"Kensuke!" cried the crowd, every man jack and woman dear there.

Cotton jumped up and rushed out to meet his pitcher. "That was fantastic!" he shouted. "That was Bobby Feller. You're not only a thrower, you're a pitcher." And Kensuke beamed and bowed, and Cotton bowed back. But then Cotton stuck out his hand and said, "Shake hands like an American pitcher," and they shook, although of course Kensuke didn't really know how, and it was a dishrag shake.

The fans roared at the gesture, though, and over on the first-base side, Endo, the town barber, stuck out his hand to his pal Kagami, who worked in the airplane parts factory, and Kagami shook it. And Sato saw that and shook hands with Inoguchi, and then pretty soon people everywhere were turning and shaking hands with their neighbors. Kato and Hiranuma shook hands with one another. Miyuki shook hands with her mother. The players shook hands. All the children shook hands. It was the happiest Tochigi had been in a long time.

Even two innings later, when the game was over, 10–1 Tochigi, the crowd still milled around. Nobody wanted to leave. Cotton just stayed on the bench, taking it all in, watching the celebration, until finally the people began to melt away, moving off under where the sun glanced onto the cherry blossoms. After a while, Miyuki and her mother joined him, and then, just when they were ready to go home, Kensuke headed over.

Cotton said: "You really were wonderful out there. I promise you, next year you'll be pitching in Tokyo. Right, Mrs. Serikawa? He'll be starting with the Giants in 'forty-two," Mrs. Serikawa smiled in agreement. "Mrs. Serikawa knows baseball, Morishita. Her son was a great player."

Kensuke bowed politely, and then he reached into the back pocket of his uniform pants, pulling out a piece of paper. When he handed it over, Cotton could see that it was a postcard. He didn't even have to read it to know what it was: the draft notice for Kensuke Morishita. That's all draft notices were, just little penny postcards.

Without a word, Cotton passed it along, Miyuki caught her breath. Mrs. Serikawa said: "You are very lucky, Heitaisan"—Mr. Soldier—"honored to report for service in the Emperor's army."

"Oh, for God's sake, Mother. He's not a soldier. He's barely out of school. He's just a boy, a baseball player."

"The opportunity to serve the Emperor is most noble. Tenno Heika celebrates his birthday soon, and you will be in uniform then."

Cotton only said: "Have you told anybody else?"

The boy shook his head. "It just came today, Drake-san."

"Well, if you can, keep it quiet till after the Oyama game." Cotton rose and put an arm around him, then watched him slip away.

"Maybe we can get him a deferral," Miyuki said.

Mrs. Serikawa glared. "I cannot believe my daughter would speak this way."

Gently, Cotton touched Mrs. Serikawa on her shoulder.

"Please understand. Kensuke has made this town so happy. To take him away, to put this one boy in the army, makes—"

Mrs. Serikawa would have none of it. She simply rose and, stonyfaced, said: "I will begin dinner."

Miyuki and Cotton watched her walk away. "I'll talk to Kato," he said. "I'm a big deal around here now that the team is a winner."

"No, I will. A thing like this, Kato could never listen to a *gaijin*."

"Is there much chance?"

Miyuki shook her head. "No. I wouldn't think. But I'll try."

"Dammit. It breaks my heart," Cotton said. He wanted to scream, but he only kicked at the ground. And softly then: "And on this most beautiful day of them all."

"Do you know what it means when the cherry blossoms come down?"

"Sure." He remembered right away what Sumiko had told him. "It's the warriors falling to their death."

"Oh yes," Miyuki said. "That too. I forgot that. But it also means lost friendship. Lost . . . love."

He looked away, out over the trees. "Of course I remember. When I was a little boy, we'd sing about it. We'd have a picnic for *hanami* and we'd sing. . . ." He didn't sing. Cotton had a terrible voice. He could even screw up a rollicking good hymn, like "Onward, Christian Soldiers" or "Hark! The Herald Angels Sing." But in the best rhythm he could manage, he repeated it: 'The red sun sets, Cherry—"

"Oh, yes, yes, I remember!" she cried, and she held up her hands, to get them in unison, and they said it together:

> "The red sun sets,
>   Cherry blossoms flutter to the ground.
>   We say 'good luck'
>   And hope we meet again."

They smiled, ironically, shyly. Instinctively, Cotton reached over and took Miyuki's hand and squeezed it. It was the first time he'd touched her since they'd kissed weeks before. But then, just as quickly, he let go and turned away. After a while, she walked around him, so she could look into his face. "I'm so sad about Kensuke," she said.

"The thing is, I can't stop thinking he'll be dead next *hanami.*"

"Please, Cotton, don't say that."

"I'm sorry. But I know. The war is coming."

"You learned that in Tokyo, didn't you?"

He didn't answer that. He just said: "I know there'll be a war unless somebody stops it."

"Who can do that?"

Cotton shrugged. "No one I know," he said.

36

The *Nitta Maru* sailing for Yokohama was delayed. It came over the public address: minor engine problems had cropped up, but work was moving ahead and the ship would surely be weighing anchor by nightfall.

In sports clothes and sunglasses, carrying a briefcase, Lieutenant Commander Tsujimura strolled off the *Nitta*, away from the docks, up King Street. He made every effort to be unobtrusive, meandering over to School Street, doubling back to Nuuanu and then over to Alakea. He saw the sign there for American Orient Export-Import, and, without hesitation, his stomach untroubled, his nerves untouched, he stepped into the office and glanced around. It was precisely, as he had planned, five minutes before five o'clock.

Tsujimura saw Sammy on the phone in his office, which opened up off the main room. He had partitioned the place in '38, when they'd added new space. Ted Palmer, his assistant, was at Sammy's old desk out front, wearing a short-sleeved blue shirt and tie, no jacket, and Nancy Marumoto, the receptionist-assistant, sat head-on from the door in a modest print dress. "May I help you?" she asked the visitor.

Tsujimura removed his sunglasses and, smiling, in his best English, said: "I was on *Kamakura* to Callao, but my company require change in my plans. By chance, you have ship going to Peru this week?"

"I'm sorry, sir, but we're strictly cargo. We don't book passengers."

"Oh well, I thought take chance. I was walking over Bishop Street, to check with NYK, when I see your sign."

"Perhaps you might get something to San Francisco or Los Angeles and connect with a ship to Peru from there."

"Yes, thank you," Tsujimura said, and he departed, went up to the corner of King Street, took a bench at the bus stop there, and, pretending to read the afternoon paper, kept an eye on the American Orient offices. Soon enough, as he'd anticipated, Miss Marumoto came out. The traffic was picking up now, as businesses let out at five, and Tsujimura felt the pace around him pick up.

Several minutes passed before the door opened again at American Orient, and Palmer came out. He turned toward Tsujimura, walking up Alakea toward King. Tsujimura buried his head in his paper until the man reached the corner, turned, and went the other way. Then, casually, Tsujimura retraced his steps to the American Orient offices, opened the door, and stepped inside. Sammy's voice called out: "I'm sorry, but we're closed for the day."

Tsujimura popped his head into Sammy's office. "I think I left my sunglasses here. Please may I take look?"

Sammy noticed that the man struggled some with English, so he politely replied in Japanese: "Certainly, look around out there."

"*Arigato,*" Tsujimura replied, and he went back to Miss Marumoto's desk, laid down his briefcase, and opened it. "Here they are," he called out, and then he went back into Sammy's office, and when Sammy looked up, the man was pointing a pistol into his face.

Sammy practically fainted, not so much from fear as from shock. Tsujimura accommodated Sammy's confusion by providing him with explicit directions. "Turn around, Mr. Ushijima, and open the safe, please."

"Oh, come on," Sammy said, flicking his hand toward the safe. "There's nothing in it. You want cash, try Matson or NYK."

"Please, don't dispute me. Open the safe." And so Sammy shrugged, went over to the cabinet in the corner, threw open the drawers, and started fiddling with the knob. When he looked back, he started to say, "You're going to be disappointed," but that was when he saw that the intruder had fitted the gun with a silencer and Sammy realized this was not about robbery but about his death. "Oh," Sammy said.

"Yes," Tsujimura replied, beckoning for him to pull out the contents and lay them on the desk. "Empty your pockets, too." Tsujimura picked up the wallet and checked out Sammy's identification as he kept the gun trained on him. It would be a terrible thing indeed to murder the wrong Issei.

"I'm Ushijima," Sammy said—and with remarkable calm. "But really, please tell Kiyoshi I'm disappointed that he wouldn't do this himself. Tell him for me that I find him most dishonorable." And his shoulders sagged and his eyelids closed as he stood there, behind his desk, waiting for the bullet.

"On your knees," Tsujimura ordered, and Sammy sank down as he saw the gun draw near to his temple. He thought about trying something, anything, remote as any chance was, but Tsujimura spoke first. "Well, you should know, Mr. Ushijima, that Mr. Serikawa is not aware of this. In fact, he's still expecting dinner with you tomorrow evening."

"Really?"

"This is my decision. I'm sorry, I wasn't prepared to risk him choosing you instead of his emperor."

"And who is killing me, please?"

"My name is Tsujimura Fukio."

"*Sumimasen*, Mr. Tsujimura. But notwithstanding, my death will bring great shame to Kiyoshi, so, if you would, please tell him that he owes no obligations to my family."

Tsujimura smiled a certain benediction. "Good for you,

Ushijima-san. You die like the Japanese you were born." He leveled the gun. Sammy tried to take advantage of this brief patriotic reverie, and with one desperate lunge he sprang toward the intruder, but he was on his knees, and he couldn't purchase any leverage. The bullet blew into his face and probably killed him instantly, even though Tsujimura added one more bullet neatly, in his brain, for safe measure.

He listened then. Nothing. He put on his gloves and peeked through the blinds. If any pedestrians outside had even heard the sounds moments before, they had already dismissed it. The rush-hour crowd ambled by. After all, nothing unexpected was expected in Hawaii these serene days.

Tsujimira locked the front door, then went back and took what money there was from the safe: $187. He stripped Sammy's wallet, and then made a great to-do about messing the place up a bit more.

Momentarily, he looked down on Sammy, bowing slightly in respect and with some apology for what he had been obliged to do. First he locked Sammy's office behind him, and, after that, the whole American Orient office. Further down Alakea Street, he tossed the keys into a trash container, ambling the rest of the way to the dock. There he flipped his diplomat's passport open to the American immigration officials—although, really, they hardly noticed. The gun and Sammy's money were hidden under a false bottom of the briefcase. Tsujimura went directly to the captain's cabin, where orders were immediately passed for the *Nitta* to set sail within the hour. It was announced that the engine problems had been corrected. The ship cleared harbor before nightfall.

Kazuko was not worried that Sammy didn't come home after work. Often, like most Japanese men, he went out drinking and neglected to call. Her concern began to grow only later that night, but she did not trouble the police till Darlene woke up in the morning. It didn't matter. Horrified, Miss Marumoto found the body at eight-thirty.

The police were mystified why someone would choose to

rob a steamship office, but it was clear that Sammy had attempted to thwart the robbery, and the intruder had panicked and fired. There was some speculation that this might have been the product of some ancient vendetta from old Japan, but Mrs. Ushijima assured the police that that was out of the question. And so the police were very quickly left with the conclusion that it was precisely what it appeared to be—a stupid robbery that escalated more stupidly into murder. The crime did not long disturb the peace and tranquility of Honolulu, and, in fact, even before the murderer walked down the gangplank, disembarking from the *Nitta Maru* in Yokohama, interest in the case was all but lost.

The one person left in Hawaii who understood what had happened kept to himself, drinking and weeping and, when he was sober, doubting his mission all the more. Slowly, then, Kiyoshi took to making tea for himself, thinking of Sammy as he drank it. He looked within himself, and he prayed that at least Sammy's spirits could meet with his brother-in-law Takeo's and sort things out on that end. "Tell him I am sorry, Takeo," Kiyoshi said. "Tell him I didn't know. Tell him . . ."

37

"I baptize you in the name of the Father, the Son, and the Holy Ghost." Cotton drew the sign of the cross in water on Mr. Nakagawa's forehead, then stepped back from the old couple. "Congratulations—now you are both the newest members of Christ's family on this earth."

They beamed. "I think we'll close with a hymn, too. But we all have to sing loud, because there's not many of us." It was Holy Saturday, the day before Easter, and only a few of the Nakagawas' friends were there—plus Hanako, of course. Miyuki was in the back. "Hymn number 263: 'In Christ There is No East or West.'"

The people found their place in the hymnals. Miyuki stepped up to the front of the church, next to Hanako. "Don't worry, it's not hard," she whispered. "I'm not a Christian either."

Cotton brought his hands up. "All together now." And his hands came down. " 'In Christ there is no East or West,' " he began, and the others drifted in. " 'In Him no South or North.' "

"Come on—louder!" Cotton cried. "Louder. Louder. You too, Hanako."

"You know I don't know this stuff."

"Don't give me that. All you have to do is read from the book. Show her, Miyuki." She thrust the hymnal over, so Hanako couldn't avoid putting a hand on it, sharing. "Okay," Cotton said. "Let's start again. Everybody. Let's let them hear us over at the baseball field." Across the river, the townspeople were already assembling for the big game with Oyama.

> "In Christ there is no East or West,
> In Him no South or North,
> But one great fellowhip of love,
> Throughout the whole wide earth."

The people going across the bridge by the church could hear the singing. They were flooding into Tochigi, because not only had the word of Kensuke's prowess spread throughout the prefecture, but most people had also heard by now that he would have to report for induction. Miyuki had spoken to Captain Kato about a deferral, and Kato had even been bold enough to approach his superiors, but they turned him down out of hand. No exceptions in Tokyo for country boys who played baseball.

> "In Him shall true hearts everywhere
> Their high communion find;
> His service is the golden cord
> Close to binding all mankind."

Miyuki and her mother had tea for the Nakagawas and the other guests, but game time was approaching, and Cotton had to leave. He called to Hanako, and they walked out of the church courtyard together, toward the baseball field. The game was still more than an hour away, but already the stands were nearly filled.

"Hey, you sang good," Cotton said. "But then, you *are* good. It meant so much to your parents, you coming up here. And look—" He stopped her.

"Yeah?"

"I was wondering. You wanna get in a little work up here?"

"Maybe. When?"

"Tonight. After the game."

"Sure, but I thought you—"

"Whoa, not me, Hanako."

"Oh." Her disappointment showed. "Who, then?"

"The boy who's pitching. Kensuke."

"You pimping for your team, huh, Drake-san?"

"Not quite. The kid's the best pitcher I ever saw in Japan. He'd be throwing at Korakuen next spring, but he got drafted, and I was just trying to think of the best going-away present I could give him."

"Sure." Hanako beamed. "Keep me from getting rusty, too. I'm staying over a few more days to help out Mom and Pop."

"That's nice," Cotton said. He filed the news away in his mind, and they resumed walking. "Why don't you stay up here?"

"Work in that factory? Are you kidding me? I'd a helluva lot rather be on my back a few hours a night than stand on my feet all day like those poor women working over there."

"Well, why not open a business here? The men are always complaining about the standard of whores we've got in Tochigi."

"Aw, come on, Drake-san. I'm like your pitcher—good enough to go to Tokyo. If you're the best at what you do"— and she winked at him—"you don't stay in Tochigi. Do you, Drake-san?"

"No," he said, shaking his head, grinning.

"No matter what happens, I'll give the boy a Tokyo time tonight," Hanako said, and she jabbed Cotton in the ribs.

The mailman brought a letter to Miyuki from Kiyoshi, but the game was starting soon, so she left it unopened in her room and walked over to the field with her mother. Miyuki wondered sometimes whether Kiyoshi could tell from her letters how she felt, for she could certainly tell from his that he loved her still and missed her terribly. That was why she hated, really, to get his letters, because they made her feel so guilty.

Today was such a glorious occasion, too. The special town festivals, in August and November, had lost their luster the last couple of hard years, but suddenly, for this moment, Kensuke had created something special in this one tiny place. "Never!" exclaimed Mrs. Nakagawa, surveying the scene. "Never anything here in all my life!"

The crowd overflowed the stands, filling out down the foul lines, and even beyond the outfield fence, by the river. Some boys climbed the trees for a look, shaking loose the blossoms, and the visitors from Oyama and the other towns who had arrived well in time for the first pitch were surprised to discover they were shut out of any good vantage. So they just packed around, hoping to catch a glimpse.

And here came Kensuke, striding to the mound, and even the umpire stood back and admired him. There would be no disappointing today, either. Kensuke struck out the side on eleven pitches in the first inning, and when the third batter went down swinging, the crescendo carried out from Tochigi, across the bright green fields with their bright yellow flowers, over the paddies and on to the purple mountains beyond. Cotton strolled over to the fence down the first-base line, where he had let Miyuki and her mother put down a large mat for themselves and the Nakagawas. "I wish Tenno Heika could have heard that," he said, " 'cause then they'd find another boy for this army." Even Mrs. Serikawa had to smile.

The Oyama pitcher was his team's ace, a good country

pitcher, and he matched Kensuke fairly well. There was no score through three innings, but after Kensuke put down the side again in the fourth—twelve in a row, now, eight of them on strikes—Tochigi got three runs when Tejiro cleared the bases with a double. Cotton went back over to the ladies and Mr. Nakagawa at the fence. "If you came to see a baseball game, you might as well leave now," he said, " 'cause there's no way in the world that these boys are gonna get three runs off Kensuke. But if you wanna see a real work of art"—he winked—"then better stick around."

Only once did an Oyama batter get a ball to the outfield, and that was a lazy fly ball that drifted foul in short right. Only twice did the visitors even take Kensuke to three balls— and both times he struck the batters out, on curves, looking. "God in heaven," Cotton said to himself, awed at the boy.

As Kensuke drew closer to a perfect game, everyone stood, and the roars rose to a new pitch. The sounds reverberated differently than anyone remembered from before. Cotton just sat back and watched, for he alone understood that Kensuke was somehow building a miracle as much as a masterpiece. The pitcher was accomplishing something that was, really, beyond his abilities. He could reach this level in time, two years from now perhaps, more likely three or four. But that would be denied him by the war, and so, mystically, he was managing to achieve on this day in 1941 what he should not be able to do until sometime in the future.

In the ninth inning, the first batter struck out, the seventeenth Oyama man to go down on strikes. The roars increased; even those who had come over from Oyama to cheer for their team were rooting for Kensuke now, hoping for a perfect game.

The next batter managed to dribble an outside pitch down to the first baseman, who took it unassisted. "Kensuke— Kensuke—Kensuke!" the fans all began to chant. He was just reaching back and firing fastballs now. But it didn't even matter that the hitters knew what was coming. They'd never seen anything like this before.

The twenty-seventh batter stood in. Strike one. Strike two.

The cheers now were in homage to the inevitable. It seemed that even before the next pitch thudded into Sakao's mitt, the teammates were upon Kensuke, pummeling him, raising him up, high on their shoulders. The crowd held its place, cheering, but with a certain reverence. Even the ones who didn't know baseball from sumo understood they'd been in the presence of genius this afternoon.

Slowly, Cotton rose and started to move to the mound. Kensuke saw him coming and called for his teammates to let him down. Gently, they dropped him to the ground and parted, so he could walk over to his coach. They met at the first-base line. Cotton was beaming so that his smile could be seen across the river. Then he bowed deeply.

Kensuke bowed.

This was the part everyone was waiting for. Cotton stuck out his hand and Kensuke took it. They held that pose, and all over the field, people turned to their neighbors and shook hands. Everybody pumped and laughed. Even the Oyama people caught on and joined in. Cotton and Kensuke shook then, up and down, and Cotton registered his surprise: what a firm handshake it was from Kensuke this time. The boy smiled. "Mrs. Serikawa taught me how to shake hands like an American."

Cotton nodded, but held on to his hand. "I want you to know something. Today, you pitched the finest game of baseball that any Japanese has pitched anywhere. In Korakuen Stadium, anywhere, ever. Do you know that?"

"Yes, I do, Drake-san."

"Good. That's even more important than pitching the perfect game. That you knew. You'll always have that." They finished their handshake. "Now, I have a present for you. Do you see that lady over there next to Mrs. Serikawa?"

Kensuke peered. "The chubby little one?"

"Yes. When you're finished celebrating with your buddies, you go with her."

"Where?"

"Never mind. Just go with her. Now, you listened to me

once, and I showed you how to be the best pitcher in baseball. Do what I say this time, too."

"Okay, Drake-san."

"Now, Morishita, this must be goodbye. Tomorrow is Easter, the most important Christian holiday, and I have much work to do. And then, something has come up, and I must go to Tokyo. So, goodbye my friend. *Sayonara.*"

The Japanese have never been much for goodbyes. There is no hugging or kissing, and of course Cotton knew that, but he didn't care. He pulled the young man to him and held him in an embrace. "Excuse me for being a *gaijin,*" he said.

"I am honored. And Drake-san, I'll see you after the war."

"I'll pay to see you pitch then." And Kensuke walked off the diamond.

The red sun sets. And now, all the blossoms have fallen to the ground.

Miyuki found Cotton sitting in the last row of the church a couple of hours later. He had his vestments on, because he was going to hold a special Easter Eve service that evening. She sat down next to him, without a word, and pretended to be as pious as he was. Finally, without changing expression, she said: "Cotton, remember you told me about Jesus saying: 'Do unto others as you would have them to unto you'?"

He turned to face her, delighted that she recalled that so clearly. "I certainly do. Why?"

"Oh, I just heard you gave Hanako to Kensuke for the night." His jaw dropped; she had him. "Is that a Christian thing to do?"

"I think it was more of a man thing to do. Are you going to tell the bishop on me?"

"No. I was just thinking about your birthday coming up."

"A necktie would be quite sufficient, thank you."

She elbowed him gently in the ribs and handed him a sheet of paper. "Here. This is for you, from Kiyoshi. It was in the envelope with my letter."

"How is he?" Cotton asked, unfolding the paper.

"I haven't read his letter yet. As soon as I saw this, I came looking for you."

Cotton started to read. It was only a few sentences. It was about Sammy. He threw his hands over his face; a sob choked him. "Oh my God. Oh my God in heaven." And then he leaned forward, his head on the back of the pew before him. Miyuki had to do something. Tentatively, she laid a hand on his neck; just kept it there to let him know she was with him. Cotton was crying so hard—deep, heavy sobs— that it was a long while before he could even find the breath to gasp: "Sammy's been killed. A robbery." She squeezed his neck, but still he didn't move.

At last he straightened himself up and wiped away his tears with his fingers. Then he dried his face on his surplice. "Here," he said, handing her the note, "you can read this." He went up to the altar, knelt before it, and began to pray.

Miyuki read the note, and then she read her letter from Kiyoshi as well. Cotton raised himself up and took a seat alone, in the first pew. After a while Miyuki walked up to him. "Do you want me to leave you now?" she asked.

"No, thank you. Please, stay with me now."

So she sat down next to him, in silence. Eventually, Miyuki said: "I'd like to pray, too."

"All right."

"But I don't know how to pray like a Christian."

"It's easy. You just kneel there and talk to God. You know how to kneel, and you know how to talk." He shrugged.

"I've never talked to your God before. I've never talked to Jesus."

"Well, you could just start by introducing yourself. Then go from there. Okay?"

"Okay," Miyuki said, and she leaned forward and knelt, holding her hands together in prayer, the way she'd seen. She prayed for a while, and then sat back. After more silence, she held up her letter. "Kiyoshi says Kazuko will bring Sammy's ashes here," she said. "He wants you to spread them."

"Oh? I would've thought Sammy'd want them in Hawaii. That was his home. Not Japan." He shrugged. "But then, none of it makes any sense." Miyuki turned to look at him. "I lived in Hawaii. Nobody kills people in daylight robberies on Alakea Street when there's no money worth stealing."

She kept looking at him. "You don't think it was a robbery, do you?"

"I said, it doesn't make any sense." He turned away from her stare. It was disconcerting of Miyuki, a very Western stare.

"You think Kiyoshi did—?" Cotton turned back sharply to her. She rephrased her words. "You think Kiyoshi might be involved?"

"God forgive me if I do."

There was silence awhile before Miyuki finally spoke again. She said: "I do."

"Why would you say a thing like that?"

"Because I think if I knew what you knew, I would think that."

"Miyuki, I don't *know* anything. I swear."

"You don't *know* Jesus either, do you?" He looked at her, uncomfortably. "You don't know Him. But you spend your life telling people to believe in Him." Cotton nodded. He wasn't at all prepared when suddenly, this time, Miyuki burst into tears and fell into his arms. Cotton held her for a long time, in the first pew of his church, under the cross upon the altar on Holy Saturday.

38

Cotton had a second sake, to gird himself. He was in Yoshiwara, at the teahouse, the Matsubaya, getting ready to walk down to the Shinyanagi and deceive Sumiko again. But, of course, as he explained patiently to himself—again—there was no wrongdoing in this. Not really. There was no . . . sin. Enjoying the pleasures of her flesh were simply required by these random circumstances. God knows—don't you know,

God?—that Cotton Drake had not asked for this role, having
to share some of his time doing the Lord's work by taking on
this odd job for President Roosevelt. And if getting laid was
the price of being called upon to play a part in a noble cause,
it was merely a pleasant irony he could joke about with old
pals someday. It's a tough job, but somebody . . . Ha, ha. Ha.

"I'm sorry, sir," the contact man told him, coming over to
Cotton, bowing and scraping, wringing his hands, pulling out
all the contrite stops. "I'm afraid the girl you wish is still with
a very important customer."

Cotton glanced at his watch. Quarter past ten. His appointment with Sumiko at the Shinyanagi had been for ten.
"Helluva way to run a whorehouse," he groused, feigning
bluster.

Of course, the real issue was not how he was deceiving
Sumiko but how much he was deceiving himself. And that
he'd only admit to on the fringes, maybe halfway down a cup
of sake, when the booze had lit him up only a little—not
when he'd done in the whole cup or more, and he was dulled
and dimmed down to where all he wanted to do was agree
with himself. "I'm a man," Cotton told himself—or, anyway,
told the Reverend Mr. Drake. "I'm a man, and to hell with
what my vocation happens to be. I'm still a man, right?"

"Yes, but you are a priest, too," the Reverend Mr. Drake
replied.

"Yeah, sure, but I'm not some damn nancy-boy Catholic
priest, accepting celibacy as the easy way out. Am I?" Cotton
asked.

"Well, no," the Reverend Mr. Drake agreed, pleasing Cotton so much he had another sip of sake.

"Damn straight. I'm of this world, and prostitution is as legal as prayer here—and look, if I happen, just happen, to
gain some natural manly gratification in the bargain of trying
to stop a war and save much of mankind, then don't play
holier-than-thou with me just because I have to . . . uh, fib a
little to the hooker." And he finished the sake and asked for
another, and while he waited, Cotton turned away from his
conversation with the Reverend Mr. Drake and glanced

around at the other men waiting there. And this time he saw himself in them, and he knew damn well that the part about him doing this to save a great deal of mankind was a lie. In fact, Cotton thought, it's bullshit, isn't it?"

And out loud—in a whisper, but still out loud—the Reverend Mr. Drake himself replied: "Yes—bullshit." So they were finally honest with each other, Cotton and the Reverend Mr. Drake. They were in agreement: it was bullshit. It was bullshit because, as the Reverend Mr. Drake reminded Cotton: You can't have Miyuki. You're going crazy living with Miyuki, but you can't have her. The whore is beautiful, a class *oiran,* and she's a nice lady, too, and maybe she even holds the darkest secrets of all Japan. But mostly she's an excuse. She reminds you of Miyuki. She's pretty, like Miyuki, and she has legs like Miyuki, and tits like Miyuki, and she fucks you like you would like to believe Miyuki would if only you could fuck Miyuki. So go down to the American embassy first thing in the morning and tell Bowersox what you do know for sure, and the rest that seems obvious, which is that the Japanese are going to attack Hawaii. And then stop playing spy, stop trying to be some Scarlet Pimpernel in clerical drag, buster, and get back to being a missionary, assuming the standard missionary position. Cotton liked that; he giggled at his play on words. And yes, soon enough find that holy biddy that Liz had in mind for you, the one with her hair up in a bun who played the organ, who could take her rightful place with you in the missionary position. He giggled some more.

The contact man came back with the waitress. "This sake is on the house, compliments of Matsubaya," he said. "Shinyanagi is very sorry for the delay."

Cotton nodded at him. He took the cup. Drink it and go home, go back to the Serikawas' house, go see Bowersox tomorrow, and then go to Tochigi and tell Miyuki, "Thank you very much for all your help, but please go. Take your mother and get your ass out of here, away from yours truly." He looked up at the contact man. "Uh—look," Cotton said, "it's late. Just tell Shinyanagi, thanks but no thanks."

The man shooed the waitress away. "Oh no, no, no. They

assured me: it'll just be a few minutes." He leaned down, beckoning to Cotton. "A general," he whispered. "A very big general. You know how these things are."

"Certainly," Cotton said. And to himself: Teshima. It must be Teshima. Well . . . He threw down the drink and sprang up. "All right, I'll walk down to Shinyanagi and wait there."

The little Japanese scurried after Cotton. "No, no, no, please. That's not the proper procedure, sir."

"It's not the proper procedure to let somebody stay with a whore past another man's hour," and Cotton stomped out the door, down the Oiran Douchou, to the side street where Shinyanagi was located. The contact man from Matsubaya had already called, and the manager, Okumura, was waiting, nervously, proffering his most obsequious apologies. "I understand your predicament," Cotton said, trying to put the German accent back into Otto's Japanese. "General Teshima is a powerful man."

"Yes, yes," Okumura mumbled, bowing. So, it was indeed Teshima. Cotton was ushered into the manager's office, where Okumura assured him he could wait in comfort. Alas, though, more time passed, and Okumura grew more embarrassed. "Cannot I offer you another girl? We have many fine *oiran*—"

"All right—Hanako!" Cotton thundered. "I hear she's terrific." What the hell, he knew she was staying in Tochigi with her parents—that was the whole reason he'd arranged to come down now—but he might as well put in a good word for her with the boss.

That completely rattled Okumura. "Oh, I am sorry, but Hanako is away for a few days. But we have several more—"

"No, no. If not Sumiko, only Hanako." The poor manager was distraught, shamed. Cotton was afraid he was going to go out and commit seppuku. "So, I wait for Sumiko," he said quickly.

And before much more time passed, Cotton heard some commotion down the hall, and when the manager popped up and ran out, Cotton peered through the *noren*, and there stood

Yoichi Teshima, smart in his general's uniform, but also drunk and smirking.

Cotton couldn't help himself. He brushed past the manager into the corridor, so that Teshima would at least have to consider him as he passed by. Then Cotton looked down on the stocky little man, enjoying the view.

Still, Teshima managed to look back up at Cotton uncowed, with presence. "I keep you waiting, *gaijin?*"

The manager covered his face in fear. "Yes, General, you did," said Cotton.

Teshima took out a cigarette and measured Cotton as he lit it. "I went twice," he said, and he laughed loudly.

Cotton offered no response.

"So what are you, *gaijin?* What country?"

"German."

"Ah." Teshima brightened at this, and he clapped Cotton drunkenly on the shoulder. "Our great ally. I'm sorry. I wouldn't have kept a German waiting. I thought you were one of those goddamn Americans."

"Nein, mein General," Cotton replied. He was feeling rather devilish.

"Ah, ja, ja, Freund—" Teshima held up a finger, indicating that he had more to say. But he was too drunk, and after a moment or two he gave it up and went back to Japanese. "Oh shit, it's been three years since I was in Germany, and I can't remember anything else."

"I understand, General Teshima," Cotton said, retreating back to Japanese himself.

"Well, listen, German, you like good Scotch?" Cotton nodded. "Okay, you tell Sumiko to give you a drink of my bottle. This is a great honor for her, to be able to fuck a German. You"—he waved a finger in Cotton's face—"you got all that hair on your body. Japanese girls love all that hair. Of course, I got a better prick than you!" He roared, and Cotton did the best he could to fake laughing with him. Uneasily, then, Teshima fell a little to the side, so that he had to reach out to grab Cotton to hold his balance. *"Danke schön.* And what is your name, German?"

"Otto. Otto von Kohorn."

"Otto. Otto. And what business are you in?"

"Shipping." And Cotton added gratuitously: "I was in Hawaii." He paused then, carefully examining Teshima's reaction.

For whatever it was worth, Teshima drew back. "You're in Hawaii now?"

"No, in the past. I'm mostly in Nagasaki now."

That was enough of the institutional niceties for Teshima. He was really quite drunk. And so, loudly, with a final flourish: *"Auf Wiedersehen, Freund Otto."*

"Auf Wiedersehen, mein General." And Cotton turned down the corridor toward Sumiko's room.

She was waiting just inside the *noren* in a sunset orange and jet black kimono. She'd heard his voice, and changed and primped, and now her eyes lit up, as she turned her face this way and that to show him it was smooth and pretty again. "You said you wouldn't be here for another week."

"Things moved quickly," Cotton said, and he took her in his arms, and first he kissed that side of her face where Teshima had belted her, and then he kissed her on the lips, full and long. He wanted to take her right then, but he made himself wait, and so he told her how Teshima had invited him to share his Scotch. Sumiko opened the cabinet and she took a drink with Cotton. They both cooed and flirted, and then Cotton opened her kimono and drew his fingers all over her body, as if he were somehow tracing Miyuki. And then he kissed her, tracing her the same way with his tongue, starting at Sumiko's mouth, down her neck to her breasts, kissing them both, licking them, one after another, then burying his head between them, holding her tighter, closing his eyes, trying to pretend that she was Miyuki. That was hard to do, though, because as much as he loved Miyuki, Sumiko was so beautiful, too, and, even better, Sumiko knew how to take him, right then, to a sort of place where Cotton had always been taught that only souls—and, really, at that, only the best of souls—could aspire to.

The next morning, since Cotton knew Hanako was away, he went to pick up Sumiko at the apartment. She met him in a wonderful *moga* outfit, a spring dress of gray and maroon, shoes that matched the gray, and a hat with a long feather in it, as fashionable as anything Cotton remembered from the States. He thought, Oh, how I'd like to see Miyuki in this! But then he told himself: You must not do that anymore. It's not fair to Sumiko. You will never think Miyuki's name when you're with her.

And, of course, that was easy. It was like that ancient tale about how easy it is to turn lead into gold: you simply put the lead into a large pot and bring it to a boil without ever once thinking of the word "hippopotamus." So as soon as he held Sumiko and kissed Sumiko, he thought: Miyuki.

They caught a cab down to the Ginza, the driver hooking on to the streetcar tracks when he could and driving like a madman when he could not. Cotton was convinced that Tokyo taxi drivers must have considered it a matter of face ever to downshift. But then, by now the streets were all but empty of private cars, and the cabs weaved in and out of the bicycles and ox carts and *jin-riki-sha* that had suddenly reappeared lately, as the bad times grew even worse.

In the department store they went to, the salesgirls flitted around what few shoppers there were. Cotton and Sumiko had tea, and he bought her a flower parasol that picked up the maroon in her dress. They strolled some more and stopped for lunch, and he let her tell him all about Japan, because, of course, Otto was from Germany. She was so excited. "Do you know what this is?" she asked, as they left the restaurant.

"What is?"

"What you and me are doing?" He shook his head, not understanding what she was getting at. "I have seen it in the American movies. It is called a date." She said the last word in English, because, of course, there was no such word in Japanese.

"Date?" Cotton repeated.

"Date. We are a date," and she took and squeezed his hand with joy—forgetting even to make sure no one saw her couple openly with a *gaijin*. Cotton grinned happily. It was a crazy thing to think about a whore, but Sumiko was so wonderfully, well, innocent.

Just then, they happened upon a Shinto shrine, where some special ceremony was under way. Sumiko took her hand from his, put it to her lips, hushing him, and then she showed him in, directing Cotton to seats in the back. They heard a big drum and turned to see the man who was beating it leading other musicians in, all of them wearing robes of orange silk covered with green gauze. "What is this?" Cotton whispered. He wasn't pretending; he didn't have a clue. But then, neither did Sumiko; she shook her head.

Priests followed, performing a great deal of ritual purifying. "Who are they?" Cotton beckoned to the men seated before the altar. Sumiko shook her head again. Then the chief priest passed out the most spectacular variety of vegetables— daikons, sweet potatoes, the long Japanese carrots, all sorts of bounty—and sake too. Everybody there was brought the feast, even the two strangers on a date in the back. It had overtones of communion, Cotton thought, except it was altogether joyful here.

Only when the priests started chanting, then, did Sumiko and Cotton catch onto what it was about. The men in front of the altar were all from the poultry trade, from the shops and restaurants that featured chicken dishes, and this was their annual ceremony for the repose of the chickens whose grateful deaths had kept these gentlemen so prosperous. "It's for chickens," Sumiko whispered.

Cotton had broken the code himself, but he had to play dumb. "Chickens?" he asked, flapping his arms like wings.

"Yes. These are the men who make their livings with chickens, so they are praying for the chickens they slaughter." Cotton screwed up his face. "It's very Japanese," Sumiko acknowledged. "All spirits, all over Japan. There are so many spirits."

"Even chicken spirits?" She smiled and briefly took his

hand, yanking him out of the shrine. "Hey, where're we going, Sumiko?"

Outside, she said: "In the movies, the American date ends with love." She reached up and pecked him on the cheek.

"Fine with me."

"You are my *aijin*." She couldn't believe she had said that, but, of course, Otto probably wouldn't know the word. It meant "lover."

"What's an *aijin?*"

Sumiko handed her parasol to Cotton and put her right hand over her heart and her left hand over it. "It's very *moga*," she explained.

They took a taxi back to her apartment. It was a third-floor walk-up, small and spare, tight for one person, let alone for Sumiko and Hanako both, but in comparison with the accommodations that most whores—or female factory workers, for that matter—could expect in Tokyo, it was a *suite royale*. Indeed, many of the poor whores in the standard Yoshiwara brothels still lived secluded ghetto lives, barely able to escape their rooms, but Sumiko and Hanako and their other colleagues at the Shinyanagi were the top of the line, the most elegant or entertaining *oiran* that Yoshiwara could offer the carriage trade.

Proudly then, Sumiko swept her arm around her room, past the one *kakejiku*—an old charcoal brush painting—on the wall, past the one dresser, the one large mirror. She beamed. "Neat, you see," she said. "We just had *oosuiji*, the big spring cleanup, the other day."

"Very nice. You earned a white paper."

"Yes." She pointed to the door. "You know Japanese customs so well. Would you like some tea?"

Cotton shook his head. "I only want you now, Sumiko." She smiled back, shyly, and since she still held her new parasol, she opened it up and played the coquette, twirling it before her face. Cotton stepped toward her, and she peeked out at him. He took her by the hips and looked deep into her eyes.

And then Cotton stopped abruptly. He took his hand off her and turned away. "I'm sorry, but I'm still very angry."

Sumiko went undone, aghast. What could she possibly have done to offend him so? "Otto, what did I do?"

Cotton turned back, but he kept his face grim. "No, I'm not mad at you. I'm mad at General Teshima."

Sumiko looked even more stricken at that. "Because he made me late for you last night?"

"I didn't like that, but it is my great anger that when I saw him at Shinyanagi, I remembered again he hit you, and I wanted to hit him." And he drove his fist into the palm of his other hand.

Sumiko grabbed for the lapels of his Norfolk jacket. "No, no, Otto, you must never even think that. General Teshima is such a powerful man, and he is so mean."

"But he hit you, Sumiko, and I—" He caressed her cheek, sensing her soften at his touch, and pleased that she did, too. She was so sweet; there was so much of Cotton that had grown proud and happy that such a lovely thing could love him.

"Please, I told you, Otto, he didn't mean to hit me. He was having an argument with Admiral Sakamaki—"

"Why do you protect Teshima?" Cotton twisted away from her again, tormenting her, playing on her emotions.

"No, no. I promise, he—"

Cotton turned back, his face angrier yet. "Then you tell me now: why is this argument so important that Teshima would fight the navy captain?"

He could see: he had her. She was on the defensive, so smitten with him, her dear *gaijin*, that she was unable to see through to what he was really after. "It was just some stupid military argument, Otto," she began. She must not let Cotton stay angry, for he was a man first—a customer—but he was also the one man she wanted to please. In all her life. Besides, what subtlety had Sumiko ever encountered with any *gaijin*? Her only experience was with men, cash on the line—fuck me, Sumiko, suck me, do it on top, on bottom, this way, that way. It was the curious, perverse truth that this prostitute from the Tokyo demimonde actually knew little about the kind of lying and deception that most people are trained to anticipate.

"So? What?" Cotton growled.

Sumiko tried to remember. Whores—women—heard things they were conditioned to pretend they didn't hear. "They were both so drunk, and the admiral was teasing the general, which is not a very wise thing to do."

"Tease? This caused a big fight? You'd make a fool of me, Sumiko."

"No, wait. It was about how the navy had this major plan going. I remember. General Teshima screamed that the whole operation was crazy, bad for Japan. And Sakamaki-san kept laughing that the general was just mad because it was the navy in charge and—"

"Why?"

"Why's what?"

"Why the navy in charge?"

Sumiko searched her mind. She didn't know. If anything, she was pleased with herself that she had recalled even this much. "I don't remember, Otto."

Cotton wouldn't let up. He had her on the run. "I can't believe this. You protect Teshima. He just hit you. There was no argument with Admiral Sakamaki."

"Yes, yes, there was." She reached out to touch him. Why did he have to ruin her wonderful date with all this old, unimportant fuss between two drunks?

"You care too much for Teshima."

"No, no, I hate him, Otto. But he is just such a good customer. I—wait. Wait." Something came back to her. "I remember now. General Teshima kept saying, 'It's crazy, it's the wrong way.'"

Cotton grabbed her shoulders. "The wrong way? The wrong way from what?"

Sumiko thought hard. "From the oil, from the rubber. Operation Z—I remember, that's what it was called—was . . . it was seven thousand miles the wrong way from the oil."

"Operation Z?"

"Yes."

"And then they fight?" She nodded.

"Yes, I told you that. They were drunk. They are always arguing silly military things. And I just got caught in the middle. You see?"

Cotton had squeezed enough out of her. He backed off now. At some point, even the whore would grow suspicious of his questions. "Okay. But if Teshima hurts you again, I'll hit him."

"He won't, I promise. Please." And she fell against his chest and let him hold her. She had him back to herself, returned from all the military foolishness. Cotton smoothed her hair back, and then they kissed, standing up, in the middle of the room, and she could feel his ardor, matching hers, hard against her body, and she fumbled to open his belt and the buttons on his fly, just as he reached around her to pull the zipper down the back of the maroon and gray dress.

Cotton took her hand from his fly, but Sumiko had only a moment to look hurt. "No, no, Sumiko," and he held her gently by the shoulders. "You always must undress men. Let me undress you this time." And he did, every stitch—the maroon and gray dress falling off her shoulders, down over her hips to the floor. She started to step out of it, but Cotton laid a hand on her arm. "Now, please—I said let me," and this time she followed his orders and stood still, as he took off her bra next, and then her slip, and the moga high heels after that, Cotton falling to his knees to remove them. And from where he knelt, he pulled down the panties and the stockings, until there she was, naked, as he looked up to her, only golden skin and ebony hair, this gorgeous brocade of a woman before his eyes.

Cotton rose to his feet, and though they stared at each other, it was only for a moment, for then he swept her up in his arms, carried her across to the bed mats, and laid her gently down. Sumiko had to catch her breath. Why, this was even better than the dates in the American movies! Cotton knelt before her, watching her while he removed his coat and his tie and his shirt, throwing them aside. Then he leaned over her, softly rubbing both her breasts at once. Sumiko closed her eyes and sighed.

"All right," Cotton said. "You can help now." And even as he kept both his hands upon her breasts, she opened her eyes and reached for his fly again. Soon they kissed, and they made love all the rest of the afternoon, the noise from the streets below drifting up, the vendors and the newsboys, and once, as if on cue, exactly as they came to climax, the drums and the saxophone of a *chindonya* band, suddenly playing outside, trying to summon attention to some new shop down the street.

"I make love to Sumiko, I hear music," Cotton laughed.

She clapped her hands, like cymbals, and nestled in the crook of his arm, so happy, she was sure, that he could hear her smile. Maybe he could even smell her smile, too. Surely it smelled like the magnolias, which were just blooming now. "Otto?"

"Yes?"

"Do you think you can hear a smile? Can you smell a smile?"

"What? My Japanese isn't that good."

"I think so," Sumiko went on anyway. "If someone is that happy."

He swallowed. She loved him even more than he had imagined—and all the worse, Cotton had come to like her so much—not for reminding him of Miyuki—but just for being Sumiko. Silently, Cotton prayed for Gods' forgiveness—or at least His understanding.

She interrupted his thoughts. "You know what?"

"No."

"In the mornings now, when I wake up, I can tell you right away how clear the air is outside."

"How?"

"Just by listening."

Cotton pinched her gently in her cheeks. "You *hear* the smiles *outside?*"

She laughed. "No. But almost. If the voices on the street are loud and easy to understand, then it means that the peo-

ple have not put on their *masuku* yet. So, no masks, no bad
fumes. Not yet, anyway. When the voices are muffled,
though, I know everybody has their *masuku* on, and it'll be an
ugly day, especially hard to breathe."

"I see."

Sumiko rolled over then, resting on an elbow. With her
other hand she brushed his hair back. "You are so handsome,
Otto. I like you even better when you take your eyeglasses
off."

"I like you even better with your clothes off."

She giggled, and turned back over, lying with her head on
his chest. After a while she said: "You know, it's hard to remember, but when I first came to Tokyo, the air didn't used
to be that bad."

"Where're you from?"

"Fukuoka. You know it?"

"No," he lied.

"It's on Kyushu. You should know Fukuoka. The train goes
through it to Nagasaki."

"Oh. Oh yeah."

"Kyushunjin are the best Japanese. We're the nicest. We
have the most patience. The people from Osaka are the worst
Japanese. Work, work, work. 'Are you making any money today?' That's all they say. And Tokyo, the people here are the
most active. Hurry, hurry, hurry, all the time. Kyushu—we're
the most relaxed."

"And the sweetest," Cotton said flirting.

For that, she turned over and kissed him on his chest. "We
have the roundest eyes, too. See? And we're the darkest." She
picked up his arm and wrapped hers in it, intertwined.
"Other Japanese girls you sleep with are lighter, aren't they?"

"I don't sleep with any other Japanese girls anymore," Cotton said, and for that she snuggled up and kissed him on the
cheek.

After a bit she raised her head and looked into his eyes. He
could tell she was nervous. "Can I ask you a moga question?"

"Uh-huh."

Sumiko caught her breath. "Are you married?"

"No."

"I mean, nowhere in the world?"

"Marriage is everywhere," he laughed. "I'm not married anywhere."

She smiled at that and put her head down next to his again. "I wanted to be married by now," she said. "When I came to Yoshiwara, I thought it would only be two, three years, maybe, make some money, and go back to Kyushu before I became a Christmas cake, an old maid. But then, so many things happen, and all the men are in the damn army, they're all in China or in Operation Z." She lifted up her head and winked; she knew he'd like that. "And so, I stay."

"How long will you stay?"

"I don't know. Once, last year, there was a businessman here, very prominent in a large *zaibatsu*, and he wanted me to be his *omekakesan*, his second wife. It was all arranged. He was very wealthy—he could afford an *omekakesan* easily. But then, at the last minute he told me the war was getting too big, the economy bad. It was too risky, taking me on."

"Big mistake, to pass you up."

"Maybe if you stay in Japan and find a first wife and war doesn't come and you keep making money, maybe you can take me as an *omekakesan*."

Cotton closed his eyes and asked again for God's forgiveness. It wasn't easy, stopping war. But then Sumiko reached down and caressed him and, when he was hard, took him in her mouth, and once again Cotton forgot altogether about God and war, both.

There was something particularly dirty about leaving Sumiko's and going directly to the American embassy. Cotton walked a long time before he looked for a streetcar. To report on anything that went on between himself and Sumiko seemed so tawdry, so . . . so un-American. It distorted the one thing in his life that should have been so uncomplicated and lovely: the two of them, the priest and the whore, finding in each other now what they couldn't get from anyone else.

There was even a part of him that was relieved, then, when the receptionist with the southern accent told him that Mr. Bowersox was away. Still, he felt obliged to ask for his secretary, to find out when Bowersox would be back. Damn it, it must matter a great deal that a Japanese naval captain and a Japanese general have been arguing about a major operation that was pointed to hit seven thousands miles away from oil and rubber—from Southeast Asia. Even allowing for hyperbole, where could the navy be landing? In inland Siberia? That must be about seven thousand miles. Africa? Come on, nothing fit—nothing ever fit except Hawaii.

"Mr. Drake?" Bowersox's secretary had come out to meet him.

"I was just wondering when Saint would be back, when—"

"I'm sorry, but Mr. Bowersox is on a mission out of town, and we don't know when he'll return."

"All right, thank you. I'll call the next time I'm back in Tokyo." Cotton turned to go, but then he swung back. "Well, perhaps I could see Ambassador Grew for a few minutes."

"I'm sorry, Mr. Drake, but the ambassador and Mrs. Grew have stolen off to Karuizawa for a few days' holiday." That was a resort, northwest of Tokyo, up in the mountains, favored by foreigners. "Would you like me to leave word with Ambassador Grew's secretary?"

Cotton shook his head. "No, never mind, thank you. It's nothing that can't wait till Saint returns." So there was nothing more he could do about it now. He knew he would go back to Sumiko and try to learn more from her about General Teshima's information. What else could he do? After all, more deceit on his part could only be a technical matter of degree. His duplicity was already established—even God was in that loop.

39

It became a routine for Cotton, then. His baseball team had no games scheduled Mondays or Tuesdays, so almost every week he would say goodbye to Miyuki and take the train into Tokyo on "church business." Miyuki would leave the kindergarten and watch him start his walk to the station, swinging his arms as he stepped out, striding down the Street That Goes Along the River. Whatever it was, it wasn't the way a man went off on church business. Miyuki knew that much.

She missed him as soon as he left her, and always that evening, Monday, she would leave the rectory after dinner with her mother and walk by the river herself, and stand there at the one place in all the world where Cotton Drake had taken Miyuki Serikawa in his arms and kissed her.

By then, Cotton would already be with Sumiko. First, when he got to Tokyo, he would go over to the Serikawas' house, become Otto again there, then go meet Sumiko at the Shinyanagi, paying for her services just like any customer (though getting somewhat more attention, and some of General Teshima's Scotch as well). The next morning, Sumiko would come meet him at the Serikawa house—he told her his company was renting it—and then they'd do the town together, all day, just another moga and mobo out on a real date.

Sometimes Cotton would find a way to ask her about General Teshima. "Why do you always want to know about him?" she replied—not mad, not curious really, only teasing him.

"I just want to check on him, make sure he never hits you again." He was her protector. Someday, he knew, she would tell him something else. It was a fair bargain, wasn't it? As long as Bowersox wasn't available for Cotton to report to, it didn't seem so dishonest. It didn't hardly seem like sinning. She was just a contact, and it was just . . . dates.

Each Tuesday they'd do something new, something distinctly Japanese. Once he let her take him to the Kabuki, another time to the doll theater. One particularly beautiful afternoon Sumiko decided that it was time that her German saw a baseball game, and so she took him out to Korakuen to watch the Giants. How pleased she was when a foul ball came their way and Otto snared it with one hand! Then afterwards, they would stroll in the spring sun and go back to the Serikawas' house and make love, until it was time for Sumiko to go to work at the Shinyanagi. And then he would go grab the train to Tochigi, back to his parishioners.

That particular Tuesday, after the baseball game, when it was time for her to leave him, she said: "Will you be back in Tokyo next week, too?" He always told her that he traveled most of the week—Kobe, Nagasaki, Shanghai, and so forth.

"I think so."

She shook his face in her hands. "Will you stay all night with me, Otto? I want to wake up with you one morning, like a real *aijin.*"

"But you need to work nights."

"I'll call in sick."

So that next Tuesday evening he stayed over, and they went out to a Yose, a special Japanese comedy, and then afterwards, he took her to the Mimi Bluette, which was the most intimate bar in the Ginza. Sumiko felt more like a moga that night than at any other time. And when she heard the birds sing in the morning, she remembered where she was, and she snuggled into Cotton's arms and glowed.

Unfortunately, when Sumiko tried to pull the same trick two weeks later, Mr. Okumura, the manager of the Shinyanagi, didn't believe her. Someone had already told him about how they'd seen Sumiko running around town with her *gaijin* customer. Mr. Okumura wasn't born yesterday. He had somebody tail Sumiko, picking her up at her apartment, following her to the Serikawas' house, where she met up with

Cotton, and then, this day, onto the Sanja Festival at the
Asakusa Shrine at Sensoji. The tail got the goods on her.

The next morning, when Sumiko showed up at the Shinyanagi, Mr. Okumura confronted her. "I'm sorry, Okumura-
san," Sumiko said, putting one hand to her forehead, "but I
was so sick all yesterday, and even now I still feel a little
weak."

Whereupon, the manager signaled to the man who had followed Sumiko with Cotton all day yesterday, and he immediately began to recount her adventures; he even held up a
snapshot he'd made of them in Sensoji.

Sumiko was mortified, but even before she could apologize,
Okumura hauled back and slapped her full across the face.
Sumiko bowed, holding back the tears; and as she kept that
position, head down, Okumura went on to say that not only
was he docking her full pay for the week but he would fire
her if she ever pulled a fast one again. In fact, he would have
booted her out right on the spot, but the Shinyanagi made
more money off Sumiko than any other whore.

Sumiko never told Cotton what happened. They just went
back to sharing days. In fact, it was somewhat ironic, for the
next Tuesday, May 27, was the thirty-sixth anniversary of
Tsushima, of the Z signal. There were flags flying everywhere
in celebration, bands and parades of military might. Sumiko
and Cotton went back to the Serikawas' house, just as it
started to pour. The baiu, the rainy season, was coming to
Tokyo.

"Guess what?" Sumiko asked, as they lay on the tatami after love, listening to the rain. "General Teshima is going
away."

"Oh?"

"You always care so much about him. He's leaving for
Kagoshima."

"Where's that?"

"Kyushu, but the farthest south." Cotton knew. He'd been
to Kagoshima once. It would be the equivalent of Miami in
the United States.

"What's down there?"

"Maneuvers." The way she said that, though, it was more of a question. She couldn't explain what the maneuvers were for, or, really, what maneuvers were. But Cotton was delighted that she'd brought the subject of Teshima up. All his pressuring her had paid off again, just when he'd given up hope.

"So," he asked, as naturally as he could, "what makes Teshima angry now?"

"Oh, that's easy," she laughed. It was fun making fun of Teshima. "Torpedoes. Torpedoes. He's always bitching about our torpedoes."

"What about them?"

"Something doesn't work just right. They go too deep in the water." She shrugged. "Do you know, I'm not even sure what torpedoes do! Do you?"

He took a finger and traced it up her body. "They're water bombs. They go along right near the top of the water, and when they come to a ship"—his finger came softly up her stomach, past her belly button, till it reached the base of one of her breasts—"it goes boom!" And he made the noise and drummed his fingers all over her breast. She giggled. "So, if the torpedoes are too deep"—he started his finger up her belly again—"they"—and he lifted the finger off of her and drew it in the air, over her breast—"miss the target."

The planes, Cotton thought: they would be firing torpedoes at the American ships. The Japanese are experimenting, trying to get the right angle for the torpedoes, coming out of the sky instead of out of submarines.

She took his hand and laid it on the breast it had bypassed. "I can see why the General Teshima is angry. I don't like the torpedoes that miss the target either."

The Serikawas' was their love nest, each Tuesday. Before she left the house that particular day, Sumiko even searched the closets. Then, she took down from the walls the pictures of the snow-covered branches and the pine trees on the mountain and put up the summer ones she found, one of huge camellias with their scarlet blossoms, the other of a moon shining on a bridge over a river. "There," she said.

"Even if you just rent our house"—she said that so naturally, in the first person *plural*—"you still have to put the summer pictures up." And she kissed him and said, "I'm trying so hard to make you Japanese, so I can keep you forever, Otto," and took her umbrella and went off to her job, just like any working girl.

Cotton always would call the embassy then, before he headed over to the Asakusa station for the train back; but each time, he found out that no, Mr. Boxersox hadn't returned from his special assignment, and each time, Cotton still wasn't sure that he wanted him back.

Early in June, after his usual weekly trip into Tokyo, Cotton came back to Tochigi and had dinner with Miyuki and Mrs. Serikawa. The electricity had been reduced in most of the perfecture, though, and he went to bed early, as soon as it was dark. But he couldn't fall off to sleep, so he heard Miyuki when she got up and came down the steps and stared at him.

Miyuki had decided she must talk to Cotton alone. Of course, she always wanted to talk to Cotton alone. But this time she had been thinking: I can be a Christian. I want to be one, and I can be one. If I can't have Cotton, at least I can be in Cotton's flock. I can be that part of Cotton, anyway, I can be baptized.

At first, when he saw her coming down the stairs, he played possum. But he couldn't stop himself and he opened his eyes and called softly to her. "Hi, Beautiful Snow," he said.

She padded over and crouched down next to where he lay, propped up on one elbow. "I'm sorry, Cotton, I didn't mean to wake—" She stopped. She didn't have the nerve to just start right in about baptism—all the more so now, as she crouched beside his bed. She had to drop her eyes from his face, and that was worse, for her vision fell upon his broad, bare shoulders, coming out from under the sheet, and she knew he had nothing on under that sheet, and she could not get that out of her mind.

"You didn't wake me," he said. "I couldn't sleep. It's so hot."

"Yes. I guess it's going to be a hot summer."

And then Cotton pushed himself up, decorously keeping the sheet as cover. It fell into his lap, and he was bare to the waist, the moonlight coming over his shoulders. He brushed his fair hair back, and Miyuki caught herself and tried to start again. "I just came down because—"

"Yes?"

"I hope I'm not being nosy, but you, uh, just seemed so worried when you came back from Tokyo today."

She could feel his eyes going over her, even though there was just a pinch of moonlight sliding through the windows. Maybe it was the dark that emboldened Cotton. "You know me too well," he said.

"Perhaps."

"Well, really I wasn't worried," Cotton went on. "But close enough. I was upset. Or maybe angry. At myself."

Miyuki hesitated again, angling her eyes just away from his. Finally: "You're seeing someone in Tokyo, aren't you?"

"Women's intuition, huh?" Cotton said.

No, she thought: lovers' intuition. Jealousy. She lied nicely: "It's good you have a girl. You need a girl. I thought maybe you were just snooping around Tokyo, being dangerous. A girl is better. So, why are you upset?"

"It's complicated."

"Not more of that Christian guilt, is it?"

"No. It's just that I really haven't been fair to her. I haven't been honest."

"Oh?"

"I don't love her," he said. "I care for her very much, but I don't love her." He paused just short of saying "like I do you," but Miyuki heard it anyway. Her heart raced, catching up with dreams: *He still loves me.* Cotton ground his teeth in the dark, furious with himself. Here he had a chance to distance himself from Miyuki, to let her know there was another woman; and what did he do? He diminished the other woman. Because: *I still love her.*

They stared at each other, and for just a moment he began to move toward her lips. But he stopped. "Go away, please, Miyuki. Go away now."

She nodded, stood back up without a word, and headed up to her room. At the steps, though, she turned. She knew he was still watching her.

"Please," Cotton said in English. "Please, Beautiful Snow."

"Do you ever see me in the back of church Sundays?" she said.

"Yes, I do."

"I listen to your sermons. Sometimes, I go get them off your desk after church, because I can understand them better if I read them. And I read the Bible each night. I pray, Cotton. I pray all the time."

"What do you pray?"

"Never mind. But I know God is listening to my prayers, and He wants me to be a Christian."

"You're sure?"

"I want you to baptize me."

Cotton sighed. "We have to wait till Kiyoshi comes back, so we can discuss it with him."

"Why?" She put her hands on her hips. "Kiyoshi can't tell me anything about Jesus."

"I know, but—"

"Am I the only person in Japan you *don't* want to be a Christian?"

"Please, Miyuki. Please."

"You are destroying me every way, Cotton," Miyuki said. "First my heart. Now my soul." And she went back on up the stairs.

At least his team kept winning. But even that was different now, since Kensuke had gone away. Two more of the older players were drafted, and another two had their notices. Cotton scared up some older men and even brought in a precocious fifteen-year-old to fill in, and Tochigi somehow stayed in first place. After all, the other teams were all losing players to the army, too. Finally, Tejiro and Sakao came to Cotton at the rectory one day and asked him to play as well as manage, and when he was sure the whole team wanted him, he took over at third base. In his first game, he homered to left center with a man on and started an around-the-horn double play that ended the game, 8–7.

So Cotton became even more of a hero in Tochigi. The people waved to him in the streets, bowed to him in the bath, and even came to try out the church. To the absolute amazement of the Episcopal Mission District of Tokyo, the little church up in Tochigi was actually increasing its rolls, while the membership of every other Christian parish throughout Japan was plummeting.

Unfortunately, Cotton's star status distinguished him only so far as Tochigi and the church were concerned. His movements were monitored, he knew, and his mail and telephone calls checked. Poor Mrs. Serikawa couldn't even make a harmless call to her sister-in-law down in the little town of Aimoto without being eavesdropped on, and when Liz Taliaferro sent Cotton a photograph of herself with her new baby boy, the censors did such a sloppy job of opening the letter that the photograph was slightly torn.

Oh well, he took out the picture and studied it. Glanced at the baby, studied Liz. She still seemed so pretty to him—there was a pang for having given up anyone so good-looking. But mostly he only mused on how long ago she seemed to have been in his life. And Liz was, now, long ago—five years. And how far away she seemed! But that was only because Miyuki was close. It wasn't a matter of the time gone by, he knew. The years had nothing to do with it. Liz could have seemed like yesterday if it weren't for Miyuki.

He tossed the photograph into a desk drawer and went over to the church to meet with the ladies of the altar guild. They were already gathered in the front pews, fanning themselves from the heat. "Would we be cooler outside, by the river?" Cotton asked, and they all looked at each other and decided to stay.

"The sun is even more hot," Mrs. Uchida said.

It was mostly a refresher course on the altar duties, so Cotton began talking about his vestments and how he wanted the communion silver handled. But then he heard footsteps in the back and looked up to see Captain Kato and Chief Hiranuma enter. Maybe the women would have turned around anyway, out of curiosity; but when they saw the worried expression on Cotton's face, they all swiveled about immediately.

"It's all right, Mr. Drake—we'll wait till you're finished," the chief called out, and they took seats.

Cotton began to speak to the ladies again, bringing out the chalice. But immediately he could tell he had lost them. There was not a person left in Tochigi who would not be concerned if either the army or the police arrived on his doorstep. The altar guild ladies kept looking back surreptitiously, then glancing over to one another. Cotton could see it was useless. "You know," he said as casually as he could, "I think it's very rude for us to keep Captain Kato and Chief Hiranuma waiting. They're such important men. So let me discuss what business they may have, and then I'll return to finish our meeting."

The women murmured their approval, and Cotton strode down the aisle, then escorted the two men across the yard and over to his office. They looked very grim indeed, even passing on his offer of tea. "I hope this is important," Cotton said. "Some of these old ladies walked a long way in the heat."

"Yes, it is important, Drake-san," Kato replied, his tone as grave as the manner both men presented.

"Well, then, what is it?"

"I am sorry, but there have been complaints, and"—a long pause—"and you will not be allowed to play on the baseball team anymore."

Inwardly, Cotton sighed with relief. He'd come to expect nothing short of being expelled from Japan. The baseball team, for God's sweet sake! But he kept his own severe countenance, only switching it from concern to irritation. "What? I live in Tochigi. The people here asked me to play."

"That's true. But you are a *gaijin*, and though we may know you, the people from the other towns in the league don't."

"But isn't it better for the league to have as many good players as possible in these difficult times?" Cotton had learned by now that it was always wise to say "in these difficult times," or some sympathetic variation thereof.

Hiranuma nodded vigorously, but he also looked away, and Cotton could tell there was more. "This is true, Mr. Drake, but I would humbly recommend that you do not protest. You see, there has also been a complaint about Mrs. Serikawa."

"Miyuki?"

Hiranuma was embarrassed. He glanced over to Kato. "Well, both Mrs. Serikawas."

Cotton actually said: "Huh?"

"You see, one of the officials from Oyama demands that I report both the ladies to the *tokko*, the secret police, so that they will have their citizenship taken from them."

"What in the world are you talking about?"

Kato stepped forward. "It's a very sensitive point, but the new National Defense Security Law stipulates that any Japanese woman living with a *gaijin* must forfeit her status as a Japanese."

"You can't be serious."

"That is the law, Drake-san. Passed last month, in force now. These are perilous times for our country."

"Kato-san, I do not dispute that that is the law, but surely it was never intended to refer to a woman simply residing in the same building with a *gaijin*. Certainly, it means marriage, cohabitation, not—"

"I would think so," Hiranuma said. "But I have read the law, and it is not clear on this matter. And the official in Oyama is persistent."

"I should never have gone three-for-four against them over there the other day," Cotton said ruefully.

The both smiled, grateful for a little humor. "Exactly," Kato said. "But if you step down from playing, and if you move out of this house, I'm sure the gentleman from Oyama will be satisfied."

"Move out of here? Out of the rectory?"

"You can sleep in the church. That will satisfy the *tokko*."

Sullenly, Cotton leaned forward. "There's not toilet in the church. Does the guy in Oyama know if the National Security Defense Law allows Miyuki and her mother to maintain their citizenship if a *gaijin* goes over and pees in the same house?"

"That is permissible," Kato declared, trying to maintain his military bearing.

"Thank you," Cotton said.

But Hiranuma cleared his throat and said: "There is one more thing."

"I'm all ears."

"Another teacher in the elementary school has been drafted, and we will need Mrs. Serikawa to take his place."

"I am not Mrs. Serikawa's husband. As you know, I don't even live in the same building with her. You'll have to take this up with her."

"I'm afraid it is required," Kato replied, and this time without so much consideration in his voice. "Or if she prefers, she may go to work in the geta factory." That's the way they still referred to the airplane parts factory.

Cotton bowed without disputing that amiable fraud. "I'm sure she'd rather teach than work in the geta factory. I'll teach the kindergarten here myself." Or close it down, he thought.

The two officials bowed and departed. Hiranuma, though, turned back at the door. "I do want you to know, Drake-san, that this is not the feeling of Tochigi. We are not unhappy that you are staying with us, and when these painful times are over—"

"*Arigato*, Hiranuma-san. Thank you, Kato-san. Tochigi is my home now, and I hope there is no greater war, so that I may stay here many years with all my good friends."

Kato looked him up and down. "You really mean that, don't you?"

"Yes, I do, Captain," Cotton said.

"Behave yourself, then, Drake-san."

"And sleep in the church," Hiranuma added.

"Yes," Kato said. "Make sure you sleep alone in the church."

40

"Well, well, Cotton, good to see you again," Bowersox said. "Sorry I left here like a thief in the night, but it had to be *beaucoup* sub rosa." He fanned himself. The summer of '41 was turning out to be exceptionally hot, with the charcoal fumes all the more asphyxiating in the oppressive air. What Westerners who could escaped up to Karuizawa, there to drink gin and play tennis under the cool pine trees.

Bowersox had all the windows in his office thrown open, with the extra floor and table fans he'd appropriated from vacationing colleagues going full blast. "You think it's bad here, spend three months in Chungking."

"Oh, so that's were you've been," Cotton said.

"One big piss pot. Pardon my French, Reverend Doctor. Got there late in April, it was like winter had forgotten to leave. Foggy from the snow still melting. Then, bingo, overnight, sweltering. And open sewers. You can't believe the stench."

"Funny place to choose as a capital."

Bowersox stopped dead, then made quite a drama out of lighting his cigarette. "You know, Cotton, that was cheap of you. Being patronizing doesn't befit a man of the cloth."

"Come on, Saint, you're the one said it was a stinkhole."

"Yes, yes—but you know damn well Gimo didn't have any choice in the matter."

"Gimo?"

"General Chiang. Chungking was the best he could do, thank you very much. The Japanese army didn't leave him much alternative."

"Can I ask? What you were doing there?" Bowersox's secretary brought in a pitcher of lemonade and poured the men two tall glasses.

"I don't see why not. Ambassador Johnson was being replaced in China, and before he headed back, State thought maybe we ought to get ... well, a second opinion. So Gil Adair—he's the number-two man at FE—was sent over, and they asked me to accompany him."

"And? How're things going there?"

Bowersox shook his head mournfully, emerging from that studied melancholy with a passion Cotton had never witnessed before. "Oh, if only you could have seen, Cotton! If only all good Americans could. You talk about London, you talk about the blitz. I bow to no one more in admiration. But what Chungking is suffering from the Japanese every day only makes London pale." His voice rose in timbre and emotion, the words alone seeming to lift him to his feet. "By God, every day—bombs, bombs, more bombs. Why the entire time I was there, more than two months, and there wasn't one day we were spared! One day, hell, there wasn't a period of more than five or six hours when we were safe from the Jap bombs."

"It must have been awful."

"Awful? Awful?" Bowersox was beside himself. He used every melodramatic gesture short of lowering his forehead onto his wrist. "Those brave souls, those magnificent Chinese—the refugees flooding to Gimo, spilling into the city, then out over the walls when the bombs came. And the general and his lovely lady, holding their heads high, giving hope to a whole nation." He leaned down onto his desk, peering across at Cotton. "We will not let America forget them."

"No," Cotton said.

Boxersox sighed. The fans suddenly seemed to roar in the fresh silence. Then, in a flash, without warning, Boxersox rose and marched past Cotton to his door. He closed it. "The heat's on here, too—and that's no pun."

"Oh?"

Bowersox came back and sat on the desk, looking down on Cotton. "I think it's time you left Japan," he declared.

"I think about that, Saint. It crosses my mind every day."

"It's past thinking. Savvy? It's time for any sensible Joe to cut and run. The time for Christian martyrs is past."

"Don't worry. I don't fancy being on anybody's rack."

Bowersox scrutinized Cotton anew. "Can you hold a secret?"

"Part of my job, keeping confidences."

"Okay. It's just for a day." With that, Bowersox went back around his desk, where he unlocked a drawer and pulled out a paper. "Arrived just two hours ago. Absolutely top secret code. We've sent for the ambassador to return on the double from Karuizawa." He flicked the corner of the sheet with his index finger for emphasis. "Tomorrow, 26 July, the year of our Lord nineteen and forty-one, we're freezing all Japanese assets in the United States of America. No more of our Texas oil, Mr. Hirohito."

Very softly, Cotton said: "Good lord. That really is serious."

"You're telling me. I don't think you should be surprised to see both the British and the Dutch join our party. FDR is finally just fed up taking crap off these guys. Savvy?"

Cotton rose himself, moving closer to a fan. "This'll back them into even more of a corner, won't it?" Bowersox nodded, grinning smugly. "Well, then, Saint, that's all the more reason you should listen to me now."

"Ah, you've been moonlighting as a secret agent again, hug?"

"That's why I needed to talk to you."

Bowersox lit another cigarette, off the previous butt. "I told you, Washington put no credence whatsoever in that rumor of yours from the cook. The Japs'll go south. It's all falling into place. Vichy's already invited them into Indochina."

Cotton stepped over to the window. With the door shut, the sweat was pouring off them both now. "You know, Saint, you're the one always telling me how sneaky the Japanese are. But here I am, trying to give you evidence of that very thing, and still I can't budge you from accepting the same old conventional wisdom you'd hear at every cocktail party at any embassy in town."

"So, I should accept your unconventional wisdom?"

"I have the evidence."

"Oh you do?" His eyebrows raised up.

"All right, it's all circumstantial, but altogether it's pretty damn convincing."

Smugly as he could, Bowersox said: "Says who?"

Cotton ignored him. "All right, first we already know that Admiral Yamamoto's own cook has told his brother that an attack on Hawaii was in the works."

"Scuttlebutt."

"Rationalization isn't any more attractive when it comes from an esteemed member of the diplomatic corps. Would you prefer me to write my congressman?"

"Go on." Bowersox poured them both more lemonade. "God," he said, "it's so hot you gotta fuck in the bathtub."

It was supposed to elicit a big laugh, so Cotton cracked a smile. Then he got very businesslike, speaking as if he were delivering a report. "Okay. Point two. I mentioned this to you before. I have a good friend. Japanese. He was sent to Honolulu, allegedly on commercial business. But there is no logical professional reason for him to be there. Only I happen to know that the man who sent him was an old family friend. His name: Admiral Isoroku Yamamoto."

"So you presume your buddy's some sort of a spy."

"Yes, I *presume* exactly that. And I also had another good friend in Honolulu. Issei. He was murdered. I *presume* he knew something."

"Your spy friend killed him?"

That stopped Cotton. He held his face up to the fan, letting the wind blow right on him. "I can't believe that, no. Don't make me speculate. . . . I'm only sure *why* he was killed."

"All right, what's his name—your spy friend?" Cotton paused, just an instant, but Bowersox jumped on him. "You're not going to tell me?"

"No, I am. This time I am. He should be expelled and sent back to Japan." The words "to his wife" followed, as clearly

articulated in his mind as the foregoing had been on his lips;
but he moved on, quickly putting the thought behind him.
"His name is Kiyoshi Serikawa. Write it down." Cotton
spelled it out. "He's officially employed by NYK. He should
be followed. Maybe his place should be searched."

"You understand. If certain, uh, indiscreet things were
found, your friend might not only be expelled."

For a fleeting instant, Cotton saw an old Bible picture of
King David, plotting to have Bathsheba's husband killed
while in the background, Bathsheba, at her most fetching,
was having her hair combed. "I understand the possible con-
sequences to Kiyoshi. I—"

"All right, fine. He's worth a look." Bowersox tossed his
pencil back down and clapped his hands.

"Hold on, Saint. I'm not finished. Not by a long shot."

"Oh?"

"A couple of months ago, shortly after you left for Chungking, there was a rather violent argument in a house in
Yoshiwara."

Bowersox looked up, grinning foolishly. "Oh, was the
handsome young parson there?"

"No. But I heard about if from someone who was."

"A whore?"

"Yes, in fact."

"My, I wouldn't have known you kept such company!"

Cotton let the smirk run its course. "I slum a little, Saint.
Whorehouses, embassies . . ."

"So what did the whore tell you?"

"That there were a couple of very high-ranking officers
there one night. One army, one navy. And they were pretty
drunk and they got into an argument. Big argument. Punches
were thrown and—"

"About what?"

"You know what the Z signal was?"

"The what?"

"Z, as in 'zoo.' It was probably the most famous battle
message ever given in Japanese history. By Admiral Togo at
Tsushima. Hell, I learned about it in school. The admiral

said: 'On this one battle rests the fate of our nation. Let every man do his utmost.' May twenty-seventh. Every year we heard the tale again, had to perform little reenactments in class, all that. It's as sacred as you can get in the Japanese military."

"All right. Z."

"So the general and the navy captain were having a knock-down-drag-out fight about something known as Operation . . . Z. Now, Saint, we don't have to know what exactly Operation Z is, but you can be absolutely sure that the Japanese are not going to name something after Admiral Togo's Z signal unless it is very, very important indeed. They are not going to name any nickle-dime training maneuvers Operation Z." He couldn't resist: "Savvy?" Cotton added.

Bowersox didn't exhibit any recognition of the parody of himself. He just said. "So, all right, what is Operation Z?"

"I don't know—"

"You don't know?"

"No. Not for sure. Not yet. But what I do know is that the general in the whorehouse was angry for one reason—and that is that Z was basically a naval operation, it was taking money and emphasis away from the army, and—get this—it was pointed toward a location seven thousand miles away from Southeast Asia, where you're so sure they'll strike. That's what pissed the general off."

Boxersox only mumbled "Hmmm," but Cotton could tell he was listening.

"Now, you put that together, and it comes up Hawaii. Every time. The only place."

"Okay, okay. Anything else?"

"Well, torpedoes."

"What about 'em?"

"I don't know for sure. Damn, I can't give you every answer."

"The torpedo information come from the whore, too?"

Cotton took his time pouring more lemonade before he looked up and answered. "What do you expect, Saint? You want Hirohito to send you a personal letter with all the plans?

You want Tojo to drop by the embassy for breakfast some morning and lay it all out for you? It's whores and cooks and friends where you learn this kind of stuff. And taken together, it's pretty damn good stuff."

"All right. All right. Don't be patronizing with me. So when is Operation Z?"

"Sorry, I don't have the foggiest. Not for a while, though. Right now, there's some sort of maneuvers going on down in Kagoshima—"

"Where's that?"

"City in the south. Port. But listen to me now. Personally. I was in the shipping business. I know the routes, the Pacific lanes. Know them just as well as my old friend"—Cotton pointed to the pad on Bowersox's desk—"Kiyoshi Serikawa. And if Japan is indeed going to send an armada to Hawaii— *if*—there's really only one way and one time of year when it wouldn't be detected immediately."

Bowersox held out his hands. "I'm in your class, Professor."

"Well, they can't come to Hawaii from the south. That's the logical route—below Wake Island, swinging up, past the Marshalls. Even as vast as the Pacific is, though, the odds are that any operation big enough to attack Hawaii—carriers, troopships, support—is almost surely going to be detected coming that way. But north, Saint—nobody hardly ever goes that route, and especially nobody tries it once the summer's over. Come October, November, the traffic just disappears up there. Too cold. Too rough. Maybe the odd Russian ship out of Vladivostok in the autumn, but by wintertime there's nothing up there. Just too risky. High waves. Very dicey. Yamamoto would never chance that after the first of the year."

Bowersox was listening intently. Even as he lit a cigarette, he kept his eyes on Cotton. "So everything I can deduce tells me that they'll have to go north, and the best time up there is the fall—November, say, maybe December."

"Christmas. It'd be just like the bastards to attack Christmas."

"I thought about that myself. But the fleet'll be docked in

Pearl then. If they're going to try and take Hawaii, they'd obviously want to come in when the fleet's out to sea."

"Good point. Pretty good for a preacher in his spare time."

"It isn't hard, Saint. It all adds up when you lay it out."

"All right, here's what I'm going to do. Number one, I'll cable Hawaii pronto and have somebody run a check on—uh"—he glanced down at his notes—"Serikawa. NYK."

Cotton ducked his head. Hearing Bowersox say Kiyoshi's name made him more nervous than ever. He had crossed a line. "Right." he said.

"And then I'm going to snoop around, troll a little off the back of the boat, see what I can come up with."

"Wouldn't it be more, uh, prudent, just to report this directly to Washington?"

Bowersox savored more lemonade. "You said we have time. Let's see if we can't come up with even more persuasive intelligence."

That made sense to Cotton. "Okay," he said.

"Who else have you told this to, anyway?"

Cotton shook his head. "No one. Who the hell can I tell? I can't call out of the country or write—"

"You can't?"

"Are you kidding? They monitor every *gaijin* left in Japan. And I'm a little more visible, a little more, uh . . . controversial. I was just waiting for you to get back."

"So you had to keep going back to that whorehouse for updates, didn't you? Heh, heh."

"Oh, come on." Damn Bowersox.

"All right then. Not a word to another soul. I'm your contact, and I'll make sure that nobody knows who's feeding me this information. I don't want to jeopardize you." Bowersox paused for a moment. "By the way, where was it in Yoshiwara? Who are the officers with the loose lips?"

"Oh no, Saint. I'm not jeopardizing *my* contact."

"As you wish. I understand. You're getting good at this, Cotton. Maybe you missed your true calling." Cotton shrugged. "You'll check back with me?"

"A couple of weeks. I, uh, often get in Mondays. And anything comes up, you come to Tochigi. Hey, we got the best baseball team in the prefecture." He saluted Bowersox, picked up his jacket, flung it over his wet shoulder, and walked away, down the corridor.

Bowersox took another drag on his cigarette; then, sweltering as it still was, he closed the door again and went back to his desk. First, he wrote out a cable, to go by code to the FBI in Hawaii, asking for a cursory background check on one Kiyoshi Serikawa of NYK Lines. Bowersox made no request that he be followed or investigated—only ID. Then, even before he went down to the cable room, he called the office of General Yoichi Teshima. The general was out of town. In the best Japanese he could manage—and that diminished by his months in Chungking—Bowersox inquired if someone who spoke English could be put on the phone. He said it was important. Soon, a Lieutenant Nishida picked up the receiver.

"Is it possible for me to speak to General Teshima?"

"He is away, Mr. Bowersox."

"When will he return?"

"I cannot tell you that."

"When you speak to the general, please tell him that it is most critical that I talk to him."

"Yes. I will tell the general."

Bowersox gave out a telephone number. "That is my home number, Lieutenant. Tell the general to call me there in the evening."

"I certainly will."

Bowersox paused for a moment. Then he said: "May I assume General Teshima is still in Kagoshima?"

There was only silence on the other end of the phone. Loud, stunned silence, Bowersox thought.

41

Sumiko always knew she would hear this sometime, but, when finally he told her, she bit her lip and fell into Cotton's arms. "I must leave Japan," he said. "My company is sending me back to Hawaii."

He rubbed her hair as she buried her face into his shoulder. "I went to the shrine every day and prayed to all seven deities of good luck that you would stay."

"Yes. I never wanted to leave." Cotton didn't want to say any more, for he wasn't a good liar. The priesthood was a good profession for him, because the lies there only had to be nice little fibs, false comfort, innocent, uplifting, mumbo-jumbo. He wasn't at all cut out for this scale of deception that he had fallen into. And really, now he knew that the true reason he couldn't come back to Sumiko anymore was not Deception, the principle. It was deceiving Sumiko, the person. The lady.

She pulled away abruptly. "I'll be with you all night."

"But you must work at Shinyanagi tonight."

"I'll call." She did not try to lie to Okumura, only begged him to let her have this one night to herself. She promised to work her nights off for the next month, even to come in when next she had her period and help out around the house. Okumura checked her customers for the evening. None were bigwigs. He relented. "Oh, thank you, Okumura-san," Sumiko cooed.

"But no nonsense tomorrow. General Teshima just called. He is back in Tokyo and has scheduled you for tomorrow."

Sumiko assured Okumura she would be there. When she hung up, she turned to Cotton and put on her saddest face. "It's not my lucky day. You leave, and General Teshima is back from Kagoshima." Then she beamed. "But I have the night with you, Otto."

They made love then, in a pool of sweat, laughing and sliding. Tokyo was a cauldron now. When they went out afterwards to shop for dinner, the city seemed deserted. Children ran about nearly naked; well, not even the children ran. One little boy was selling newspapers. *"Gogai, gogai!"* he called. "Extra, extra!" The kid looked like he was ready to faint from the heat, and since he had only three papers left, Cotton bought them all and told him to go home and cool off. He asked Sumiko to read him the big news, but it really wasn't that much, just that General MacArthur had been placed in command of the entire American army in the Far East, with headquarters in Manila. Everything was important in the news now, though, just as every report, in the papers or on the radio, was hideously slanted, the most blatant propaganda.

But it was even too hot for patriotism. The most formal Japanese had stopped wearing jackets to the office, and the poor workmen all wore cold towels wrapped about their heads. Families dipped together in the Sumida among the junks, and never mind how dirty it was. The shops were empty, and after Cotton and Sumiko bought their food, he pulled her into a little women's clothing store and bought her a glorious kimono of royal blue and silver. Hot as it was back at the Serikawas' house, she wouldn't take it off.

She bathed him, and he found some quinine water and introduced her to gin and tonic. "It's the coolest drink of all," he explained. "The British drank this whenever they went to the tropics." The more Cotton was with Sumiko, the more he wanted to show her things, to share his things—even more so, perhaps, because there was so little of his real self that he could give her. This was the last night, though, and there was little time for talk. Quickly, they threw themselves on each other, and Cotton began to kiss her, everywhere. She was surprised when he did not stop when his mouth reached her deepest parts. "Otto, men don't kiss whores there," Sumiko sighed.

He took his mouth away just long enough to say: *"I* kiss Sumiko there." And softly then, in English, just as he returned to her: "Cotton does." Sumiko was already crying tears for what he meant to her, and now she cried out in rapture for what he gave her. And soon, they fell asleep in each other's arms, the heat be damned. Her heart was broken that he was going, but so was his own—more torn than Cotton would admit.

Bowersox would have preferred that Teshima meet him alone, but the general maintained the posture of nonchalance and invited Bowersox to the geisha house. In fact, ever since his office had informed him that Bowersox had known he was in Kagoshima, Teshima had been on pins and needles, cutting short his tour there by two weeks to return to Tokyo.

Face must be maintained, though. Calm. Business as usual. They drank together, they even played some *yo yo ye* with Sai and Midori, the poor geishas sweltering in their fancy kimonos, even as Teshima and Bowersox stripped down to their underwear.

"So," Teshima said at last, as casually as he could manage, "what did you call me about last week?"

"You won't like it, Yoichi." Teshima shrugged, too unconcerned by half. "But it's important, so—" Bowersox yanked his thumb in the direction of the geishas, and the general told them to leave some sake behind and clear out.

"So what's up?"

"I've been in Chungking," Bowersox began.

"Not a nice place to be."

"No, you bastards bombed us every day."

Teshima chortled. "How did we miss you, Saint? We must need more practice."

"Are your pilots getting that in Kagoshima?"

The grin dropped off Teshima's face. "You're very pleased with yourself for knowing where I was."

"It should be of concern to you."

"It is. I'm here." He offered Bowersox more sake, but the American put his hand over his cup. This was too crucial to be clouded by any more liquor.

"I heard a lot more about Nanking over there. You were very bad boys. Very naughty."

"Don't be pious, Saint. We're at war. When you're at war, you'll—"

"I'm ready for war, Yoichi. I look forward to war with you, every bit as much as you dream of war with us. So, if war's your pleasure, then tell your stupid colleagues to be careful."

"What the hell does that mean?"

"It means that as much as you control everything now—the newspapers and radio, business, religion—Admiral Perry has landed. Savvy?" Teshima was puzzled; Bowersox went on. "You're not isolated any longer. You can't expect geishas and whores and shopgirls and waitresses and everyone not to hear—"

"Saint, what are you driving at?"

Bowersox had set him up nicely. Smugly now: "Operation Z is what I'm driving at, General."

Teshima did not even attempt to conceal the fright that came to his face. He did not look off. He simply composed himself, in full view of Bowersox, straightening himself up, wiping his cloudy eyeglasses, turning all business again, controlled, even cold sober, it seemed. "You know?" he began.

"A great deal, yes."

"Then help me," Teshima said. "Where's the leak?"

"Honestly, I don't know, Yoichi. You people have got to be more careful."

"I'd like to cut off somebody's nuts."

"Might be tough. Whoever it was, was a big cheese."

"A what?" Teshima asked.

"A high-ranking officer."

"Navy?"

"Well, no. But in fact, he was with someone from the navy."

Teshima's brow crinkled, and he wiped the sweat off his face, mopping his whole pate. "Where was this?"

"Yoshiwara. A few weeks ago, I gather. I don't know what house up there. All I know is: army officer, navy officer, came in together." Teshima's face flushed, and the sweat began to rise again. "They get into an argument. Had a lot to drink, both of them. And they're arguing about . . . Operation Z. The army officer was against it."

"Damn, it's hot," Teshima said, trying to keep the panic out of his voice. He reached for the bell and rang it, and Sai and Midori entered with cold towels and matted the two men's bodies. Teshima caught his breath, waiting till they finished and left. "So someone overheard the argument. A whore?"

"Yes. And she told somebody."

"And he told you?"

Bowersox nodded.

"Who is he?"

Bowersox shook his head and grinned. "Don't worry. He's not telling anyone else—not as long as nobody bothers me. Don't you fret about my end, Yoichi. I'm just telling you to warn your people to be careful."

Teshima nodded his thanks, and more sweat poured off him. "Such heat, Saint," he said. "Such heat."

"You're almost like a white man, you're so red," Bowersox said, laughing.

In the morning, after they pulled apart from each other for the last time, Sumiko knelt before Cotton. They smiled at each other, and then he reached up and took her hair, matted down on her forehead, and gently combed it back with his fingers.

"Please, Otto, you must not touch me anymore. I have to go now."

"But I want to tell you something."

"Yes?"

"Besides goodbye, something."

"You really are married."

"No, no—"

"But I don't care."

"No, Sumiko. No. I promise." He drew his breath in. "But yes, there is a woman."

"Where?"

"Somewhere. It doesn't matter. And I fell in love with her. But she—"

"She didn't love you? I can't believe that."

"Sumiko, please let me finish. Don't be such a moga." She pouted, so he smiled and laid the back of his hand on her cheek to show he was only kidding her. "She did love me. Only she is the one that's married. And that was very painful to me, because I saw her often, and when I met you I wanted you because you were able to help me forget her."

"That's all right."

"No, no, it isn't," Cotton said. He had to let her know how guilty he felt, even if he couldn't tell her all the real reasons why. "But then, you came to mean so much more to me."

"And you forget her?" Sumiko cried out.

He reached over and took her hand. Easy as it could be, there must be no more lies. "No, Sumiko. No, I've never forgotten her."

"Oh."

"But I have come to have much love for you."

"You could love a whore? Western men don't—"

"No, no." She stopped talking. "I could . . . love you, Sumiko." He knew that now. If there were no Miyuki, there would be Sumiko. Whatever of love, for Liz first, and now Miyuki, no one else had ever charmed him the way this dear little doll-woman had. But love, Cotton knew—real love could follow in the path of charm. Sumiko ducked her head, and tears rolled out of her eyes, flowing down her face to where they mingled with the perspiration, so that her whole face glowed gold. Cotton would always remember that. He lifted her face up with a finger under her chin. "Sumiko, these are bad times for everyone, and I'm sorry I must leave Japan. But maybe, maybe when war is over, I can come back and find you."

She bowed again. "I would be proud to be your *omekakesan,* your second wife."

"No, Sumiko. I would be proud to have you as my *oku-san,* my only wife."

She stared at him, taking the words and rolling them around between her mind and her ears to make sure she had heard them correctly. Finally, when she was sure, she put her hand to her breast to calm her beating heart. "You are so sweet."

"You are sweet, Sumiko. I am only truthful." At last.

"Ai shite imasu," she whispered. It was the closest the Japanese language could come to "I love you." And then she leaned forward on her knees, and Cotton rose up on an elbow, and their lips came together, barely meeting, their eyes barely closed, their bodies barely touching, kissing as sweetly and gently as any man and woman could, more in the way we say that the moonlight kisses us, or a zephyr, or the morning dew kisses a flower. That's how they kissed.

At last Sumiko drew back, placing her fingers as softly on Cotton's lips as her lips had been on them. "Not another word," she said. Then she moved her fingers up to his eyelids and carefully brought them closed. "I don't want you to see me anymore. I only want you to remember kissing me."

"Yes," Cotton said.

"I *said*, not another word."

He smiled. She helped him lie back down. He kept his eyes shut. He really did. He heard her moving about, dressing. He heard her shoes, then, moving across the floor. "Dream of me, Otto-san," he heard her say from across the room. And then he heard her go, he heard her gone . . . and when he finally opened his eyes, Sumiko wasn't there anymore.

Bowersox came out to the reception area to greet Cotton. He had a wet handkerchief around his neck; his shirt was wringing wet. "Good you came. I had something to tell you," and he steered Cotton to a place right under a ceiling fan.

"What's up?" Cotton said.

"Coolest spot in the compound. See? Cross-ventilation." He lit a cigarette. "Let's see. Of course, I reported everything you said to Ambassador Grew, and he was extremely interested. I assured him that you—my contact—would keep me posted. Anything new?" Cotton shook his head. "Nothing from the little cunt up in Yoshiwara?"

Cotton bit his lip. It had hardly been an hour since he had left Sumiko. "That contact is finished."

"Well, we're at a standstill, then, because what I had to tell you was about that Jap you wanted me to check on in Hawaii."

"Yes?"

"The one at NYK."

"Yes. Kiyoshi Serikawa," Cotton said. "What is it?"

"He's not there anymore. Vamoosed."

"What do you mean, Saint? That can't be." Cotton's head was spinning. Kiyoshi wouldn't take off and not advise Miyuki, would he? Or would he advise her and she not tell him? Neither made any sense.

"Well, it can be. The cable came in late yesterday and was decoded this morning." He took a piece of paper out of his back pocket and handed it to Cotton. "See, he sailed three days ago."

Cotton looked up from the cable. "He's coming home. Back to Yokohama."

Bowersox pointed back to the paper. "The funny thing is, too, he's on the *President Coolidge*. Paid full fare. The *Asama* sails tomorrow, but he couldn't wait. Whatever it is, they must want his ass back here in a hurry." Cotton handed the cable back to Bowersox. "Any idea what's up?"

"Not the foggiest."

42

Cotton saw the Nakagawas hanging about shyly after the service Sunday, and when the other parishioners moved off, he approached them, and they talked about the weather. It was the summer everybody in Japan talked about the weather. The heat wave had finally broken.

"No, this has not been a Japanese year, has it, Drake-san?" Mrs. Nakagawa said.

"Well, certainly not a Japanese summer. Maybe now it'll be a Japanese year again." He paused for the moment. "Maybe now everything will be fine again in Japan."

The old couple nodded. That about did it with the weather conversation, and it was apparent to Cotton they didn't know quite how to tackle whatever real subject it was that was on their minds. Mrs. Nakagawa played with a piece of paper in her hands. "Is there anything I can help you with?" Cotton asked.

"Yes, Drake-san. May we have a special prayer in the church with you?"

"Of course." He pointed to the door and stepped in that direction. "Who is it for?"

"Hanako."

Cotton wheeled back sharply. "Hanako? Is something wrong with her?"

"No, not Hanako, Drake-san. It is her friend."

Instinctively, Cotton blurted out: "Sumiko?"

"You know Sumiko?" Mrs. Nakagawa asked.

"Well, yes, I've met her. Is, uh—" He stumbled.

"Yes, it is Sumiko," Mrs. Nakagawa said, and, tentatively, she started to hold up the paper. Rudely, Cotton snatched it from her, with such a sudden burst that Mrs. Nakagawa fell back a step. Cotton didn't apologize, only held the paper up. It was a letter from Hanako:

Dear Mom and Pop,

I have terrible news. Dear Sumiko has disappeared. Yesterday she came back from being with her boyfriend, and she was so happy, and I had to go early to work and Sumiko never arrived at Shinyanagi.

I know she changed her clothes, but then we know nothing about where she went or where she is. I have reported it to the police, but they know nothing yet.

I have prayed at the temple, and every shrine I pass I put sen in and pray there too. Will you pray to your

Yesu? Please tell Drake-san about Sumiko and have him pray at his church.

Your daughter,
Hanako

Hanako had underlined the last sentence, but Cotton read the whole letter again. His hands were so tight on the paper that Mrs. Nakagawa was sure he was going to yank it apart. "Sumiko," he whispered. Miyuki was standing across the courtyard, watching. Even that far away, she could see the blood drain from his face, and the tension in his hands, pulling at the sheet of paper. She started to come over, but it was just then that Cotton led the Nakagawas into church.

By the time he came out, everyone else had gone, and Miyuki went right to him. "It's about your girl, isn't it?"

"Sumiko is her name."

"What is it? Can you—"

"I don't know. She's missing."

Miyuki said: "I'm sorry, Cotton. I hope—" She stopped. He had taken her hand and was squeezing it hard, and she didn't think he even realized what he was doing. "If you had baptized me, I could pray for her."

Cotton said: "You can pray for her without being baptized. Please, Miyuki, I have to go into Tokyo." He glanced at his watch. "I can get the one o'clock. Tell Tejiro and Sakao they have to run the team if I'm not back for the game."

"Okay."

"And Miyuki . . ."

"Yes?"

"Please pray for me too."

"Ah, Serikawa-kun, what a magnificent job you did in Hawaii!" Yamamoto said, and before Kiyoshi could bow, the admiral stuck out his hand and shook Kiyoshi's. "There. You must be feeling very Western these days."

"Yes, Yamamoto Shirei Chokan," he said, walking into

Yamamoto's office at the Naval Ministry, the one the admiral used in Tokyo when he was away from the fleet.

"But now we will return to making you Japanese," the admiral said, and he gestured for Kiyoshi to sit down on the tatami with him. A steward brought in cakes and tea. "I'm sorry that we had to rush you back on the *Coolidge*—"

"It's a fine ship, sir."

"But it suddenly occurred to me that since we're having meetings with the army this week in Meguro, it would be a good idea to have you on hand personally. You know our fine generals. Visceral types. They accept things better if you walk them through it. Eyewitness."

Kiyoshi sipped his tea. "So, a lot of people know now?"

Yamamoto shook his head. "No, it's still only a few. The prime minister hasn't even been advised yet. Tenno Heika hasn't. But, of course, the circle has had to grow."

"Has any date been set yet?"

Yamamoto didn't answer right away. After a bit, he templed his hands and spoke: "November 16. I hesitated just now because that remains highly confidential. But yes, you're the man in Hawaii—you should be one to know."

"The sixteenth? What day of the week is that?"

"Sunday. As you suggested." Kiyoshi nodded, pleased with the credit Yamamoto had accorded him. "Now, when these meetings with the army are finished, I want you to leave immediately for Kagoshima."

Kiyoshi had the teacup almost to his lips, but with that, he lowered it and looked to the admiral. "But sir—"

"Is that a problem?"

"Please, Yamamoto Shirei Chokan, I haven't seen my wife in months. I don't know what you have for me in Kagoshima, but can't it wait for a few days?"

Yamamoto held out his hands, in obvious embarrassment. "I apologize. That was very thoughtless of me, Serikawa-kun. Yes, of course Kagoshima will wait a day or two. Even better, you have my permission to bring Mrs. Serikawa along and make a holiday of it."

Kiyoshi thanked the admiral, who patted him avuncularly

on the knee. Then he got to his feet and, without a word, walked over to the window, hands clasped behind him, looking out. Kiyoshi waited, silent, until at last Yamamoto turned back. "I am aware that you are terribly distressed about the required solution to the unfortunate situation we found ourselves in a few weeks ago in Hawaii."

The tone was warm and understanding, but Kiyoshi was no less cold and firm in his reply. "Yes sir," he said. "That is an accurate expression of my feelings."

"Yes, so I know that our own relationship cannot go forward unless we discuss this matter with candor." Kiyoshi nodded to that. "So, I shall tell you flat out: it was not my idea, *but* . . . neither can I imagine any other determination."

Kiyoshi hated being on the floor, literally at the admiral's feet. Still, he didn't think he should get up. "Begging your pardon, sir, but I believe I should have been consulted and given the opportunity to deal with Sammy Ushijima myself before such—" he paused—"extreme action was taken."

"Perhaps," Yamamoto said. "I'll concede that we were not altogether considerate. But so what? That one man jeopardized the entire Operation Z—and by extension, jeopardized the fate of our empire."

Kiyoshi spoke softly: "But he was my good friend, sir."

Yamamoto pointed to his desk. "I have shown you my book. I've lost too many good friends."

"Yes sir, I know. But none of them were murdered by our—"

The admiral slammed the side of the desk. "Don't test me, lieutenant! The defense of the empire does not constitute murder. I regret with all my heart that you had to lose a friend. I cannot regret that our future was served by such a necessarily hard judgment."

Kiyoshi lowered his head. He muttered "Yes sir," although it was obvious to Yamamoto that the words came without a scintilla of heart in them. The admiral stepped over to Kiyoshi and stood above him. "Don't sulk. It's most unbecoming."

"I'm sorry, Yamomoto Shirei Chokan."

"Let me give you some wise advice—not because of my own sagacity, but simply because of what I've personally had to endure." Kiyoshi raised his head. "There is hardly a Japanese in the land—and certainly none in the army—who does not subscribe to the view that a dwarfed pine cannot return to survive in a pot once its roots have been allowed to grow.

"All of us who have lived abroad return to face that assumption about ourselves, and I can assure you that that is exactly how everyone now characterizes Serikawa Kiyoshi. Like me—or, in any event, like the me who spent so many years in America a decade ago—they believe that you have been away too much to any longer accept our ways. It will be tacitly assumed that you now see Japan through blue eyes."

"I understand that, sir."

"Then, Serikawa-kun, you must bend back over like a willow to prove those assumptions incorrect. Because, make no mistake; I have no intention of seeing resistance to Operation Z develop because of the extension of suspicion connected to one of my junior aides. You must embrace the harsh notions that war brings, and furthermore, you must embrace them publicly and with enthusiasm. Is that clear?"

"Yes sir," Kiyoshi said, stoutly.

"Good. Now I have given you the courtesy of my apologies for things past and the guidance of my counsel for things future, so we may return to the details of the present." Kiyoshi formally bowed from his position on the floor. "I gather there is no suspicion whatsoever in Hawaii of our plans."

"None. As I reported, I'm convinced the Americans don't even bother to patrol to the north."

"Curious people. They never learn. But for a single vote in Congress the other day, they would have abandoned their military draft. They have this almost innocent view of war."

Yamamoto chuckled. He was making an effort to reassure Kiyoshi that he wasn't going to remain angry with him. But even more, he was enjoying himself, having the opportunity to talk about the enemy with someone who understood them as well as he did. "You're one of the few Japanese I know, able to appreciate the semantic difference that's always applied by the Americans to distinguish between the Eastern and the Western military. Their most brilliant strategies constitute 'surprise'; ours, 'sneak attacks.' I remember one time back in Washington, at some international naval meeting, and some pompous British ass was criticizing us for being 'sneaky' at Tsushima, and I broke in and said, 'Oh, forgive me, sir, I wasn't aware that Lord Nelson was Japanese.'"

"What?" Kiyoshi asked.

"That's exactly what the Englishman said. And I replied, 'Because, sir, if you read your naval history, Lord Nelson's brilliant victory at Jutland depended much more on the element of surprise than did Admiral Togo's at Tsushima."

Kiyoshi grinned, while the admiral went on, now striding about his office, as he regaled himself and his other audience of one. "Nelson's uh, 'surprise' was no isolated event, either. Ever heard of Zachary Taylor?" Kiyoshi scratched his head. "President of the United States about a hundred years ago. Elected strictly because he was a war hero. His heroics consisted largely of leading a sneak—excuse me, a *surprise* attack—into Mexico before Congress got around to the nicety of declaring war. I will make sure that if we do hit Hawaii, we must officially declare war first."

"Forgive me, sir, but they'll still—"

"I understand. We will be the villain whatever. Americans are so damn smug, really. They think everybody in the world longs to be an American, so anyone who would cross America is taking on the whole world." He sighed. "How different we are. There isn't a Japanese who could even conceive that anybody else would want to be one of us." Kiyoshi chuckled. "Would we?"

"No, sir."

Yamamoto had gone back to his desk and was rummaging through it, so Kiyoshi took the opportunity to rise. The admiral found what he was looking for, an old art print of some sort, and thrust it at Kiyoshi. "I know you won't know him."

Kiyoshi studied it anyhow. "An American Indian?"

"Yes, a fellow named Opechanacanough."

"Opuh—?"

The admiral spelled it out in English. "Opechanacanough. I thought about naming our little enterprise after him— Operation Opechanacanough—but finally I decided to settle on Z and just keep him as my private hero."

"Who was he?"

"Powhatan Indian chief in Virginia shortly after the first English settlers arrived in Jamestown in 1607. There have been lots of interesting military campaigns in Virginia. I used to take weekends down from Washington, and I read about friend Opechanacanough and traced his best work. Same basic issues as ours today. Just tobacco then, oil now. The Americans think they're entitled and expect everybody else to settle for the hind teat. They backed the chief into a corner of Virginia, no less than they're making us settle for a bit of the world. And finally, Opechanacanough couldn't accept that any longer, and he planned an amazingly sophisticated attack along the James River for one morning, March 22, 1622. He hit several of the settlements simultaneously—"

"Sneak attack?"

"Oh, absolutely. Keep in mind that for the Americans, the only ones sneakier than Orientals are Indians. But Opechanacanough's attack was all wonderfully coordinated, extraordinarily successful. What we're planning is no more intelligent, just a bit larger theater."

"So what happened to the chief?"

"Well, he's been forgotten. The Americans always conveniently forget the bad news. So no one over there will use that history to prepare better for us, which is good for us since"— Yamamoto grinned—"we're sort of the Powhatans of 1941. But the other truth is that the Americans eventually prevailed over Opechanacanough. There were too many of them, too many resources."

"But isn't that exactly—"

"Exactly what's likely to happen now?"

Kiyoshi nodded.

Yamamoto looked steely. "Look, I never pretended this wasn't risky."

"I'm sorry, sir, I'll be the good soldier you want in public, but I still don't want any part of the United States."

"Neither do I," Yamamoto replied, reaching over and taking the drawing of Chief Opechanacanough back. "Neither, I'm sure, did our friend here. But someday, *someday*, someone will make them pay for that damn vanity of theirs. And with luck, that can be us." The admiral paused. Then, with emphasis: "A *lot* of luck. Right, Chief? Right, Lieutenant?"

"Yes sir." He knew the discussion was concluded, and he also knew the admiral didn't want to hear any more of his practical reservations, so he turned to go.

But Yamamoto called him back and punched the intercom. "Bring me that photo in," he said. And to Kiyoshi: "We appear to have some sort of security problem here. There's a general. Fellow named Teshima Yoichi. Quite brilliant, really. Very successful in China—Nanking, particularly. He's been reassigned to *jouhou kyoku*, to intelligence, and that made him one of the first in the army to have any awareness of Z. Unfortunately, however smart he may be, he's a pig. Barbarian. I think we've only begun to hear the truth about Nanking—"

"Yes, sir, I've heard rumors myself."

"Anyway, Teshima thinks mostly with his dick and spends a great deal of his spare time in Yoshiwara. For once, though, this turned out to be useful, because one of his whores told him that a *gaijin* had suddenly become very prominent in Yoshiwara."

The door opened and an enlisted man entered, carrying a folder, which he handed to the admiral. "The *gaijin* was trying to turn up secrets that might have been spouted in a house?" Kiyoshi said.

"According to Teshima, that's it. Pretty clever."

"Do we know if he picked anything up?"

"Well, Teshima says he heard there was one naval officer who was babbling one evening when he was drunk. But he could never pin it down. Who knows? We'll probably never find out for sure. Unless we can find the *gaijin*."

"You know his name?"

"That's why I'm showing you this. He says he's a German

named Otto von Kohorn. Teshima says he even met him one night before all this came to light. He purports to be in the shipping business and used to work in Hawaii. So if there's any truth to that, you should recognize him."

Yamamoto rooted the photo out of the folder and handed it to Kiyoshi. It was fortunate for Kiyoshi, then, that the admiral looked back into the folder for something else just at this moment, because no matter how much Kiyoshi tried to contain his shock, his expression surely would have given him away when he laid his eyes on the photograph of Cotton Drake.

Cotton was standing at a shop along the mall outside Sensoji, his one arm wrapped around a gorgeous Japanese woman, who was laughing. Cotton wore sunglasses and a cap on his head and a jacket Kiyoshi didn't recognize. But there was no question whatsoever: it was Cotton Drake. Kiyoshi's mind wobbled; he played for time. "Good-looking dame."

Yamamoto looked up from the folder. "Hey, I'm not handing out dirty postcards. We know who she is."

"Who? Can I ask?"

"A special *oiran* of the *gaijin*'s. Sumiko something or other."

"A whore?" Kiyoshi asked. It was almost as inconceivable to think of Cotton with a prostitute as it was to imagine him leading a double life as a spy.

"This guy obviously knows his way around. This picture was taken by somebody at her house, the . . . uh—" he searched the folder for the name—"the Shinyanagi. Know it?" Kiyoshi shook his head. "They were annoyed when she started calling in sick, and so the manager had someone tail her one day and got this shot at Sensoji with her lover boy here."

"Where's she now?"

"Vanished. Unfortunately. Just like the German. Teshima went to her apartment himself, but she was gone. He figures maybe she ran off with the guy. Or maybe he killed her."

Kiyoshi swallowed. *Cotton?* "Killed her?"

"Teshima's pretty sure it can only be one or the other."

Kiyoshi bought more time, trying to collect himself, scrutinizing the photo some more. "So, uh, please, what's the guy's name again?"

"Otto von Kohorn. But nobody by that name has ever entered the country."

Kiyoshi swallowed and shook his head. "I've never met a von Kohorn." Well, technically . . .

"Hawaii? Shipping?" This time Kiyoshi only shook his head. He couldn't bring himself to lie again to Admiral Yamamoto. He handed the picture back to him.

"Well, Teshima's going to continue the search."

"But if he's German, what do we have to fear?"

"Nothing, I hope. It's just that the krauts don't trust us any more than we trust them. If Hitler will turn on Stalin, we can't be sure where they'll be on November 16, can we?"

"No sir."

"Maybe it's all moot anyhow. Teshima's sure the whore's in the bottom of some river. My guess is, Otto took her back into the German embassy. But anyway, Teshima's thugs will keep looking for them both."

"Yes, sir," Kiyoshi said, struggling to maintain his composure. "I'll prepare for the meetings at Meguro."

He wiped at his forehead. His best friend in all the world—a spy. Against Japan. And he was living with his wife. But then, what was he, Kiyoshi Serikawa? What had become of him? He had murdered Sammy Ushijima as surely as if he had pulled the trigger himself. He could feel his legs buckle and fought to keep himself upright. He barely even heard Yamamoto telling him that he would be honorably commissioned as a lieutenant in His Majesty's navy, assigned here to Yamamoto's own staff in these headquarters.

"Thank you, sir," Kiyoshi heard someone say who sounded rather like himself.

43

At the Looking-Back Willow, Cotton put on his eyeglasses, adjusted his cap, and then walked down to the big teahouse, the Matsubaya. He ordered a sake and asked the contact man to call down to the Shinyanagi for Sumiko.

The man returned quickly. "I am sorry, Mr. von Kohorn, but I am advised that Sumiko is away. The Shinyanagi wishes to know if you will please come down right away and take another girl?"

"Of course," Cotton answered, and he stepped briskly down the street and around the corner to the Shinyanagi, where Mr. Okumura stood out front, bowing and grinning as soon as Cotton came into view. "I am most sorry that Sumiko is not here," he said. "But you have expressed an interest in Hanako—"

"Someone else."

"Of course," the manager said, and he ushered Cotton into his office and began showing him the photographs of the full Shinyanagi stable. He had forgotten to remove Sumiko's picture, and tried to quickly turn the page when Cotton came to it, but Cotton held the picture down and stared at her, remembering their last, sweet kiss, and wondering if she was still able to remember it too.

"So, where is Sumiko now?"

Okumura held out his hands. "Perhaps she went home to Fukuoka."

"No warning, no explanation? Sumiko was a most reliable girl." The manager looked away from Cotton. He was terribly uncomfortable. "How long has Sumiko been gone?"

That the manager could handle. "Last Tuesday," he answered quickly. But he remained most nervous, his eyes flitting about, till he drew the *noren* back and looked into the empty hall. "Sorry, von Kohorn-san. I thought I heard a customer."

"General Teshima, perhaps?" Nervously, the manager shook his head, then took off his spectacles and wiped them. Cotton pressed him. "My new friend General Teshima. He hasn't been here?"

"In Tokyo, yes, but not here."

"Oh? When was my friend Yoichi here last?"

"Several days now. I'm not sure."

"Well, look." Cotton's voice turned sharp as he pointed at the schedule book. Okumura froze, so Cotton simply grabbed the book himself.

"Please, Mr. von Kohorn, you—" But Okumura was so shocked by it all, so discombobulated, that instead of trying to take the book back from the *gaijin*, he only wrung his hands, mumbled, and looked out the front window. Cotton ignored him. He ran his finger down the list. This was Monday. Back he went through the nights, turning the pages. Back, back Cotton went—through the weekend, last Thursday, Wednesday. Teshima's name was down for her that Wednesday, and then Saturday, and today, this Monday. But these last two times a line had been drawn through the general's name.

The manager, finally emboldened, came back over to Cotton and tried to pull the book away. "Excuse me," he said. Roughly, Cotton shoved him away. He flipped through the book again. Teshima's name was as regular as any he saw— always with Sumiko, about every third night and usually at the top of the list, suggesting advance appointments had been made. Sometimes his name was added late, surely because he must have called at the last minute after a night of drinking at the geisha house. But except for huge gaps, when the general was obviously on duty away from Tokyo, he was always there, clockwork, always with Sumiko.

Cotton flipped back to the last week's listings. He showed it to Okumura. "Here—why was the line drawn through?"

"Please, this is none of your affair." Cotton didn't wait. He surprised himself; he took the man and grabbed him by his collar and banged him hard against the wall. "Tell me. That's

all. Just tell me, Okumura. The general canceled, didn't he?"
The manager breathed heavily. "Someone from his office
canceled? Saturday and Monday? They canceled ahead of
time, didn't they?"

Okumura's eyes widened now. Something was wrong.
Something with Otto was suddenly terribly different.

"He canceled? Right?" Cotton screamed, and now he
banged the man's head against the wall. "Dammit, answer
me. He hasn't been in this week, has he?" Cotton raised his
fist. Poor Okumura's eyes darted about. He couldn't bring
himself to answer. But he did move his head. Just a bit, up
and down. It was all Cotton needed. He let the man go.
"God damn him, god damn the sonofabitch." He said that in
English, then back to Okumura in Japanese: "Of course he
cancels. He knows where she is. He knew she wouldn't be
here . . . *couldn't* be here."

Okumura didn't answer, only shrank back. But suddenly
his eyes darted to the window, for outside, a car's lights had
appeared, shining off the pink lanterns that hung down the
street. It didn't occur to Cotton right away, but . . . how few
cars there were in Yoshiwara these days. Even what taxis
there were would stop out by the Looking-Back Willow, stay
on the main roads, save drops of fuel. And then it clicked in
his mind: they'd tipped somebody off. Trapped.

The special policeman from *tokko* was already at the door
when Cotton pushed back the *noren*. So he pasted a smile on
his face and bowed. Instinctively, the cop bowed back. Cotton
didn't wait. He yanked his right hand back and slugged the
little man flush on his chin. The guy went reeling backwards.
Cotton regarded him in absolute wonder. He'd never hit anyone in his life—maybe scuffled a couple of times when he was
a little boy, pushing and pulling, but this was the first time
he'd ever slugged anybody. He stared in shock at what he had
done, the *tokko* man down on his knees now, groaning, trying
to reach for his pistol. And Cotton's hand hurt. It had never
really occurred to him that if you hit somebody smack on the
chin, it hurt your hand as well as the other guy's chin. But his
mind was clear again, and he knew he had to get away. He

kicked the man on the floor in the face and started to jump past him, but then he saw the other cop coming out of the driver's side, already brandishing a pistol. Cotton didn't have any choice. He turned back inside. Okumura had come out of his office, wide-eyed, and Cotton didn't have to hit him to get by, only push him back, and there he went, ass over teakettle, ending up almost knocking over one of his whores, who came out of her room to see what all the commotion was.

Cotton tore down the hall, threw open the *fusama*, and ducked into Sumiko's old room just as he heard the shot go off. He didn't know where the bullet went, only that it didn't hit him. The new whore, who had been assigned to Sumiko's place, saw Cotton first. She was on the bottom. The customer twisted his neck just in time to see Cotton hurtle over them and go bursting through the paper window that took him into the Shinyanagi's pretty little rear garden.

He staggered through it, cursing himself for being so stupid, then vaulted the wall and took a turn into a small street. He'd been here only once before, when he'd walked Sumiko back to work one Tuesday. He'd even kissed her goodbye here. He heard the cops chasing him, and he rounded the corner and dashed into the *matsunoyu*, the large bath, there.

Immediately, Cotton knew why this was all so unfamiliar. He'd found the back way into the homosexual area of Yoshiwara, and when he barged into the bath, it was all men, some of them washing each other. They gaped at him, but he found a *fusama* on the other side of the bath, and when he broke through, outside, he was safe for the moment. Alone.

He whirled, then, and dashed down the street, gasping now. He was in good shape from all his baseball, but he was also scared to death and he was lost. The little streets wandered, often lit only by the pink lanterns. A few men were coming and going along the way. They stared at him. A *gaijin* running through Yoshiwara? There weren't but a couple thousand left in all of Tokyo now.

He turned another corner, and still he couldn't see the cops behind him. There was a big doghouse there. Doghouses seemed to be everywhere in Yoshiwara. He thought about climbing in. They couldn't check every doghouse in Yoshiwara. Except suppose there was a dog in his house? He couldn't just duck in. And that was when he heard them again.

So he took off once more, weaving down this block, up the other, onto the main drag, Oiran Douchou, then quickly off it again. He stopped once and listened. And sure enough, he could hear the police calling to the pedestrians—"where's the *gaijin?*"—and he could all but hear everybody pointing after him. He couldn't wait. He had to find a place to hide. Somewhere.

He scrambled down another street. There were so many whorehouses. It was like a rabbit warren, worse in this part of Yoshiwara because some of the roll-over geishas had set up prostitution fronts, too, in the hard times. One-stop shopping. A few of them were out on the street soliciting. No matter how fast he ran, how clever he twisted and turned, there always seemed to be someone there to direct the soldiers after him.

One more corner. A quieter street, no lanterns here. He dashed down it. Wait—there. What is it? The Shinto shrine. He knew where he was. Yoshiwara had its own temple and its own shrine for all its whores. One of them was leaving right now, ringing the bell, praying for a good night's bounty of customers. He ducked across the street and hid in the shadows behind a willow. He was exhausted now. And then, cowering, silent, he heard the *tokko* men again, grilling another pedestrian. They couldn't be but a block away. Luckily, though, the man hadn't seen Cotton, so both *tokko* men cursed, and one said: "Look, let's split up—you go that way, and I'll head down here."

Cotton froze, praying the whore wouldn't cross over to his side when she came out of the shrine. His luck held this time, and as soon as she reached the corner, he dashed across the street behind her, under the *torii*, the entrance gate and into the garden of the shrine. He just made it. Hardly past the *torii*, he could hear the policeman shouting "*Gaijin?*" at the whore. But she hadn't seen him. She said no and moved on.

Then Cotton heard his footsteps begin again. Toward the shrine. There was no getting away. He had to hide. Wait. He looked up. It was a large, ornate Shinto *torii*, surrounded by massive animal statues, *tourou*. The footsteps . . . the footsteps were coming toward him.

Quickly, Cotton clambered onto the *tourou* closest to the gate, and then, springing with all his effort, he caught hold of the top of the *torii* and pulled himself up the rest of the way. He lay there still, across the roof of the great gate, exhausted, terrified. The footsteps came closer. Cotton lay flat. Be still, be still . . . don't breathe. He'll be past the shrine in a moment.

Instead, the *tokko* man stopped. And Cotton stopped breathing. The soldier was on the sidewalk, right by the gate, almost directly under him. Cotton couldn't watch, but the man looked around, and then he headed off again, down the street. Cotton could hear his steps receding enough so that he dared to raise his head and peek down. The *tokko* man held a rifle at port arms. Cotton caught his breath; he could see the bayonet gleaming in the pink light.

He started to lower his head, but that was when he saw another woman coming down the sidewalk toward him. The soldier stopped and put up his rifle. She bowed. He made a lewd remark, but she refused to acknowledge it. Instead, she passed by him smartly, then executed a turn at the *torii*, into the shrine, going right under where Cotton lay, into the garden, up the steps to the sen box.

The soldier followed. He stood directly under the *torii*, under Cotton, smirking. She tried to ignore him. She washed her hands—left first, right. She washed her mouth. She rang the bell, clapped twice, and prayed. Then she threw in an offering. When she turned back, he held up his gun and stopped her. "Can't a girl pray?"

"Let's fuck instead."

"All right. I'm through praying. I can work now."

"How much?"

"Five yen."

"Not for *tokko*, it isn't."

She assessed the situation. She got the drift. "All right, for *tokko* a special price, three yen fifty."

"Too much," he said.

"Come on, a girl's got to make a living. These are hard times."

"All right. I like you, and I've got to get on with my own work. How 'bout a quick blow job?"

"Two yen usually, but you right here, one yen."

"Seventy-five sen."

The whore could see she was up against it. She took his hand and guided him behind a statue.

Cotton peeked. He saw the cop put aside his rifle and unzip his fly, prop himself back up against the statue of a monkey there, his legs spread, the whore moving down on him. Cotton positioned himself to jump. Then—damn—he knocked some pebble, some branch, some loose part of the *torii*, some something. He never knew. All he knew was that it hit the ground with what sounded to Cotton like the bang of cymbals. But the *tokko* man was too preoccupied; only the whore heard it and raised her head.

"What was—"

"Come on, come on," the *tokko* man growled, grabbing her hair, forcing her head back down on him. Then Cotton only had to hold on a few moments more, waiting for the man's first low growl of pleasure. Cotton rose up on his knees, braced. He leaped. The cop never saw him until Cotton landed right in front of him. In one fluid motion, then, Cotton threw the girl aside, where she lay dazed, in confusion.

Then, with one roundhouse right, Cotton came up and hit the *tokko* man in the balls, and when he fell back, screaming still, in surprise as much as agony, Cotton kicked him there again. The cop crumpled to the ground, and before he even understood it—in fear for himself and anger for Sumiko—Cotton had grabbed the *tokko* man's head with both his hands and begun to pound it onto the monkey statue, again and again, until the body fell slack, the eyes vacant, blood oozing. Cotton stared at the head, between his hands. "My God, I'm going to kill this guy!" he said out loud—whispered, but out loud—and, horrified, he let the head fall from his hands as if it were unattached, and the whole body slumped back to the ground.

Cotton turned to the whore, who lay there whimpering. "Clear out of here," he said, and then he turned and ran away, under the *torii*, back out into the street.

Cotton was completely composed now. He saw a cab a block away. He waited. Two admirals alighted, come into Yoshiwara from Meguro after a day of meetings. Cotton ran out and called for the cab, ordering the driver to the Imperial.

It was only then, after a stiff drink in the bar, sure that he wasn't being tailed, that he went outside, found another cab, and took it back uptown to the Serikawas' house.

But all for nothing. As soon as Cotton slid back the *fusama* and stepped inside, he could see the figure in the dark across the way. He knew he must have a gun, and so Cotton only lowered his head and waited for whatever there was to come.

44

"I'm sorry, it's only me," the voice said. It was a woman.

"Are you alone?" Cotton asked.

"Yes. It's all right, Drake-san." When he flicked on the light, he saw Hanako standing there. "I knew you stayed here at the Serikawas' when you were in Tokyo," she said.

It hadn't even occurred to him to wonder how she happened to be here. He only knew right away it must be some important thing that brought her. Some terrible thing. She was still in her fancy working clothes, but her face was so red and her eyes puffy, her dress even streaked dirty from the tears wiped all over it. She started to sniffle again. Cotton asked only because he was obliged to hear it: "It's about your friend Sumiko?" *Your* friend.

"She's dead." And then Hanako stumbled across the room

and fell against Cotton. He supported her. Well, he tried to. Can there be anything more unfair than not being able to show you're upset when you are? There is nothing so hard to keep inside as love, except maybe guilt; and both rolled together in Cotton, so much that he wanted to scream. Instead, he only stood there, holding Hanako, playing the priest. "Oh, Hanako, I'm so sorry."

"I was working at Shinyanagi when I heard."

Cotton nodded and gave her his handkerchief. He felt ill. "How?"

"She was killed."

"Who?"

"They beat her to death. The bastards."

"Oh God." Cotton turned away and pulled at his eyes with the back of his hands, hoping she didn't see him cry.

"The Sumida. They threw her in the river." Hanako started to cry again. "The only way they were sure—" But she couldn't go any further.

"Sure what?" he finally asked.

"The only way the cops were sure it was her—" She stopped again and turned away. "Sumiko had a boyfriend, a mobo. He was a *gaijin.*"

She paused again, so Cotton said: "Yes?"

"Her mobo gave her a new kimono. Oh, you should have seen it! It was blue and silver. She loved it so." She paused. "Yes."

"That was how they identified her." Cotton gasped in spite of himself. "It was still on her. Caked in blood, but still on her." They beat her and they strangled her, and—"

That, at last, was too much. He couldn't pretend anymore. He brushed past Hanako and ran into the bathroom and threw up. He tossed a lot of water on his face, but he couldn't look at himself in the mirror when he did that. Not at all. When he came back out, Hanako said: "I'm sorry. I didn't mean to upset you so. I thought priests could deal with things like this."

Cotton just ignored that. "Why did they kill Sumiko?" he said. "Because she went around with the *gaijin?*"

Hanako had sat down on the tatami. Cotton put some water on for tea. "No. I think they thought she knew something.
I think they thought she knew something and maybe told that
to the *gaijin.*"

"What would a whore know?"

"We're with a lot of men who think theirs dicks are so wonderful we'll never pay attention to their mouths."

"Oh, yeah."

Hanako lit a cigarette. "Will you pray for Sumiko in your
church, Drake-san?"

"Of course I will. I'll pray for her wherever I am."

"We'll bury her ashes tomorrow at Kokanji. All the girls
are paying."

Cotton reached into his pocket and handed a lot of yen to
Hanako. He kept only enough to get him back to Tochigi.
"What's Kokanji?"

"Oh, it's just the temple in Yoshiwara for the prostitutes.
There's an old monk there—been there forever, taking care of
us. He was even there during the earthquake. So many of the
girls had to be buried then. The old monk buries us all,
whenever we die. Sumiko came from Fukuoka, and she still
has family there, but I want her ashes to stay here with her
friends. You're a priest, Drake-san. What do you think?"

"I think that's right."

"Good. Maybe you'll come with us to Kokanji tomorrow?"

Cotton didn't wait; he shook his head right away. Since he
knew Teshima's men were trying to catch him they'd surely
be looking for him at Sumiko's funeral. Even in his priest's
collar, there'd be no doubt who the *gaijin* was. Maybe, Cotton
thought, maybe they even threw the body in the Sumida so
that it would surface as bait for Otto. "Hanako, I can't
come."

"You have a baseball game?"

"If it was just a baseball game, I would be there with you.
But it's something else much more important, and you must
believe me." She nodded her head. "I'm going back to
Tochigi tomorrow."

"I'm going back too," Hanako said. She kept wiping at her

eyes, but for moment, anyway, she was in control of herself again.

"When?"

"Day after tomorrow. I can't ever go back to Yoshiwara. No more. Not after this. I don't care what—I'll work in the geta factory now."

"Airplane parts factory," Cotton said, permitting himself even the first glimpse of a smile.

"Yes, well, but someday it'll be a geta factory again. Someday." And now she allowed herself a little smile too. "Any of your baseball players want a wife, Cotton-san?"

He brought the tea over and sat down next to her. "Hey, they'd all want you, Hanako. But there's not many of 'em left. Too many draft postcards. We'll be lucky to get through the season."

She sipped her tea and smoked, and suddenly, almost subconsciously, it seemed, Hanako started talking about Sumiko. Not about her death, and the horror and the sorrow. Just about Sumiko. And Cotton couldn't take that. He couldn't pose anymore, and when he wanted to cry, he let the tears flow. If Hanako noticed, she didn't let on. She just kept on talking ... about how pretty Sumiko could be and what she enjoyed and what her family was like and how she become a whore and what she wanted to do with the rest of her life. Hanako told Cotton what a good professional Sumiko was, and what a good friend she was to all the girls, and what a good wife she would have been. She said that Sumiko would have been happy to have been a second wife for somebody rich, or maybe she would have gone back to Fukuoka and made some boy a fine first wife. Either way, she would have been a wonderful mother, Hanako said.

Finally, Cotton dried his eyes, and they sat in silence for a while, until he reached over and took her hand, and he said: "I think you're about the luckiest person in the world to have had a friend like Sumiko." And that made it Hanako's turn to cry.

When she stopped, she looked directly at him and said: "You were Otto, weren't you?"

"Yes. Of course I was," Cotton answered straightaway.

"I was pretty sure all along. That's why I come here to-night. Can I ask you a favor?"

"Sure."

"I'm very lonely, Cotton. And I hurt. I came here because I'd like to spend the night here with you. I can't go back to my apartment."

"I'd love to have you stay."

Cotton found her a nightshirt of Mrs. Serikawa's and laid out the futons. When he turned out the lights, he reached over and took Hanako's hand, and after a while he asked her: "Did you ever tell Sumiko you thought I was her mobo?"

"Oh no."

"Never?"

"No. If I'd told her who you really were, I'd have had to tell her that you were just with the whore because you loved your friend's wife but couldn't have her."

Cotton scratched his head. "I didn't know you knew that."

"Everybody in Tochigi knows that, silly. My parents told me. Kensuke told me the night you gave me to him. She loves you too, of course. Everybody knows that, too."

"Oh," Cotton said.

"So I didn't want to tell that to Sumiko. It was better for her not knowing things."

"It's funny. The last time I saw her, last week, I told her everything."

"You did?"

"I told her maybe, after the war, maybe if I came back, she could be my wife."

"Your *oku-san?* "

"Why not? If I can't have Miyuki—and I can't."

"No wonder she was so happy before she died."

That made Cotton start to cry again, but he managed to say: "Can you do me a favor, too?"

"Yes, Cotton-san."

"Would you take just a little of Sumiko's ashes, just a tiny little bit, and bring them with you when you come to Tochigi? Then we can have a service for her at my church."

"She was never in Tochigi. Nobody knows her."

"That's okay. You do, and I do." After a bit, Cotton could hear Hanako moving, and she came over and kissed him on his forehead. The rest of the night, each time the one would back up, the other would be crying.

Even when Cotton arrived back of Tochigi the next afternoon, he couldn't go straight home. He knew that right now they were burying Sumiko's ashes back in Yoshiwara, and so he left the station and walked wide of the town, where he could be by himself. He'd been scared in Tokyo, a *gaijin* enemy. He put on his clerical collar to come home. But now he wasn't frightened anymore. He was a missionary, safe, back in Tochigi where his parish loved him and everybody else in town cared.

Still, even that didn't matter now. All that he could think about was that he had killed Sumiko, murdered her in God's eyes as neatly as if he had been the one who had beaten her and strangled her, squeezing till the last of the breath went out of her body and her body into the Sumida.

It was the hardest for him as he neared the church and had to walk alongside the Uzuma. He had to look away, lest every time he looked in the river, he see Sumiko's body in the water, trailing blue and silver.

When at last he got to the church, he took a seat up front and tried to remember Sumiko. He tried to remember how bright and beautiful she was, but he could only hold that vision for a while, and then he'd have to stop and pray for her soul and pray for his sins again. He didn't even hear Miyuki come in. She'd seen the door open. It was a long time before she dared approach him, and then she was glad that the floor creaked and gave her away. Cotton turned around.

"Is everything all right?" Miyuki asked.

"No. Nothing. Nothing is right." He didn't even realize what he was doing, but he rose then and started walking down the aisle toward her, toward her embrace. He lay there upon her shoulder for a long time before he spoke at all. "She is dead" was all that he said, and then, once again, the tears poured out, and he started crying so hard that he had to struggle for breath. Miyuki just held him. "Sumiko is dead."

"Oh, Cotton." She waited a while longer. "How did it happen?"

"She was killed. It's the war already. It's the war."

Miyuki flinched. "Why?"

"I can't tell you, Miyuki. I want to, but I can't tell you."

"You did love her, didn't you?"

He lifted his head off her shoulder. "No, I told you: she was wonderful, Sumiko was, but I love you. I only killed her."

Miyuki knew enough not to take all that at face value. "I love you, Cotton" was all she said to him. And this time, when he started to cry, she snuggled deeper into his arms. "I'm here with you. I'm here . . . I'm here, darling."

They held each other for the longest time, pressed so tightly that they didn't hear the man come through the door, or see him stand there and stare at them.

And when they finally realized that they weren't alone and looked up, at first neither Cotton nor Miyuki recognized him, for he was in his naval lieutenant's white uniform, and they had never seen him wearing that before.

Miyuki started to say, "Kiyoshi, it's not—" But she stopped. Cotton held out a hand to him, and then he dropped it.

Still Kiyoshi only stood there. It was a long time before he spoke. Then what he said was: "Miyuki, when you're through here with the priest, I'd like very much to talk with you."

1941
KANO TO MI
THE YEAR
of the
METAL SNAKE
Kannamesai, the
Harvest Festival

45

What is more maddening; to believe the worst yet not know, or to see what appears to be the worst but be assured that what you saw was really not so?

So it was with Cotton and Kiyoshi. Every rational bone in Cotton's body told him that Kiyoshi had been sent to spy, in some fashion, in Hawaii. More's the agony, every fearful fiber in Cotton's body kept telling him that Kiyoshi was also somehow involved—even responsible—for Sammy's death. He had no proof, nothing that you could call evidence; but even so, Cotton could not think of Kiyoshi, could not look at him, without thinking that.

And Kiyoshi. He had seen his wife in Cotton's arms. And no matter that Miyuki had run after him from the church and told him no, no, Kiyoshi, you did not see me loving your friend, you only saw me consoling him. And no matter that Cotton had followed them to the station and grabbed him by the arm, pulling him away from Miyuki and her mother even as the train came down the track. "Don't think those things, Key."

"Miyuki has already told me the story," Kiyoshi replied, coldly.

"It is not a story. It is true. You must believe me: I had just learned that my girl had—" He stared to say "been killed." Instead he said: "—died."

"You had a girlfriend?"

"Yes. For some months. Almost since you left." And Cotton dabbed at his eyes again, drawing the backs of his hands over both of them.

"What was her name?"

"Her name was Sumiko."

Cotton could see that mattered to Kiyoshi, the name mattered, and he couldn't imagine why. Kiyoshi stared back at him. He saw the photograph. He heard Yamamoto speaking: "A special *oiran* of the *gaijin's*. Sumiko something or other."

Cotton was trying to tell him that he and his wife were snuggling up because something happened to some whore? *What kind of a patsy do you think I am?* Kiyoshi started to throw that in Cotton's face, to call him a lair, but the train was coming, and Mrs. Serikawa was calling him. "Take the luggage, Kiyoshi." So he only looked back at Cotton and said "All right" to be polite.

"No, it is true, Key. Tell him, Miyuki," he cried, grabbing her, pulling her back. "Tell him."

"I have, Cotton," she said, and she swung back to her husband. "It is true, Key. He lost his girl. And he needed me. And he needs . . . you. Now."

The train pulled to a stop, and the conductors came out. The other passengers began to board. Kiyoshi started to pick up his bags. He managed somehow to look at Miyuki and Cotton both, the one after the other, and yet never look at either. "I'm sorry," he said. "He doesn't need us. He has his church now. He has his Christians." And he bade the ladies go before him and followed them on.

Miyuki did not look back. If she had at all, she only would have convinced Kiyoshi that she was leaving her lover behind. But if she had looked, if she could have, she would have seen Cotton on the platform, and when the train was gone, and all the passengers departed, she would have seen him bury his head in his hands and begin to sob again.

So the Serikawas settled back into their house in Asakusa, with Kiyoshi leaving every day, going down to the Naval

Ministry, or to the Army War College, where he was assigned as an observer on the most advanced plans for Operation Z.

And every night he would come back to the house, and they would have dinner, and then Miyuki would make sure that he fucked her before they went to sleep. And that's what it was—strictly fucking, not loving, not making love. All she cared about now was conceiving, bearing a Serikawa child—the spirits willing, an heir, a son. She had grown more preoccupied about that now, more even than her mother—and notwithstanding that even with all the increasing deprivation, Mrs. Serikawa had still somehow found some dried herring eggs and purchased them for her daughter. As everyone in the Sun-Begot Land knew, herring eggs were the secret to fertility.

As much as possible, Miyuki tried to keep Kiyoshi happy, assure him that it was he she loved and wanted. She fawned over him, fed him well, plied him with drink, rubbed his back, agreed with his complaints, soothed his mind. And all that she asked in return was that he fuck her. Which, of course, he was happy to do.

Also, of course, she did not fool him one bit.

They did not even talk about Cotton at all for the first couple of weeks after they returned. Then one night Kiyoshi came home moody and preoccupied. He had been on the spot that day himself, testifying before a high council of generals, explaining how utterly unprepared the Americans were in Hawaii. He had detailed the lack of vigilance, the predictability of the American actions, the simple pattern of their fleet's movement. "They take off to sea Monday and come back Friday—every Friday. They anchor the ships, and then the men go into town and get drunk and line up before the whorehouses on Hotel Street. Then the mornings, Saturday, Sunday, they sleep it off, go to the beach, play golf."

"It cannot be that easy, Lieutenant," one crusty old general piped up.

"It can, sir. I've seen it. I've sat on the hill overlooking Pearl. I've sat where our planes will come over. I've seen the fleet moored there, unguarded. The Americans have an expression. They say something is 'like shooting ducks in a barrel.' "

" 'Ducks in a barrel'?" the general asked, chuckling. "I like that."

"Well, you ask me, sir, that's what this can be."

Maybe it was this day, hearing his own vital testimony, that finally convinced Kiyoshi that, really, only some extreme, unforeseen circumstance could waylay Operation Z now. And so he went home and drank too much with Miyuki, and he grew morose and started talking about things American and, at last, about Cotton. Still, she didn't encourage him, volunteering as little as she could.

"Did you ever meet the girl?" he asked her.

"Oh no. She was in Tokyo. He barely mentioned her."

"Did you know her name?"

"Yes. Sumiko," Miyuki said. "He did let that slip once. But nothing else about her."

Kiyoshi thought for a moment. "He must have loved her a great deal if he was so upset."

"No," Miyuki replied, instinctively. Because, of course, Cotton loved her. He slept with Sumiko, but he loved her.

Kiyoshi caught that right away. "No?"

"I mean, I think he cared for her a lot, but it wasn't just that."

"Then what was it?"

"Somehow—and I don't have any idea why—but somehow he thought he was responsible for Sumiko's death."

"How did she die?"

"I have no idea. He'd just told me, only right before you came into the church. He said: 'I killed her.' "

"He killed her?"

"No, no, no. He only meant . . . figuratively. But he felt so guilty, so responsible." She paused, and then she said: "Oh, Key, can you just imagine what it would be like for someone you care for, someone you might even . . . love, someone like that to be killed—and for you to feel responsible?"

Miyuki had no idea, of course, how the words would cut through Kiyoshi like the bullets that took down Sammy. "Yes,

I can imagine" was what he managed to say, and everything else she said was lost on him, and soon he struggled up and stumbled to his futon. He was asleep before she got there herself, so this night she excused him of his marital duties. Instead, Miyuki only lay there and thought of Cotton, for whom she still yearned.

The Serikawa residence was hardly the only household in Japan where the pressure to bear fruit and multiply was felt. Miyuki was not alone in sensing—fearing—that a greater war was near, and the chance for children soon would be gone. There was hardly a hotel ballroom left unbooked for a wedding, and the government's Marriage Encouragement Association even offered a thirty-yen bounty for those who tied the knot. Plans for propagation were, in the land, second only to plans for invasion.

Oh, a few fool dreamers still dared believe in the whimsy of peace. Hirohito, for one, yet held out. When his military men came to the Imperial Palace to advise him about how grave the situation was growing, he listened patiently, and when finally he replied to them—really, formally for the first time in five years, since the incident of *ni/ni-roku*—he asked them point blank: "Why don't you put more faith in what diplomacy can achieve today, rather than what war *may* bring us tomorrow?"

No one spoke up. No one even seemed to shuffle his feet. "Why don't you answer me?" Hirohito asked, but the generals and admirals only sat aghast, shocked at His Majesty's blunt challenge to them.

So the emperor responded to himself by shaking his head in sorrow and reaching for a single piece of paper that he had brought with him. "This is a poem my grandfather Meiji wrote," he declared. At that, the hall grew so quiet that it was beyond silence, under silence.

" 'All the seas, everywhere/Are brothers one to another,' " Hirohito read. " 'Why then do the winds and waves of strife/ Rage so violently through the world?' "

The soldiers and sailors gulped and assured Tenno Heika that, of course, they would continue to place war in the lee of diplomacy. Among themselves they agreed that November 16 would indeed be the best Sunday to hit Hawaii.

Within a week, in fact, a yeoman second class, one Mitsuharu Noda, was handed a large, nondescript package and ordered to take it down to Kure, where a large part of the fleet was anchored. He and his assistant simply dropped over to the Central Station, purchased third-class seats on the sleeper, and used the bundles as head rests. Somewhere along the journey, Noda grew curious and opened the package up—well, nobody had told him not to. There were a bunch of black manila folders, maybe a hundred of them, with mimeographed pages stuck in them. Idly, the yeoman peeked into one, where he saw that the first page opened with this statement: "Japan is declaring war on the United States, Great Britain, and the Netherlands." The rest of the document outlined the specific plans of attack. Noda's eyebrows arched a bit, but then he just slid the one copy back into the package, snuggled up on his makeshift pillow, and fell back to sleep.

Like that, one way or another, more and more people were being brought into the circle. Two of Yamamoto's most distinguished admirals, Yamaguchi and Nagumo, almost came to blows, cursing loudly about details of the attack. But at least it wasn't in a whorehouse, and, somehow, no one who shouldn't have heard about the fight did.

Yamamoto heard, though. He was furious at this stupid breach, and so he called together a joint army-navy intelligence meeting for the express purpose of discussing the vital secrecy of Operation Z. And he began with Kiyoshi. "Serikawa-kun?"

"Sir?"

"We should have no difficulty, and we should deserve no credit for, holding even the deepest secrets on our home islands. Should we?"

"No sir. There should never be any betrayal of confidence here."

"I agree," Yamamoto said. "Don't we all?" And with all

the loud murmurs in the affirmative, no one, not even Kiyoshi, noticed how Yamamoto gently lifted his eyes and looked across the table toward Lieutenant Commander Tsujimura—the man who had murdered Sammy Ushijima in cold blood. Tsujimura himself arched his eyebrows, nodding back at the admiral, who proceeded smoothly. "I particularly inquired that of Lieutenant Serikawa because he, amongst us all, has faced the most difficult covert job, being in the lions' lair itself in Hawaii. So, may I ask, Serikawa-kun—and be absolutely candid—do you remain confident that no American—that no one—in Hawaii suspects our designs?"

"There was only one, sir. An old friend of mine, as a matter of fact," Kiyoshi began. "But wisely"—he paused and glanced first at Yamamoto, then over to Tsujimura—"wisely, it was concluded that he must not be given any opportunity to upset the plans of an empire."

There were murmurs of assent. Yamamoto continued: "And am I correct that neither is there any evidence here in Japan that any information has been picked up by the wrong people?" He shifted to look directly at Teshima. "Do we know any more, General, about that young German who was snooping in Yoshiwara?"

Teshima straightened up. "No, sir. He's disappeared. The whore he was trying to use as some kind of an informant was killed."

Kiyoshi took in a breath. "May I ask how, sir?"

Teshima looked to the junior office with irritation. "She was fished out of the Sumida."

Yamamoto followed up. "So, Teshima Taisho, who killed her?"

"Well, the kraut—von Kohorn—obviously."

Kiyoshi had to drop his head. He knew Cotton was von Kohorn, and he knew Cotton had *not* killed her. So who had? And why?

"In any event," Teshima continued, "we have no reason to think that the kraut ever did learn anything."

"How can you be so sure, Teshima Taisho?" Kiyoshi had

snapped his head up and said that before he realized it. He was terribly out of order.

Teshima slapped the table. "Yamamoto Shirei Chokan, if you would have your young man take care of Hawaii and leave—"

Yamamoto raised his hand, then patted Kiyoshi's. "I appreciate your irritation, General, and I chastise Lieutenant Serikawa for a moment's impetuous discourtesy." He hesitated, and Kiyoshi took his lead:

"My apologies, Teshima Taisho. It's just that this whole affair is so sensitive. It occurred to me that *if* the German killed the whore, it would be because she *did* pass on some information to him that she'd learned at the house, and—"

"Excuse me, Serikawa-kun, but there is no evidence whatsoever that anyone in the army . . . or navy . . . has been guilty of spilling secrets anywhere with regard to Operation Z." Teshima's voice was almost shrill. "Clearly, the German killed her because she was unable to provide him any information, but she was growing suspicious of his inquiries. He began to press her . . . uh . . ." Hastily then: "We can imagine. And so he began to fear that, as a loyal daughter of Japan, she would turn him in to the authorities, so he . . ." Teshima drew a forefinger across his neck.

Kiyoshi's eyes jumped around the table. Was he the only one who thought the general was overreacting, was too sure by half? His gaze stopped on Tsujimura. Good grief, Tsujimura suspected everybody. But Tsujimura was playing with a pencil, completely satisfied. No one else spoke up. So: "Yes sir. Of course," Kiyoshi said. "The German."

Yamamoto carried on then. "It's gratifying to know, General Teshima, that *jouhou kyoku* is so confident that no secrets have been lost, so on behalf of us all, may I commend you and your people." Teshima bowed deeply from his seat, smiling. "But as we draw closer to November 16, the task will be ever more daunting. Let the word go out to all: If your subordinates are not required to know, don't whisper a word to them. Nothing to mistresses, nothing to geishas . . ." He didn't have to mention wives, of course. Who would tell them anything?

Yamamoto rose then, looking down at them all. " 'Behold the frog,' " he declared, recalling an old epigram. " 'Behold the frog, who when he opens his mouth, displays his whole inside.' "

They all laughed. Except Teshima.

46

That evening, before he left Tokyo to return to the fleet, Admiral Yamamoto hosted a small party with Kikuji, his mistress. It was very sophisticated, only for those who had ever lived in the West. Kiyoshi and Miyuki were the youngest invited, and although Kiyoshi was afraid the older women might be in kimono, he didn't argue with Miyuki when she picked out her favorite summer dress, a terribly stylish one, white, with red trim and flower patterns at the shoulder and hip. Kiyoshi needn't have feared, though. It was not what Miyuki wore—the other women were in Western dresses, too—but it was how she looked, so stunning that Kikuji herself told Miyuki: "You are the problem. You are too pretty to be a wife, and yet you make all the mistresses jealous because you are a wife."

Yamamoto came over gently, directed Kikuji toward some of the other guests, offered Miyuki his arm, and escorted her into the garden, where they stood on the moon-viewing platform. It was just now heading into autumn, the terrible strange heat of the summer of '41 gone, the evening perfectly cool for the admiral in his naval suit and perfectly warm for Miyuki in her cotton dress. The last of the crickets still chirped (if perhaps a bit wearily) under a new moon that hardly gave off more light than a bright star.

"Next week will be Moon Viewing Festival," Yamamoto

said. "Oh, how we used to enjoy that when I was a little boy! Do they still celebrate that out in the country? In Tochigi?"

"Certainly, they're already talking about the festival. But I'm living here with Kiyoshi now, and I imagine we'll stay in Tokyo."

"Yes, I think it's likely he'll remain posted to the Naval Ministry," Yamamoto said. "But I did want to tell you how much I regretted taking him away from you all these months past."

"I understand, sir. Don't worry, we're trying to make up for the lost time. My mother has filled me with dried herring eggs, and I thank you again for letting me accompany Kiyoshi to Kagoshima."

"I'm glad to play a small role in this partnership." He winked, then looked off into the dark sky. "It is important for you to know, Miyuki, that your husband is an *aikokusha*—a patriot. You're aware of that?" She smiled again, but this time with a different, more polite, more Japanese smile—a more Japanese *woman* smile. "He is. It's most difficult for us who have been in the West, who have friends in the West, to even contemplate, uh, hostilities with the West. Unfortunately, that's all too easy to accept if you're some wet-eared farm boy." Miyuki didn't smile this time. She only nodded. "We are the ones, Kiyoshi and myself and our kind, who must save Japan for the Emperor. I hope you understand, Miyuki."

"Have you heard that I don't, Admiral?"

"There is talk. There is always talk. And in these difficult times, talk often finds its way into personnel files." He turned to look at her, and she had the courage to face him. "I have heard that you are very close to an American."

Miyuki gripped the railing of the platform. She had not anticipated that, and she was glad that it was such a sliver of a moon, with so little light to catch her expression. There were no secrets left, were there? All right, she would meet it head-on. "He is not my lover," she declared, flat out.

"Fine, but that's Kiyoshi's concern. I worry only that the American is your conscience." Miyuki blinked. "Japanese do not own that luxury anymore."

"You're saying we can no longer possess a conscience, Admiral?"

"I'm saying: not a borrowed one," Yamamoto replied. "Not a conscience borrowed from the West."

Kiyoshi seemed distracted to Miyuki, and he was. Even at times during the party, he could not get his mind away from the afternoon's meeting. As soon as they returned home, he turned to Miyuki with urgency. "You must tell me what you know about Cotton's girl."

"I told you. I only knew her name. Just Sumiko. Nothing else. Ever. I swear, Key."

"Please. It's important. I need to know."

"I don't know any more. What is this? At this hour?" She moved close to him, ran her hands over his chest, and cooed. "Come on, darling, let's go to bed. I think it's my perfect time for a baby."

He only brushed her hands away and stepped back. "All right," he said after a moment. "Did you know this? Sumiko was a whore. In Yoshiwara."

He watched the expression on Miyuki's face. She looked genuinely puzzled. "Cotton was going with a whore?"

"Yes." Kiyoshi smiled. In his mind, he saw again the snapshot of Cotton in his sunglasses and his little cap, standing and laughing with the girl at Sensoji. He wished he'd studied her more closely, but he'd been so shocked that Cotton was the man in the photograph that he never really looked at the woman. Not much. Just this: "She was very pretty."

"How do you know, Key? How do you know all this?"

"There's a lot of things about Cotton you know, and I trust you, and I haven't pressed you. So, now it isn't for you to ask me what I know about him. I only thought maybe you could help me." Without another word, he went directly to his closet, took off his civilian suit and tie, and put on his uniform. Miyuki only stared at him, keeping her wifely place. "I don't expect to be more than an hour or two," he said, brushing past her out the door. "Our baby can wait that long."

When he was finally able to find a cab, Kiyoshi said "Yoshiwara," and then he walked directly from the great gate to the Shinyanagi.

Mr. Okumura greeted the new officer. "You are Lieutenant—"

"Yano," Kiyoshi replied.

"Yes, how do you do, Lieutenant Yano? Did you make an appointment?"

"This is business of another nature," Kiyoshi said brusquely, beckoning Okumura to enter his own office. Inside, although Kiyoshi lowered his voice, he diminished none of its sharp formality. "I apologize for arriving at this busy time, but I'm working for General Teshima on the von Kohorn matter, and something has come up."

The manager held out his hands. "But Lieutenant Yano, I have answered so many questions from so many officers."

"I only need to know when von Kohorn first started coming here."

"The spring sometime. I—" The phone rang.

"Just let me see your appointment book for that period, then."

Okumura reached for the phone. "Yes, she is available now. Please send the gentleman over." With his other hand, he opened a drawer from the cabinet and handed Kiyoshi a ledger marked "1941, JAN.—JUNE," and as the phone rang again, Kiyoshi took the book himself and started reading it, from back to front, June 30 first.

Von Kohorn's name popped up soon enough, and, as Kiyoshi traced it back, there it was on most Mondays, through June and May, into April. It was always with Sumiko. And then the name dropped off. Curiously, the last entry Kiyoshi came to—the first one for von Kohorn, early in April—wasn't for a Monday but for a Tuesday.

Kiyoshi picked up a pencil and put it to his lips. Cotton must have heard something then, he thought. I know Cotton, and he wouldn't just drop by a whorehouse for a piece of ass. He heard about something related to this one girl, and so he came to see her at this house that Tuesday. And he hit enough pay dirt to keep coming back, Mondays—day off for barbers, bartenders, and priests.

Kiyoshi borrowed a sheet of paper from Okumura and made some notes. Then he pushed the ledger back.

"I hope you found what you need, Lieutenant."

"I think so, Mr. Okumura. I would hope that the next time I return to Shinyanagi it is for more pleasurable activity." They both bowed deeply.

The next morning, instead of going to the Naval Ministry, Kiyoshi caught the train to Tochigi. It was a bright September day, and when he arrived, he found Cotton high up on a ladder, on the side of the church, touching up some places where the paint had flaked. It really needed a whole new coat, but there wasn't nearly enough money for that.

Cotton never saw Kiyoshi—not until he came right up under the ladder and rattled it. "Don't worry—nothing wrong. Just gotta ask you about something," he called out, and Cotton slid down, holding up his palms where they had some paint on them.

That was unfortunate, in a small way, not being able to shake hands, for they had left each other on the train station so at odds that just to shake hands anew, just to touch one another, would have helped. Kiyoshi seemed to understand that. Purposely, he slapped Cotton on the back and held his hand there on his shoulder. "All right, I'll cut through the bullshit, Cotton."

"What's what mean?"

"It means I believe you." Cotton turned his head. "I believe that you lived here with my wife, under this roof, and you honored me."

"Yes," Cotton said. "Thank you, Key"—and reflexively he raised up his hand to slap his friend on the back.

Kiyoshi ducked away laughing. "Hey, watch it! Regulation 838-B forbids civilians with paint on their hands to touch an officer of the Imperial Navy in uniform."

And Cotton laughed, too. It was the first time in a long

while they'd laughed together. Cotton waved a hand toward the baseball diamond. "Hey, you should come up here tomorrow. Our last game. We were supposed to keep playing for a couple more weeks, but you guys have taken all our players."

They ambled along, toward the river. "Well, I'd come back up and see your swan song, but Miyuki and I've got to take off tomorrow morning. We're dropping Mrs. Serikawa off with her sister-in-law in Aimoto, and then—" He stopped. Kagoshima was classified. "Uh, then Miyuki will be with me a couple weeks on an assignment."

Cotton understood he wasn't to ask anything else. He didn't want to, anyhow. It was painful enough trying to put Miyuki out of his mind without having her husband chat on about her. He took a seat on the edge of a bathtub there, by the riverbank. In the summer, the tubs had lined the Uzuma, but most had been taken back home by now, and only a couple were left outside. "Look, I ought to tell you something, even if you'll be away," Cotton said. "Kazuko is landing in a couple of days, and she's bringing Sammy's ashes up here."

Kiyoshi had been about to sit down on the tub next to Cotton, but as soon as he heard those words he stepped away, looking off across the river. "Please give her my love" was all he finally said. He didn't move for the longest time; it was a terrible silence. . . .

At last Cotton spoke again. "I'm sorry, Key."

He turned back. "Sammy's funeral service was the hardest thing I ever went through in my life."

"There seem so many things so hard for us to talk about all of a sudden."

"No, we don't own ourselves anymore, do we?" Kiyoshi asked. Cotton nodded his head. "Okay, but I need your help. I need to know something."

"Shoot."

"Sumiko," Kiyoshi said. Cotton got up off the tub and took a step away. "Tell me why she was killed."

"Why do you know about Sumiko?"

"Never mind. Just give me a chance to hold your trust this time."

Cotton crossed his arm and stared over to the baseball field. Finally he turned back. "All right. Sumiko was killed because she heard something by mistake from the wrong person." He paused. "And then she happened to meet another wrong person."

"You?"

"Yes—all right, I was the other wrong person."

"So, who was the first wrong person?"

Cotton shook his head vigorously. "No. I can't tell you that."

"You don't trust me?"

Cotton said: "Sumiko trusted me, Key."

"You think you could be in danger?"

"You said it yourself. There are things that belonged to us that we don't own ourselves anymore. They aren't ours to do with."

"All right, can you tell me who killed her?"

"I don't know. For sure."

"But you think you know?"

"Sure. The other wrong person. But he probably didn't kill her himself. He probably had her killed."

"Same thing," Kiyoshi said. He reached into his pocket and pulled out the sheet of paper that he'd made up the night before at Shinyanagi. On it he'd written down the names of all the military men who'd plied Sumiko's trade in the weeks leading up to Cotton's first transaction with her, early in April. Kiyoshi had listed the men's last names only, no ranks or titles, one after the other. He handed it to Cotton. "Just tell me if any names here mean anything to you."

Cotton glanced at the list. "What is this?"

"Please, Cotton, just read the names."

Cotton went down the list, expressionless, unknowing, until suddenly, near the bottom of the first column, he grimaced. "There's one," he said.

"Go on, read them all."

Cotton finished the list. "No, just the one." He handed the list back, his finger pointing to that name.

"Thank you, Cotton," Kiyoshi said. "I appreciate that." He

put the paper back in his pocket. "I also think it's time you left Japan. But I know you're a stubborn sonofabitch, so if you're still here when we get back to Tokyo, come see us." Cotton put out his hand, dry of the paint now, and they shook firmly, staring deep into each other's faces, trying to pay as much attention to each other's hearts. Kiyoshi turned, then, and started walking to the train station.

A few steps and Cotton called after him. Kiyoshi stopped and looked back. "How did you know Teshima killed her, Key? How did you know that?"

Kiyoshi only shook his head and smiled. How strange it was. They were both scared, of just how much the other one knew.

47

Cotton was surprised how much Kazuko looked like a little old lady who'd spent all her life right here in Tochigi, in the paddies. Sammy's widow, the woman Cotton had known in Hawaii, although certainly never westernized, now seemed even more Japanese than ever—wizened and hunched, more sallow. Cotton reached out to give her a hand as she stepped from the train, and, almost instinctively, she handed him the urn with her husband's ashes.

"Sammy wanted you to have these, Cotton-san," Kazuko said, and Cotton accepted the package and bowed and kissed her, then grabbed her big valise, and they went back to the rectory for some lunch.

"How long will you stay with your family in Hiroshima?" Cotton asked.

"At least through the spring," Kazuko answered, stuffing her mouth with *kimpira*—fried root mixed with carrots. Cotton had gone to all the shops and markets, trying to find as many Japanese specialties as he could. There weren't many left these days.

"There may be war with America by the spring, you know."

"Nooo. Then surely I will stay in Hiroshima, where I'll be the safest," Kazuko said. "No intruder has ever reached our shores. The divine wind, the kamikaze, will always drive away the enemy."

"But it's hard times," Cotton explained. "It's difficult to find anything now. Everything must be sent to the soldiers, and if the war widens, it'll be worse."

Kazuko cleaned her rice bowl, wiping up every last particle with tea. "It's never been better in Hawaii," she said. "All the troops there, the work. Everyone has money."

"Kazuko, I'm afraid there's no place left in the Pacific that's safe. If there's more war, I'm not sure Hawaii will be safe, or that even the kamikaze can protect Hiroshima anymore."

She looked back at him glumly. Cotton had not meant things to turn so sour. "So," he said, putting on a happier face, reaching over and taking her hand, "where do you think Sammy would want us to throw his ashes?"

"The girls told me, 'Mother, tell Cotton to leave Daddy where his spirit would rest on the best of Japan'."

"All right, I know a place where the Uzuma comes down out of the mountains, and in the spring when all the wildflowers come out it's blue and white and pink and purple. It's always green up there. It's green now, and you can look down and see so far. I go up there myself sometimes just to think."

"Like the Aiea Heights above Pearl Harbor. Sammy would go up there just to get away sometimes."

"Yes," said Cotton.

"All right—there," said Kazuko, and so that's where they headed. It was a hard journey for Kazuko on foot, but at least the ground was harder in the fall, the farm women just now moving into the rice fields for the harvest.

At one point along the road, one of those women spotted Cotton and started heading to him from out of the ooze. He didn't recognize her at first, in her universal rice pickers' uniform—broad hat against the sun, formless blue coat and trousers—but as she came closer, he could tell it was Hanako. Cotton bowed to her Japanese-style and kissed her on the cheek Western. "Hey, I thought you were going to try my church!" he said.

"Too damn much work now," Hanako said. "I told Mom and Pop I'd help 'em out." This year, too, everyone seemed to know that the rice crop was more important than ever. What else would get them through this winter? "Just too tired, Drake-san. Fucking men all night is easy—pulling rice all day is hard. After Niiname-sai I'll come to your church. I promise."

Niiname-sai was the Japanese Thanksgiving, November 23, when the Emperor offered the new grain to his family forebear the Sun Goddess. It was the second harvest holiday. The first, Kannamesai, came October 17, when Tenno Heika went to the Great Shrine at Ise and prayed for a successful harvest ahead. All the burgeoning industry, all the great manufacturing *zaibatsus*—but agriculture still meant so much to Japan. "So, I'll worship your Christmas with you," Hanako said. Cotton nodded, like a benign old priest. "And anyway, Drake-san, we all still pray Christian at home for Sumiko's soul."

"So do I," Cotton said, the tears welling up, and he embraced Hanako—and never mind what a wet mess she was from the paddies.

On, then, Cotton and Kazuko moved, the road winding back to the river, and over the bridge where old Kadota, the toll keeper, lay fast asleep. They laughed, and when Cotton woke him up, Kadota immediately waved them on, but Cotton pressed a few sen on him for Mrs. Ushijima. After all, she wasn't local.

In time, Cotton steered up off the road, and though Kazuko struggled, soon enough she saw the hill crest and the beautiful, sloping green field there. Beyond it were trees, and mountains beyond them, and below: the river and the paddies and the little town all laid out. The stubby steeple of the mission stood up just enough, so that Cotton could point out to Kazuko where they'd walked from. One black butterfly sailed by, the last sign of summer.

"See," Cotton said, sweeping his arm. "The best of Japan."

"Yes, Sammy would be very happy," Kazuko said. "He's not Christian, but he wanted you to spread his ashes in the land of his birth. He said that to me the night before the robbers got him. 'Kazuko, if anything ever happens to me . . .'"

Cotton touched her arm. "Why did he want *me* to do this?"

"Once Sammy told me: 'Kazuko, it's easy to love your country. It's easy for Japanese to love Japan and Americans America. But I think maybe I love America more because I came to America and learned to love it. And no one knows that better than Cotton, because he learned to love Japan even as I learned to love America.'"

"That's lovely," Cotton said. He laid the urn down. "Let's pray."

They stood silently for a long while, holding hands. It took Cotton back to that day five years ago, when he stood in Honolulu in a circle, holding Sammy's hand, praying for Takeo. "I loved you, *wagatomo*—my friend," Cotton said at last, raising his head to the sky. "Thank you for inviting me to be the one to help bring you back to the land of your fathers. Please watch over us and see that we keep peace in our two lands." And then Cotton opened the urn and offered it to Kazuko. She took out a handful of ashes and tossed them up, softly. Cotton followed suit, and then they walked about together, scattering handfuls over the high grass. There was a little breeze, and some of the ashes fluttered before they fell. Kazuko started to hum a little. The sun was out, and a flock of swallows flew by.

Cotton reached back in for the last of the ashes. He felt something different and loose at the bottom of the urn. "There's something in here, Kazuko."

"Yes, it's for you," she said, and purposely, she turned away from him and headed a bit down the hill, where she sat in the grass, looking off, toward Tochigi.

Cotton pulled out an envelope. His name, in English, was all that was written on it, just "Cotton." He sat down, and when he opened it, he saw that it was from Sammy, dated in April, the day before he died. And he read:

Dear Cotton,

I don't know now how I'll get this to you, but somehow I must try, because I know now that it's not safe for you in Japan, and you must get out NOW!

Also, you must know that Kiyoshi is a spy. Yes. That's why he's come back here, just to spy. I found him in the Heights, studying Pearl, so I guess they're going to attack us here. Of course, Kiyoshi denies all this, but I could tell he was lying.

I'm having dinner with him day after tomorrow, and the way I'm thinking now, I'll wait till he clears out, back to Japan, and then I'm going to see General Short himself and tell him what's up.

So things are OK on this end. The reason I'm writing you is to let you know what's with K. Be very careful around him, and also Miyuki and Mrs. S. because who knows what they are up to? DON'T TELL KIYOSHI ANYTHING when he pals up to you.

And please, get out, because even if we stop them from attacking Hawaii, you know they will strike somewhere and then right away, you will be a prisoner. Get out.

Your friend,
Sammy U.

P.S. The enclosed here is what K. was doodling when I caught him. Remember Yoshitsune from school? He surprised the enemy by coming a totally unexpected way. Do you see?

Cotton picked up the other sheet. Even if Sammy hadn't written that postscript, he would have known that the sheet was obviously Kiyoshi's. He'd doodled the same way all his life.

Then Cotton ducked his head. He would have cried, he

thought, but that he was too shocked to do anything at all. This was the final confirmation: Japan would strike Hawaii. . . . But it hardly seemed to matter at this moment on the hill, for all that Cotton's mind could absorb was that his oldest friend, Kiyoshi Serikawa, was a spy in the service of the Emperor against Cotton's country, and . . .

A murderer who had killed their friend.

Somehow, Cotton lifted the letter back up and read it again. "DON'T TELL KIYOSHI ANYTHING." And here Kiyoshi had come all the way to Tochigi the other day and sweet-talked me about trust and love and picked my brain clean. I'm as dead as Sammy. Cotton buried his head again, but each time he shook it, the same awful truths tumbled out. So, at last, he picked up the empty urn and headed down to where Kazuko still sat, taking in the sun, looking down on the earth.

Cotton held up the letter before her. "You know what's in here?"

"Come on, Cotton, you know I can't read English."

"But didn't Josephine or Darlene?"

I found it just like that, when I was cleaning out his desk drawers a couple of weeks after he died. He'd told me he'd written you a letter, that last night, but he told me he didn't know how to get it to you. So I hid it when I found it, and then I put in the ashes when I came." He nodded. "Is it bad, Cotton? It's about Kiyoshi, isn't it? He was very upset with Kiyoshi right before—"

Cotton said: "Sammy thought a war with the United States was coming. And so do I."

"Well, so, I will want to be with my family in Hiroshima."

Cotton looked her dead in the eye. "Kazuko, it would not be your husband's wishes for you to stay in Japan."

She wasn't intimidated; she didn't duck away. "Cotton," she said, "all our life together, Isamu complained: 'Be more American, Kazuko. Be more Western, more moga, be more independent, like our daughters.' So now, thank you very much, I choose to honor *that* wish of my husband." A slight but very proud smile crossed her face. "I will stay."

Cotton sighed. "All right, Kazuko. Sammy would like that. I'll take you into Tokyo tomorrow and put you on the sleeper for Hiroshima."

He helped her up, and they started back down to Tochigi. They hardly spoke; Cotton was thinking only about what he must do. When he took Kazuko into Tokyo tomorrow, he must himself then go directly to the American embassy and lay it all out. There was no question left anymore. Never mind just Bowersox—he would report to Ambassador Grew himself. Cotton knew everything now. He *knew*. Well, not the exact date. But he even knew the exact route now. For sure. North. They'll sail from Hokkaido, Cotton thought. He hadn't worked years at American Orient not to know how few ships ever plied that route. Soon, none at all, as the fall wears along. Only Kiyoshi was as familiar with that as he was. Only Kiyoshi.

But as they walked on in silence a bit further, Cotton could feel the flush coming to his face, his heart beating faster, and his head spinning, and he wanted to scream that what he was thinking couldn't be; but he knew it was, and he knew there wasn't anything he could do about it, not right away. Because, no—he knew: he wouldn't alert the United States of America until first he had found the woman he loved with all his heart and taken her safely away from the monster she was married to, away from Kiyoshi, away from Japan, and away to wherever they could be, together, forever. There would still be time for the rest of the world after that, after he got Miyuki for himself.

48

Kagoshima is the southernmost Japanese city, subtropical— "the Naples of the Orient," some European, homesick and hyperbolic alike, had once called it. Now, in the autumn of 1941, it was even more distant from the heart of the islands.

The number of trains to Kagoshima had been reduced, and those that did still run only jogged in on limited fuel. In fact, it was the middle of the night when Kiyoshi and Miyuki arrived into West Station on the last leg from Fukuoka, and past two before they fell asleep at their hotel, exhausted from their journey.

The sun was barely up, then, when the windows rattled, with an ear-pounding roar that all but tumbled them both out of their skin. "Earthquake!" Miyuki shouted, burying herself in her husband's arms.

But just as quickly the room stopped shaking, and it was as peaceful as any dawn, the sounds that had awoken them receding into the distance. Kiyoshi shook out the cobwebs. "We're all right, honey. It's just the maneuvers."

"Maneuvers? In Kagoshima? In a city? Maneuvers?" She rolled off the futon, wrapped in the covering, and peeked out the window.

Kiyoshi lit a cigarette and chuckled at her. "There's a special reason it has to be Kagoshima."

"It must be important—" Miyuki couldn't finish. Reflexively, in fact, she even ducked. The next flight of Zeros came that close, zooming down the Kotsumi River Valley at three hundred miles per hour, then diving down, barely above the buildings. From her window, Miyuki saw them pass over the big sign on top of the Yamagataya department store, so low she was sure she saw the sign wiggle from the planes' drone. The sound was so awful that Miyuki put her fingers to her ears, and she could see citizens down on the streets of Kagoshima, waving angry fists at the pilots. Miyuki turned back to Kiyoshi. "How long has this been going on?"

"Most of the summer, I'm afraid." The citizens of Kagoshima were furious. The hens had long since stopped laying, and the fish in Kagoshima Bay had all but disappeared. Even the whores of Kagoshima had petitioned the town fathers that this kind of stressful activity was disturbing their business. Everyone was on edge.

And now, explosions started going off in the harbor. From her hotel, Miyuki could actually see torpedo trails in the water, heading away toward a target breakwater a few hundred yards out in the harbor. She was so fascinated she didn't even realize that Kiyoshi had come up behind her, looking out over her shoulder. God, they work, he said to himself. The torpedoes do work. There's nothing else to stand in our way except the diplomats. And they won't; they can't.

In the distance, the Zeros curled around, heading back up to their bases. The pilots were still laughing; it was another good run over Kagoshima. None of them knew yet exactly what they were planning for, only that it was something very big. Most of the rumors at Saeki Air Base had it that it would be Hong Kong. Hong Kong had a mountain at the base of its harbor, just as Kagoshima had Tenpou standing up on one side, by the race track, and Sakurajima, rising even higher, up to four thousand feet, across the way.

Other days, though, the pilots heard it was Manila Bay they were practicing for. They knew that General MacArthur himself was staying at the Manila Hotel; nights, when they were drunk, the pilots all vowed to be the one to get MacArthur ... if it was Manila, of course. But then it was supposed to be Singapore. And last Tuesday, for some reason, the guaranteed word was that it was Sydney.

Kiyoshi went into the bathroom, but Miyuki stayed transfixed at the windows. The noise was higher now, more a rumble, and she strained to look up. But there they came, way high: bombers. She traced them as they started to come down, steering away from downtown, out of her view. If Miyuki could have followed the bombers, though, she would have seen them cut above Kagoshima Bay to a deserted stretch, where, on the beach, an outline approximating the battleship *California* had been drawn in lime. This morning, five of the six bombs hit the target. Regularly now, the Japanese bombardiers were up to eighty percent accuracy.

Miyuki started to pull her head back in, but one more plane screeched down the valley, some fighter *ronin* who had been delayed at takeoff. He made up for his tardiness with even more bravado, coming in so low, so close, that Miyuki could actually make out his face as he flashed by; she even thought she saw him grin and offer her a little wave. She watched him go the whole way till he passed out of sight over some fishing boats.

When she finally pulled the window shut and turned back, Kiyoshi already had his trousers on and was reaching for his blue jacket. "It's Honolulu, isn't it?" she said, utterly matter-of-factly.

Kiyoshi tried to be casual, fussing with his jacket buttons. "What's that? Honolulu?"

"Kagoshima. They're pretending this is Honolulu. For practice." She gestured back out the window. "I can't quite remember. Diamond Head. Where would that be? That mountain over there?"

"Oh, really, Miyuki!"

"It isn't hard to figure out. They're practicing down here for some specific reason, and they bring you in, and you've been working in Honolulu. A fool could put it together."

Kiyoshi made a great to-do about picking up his change and cigarettes. "If we'd known you fancied yourself a military expert, Yamamoto wouldn't have let me bring you down here."

"Come on, Key. I can't close my eyes. Not when everything is going to hell."

Kiyoshi picked up his hat and played with the brim, taking his time. When he raised his head, he said: "You know I didn't ask for this job. My country obliged me to do my share."

Miyuki wrapped herself tighter in the bed sheet, as if somehow that might protect her. "Maybe your country is wrong."

"*Oi!*" he said, shocked. "Who got you thinking this way? Cotton?" As harshly as he stared at her, though, Miyuki could see clearly that he was covering something up. Kiyoshi was scared. Everything was ready now; but still, Kiyoshi was so scared that Japan was wrong. Japan would lose.

"I'm only saying to you what so many Japanese think but are too damned frightened to say," Miyuki said.

"I trust that you have the good sense never to say these things to anyone but me."

"Only Cotton," she said. And then her steady voice took it a step further, almost goading him. "Cotton and I have talked about things."

Measuring every word, Kiyoshi replied: "Then you should be advised that Cotton is an American spy."

"Don't be ridiculous."

"Oh, you're so sure?" He lit another cigarette. "You asked me the other night how I knew about Cotton's girl, that she was a whore. Girlfriend!" Kiyoshi snorted. "He had no affection for her. Part of her business was sleeping with generals, and Cotton was trying to get information out of her that she may have picked up from her customers. He's more of a whore than she was."

"I don't believe that," Miyuki said, but her voice broke a little. Kiyoshi had rattled her.

"Oh, you believe him rather than your husband?"

"He's a priest, Key, a man of God."

"So what? It's just a good cover." Miyuki looked away. "Listen to me," he said. She didn't budge. "I said, listen to me," and he grabbed her and yanked her around to face him. "Now, I advise you—excuse me, I *order* you, as my wife—that you are never to mention to anyone what you said this morning about Honolulu, about Pearl Harbor."

Miyuki hadn't mentioned Pearl Harbor; she didn't even remember that name. That's when she knew she was right. "That's what Sammy knew too, didn't he?" Kiyoshi turned back at the door, glaring at his wife. "Will you kill *me* for the country, too? Well, will you, Key?"

Even before the words were out of her mouth, Miyuki regretted them. They were cruel and unfair. She would have said that she was sorry—except that before she could, Kiyoshi put down his hat, stepped purposefully toward her, drew back his hand, and slapped her hard, flush across her cheek. The pain rushed into her brain, but Miyuki didn't utter a word as she crashed to the floor.

Kiyoshi stood over her. There was no concern in his face, no compassion whatsoever. In fact, all he was waiting for was to make sure that she was conscious. Satisfied that she was, he spoke. "Whatever you think of me, I don't care, so long as you know that the only thing I regretted more than Sammy's death was that they didn't kill me too."

Miyuki managed to nod her head.

He picked his cap back up, and when he reached the doorknob, he hesitated with his hand on it. "Miyuki, I will continue to try and provide you and the Serikawa family with a son. I only ask you to provide me with the honor I deserve."

"Yes, Kiyoshi."

"Let this teach you something. You obviously do not know Cotton, and neither do you know me." As he stepped through the door, she thought she heard him add: "And I don't want you to anymore, either."

The next two mornings Kiyoshi watched the First Air Fleet fly into Kagoshima again. The first day he was on a small boat in the bay, and the next morning he joined Admiral Yamamoto, who was viewing it all from a building high on Sakurajima. Both times what the grumpy townspeople called "the Circus of Sea Eagles" was no less impressive. Then, late in the week, Kiyoshi left Miyuki behind in Kagoshima and was escorted to Saeki Air Base, the chief flight depot in the area.

He was ushered into a conference room where only five officers awaited him? Yamamoto himself and two close naval aides, as well as Genda and Fuchida, the two brilliant young air commanders whom the admiral had selected to both formulate and lead the air component of Operation Z.

Indeed, Yamamoto permitted Genda and Fuchida to grill Kiyoshi at length. They had memorized photographs of Pearl, maps, contour lines, weather reports, all the notes that Kiyoshi and Morimura, his counterpart at the consulate, had sent in. Still, this was the first time they had ever been able to talk to anyone who had actually been to Hawaii, been to Pearl Harbor. And so, over and over again: Was Kiyoshi positive the Americans didn't patrol north? Was security really that lax? Why would they keep mooring the ships together, targets, side by side? When? How? Why? On and on.

"Listen," Kiyoshi said. "Pearl is an even easier target than Kagoshima. Here, you have to contend with Sakurajima, maybe fifteen hundred meters. Ford Island is flat."

"Yes, we know," Genda said. "Still . . ."

"Hell, from what I've seen here," Kiyoshi said, "the people in Hawaii won't be as angry at you as the folks here. Another week and I think the Kagoshimans will be firing back."

They all laughed. Then Fuchida, who was scheduled to be the leader of the actual first assault wave, the man who would drop the first bombs on Hawaii, said: "Lieutenant, you are certain there are no unforeseen likelihoods? It just doesn't seem possible."

Kiyoshi straightened up, looking around to all the others. "If you are all still sure that this game is worth playing, then, yes, I am sure that this is where we make the first pitch."

Yamamoto reached out and touched Fuchida's arm. "You should know, that of everyone who is aware of Operation Z, my friend Serikawa least desires it. The reticence of his heart makes the enthusiasm of his viscera even more convincing."

Kiyoshi ducked his head. "I'm sorry, gentlemen. I've lived in America for many years. Sometimes, forgive me, but I even feel a little American."

They all rose. Genda said: "If it remains the way you say it is in Hawaii, Lieutenant, we will make it a short war."

Kiyoshi bowed. He started to leave with the others, but Yamamoto beckoned for him to come back. "Yes sir?"

"Everything is in place now. Even the torpedoes."

"I saw. Yes sir."

Yamamoto shrugged. "I'm sorry, but unless there's a miracle in Washington . . ." Kiyoshi shrugged. "All right. One other thing you can help me with. I'm ordering a liner, probably the *Tatsuta*, to keep radio silence on its regular trip to Hawaii. I want to see if it can make it, undetected, looping north. I'll order this voyage sometime late in November."

"But I thought the date we had in mind was November 16."

Yamamoto shifted in his seat. "That turned out to be too ambitious, I'm afraid. So we'll wait a bit longer, and perhaps there will be that diplomatic miracle." He drummed his fingers on the table, and Kiyoshi noticed the two missing fingers again. Sometimes he forgot. Although Yamamoto might be a man of peaceful instincts, his profession was war, his memories of glory grounded in Tsushima. "Actually," he went on, "I'd wager that diplomatic conditions are more likely to deteriorate than improve. The army grows more and more insatiable . . . and impatient."

"So . . . when?"

"Exactly. Help me with that, Kiyoshi. I've convinced myself that I must decide in a couple more weeks, by Kannamesai, say. We'll go sometime after Niiname-sai. What's the latest in December I can reasonably contemplate sending the fleet?"

"Well, sir, it's chilly up there then, but barring a bad storm, you'll have a month or so—to mid-December, I'd say."

"How high are the waves? The swells?"

"It's choppy. But not so you couldn't refuel if you had to."

"We will."

"And the advantage is that the later you go—"

"*We* go, Kiyoshi."

"Excuse me, sir?"

"Not 'you go.' *'We* go.' "

They both smiled, Kiyoshi forced. "Yes sir. The later we go, the less chance of detection."

"I know."

"Yoshitsune would be pleased, sir."

"Well put," the admiral said. "Okay, I'll make a few final checks, just to be sure, but you've assured me. One date looks firm. December the eighth. Even the moon is good for us then."

"That's a weekend?"

"Well, it's Monday here. It's Sunday, December the seventh, where we're going."

"So, that'll be the date, sir?"

"Yes. You're the first to know, Serikawa-san. As the Amer-

icans always say"—and here the admiral smiled and switched
to English—"please mark that on your calendar."

Kiyoshi saluted.

49

Softly again, Cotton rapped on the *amado*. Every Tuesday, for
weeks now, he'd taken the train from Tochigi into Tokyo,
gone to Asakusa, and walked to the Serikawas' house and
knocked. But Miyuki never was there. And never did she
write, and never did she call. So each Tuesday, all day, Cotton would wait, but the house remained empty. Once, in the
middle of the day, he did see Kiyoshi walking home. Cotton
ducked away, considered going in and confronting him; but
before he could make up his mind, Kiyoshi rushed back out.
He had something in his hands, something he'd obviously forgotten, and he hurried off, back to work.

And Miyuki never came to the door. She never came back
home.

Kannamesai, the harvest festival, came and went, and,
soon enough then, all of October. So too this autumn did
Prince Konoe, the prime minister, depart, as General Tojo—
Razor Brain, they called him behind his back—took over the
government. Now the army ruled, unchecked. Surely, soon
the fleet would be leaving for Hawaii.

Cotton was growing more desperate. How could he put off
going to see Bowersox again, to see Ambassador Grew himself, to see the whole damn embassy any longer? Last week he
even went down there, but when he reached the embassy,
he stayed outside the gates, pacing back and forth. And then
he went back to Asakusa, back to Miyuki's, and waited there
some more.

He had to see Miyuki first. He had to take her from
Kiyoshi, and then somehow take her from Japan.

But now, this would have to be the last Tuesday he would

wait for her. If she weren't here this time, he'd have to stay till Kiyoshi came home and try to learn her whereabouts from him. Sometimes, in his worst moments, Cotton thought perhaps she was dead. He carried Sammy's letter with him to show Miyuki. "Be careful around Kiyoshi when he comes back." But no, he refused to believe the worst. Kiyoshi could kill Sammy for the Emperor, but surely he couldn't kill Miyuki. He couldn't kill his wife ... could he?

Cotton realized he couldn't wait any longer. He had to find out how much Washington had acted on what he had already told Bowersox. Or were they still ignoring him, still unconvinced, still waiting for the perfect proof? Already it felt like war in Tokyo. One time Cotton saw Tojo himself, out in the streets on his white charger, urging the people on, driving them to work harder. For just a moment Cotton thought Razor Brain looked directly at him in the crowd. It was possible. What few *gaijin* were left kept inside to themselves now. But then, nobody much went out if they didn't have to. Food was scarcer still, and now the lack of fuel hurt all the more on the first chilly autumn nights. It seemed as if every hotel Cotton walked by was hosting a wedding, as the young people scurried to build even a brief future together. Hirohito's own oldest daughter, Terunomiya, Princess Sunshine, was betrothed, age fifteen. Time was short. And still: where was Miyuki?

Meanwhile, the fleet, *Kido Butai*, twenty-five warships, moved up the coast for Hitokappu Bay, in Hokkaido. Thence, to Pearl. The *Tatsuta Maru* had sailed to Honolulu a few days ago, taking its curious path north, maintaining radio silence the whole way. Nobody ever saw it, and nobody even knew where it was till it slipped down, to the warmer latitudes, to dock in Honolulu. The Southern Fleet got ready to depart too, leaving the Inland Sea for the Philippines. Almost nobody knew these things, of course. Just as everybody did know rumors.

But this Tuesday, November the eighteenth, 1941, when Cotton knocked, Miyuki answered. They gasped at each other.

Where have you been?" he said. He had no idea how urgent he sounded.

"With my mother, in Aimoto." He nodded vacantly, trying to take it in that he was finally there with her again. "Kiyoshi was traveling a lot. I'm back now."

At last Cotton came to. "I've missed you so much, my darling," he said. All those other Tuesdays, waiting, he'd imagined saying those few simple words whenever he saw her again.

Miyuki ducked her head, but she replied straightaway, "I missed you too, Cotton"—even if she had to blush and bow to get them out.

He stepped in then, taking her hand as he did, bringing her closer to him. He had to touch her.

She sighed. She had sensed he was going to say something more difficult for her to deal with. Relieved, she replied: "Before Aimoto, I took a trip with Kiyoshi. He was on business."

Cotton arched an eyebrow. "Oh, Kagoshima?" It came out of his subconscious, tumbling from his lips before he'd thought about it.

Miyuki withdrew her hand. "How in the world did you know that?"

"A good guess."

"But you shouldn't know that."

"It's Honolulu, isn't it? They're using Kagoshima as Honolulu?"

Miyuki turned away, so she could say "I guess" without looking at him. He put his hand on her shoulder and softly spun her back to him. Miyuki didn't resist, even though she felt that she'd never been so scared in her life. She wanted everything. She wanted Cotton to grab her and kiss her, and she wanted him to turn and walk away.

"It won't work, you know," he said.

"Why not?"

"Oh, because I know, and I'll tell. I'm the only one, but I'll tell."

"What do you know?"

"Everything. Well, everything but when. *When*, Miyuki? When?"

She only shook her head softly, looking into his eyes, looking for a way out. There was none there. "Oh, Cotton, why did you come back?" He took one of her hands in his. "Did you come to baptize me?"

He shook his head. "No, not today."

"So, why did you come?"

"I came here because I want you to marry me."

Miyuki's gasp became a whole loud cry. She fell away, and her bosom heaved so instinctively she put a hand there as if to keep her pounding heart from jumping out. "Are you crazy, Cotton? Have you lost your mind? I am married to Kiyoshi."

He took her other hand, holding them both now. "Listen, you must leave him. You must tell him to get a *mikudarihan.*" Divorce was virtually impossible for any woman, but a breeze for any husband in Japan, and of course Miyuki knew that. But ask Kiyoshi to fill out a *mikudarihan?* She slumped.

"Dammit, Miyuki, you must leave him! Kiyoshi killed Sammy Ushijima. He killed Sammy!"

They were both shaking now. But slowly, with that, she raised her head and took her hands from his. "How can you say that about my honorable husband? You, a Christian!"

Cotton took Sammy's letter out of his pocket. Then he stood back and let her read it herself. She struggled with the English but took it all in. At last she looked up at him. "This does not say he is a murderer, Cotton. It says he's a spy. But I know he's a spy. You know he's a spy. So what? You're a spy."

"I'm a spy?"

"Kiyoshi says you are."

"What does he know?"

"He knows you used the whore to get what information you could from some officer she slept with."

"God, Kiyoshi knows everything, huh?"

"So, it's true."

Cotton took Miyuki by the shoulders. "All right—so how do you know it's not true when I say he killed Sammy?"

"Because I asked him."

"That's all?"

"How do I know you didn't kill Sumiko?"

Cotton took his hands from her shoulders. "I didn't."

"I know. Because you tell me, and I can see. And now you know Kiyoshi didn't kill Sammy, either. Because he told me so, and I could see."

"Yes," Cotton said. He walked about the room aimlessly, here and there. His voice thickened. "God, I'm so awful. I wanted to believe Key killed Sammy because then I had a reason to take you away from him." His arms fell limply by his side. "Oh, damn, I love you so much."

"And I love you, Cotton. You know that."

"Then ask him, Miyuki—ask him: fill out the *mikudarihan.*"

"No. No." Softly, she shook her head. "I cannot do that. I cannot dishonor my husband."

Cotton started to her, but he stopped. He knew if he came any closer to her again, he would grab her and never let her go. "Then, look, just do *me* this honor. Think about it. You love me. Think about me for a few days. And maybe then . . . maybe you . . ." He shrugged.

She only bowed. She wanted to run to him and embrace him, but she made herself stay still. She made herself stay Japanese. "All right" was all she said, and Cotton knew he couldn't expect any more. She could never leave Kiyoshi. Miyuki's husband, the Serikawas' *yoshi.* Their seed. So Cotton would go see Bowersox, and then he would leave the Sun-Begot Land, either for the time being or forever. Either one; it really didn't matter which if Miyuki wasn't with him.

All day after Cotton left, Miyuki thought. Sometimes she read from the prayer book she had taken with her from Tochigi. Sometimes she dreamed about being with him. It was a funny combination. Finally, she sat down and wrote a note. It required several versions before she was satisfied. Then she went over to the nearest Buddhist temple and prayed. She didn't have the nerve to go to a Christian church alone. She wasn't sure if you needed a pass to get in, or something like that, so she went to the temple, where she was comfortable, and prayed in every way she knew, Shinto, Buddhist, and Christian. It didn't matter much how. What she prayed was Japanese. For Japan.

The next morning, after Kiyoshi left the house, Miyuki went to her closet and found her most traditional kimono, the gold one that she had been given years ago to dress up for Tenno Heika. She took off her moga bra and panties and put on the red shirt that was the only proper underwear, then put on the gold kimono, laboriously tying all six sashes, fitting the obi around her, fumbling to tie it tight in back, all but stifling herself. It was just a little too tight. Then, on her feet she slipped into her finest silk *zoori* and shuffled off to the trolley stop, sweating on what was an uncommonly hot and foggy November day.

She had to transfer twice to get to the palace. Tenno Heika will see me, Miyuki thought. He must remember me. He remembers my father, and of course he remembers my brother. Both, in one way or another, died for him. So he will at least see me, and I will tell Tenno Heika that it is too late, an American is about to alert his country, so then he will call back the fleet, and the moment will be lost and peace will be saved. For now, for sure; maybe forever. I can do it. I am Japanese, and I am only a woman; but no, Cotton Drake is not the only one who can avert a war. I am the other. And I am even better, because I can stop it before it happens. Once Cotton alerts the Americans, they will be mad, even after they stop it. I am the better one.

Alighting at the Sakuradamon gate, as the other passengers bowed, Miyuki made her way down to the guardhouse that overlooked the moat. The guards had already spotted the beautiful woman in the gold kimono coming and had made the appropriate observations common to guards everywhere who espy a beautiful woman. Then the sergeant stepped down from the sentinel box and blocked Miyuki's path.

"I know this is most unusual, but I would like to meet with Tenno Heika himself," Miyuki declared straight out.

The sergeant suppressed a laugh. "As you know, that is impossible."

"I have known Tenno Heika," Miyuki continued. "Please, call for the officer in charge. I will have him contact the Imperial Household Agency for me." Not for nothing was she a soldier's daughter. The sergeant hesitated. "Go, quickly, sergeant. This is most important. This concerns the war." The guard still looked dumbfounded. Miyuki made a shooing motion. "Go, go. Get me the officer."

"What is your name?"

"You tell the officer that my name is Serikawa Miyuki, the daughter of Colonel Serikawa Shinji, the hero of Manchukuo, and the sister of Captain Serikawa Takeo, the leader of the *ni/ni-roku.*"

Well, that was good enough for the sergeant. Returning to the box, he summoned the officer, a young lieutenant, who arrived soon enough, on a bicycle, hurrying through the fog down the gravel path.

Patiently, Miyuki repeated her petition. "I was invited here at Kigen," she said. He took that in. The lady wasn't crazy. The lieutenant couldn't quite figure her out, but she wasn't like the other lunatics who appeared periodically, asking for His Majesty. "And I was to be Tenno Heika's concubine," Miyuki added.

"Everyone knows Tenno Heika took no concubines."

"Yes, but if Her Majesty hadn't given birth to Prince Akihito, I was the virgin Tenno Heika had chosen."

"Oh," said the lieutenant.

Quickly, then, Miyuki held up the piece of paper she had written on at home. "Please pass on this message to the colonel of the guard, and advise him that this matter concerns the imminent war against the United States. Will you do that . . . for me?"

He hesitated, but only for a moment, and then took the paper from her. Miyuki bowed. She knew that for now this was the best she could hope for.

The lieutenant unfolded the paper and read it. It contained Miyuki's name, address, and phone number, the family history she had already repeated, and a simple plea that she be allowed to see Tenno Heika for a few minutes "to discuss utmost matters of immediate concern involving war with the United States of America." And then Miyuki had added one more thing: a crude representation of the Hawaiian Island chain, with a star at Pearl Harbor. It was barely more than a series of dots and circles, but they were laid out in the slant that the islands describe. Miyuki was positive that anyone with knowledge of Operation Z would instantly appreciate her knowledge.

The lieutenant folded the paper back up. "You will pass this along?" Miyuki said. "It is most urgent I see Tenno Heika."

"Yes, ma'am," he answered. He was still dazzled by this magnificent beauty who had appeared out of nowhere dressed in the most extraordinary gold kimono asking for His Majesty himself. Even before Miyuki bowed and turned, to start walking across the bridge over the moat, the lieutenant had scrambled back aboard his bicycle and was pedaling furiously down the gravel path toward the headquarters of the Imperial Guard.

By the time Miyuki got back on a streetcar, the fog had lifted.

50

Even by their own excessive standards, they'd had a great deal to drink, Scotch and sake, Bowersox and Teshima. Occasionally, a whore would peek through the *noren*, and Teshima would send her away or ask her to pour him another drink.

This time, after he got his drink, Teshima poked and squeezed his whore, before he shooed her back out, to wait in the other little room with Bowersox's girl until they were ready. The international situation had grown too tense for the two men, the Japanese general and the American diplomat, to be seen together. No longer, even, could they meet at the geisha house or go up to Yoshiwara in each other's company. Instead, Teshima had a couple of whores brought to a small apartment in Ueno that he used for assignations and other private meetings, and then he and Bowersox rendezvoused there for the evening.

"Well, if anyone ever spotted us, we could tell them we're part of the secret diplomatic negotiations," Bowersox said.

"Yes, but your President would like that more than my prime minister."

Bowersox snorted. "Roosevelt wants war as much as Tojo does, I'm sure. It's the only way to decide matters."

"I heartily agree, Saint-san," Teshima said, and he raised his glass, tilting it, splashing it. "We're the only honest bastards on either side."

"To war against Japan," Bowersox said, raising his.

"To war against America," Teshima roared. Bowersox winked at him. "When the war is over, and we've won, we'll be gracious to you, Saint, I promise. You and I will drink and whore together again . . . in San Francisco."

"I'll tell the Chinese who run the prison camp you're in to give General Teshima special treatment."

They clinked their glasses and laughed again. Teshima's whore stuck her head through the *noren* again, but he waved her off. "Stay back there with the other cunt, and let my good friend and I say goodbye to each other, because soon our countries will be at war." He slapped Bowersox on the back. "Who knows, we may even kill each other." And they roared again.

Nervously, though, the whore started to duck back. "Wait," Teshima said. "Help me off with my coat. I gotta show one thing to my friend here."

The whore unbuttoned Teshima's jacket and pulled his arms out of his sleeves. She started to hang up the coat, but he took it back from her and fished something out of a pocket. Then he turned to speak to Bowersox, who was struggling to his feet. "Maybe you can help me, Saint. You know all the *gaijin* worth shit in Tokyo. Ever see this guy? He's a German." And he handed Bowersox Cotton's picture. It was only half of the original photograph taken at Sensoji, Sumiko having been cut off.

Of course, Bowersox recognized Cotton right away, even behind his sunglasses. Immediately he yanked his thumb toward the whore, and Teshima slapped her on the rear and told her to come back in a couple more minutes. "Why do you want to know about this guy?" Bowersox asked, parrying for an opening.

Teshima perked up. "You know him?"

"I said, why?"

"He found some things out he had no business knowing. Then he disappeared. When the Sorge spy ring was uncovered last month, we figured he was part of that." A German, Richard Sorge, had run an amazingly effective catch-as-catch-can Soviet spy operation that had finally been tripped up. It was really incredibly easy to find things out in Tokyo then, if only you made any sort of an effort. "But the best we can tell, Sorge never laid eyes on him." Teshima kept on, taking off his socks and shoes. "So, we figure he must be out of the country by now."

Bowersox handed the picture back. "He isn't," he said, sotto voce.

Teshima froze. "Who is he?"

"Well, he's not German."

"American?" Teshima studied the photo again.

"Uh-huh."

"Is he a spy?"

Bowersox shook his head. "No, only a do-gooder. But he's clever at meddling."

"Obviously." Now Teshima was growing testy. "So, who is he?"

Bowersox laughed, enjoying the game. "Well, as a matter of fact, Yoichi, he's the one who told me about Hawaii."

Teshima flinched. "This guy? This guy's your contact?"

Bowersox nodded. But then, quickly: "One of them," he said, as if he owned platoons of well-placed confidants.

"Tell me who he is." Teshima's voice had changed; now it was harsh and steely.

"Will you kill him?" Teshima looked away. Bowersox had risen all the way up by now, and he kicked Teshima gently in his foot. "Come on, will you kill him?"

"Well, perhaps there's no need to. We'll put a tail on him. He can't phone out. We read his mail. If he's only reporting to you, maybe . . ."

Bowersox leaned down. "I don't think you understand me, Yoichi. I *expect* you to kill him. Savvy?"

Teshima laughed. "Oh. Fine. That's no problem."

"Good. I've often wondered what I would do." Teshima struggled up. "You see, as soon as you attack Hawaii, he'll understand that I betrayed him. He'll see we weren't prepared. He'll find out I never passed on his information. When the war's over, if he lives, it would hardly be good for my career." He shook his head. "Or my neck, even."

"So, who is our friend, Saint?"

"His name is Cotton Drake. The Reverend Cotton Drake." Teshima certainly never expected that. He looked back at the photograph. "A missionary?"

"Episcopal. In Tochigi."

"What the hell's a missionary doing coming to Yoshiwara?"

"An interesting man of the cloth, Yoichi. Good baseball player, too. You really ought to go see Tochigi play. The people up there love Cotton-san, and he speaks better Japanese than you do. I think he's the man my parents wanted me to be."

"This is not bullshit? A missionary? A missionary was running around with my whore?"

Bowersox took another swallow of his drink. "Well, some men of God are intrepid upon this earth, too."

"But you want his ass dead?" Teshima said. In fact, it didn't really matter what Bowersox answered. It was a done deal. Cotton Drake knew what Bowersox didn't know, that General Yoichi Teshima was in fact the officer who had indiscreetly spilled the beans before a whore. And, of course, Teshima knew he knew. As such, Teshima understood now that his future lay in the strange American's hands as much as Bowersox's future might. Teshima *had* to eliminate him.

Bowersox combed back his hair, looking carefully at himself in the mirror. "My admiration for the Reverend Mr. Drake ends where his control over my fate begins. Savvy?"

"As you wish, Saint," Teshima said.

"You wanted to see me, Lieutenant?" the colonel of the guard asked.

"Yes sir. Yesterday, when you were away, this dame came to the gate. . . ." And on and on he went, recounting the sudden apparitional appearance of this woman in gold and all that she had said, and how, however odd it seemed, he'd believed her. He handed the colonel her letter, and the senior officer examined it, even turning it over, as if there must be something more to it. Finally, he looked back up at the lieutenant. "Was she pretty?" he asked.

"Excuse me, sir?"

"Was the lady pretty?"

"Yes sir, I would say she was as beautiful as any woman I've ever seen in my life."

The colonel chuckled. "I thought so. I thought that might be the case."

The lieutenant started to protest. He knew what the colonel was thinking, and he wanted to assure him that, sure, his head could be turned as quickly as any man's, but there was more to this strange woman, that obviously she really knew something. But all he managed to say was "But sir—" before the colonel grinned and interrupted.

"I'm glad the army hasn't dimmed your appreciation of beauty." He waved the younger man off. The lieutenant paused for a moment. "Thank you, Lieutenant."

He saluted and left. The colonel laid the paper down on his desk, and pushed it over to the side when he left work for the day.

51

Bowersox actually rubbed his hands together and smirked. "It's about time you got back here. I wanna show you something."

He tossed Cotton a file marked Top Secret, and Cotton tore through it. It was as impressive as advertised: cables from both FE and State in Washington and CINCPAC—the office of the Pacific Fleet—in Honolulu. "All decoded cables, highest priority," Bowersox gushed. "I could get my tit in a wringer showing you this, except, of course, you're responsible for all this coming about—so I figure, no sense standing on ceremony."

Cotton read avidly. "Received your latest wire. . . . Doubling islands surveillance. . . . Will shift entire San Diego fleet to Pearl support, plus large numbers Army personnel from mainland to General Short command. . . . Admiral Kimmel placing entire fleet 24-hour alert and staggering fleet schedule from Pearl. . . . Adjust reconnaissance flights to all. . . ." Cotton turned the pages as fast as he could devour the information.

A final cable was a copy of a wire from Washington to Honolulu discussing the possibility of whether the news plans should be masked, in better hopes, perhaps, of suckering the Japanese to commit to what they still assumed to be a surprise attack. Or should the President himself simply frostily inform Nomura, the Japanese ambassador to Washington, that the United States was aware of the planned shenanigans? Or should Roosevelt so inform Tojo—or even Hirohito himself?

"God, Saint, this is terrific!" Cotton said.

It was, too—or it would have been if only it hadn't all been fabricated, typed up by Bowersox himself strictly for Cotton's benefit.

"Now, feel a little bit better about the boys and girls running your United States government?" Cotton swept out his hands, like a cavalier presenting a bow of respect. "So, know anything new?" Bowersox asked him.

"Well, you know where Kagoshima is?" Cotton asked.

"Sure—way down south."

"We got a consulate there?"

Bowersox shook his head. "The only one on Kyushu is Nagasaki."

"Okay, get the consul there to sneak down to Kagoshima. That's where the pilots have been practicing for the last few months."

"At a city?"

"Look." Cotton took a map out of his briefcase and laid it on the desk. "I copied this out of the library. With a little imagination, you can make Kagoshima Bay into Pearl Harbor. See?" He pointed at the map, drawing lines with his finger where the Zeros might go.

"And they've been practicing in the open down there?"

"Yeah—it's like if we tried to use New Orleans for some secret exercises. But anyway, I imagine the practicing has stopped now, and if it has, that almost surely means the planes are on the carriers. Wherever they are."

"When's the date?" Bowersox asked.

"That I don't know . . . exactly. But soon."

Bowersox shook his head. "You don't know? Jesus, you know everything else."

"Well, I'm glad you finally started taking me seriously."

"Hey, Padre, I always took you seriously." He put out one cigarette and immediately shook another out of the pack. "It's just that the geniuses back home needed some convincing." Then he lit the Lucky and blew a lot of smoke. "Of course, there's a lot of people also taking the Reverend Mr. Drake more seriously these days."

"What does that mean?"

"Keep an eye in your rearview mirror."

"I'm being followed?"

"Someone from *jouhou kyoku*, I suppose. Intelligence." Cot-

ton leaned back in his chair and sighed. "Look, don't be surprised. There's hardly two hundred Yanks left in Tokyo. And
if you're the Japs, you can ignore a lot of 'em. Women. Children. Old people. It isn't any great test of their manpower to
cover what's left."

"Somebody reported me?" Cotton asked. Kiyoshi, of
course.

"Probably. But all the bastards are jumpy now, and any
American is prima facie fair game."

"Ipso facto," Cotton said.

"Exactly."

"So, what do I do?"

Bowersox leaned in closer, across the desk. "You want my
advice?" Cotton shrugged. "You've never taken it before."

"So?"

"Go back to your church and sit tight. Don't do anything
out of the ordinary."

"What could they do to me?"

"Oh, they could slap you in the hoosegow like that,"
Bowersox said, snapping his fingers. "Understand, your association with the Heavenly Father doesn't count for shit anymore." Cotton nodded. "And make no mistake—anybody
you talk to, anybody you see, you jeopardize as much as
yourself."

"Anybody?" Miyuki, Cotton thought.

"Anybody. Look, if you've got to talk privately, if you stum-
ble across anything new, you get in touch with me. Pronto."
Bowersox scribbled out some directions. "Meet me here."

Cotton studied it. "What is this?"

"It's just a place. Apartment up by Ueno Park. You call
me, I'll meet you there."

"Won't the Japanese be watching it? I mean, if they're tailing me, they must be doubling on you, any American official."

"Don't worry. This is supposed to be a little love nest
where somebody is poking his mistress. The Japs understand
that sort of thing. Savvy? Just call me, go there. I'll come."

"Okay."

Bowersox smiled. Perfect. Until Teshima's goons got Cotton, he had him pinned down: don't go anywhere, don't talk to anyone else, and if you learn anything, go to the apartment near Ueno Park—General Teshima's. "Good," Bowersox said.

Cotton stood up. He hesitated. "Saint?"

"Yes?"

"Suppose I wanted to go."

"Go where?"

"Leave Japan."

"Oh, finally."

"Just suppose. Is there anything out anymore?"

Bowersox took a drag. Cotton Drake was never leaving Japan alive. But as long as he was still alive, he would humor him. "On the QT?"

"Sure."

"Okay. This just in. The Japs want the *Tatsuta Maru* to make a special run. Almost nobody knows about it yet. The ambassador just requested Washington approval. It'd leave here December second. That's a Tuesday. Honolulu a week later."

"Eight days," Cotton said. The schedules from American Orient were still in his head.

"Okay, so it gets in the tenth. Then on to San Francisco, Manzanillo, and Balboa. Leaves there"—he checked a sheet on his desk—"December twenty-seventh. It picks up all sorts of Japanese nationals posted overseas, then swings back here."

Cotton thought that over. "You say it leaves the second—Tuesday a week?"

"Right. You want your little red ass on that schooner?"

"Is there space?"

"For you, of course." Cotton didn't reply, just stood there looking out. "Well, you want a ticket?" Bowersox asked him.

"I'll get back to you. Maybe I do. But if I go: two tickets."

Bowersox's head flipped up. He was flustered. "Oh?" was all he said. Drake had surprised him again. Someone else going out with him—that could only mean another snoop, another American with all this knowledge. Damn.

Somehow, though, by luck or by instinct, Bowersox had the presence of mind to ask the one right extra question. "Is that just two tickets or two cabins?" And now it was Cotton who hesitated. So Bowersox jumped in. "Hey, I'm not being nosy, Padre. I have to know. The boat's gonna be—"

"Two tickets, one cabin," Cotton said. "I'll let you know."

Outside the embassy gates, Cotton turned right and walked briskly for two blocks. He wanted to look back, but he restrained himself. suddenly, then, at the light, he made an almost military about-face and started retracing his steps. Sure enough, halfway down the block, a thin young Japanese man turned quickly, off guard, and started examining the store window there. Western ladies' chapeaus: he was studying them intently as Cotton crossed behind him.

Cotton headed back into the embassy grounds, as if perhaps he'd left something behind, and strolled about for five minutes, then came back out, turning the other way this time. He saw a newsboy across the—"*Gogai! Gogai!*"—so he cut over and bought a paper. He glanced at the headlines—more negotiations, no more hope—then skimmed through the rest of the front-page propaganda, turning to the scandalous page three, HIGH SCHOOL PROSTITUTION RING UNCOVERED IN OSAKA!! Cotton peeked over the top of the paper. Sure enough, across the street, down a little way, the same thin young man stood, pretending to read a paper himself. Bowersox was right. They did have a tail on him.

Actually, too, although this Cotton couldn't know, the fellow was a bit more than that. He was an assassin.

52

Bowersox was already at the apartment in Ueno when Teshima arrived. The American was beside himself; he'd actually taken an embassy limousine.

"What the hell is it, Saint?"

"Drake."

Teshima calmed him down. "Don't worry. Don't worry. We're getting him today. We would've had him already, but he went to see you."

"I know. I know."

"What do you want—we grab him at the American embassy?"

"No, but—"

"You brought me here for this, Saint? I guarantee you, we're tailing Drake now, and as soon as we get him some place quiet, we'll . . ." He shrugged, grinning. "The Reverend Drake will not be alive tomorrow morning."

"You can't do it," Bowersox said.

Teshima frowned, irritated. "What do you mean? You're the one wanted him dead."

Bowersox sighed. "There's someone else."

Teshima slammed the wall. "Someone else knows?"

"Yeah. Some dame."

"Who?"

"I don't know who, Yoichi. It was just that Drake was talking in my office about maybe leaving Japan—he never did that before—and I played along, told him the *Tatsu* was probably going out, and all of a sudden he said all right, but two tickets. One cabin, two tickets."

Teshima paced the apartment. It was strictly utilitarian, all but empty except for one desk and two futons. He kept banging the thin walls. Bowersox was afraid he'd put his fist through. "Shit! And you don't know who she is?"

"No idea. He's never mentioned a woman. Except the whore."

Teshima stopped and took the new cigarette away from Bowersox and stuck it in his own lips. "All right, we'll try to catch up with the guy following him."

"Tell them just to keep following him and find the dame."

"I know, Saint, I know," Teshima said, reaching for the phone. Damn—how many of Drake's women was he going to have to kill to keep protecting himself?

Cotton began to walk, faster now. The man followed. Cotton grabbed a streetcar downtown. The tail popped on just behind him. So Cotton hopped off at the next stop, dashed behind a taxi, around an ox cart; and then quickly, precisely as the light turned, he jumped back on again. Just made it. He'd lost him. Easy. He looked up, and there, peeking from behind the red-collar girl, was the tail. This time, too, the thin man acknowledged him—just enough, smiling. Cotton smiled back. Who the hell am I kidding? he asked himself. He was whipped. He looked around. There wasn't another white man on the streetcar, on the street. So what if he was able to escape from the guy? How long would it take to spot him again? So he relaxed, and when the streetcar reached the Ginza, Cotton not only signaled to his tail that he was getting off, but even pointed to the phone booth where he was going to call the Serikawas'.

Miyuki answered almost before the first ring had started. She grabbed every call that way, sure that the next one would be from the palace guard, inviting her down to see Tenno Heika. "Hi," Cotton said, and even though it was Cotton, she couldn't hide the disappointment in her voice.

"Hello, Cotton."

"Listen, I'm down in the Ginza, but I can't come up to see you. There's a guy from the *tokko* following me, and I don't want to come to your house."

"Why?"

"I don't know exactly why. Just these guys are so jumpy, and it might implicate you in some way. Okay?"

"Okay."

"Now, the next time I come in, I'll call you from Asakusa, and you'll meet me in Tsukiji." That was the section of town best known for the fish market, but Trinity Cathedral was nearby.

"At the cathedral there?"

"Yes. It certainly wouldn't raise anybody's eyebrows for a priest to meet someone there."

"No," she said. "And Cotton . . . ?"

"Yes?"

"If we meet there, at the cathedral, will you baptize me?"

"You're sure?"

"Yes, I am. I want to be a Christian."

"All right, if we can meet there, I'll baptize you."

"Thank you, Cotton."

And he waited. He was not the least bit interested now in matters spiritual. All that counted in the world was them, was her. But Miyuki didn't say anything else then. So Cotton said it: "Did you think . . . about us?"

"I always think about us."

Cotton made himself stay cool. "There is one last boat leaving for the States, Miyuki." No answer. No nothing. He thought he heard her breathing. "Miyuki?"

"Yes, Cotton?"

"I will ask Kiyoshi myself to give you a divorce, and we can marry, and be on that boat." No answer. No nothing. "Miyuki?"

"Yes?"

"Miyuki, I love you." Silence. "With all my heart." Silence." And soul." Silence. "Miyuki, I love you." Silence.

"Cotton . . ."

"Yes?"

Silence. And then: "Kiyoshi is an honorable husband" was all that Miyuki said.

"Yes," Cotton said. "He is."

"Yes," Miyuki said. She was crying, so that she didn't hear

him say he would call again. And when Cotton didn't hear
her anymore, he put the phone up.

Still, it was a long time before he came out of the booth.
He just stood there, staring at the phone. He never even
should have asked her. Maybe it would be best just to get on
the *Tatsu* himself and start again somewhere else—find Liz's
organist, the one with her hair up in a bun.

And when he finally came out of the booth, he didn't even
see the tail, the skinny guy. He didn't even look back. Cotton
just walked through the Ginza. He didn't even notice all the
people staring at him, sneering at the *gaijin*.

He passed a theater. That caught his attention. A new play
had just opened: *A Day at Sengaku-ji*. That was the temple
where the forty-seven *ronin* had committed their mass seppuku. Around the corner was a movie theater. Just opening!
Today! A wonderful new patriotic drama—*Chushin Gura*—
about . . . the forty-seven *ronin*. "I don't think so," Cotton said
out loud.

But down the street at the Hibiya Theater, what still should
be playing, of all things, but an American film entitled *I
Wanted Wings*, starring Veronica Lake, William Holden, and
Ray Milland, Incredibly, it was about the U.S. Army Air
Corps training for a coming war. Cotton stood before the
ticket window. He needed escape. When was the last time
he'd even seen a movie—any movie? There was a sign there
announcing that the Hibiya Theater was instituting a new
policy and, starting tomorrow, November 20, for the better-
ment of the Japanese people, only movies made in Japan,
Germany, or France would be shown. "Well, last chance,"
Cotton said, and he put down his fifty sen and bought a
ticket. If he'd looked behind him, he'd have seen his tail come
in shortly afterwards. But Cotton didn't care. Mostly, he concentrated on Veronica Lake. She was a new star, but she reminded him of Liz, of all those times when he'd made love
with Liz, and her blond hair had fallen over her forehead,
much like Veronica Lake's blond hair did for William
Holden. Cotton hadn't thought about Liz in a long time, and

he knew that meant that in his heart, he had accepted that Miyuki must truly be lost to him forever.

The tail took a seat a few rows behind Cotton. His name was Takahashi. He was Teshima's best man. It was he and his partner who had killed Sumiko. It'd been good duty. They took turns raping her first. It did not bother Takahashi, killing her, because he had been assured that she was an enemy of the Emperor, just as the *gaijin* watching the movie was, too.

Slowly, as his eyes adjusted to the dark, Takahashi took them off Veronica Lake and looked around. There were only three other people in the whole theater, and two of them were a young moga and mobo furtively necking, and the other was an old man half-asleep.

Takahashi saw an exit door down the aisle from where Cotton sat, near the front of the theater. He got up and went back up to the lobby, and then down the secluded alley alongside the theater. Sure enough, the exit door opened out there, next to a row of large trash bins—any one good enough for holding a body.

Takahashi went back inside and took the same seat a few rows behind Cotton. On the screen, William Holden was flirting with Veronica Lake at the air base. After a few minutes, Takahashi reached under his jacket and pulled out a thin, sharp knife from its sheath. He waited for the noise of the planes taking off. The propellers were starting up. Takahashi began to rise. It would be very easy, grabbing the *gaijin* from behind, cutting his throat. Very quick. Very bloody, of course. And some gurgling. But out the side door, into the trash.

Takahashi rose up and began stepping forward. His left hand was poised to grab Cotton, and his right held the knife to—

That was when the lights went on.

The moga and mobo broke apart, embarrassed. The old man woke up with a start. Takahashi sank back down into a seat just as Cotton turned around to see what was up. The manager of the theater, a dapper little man in a polka-dotted bowtie, was striding down the aisle. He carried a film can with him and took a position at the front of the theater, under the screen.

"Ladies and gentlemen," he cried, "I possess such accumulated shame that the Hibiya Theater continues to show this movie about American warriors that I have decided, for the honor of Tenno Heika and the many brave Japanese soldiers defending us in China, to conclude this disgraceful film immediately and replace it with *Genroku Chushingura*, a Japanese story both appropriate and glorious, which has just been delivered. Please remain seated and this wonderful new movie that pays homage to our great heroes will begin."

The moga and mobo, the old man, and Takahashi applauded. Cotton merely rose. He'd noticed the tail when he turned around, and now he addressed him as he left: "Hey, I'm sorry, pal, but I only wanted to see Veronica Lake. I'm just going up to Asakusa now to get the train back to Tochigi, so you can catch up with me back there if you wanna see the new show."

Takahashi grinned foolishly and bowed his head. The knife was back in its sheath in his pocket, so he followed Cotton out of the theater, up to the Asakusa Station. When cotton got into the ticket line, Takahashi popped into a phone booth and called the office. "We've been trying to get hold of you," the desk man said. "Change in plans." Sorry, they didn't want to kill the *gaijin*, but keep following him and see if he ever meets a woman. "Okay," Takahashi said.

Cotton took his ticket and headed for the train. It was exactly four o'clock. Cotton knew it was four o'clock because every day now, eleven and four sharp, over the loudspeakers that were set up everywhere in the land, the martial music was suspended for a couple of minutes and everyone stopped while the national anthem was played. This time, on the platform, as Cotton stood respectfully, looking at the flag of the rising sun that was posted across the way, he could see all the people around him staring at him, and he could sense all the people hating him.

So when the "Kimigayo" was finished playing, he walked

over to Takahashi and made a great show out of throwing his
arm around him and acting like the man was his best friend
in all the world. Takahashi was furious, but what could he
do? All the people on the platform glared at him, too, and
some displayed purer patriotism by walking away, leaving
Cotton and Takahashi standing there alone, the hunter and
the hunted, waiting for the next train to Tochigi.

It was about that same time that Bowersox was finally able to
get in to see Ambassador Grew. He waved off the offer of a
chair. "Thank you, sir, but this won't take but a moment."

"Yes?"

"Our missionary detective, Mr. Drake, came by my office
again today. He bothers me rather regularly now, I'm afraid."

"He seemed a nice enough young fellow."

"Well, he's getting a bit hysterical with it all. I strongly recommended he be out on the *Tatsuta.*"

"Good idea for any American, really."

"Each time I see Mr. Drake he's unraveled a little more,
and he has a new rumor for me. Then he gets rather testy
when I won't personally try to get President Roosevelt on the
phone."

Grew chuckled and played with his big mustache. "It was
Hawaii, wasn't it?"

"Well, at first, yes. But then he assured me it was Hong
Kong. He had that on best authority from some parishioner.
Then, just today, it was Russia. The Japs were going north,
for sure, because one of the sons of the local mailman had
been shifted in his basic training."

"And?"

"Well, sir, I just wanted to warn you that Drake seems to
grow more and more impatient with my failure to alert Washington, so he's talking about calling you for an appointment.
He's very well-spoken—"

"I remember."

"And a vessel of the Lord. Impressive. So I'm just forewarning you, should he call, I'd advise your office not to allow him to make an appointment."

The ambassador brushed back his mustache. "I appreciate your being so solicitous on the boss's behalf, Saint, and I promise you, I'll avoid Mr. Drake like the plague. God knows I've got enough people I *have* to see."

"Thank you, sir," Bowersox said, and he started to leave.

"By the way, Saint, what's your best guess now where they might strike?"

"Singapore, probably," Bowersox replied. "Southeast Asia for sure. Nothing else makes any sense."

"Yes, my view completely," the ambassador said. "And we'll continue so to advise Washington."

The two captains of the guard came into the colonel's office and began to go over plans for Gishi-sai, the annual memorial festival of the forty-seven *ronin*. Reports had already come down that Tenno Heika himself might visit Sengaku-ji for Gishi-sai, and so at least initial preparations must be made for that contingency.

Satisfied that the guard was sufficiently on line, the colonel thanked the two captains, but as one rose from his seat by the desk, he knocked some papers to the floor. He grabbed them up, apologizing, straightening them back in a pile. "Hawaii?" he said.

"What's that?" asked the colonel.

The captain held up Miyuki's sheet of paper. "What is this? Some kind of map of the Hawaiian Islands?"

The colonel took back the piece of paper and glanced at it. "Damned if I know. This is from some good-looking, goofy dame who came out to Sakuradamon the other day, demanding to see Tenno Heika. Lieutenant Tsunoda fell in love with her, I think."

They all laughed, and the captains turned to leave.

This time, the colonel wadded Miyuki's letter into a ball and pitched it into his wastebasket.

53

All night Miyuki felt Kiyoshi shifting about. Twice, when she woke, he'd gotten up to smoke a cigarette. He'd seemed distracted, distant even, when they'd made love earlier. It was still pitch dark out, with only the glow from his cigarette, but Miyuki got up, slipped on her *dotera*, and went over to him.

"What's the matter?" she said. "And don't say 'nothing.' "

"Nothing," Kiyoshi replied—but, anyway, that did get a little laugh out of him. "Well, how about 'everything'?"

"So, besides everything, what is it?"

"Oh, just the war. You know, the war is coming." The tip of his cigarette glowed brighter in the dark when he dragged on it.

"I know."

"All right, I have one question for you, Miyuki, and this is a good place to ask it, in the dark." The brighter glow, again. He was smoking more these days, Miyuki thought. "Tell me—in Tochigi, what happened between you and Cotton?"

"I told you." The brighter glow. "And Cotton told you, too."

"Tell me again."

"Nothing."

The brighter glow. "Nothing at all?"

"Why must you ask me again?"

"Actually, I'm really only interested in what Cotton did."

"And not your wife?" The brighter glow.

"A woman who cheats on her husband only betrays him. A man who screws his best friend's wife betrays everything in his life."

Miyuki bit her tongue. "And he isn't worth anything," Kiyoshi added. He took another drag and put the cigarette out, and now there was nothing but the darkest dark and their voices. "So?" he said.

"I told you. Nothing."

"Nothing at all? The whole time?"

"All right, all right." The match fired, and Miyuki could see Kiyoshi as he lit another cigarette. His face looked sad and faraway, so different from the intensity of his voice. "One night, Key—late, like this—I woke up and I saw Cotton standing outside, by the river, and I knew I shouldn't do it, but forgive me, I went out there—"

"Why?"

"I'm not sure. I think in order to seduce him." No answer. The cigarette glowed. "And so we talked, flirted. I flirted, and then I made him kiss me."

"You *made* him?"

"More or less."

"To seduce him?"

"What does it matter? You told me you weren't interested in what I did, only Cotton."

She heard him chuckle. "Good for you. You got me."

"Well," Miyuki went on. "That was all. We kissed in the moonlight." The brighter glow. "And then he backed away and left me. And that was the most that happened between us. We were both very lonely, Key. But that was all. I think Cotton is the best friend you could ever have."

Kiyoshi took another long drag. "Thank you. That's what I think, too."

Kiyoshi may have slept only a little the rest of the night, but still he was up at dawn. He was already dressed in his uniform and having coffee when Miyuki woke again. "My, gracious—coffee!" she said. It had become a great luxury these days.

"Life's little pleasures," Kiyoshi said. "I read in the newspaper yesterday that they're going to allow everybody one mandarin orange and one bottle of beer for New Year's. There's something to look forward to." He lit a cigarette and coughed.

"You're smoking too much, Key."

"I know."

"Key?"

"Yes?"

"I do want to become a Christian. I want Cotton to baptize me."

He took a swallow and a drag, but even then he didn't respond. Finally, he just said, "All right. Fine."

"That's all? *'All right.'* "

"I see Cotton with Jesus sometimes, and I think, maybe that's good to have. And so, if you . . ."

He shrugged.

"Would you come to the cathedral when he baptizes me?"

"Sure. If I can."

He came over to Miyuki then, and knelt down beside her, and lifted her up next to him, and held her as tight as he could for a long time. It was funny; Miyuki thought she felt closer to Kiyoshi at this moment than all those times they tried to make a baby. Then he gently let her back down and stood up, straightening his blue jacket. Miyuki thought: how handsome he looks in his uniform. She hated all the men in uniforms on the street, but she liked Kiyoshi in his. She'd grown used to him this way. "Isn't it awfully early?" she asked.

"I have a meeting first thing today. At the War Ministry." He blew her a kiss.

But she was right. It was so early that he walked all the way down to War, which was just across the moat from the Palace. Even then, Kiyoshi waited for a half-hour in the anteroom before General Teshima arrived at his office and called him in.

He nodded at Kiyoshi, not to him, and neglected to grant him even the most cursory greeting. This did not trouble Kiyoshi, though, for he expected no more from Teshima, and it would make it easier for him to respond in kind. Except for a grunt that was meant to pass for "Good morning," Teshima went right to the heart of things. "Have you spoken to Admiral Yamamoto this morning?"

Kiyoshi replied: "No"—not "No sir"—"he's on the Inland

Sea, aboard the *Nagato*, and I wouldn't imagine there would
be any need for him to contact me."

"I *know* where the admiral is," Teshima snapped. This was
going to be terribly unpleasant. "And I also know damn well
that the fleet, *Kido Butai*, arrives tomorrow in Hitokappu Bay,
primed for final orders from the admiral to strike out for
Hawaii."

"Yes . . . sir, I'm aware."

"And do you also know that the entire mission is jeopardized because two *gaijin* have learned of Operation Z?"

Well, Kiyoshi thought to himself, this is moving even faster
than I imagined. But he played coy, responding legalistically.
"I am not personally aware, sir, of two *gaijin* cognizant of Operation Z."

"No?"

"No." Kiyoshi lit a cigarette without asking permission.

"No sir."

"No sir. Teshima Taisho." General Teshima.

Teshima was infuriated. He despised everything about
Kiyoshi. He was navy. He was Yamamoto's boy. Handsome.
Cultured. At ease with anyone. And this morning he was
smug, to boot. But Teshima restrained himself. If Kiyoshi
would be as disagreeable as he was, he would try to be as
cool as Kiyoshi. Without a word—even, the general hoped,
without expression—he simply turned over a photograph on
his desk and flipped it toward Kiyoshi.

Kiyoshi saw it right away. He expected it. He didn't even
pick it up; and before Teshima could begin any interrogation,
he simply declared: "That's the Reverend Cotton Drake, an
Episcopal minister presently stationed at the mission in
Tochigi."

His voice dripping, Teshima said: "And is this perhaps the
first time you ever saw this photo?"

"No," Kiyoshi said evenly. "Admiral Yamamoto asked me
about it some time ago."

"I see. And you—"

Kiyoshi's eyes did not waver, peering dead into his inquisitor. Without so much as a blink: "Well, I lied, General. On that occasion, I denied ever knowing this person."

"You lied to Admiral Yamamoto?" Teshima said gratuitously, unable to resist the repetition.

Kiyoshi kept staring at him. Then, rather like he was at a cocktail party somewhere, he simply crossed his legs, said "Uh-huh," and drew on his cigarette. Most of all, he hoped his contempt showed. He hated Teshima every bit as much as Teshima hated him. Army, a peasant. Crude. One of those half-formed Japanese who managed to achieve the worst of both worlds: old Eastern traditionalism without grace on the one hand, modern Western science and materialism without subtlety on the other. And still he kept looking at Teshima, forcing the general to ask him directly:

"So, why did you lie to the admiral?"

"I lied because Cotton Drake is my oldest buddy in this world. He was a business associate and remains my dearest friend. And he is a priest—not of our faith, but a man of God. I trust him. Indeed, when I first was shown this photo, my own wife and mother were living with him at his mission. And so, I was so shocked that I instinctively denied any knowledge of him."

"Is Admiral Yamamoto aware of your deceit?"

"In fact, I've written him a letter. I haven't mailed it, yet. I think the admiral's got enough on his mind right now. But"—he shrugged—"in time."

"You'll be court-martialed," Teshima announced, delighted.

"I imagine," Kiyoshi said, his voice still flat. "Any member of His Majesty's military who jeopardizes Operation Z should expect that." He stopped, the last words tumbling onto Teshima's desk as if someone had spilled something there. Kiyoshi watched. The general ducked his head and cleared his throat, and Kiyoshi permitted himself a sly smile, safe that it wouldn't be seen.

Now Teshima lit a cigarette, and, trying to regain the offensive, he reached over and drummed a forefinger on Cotton's face on the photograph. "Needless to say, Mr. Drake is one of the two Americans familiar with the existence of Operation Z."

"Yes. I'm not really surprised."

"That's all you say, Serikawa-kun?"

"Look, I'm sorry. You tell me what to do to atone?"

Teshima glared at him, but really only for lack of knowing what else to do. He had been sure the guilty man would obsequiously petition him for clemency, bow and scrape, squirm for mercy. Instead, here was Kiyoshi acting with as much stoicism and responsibility as the first textbook imperial soldier. So Teshima took on a more benevolent air. "You know, you're really quite lucky, Serikawa. By coincidence, the one American Drake selected as his go-between, a man named Bowersox, is a friend of mine, and he elected to pass this information on to me."

"Bowersox?"

"He's in the American embassy."

"A spy—in the embassy?" Kiyoshi was incredulous.

"A traitor."

"Oh."

"Well, I should say, of course Bowersox views himself as *aikokusha*, a patriot. He believes the greater good of the United States will be served by war, and the greatest good by our attack on American territory. For the more emotional response it will engender over there. The United States will then rise up and save China from us. What do you think, Serikawa-kun—is it ever possible for a man to place his judgment above his nation's?"

"Are you intimating that I made that sort of decision when I denied knowing the man in the photograph?"

"No, I'm only framing the question."

Kiyoshi ground out his cigarette. "It's different, the West and East. Americans have some latitude—some—but . . ."

"Japanese?"

"Japanese must accept our consensus or"—Kiyoshi shrugged—"prepare to depart Japan."

Teshima rose from behind his desk. "And now you would atone for your error?"

"I said so. Yes."

"Good," Teshima replied, and he hesitated, but altogether for effect, adding a smile to his face with the same studied manner and purpose he showed when he strapped on a sidearm. "Good. Then I want you to kill both the *gaijin*—both Bowersox and your missionary."

The horrible bluntness of the remark came as no surprise to Kiyoshi, and he could respond as coolly as before: "I'm sorry, Teshima Taisho, but I am not capable of murder."

"Yes, we know you shrink from the hard work. Someone else in Hawaii had to take on the task when your old business associate started to turn traitor."

"Sammy Ushijima was a very old friend of mine."

"That's not the point, Serikawa-kun. We're not talking homicide here. We're talking about war. We're talking about the very existence of Japan. Two weeks from now those pilots of ours will turn their guns on Hawaii. And people will die. *Enemy* will die. The pilots understand what they must do, and they will be no more guilty of *murdering* Americans than you will."

"I don't care. No man should ever be asked to kill his friend to prove his honor."

"A difficult mission, to be sure. But hey, Serikawa-kun, it is not me that has placed you in this predicament. It was not me that lied to Yamamoto Isoroku, the admiral of the fleet. It was not me"—Teshima was really rolling now—"that jeopardized Operation Z, and with it, the fate of the Pacific War."

Steely, Kiyoshi stared back up at Teshima. He waited as long as he dared, and when he finally rose, he took his time, unwinding, stretching to his full height. And then, looking down on Teshima, as directly and icily as he could, he declared: "It . . . was . . . too."

At first, Teshima really didn't understand what Serikawa had said—or, anyway, what he had meant. He was rattled; he should have pulled rank and shouted at Kiyoshi for his insubordination. Instead, all he did was plead for clarification. "And what does that mean?"

"It means very simply that I know it was your drunken

ramblings in Yoshiwara one night with the whore Sumiko at Shinyanagi house that eventually provided Drake with the information that allowed him to make the proper deductions that we would strike Hawaii." Pause. "That's what it means."

The blood drained from Teshima's face, and he looked for a way out. He spied his teapot across the room and retreated from Kiyoshi to it. But Kiyoshi did not just continue his lacerating attack; he followed the general, taking up a place directly before him even as he poured the tea. "Look, okay, I protected Drake. But so what? The cat was already out of the bag. But you—you were the one who let it out." He pointed his forefinger straight at Teshima's chest, jabbing, stopping only just short of touching him. *"You* created this problem. *You* let the secrets slip. And so what are *you* going to do to atone?"

Teshima sipped his tea, trying to buy a clear head and consider his retort. It was hard for him, though. It wasn't just that his career was in jeopardy. Kiyoshi's damn manner, his laughs and smiles, his command, were almost as maddening as what Kiyoshi was saying. Teshima put the tea down and tried to purchase a grip back into this match. "You know, Serikawa-kun, you shouldn't be so cocky. You protected Drake. But who else has he told?"

"Oh, I wouldn't worry about that," Kiyoshi said— suddenly, more the good cop. "The whore's death sent a powerful message. Besides Mr. Drake, surely, I'm the only one you have to worry yourself about."

Teshima chuckled, delighted that at last he'd turned the game on Kiyoshi. "I wouldn't be so sure about that, Serikawa. There's a dame."

Kiyoshi gave a little laugh. "Oh, never mind that, Yoichi." "Yoichi" now—just "Yoichi." The first name—Western-style. Teshima was seething.

"No? Why?"

"Because the dame's my wife."

Teshima was incredulous. "Your wife?"

Kiyoshi said: "Yes."

"He wants to take her with him on the *Tatsu.*"

"Well, after all, he loves her," Kiyoshi said, lighting another cigarette.

"That doesn't bother you?" Teshima was going crazy. Every time he played another face card, Kiyoshi trumped him.

"Don't worry, she's not going anywhere."

"How do you know?"

"I know, because she's my wife, and because I wouldn't permit it."

Teshima tried to sort all this out. Kiyoshi helped him: "Look, Yoichi, don't let any of this give you ideas. My wife doesn't know anything about you, and neither does anyone else except my friend Drake and, I guess, your friend Bowersox. And just so there is no mistake: the letter that I wrote to Admiral Yamamoto—that statement of atonement that gratified you so . . ."

"Yes?" Teshima asked, even if he could guess what was coming.

"That letter isn't limited to a confession of my own transgression. There are other pertinent facts revealed. Any foul play that should come to me, or to my wife"—he added that quickly—"or to—"

"I understand."

"Good. So long as you play ball with me, Teshima Taisho."

Teshima still wasn't completely buying, though. "You'll ruin me, won't you?" he asked, a plaintive tone, almost pitying.

"No, not . . . necessarily," Kiyoshi replied, and he walked back over to Teshima and poured himself a cup of tea. "All I want is for you to trade me a guarantee of Mr. Drake's life for my guarantee that I won't expose you and ruin your career."

Teshima slumped down the wall, onto the tatami. "Go on," he sighed.

"First, I need some simple help from you. Some forms signed and whatnot. You already told me you know that the *Tatsuta Maru* departs Yokohama Tuesday next." Teshima nodded. "Perhaps you're not aware that the ship will never reach any destination."

Teshima looked up, the intrigue in this revelation even relaxing, for the moment, his own personal anxiety. "How's that?"

"It's a shadow ship, a decoy. So long as the *Tatsu* is headed out, the Americans will be inclined to believe that hostilities won't be imminent. After all, the ostensible purpose of the ship's voyage is to take Americans out of Japan, and for us to bring back our diplomats and businessmen, *before* war starts. The *Tatsuta Maru* is our Trojan fish."

"Very clever," Teshima said.

"Yes, I'd say the navy *is* very clever." Teshima grumped. "Now, it is simply my intention to have Cotton Drake board that ship for Hawaii."

"But why should he agree to go?" Teshima asked. "He still believes—completely—that Bowersox has transmitted all the vital information that he's passed on. America has been alerted. There will be no war. He can stay here at his mission."

"Exactly. So I will tell him the truth—that Bowersox has deceived him." Teshima frowned. "You've already marked Bowersox for death," Kiyoshi said. "What does it matter?"

"Well, yes—nothing. Bowersox matters nothing anymore."

"Exactly. He's yours. But I will make it very clear to Cotton what is also true: that he cannot phone out or write out of Japan, and that he is being followed wherever he goes—that, in effect, he is under house arrest."

"That is true," Teshima said.

"And so, as Cotton will see, his only chance is to leave on the *Tatsu*. And why not? I'll tell him I'm betraying Japan, and—"

"Will he believe you?"

"He'll believe me. He trusts me. And he'll see how I need him as my instrument to get the word out. It makes sense. I stick my head in a noose if I tell. And, of course, I'll make him think he's still got plenty of time when he arrives in

Hawaii to go warn the Pacific Command that we're planning to attack."

Teshima grinned. "Only, of course, he never reaches Hawaii."

"Exactly. The ship will have turned around and will still be floating back to Yokohama when we hit Pearl on the seventh. You need have no fear that Cotton'll spill the beans." Teshima nodded again, even grinned. Kiyoshi went on: "And since Operation Z should work, your career is safe. You have my word on it, Teshima Taisho. I will tear up that letter to Admiral Yamamoto and forget the whole business. I will make sure that Cotton Drake understands your, uh, kindness, in his behalf. Then he'll be repatriated at some point and sent to some new mission far away from Japan. That's all I desire. I don't want your epaulets, only the life of my friend."

Teshima said: "Okay. I got it."

"Well, not quite *all* of it," Kiyoshi said, with something of a twinkle.

"Oh?"

"I want him my *on* man. I want him to know I saved his life."

"Why's that?"

"Because I don't want ever after to worry again about his chasing after my wife. But that's between you and me."

Teshima grinned; he liked being included in such devious intimacies. "I understand perfectly now."

"Good," Kiyoshi said. "Do I have your sacred word on the bargain?"

Teshima looked away. He was still cross-legged on the mat. He took a drag on his cigarette, and as the smoke came out of his nostrils in a great swoosh, he lowered his big, shiny head and, in his best general's voice, declared: "It's a deal, Serikawa-kun."

54

"Are you going to be a frequent guest?" Cotton asked Kiyoshi. He fixed tea, this Monday, the twenty-fourth of November.

"Did I get you at a bad time?"

Cotton laughed. Since Miyuki had left, there was no kindergarten anymore at the mission, and Cotton's days were usually so empty now that he often just helped around town—especially since in so many houses there wasn't a man around the house anymore. "I'm sort of a professional Good Samaritan," he explained.

"Will you stay in Japan?" Kiyoshi asked. "Is there any point in it?"

"I'm beginning to doubt it. They have a man following me now, I'm sure you know."

Kiyoshi dropped his eyes. "Oh? Who?"

Cotton shrugged. "We haven't been properly introduced, but the *tokko,* I guess. He's out there now. Two guys, really— day man, night man. They must be bored stiff. I got somebody to invite the day man into the service yesterday, but he wouldn't come in."

Kiyoshi lit a cigarette. "They think you know some things."

"They must. They put good men on me. I tried to dodge the one guy in Tokyo the other day, but no luck. Pretty hard, a *gaijin* getting lost these days in Japan."

"Come on, let's take a walk," Kiyoshi said all of a sudden, and Cotton shrugged okay, and they fell in step, heading down the Street That Goes Along the River. Cotton jerked his thumb over his shoulder, and they glanced back at the man following them. "I'll take care of him, Cot."

Kiyoshi went back and introduced himself to the *tokko* man, pulling his credentials out of his pocket. He handed over a letter signed by General Teshima. Takahashi read it carefully, folded it up, saluted Kiyoshi, and went to get some lunch.

"Well," Cotton said, when Kiyoshi caught up with him again, "you *do* swing some weight around here."

Kiyoshi didn't respond, though. He was very serious. He said: "Would you take me up where you spread Sammy's ashes?"

"It's a long hike."

"I don't mind, Cot. I have all day for you. This is the most important day of my life." Cotton stopped dead when he heard that, and Kiyoshi put a hand on his arm. "It is. I've come here with the express purpose of betraying my country for you."

He said it flat out, just as simple as that, just the way he told General Teshima he would.

Cotton put his hands up to his head, almost a stage double take. "Key?"

"Yes, that's what I said."

"Then, yes, let's go up with Sammy."

"Yes," Kiyoshi said, and they took off again. It was a glorious day for walking, unseasonably warm, the countryside still green, with the maples turned where Cotton and Kiyoshi started up into the hills. They never said a single word the whole way, although sometimes Cotton turned and looked at Kiyoshi. At the little bridge over the Uzuma, Cotton roused Kadota and gave the old man the toll for Kiyoshi. Kadota jumped to his feet and saluted when he saw the uniform, and Cotton and Kiyoshi laughed. It felt good to have a little laugh.

But then they returned to silence, even when they got to the field. Finally Cotton spoke. "Do you approve?"

"Oh, it's a beautiful place for Sammy."

"Yes."

"Listen, you do most of the praying, Cot, so let *me* pray for him this time."

"Sure."

Kiyoshi bowed his head. When he was finished, he raised his eyes and said: "I want you to know, I didn't kill him."

"I know that, Key."

"How?"

"Oh, because I accused you of it before Miyuki, and she assured me that you didn't. And that's good enough for me."

"Thank you." They collapsed down onto where the sun had warmed the ground. "But I might as well have killed him."

"I can imagine how you feel."

"Yes, but it's important for me to tell you all about it," Kiyoshi said, and he began, "I was a spy in Hawaii, and Sammy suspected . . ." and he went on from there, all of it. By the end, he was crying. Ashamed, he stood up and walked away, looking out over the land.

Cotton went right to him and put an arm around his shoulder. "It's okay. In all the world, I'm the one person who knows how you feel, because I caused the death of my friend, too."

"Yeah. The whore. I know."

"All of it?"

"The most, I suppose," Kiyoshi said.

Cotton took his hand off his shoulder and squeezed Kiyoshi's neck. "It's a great world, isn't it, Key? And next we'll be at war, won't we?"

Kiyoshi nodded, then spoke with the same sort of emotion as if he were reading a commuter train schedule: "Sunday, December fourteenth, at approximately seven-thirty in the morning, we'll hit Hawaii."

"You're telling me that?"

"I told you, I came to see you in order to betray my country."

"So is everything ready?"

"The fleet is rendezvousing in Hitokappu Bay right now."

"And do the torpedoes work in shallow water?"

"My, you do know everything."

"The date," Cotton said. "I didn't know the date. But I've already passed everything else on; it's too late. You didn't have to betray Japan, so we can forget that you did." Cotton winked. "We know it all, and we're waiting for you."

Kiyoshi shook his head. "I hate to tell you this, pal, but they don't know." Cotton twisted his head. "You know. Bowersox knows. But the United States of America *doesn't* know."

Cotton's mouth flew open. "Bowersox! How the hell do you know Bowersox?"

"Well, he's a traitor, Cot. Just like me. Birds of a feather."

"He can't be."

"He sucked you in completely."

Cotton was horrified, his foolish pride hurt as much as he was shocked. "It can't be. Are you conning me? You still the spy?"

Kiyoshi held out his hands. "I'm sorry, Cot. Let's see. Did Bowersox give you a contact place?" Cotton only stared back. "Come on, did he?" Cotton nodded. "Ueno Park?" Cotton cursed. Kiyoshi reached into his pocket and pulled out the directions to the apartment. He handed it to Cotton. "See?"

"I can't believe it," Cotton said.

"It's Teshima's place."

"Teshima is Bowersox's . . . ?" The words drifted off.

"Oh yeah, they're asshole buddies."

"Shit!" he screamed, Screamed it out over the hills. "The dirty sonofabitch."

Kiyoshi even laughed a little. "All right, take it easy! You're in the big leagues now, but I'm going to take care of things for you."

"But why?" Cotton persisted. "Why did Bowersox do it?"

"Oh, come on, that's not hard. He's shrewd on the one hand, amoral on the other. He's a China man, and he wants us to fight you because he's convinced that if we attack you—especially Hawaii—then you'll come back at us with everything you got." Cotton sank down to the ground, lay back, and listened. "And of course"—Kiyoshi sighed—"he's right."

"He is?"

"Look, Bowersox may be evil, but I think he's got it figured. Yamamoto's wrong, Cotton. The admiral is honorable and Bowersox is a snake, but the admiral is the one who's wrong. We can't beat you—no way."

"I agree," Cotton said.

"Exactly. So the worst thing Japan can do is fight you, attack Hawaii. And I'm sorry, but I can't just let this happen to my country. You understand?"

Cotton raised up, wrapping his arms around his knees. "Oh, sure, I understand what you're thinking. Except, why bother with me? All you have to do is walk into the American embassy and tell the lady at the desk with the southern accent that you would like to see Ambassador Grew. And then you tell him exactly what you just told me. Cut out the middleman."

"Come on, Cotton. Because I'm Japanese. Because I can't bring myself to do that. And I have you, so I'll use you." He flicked his cigarette butt as far as he could. "I have a personal reason, too."

"Oh?"

"I want your ass outta Japan, and you'll never leave unless I make you."

"What's that mean?"

"Look, it's going to be hell for Americans around here."

"Thanks for the tip."

"That's my point, Cot. And it's gonna get worse, and you're too damn blockheaded to understand that. You think you can keep on preaching that love-thy-neighbor bullshit, but the world is still run by the Bowersoxes and the Teshimas, and Jesus himself couldn't get down off the cross and change that." Cotton only buried his head into his knees. "Do you understand?"

Cotton raised his head just enough to say "Maybe."

"All right, listen to me. The *Tatsuta Maru* is going to leave for Hawaii on the second—that's Tuesday, a week from tomorrow. It'll arrive Honolulu December tenth. It's easy. You walk off the damn boat and take a cab over to CINCPAC, and you knock on Admiral Kimmel's door, and you say, 'Good afternoon, Admiral, my name is Cotton Drake, and I just arrived from Japan, and I'd like you to know that a fleet of twenty-three of the emperor's finest ships, with 350 attack planes on their decks, is bearing down on us as we speak, and the Japanese will attack us this coming Sunday morning, December fourteenth, in the year of our Lord 1941. So Admiral Kimmel, hey, let's you and me get some of the other Yanks and sneak out Saturday night and catch them by surprise and end the war before it starts.' "

Cotton had to chuckle a little. But he still appeared a bit puzzled. "Wait a minute. You said Sunday."

"The fourteenth."

"But all the ships are at berth then. At Pearl. What sense does that make? You want to land on the island when they're dicking around out at sea."

Kiyoshi said: "Hey, Cot, we don't want to *take* Hawaii. I don't think we could, anyhow. That's moving too much manpower too far. We don't want Hawaii. What we want is the fleet. That's the idea. Cripple it, destroy it, and we own the Pacific."

"God, I never thought about it that way."

"No, neither did I, at first. Kagoshima wasn't Honolulu. Just Pearl."

Cotton lay back on the grass, staring up to the clear autumn sky. Kiyoshi let him take this all in. He lit another cigarette. "You smoke too much," Cotton said.

"You sound like my damn wife."

Cotton went back to thinking. "All right," he finally said. "Why in God's name are they going to let me on the *Tatsu?* They're already suspicious of me."

"Very."

"Right. They got Tweedledum and Tweedledee, one or the other, on my tail every moment of the day. They're going to let me waltz onto the *Tatsuta Maru,* off to Hawaii?"

"I'm going to take care of the guys tailing you. I know how to handle that."

"Fine. But Teshima's gonna let me leave Japan two weeks before the attack? Bowersox?"

Kiyoshi knelt down next to Cotton. "Of course they won't let you go. *If* they know. But they won't."

"Why not?"

"Because, hey, I worked for NYK. And I am a lieutenant

in the Imperial Navy, on Admiral Yamamoto's own staff. I have contacts, and I have authority."

"So?"

"So, don't you worry. I can get you on that manifest under another name."

"You're sure?"

"Don't you trust me, Cotton?" He stood up and looked down at him, arms crossed.

That irritated Cotton. "Of course I trust you, Key," he said, his voice rising. "I just don't see how you—"

"Just you gimme your passport and your papers when I leave here today, and I will take care of things, and there will be no Reverend Mr. Cotton Drake listed on that ship. Okay?"

"Okay." Cotton said. "I haven't got much choice anyhow, have I?" He held out his hand.

"No, you don't," Kiyoshi answered, and he pulled him to his feet.

Cotton dusted off his clothes. "The fourteenth," he said then. "I should have known it would've been the fourteenth. Gishi-sai. Perfect. The *ronin* come back to life."

"Yeah," Kiyoshi said. And he chuckled to himself: Amazing, nobody among us Japanese ever thought of that, or maybe we would have actually planned it for the fourteenth instead of the seventh. Cotton knows us better than we know ourselves.

He stepped closer to Cotton. "Okay, now I want to be totally honest with you, so there's one other thing you must know—one other reason I want you to leave the country."

Cotton knew that answer, but he said "What's that?" anyway.

"Because I want you away from my wife."

"I swear we never—"

"I know that. I told you, I really *do* believe you. And that's hard." Cotton swallowed. "There's a part of me that still wants to think that you took advantage of my wife and tricked her and screwed her—"

"Stop!" Cotton yelled that. "Why would you want to think that?"

"Because then I could hate you."

"But why, Key?" Cotton held out his hands. "Why would you want to hate me?"

"Because my wife loves you. I love her, and she loves you, and I want to hate you for that, Cotton. I want to hate you, but . . ." Kiyoshi stopped, looking back down at the land spread out below. At last: "I love you. I still love you."

"I know, Key. I love you, too."

"Okay, fine, but I want you on that boat, Cotton. The only two things I dream about in my life now are to stop this damn war and to get my wife back. And"—he smiled—"sending your ass outta here serves both those purposes."

Cotton had to laugh out loud, but this time, spontaneously, he also threw out his arms and embraced his oldest friend. "You know, you're noble, Serikawa Kiyoshi. You are. I'm honored to be the best friend on earth of a man such as you."

"Thank you," Kiyoshi said, in barely a whisper. Then they let go each other and stood back. "Now," Kiyoshi went on, "I have a favor, too. I'd like you to go on ahead. I'll meet you down at the bridge, but I'd like a few moments alone with Sammy."

"Of course," Cotton said, bowing, and Kiyoshi watched after him, as he wended his way down the hill, disappearing into a chaparral of *kaki* trees by the path.

The afternoon sun was still high above the maples, warm and bright upon the hill. There wasn't but baby blue in the sky. "What a glorious place Cotton left you, Sammy!" Kiyoshi said, out loud and in English. "I could stay here forever myself." He sank to the earth, cross-legged, his back as straight as he could make it. He took his left hand, next, and laid the back of it in the palm of his right hand, and then he gazed down for a long time, meditating. At last, calling out, Kiyoshi spoke these words: "Forgive me, Sammy, for all I've done. But I do feel your spirit here, and I trust you'll believe me when I say I'm trying to set things straight. Goodbye, for now, Sammy."

55

Teshima's aide had learned enough to inform the general immediately of Kiyoshi's arrival. Promptly, an angry full colonel was obliged to vacate Teshima's office to be replaced by a mere naval lieutenant. And Teshima even immediately offered Kiyoshi tea and cigarettes.

"I've just been advised that up in Hitokappu, the last of the fleet officers have been told where the strike force is heading," he said.

"So *Kido Butai* departs tomorrow?" Kiyoshi said. Wednesday the twenty-sixth.

"It will if our missionary friend—"

"There is no problem with that," Kiyoshi interrupted. "His silence and your reputation are secured."

Teshima smiled his toothiest. "You know, Serikawa-kun, I must admit, I had no idea you navy types could be so cunning."

"Don't forget, Teshima Taisho, I'm a *yoshi* in one of the bravest *army* families of our time. No doubt some of your army has rubbed off on me."

Teshima liked that. "So Drake agreed to leave on the *Tatsuta* next week?"

"Wouldn't you? He knew full well he was being followed. He was appalled to learn, from me, that he had been betrayed by his contact in his own embassy. But he trusts me, of course, and he accepts my story that I'm betraying Japan. Besides, if he goes to Hawaii on the *Tatsu*, he'll become a hero for saving his country—and he's safely on American soil, to boot. It required no magic powers of persuasion on my part. Here." Seamlessly, as if it were all of a piece, Kiyoshi brought out some papers and shoved them at Teshima; he even handed him a fountain pen in the same motion. "All I need from you, Teshima Taisho, is to sign some paperwork to get the American on his way."

"More?"

"Lots more. Priority endorsement for a ticket, approval for a *gaijin* to enter the Yokohama harbor area, et cetera, et cetera, et cetera. Duplicates, triplicates. War is inconvenient, sir. Paperwork exceeds ammunition."

Teshima grumbled. He had a cigarette in his mouth, and Kiyoshi lit it so as not to distract the general as he scribbled his signature, here and there and wherever Kiyoshi pointed. He slapped another sheet down. "Starting Monday, the new month, a *gaijin*'ll even need papers to travel from Tochigi into Tokyo."

Teshima scrawled on that, too. "We'll even need permission to fuck soon," he groaned.

Kiyoshi made sure to laugh, snatching up all the papers. "Oh, the horrors of war," he said.

Teshima sat back. "So much for Drake. What about Bowersox?"

"If he, uh, vanishes," Kiyoshi said, tucking all the papers into his briefcase, "do we risk raising American suspicions? Is it possible he's left some sort of message with a colleague that should be opened in the event of his disappearance?"

"Ah, a page from Lieutenant Serikawa's book of intrigue." Kiyoshi smiled, accepting that as a compliment. "I wouldn't think so, though. Bowersox is a loner, and when your game is betrayal, it's not likely that you share any confidences."

"But General, he's an important diplomat, and once he fails to come into his office, the Americans are bound to start asking questions."

"Yes, but the man isn't popular. The ambassador, in particular, can't stand his ass. There's no wife, no girlfriend, no close colleague. Plus, it's well known that Saint is a habitué of the demimonde. He's incorrigible—whores, drinks, gambles." Kiyoshi couldn't suppress a smile at that assessment, but Teshima accepted that in good spirits. "So, Serikawa-kun, you see why he's made such good company for me off-hours."

"Yes sir."

Good-naturedly, Teshima even laughed again. "And so, should Saint, uh, disappear, any reasonable person will first conclude that he encountered difficulty—perhaps, even, his demise—in some personal contretemps. Should the Americans inquire about his whereabouts, I'll make sure that some diverting tale finds its way back—the usual lust and liquor."

Kiyoshi concurred. "Someone will, uh—" he searched for the right word—"uh, swipe Bowersox?"

"That's no trick. He'll come to the apartment near Ueno Park on request. I suggest you meet him there."

"Me?"

"Listen, Serikawa-kun, you bargained for your friend's life with me. Bowersox never agreed to that deal. On the contrary. I promised him Drake dead." Teshima looked coldly at Kiyoshi. "But *you* promised me Bowersox likewise, and I'm holding you to that promise."

"I'll see Bowersox," Kiyoshi snapped.

"He can't be allowed to run free. He's really the worst kind of nuisance. He's a rogue on one hand and a zealot on the other."

"I'll talk to him."

"You'll take care of him?"

"If it's necessary."

"It is."

"If it's necessary, and I can't, I know you have someone else who can."

"Just as in Hawaii, you pass the difficult responsibility on."

"Yes," Kiyoshi said, his blood starting to heat up again.

"You walk a fine line, Serikawa-kun. I'm just warning you. The longer you play these games, the more risk you create for Drake."

Kiyoshi straightened up. "It's a week from today the *Tatsu* sails. Our deal was that you will protect Cotton."

"No. Our deal was that I will *not* have him killed. But protect him? I cannot protect him from Bowersox, and I cannot protect him from himself."

"Sir?"

Teshima waggled a finger. "Just so there is no misunderstanding."

"What?"

Teshima sat back in his big chair. "Does your friend, Mr. Drake, know cormorant fishing?"

"We did most of our growing up together in Gifu prefecture."

"Oh, yes, the masters down there." Cormorants are great, rapacious fishing birds, fitted by their handlers, the *ujo*, with a ring at the base of their long, thin necks. Set out by the *ujo* from rowboats, the cormorants can pass the small fish they catch down through the neck rings into their happy stomachs. The larger, juicier fish can't fit through the ring, though, so they must be handed over to the *ujo* and his assistants for human consumption. "So understand—Mr. Drake, he is the cormorant."

"And you are the *ujo?*"

"If you like," Teshima said, pleased with the thought.

"Drake has a ring around his neck, and we'll only allow him tidbits. The other day he intentionally tried to escape from the gentleman following him. This isn't a game, Serikawa-kun. The men from *tokko* have been advised that now they are only Drake's watchmen, not his assassins, but they also understand that they are not to tolerate any more mischievousness on his part. Until they deliver him safely to the *Tatsuta*, he is not to try and phone or write or contact a soul besides those fool Christian peasants he ministers to in Tochigi."

"I will advise him to be careful."

"You better, Serikawa-kun. If he even tries to go for a wrong fish again, his neck will be squeezed."

Kiyoshi saluted.

The smile returned to Teshima's face. "My regards to Mr. Bowersox," he said. "My apologies as well." He winked.

"Yes sir," Kiyoshi replied.

* * *

There was so much for Kiyoshi to do. First thing the next day, Wednesday, he took the train down to Yokohama, not only to stop by the NYK offices there but to go to the other shipping companies as well. He visited his old buddies from his days at American Orient, and his friendly rivals at the Blue Funnel Line, at TOA, P & O, and the Messageries Maritime Mail Service. All their livelihoods had been devastated, with so few routes still running, and most of the captains and sailors alike more or less shanghaied into His Majesty's navy. An odd combination of aimlessness and tension filled the port.

Ah, but the *Tatsuta Maru* was there, berthed and waiting for its much-publicized departure Tuesday, its two great smoke-stacks shining. Official announcement of the ship's trip had been made and reservations were fast filling up, but one of his old colleagues took the time to escort Kiyoshi on board and personally show him the cabin that his friend Mr. Drake had been assigned. More paperwork. Done.

Back to Tokyo, to the railroad station. The people milled everywhere, not just coming and going to work but pushing and bitching to get out, go anywhere. No one said it, but everybody knew: soon, it would not just be China spilling their Japanese blood. Couples poured through the station, trying to find a train that would take them off two or three days, alone, where they could lie down together again. Kiyoshi passed in all the necessary papers, and the passports, revalidated, and permission cards. But after an endless wait, they all got stamped. Done.

Next, the Bank of Japan. More forms. And the police station. Somewhere, he remembered, he had to get a gun. Maybe back at the Naval Ministry, if he had time. But City Office was next. That too, done. He coughed from the charcoal fumes. He had to remember to buy a *masuku*. Sometimes, now, the air was so foul that when his phlegm came up, it was dark and spotted black. The city itself, all of it, grew dimmer each day, the lights lowering, the people's spirits puffed up false with bravado and ignorance. At quarter past seven that night, when Kiyoshi finally got off the streetcar in Asakusa and started walking home to Miyuki, he could still hear the voices of the generals and the cabinet officers spewing pep talk out of the loud-speakers, because now it was Government Hour, and everybody in the streets listened dutifully, perking up at all the right places and cheering out loud right after the correct number of perked-up places.

He got drunk with Miyuki that night, and they made love sloppily and inconsequentially, not happily at all. But: done.

"Where's Yoichi?" Bowersox said, as soon as he came into the room near Ueno Park.

It was the next morning, Thursday the twenty-seventh.

"I'm sorry, Mr. Bowersox, but General Teshima has been detained, and asked me to see you."

Bowersox hesitated by the door. It was the language that held him, the perfect, unaccented English coming from the mouth of this man, impeccably turned out in the uniform of His Majesty's Imperial Navy. Kiyoshi took advantage of the slight, uncertain pause and put out his hand. "I'm Kiyoshi Serikawa, sir."

Bowersox looked at the hand before he took it. "Hello." Then quickly: "I'm only supposed to speak to Yoichi."

Kiyoshi ignored that. "I've spent a great deal of my life in the United States. I went to Harvard."

"Kiss my ass," Bowersox said.

"And I'm an old friend of Cotton Drake's."

That caught Bowersox's attention. His eyebrows arched up. A moment more: "Sure. You're the one who was in Hawaii."

"Yes. That one."

Bowersox circled into the room. He took out a pack of his Luckies, flipping some of them up toward Kiyoshi, lighting both their cigarettes. They were both still wary of one another. "So, this is about Drake?" Bowersox said, and Kiyoshi nodded his head. "Have you taken care of him yet?"

Kiyoshi leaned back on the desk. "In a fashion."

"What's that mean?"

"Later on this afternoon, when you get back to the embassy, you'll receive, from NYK, a ship's manifest for the

Tatsuta's sailing Tuesday. The Reverend Drake's name will be on it."

Bowersox lurched. "What?"

Kiyoshi held up his hand. "Exactly. That's why I'm informing you. That's why I asked you here."

This did not placate Bowersox. "You get Yoichi over here right away." He pointed at the phone. "Go on, call him up. I am risking my little red ass for the glory of your Emperor, to save you from the mischief of Cotton Drake."

"We're all cognizant of that, and we're all most appreciative."

"Oh, sure, so you let Drake waltz away, and as soon as he finds out the U.S. isn't expecting an attack on Hawaii, it'll take him about five seconds to figure out that I withheld his information. And then I'm ruined. Savvy?"

Bowersox looked like he might grab the phone, so Kiyoshi gently laid his hand on top of it. "Do you really think General Teshima would let Drake go to Hawaii before we attacked Hawaii?"

Bowersox stopped, considering that. "What's up?" he asked.

"Cotton is boarding a ship to nowhere."

"How's that?"

"The *Tatsuta Maru* is our decoy. We're sending her out to show the world that, never fear, it's business as usual."

"The attack will occur when she's at sea?"

"I think you can safely conclude that," Kiyoshi said. Then, unaccountably, he started to laugh.

"What the hell are you laughing at? You think this is funny?"

"I'm sorry, Mr. Bowersox. It's just so bizarre discussing this with a member of the American embassy."

"I hope you don't think I'm some goddamn traitor, Lieutenant. I'm not *for* you sons-of-bitches. In fact, I want to cut your balls off. Savvy?"

"Well, sort of."

"Look, you've lived in America. You know very well that there are a helluva lot of Americans, starting with the President himself, who would applaud my decision in their hearts, even if they'd have to condemn it before the world."

"I believe that."

"Where the hell is it written that patriots have to die, nobly, in lost causes?" Bowersox asked, and he mumbled something further that Kiyoshi couldn't make out about Nathan Hale.

"You'd be surprised how much I understand you," Kiyoshi said. "But help me with one thing."

"Shoot."

"When we attack Hawaii, a lot of your countrymen will die. Cotton would have saved those lives if he stopped the attack."

"Sure," Bowersox said. "But I don't know those men." He stepped over and put out his cigarette. "And neither do I know the ones who will *not* die later in China for what I do now. Savvy?" There was such a smugness to Bowersox that Kiyoshi thought that he could hardly have tolerated him ... except that he agreed with him. "You see my point?" Bowersox pressed him, smiling. "You do, don't you?"

"Granted, Mr. Bowersox, there's probably a lot of truth in what you say."

"Aha!" Bowersox shrieked, giving his best performance from a melodrama. "Eureka! I've found one! I've smoked out a Japanese who actually admits doubt." Kiyoshi ducked his head. "Goddamn, don't be embarrassed, Lieutenant. The truth is rarely discovered unless we doubt."

"You overstate my natural caution."

"Aw, bullshit," Bowersox went on, chortling a bit. "Now I know why you find this so curious. It isn't just you, the Japanese, discussing these matters with me, the American. No. It's more than that. It's: I, the American, who welcome your attack, and you, the Japanese, who regret it. Huh? Huh?"

Kiyoshi turned away and walked across the room. When he turned back, he said, "Yeah," but so softly Bowersox could hardly make it out. Then, louder: "I wanted to meet you, Mr. Bowersox. I really did."

"Hey, don't worry," Bowersox said. "I'll keep your secret,

pal. As one patriot to another." But the smile went right away, then, and he slapped the desk. "But enough of the damn philosophy. Let's get back to our mutual friend."

"There's no need for anybody to die," Kiyoshi said. Bowersox didn't know it, of course, and Kiyoshi couldn't tell him, but it was really Bowersox's own life he was seeking to save. Cotton already had his safe passage.

"I'm afraid there is," Bowersox said. "That was the deal. The missionary may be a nice man, but he must be killed."

"If the *Tatsu* sails and we attack Pearl Harbor, what do you care?"

"Because the *Tatsu* comes back, doesn't it? And Drake will get repatriated. They'll trade us all for Japanese nationals in the U.S., and then he blows the whistle on me. Nobody is going to appreciate the niceties of my situation like you have."

"Cotton will never talk. I swear. He'll never mention your name."

"Why?"

"Because I'll tell him: 'In Japan, Bowersox let you live. Now, you must let Bowersox be, ever after.' That's good enough for Cotton. He's not vengeful."

"I'm not vengeful either, Lieutenant. I'm only careful. And I can't have anyone walking around God's green earth holding dark secrets about me for the rest of my life."

"Cotton will never give the secret up. I swear."

"I'm sorry. I don't buy it. If you guys are too squeamish to kill him, I'll make sure it's done myself."

"No."

"Don't you tell me *no*, Lieutenant. The only one who can do that is Yoichi, and I don't think he will. I don't think he gives a rat's ass about your friend." He reached over and picked up the phone.

"Put it down," Kiyoshi said, stepping toward him.

"Listen, stay out of this, Lieutenant. Either Teshima does what he promises and kills the missionary, or I get it done. It's really no affair of yours." He dialed the first digit of the telephone number.

"Put the goddamn phone down, Bowersox." He dialed the

second digit. Kiyoshi stepped quickly to the other side of the desk, yanked open the top drawer there, and pulled out the pistol. Bowersox stopped with the third digit. He saw the gun out of the corner of his eye. Then he saw it even more clearly as Kiyoshi stepped in front of him, aiming at his heart. Defiantly, Bowersox finished dialing the third digit. "Put it down. Put it down. I don't want any killing. Just get lost, Bowersox. Can't you see? Get 1—"

The phone came hurtling toward Kiyoshi, the black receiver slamming into his shoulder. He wasn't ready at all for that action. This wasn't Kiyoshi's business, guns. It never occurred to him that somebody would charge into the face of a gun, but here came Bowersox, taking advantage of his surprise, flying full force into Kiyoshi, driving him back into the wall. Bowersox fell onto him there, pushing Kiyoshi's gun away, smothering his reach, kneeing Kiyoshi so sharply that he crumpled to the ground, forcing him to use all his strength just to hang onto the weapon.

Bowersox fought far better than Kiyoshi would have imagined; but still, the older man had to devote most of his energy to wrestling for the gun, so he couldn't press his advantage effectively. And he was starting to grow weary. Bowersox was breathing hard; he knew he couldn't hang on much longer. And so, calculated as ever, he suddenly rolled off Kiyoshi and threw all his weight onto Kiyoshi's arm, trying to wrench the pistol away. He had both hands on Kiyoshi's wrist when the gun went off.

Both men cried out in shock and caught their breath: they hadn't been hit. Somehow, then, in that second, Kiyoshi was able to take his free hand and whack it up the side of Bowersox's face. The American winced, loosened his grip for an instant; and although Kiyoshi was still on his back, he was able to take the heel of his left hand and jam Bowersox's head back. Bowersox was losing his hold on Kiyoshi, losing his will, and when Kiyoshi brought his knee up, Bowersox felt the blow enough to relax his defense, and Kiyoshi was able to bring his free hand down hard into Bowersox's stomach.

That was all he had to do. Bowersox cried out and his

hands fell away. Kiyoshi could actually see the fear and the regret both in the man's eyes in that instant when he pulled the trigger. The bullet slammed into Bowersox's chest, near enough, it seemed, to his heart.

"I wanted to save you," Kiyoshi mumbled. Then he shot one more bullet into him, to be sure. They were the first two bullets he had ever fired in his life.

Bowersox was dead; Kiyoshi stood up, put the safety back on the gun, and brushed himself off. He was crying—deep, breathless sobs—until at last, he forced himself to retrieve the phone and dial. Never once could he bring himself to look over at the bloody body on the floor. "I just killed Bowersox," he said into the receiver.

"Where are you?" Teshima asked.

"In your place in Ueno."

"You killed him there?"

"He tried to attack me."

"Is it a mess?"

Kiyoshi still couldn't look back. "I don't know how much of a mess murder is supposed to be."

"All right. Well, just leave everything alone. I'll send someone over."

"Okay."

"You know, Serikawa, you make me proud of you. I didn't think you had this courage. Your father and your brother— their spirits cheer you today for what you've done for Japan."

"Thank you," Kiyoshi said, and he put down the phone. He couldn't avoid Bowersox now; he lay too close to the door. So when Kiyoshi picked up his navy cap, he laid it over his heart and spoke to the dead man: "I'm sorry, Mr. Bowersox. You could have gone away for a couple weeks. Then you could have trusted Cotton forever. You could have." And then he left, walking haphazardly down the streets toward the park.

He remembered, too, vividly: the first time he ever came to Tokyo, it was spring, and his father took the whole family to Ueno to see the *hanami*. "If you are Japanese," he told Kiyoshi, "the only two things you absolutely must see are

Ueno Park when the cherry blossoms are out and Fuji-san anytime."

"I've seen Fuji-san already, Father," he had said.

"Yes," Mr. Okuno laughed. "So here is Ueno, and now you can die."

Kiyoshi smiled at that memory now as he retreated as far as he could into the park, trying to escape from the ubiquitous loudspeakers.

He put his hands over his ears. "Aikoku Koshinkyoku," the favorite patriotic march, blared out next. Hardly an hour could go by any longer without "Aikoku Koshinkyoku." The loudspeakers must be multiplying these days; they seemed to chase after him. "To all citizens: By devoted order of His Majesty Tenno Heika, next Tuesday, the second of December, will be set aside as a special *Houkoubi*, an appointed day of sacrifice, when we will all be privileged to give more of ourselves to our great land."

Only well into the park could Kiyoshi finally find some quiet. He walked in little circles, surprised at how little he was actually thinking about how he'd just killed Bowersox. It all seemed to flow together, one big mess, and so he just gave up and thought again of the things ahead he still had to do.

When he came out of Ueno, he called Miyuki at home and asked her to meet him at the Yasukuni shrine. It was late autumn now; and so by the time they met, under the great *torii*, it was dusk.

"Why did you want to meet me here?" she asked, as they moved down toward the shrine.

"I'm not sure, really. I think it's just because all of a sudden I felt very Japanese, and so I wanted to talk to all the great spirits . . . your father, your brother."

"I'm sure they're here, and they'll be with you. I'm not sure they can reach me any longer, since I think like a Christian now. Even if I'm not baptized yet."

Kiyoshi said: "Oh, with spirits, I don't think it matters how a person worships." He paused and threw some coins. "I'm sure the Serikawa spirits are still with you." Then he bowed and prayed. So did Miyuki. When she finished, he asked her: "If you'll tell me, what did you pray?"

"That we have peace. That's all," Miyuki said.

Softly, when she looked back over at him, Kiyoshi said: "Me too."

"This is a military shrine," Miyuki said, smiling a little at the irony. "I'm not sure many of the people who come here send those thoughts up."

"No," Kiyoshi said, and he took her hand. "But the two things that mean the most to me are my country and you, and so it suddenly was very important to me this afternoon that I be together with you both." Miyuki squeezed his hand, and then she stretched up, on her tiptoes, and pecked her husband on the cheek. Miyuki knew then that things were moving even more quickly than she understood, and the worst she could do to Kiyoshi was cheat him by withholding any of those little spontaneous moments that add up to the best of love and memory.

On the gravel path, then, they walked hand in hand out of Yasukuni, toward home, and Miyuki knew that she felt closer to him than she had in months, maybe even since Kigen. "Come here, Kiyoshi," she said when he turned out the lights, and this time, she took all of him to her, and not just the part of him that might give her a baby. This night she took Kiyoshi.

He could sense it, too, that at last she was holding all of him tightly again. "Oh, my Miyuki!" he cried. It wasn't just that she wrapped her arms and legs around him, it was that this time he could feel her within *him*. How long it had been since he'd felt that way! "Thank you for this, Miyuki," he said, and she kissed him, thrusting her tongue into his mouth, and Miyuki tingled. She hadn't tingled in so long, either, but now she was sure that all the Serikawa spirits were with them, helping them to form a new Serikawa generation that she and Kiyoshi hadn't been able to create by themselves.

Kiyoshi felt that way, too, which made it so much easier for him to steal away the next morning while his wife still lay there, asleep and beautiful, and still his. For now.

56

The fleet for Hawaii was well out from Hitokappu now, this day, Friday. Monday would mean a new week and a new month as well, and the ultimate decision would be placed in Tenno Heika's hands that day. But it was understood. What could stop Operation Z now?

At the Naval Ministry, no one could work; everything was suspected, everything anticipated. At ten o'clock, Kiyoshi straightened out his desk, and when it was neat as a pin, he told the secretary for his section that he had to go out to the Naval Staff College. The only specific message Kiyoshi left behind was for General Teshima: Should he call, tell him that Kiyoshi would come back up from Yokohama directly after the *Tatsuta Maru* sailed on Tuesday in order to give him a full update.

Then, outside the ministry, Kiyoshi went through the motions of heading to the bus stop. Instead, though, he turned down a side street and cut the other way, walking the few blocks to the Tokyo City Office. There, he entered, found the correct room, took a seat, and when his time came, declared his intention to divorce his wife, Serikawa Miyuki.

It was not difficult for a Japanese man to obtain a divorce, a *mikudarihan*. Hardly. There was no chivalry involved; husbands routinely divorced sickly wives, getting on with their own honorable lives. The state only required Kiyoshi to write out a formal statement, three and a half lines precisely, rather like some bureaucratic haiku. "What is the reason?" the clerk asked, hardly glancing up.

"The woman is barren," Kiyoshi declared, and the fellow nodded and advised him to take a seat again, which Kiyoshi did, but he was barely into the first few pages of propaganda in this morning's *Asahi Shimbum* when the clerk came back with the divorce decree, stamped and filed in duplicate.

Kiyoshi left for Asakusa to get the train to Tochigi, a Serikawa no more.

He walked casually up the Street That Goes Along the River. The sun shone brightly, and Okuno Kiyoshi could even see some carp gliding through the Uzuma. Without even realizing it, he said this aloud, to himself: "What a glorious day to be alive!" And he stopped here and there, paying his respects to the people of Cotton's town. It wasn't nearly as bad outside of Tokyo.

Where the river came up by the school, Kiyoshi spotted Cotton's day guard, Takahashi, sitting on a bench there, comfortably taking his ease, with only one eye on the mission compound. Of course, as soon as he saw Kiyoshi approaching in his naval uniform, Takahashi jumped up and saluted.

Kiyoshi gestured for him to sit back down, and there he brought out a sheaf of papers and handed them to him. "I bring these personally from General Teshima. Read them carefully."

Takahashi studied the orders. "But I thought I was following Drake to Yokohama."

"Exactly. This is what is amended. Instead, you will make sure he goes to Central Station and is on that express to Osaka." Kiyoshi pointed to that line in the orders. And the others, one by one. "You understand? There is no confusion?"

"No sir."

"Good." He took out another letter and opened it up. "Now, what time does your night relief"—he glanced at the orders—"Sakai. What time does he come on?"

"Five o'clock."

"I assumed that, and I won't be able to stay around till then. You must pass this on to him. Read it." Takahashi did. "Any questions?"

"No sir. It's quite clear. Sakai follows Mr. Drake into Asakusa tomorrow and guards that house till I report at dawn."

"Exactly." Kiyoshi looked directly at the guard. "Now, Takahashi-san, I cannot impress on you how important this matter is to General Teshima. The utmost secrecy is required. You will not even share your own instructions with Sakai. Is that understood?"

"Yes sir."

"You may, however, advise Sakai that once his duty is completed Sunday morning, General Teshima has awarded him a full three days off. Likewise, after Drake gets on that train, the general's gratitude for your service manifests itself in a three-day holiday for you. Both you and Sakai need not report back to headquarters till Wednesday morning."

Takahashi beamed. "Why, thank you, sir."

"Your gratitude goes not to me but to General Teshima. He expects in return only your fullest devotion to these orders and to the secrecy of the mission."

"Yes sir!" Takahashi shouted, and he rose and bowed deeply.

Kiyoshi turned to the mission. There, he found Cotton at his desk, going through his papers, saving some, tossing out others.

"Hey, you're a couple days early, Key," he said, clasping his hand with both of his. "Or . . . uh-oh, is there a problem?"

"Just a shift in plans. Which is a nice way of saying I lied to you the other day."

"Oh?"

Kiyoshi threw that off so blithely, Cotton couldn't tell whether or not he was kidding.

"Well, can we discuss this over a drink?" Kiyoshi asked then, and Cotton gave up trying to analyze him and got into the spirit of just-us-pals:

"Why, Serikawa-san, the sun hasn't gone over the yardarm yet." And he laughed and reached for his Scotch bottle. "Or is it under the yardarm?"

"You're asking me about . . . *yardarms?*" Kiyoshi said. "What the hell is a yardarm?"

Cotton shrugged and held up the Scotch. "I was saving this to share with a lady named Hanako," he said. "She was Sumiko's best friend, and we were gonna toast Sumiko before

I left. But"—he presented the bottle—"for you, Key. Hanako and I'll make do with something else." So Cotton poured, and they sat on the tatami and sipped their drinks. "Well, did you really lie to me, or did you—"

"Fib?" Kiyoshi said facetiously.

"You fibbed?"

"No, I'm sorry—I lied. I lied to you."

"Oh," Cotton said, and for the first time he understood how serious Kiyoshi really was.

"Yes, the date for the attack—"

"Gishi-sai."

"No, that's just it—it isn't Gishi-sai. That's the lie."

"Oh, so when is it? The next Sunday? Christmas?"

"No, Cot—it's the Sunday *before* Gishi-sai. The seventh."

"The seventh?" Kiyoshi nodded, while the anger washed the surprise out of Cotton's voice: "What kind of crap is that? The *Tatsu* will still be out in the middle of the Pacific Ocean on the seventh."

"I know," Kiyoshi said. "Only you—you won't be on the *Tatsu.*" Cotton's head jerked up. "And I'm sorry, but I needed your papers to work things out."

"What things? What the hell is going on?"

"The *Tatsuta Maru* isn't the only ship leaving Japan."

"Really?"

"As you wily Occidentals like to say, there's more than one way to skin a dog."

"A cat."

"That too. You see, there's still a couple boats working Shanghai. Mail service every day, business as usual. And the TOA line is still running the *Nagasaki Maru.*"

"Shanghai, huh?" Cotton took a sip of his Scotch. "I thought anybody with half a brain was getting the hell *out* of Shanghai."

"Yeah, pretty much. But the U.S. Marines are still there. And the port's still open. There's still ships going out to Manila and Hong Kong."

"You want me to go out that way?"

"I don't *want.* You have to, Cot. It's the only way left out."

"If you say so."

Kiyoshi nodded vigorously. "You also have to play this strictly by my book. Teshima is prepared to have the *tokko* grab you—kill you—the instant you stray off line. He calls you his cormorant, and he's got a ring around your neck until the moment you step on the *Tatsu*. Except, of course, you're not going to."

"Step on the *Tatsu?*"

"Right."

"Okay," Cotton said, scratching his head. "Walk me through this."

"You go into Tokyo tomorrow night, and—"

"Tomorrow night? Saturday? I got services Sunday. I can't—"

"Cotton, please—I'm sorry, but the war is not operating on a church schedule right now." Cotton nodded, smiling ruefully. "Good. Now you spend the night with—uh, you spend the night at our house. Catch the eight o'clock express the next morning. Our friend"—Kiyoshi gestured outside to the guard—"Takahashi will dutifully follow you to Central Station. He thinks you're going to Osaka. But you stay on to Nagasaki."

"I have a ticket to Nagasaki?"

"Ticket, papers—everything. I'll show you all that."

"You're thorough, Key."

"Yeah. The train gets into Nagasaki late Monday afternoon. Okay?" Cotton nodded. "Get a hotel. The *Nagasaki Maru* sails noon Tuesday, docks Shanghai Wednesday morning. You're booked passage several hours later on the *Saigon Voyageur*. Vichy ship. It arrives Manila Sunday afternoon."

"That's cutting it close."

"Sorry, best I can do. But you've got enough leeway. We don't hit Hawaii till the next morning—Sunday back there. So you sashay up to the Manila Hotel and report to General MacArthur. There'll still be plenty of time for the Americans to get the fleet out of Pearl. And you're safe, no matter what happens. You're safe. On American territory."

Kiyoshi got to his feet and went across the room to fetch

the last splash of the Scotch. Cotton followed him. "You really want me out of Japan, don't you?"

Kiyoshi nodded. "We've gone through all this, Cotton."

"Miyuki?"

Kiyoshi held up his glass in the manner of a toast.

"But I told you," Cotton said. "I promise I'll stay away. I don't have to leave. If you can sneak me out of the country, then you sure as hell can get me into the right place in Tokyo. The British Embassy. The Dutch. There's still a few Western newspaper guys around. There's still lots of people here to tell."

"No, no, no, Cotton." And Kiyoshi held up his hands. "You are just not listening to me. I want you outta here. All right?" Cotton shifted as if he were going to argue, so Kiyoshi held up his hands again. "No, no, no. If that's too difficult for you to deal with, then please understand—you owe it to me to get outta here."

"What?"

"You're my *on* man. You owe me."

"Don't give me that crap. I'm not Japanese."

Kiyoshi shrugged. "Okay, I'll be American. Because you're my brother and I'm your keeper." He paused and drew on his cigarette. Only after he turned back from blowing the smoke away did he look directly at Cotton and say: "I killed Bowersox yesterday for you."

Cotton gagged. He tried to put the glass down on the tatami next to him, but he botched it, and it fell over. "What?"

"Yes."

"Killed?" Kiyoshi nodded, without expression. "You killed him? For *me?*" Cotton struggled to his feet, went over to his desk, laid his hands far out on it, opening up his lungs as best he could, grabbing for air.

"Look, if I didn't kill Bowersox, he was gonna kill you."

"So you saved my life—with murder?"

"Yes."

"Key, Key—that goes against everything I am!" Nervously, he brushed his hair back, leaving his hands over his eyes, and sat on the desk. Kiyoshi poured the last couple of ounces of

Scotch and gave it to him, and when Cotton threw it back, neat, it occurred to Kiyoshi he'd never seen him do that before. He came over and took a place next to Cotton but talked away from him, looking out to the room almost as if Cotton weren't there. "It's funny. I pulled the trigger. Twice. I shot him right here"—he tapped his chest—"very close range. It all happened very fast. We were fighting, and suddenly I had my chance. I didn't want to kill him." He turned to Cotton. "I do want you to know that."

"Okay," Cotton said.

"But"—looking away again—"maybe it doesn't even matter. Bowersox was a traitor. Traitors are supposed to die. No matter how well intentioned, traitors are supposed to die. Right?"

"I don't know," Cotton said. He shook his head. "Frankly, I'm not sure of much of anything right now."

"Well, don't worry about me. I'll tell you this: I don't feel much. It's only been a day since I shot him, and I don't feel much at all."

Cotton swung to look directly at Kiyoshi. "You don't feel? You kill a—" But Kiyoshi was staring out again. "My God, Key, what is this doing to you?"

"No, no, you're not listening. Sammy. I didn't pull any trigger that time. I was miles away. And in my heart I still feel I killed him." He shrugged. "But Bowersox? I pulled that trigger. Bang! Bang!" He pantomined shooting. "But so what? I didn't have any choice. If I didn't kill Bowersox, he would've killed you. And I couldn't stand that. I already had the one friend's death on my conscience."

"Yeah," Cotton said. "I know how that works"—and he wrapped his left arm around Kiyoshi. They were sitting there together on the desk like lovers, Kiyoshi with his right arm around Cotton's shoulder, Cotton with his left arm around Kiyoshi's waist. They held each other for a long time. Finally, Cotton said: "Well, okay—thanks. I guess."

Kiyoshi squeezed him good-naturedly as he got up. "No, no thanks necessary. I just made a choice, and in the bargain I happened to save your life." Then he winked and threw back the last of his Scotch. "And now, if you'll excuse me, Reverend Drake, I think it's the time when I should go over to your church and pray awhile about some things on my mind."

57

It had never even occurred to Cotton. The possibility had never once crossed his mind. And that fact proved ultimately that no matter how long he lived in Japan, no matter how deeply he embraced the land and its people and their culture—no matter—he could never be Japanese. No, otherwise Cotton would not have been utterly, completely shocked when he entered the church a few minutes later and found Kiyoshi sitting there, expressionless, cross-legged, bare-chested, a dagger in his right hand, preparing to commit seppuku.

"I thought you'd never come," Kiyoshi said, breaking a little smile.

Cotton cried out. Gingerly, then, he stepped toward Kiyoshi, a hand out in some involuntary supplication. "God, Key, you can't do this!"

Kiyoshi spoke dispassionately then, so without inflection, so rehearsed that it sounded like some form of a recorded announcement. "No, Cotton, I've thought this through very carefully, and once I started down this path, this really could be the only destination."

"But if you can get me out of the country, surely you—"

Kiyoshi held up his hand with the knife in it. It was the same dagger Takeo had used five years ago for these same raw purposes. "Perhaps I could. But I don't want that. I'm Japanese, Cot. Forever. And just because I disagree with my country now doesn't mean that I reject her. On the contrary. I'm acting to save her. But"—a slight shrug—"all that Japan means, and all that is good about her, must reject me." He sighed. "And I understand that, and I accept it." So Cotton nodded. He knew enough not to argue now.

Kiyoshi went on, almost maddening in his dry, level tone. "So, don't try and stop me. If you make any move toward me, all I'll do is sink this into myself, and you'll gain nothing. In fact, Cot, you'll mess things up, because I have a few matters to go over with you." With his free hand, Kiyoshi patted some papers lying to his side.

"Okay."

"Good. Now, first the last. I will need you to apply the coup de grace."

"Please, Kiyoshi, not—"

"I've provided you a choice." He pointed to his other side. "I brought a gun as well as Takeo's sword. I understand if cutting my head off is a bit too grisly for a *gaijin*, even for you. I'd prefer that, but if the gun must suffice . . ." He shrugged. He might as well have been talking about chocolate or vanilla. "The gun works. I know. It was what I used on Mr. Bowersox."

"You know it's against my religion to kill."

Kiyoshi shook his head and waggled a finger, like mother to a naughty child. "Cotton, Cotton—there you go, being vocational again!"

"You leave me no options?"

"I think it's a very clear choice: put me out of my misery, or watch while your best friend dies a slow, agonizing death." He shrugged. "Anyway, take a seat now."

Kiyoshi was in the middle of the rear aisle, just to the right of the church entrance. He gestured to the last pew, and Cotton rested there, sitting on the back. Kiyoshi started to talk again, but Cotton threw up his hand to stop him, then put both hands to his face, bowing his head in silent prayer.

Kiyoshi waited patiently until Cotton raised his head again and brushed away his tears. "Are you ready to, uh, take this all in now?" Kiyoshi asked.

"I guess."

"Okay. It isn't that complicated." Kiyoshi reached over to

his left, and from the top of the pile of papers there he slid the first document off. "This is a copy of my *mikudarihan.*"

"What?" Cotton flew up off the pew, hands out.

"I divorced Miyuki earlier today at the Tokyo City Office. It's all there." Cotton started to lean down and pick it up, but Kiyoshi waved him off, quite irritably. "I said, it's all there, in order. Let's go through everything first, and then, if you have any questions . . ."

"Will you stop being so damn businesslike?" Cotton suddenly snapped. He threw his hands up in the air, then turned around and rested with them, this time leaning forward on the back of the last pew.

"I'm sorry. It wards off emotion. Old Oriental trick."

Cotton turned around and sat back on the rear of the pew, arms akimbo. "All right, why did you divorce her?" They'd been speaking in English so far. He asked that question in Japanese. It was instinctive, but even so, Kiyoshi stayed in English.

"Two reasons. First, Miyuki and I went to Yasukuni yesterday. We visited the spirits of Colonel Serikawa and Takeo. It just wouldn't be fair to them to have to suffer a traitor in the family. Takeo wanted me to be a Serikawa. I couldn't repay him doing what I have. It would have to be Okuno Kiyoshi and not Serikawa Kiyoshi who betrayed his country and his Emperor."

Kiyoshi fidgeted a little; he'd been sitting this way for a long time. But he never let the knife in his hand wander far from where it was pointed, at the left side of his belly.

"And . . ." Cotton said.

"The second reason is a great deal more practical. You see, Miyuki will be a widow momentarily, so you'll be free to marry her in God's eyes. You'd lack state approval, but frankly, Cot, living in sin isn't what concerns me here." He chuckled. "What I am concerned about is Miyuki getting a visa into the Philippines—and the *mikudarihan* makes that possible.

"Now, when you reach Nagasaki, you take Miyuki's passport—" He reached over and tossed that on top of the divorce decree. "Luckily, she had this from our honeymoon in Hawaii. I got it revalidated with Teshima's forged signature. You take that and the *mikudarihan* to the American consulate. A visa for the Philippines for your wife should be pro forma to obtain with a passport and wedding license. Easy. And you'll have plenty of time to get married that morning in Nagasaki."

"You're very thorough, Key."

"Well, for God's sake, if you're going to commit treason and seppuku, you don't want to leave any loose ends. It'd be absolutely stupid to do this to no avail, wouldn't it?"

"Yes, it would," Cotton replied. By now, he was speaking in much the same dry tone as Kiyoshi. He was right; it was easier.

Kiyoshi shifted his back a bit. "Now, I'm sorry to have to go over the rest of this stuff—it's all bureaucratic nonsense. But you know how it is when Japanese run anything, even a war." One by one, he took the papers off the pile, glanced at them, and flipped them over toward Cotton. "Let's see here. First. This is Miyuki's ticket on that same train with you— eight o'clock Sunday to Nagasaki. Here's the police permission for her transit. And her steamship tickets—the *Nagasaki Maru* to Shanghai, and then the *Saigon Voyageur* to Manila. And likewise, uh, here's the police permission for her to leave the country—all further thanks to the good General Teshima's ignorant authority."

Cotton nodded, but that made him start to cry a little again, and so Kiyoshi resumed his stoic posture and began to sift through the remaining papers, like a bored clerk in a store. "Okay, let's see what's left. This is the departure permission duplicate I also had to file with the Bank of Japan. Easy to do, inasmuch as I was still her husband then. And this is a tax clearance I had to obtain for all her personal effects."

"Is that all?" Cotton leaned down and began to scoop up the papers.

"You know, Cotton, it'd probably be a good idea if you got

a big envelope for all that stuff. There's a lot of other odds and ends in there. You got to read it all carefully."

Cotton stopped in mid-stoop. "Will you stop being so damned efficient?"

Kiyoshi permitted himself a smile. "I'm sorry. That takes care of business, I think."

Cotton sighed. "Does Miyuki know?"

"No, I couldn't tell her. I do have a letter for her here." He'd kept that on the other side, by the gun and the sword. "But if you would, please . . ."

"Yes?"

"Tell her yourself that I loved her with all my heart, and tell her that I also loved you, and that my spirits will watch over you both . . . and your children, too."

Now Cotton began to sob. Deeply, desperately. Kiyoshi only sat still, and when the tears welled up in his own eyes, he assured himself that it was all right, that he was not crying out of sadness for himself, but only to be polite for Cotton, to show him how much he would miss him. When Cotton covered his eyes, Kiyoshi surreptitiously swept a hand up and brushed his own little tears away. "Sometimes," he said, "I mean sometimes before I decided to be a traitor, sometimes even then, I thought, well, I'd divorce her and let you take her away. But I was never that . . . gracious. I was so jealous of you, Cotton. Hell, I still am."

"You don't have to talk about this."

"No, you should know. I couldn't bear to give her up on my own. I had to keep trying. There was a part of me that always wanted war, because then you'd have to leave. But then, in the end, I knew what I had to do." He shrugged. "And you get her. Is that fate?"

"I don't know, Key. I've never put much store in fate. I think fate's just people trying to make luck appear responsible."

"Yeah," Kiyoshi said. He was afraid they both were going to start crying again. So with a friendly salute with his left hand, he said: "And give my personal regards to General MacArthur, too."

Cotton stepped forward then. For just an instant Kiyoshi tensed, gripping the knife more tightly. But Cotton only held out his hands in a benediction.

"Oh God," he cried out, putting his hands on Kiyoshi's head, "that God of mercy whom we all worship, whatever we may call Him, please watch over the soul of Se—uh, Okuno Kiyoshi, the best friend I have ever had. And, Lord Jesus, help me live up to the faith he has placed in me, to care for his wife and to help save our two lands from war. Amen."

"Amen," Kiyoshi added.

Cotton stepped away. "I'll leave you alone now, Key."

"I hope you use the sword," Kiyoshi said. "Really, it should be easy for you. You were always a good line-drive hitter."

Cotton bowed, deep, from the waist. *"Korede owakare,"* he said. Goodbye forever.

"Goodbye forever," Kiyoshi said.

Cotton turned and walked up the aisle, to kneel before the cross. He hadn't been praying long for Kiyoshi's soul when he heard a cry and a gasp—more a gurgle, really. It was not loud. Cotton looked up to the altar. "Forgive me, Father, for what I must do now to the man who saved my life." He stood then, and without ceremony he strode to the back of the church. Near the last pew, he saw Kiyoshi on the floor, spilling out of himself, bloody and gruesome and so in pain. Quickly, Cotton reached down and snatched up Takeo's sword. Somehow, Kiyoshi managed a slight, fond smile as he saw Cotton raise the great weapon and start to come around and bring it down upon him.

Early the next morning, before dawn, when Tochigi lay still and only Sakai, the night *tokko* guard, seemed awake, Cotton moved out of the rectory and across the courtyard. He waved to Sakai, outside, and unlocked the church. He had washed it down earlier. Now, he brought in a cart he'd borrowed, and placed Kiyoshi's body in it, wrapped in an old canvas. His head he placed in the thin black shroud the church used to cover the cross on the altar during Lent. Then Cotton piled some leaves and branches over his load, and, just past the *asahi*, he pushed it out of the mission.

First he walked over to Sakai. "Now, I know you must watch me," Cotton said, "but I must attend to some of my religious business, and so, when we get up there in the hills, I hope you will be kind enough to give me some privacy."

It was a small lie, and the guard considered it, following Cotton and the cart at some distance through the town.

On the road, outside Tochigi, Cotton stopped by the Nakagawas' and told Hanako that he had to leave that day if he was to make the *Tatsuta Maru*. "Is war really coming now?" she asked.

"Maybe someone can still stop it," Cotton replied. "Anyway, whatever happens in the world, I'll be back here someday. I still have to make a Christian out of you." She hugged him, and he went on his way.

At the tolls, old Kadota had just come on duty. "*Ohayo*, Kadota-san!" Cotton called out.

"What are you doing with the cart?"

"Oh, I'm just doing a favor for a good friend," he said, and he laid down a few sen and pointed to Sakai, coming up the road just behind him. "This is for him, the *tokko* man." He called back to Sakai: "I'm going up on the hill to worship now. Please wait here with Mr. Kadota."

Sakai looked very dubious. Kadota said: "Drake-san belongs to Tochigi now, and you must trust him. If he says he will be back, he will." And he offered Sakai some of his breakfast.

So Cotton was able to go on alone, around the bend and off the road, up to the crest of the same hill where he had let Sammy's ashes fly, where Kiyoshi had come to visit only five days ago. The ground wasn't frozen yet, but still it was hard work, digging a grave, and soon Cotton was sweating through his shirt. But finally he laid Kiyoshi's body down in a little trough about two feet deep. More carefully, then, he placed his friend's head with it, nestling it into the soil, and then he pinned a small card on the canvas. On it he had written,

"Okuno Kiyoshi—November 28, 1941," and then had added one other word: *"Aikokusha."* Patriot.

Then he shoveled the dirt over Kiyoshi and laid leaves and branches upon the grave. At the head, to mark the spot, he placed some *sotoba,* the sticks he had picked up from the Buddhist cemetery yesterday.

When he was finished, Cotton sat there for a long time with Kiyoshi. "Sammy, he's here with you now," he said once, out loud. And later: "I must go now, Kiyoshi. Sometime I'll bring Miyuki, and we'll come back for you." He cried a bit more before he finally started pushing the empty cart back down the hill. It was time to get on with all that Kiyoshi had planned for him.

Sakai was waiting for him anxiously at the tollbooth.

"See," old Kadota said, "Drake-san is most honorable."

1941

KANO TO MI

THE YEAR
of the
METAL SNAKE

Gishi-sai, the Festival of the Forty-Seven *Ronin*

58

Miyuki was her best moga self when Cotton arrived that Saturday evening, all Western dress and makeup. Western girl. She stretched up and pecked Cotton on the cheek. "Kiyoshi said you'd probably be here tonight, but now I don't know where he is," she said. Cotton had to turn away. "I haven't heard a word from him since he stole out of here yesterday morning." Cotton made a fuss out of putting his bags down. "But I imagine things are going fast now. Maybe he's with Admiral Yamamoto or—"

Cotton couldn't let her go on any longer; he turned back to her. "It's okay," he said. "I know where he is."

"You do?"

"Yes." And Cotton stepped forward then and took both her hands in his. The whole way from Tochigi, packed into the red seats, he had thought about this moment and what he must say, but everything he tried out seemed forced and rehearsed. So he only looked Miyuki square in the eyes and took a little breath, and this is what he said: "Kiyoshi came to see me in Tochigi yesterday afternoon, and after we talked together for a while, he went over to the church and committed seppuku there."

It was not unexpected for Miyuki—not, anyway, by the time Cotton got to the last words. In fact, all she said was "Oh." But then Miyuki began to squeeze the hands that held hers—harder, harder. So he just went on:

"I tried to talk him out of it, Miyuki. I did. I promise. But he was determined, and in the end, I . . . I . . ."

"Yes?"

"He'd asked me, and—"

"Yes." She consoled him now. "I did that for Takeo."

"I remember. And then, this morning, first thing, I buried him up on that hill with Sammy's ashes."

Only then, silently, did Miyuki fall apart. Cotton held her. "There is a letter for you," he said. He wanted to make sure she knew that before she collapsed. And she did, crying. He just held her then and didn't say any more.

At last Miyuki broke away from Cotton and walked over to the shrine in the corner, standing before it without a word for a long time. "My poor Kiyoshi," she said at last. Then she turned her head to Cotton. "Yours too."

"Yes, mine too."

"He was a wonderful man."

"The best I ever met on this earth," Cotton said.

The tears welled up in Miyuki's eyes again, and then she even began to cry once more, this time in great sobs. Finally she turned back to face Cotton. "Tell me all about it now," she said.

"Well, there's a lot to say," he began, and they sat down together on the tatami, and Cotton went over everything he could remember, straight through to going to the Philippines. Miyuki barely spoke, until at last, when he was done, when they had reached the Manila Hotel, and were there informing General MacArthur of the impending attack on Hawaii, only then did Cotton hand Miyuki the letter Kiyoshi had written her. He went upstairs after he gave it to her, so she could be alone when she read it.

It was about a half-hour later, and he was just sitting on the floor, staring at the dark walls, when she came back up, with tea. "I only have one question."

"Yes?"

"Do you think that if I hadn't fallen in love with you, he still would've done this?"

"Don't worry about that," Cotton said. "This only had to

do with betraying his country. We broke his heart. But we
didn't kill him."

"Are you sure?"

"Well, pretty," Cotton said after he thought it over.

Miyuki sat down next to him, and they sipped their tea. At
last she said: "All right, let's you and me talk about Kiyoshi."
And they did, remembering all that they could, crying, but
laughing some too. Finally, Cotton prayed for Kiyoshi, and
when he finished, Miyuki rose. "I'll have to pack now," she
said. "We have to leave early for the train tomorrow."

She moved about, tidying up the house to make sure it
would look very neat for whoever lived here next. She wrote
a letter to her mother, too. "I do not know when next I will
see you," Miyuki finished, "but when I do, I hope I will return to you with a grandson as well." When she was sure that
everything was taken care of, she turned off the light there
and went upstairs, to where Cotton was lying on his futon in
his pajamas.

"But where do I sleep?" Miyuki said.

"I wasn't sure where you'd want to be."

"Why, I am with you now, of course," she said, and she
gestured to the spot next to his futon.

Cotton got up and went across the room to where her
futon lay, rolled up. When he brought it back, she had let her
dotera slip off her, to her ankles, and she stood there before
him—unashamed, Cotton could not help thinking. "Unashamed" was always the way this was in the damn Bible.

Gingerly, he put her futon down approximately next to his.
"Look, do you really think . . . ?" Cotton began.

"Why not?" she said.

"Well, you know. . . . It just doesn't seem right, in Kiyoshi's
house."

"Is it really because you made love to Sumiko here, too?"

Cotton blushed, and for lack of anything better to do, he
lay back down on his futon. "Right now I'm only thinking
about Kiyoshi."

"Well, I would think he'd want you to have me here for
first time, where there is so much of him everywhere."

Cotton gulped a little. "I'd like to believe that," he said.

"Good," she said, kneeling down next to Cotton. "I made love to Kiyoshi the first time here, right after Takeo did his seppuku. And the last time was night before last, just before Kiyoshi did the same. What does that mean, Cotton?"

"I don't know. What do you think?"

Miyuki shrugged. "I just think it means it is time for us, now," she said, and she smiled and took one of his hands and placed it on her breast and held it there for what seemed the longest time, frozen, a tableau. "Now, we kiss," she said, and she leaned forward and their lips touched.

He started to pull her down to him, but Miyuki stopped him and helped take off his pajamas first. She kept kneeling over him, and when he was naked she caressed him, pulling softly on him, and then she took his hands and placed them back on her breasts. Miyuki arched her back and closed her eyes, holding his hands on her. "I've dreamed so often about this moment," she sighed, her head still tilted back, looking up.

"Me too, darling."

She turned down to look at him. "No, no. I mean I would think exactly how I wanted it, our first time."

"Like this?"

"Yes, I wanted you to see me."

"You're so beautiful."

"But I'm always beautiful to you, aren't I?" she teased him.

"Always."

"So it wasn't that I just wanted you to see how beautiful I was. I wanted you to watch me, to see how *happy* I was." And she increased the pressure on his hands on her breasts, making him massage them, and with it she turned her head side to side, murmuring. "See?" she said. "See how happy you make your Miyuki?"

"Yes." And she leaned down upon him then, so that he could kiss her nipples, and then her mouth; but as Cotton's ardor grew, and he tried to pull her all the way down with him, on the futon, she pushed herself back up.

"No, no—not lying down. I said: the first time you must

see me clearly, in the light." And she held up her head again
and sighed, reached down for Cotton between his legs, and
put him in her—and in that instant they were at last one together, consummated, and Miyuki called out, for love and for
bliss, for rapture, and only then, only after she knew he could
see how happy she was, only then did she begin to move, and
then Cotton, and then both together, laughing, crying, perfectly, exactly the way they knew it was always supposed to
be.

59

Even as they came into the station, Takahashi just wouldn't
keep up with Cotton. No, he felt that he had to play the tail,
lurking, moving behind at a proper distance—and never
mind that Cotton knew he was following him. Never mind,
for that matter, that Cotton *wanted* Takahashi to tail him, to
verify—if it came to that—that Cotton had boarded the express to Osaka. Alone. "Come on, Takahashi-san," Cotton
called back to him. "You can help me carry this." He held up
one of his suitcases. But the *tokko* man hung back, artfully
shadowing Cotton by a few steps.

Central Station was a madhouse. Cotton hadn't been here
since Kigen, more than a year ago, and as bustling as it had
been on that day of days, now it was an altogether different
crowd—frantic in its movements, unsure, even scared. The
soldiers made the difference. The station was jammed with
them, boorishly shouldering the civilians aside whenever it
suited them.

Kiyoshi had left Cotton instructions that he should leave
home ahead of Miyuki—drawing Takahashi away so that his
suspicions wouldn't be aroused if he saw her leaving with luggage, too, and with the *gaijin*. Now, though, Cotton began to
fret. Maybe they hadn't allowed enough time. He couldn't see
Miyuki. And the inspectors were giving some of the travelers

a real going-over; even, sometimes, Cotton would see someone sent away, their papers not in proper order. He kept
glancing around, but there was no sight of her. There'd been
no cabs, and the streetcars had been so crowded. Maybe they
hadn't even let her on the streetcar with her heavy bags.

And then he was at the head of his line for the Nagasaki
Express. The sergeant looked Cotton over warily. Cotton
handed over his ticket, his permit to travel, his ID, even his
passport for good measure. And although the sergeant grumbled, all the papers were perfectly correct, and so he could do
nothing but jam them back to Cotton and wave him on.

Still, he couldn't resist a parting shot (sure Cotton couldn't
understand him). "Get your hairy ass out of our country," he
snarled.

Cotton bowed, replying in his impeccable Japanese: "It is a
wonderful country, Japan, and my heart will always stay here,
no matter where I may be on this earth." The sergeant's
mouth flew open, and he was so flustered, he turned to the
next man in line without another word.

Cotton went over and bowed to Takahashi, deftly dishing
him a ten-yen bill. Takahashi shook his head as he neatly
slipped the bill into his pocket. "It's Sunday," Cotton said.
"Take your family back to the Hibiya and see the new movie
there we just missed."

Takahashi blushed. He'd come to rather like the *gaijin*, and
it embarrassed him to think he'd almost killed the poor fellow
in that very theater. He bowed very quickly and hurried away
before anybody could see him consorting with the man he
had orders to follow.

Cotton headed for the train, but there was still no sign of
Miyuki. He had to get on, though. It was only another twenty
minutes before the train left, and he was lucky to find one
seat. The soldiers took up most of the best places, leaving the
civilians to scramble for what space was left. The old folks
could only shuffle, just fighting to hold their own. They were
so tiny, some of them born even before Meiji ruled, before Japan was really part of this world.

The train started up in place, ready to go. There were no

more seats, and Cotton had to keep explaining that he was saving his for a woman. But where was Miyuki? Where was she? He looked at his watch. He looked out the window. Barely ten more minutes . . .

"Why are you leaving the country?" the guard snapped at Miyuki. It was already past quarter to eight. The express pulled out at eight sharp.

"You have my papers, please," Miyuki replied. "They are endorsed personally by General Teshima Yoichi. Himself."

"Yes, but I would like to know why a Japanese woman would leave her country at such a time when our nation is threatened, and Tenno Heika calls upon us all for sacrifice."

"It is certainly not my choice to leave," Miyuki said. "But as with any good Japanese woman, I am obliged to follow my husband."

"And who is your husband?" He played with the papers, not really studying them, only turning them over as if they were playing cards.

Miyuki pointed to the right places. "You see, he is Lieutenant Serikawa Kiyoshi of the Imperial Navy, and he has been posted to Shanghai."

"A wife goes on duty with a naval officer? Army officers must endure such separations from their families."

"My husband volunteered to be sent to sea, but he has been ordered personally to the embassy in Shanghai by Admiral Yamamoto, and I am required there to serve as a hostess."

The departure announcement came in the background. The people in line behind Miyuki shifted on their feet and sighed anxiously, and one young man to the rear called out: "Hurry up, please. We will miss our train."

The soldier stiffened. "Wait here," he told Miyuki, and, taking his good time, he strode back to the offender. "This is no way to speak to a member of the Imperial Army," he told him.

The young man didn't argue. He bowed. "I am so sorry for my impatient behavior, Sergeant."

"Apologies will not suffice. We are all doing what *we* can in this effort, but you, by insulting me, are insulting the Emperor as well."

"I didn't mean to do that."

"Well, you go to the end of the line and think about your anti-Japanese actions there."

"But then I will miss the train."

"So, you will get the next."

"But I don't have permission to travel the next."

"I cannot help that."

The PA boomed out: "All aboard for the eight o'clock express to Nagasaki."

"Please," the young man said.

The soldier placed his arms akimbo. "We will wait until you move. And if you do not move, you will only serve to punish your fellow citizens in line as well."

The young man looked up at the others. They beseeched him with their expressions until, hangdog, he turned and headed to the rear. Only then did the sergeant return to Miyuki . . . and started going through her papers all over again. The bastard, she thought, keeping a smile on her face. Forgive me, Father. Forgive me, Takeo. Your army is all bastards now. Finally, in slow motion, the sergeant stamped Miyuki's ticket and let her pass.

She snatched up her bags. An extra hat she was carrying dropped, but already she could see the gate closing ahead, and she didn't even slow down. She and an old couple from Okayama were the last ones through the gate.

"Find a seat," the conductor ordered her. There were no seats left. The soldiers overflowed the train. Miyuki couldn't even get beyond the last car, struggling with her luggage. The ones with seats cursed her as she struggled by them. Finally, in the well at the end of the car, she found a little spot, plunked her suitcases down there, and sat on them. She could hear the soldiers laughing that the lady in the green hat could maybe have a seat part of the way to Nagoya if she would only engage in some spectacular physical activities they described in even louder voices. Miyuki just pretended not to hear. Nobody else on the train objected, either. Nobody in Japan crossed soldiers anymore.

Ahead, in his car, Cotton was sitting next to a civilian. He turned and said to him: "I'm looking for my friend who's supposed to be on this train. Will you watch my place?"

"Are you American?" Cotton nodded. "I thought so. I don't want any butter eater next to me."

Cotton refused to take the bait. As evenly as he could, he simply replied: "Well, I'm looking for this absolutely beautiful Japanese woman, and if I find her, she'll be the one to sit here next to you, and you'll be rid of me. Not a bad trade."

The man only grumped, so Cotton laid his hat on the seat and set out to look for Miyuki.

In a way, of course, what did it matter? If she hadn't made the train, he couldn't go back for her. He was a fugitive now, traveling with forged papers. He was supposed to be under guard in Tochigi, leaving on the *Tatsuta Maru* Tuesday. His only hope now was to push on, catch the *Nagasaki Maru,* and get to Manila by himself.

What upset him so now, as he plunged through the cars, was how scared he was—scared that if Miyuki wasn't on the train, wasn't with him, he would get off and go back for her. Somehow. To hell with America. To hell with the war. To hell with Kiyoshi's life, sacrificed for nothing. It frightened Cotton that he would even think that way. But he ached for Miyuki. In his love, and in his lust, he hadn't thought about anything but her. And now he was thinking about giving up the whole damn world for her. Literally.

I have blood on my heart, Cotton said to himself. I have my best friend's blood on my heart.

Only one more car, and still he couldn't find her. He wanted to scream for Miyuki. He could see the end of the train ahead. In fact, he was so upset that he almost missed her there, tucked away on top of her luggage. "Hi, blue eyes," the voice whispered, and the wave of relief that fell over him was only tempered by the fact that he couldn't sweep her into his arms.

"Hi there," Cotton said, and took her bag. He could hear the soldiers near Miyuki swearing at them both, calling her a cheap whore and a Korean and worse as she went back with Cotton to where his seat was. He gave it to Miyuki, and the grumpy gentleman seemed pleased, even if he didn't say anything.

After Osaka, Cotton found a seat himself in another part of the car. And then, later, not long after the express pulled out of Hiroshima, Cotton happened to glance at his watch. It was three-thirty in the morning. Monday morning. "My God," he thought. "Exactly a week from this moment. It's eight o'clock Sunday morning in Hawaii now. If I don't get out to MacArthur, exactly a week from this moment they'll hit Pearl."

Back in Tokyo, a short while before the express finally came into Nagasaki, at just after two o'clock that Monday afternoon, December 1, Premier Tojo and his military chiefs entered Room 1 East of the Imperial Palace. There, without preamble, they explained to Hirohito, who sat attentively on the dais, why there was no longer any choice but to start war against the United States, Great Britain, and the Netherlands. "The American demands that we vacate China are impossible, Your Majesty," Tojo said. "They insult the Emperor. They insult the empire."

Hirohito didn't utter a word. At last, he only nodded impassively, rose, and departed the room. The others went about the business of signing the papers, and then those documents of war were brought to Hirohito in his quarters, to that same room where he had met Takeo almost six years ago, during that week when Hirohito had first begun wearing his military uniform.

The Emperor bade Marquis Kido, the Lord Keeper of the Privy Seal, to stay so that he might talk to the wise old man who had become his friend. At last, though, Tenno Heika nodded his head wearily and said only, "It is too humiliating, what America asks of us," and with that the marquis nodded, and Hirohito reached for his seal and stamped the papers with the authorization for Operation Z to strike the flint of World War II.

60

The Nagasaki Express came over the mountains from Fukuoka and glided into the station where the Urakami River widens into the harbor. There was a crush to get off, so only when almost all the other travelers had pushed their way out did Miyuki and Cotton hoist their bags and head out of the station for a hotel.

Of course there were no cabs, but Kiyoshi had told Cotton where to go—up to the Omura-cho district, by the Dejima, the old Portuguese trade center, where the first foreigners to Japan had been sequestered. Nagasaki was the closest port to the mainland across the East China Sea, and had always been the most open Japanese city, the one little side window on the world that the shogunate had permitted. It was here that Madame Butterfly had waited for her lover to return.

"Come on, there'll be hotels up there, used to the foreign trade," Cotton told Miyuki, and they started plodding up the sidewalk by the docks.

Suddenly: "There it is!" Miyuki cried out—and there it was, the *Nagasaki Maru*, berthed. A notice said that it weighed anchor for Shanghai tomorrow, Tuesday, December 2, at 2:30 P.M. All aboard no later than one-thirty. "Our baby," she said.

"You bet—the owl and the pussycat go off to sea in a beautiful pea-green boat," Cotton said in English.

"What?"

"Never mind." And that's when he saw a streetcar, and they ran for it as best they could, struggling with the luggage.

For just an instant Cotton didn't think they were going to let him on when they saw he wasn't Japanese, but Miyuki had a foot up, and they both clambered aboard. Up in Omura-cho, she spied a little hotel, the Saiwaiso. "That's appropriate," she whispered, and they got off. "It means 'Happiness Place.'"

Cotton signed the register "Rev. and Mrs. Cotton Drake," the clerk eying him with the same expression of disgust that Cotton had come to expect from almost all Japanese these days. He noticed, too, that, if anything, the man looked at Miyuki even more censoriously, horrified that she could have married an American. "It'll just be the one night," Cotton added quickly. "We're sailing for Shanghai tomorrow."

"Good," the clerk said. He didn't offer help with their luggage.

In their room, as soon as he closed the door, Cotton took Miyuki in his arms and kissed her feverishly. Then his hands began to reach for her breasts. She pulled away. "No, no, you. We have things to do."

"Come on, just once."

"We have all night, bad boy." And she thought wryly: My, so much for Kiyoshi's sacred memory . . . at least in matters libidinous. "Here," Miyuki said, her fingers drawing down through the phone book. "The City Office number is 62-4711." Cotton called it, but they were too late today; they could not get married till the next morning. "That's okay," Miyuki said. "I know what we'll do instead. Come on," she told him, taking him by the hand to the door.

On his ship, anchored in the Inland Sea, Admiral Yamamoto received word from Tokyo that the Emperor had formally sanctioned war. The *Kido Butai* was just about passing the international date line now, a thousand or so miles north of Midway, perfectly on schedule. In an altogether new code, the admiral cabled his task force: *"Niitaka yama nobore ichi-ni/ rei-ya"*—Climb Mount Niitaka, twelve-oh-eight." That meant the attack was on, as planned, for December 8, Tokyo time. Mount Niitaka, in Formosa, was not nearly so famous as Fuji-san, but now that Formosa was part of His Majesty's empire, it was the tallest peak under the *asahi*—and this particular business wasn't about beauty. This was about supremacy.

That done, Yamamoto prepared to leave his ship and go up to Tokyo, where he had been summoned to meet with Tenno Heika himself at the Palace on Wednesday morning, the third.

Tenshudo, the Little Church of the Heavenly Master, was stark and empty. It was dark, late of the afternoon, the pitch of winter, and when Cotton finally found some light switches, they only dimly lit up the exterior aisles.

But they found a decanter of water, and Cotton carried it over to the baptismal font, down in front of the altar. He poured a bit in. "Are you ready, darling?"

"You will marry a Christian," Miyuki replied.

"There should be two witnesses here, but God makes allowances for unusual times," Cotton declared, speaking out past Miyuki to the whole church, even if no one else was in the church. He picked up a copy of the *Book of Common Prayer* from the first pew and handed it to her, marking the right page, then opened his own, which he had brought with him, and began the service—"Dearly beloved . . ."—the two of them alone in this church as they were alone in the knowledge of what other men were about to do with the world.

Cotton proceeded, his voice rising to the ceiling, echoing a little off the walls—sharper, it seemed, now that there was no light left to shine through the stained glass windows and compete with the words. "Dost thou renounce the devil and all his works, the vain pomp and glory of the world, with all covetous desires of the same, and the—uh—sinful desires of the flesh, so that thou wilt not follow, nor be led by them?"

Miyuki looked at him, and he looked back, but they both kept their faces straight, even if the reference to the sinful desires of the flesh tried their solemnity. And Cotton nodded to her. "I renounce them all," Miyuki spoke out, from the book, "and by God's help will endeavor not to follow nor be led by them."

He nodded again, continuing the reading until he came to the part about the naming. "I'm supposed to ask the witnesses, 'Name this person,' " Cotton explained. "Excuse me"—he glanced up for effect—"but since we don't have any witnesses, I'll have to improvise a bit."

"Okay."

"So, what is your name?"

"Miyuki Serik—"

"Just your first name. Not your family name."

"Well, Miyuki."

Cotton nodded. "We receive—"

"Wait a minute," Miyuki interrupted him. "I have a question."

"Yeah?"

"What's a middle name?"

"Well, darling, you don't have one."

"But you do."

"Yeah, most Westerners do. Even if we don't use it, most of us have one."

"What's yours?"

"Drewry." He spelled it out. "It was my mother's maiden name. Cotton Drewry Drake."

"How do you get one?"

"A middle name?"

"Yes."

"Well, you're baptized with it."

"I thought so," Miyuki said. "I'd like one too."

"A middle name?"

"Yes."

"Well, actually, you'll sort of get one tomorrow another way. You'll be Miyuki Serikawa Drake after we get married."

"Can't I have one now, too?"

Cotton shrugged. "This is highly irregular, madam," he said, smiling broadly. "First, the minister forces you to denounce the desires of the flesh just before your wedding night—to that selfsame minister—and now you come up here to be baptized and don't have your name chosen yet."

"Well, I'm sorry, Reverend Drake, but I didn't know quite how this worked."

"It's okay, I guess," Cotton went on, pretending to be grave. "Now, you know what middle name you want?" Miyuki nodded. "Good. Okay, name this person. Name yourself."

Miyuki looked up from her prayer book straight at Cotton. "Miyuki Kiyosho," she declared in a loud, crisp voice—the middle name the female version of Kiyoshi.

The words pounded into Cotton, and he caught a lump in his throat. He tried to go on, but "We receive this person" was as far as he got before he broke down. First he tried to blot the tears, but he gave up when he saw that Miyuki was crying too, so he just put his arms around her. "All right," he finally said, stepping back, trying to find a smile again, "all right, this certainly is a very unconventional baptism. But"— and he reached over, took her hand, and squeezed it. "Don't worry," he said. "It still counts." Then Cotton made a half-turn away from Miyuki, and, as if he were addressing a full church, he spoke out loudly: "We receive this person, Miyuki Kiyosho, into the congregation of Christ's flock, and do sign her with the sign of the cross"—and he dipped his other hand into the font, letting the water run through his fingers, until he pulled it out and drew his forefinger across her forehead and down, in the sign of the cross. Then he smiled at her, as adoringly as Cotton could upon this woman, who was his, before him.

"I am a Christian now?" she asked.

"Yes, you are Miyuki Kiyosho of Christ's army on earth." He led her down to the front pew then, and they sat there for a long time in the still, dark church, never saying a word, until finally Cotton declared: "*Ai shite imasu*, Miyuki Kiyosho."

"I love you too, Cotton-san," she replied.

Ensign Oda knocked on Yamamoto's door and saluted. "All of the arrangements are completed, sir. We will depart the ship at eleven hundred, the car will take you to Osaka, and the train from there, arriving Tokyo nineteen hundred thirty hours."

"Good."

"Kiyuki has reserved the room for dinner."

"Fine."

"I was able to contact all of the gentlemen you wanted for cocktails except for Lieutenant Serikawa. He left his office midday Friday and has never returned."

"Hmmm. Did you try him at home?"

"Yes sir. But there's no reply there. I called back to his office and spoke to another officer, who advised me that Lieutenant Serikawa had been working on some security matters with *jouhou kyoku*, with General Teshima Yoichi—"

"I know Teshima."

"Yes sir. The lieutenant left word that he'll be speaking to General Teshima Tuesday afternoon. I called the general's office, but he'd already left for the day."

"Hitting the whorehouses early," Yamamoto grumbled.

"Excuse me, sir?"

"Never mind, Ensign. Telephone Teshima tomorrow morning and have him make sure that Serikawa calls me in the afternoon when he gets there. I want him to join me with the others Wednesday. I want him there to celebrate. You know, it's really quite extraordinary what we're about to pull off, Ensign."

"Yes sir."

Yamamoto beamed. "Hell, son, I might even raise a cup or two of sake myself."

61

Cotton walked away from the clerk, brandishing their marriage certificate. "First thing in the Philippines, we'll get married in a church," he said. "But for now, this makes an honest woman of you."

Miyuki cocked her head. "What?"

"The owl and the pussycat got hitched," he said, and he kissed her on the cheek and called her *oku-sama*—honorable housewife. None of it was terribly romantic. She had just kept Kiyoshi's wedding band on, and the whole business had taken less than an hour—most of that waiting behind other couples. Then: fill out the forms, stick your right thumb prints on an ink pad and onto the certificate. Cotton thought: It takes longer to pay a parking ticket in the States than to get married in Japan.

Of course, usually after the legal formalities, most Japanese couples went on to a Shinto ceremony and then to a magnificent hotel celebration, the way Miyuki had married Kiyoshi five years ago. So, outside the City Office, Cotton yanked his bride into the first restaurant they came to, and when the waiter finally deigned to come over to the *gaijin*, Cotton said: "I know it's early, but we'd like sake, and three cups. You have lacquered cups?"

The waiter stared back at them. "Don't you Westerners know? The emperor has deemed today *Houkoubi*, a day of sacrifice for all Japanese people."

"I know these are difficult times," Cotton answered, "but"—and he held up his inked thumb—"we are just married."

The waiter didn't reply. Miyuki held up her thumb, too. The waiter scrunched up his nose, that this gorgeous Japanese woman would marry some hated American. But despite his surly silence, he returned with the sake and the three lacquered cups.

Cotton lined up the three cups, pouring some sake into each of them. The tradition called for both the bride and groom to take three sips from each of the cups—"thrice three, nine times"—and so they went down the line, as the waiter eyed them with rising indignation. When Cotton held the third cup up before his ninth sip and said, "I will love you and honor you and care for you as long as I live, Miyuki," that was too much for the waiter, and he turned away in disgust.

"And I, you, Cotton," Miyuki said, her eyes shining.

And together: "Thrice, three, nine times."

Then Cotton leaned in closer: "Now, darling, I guess it's back to business. Sorry."

"Me too." She shrugged.

"We'll go together to the consulate to get you the visa, then back to the hotel." She nodded. "Then I want you to get to the boat."

"Alone?" She screwed up her face.

"Look, we're almost out, but I'm still fair game. If Teshima finds out I'm not on the *Tatsuta*, they'll be looking all over Japan for me. But"—and Cotton took her hands, drawing even closer across the table—"no one is looking for you. No one really knows you exist. Whatever happens to me, you can get through."

"I don't want to get through without you."

"That's very sweet. But let's be more practical. You go to the boat by yourself, you stay in your cabin, and even *when* I make it on board, you never acknowledge me in any way. Not till we arrive in Manila."

"Okay."

"Now, you know where to go?"

"General MacArthur, Manila Hotel."

"And you know what to tell him?"

"I think so. Tell me again."

"Okay. We'll—you'll—arrive Manila Sunday afternoon, the seventh. You tell him that the next morning, at eight o'clock in Hawaii, the Zeros'll hit. That's Sunday, December seventh, Hawaii time. All right?" Miyuki nodded. "The fleet is arriving by a northern route. The planes will come out of the north. Tell General MacArthur the Japanese don't want the islands. They only want the fleet. Get the ships out of Pearl Harbor and go after the Japanese fleet."

"Yes. I know that."

"Now, also," Cotton went on, "I don't know the details, but they're bound to hit the Philippines, too."

"The Philippines?"

Cotton had to laugh. "Yeah, we're heading into the teeth of the storm. But we're going to stop the storm. Us. You. Okay?"

"Please, Cotton, I won't have to do this. You will. Won't you?"

"I hope so." But he saw the fear on her face. "Look, don't worry. If they catch me, they won't hurt me. I'm only a temporary nuisance to them, and once December seventh passes I lose all value. Then I'm just another American to be sent home—and probably with benefit of clergy, too."

"Yes, I see," Miyuki said.

To himself, Cotton thought that Teshima would in fact have him killed straightaway—well, after torturing him some first. "There's nothing to worry about," he assured her.

At that moment, in his office in the War Ministry in Tokyo, General Teshima answered his phone. "General," said the voice, "this is Ensign Oda, Admiral Yamamoto's aide. The admiral wishes to meet with Lieutenant Serikawa tonight when he gets to Tokyo, and while we've been advised that the lieutenant is on assignment, we understand that he'll be reporting to you this afternoon."

"Yeah," Teshima said. "He's calling me from Yokohama."

"Oh, just phoning you?"

Teshima shuffled papers on his desk with his free hand. "Yeah, soon as the *Tatsuta Maru* sails."

"I'm sorry, sir. And when is that?"

Teshima glanced at his watch. "'Bout an hour and a half from now. Leaves at noon."

"Fine—well, will you please have the lieutenant call me about this evening?" Oda gave the phone number.

Teshima scribbled it down and hung up. Then he swirled about in his chair, and for no good reason but that he wasn't busy, he yelled for his assistant. "Hey, Yukio—call down to NYK in Yokohama and find out if everything is okay with that damn boat."

"What boat is that, sir?"

"The *Tatsuta Maru*. What other boats are there?"

Right down the street from the main police station, flanked by the Chinese and British consulates, sat the consulate of the United States of America in Nagasaki. It was set back off the street, a small courtyard before it, with the rear of the property ending at the harbor. There was even a little dock there, with a speedboat that American officials could use to run directly to the train station or out to any American vessel that came into harbor.

Cotton and Miyuki came round the corner to the consulate, but drew back immediately before the sight of a whole squadron of Japanese troops posted there. "My God!" Cotton said. "They might even be looking for me."

Miyuki risked a peek. "Don't worry. I'm sure it's just a precaution, watching the embassies," she said. And then: "Let me go in by myself."

"That's crazy."

"It is not. You just told me nobody knows I exist."

"Well—"

"Besides, I'm the one picking up the visa. The consulate's expecting me. Whether or not you come, I have the wedding certificate. I have the proof."

Cotton mulled that over. But really—what choice was there? "Okay," he said, and he handed her the marriage certificate and her other documents. "But any problems, get the hell out. If I'm not here, go to the hotel. If I'm not there, make the boat." He took her by the shoulders. "Whatever you do, make that damn boat."

"All right," she said, and she pecked him on the cheek and popped round the corner, heading directly toward the consulate, weaving through the gauntlet of leering soldiers in the courtyard. Cotton pulled his head back and tried to look inconspicuous, leaning up against the wall. He wished he smoked; this was the sort of occasion when people who smoked could get away with doing nothing, while people who didn't smoke looked like they must be up to no good.

Amazingly, though, it took only a few minutes. When he dared peek around the corner again, he saw Miyuki, emerging from the embassy with a smile so big he could make it out even from that distance. "I got it," she said, as soon as she came around the corner, and he hugged her, whirling her feet clear off the ground.

"I can't believe it was that easy," Cotton said.

"Well, there was nobody else there, and everything was already all drawn up for the new bride. They just looked at my papers and showed me where to sign." She showed him where the visa to the Philippines had been placed in her passport.

Cotton hugged her and then grabbed her hand, yanking her in the other direction, away from the troops.

"Uh-oh," Miyuki said after they'd gone a few steps. "That's the police station up there."

"Okay," Cotton said, "take the right here," and they ducked into the narrow street behind the building. Bad luck. Straight ahead, a half-block away, no more, marching directly at them, came another whole squad of soldiers—stepping smartly, snappy holsters, shiny boots. The *kempeitai*—military police. "Dammit," Cotton said—and, instinctively, he did the stupidest possible thing, which was to jerk Miyuki back and try to double around, out of the little street and back up toward the police station.

It was the most suspicious of gestures, and hardly had they ducked around the corner when they heard footsteps chasing them, and after a moment, one voice calling: "Stop, Drake, stop!"

Cotton stopped Miyuki, reaching into his pockets for all their papers. "Go," he said, shoving everything into her hands. "Go, get away from me." She took off, striding.

"Stop, Mr. Drake. Wait." The voice was closer, the footsteps pounding. There was no getting away. Better to go back around the corner, get arrested there; maybe Miyuki would have gotten away. So he came back around—and smashed headlong into the first Japanese MP. In fact, it was all Cotton could do to keep his balance, and he tripped, falling back hard against the building. The soldier's own momentum carried him into Cotton, slamming him, so that Cotton's head banged hard. The soldier was a giant of a Japanese, too, and the nightstick he carried somehow speared Cotton in his chest. Cotton cried out, his head ringing. But then: "Drake-san!" said the Japanese.

The words rang strangely, and Cotton made himself look up. "My God—Kensuke!" He said it again—"Kensuke, Kensuke!"—and he was so relieved, he threw himself onto the boy and hung there, his heart still racing for fear even as he laughed. Then he remembered; he grabbed Kensuke and yanked him back around the corner.

Miyuki was still in sight, scurrying up by the police station. Cotton screamed after her: "Miyuki! Stop! It's Kensuke."

She slowed, but she didn't dare look back.

Cotton nudged Kensuke. "It is me, Mrs. Serikawa!" he hollered. "It is."

Hearing that, she stopped altogether and, tentatively, swung back, risking a peek. Only when she could see with her own eyes that it really was Kensuke did she throw up her hands and begin to hurry back. "Kensuke! Kensuke-san!" she cried.

Kensuke beamed. The Japanese army tailors had tried their best, but still his uniform was a bit too small for him— serving to make him appear somewhat foolish yet, as well, all the larger and more menacing. Cotton threw an arm around his shoulder. "What in the world are you doing here?"

"They made me military police, Drake-san. Too tall—I'd catch a bullet in battle." Cotton laughed. "Hey, this is better than going to China."

"Sure is."

"This week I'm assigned to the British consulate."

Cotton cocked his head. "You mean there are always soldiers on guard at the consulates?"

"Oh, sure," Kensuke said. "They usually even post two squads at the American. Some at the Dutch, too."

Cotton nodded. Miyuki's guess was right—and that was good news. The army wasn't looking for him. He tapped Kensuke on his pitching arm. "You taking care of that?"

"I'm afraid there isn't much call for baseball these days, Drake-san."

"No. But maybe in the spring," Cotton lied.

"Yes, perhaps everything will be fine again by the spring."

Miyuki reached them now from one direction just as the rest of the troops arrived from the other. There was much bowing, and all the other young soldiers ogled Miyuki so that Kensuke had to call their attention back to the *gaijin*. "Hey, this is the American I told you about, the one who coached our baseball team in Tochigi."

They all said "Aah," and when the sergeant bowed deeply, so did all the others. How strange it was: the first courteous treatment Cotton had received for days, and here it was from the army—from the army *police*. Cotton bowed. *"Ohayo, ohayo,"* he said. "And this is Mrs. . . . uh, Mrs. Serikawa." She glanced quickly at Cotton, and then everybody bowed some more. "Mrs. Serikawa's husband is a lieutenant in the navy."

"Aah."

"Lieutenant Serikawa works for Admiral Yamamoto himself."

More aahs. Miyuki blushed and bowed again. Cotton grabbed Kensuke by his bicep. "And I want you all to know that Kensuke is good enough to play for the Giants." The others all stared at him quizzically. Kensuke himself was mortified. "No, he is," Cotton said. "Whatever happens, I want you to remember that." They all nodded. "Kensuke is so good he could play in the United States."

Kensuke couldn't handle the attention any longer. He stepped forward. "Sergeant, may I request permission to stay with Mr. Drake for a while before I rejoin you back at the base?"

"Yes, Private Kensuke Morishita, great baseball star," the sergeant said, feigning deep homage, and all the others laughed heartily. And the sergeant saluted Kensuke in good humor and took the rest of the squad on its way.

Cotton reached into his pocket and pulled out some yen. "I'd like to treat you to lunch," he said, "but—"

"It is *Houkoubi*, a day of sacrifice, so we couldn't enjoy a good lunch anyhow."

"So here—" Cotton handed him the bills—"you have a good meal on me sometime."

"Oh, thank you, Drake-san! We have so little money, and so little to eat."

"Perhaps you could do me a favor, too," Cotton said.

"Anything for you, Drake-san."

"You're off duty for a while?"

"Yes, now I don't have to be back to the consulate till two."

"Good, Mrs. Serikawa is taking the *Nagasaki Maru* this afternoon, to join her husband in Shanghai." Kensuke nodded discreetly. Cotton went on: "I'd hoped to be on the ship myself, but I may be delayed at the church. If you met Miyuki at her hotel around a quarter after twelve, could you escort her to the *Nagasaki*, help her with her bags?"

"Of course, Drake-san."

Miyuki joined Cotton in bowing thanks, and Cotton gave Kensuke directions to their hotel, the Saiwaiso. And then, even before Cotton could do it himself, Kensuke stuck out his hand and gave the *gaijin* a good, strong shake, just the way it had been with them back in their spring, the one that now seemed so very long ago.

As soon as Cotton and Miyuki were on their way, Cotton said: "I don't think it'll hurt things any if you show up at the ship in the escort of the *kempeitai*."

She grabbed his right arm in both her hands and snuggled up to him as they walked along. "Yes, my smart blue eyes," she said, and Cotton couldn't help himself. Right on the street there, he stopped and took his other arm and wrapped it around her, hugging her. It wasn't just that he loved her so. It was the first time he really believed they were going to make it out, together. *Really* believed that. And in just that moment, Miyuki reached up and kissed him in his ear and whispered: "It's going to work, darling. I know, it's going to work."

General Teshima lit a cigarette and called up to Yoshiwara to make an appointment that evening with a new girl he'd heard about. Then he yelled out to his aide: "Dammit, Yukio, it's almost twelve-thirty. Hasn't Serikawa called yet?"

The sergeant hurried in. "No sir, not yet."

"Well, then, stop sitting on your ass and call NYK yourself."

It took a while, then, before there was finally a clear line to Yokohama; but when Yukio got through, he buzzed the general, and Teshima yanked up the receiver. "The *Tatsuta* has left, sir," the NYK man said. "In fact, it's already well out in the bay, almost to Yokosuka."

Teshima smiled. "Good. And every berth is taken?"

"Yes, General. The ship was completely filled." Teshima nodded to himself, shaking another cigarette out of the pack. In fact, he was about to lay the phone down when, almost as an afterthought, the NYK man added: "Yes, only three reservations failed to show, but there was great demand, as you know, and it was easy to fill those spots."

Teshima froze, his mouth agape, as he dimly realized what the man had said to him. "What? You mean three passengers didn't make it?"

"Yes sir. But don't worry—we were able to fill those berths."

"I don't give a good goddamn about that. I want to know who those passengers were."

"The ones who didn't make it?"

"Yes, yes. Their names."

"Just a minute, General. I'll have to get the manifest."

Teshima snorted. He lit his cigarette, then drew his other hand back over his shaved head and banged his fist on his desk. "Yukio, Yukio—get your ass in here!"

The sergeant came running. "Yes sir?"

"What the hell was the name of the guy from *tokko* who was following Drake?"

"There were two of them, sir—round the clock."

"Yeah, well, get them on the phone!" He heard the NYK man come back on the line. "Yes, yes?" Teshima screamed.

"I have those names, sir," the man said.

"Yes, yes."

"The ones with reservations who didn't make the sailing."

"Yes, yes, I know! Who the hell are they?"

"Well, there's a Mr. and Mrs. Ralph Tripstead . . . and, uh, let's see here . . ."

"Yes, goddammit?"

". . . and, here—the Reverend Cotton Drake."

Teshima knew that was coming. Still, he bellowed: "You're sure?"

"Yes sir, I am. We gave that cabin to—"

"Shit!" Teshima hollered, and he just let the receiver drop, so that it rattled onto his desk and dangled off it. "Yukio—Yukio!"

The sergeant rushed back in. "Yes sir. The day guard's name is Takahashi and the night man is Sakai."

"Well?"

"Neither one is in the office."

"Well, where the hell are they?"

"Takahashi should be coming back from Yokohama, from the *Tatsuta*—"

"Yeah—my ass."

"Sir?"

"Never mind. And the other guy, the night man?"

"Sakai. We'll call his home," Yukio said.

Teshima stood up, sweeping the phone itself off his desk for effect. "You call both their homes. You tell the *tokko* to find their asses and get them over here right away."

"Yes sir."

"I mean *right away*. And I don't want to hear any shit about using gasoline. I don't care if they use Tojo's car. You get them here right away!"

62

"It's late, darling," Miyuki said, when Cotton put his arms around her. "Kensuke will be here soon."

"So he'll wait," he said, and he laughed devilishly, nuzzling her.

"We lived together for months and you restrained yourself."

"*Oi*, you weren't my wife then."

"Don't you ever say '*oi*' to me again." She pretended to pout.

"Don't you ever refuse to make love to me again." They looked into each other's eyes. It was quite amazing, really, how long they just stared, their eyes locked and loving. Finally, she could tell he was going to kiss her, so she spoke:

"You know, *gaijin*, I don't understand how I ever could have believed there was a world where girls couldn't love a man like I love you."

"I never loved anyone like you, either."

"But you *could* love. Japan thinks it's modern, but it isn't. Not yet. Not if we aren't smart enough to know about your love."

They looked at each other some more, both of them afraid that they might never have the chance again. It was as important to look and love as to make love. Only after a long while did Cotton press his mouth on hers, and kiss her, as if he would never stop. Miyuki had to pull away. "If you kiss me any more there will be no time left for the rest," she said, hurrying to undress. They tumbled onto the futon. "When we get to the Philippines, we'll stay in bed for a whole day," she promised him, laughing.

"For a week."

"No, we must go to church on Sunday. Remember? I'm a Christian now."

"And I'm your husband now," he said, wrapping his arms around her, falling upon her lips once more, and on her body, and imagining that this would go on and on and on and . . .

"What the fuck is this?" Teshima bellowed. He held out the piece of paper Takahashi had given him.

"It's your orders, sir."

Teshima studied the paper. He saw his signature. It *was* his; there was no question. So: "What the fuck is this?" he screamed again.

Takahashi was shaking. They'd found him in the park, with his little boy. They couldn't locate Sakai. They'd brought him straightaway, even with his son, who was outside in the anteroom, cowering as the general yelled at his father. Takahashi tried again: "But please, sir, look, it's the orders you signed for me to escort Mr. Drake to the station."

"Station? He was supposed to go to Yokohama."

"But the orders . . ." As much as he dared, Takahashi gestured back to the paper.

"What station?" Teshima yelled.

"Central."

"When?"

Takahashi thought. "Sunday morning."

"So, who gave you the orders?"

Takahashi hesitated. They were back to that. He tried again. "But, but . . . *you* did, sir." And again he nodded toward the paper.

Teshima balled up the paper in his fist and shoved it into Takahashi's chest. "I didn't say 'Who *signed* the orders?' I said 'Who *gave* them to you? Gave? *Gave?*'"

"Oh. Serikawa, sir. Lieutenant Serikawa did."

Teshima threw the ball of paper onto the floor. "Damn. Damn. I should have known." Then he leaned back across the desk. "When?"

"When what, sir?"

"When did he give you the orders? What other when is there?" He punched him in the chest again, and Takahashi had to struggle to keep his feet and hold his military position before the general.

"Friday afternoon, sir. As soon as he arrived in Tochigi."

"And where is he now? Where is Serikawa?" Takahashi shrugged helplessly. Teshima whirled to Yukio: "Where he is, Yukio? Where is that cocksucker now?"

"He never reported back to his office, sir."

"Did you check at his home?"

"No answer, sir."

"Shit!" Teshima thundered. He paced, lighting a new cigarette. "So, where can he be, what's-your-name?"

"Takahashi, sir."

"I don't give a shit what your name is! I just want to know where Serikawa is."

Takahashi sucked in a breath. "Sir, I don't know where he is, sir. The last time I saw him was Friday. He gave me the orders and went into Mr. Drake's place."

"And when did you leave with Drake?"

"We went to Tokyo late the next day, Saturday."

"But you never saw Serikawa again—after he went to Drake's?"

"No sir, I never did."

"Shit—he killed him!" Teshima said, pacing some more, pacing and smoking. "The priest killed him! You think?"

"I don't know, sir. Lieutenant Serikawa had already given me those orders"—he pointed to the ball of paper on the floor—"to take Mr. Drake to the train station."

Teshima mulled that over. "All right. All right—who knows? To hell with Serikawa for now, anyhow. Drake. Drake. Where the hell is Drake? He's the one who matters. Right?"

"Yes sir," Takahashi said, happy for the chance to be agreeable.

"So, you put him on the train?"

"Yes sir."

"Well, where was he going?"

"Osaka."

"You put him on the Osaka train?"

"No sir. It was the Nagasaki Express. It was just that he was going to Osaka."

"And he got on?"

"Yes sir. I saw him go through the gates. He had a travel pass signed by you."

"The hell I did!" Teshima screamed, and this time he turned around and swatted Takahashi hard across the face with the back of his hand, full power. The *tokko* man went reeling backwards, crashing to the wall, right across from where his little son, sitting in the outer office, could see. The boy stood up, frightened, and started to move toward his father. Takahashi looked over to him, trying to look reassuring. Teshima slammed the door shut in the little fellow's face and threw Takahashi back down just as he started to struggle to his feet. "Now, you stop worrying about your kid and listen to me! I didn't sign any pass for Drake. You understand?"

Takahashi held his head. "I'm sorry, sir. It was my mistake. Somebody signed your name."

"Yes. Now, get your ass up." Takahashi found his feet. "All right. Osaka?"

"Yes sir."

"Why Osaka?"

"Well, sir, he told me he lived down there, near Kyoto, growing up."

Teshima sneered. "What, did you have chats with him? Were you following him or hanging out with him?" Takahashi ducked his head, but Teshima ignored him now, and when he spoke again it was really only to himself. "Where would he go? He wouldn't go home now. He's not some goddamn carp. Where would he go?" He kept on walking around the room. He saw Takahashi rolling from foot to foot. Generously, he waved to him. "Sit down. Sit down and think, you dumb sonofabitch. You too, Yukio. Think."

"Well, where else does the train stop?" Yukio said.

"Yeah, yeah. Where?" He turned to Takahashi, who had slumped on the floor.

"Well, Kobe."

"No, no, not Kobe."

Takahashi tried to think. "Oyama."

"No, no. Nothing there."

"Hiroshima."

"No. How about Fukuoka?" Teshima asked. "It stops there."

"Yes sir, I'm sure."

Teshima brightened. "That's it. There's the airline that flies out there. The one airline."

"Dai Nippon," Yukio said.

"Yes." He began to pace again. "Where's it fly to?"

"China," Takahashi said.

"I know China, you imbecile! *Where* China?"

"Canton, I know," Yukio said. "And I think Taihoku first."

"Right," Teshima said. "Find out if the butter eater was on any of their flights. And if he's in the air now, either bring it back or shoot the goddamn thing down!"

Yukio threw open the door. Takahashi's little son was standing there, quaking. With disdain, Teshima waved to Takahashi to clear out of his office. Relieved, the man grabbed his son and hurried away as Teshima continued to yell obscenities after him.

63

For Miyuki to board the *Nagasaki Maru*, it was necessary first for her to pass under the arch that led off the main street that ran by the harbor. Beyond the first checkpoint there was a broad, open quandrangle for her to pass through, with only one small guarded entrance at the other side.

At the first outer gate, to her surprise, a military policeman barely glanced at her papers, then waved Miyuki on. Kensuke picked up Miyuki's larger bag again, and they crossed the empty square together to the final checkpoint, where he thrust the papers at the police officer. "I trust you will take the most expeditious care of Mrs. Serikawa," Kensuke said.

The constable and the ship's officer both nodded, smiling with favor on the beautiful woman in the fashionable mauve overcoat with its fur collar and the stylish green hat with the feather on it. They flipped through her ticket and passport and all the various permissions—tax clearance, police approval, Bank of Japan endorsement—murmuring almost apologetically to both Miyuki and Kensuke about even this cursory inspection.

"Of course, I understand," Miyuki purred. "These are such difficult times."

"Unusual times," the policeman added.

"Trying times," the ship's officer put in.

"Yes," said Miyuki, and she smiled her brightest when the policeman came to her passport photo and looked up, checking it with the real face before him. He flipped through the rest of the book, stopped at the American visa for the Philippines; but it was obvious he couldn't read English, and he didn't want to make any fuss, so he merely handed it and all the other papers along to the other official. "Everything is in order," he declared. And bowing: "I hope you have a pleasant journey, Mrs. Serikawa."

The ship's officer simply stamped the ticket to Shanghai with no more concern than a red-collar girl punched a streetcar ride into the Ginza. All he said was: "Will you need any help with your luggage, Mrs. Serikawa?"

"No, thank you. I can manage these two little bags. My, uh, trunks are being sent."

"Please see the steward at the top of the gangplank, then, and he'll show you to your cabin. Two-eighteen."

Both men bowed profusely. Kensuke did, too. But Miyuki reached out and took his hand. "No, no," she said, and she fetched up on her tiptoes and pecked a little kiss on his cheek.

Even this most modest expression of affection threw the officials, though, and they bowed their heads in embarrassment. Miyuki didn't care; she kept hold of Kensuke's one hand and so softly, so dearly, she said: "*Sayonara,* Morishita-san."

"*Sayonara,*" he replied, blushing, unable to look at her.

Up the gangplank she walked, then, carrying her own small

bags, each in one hand, the feather in her hat waving a bit in the little breeze. "Moga," the cop said as soon as she was out of earshot.

Kensuke smiled. Boldly, he suddenly called out: "Hey, Mrs. Serikawa!" Miyuki stopped halfway up the gangplank and looked back, and when she did, Kensuke went into his windup and pretended to throw her a pitch. She laughed and put down her bags, bent her knees a little, put up her hands before her, and caught the imaginary ball he threw. Then she and Kensuke laughed out loud. *Sayonara*.

Sergeant Yukio came back into General Teshima's office. "Good news, sir. The Dai Nippon flights were all suspended three days ago. There's no more commercial air traffic anywhere out of Japan."

"Ah, that is good news," Teshima said, and he raised his cup of sake. It was, in fact, his second cup. The day of sacrifice had gone quickly by the boards with the general. "So, where did Drake go on that damn train?"

"Nagasaki was the next stop after Fukuoka," Yukio said.

Teshima scratched at his shiny head. "But there's no more ships out of there, are there? The *Tatsuta*'s the last."

Yukio stepped closer. He was carrying a newspaper, the morning *Yomiuri*. "Across the Pacific, yes, sir. But there's still some China traffic." He turned the paper around, laying it down before the general. "Look." The advertisements bracketed the shipping announcements. "See, sir. The TOA Line is still operating Daily mail ships—"

"They take passengers?"

"Usually, yes, sir. And you can see, there's still regular traffic to Shanghai from Nagasaki."

Teshima frowned, pouring back the last of the sake. "Okay, let's see. If Drake left here on Sunday morning, when would that train get into Nagasaki?"

"Yesterday afternoon."

"All right. Check. Any boats out of there. Liners, mail, cargo—I don't give a shit. Anything he could get on. I want every passenger manifest. It shouldn't be difficult. There can't be that many *gaijin* traveling these days."

"Yes sir." Yukio saluted crisply and turned to go. He paused at the door.

"What is it, Sergeant?"

"I'm sorry, sir. What do I tell them in Nagasaki?"

"What do you mean, 'tell them'?"

"If we do catch Drake, sir? What do they do?"

"Hold the sonofabitch!" Teshima said. "Hold him. Hold him under twenty-four-hour watch. In isolation. Try to get him to tell us where Serikawa is." He leaned back and lit a cigarette. "After that, they are to use their own discretion. But you are to advise them that it is war now—"

"With the United States, sir?"

"Yes, Sergeant. It is war with the United States now, and Mr. Drake has conducted himself like a wartime spy. You understand?"

"Yes sir."

"And that charge is to be communicated under my signature to whoever catches Drake." Teshima took his right hand, then, and slid it up by his jacket front till he fit his own neck neatly into the valley between his thumb and forefinger. With that, he yanked his hand up under his chin, snapping his head back.

"Yes sir, I understand," Yukio said, and for good measure he saluted again. These were difficult times.

Cotton checked out of the Saiwaiso, the Happiness Place; but there was yet some time, and so he detoured back up to the Little Church of the Heavenly God, where he sat and prayed for all of them. For Japan. For America. For Kiyoshi's soul. And for Miyuki and himself, that they would survive all this together. Then he headed back down toward the docks, cutting this way and that to stay off the main road until he spied a streetcar and hopped on for the last mile or so. He could see where the *Nagasaki* was berthed, because smoke had already started coming out of her one big stack. The tugs were getting ready to push her back and escort her out of the harbor, up around the base of Mount Imasayama across the way and into the safety of the East China Sea and, beyond, to Shanghai.

Cotton's mind was churning, thinking and rethinking the plan. To hell with waiting for MacArthur in Manila, he told himself. There must be scores of Westerners I can find in Shanghai that I can tell. I'll have Yamamoto's fleet turned around and heading back to Japan long before Miyuki and I even reach the safe shores of the Philippines. Maybe then there would be no war between the United States and Japan, and he and Miyuki could come back to Tochigi, to run the mission and raise a family. Just make the boat, get on the *Nagasaki*. . . . He jumped off the streetcar and strolled toward the dock, swinging his suitcase.

Miyuki saw Cotton before he spotted her. She was leaning over at the rail, but the other passengers were crowded on either side of her, and he couldn't make her out right away. Cotton didn't want to look up there too long. Casual, he told himself. Easy now. He ambled up to the quadrangle and handed over all his papers to the soldiers at the first checkpoint. "Good afternoon," Cotton said, positively jaunty; and when the officer started inspecting his documents, Cotton glanced back up at the decks again, and this time he saw Miyuki at the rail, the mauve overcoat with the fur collar and the feather sticking up out of the green hat that Kiyoshi had given her. *She made it! She's safe!*

Immediately, he looked away again, bringing his eyes back to the soldiers who were checking his papers. Cotton didn't even spot Kensuke way over to the side of the square, lounging there with a couple of longshoremen, enjoying a smoke.

At the desk, the officer looked to his colleagues, and one of them took off his cap. It was a signal, but artfully managed, and Cotton didn't have any idea. Miyuki didn't spot it, either. It didn't even register with her that when she came through that first gate, there had been only one soldier there, and now there were three. Kensuke didn't notice anything, either. He was just glad to see that Cotton had made it. He ground out his smoke on the pavement. "Got to take care of my *on* man," he said; and as he started over toward Cotton, he scanned the decks for Miyuki. When he spied her, he called out gaily: "Hey, Drake-san made it!"

Cotton heard that. He turned to catch sight of Kensuke just as the officer handed him back his papers.

Miyuki shrunk down, crossing her hands in front of her, signaling to Kensuke: No, no. Not another word, Kensuke, please, she thought. Don't let them connect me to the *gaijin*.

She would have ducked away, hidden in her cabin, but that was when she saw all the soldiers running. From everywhere. They came in four different squads, from behind Cotton, and from the buildings on either side—one, as a matter of fact, from right behind Kensuke—and even from off the ship itself, five men pounding down the gangplank, port arms.

Cotton had hardly taken three or four steps away from the desk when the three soldiers there jumped up and pulled out their guns, screaming for him to stop. He dropped his valise. He knew he was trapped, and his eyes darted about. They fell again on Kensuke, who was well across the quadrangle. Desperately, Cotton tried somehow to signal him, to tell him: "Say nothing, Kensuke. Show nothing." And then, in the next instant, Cotton glanced up, allowing himself a last glimpse of Miyuki. She was still there, under the green hat with the feather, but now her hand was drawn up across her face. He saw that.

Only then did he turn and run. He expected to be shot. Even after he heard the officer at the desk scream "Don't shoot him!" he still expected to be shot. And what was the point in trying to escape, anyhow? The soldiers were closing on him from all sides. The closest ones flew past Kensuke as he stood transfixed. Cotton whirled the other way, rushing back past the three soldiers at the desk. Any one of them could have shot him point blank. The one nearest even grabbed him for an instant, but Cotton shook himself loose. The others tore after him.

Get back into the streets, Cotton thought. Get away from

the boat. Fight them. Distract them. Get away. Away, away, away the ship, away from Miyuki.

Miyuki couldn't move. She was rooted there at the rail, terrified. She watched Cotton run, even feeling a worthless kind of pride that he could run so fast. But for what? She could see the scene all laid out before her—ever more troops, converging on Cotton, like pincers.

Still, somehow Cotton managed to escape the quadrangle and get all the way across the street before the soldiers finally managed to cut him off. They grabbed him just there by the building—the one where the NYK offices were located—but Miyuki could see that Cotton kept on struggling, so that two men jumped on his back, and their momentum carried Cotton on, past the edge of the building, and around the corner and out of her sight.

That was when she remembered Kensuke, and she looked back down to where he had been. There he was still, standing frozen, baffled, all alone in the middle of the empty square. And just at that moment, he glanced up to her. It was only for an instant. Somehow, Kensuke understood. Something. And somehow, he understood that whatever that something was, Kensuke was not to involve Miyuki. It was their secret. He nodded toward her, almost imperceptibly. But she saw, and she knew what he was telling her. She was safe with him.

And then Kensuke turned back, away, back toward where Cotton had disappeared, across the street, around the corner of the building. Without warning Kensuke dashed across that empty piece of pavement, his great, long Japanese legs eating up the yardage, passing the slowest of the troops. They all were running that way. And if Miyuki could have seen, there were already a dozen or more men there who had caught up with Cotton, and they were holding him down, thrashing him, pummeling him harder, the harder he fought back and screamed at them.

Miyuki couldn't see that from where she was, though. She could only see Kensuke, and her eyes followed him, watching him sprint across the square—so fast that it was easy to believe that he could save Cotton. She could even hear

Kensuke, too, because all the time he was running, he was hollering out "No, no, no!" and "Stop, stop!"

Kensuke couldn't see Cotton, somewhere in the soldiers' midst, when he arrived at the edge of the NYK building. But he didn't even break stride; he just threw himself out in a great, long leap. Miyuki could see him take off, but then he was gone from her sight. She could see the soldiers, though. She could imagine that wherever Kensuke had landed, Cotton was there at the bottom of the mass, broken and bleeding . . . maybe even already dead. Maybe.

Then she didn't hear any more. The soldiers began to scatter. Some came back her way, toward the ship. But there was no sign of Cotton—or of Kensuke. She never saw either of them come back around the corner. And so soon enough, when the *Nagasaki Maru*'s smokestack blew, Miyuki began to tremble. She knew then that Cotton wasn't going to come back from around that corner. She was alone. She bit into her hand to keep from crying there at the rail, but the other passengers were looking out to where all the excitement had just taken place. Nobody noticed the lovely woman in the mauve coat with the fur collar and the green hat with the long feather, moving away from the rail, holding back her tears, fleeing to her cabin.

The smokestack blew again, and the ship weighed anchor, heading out and away, round where Imasayama rose, and into the open sea beyond, carrying Mrs. Drake Miyuki away from the Sun-Begot Land all by herself.

64

Sunday was the worst, the last day on board the *Saigon Voyageur*. Only then did Miyuki learn that the old ship had lost so much time out of Shanghai that she might not be able to make Manila by nightfall. The deck officer she asked only laughed and said it would surely be even worse for the rest of them on the Indochina leg; they almost *never* made that on schedule. "But must be Manila today," Miyuki said, in the best English she could manage.

He shrugged. It would be close. The sun would go down behind the Zambales Mountains before six, and if the *Voyageur* lost any more time, she'd have to anchor in the bay then, in the shelter of Corregidor, and dock tomorrow morning.

The officer tried to commiserate with her. He said he had a girl in Manila, and you could bet that he wanted to get there as much as Miyuki did. Compared with the other two points on his route, Saigon and Shanghai, which were both controlled by the Japanese now, Manila was choice. "Good place, Philippines," he explained to Miyuki, in his best English. "Like Switzerland maybe. You and husband stay there. Safest place come the war."

"Only must get there today." She had already calculated the time. It would be three-thirty Monday morning in Manila when the Zeros hit Hawaii at eight there Sunday. Already, that was less than twelve hours away.

She went back to her cabin and prayed. She made herself pray out loud in English. She had tried to practice English the whole trip from Shanghai, but she had to work by herself in her cabin, because it was a French ship with almost no English speakers. Besides, whenever she ventured out, the Japanese men on board bound for Saigon tried to pick her up, asking her all sorts of questions she didn't want to answer.

And now she took out a pad, and with the careful help of her dictionary she wrote this:

My name Mrs. Miyuki Drake, wife of the Reverend Cotton Drewry Drake of American citizen. Japanese to attack Hawaii 7 December of 8 hours morning. Thank you.

She put that in her brassiere and left her cabin, and when she did, she could see the Bataan Peninsula almost dead ahead, the *Voyageur* cutting briskly through the channel of Manila Bay. "Go to land?" she asked the first crewman she saw, rushing by.

Oui, oui, madame," he called back to her.

The captain hit it right on the money. The *Saigon Voyageur* tied up at Manila at twenty minutes past five. Not a half-hour later, the sun fell behind the Zambales, and by the time Miyuki had picked up her bags and the passengers were allowed to leave ship, the winter night had come, the dark making Miyuki feel that much more lost, that much more hopeless.

And now the real problem. She had to speak English, and hers had deteriorated so. Besides, when she had spoken in English with Kiyoshi or Cotton, they'd always been patient, spoken slowly to her. The only time she'd ever been out of Japan before—on honeymoon in Hawaii—she hardly spoke English at all, except to be cute for clerks and salespeople, who were obliged to congratulate her profusely for trying.

But now, as soon as she alighted from the *Voyageur,* she had to endure the immigration officials, screaming at her. She barely could make out a word. It was horrible. Why is the visa in a different name than the passport? Who is Cotton Drake? Where is he? Why have you come to the Philippines without him? What is this shit (holding up her Japanese divorce papers)? Don't you speak English any better? What? Why not? Where will you stay? When is your husband getting here? Why is the visa in a different name than the passport? Who is Cotton Drake? Where . . . ?

It was hot and sticky. It was December, but it felt like July. Miyuki had tried to keep her clothes clean, but she'd brought so few—just two good dresses, and she had to save the clean blue one for when she got to the hotel and met with General Douglas MacArthur.

And please, she kept saying to herself, make me remember not to say "prease." If I say "prease," they will laugh at me, as well as hate me. She could tell they hated her, the Filipinos. The Filipinos hated all the Japanese. Prease. Prease. She tried, but it kept coming out "prease" when she didn't concentrate, and when she did concentrate, *all* she could say was "please"—but she forgot everything else. Please. Prease. Either way, they all laughed at her.

But, at last, the last official stamped whatever he had to stamp last on the last document and waved her on. And there Miyuki was—nowhere. The place was chaotic and intimidating, the usual sort of madness that attends the arrival of every boat everywhere. Rough, greedy men pushed upon her, saying things she didn't understand in English thick with Tagalog inflections. She knew how terrified she looked, too, she recognized what an easy mark she must have been. So she grasped her purse tighter, even discreetly touched her breast to make sure that the note she had written was still there. That was when her eyes fell on the big clock above the wharf: seven-forty-five. A quarter to eight, less than eight hours till the Japanese started the war. Miyuki was scared to death.

She finally fought her way past the first wave of hustlers and scoundrels, and found a momentary peace standing under a streetlight. She looked around. Maybe she could even see the Manila Hotel from here. But no. She did see the moon, though. Couldn't miss that—nearly full. And the simple truth struck her that it was also nearly a full moon over Honolulu. Somewhere, north of Hawaii, there would be plenty of good moonlight for the fleet to see by before they took off at the next dawn. The moon—the same moon—made Hawaii seem even closer and her mission even more urgent.

An empty cab rushed by. Miyuki reached into her purse and pulled out a five-dollar bill, American. She'd put all her yen away and had only dollars in her pocketbook. She waved the bill. The next cab screeched to a halt. "Please—Manira Hotel," Miyuki said.

"For that?" the driver asked, making sure, gesturing to the fiver. Miyuki nodded. "Get in," he said.

It was a forty-cent ride to the hotel, but Miyuki didn't care. She didn't even notice the meter. She was just so relieved to see the hotel, its bright lights where the cab drove up, the Philippines and American flags flying side by side on the roof, above the penthouse where General MacArthur resided with his wife and young son.

She approached the desk, negotiating warily through the crowd, feeling the preying eyes of all the men there upon her. A lot of them were reporters, any one of whom would have had the scoop of the century if only he'd known what lay under the brassiere of this frightened little Japanese flower who stumbled through the lobby. A bellboy rushed up to her and tried to grab her bags, but Miyuki clung to them as if he were a thief. He laughed and steered her to the reception desk.

She heard more laughter behind her, but she didn't look back, sure that it was directed at her. It wasn't though—just a tipsy bunch of Army Air Corps officers, piling out of the lobby bar. They were all in their gaudy tropical civvies, preparing to begin what promised to be the biggest bash of the year: a party honoring MacArthur's Air Corps commander, Major General Lewis Brereton, who was flying out early tomorrow morning to Java on his way to hitch up with Chiang Kai-Shek's air forces in China.

So, except for a skeleton guard at the bases, there was hardly an airman who wasn't there for the party, for the music and food and drink, and for the finest that the Manila demimonde could offer. "BETTER THAN MINSKY'S" was what all the party posters promised.

Miyuki placed her hands gently on the reception counter, afraid to speak, yet knowing she must. Please.

"Yes?" said the clerk. He was the sort who treated everyone he didn't recognize in his most condescending manner, and the opportunity to intimidate a nervous Japanese bitch encouraged his rudeness all the more.

"Please, room," Miyuki whispered, although even as the words left her lips, she knew that it sounded all wrong: "Prease, loom."

"Do you have a reservation with us?" She looked back blankly. She didn't understand. But she took a guess and shook her head, no.

"What are you, one of the B-girls with the party?" the clerk snapped next—and, of course, Miyuki didn't know what he had asked her, so she shook her head again, halfway between "I don't know" and "What?"

Quickly, then, she reached for her passport, opening it to the page where her visa was stamped. "American wife," she said. And she put some American dollars on the counter too. The clerk deigned to examine her passport, shrugged, and pushed the register over. Proudly, Miyuki signed in the English letters she'd practiced diligently on the boat down. The clerk took her cash and signaled for a bellboy.

Miyuki felt confident. "Question, prease."

"Yes, what is it?"

"I wish talk General MacArthur. Prease. His loom number, prease, sir."

This took the clerk to even greater heights of sarcasm. "Oh, *you* wish to speak with *General* MacArthur?"

"Yes," Miyuki said, brightening, taking him at face value, missing all his ugly inflection.

"The general is not to be disturbed by strangers . . . like you," he snapped, turning his back upon her.

"Prease—"

He'd hoped she would continue her petition, and he whirled back on her. "Madam, if you make any effort whatsoever to bother General MacArthur, you will be promptly removed from these premises. Do you understand?"

Miyuki didn't, of course; but there could be no doubt about his tone this time, and so Miyuki bowed and left with the bellboy.

At her room, she pulled out a dime to tip him; but as he started to leave, she got an idea, and she lifted up a dollar bill. "Hey," she said, and he looked with sudden attention upon her—or, rather, upon the substantial legal tender she waved. "Tell where General MacArthur."

"What room he's in?" She nodded. He pondered—not whether to take the money but how to handle this situation. "Okay," he said, snatching the bill. A U.S. dollar was a great deal of money. "The general's in the penthouse."

Miyuki didn't understand, but she did make out the last syllable.

"Not in hotel? In *house?*"

"Yeah, in the *pent*house." She shook her head. But he tried to help her. "Penthouse," he repeated. "Top floor"—and he jerked his thumb up to the ceiling.

"Ah, roof?" Miyuki asked, only it came out "Loof," and the little Filipino laughed.

"Yeah, loof," he said.

"You me take." He shook his head. Miyuki went back to her purse and held up another dollar.

The bellboy's eyes widened, but he retained sufficient presence of mind to negotiate: he held up two fingers. Miyuki dug out another bill. He took it and led her back down the hall and pushed the elevator button. When it came, he spoke in Tagalog to the operator: "Hey, Basket, take this lady up to the penthouse."

"Whatdya mean, the penthouse? Nobody goes up to see the general without orders."

The bellboy turned to Miyuki and rubbed his thumb and forefinger together. She held up a dollar. Basket looked from the buck to the bellboy. The bellboy held out two fingers at his belt, like a catcher calling for a curve ball, so Basket said, "Two." Miyuki nodded and went back into her purse. She was out of singles, but she gathered up all her change. Basket accepted that extra eighty-nine cents and beckoned Miyuki to step inside. Several floor lights were calling to him, but he jammed the elevator into gear and rode it straight to the top. There, he all but shoved Miyuki off, quickly closing the door behind her and whipping the car back down.

Tentatively, Miyuki looked in either direction, but she'd hardly had a chance to guess which way to go when a swarthy American soldier suddenly loomed from around the corner. "Halt!" he called out, in his most menacing military voice. "Who are you?"

Terrified, Miyuki couldn't speak. She only gasped for breath, as he held up a billy club and fired questions at her. "I said, who are you? How did you get here? What are you

doing here? What's your name? Are you a Jap?" She managed to nod instinctively when she heard the word. "Yeah, I
figured, I thought so," said the guard. "You sure look just like
a Jap to me."

Finally, actually closing her eyes to concentrate, Miyuki
managed: "Prease, General MacArthur."

At first, the guard only stared at her. Then: "What?"

"Gener—"

And he roared. Then he got back in character. "Get outta
here!" he bellowed.

"Important, prease. War—" But the corporal had had
quite enough. He grabbed Miyuki roughly by the wrist, turning her around, facing her roughly up against the wall as he
pressed the elevator button.

"Jap!"

"Me American wife," Miyuki managed.

"Yeah, and I'm the Emperor of all the Japs." This rejoin-
der of his amused the corporal greatly, and he chuckled to
himself. It was clear to him that his vigilance had brought the
dangerous situation under control, so he relaxed his grip on
her and turned her around, checking her out. "You a
whore?" he asked. Miyuki looked puzzled. He stuck his forefinger through a circle he formed with his thumb and forefinger on the other hand. "You a whore with the party? Fuckee,
fuckee?"

Miyuki got that drift. She shook her head vigorously. "Me
American wife," she said; and remembering her passport with
her visa in her purse, she thought to show it to him. But even
better, then, her mind rolling now, she remembered the paper
she had written. At least this soldier could take that to
MacArthur. Instinctively Miyuki brought her hand up and
started to reach inside her blouse. The corporal had been
forewarned about tricky Oriental vixens, though, and even as
Miyuki's hand reached the paper, the soldier's hand flashed
out, grabbing her at the wrist again. "Goddamn, you got a
gun in there?" he screamed, and he banged her whole body
hard against the wall, so that her head flipped back, banging
hard. She saw stars.

"Fuckin' Jap cunt!" the corporal said, unbuckling his pistol, waving it at her. He began to pat her body gratuitously, starting with her breasts, searching for a weapon. Miyuki only held up her hand, offering him the crumpled note.

"Take, prease," she said, but he slapped her hand away; and when suddenly the elevator arrived and the door opened, the corporal pushed her back into it, so roughly that she lost her balance, stumbling all the way to the back wall, crashing there, slumping to the floor.

The corporal waved his billy club at Basket.

"Get the fuckin' Jap cunt outta here and don't bring no one else to this floor—you hear me?"

"Prease," Miyuki said, holding the piece of paper up.

Basket closed the door. "What I tell you?" he said. "You can't see General MacArthur."

Miyuki struggled to her feet and got off at her floor, the eighth. In her room, she threw herself across her bed and cried. She hadn't cried till now. Cotton—and Kiyoshi—would have been proud of her so far. And she didn't cry for long, either. "I will try again, Cotton," she said out loud, in Japanese, and she rose from the bed and began to lay out her best clothes, the clean blue dress she had saved. Then Miyuki took a shower. She looked at her watch. It was already past nine o'clock.

Somewhere in the Pacific, under the moon north of Hawaii, where it had just struck three o'clock Sunday morning, the first attack pilots on the carriers were already up, after tossing and turning in their bunks most of their short night. Like Miyuki, they were dressing in their finest clean garments, recalling the noble samurai of old when they went off to battle. In the pilots' mess, the music coming clear over the intercom was from a radio station in Honolulu.

Putting on her makeup, Miyuki peered into the mirror. Someone will listen to me, she thought. I am a Jap, and I can't speak much English, but there are all those men down-stairs, and one of them will listen to a beautiful woman. I am a beautiful woman, she thought. I know that. Even if she couldn't reach General MacArthur himself, some American man would listen to her. She picked up the note as she left the room, but this time she decided she didn't have to hide it anymore, so she just put it in her purse, with the rest of her cash, and her passport and room key and the one photograph she had of her husband.

65

The lobby had thinned out even more now, only a few older people left—rich Filipinos mostly, taking their ease in the plush chairs under the palms. Miyuki sized up that scene quickly and turned to the bar.

The panic seized her there again right away—the place was so fearful, so forbidding, so alien. Sure, she'd been to American bars a few times, but always with Kiyoshi—in Ha-waii on their honeymoon, to the Imperial a couple of times—but now she was alone, and she wasn't sure what to do. There were a few men scattered around the big mahogany bar, but only two women, and they were both seated deco-rously at tables with gentlemen escorts. Her mind raced. Maybe women weren't allowed at the bar. Better play it safe—even if the whole point was to be conspicuous and at-tract some American she could tell about Hawaii.

So Miyuki went to a little cocktail table to the side and sat there, hands folded on it like a debutante. And she waited. She saw the men turn from their drinks to look at her. She wanted to leave. She wanted get up and run away. To where? Nothing in her whole life had prepared her for this.

"Yes?" said the waiter.

She was ready, rehearsed with what to reply. "Gin and tonic," Miyuki declared in a loud, clear English voice.

She had taken two sips when a guy she'd eyed finally came from around the bar. She had already noticed him staring, the worst of the lot: a large Westerner, surely American, smoking a big cigar and talking loudly. He was wearing a Philippine barong shirt with the false air of a man gone determinedly native. Also, he was obviously drunk.

"You waitin' for anybody, little lady?"

Miyuki got the drift if not the words. She just beckoned to the other seat at the table, and the man fell into it. "I'm Earl," he said.

"I Miyuki Drake."

"Drake? Drake? Aren't you a Jap?"

"American wife. Christian. Husband in Japan."

Earl looked at her, totally puzzled. Was this some sort of scam? "Yeah?" he asked.

"You American?"

"Of course I am."

"Help me, then," Miyuki said, and she leaned forward, a hand on his big hairy arm. He drew back some. "You tell General MacArthur. Japanese attack Hawaii."

"Wha—?"

"In"—she looked at her watch—"only five hours."

"What is this shit?"

Quickly she reached into her purse and pulled out the paper. Earl took it as if he were handling an explosive. He read it with his nose scrunched up the whole time. "What is this shit?" he said again, throwing it back on the table. "What is this? Is this some Jap shit?"

"Please, tell General—"

"You want to fuck, or what?"

Miyuki picked up the paper and pointed to it. "Prease, prease. Help. Tell General."

"This *is* some Jap shit, isn't it?" Earl said. "Don't give me any Jap shit." He got up and stormed away. "You shouldn't even let any Japs in here, Rabbit," he said to the bartender. All Filipinos seemed to have nicknames. Rabbit only nodded, but Miyuki could see all the customers looking at her now. The big man went back to his friend and began to grouse loudly, but all Miyuki could make out was "Jap" and "shit." Nobody else came near her.

Miyuki sipped on her gin and tonic. It tasted good. She'd always liked gin the best of all the Western drinks. And she knew the alcohol would embolden her a little. She thought about ordering another, but when the waiter came back, she paid the bill quickly and hurried away.

The lobby was deserted. But she could hear music, and she steered toward it, across the lobby and down the hall. Louder it came, the big band sound without quite so big a band, but then voices with it, singing and talking and calling, the raucous noises that herald parties everywhere in the world. A couple of Western men were coming at her, like advance scouts, and they passed by, carrying their glasses, on the way to the men's room. They were only just a step past her when one loudly advised the other he'd "like to fuck that." And they both laughed. She paused. She went on. The gin gave her a little courage.

And suddenly the doors to the pavilion were there, and beyond was this crush of people—men, mostly, all Western, in bright sport shirts. Only here and there were a few men in uniform. In fact, although Miyuki couldn't know it, almost every man at the party was in the U.S. military. This was the going-away party for General Brereton, and only those few airmen who hadn't been able to get off duty early had come directly to the hotel in their uniforms. But Miyuki was looking for a soldier, and she searched for the most impressive-looking soldier she saw.

There. As she drew closer to him, she saw some kind of shining insignia flash on his lapel, and although she didn't know quite what it was, she knew enough: he was an officer. He was the one.

Hardly had she stepped toward him, though, than she found herself literally lifted up off her feet—two young airmen in sport shirts behind her, each with a hand on her elbow, rushing her forward. "Come on, babe." "She's mine first." "Join the party." "Fuckee fuckee." Miyuki tried to smile politely and not to struggle, but then somebody else goosed her, and she jerked, and they laughed and put her down, leering at her, sloshing their calamansi-and-rums over her, and saying the lewdest things, she knew, even if she didn't understand the words.

She couldn't believe it. They were worse even than Japanese men.

The loudest one, on her left, said: "You lookin' for anyone, sister?"

"You American?" Miyuki replied.

"Hey, if you're lookin' to fuck American dollar, we're all American."

The man on the other side turned her back to him. "What are you, Chinese?"

"Chinese the ones got their cunts going sideways," his friend said, and they both roared.

"American wife," Miyuki declared, throwing back her shoulders, and she pulled away from them.

Miyuki kept moving. Suddenly, then, a great shout went up, and Miyuki's curiosity got the best of her. She started jumping up and down on her tiptoes, straining for a view between the broad shoulders. There she made out a stage with a band on it—"Terso's," it said on the drum, though in script Miyuki couldn't comprehend—and more active decoration in the form of some strippers, bumping and grinding. The great cheer evidently had come when all of the dancers had gotten down to their pasties and G-strings.

Despite herself, Miyuki had to keep looking; she'd never seen anything like this before. But then somebody ran his hand clear up her leg, forcing her to slap at it and struggle on toward the officer. When she finally managed to reach his side, though, he didn't even notice her, since he too had his eyes on the stage. He even joined in the consensus cries of "Take it off!" and laughed at one particularly drunk corporal in a flower print shirt with beer stains who had to be continually restrained from trying to get up on stage.

Finally, Miyuki summoned the nerve to elbow the officer; and when he glanced down, his eyes lit up at this surprise package left on his doorstep. Miyuki made herself say: "Hi, I come to you."

"Yeah? Anytime, babes." And then, without a by-your-leave, he simply reached down and, with one finger, pulled Miyuki's dress out from her body and peered down her chest. "Not too bad," he told her.

Somehow, Miyuki smiled and kept her composure even as her spirits fell. This officer had seemed like her best hope, but she could tell he was probably drunker even than the two loutish sport shirts she'd had to deal with; he only looked better behaved in his uniform. "How much?" he said. Miyuki cocked her head. "How much a throw? I can't stay all night, babes. I got the short straw, and I gotta go back to Clark tonight."

Still, any port in a storm. "I must talk you first."

The officer didn't even hear that, though, for the cheers suddenly found a new crescendo, and he jerked his head up to see what he was missing. "Yeahhh!" screamed the officer when he could see, so excited he raised an arm in the old college locomotive cheer. The lead stripper on stage, an especially well endowed young lady, had begun the traditional reverse whirl, spinning the tassle on one nipple clockwise, the other counterclockwise. The crowd was so appreciative, in fact, that Terso and most of his sidemen took this opportunity to depart the stage for a drink, leaving only the drummer and saxophonist behind.

The officer turned back to Miyuki. "I seen that a lot," he advised her. "But I never seen a chink do it before." He explained, as a connoisseur: "It's torque, you understand. You people don't have big enough tits." Miyuki just nodded. Luckily, too, a new girl came out on stage, and since she was starting off dressed, the officer concentrated all his attentions on Miyuki. "So, how much?"

She shrugged, ignorant.

"All right, all right, I'll buy you a drink first," and he wrapped his arm around her and convoyed her back through the mob to the bar.

"Gin and tonic," Miyuki said when she realized what was

up. She took a big gulp of the drink, which quite impressed the officer—"You got a hollow tit?" he asked, smirking, patting her left breast.

Miyuki didn't wait any longer. She just reached over to him, caught a handful of his shirt, and yanked him a few feet away from the bar to a relative island of serenity. "Listen, please."

Her sudden solemn intensity caught the officer off guard, and he gave her his ear. "See watch," Miyuki said, pointing at her wrist.

"Sure. Twenty-two fifty-three," he said. "Almost eleven o'clock." Miyuki counted on her fingers. She'd lost him. "It can't be that complicated, sweetie. How much one hour? I told you, I haven't got all night."

"Three-thirty," Miyuki announced, getting it straight in her mind again.

"I only got an hour, honey. I told you. How much a throw?"

"Three-thirty here"

"Three-thirty what?"

"I American wife."

"What?"

"Listen, please."

"How damn much? Fuckee, fuckee, how muchee?"

Miyuki waited. She held up her hands. And then, when at least she had him humoring her, she spoke: "Japanese attack Hawaii in four and a half more hours. Three-thirty."

He just stared at her. What in the world was she talking about? "What did you say?"

Miyuki smiled. At least he was listening. She tried again, slowly: "Japanese attack Hawaii. Tonight." His watch again, tapping it. "Four and a half more hours." She held up four fingers.

The officer shook his head, incredulous. "You're a Jap, right?"

Miyuki nodded. Quickly then: "But American wife." She reached for her purse to show him her identification.

But it was over now she had completely lost him. "Look,

Charley-mama, I don't know what you're up to, but you better stop this kinda shit. You hear me?"

"Is true. Prease."

"What, you on opium or something?"

"I try warn you."

"Oh sure. Get your yellow ass outta here!" he shouted, and suddenly he thrust out his two hands, smashing Miyuki at the shoulders, sending her reeling back. Her drink spilled all over her, and she only barely held her balance. The officer, furious, just stood there, yelling: "Fuck you, Charley-mama cunt!"

Miyuki watched him turn away. She tried to wipe the worst of the gin off her dress with a napkin. The others at the bar were all looking at her, snickering. "Prease, hear Miyuki," she said. They laughed some more. Miyuki shook her head. She couldn't understand. These were Americans—American soldiers!—and they wouldn't listen to her. "I am sorry, Kiyoshi," she muttered. "I try. I try, Cotton."

She brushed her hair back with her hands and stood straight again. Okay, they're all too drunk here. I must try General MacArthur again. Maybe there's a new guard on now. Maybe. She started to leave the room, skirting the crowd at the bar.

That was when an even greater cheer rose up. Even the men who hadn't been served yet at the bar turned and rushed over to watch, pinning Miyuki in the crowd again. She couldn't even see the stage.

What she was missing was no less than Manila's most famous stripper—the Snatch Queen, as she was so delicately known in every dump in the Orient—displaying her peculiar talent, which consisted of squatting and talking all currency, bills and change alike, up her nimble lower regions. One airman had thought to bring along a silver dollar—a cartwheel, the soldiers called it—just for the occasion; and as the Snatch Queen prepared to swallow it up, the chant began: "Snatch! Snatch! Snatch!" and, in counterpoint, "Cartwheel! Cartwheel!" What a time! No one here was disappointed: this surely was *the* party of '41 in the Philippines.

Across the way, one especially exuberant group of airmen grabbed one of the whores they were with and, lifting her up over their heads, passed her along. The game spread, and all over the ballroom the men cheered and raised the women up.

Miyuki never even saw it coming. Before she realized it, she was off her feet, hands all over her. Her blue dress climbed up over her knees, up to her thighs. Once she tried to grab at it, but it was no good. The men's hands were everywhere upon her, pawing her. It was impossible to struggle, and she had to just let herself be carried along. She only clutched her purse tighter: whatever happened, she mustn't lose that. Everything was in there.

So on and on she went, scared, breathless, her head spinning. Her shoes came off somewhere, first one, then the other, and she could feel her stockings down on one side, ripped clear off her garter belt. Finally, she felt herself going back down, her feet on the floor. Uneasily, she found her footing. She raised her head up and saw where she was. Miyuki had been passed up to the stage.

She was not alone. The Snatch Queen had gone, but there were four or five other Filipinas in skimpy bar-girl outfits, who'd been passed along the way, just like Miyuki. Unlike Miyuki, though, they appeared delighted at being in the spotlight, and they were laughing and wiggling, leaning down, cupping their breasts and holding them up, brandishing them just out of the reach of the drunks who ringed the stage.

"Take it off! Take it off!" came the cries, and the most accommodating of the young ladies removed her little top and started dancing to the beat in her skirt and bra. One by one, the others joined suit, until only Miyuki stood to the side, watching.

She looked out at the men; they were hooting and laughing, pointing at her, and screaming "Take it off! Take it off!" She stared down at them. Somehow, a kind of Japanese calm came over her. As much as she hated these awful men, she had to make them listen to her, or they would die. They were soldiers, and they would be the ones to die first; and as much as she hated them now, she didn't want them to die. Wouldn't they listen? Miyuki smoothed down her blue dress and stepped forward.

Only the drummer was left from the band, pounding out his sorry, monotonous beat for the most desultory bump-and-grind. Miyuki turned back to him, signaling for him to stop; but he only looked up at her curiously, through the smoky haze, and kept on going—bang, bang, bang. So Miyuki grabbed his arm. More bemused then angry, the drummer stopped, and in this sudden, odd absence of noise she stepped back up to the front of the stage. Still clinging to her purse, Miyuki looked rather as if she were about to address the Garden Club. In the back of the huge room distant from the stage, the laughter and shouts continued to rise and fall, from a sweeping mumble to a thundering roar; but, at least around the stage, a few curious soldiers were paying attention to her.

"My name Miyuki Drake," she began. "Don't rook women there"—she gestured to the whores, topless to her side—"listen woman here!"

Shouts. Laughter. "Take it off! Take it off!" But one man, way over to the side, just leaving a bar there, looked up when he heard the woman speak. Somehow, in this din, something rang a distant bell for him. He stepped closer, keeping his eyes on the strange, beautiful woman with the blue dress and the small purse in the middle of the mean, vulgar stage.

Miyuki tried to talk again, even took the note from out of her purse and waved it, but the louts round the stage wouldn't listen, drowning out her every effort with their chant. She glared at them. "Hear me!" she cried. "Hear me, prease!"—and she held the note high. "Read—prease!"

"Take it off! Take it off!" Defiantly then, absolutely purposefully yet almost unconsciously, she leaned down and took off her torn left stocking, the one that had come loose from her garters, and threw it out to the men. They cheered. "Okay, okay? Hear me now?"

And for just a second they held their shouts, and Miyuki began again: "I American wife. I Christian, and—" But that was all. The shouts and filth rose up again. Incensed, Miyuki reached up her right leg, unbuckled her stocking, and threw it out. More cheers—but more attention, too. Miyuki tried to seize it. She needed to reach only one man, one American who would believe her. "I American wife," she began again. "I Christian. I for you."

The tall man by the bar stepped closer still. He wore a custom barong over his Brooks Brothers trousers, and he kept his eyes on her as he parted the crowd before him, moving forward, never even apologizing when the other, smaller men complained.

"Husband the Reverend Cotton Drake," Miyuki said, and the tall American caught his breath at that. "My God!" he said, as everybody around him cried another "Take it off!"

"Prease, prease, hear woman!" But no one near the stage would listen anymore.

"Take it off! Take it off!" Now even the whores on stage were laughing at her and screaming.

"Listen, please!" Miyuki shouted back, concentrating, getting her pronunciation right this time. The drummer got up and left to get a smoke; he'd had enough of this.

"Take if off! Take it off!"

And suddenly she paused, and although she kept tight hold of her purse in one hand, she put that hand on one hip, and her other hand on the other, and with her legs set apart, Miyuki threw back her head, and she stopped looking out into the whole crowd: instead, she started searching into each single face there, one by one—each leering, drunken, foolish face. And she peered into those faces, men's and boys', and her eyes flashed at them, and she grew bolder that way, taking their own ugly eyes on directly. "So," she said to them, the ones up close, the ones who could hear her voice, the ones who could see her eyes, "will you risten to me if I do?" And she raised one arm to the top of her dress.

"Yeah, yeah!" the men hollered.

She didn't care anymore. What did it matter? She was finished with trying to save them. "Yes," Miyuki said softly, and without any fuss, no less than if she were alone in her room, she reached behind her to the zipper in back, undid her dress, and let it slip off her shoulders, over her hips, and down her legs to the floor. Now the men would listen.

They roared. They didn't listen at all.

The tall American began to push now, roughly, and never mind whom he pushed aside. He yanked at the men in his path, coming closer, nearer to the stage, to the Japanese woman up there, standing alone in her bra and slip, not dancing, not singing, just trying to speak.

But Miyuki was beaten now, fool enough to have tried to beat them at their own game. They'd whipped her, and her heart raced, her skin flushed with shame. She held out her hands plaintively. "Prease—prease—hear me! Japanese attack Hawaii!" That got a few heads twisted around to her, but mostly only hoots and hollers, some Bronx cheers, lots of laughter. She wanted to cry but wouldn't. They wouldn't get to see her cry. "Prease—prease!" she called out to them. She stepped forward. "Soon—Hawaii—much soon." She looked at her wristwatch. It was gone. It was the first time she'd noticed. The watch had been lost, like her shoes, when they'd carried her up onto the stage. She forgot the crowd. She stared at her wrist. Kiyoshi had bought her that watch in Hawaii, when they were on honeymoon. It was a one hundred percent American watch—a Longines watch from the United States of America. She could feel her eyes beginning to mist up, but she would not cry; she would not touch her eyes. She just kept feeling her wrist where her watch had been. Somehow, the watch mattered. It mattered a great deal.

The tall American got closer. He started calling her name. "Mrs. Drake! Mrs. Drake! Over here! Mrs. Drake!" But Miyuki couldn't hear him. She didn't hear anything. The men had started to chant again. She held out her hands in supplication, like the saints in the Bible pictures always did. "I tell you," she began. "Attack—Hawaii. Soon." But no one heard. One of the whores started dancing again, playing with her panties.

Miyuki could feel her head spinning. How long had it been since she'd eaten anything? Hours. Hours and hours. On the ship. And the gin . . . Her eyes were unfocused now, her legs buckling. She didn't even see the corporal in the flower print shirt with the beer stains vault up onto the stage and step up to her and reach out and grab her bra right in the middle, between her breasts, and yank at it. The clip in the back gave way and it pulled off into his hand, and the men still watching in the first rows cheered Miyuki's bare breasts and her shame, and that was the last she remembered.

For just a moment more, she stood there looking out, numb. She made no effort to cover herself, just stood there, shaking her head. And then, instinctively, she began to raise her arms up, but it was too late, because her legs began to buckle and she slumped, the piece of paper she had clutched so tightly in one hand drifting away, gone. *Japanesse to attack Hawaii 7 December of 8 hours morning. Thank you.* The tall man in the custom barong reached the stage just then, just as Miyuki fainted, falling back onto the drum set, so that she and the drums together fell, rattling, to the stage floor.

In the front rows, the drunken men laughed some more, and the corporal in the flower print shirt held up Miyuki's bra like a guidon and twirled it round and round until just before Captain Win Taliaferro's right cross fetched him square on the chin and sent him stumbling back, off the stage and on top of his drunken buddies in the front rows.

66

In Honolulu all was still, in the pitch of the night, the moon gone now behind some clouds. The enlisted men had departed Hotel Street for their barracks and ships, leaving behind the dives and the bars, the whores and the B-girls, the Filipino tattoo artists and the taxi dancers. A few of the soldiers and sailors had sprung for two-bit haircuts from the female Japanese barbers, who had plied the tonsorial trade there for years. A few of them had gotten drunk and disorderly. More, though, had only played cards or seen a movie, or walked the tawdry streets aimlessly, or written wistful letters to their girls back home.

Waikiki was dark, the Pacific uncommonly calm. The band at the Royal Hawaiian had finished up at midnight sharp, and the great Pink Palace lay quiet now. Admiral Kimmel, the commander-in-chief of the Pacific Fleet, who had spent the evening at a private dinner party next door at the Halekulani, had long since taken Mrs. Kimmel home and gone to bed. So too had his opposite number in the army, General Short, who had enjoyed a perfectly lovely evening with Mrs. Short and their staff and wives at a charity dance at the Schofield Barracks Officers Club. After all, the two commanding officers had to be up bright and early, because, they had their regular Sunday-morning golf game scheduled.

Up north, though, in the ocean, *Kido Butai* had come alive by now. The tension in the fleet was hard to discern, however, because there was yet so much detail to attend to before the planes would fly south to Pearl.

Back in Japan, aboard his flagship, *Nagato*, anchored off of Hashirajima, Admiral Yamamoto awoke, roused by his personal mess steward, Minoru Wada, whose brother, Naboru, still worked as a cook at the Peruvian embassy.

The admiral got up and dressed, and then he nibbled on cakes and drank tea with his senior staff. "Have we heard yet if all is in order to officially notify the United States government that we are at war?" he asked.

Admiral Ugaki replied: "That should be set, sir. The full ultimatum was sent yesterday to our embassy in Washington."

Yamamoto sipped his tea: "Well, let's cable Tokyo to be sure. I'd like my mind put at ease about that."

A captain left the room to check out that situation. The steward, Wada, poured some more tea, and they all made small talk, anxiously awaiting the word from over Pearl Harbor.

Taliaferro bent over, disentangling Miyuki from the drums.
She was still out, for her head had bounced hard on the stage
floor. Now he lifted her up gently, cradling her head in his
lap. Not ten feet away, the party went on, undiminished; very
few men even bothered to look up at them, and Taliaferro
had to scream twice at one of the whores to pick up Miyuki's
dress. He grabbed it and draped it across her chest.

Only one other man jumped up on stage. He saluted.
"Captain, Sergeant O'Reilly, First Wing."

Taliaferro looked up. "O'Reilly, yes. Get me some water up
here. Ice. Some napkins or something."

"Yes sir." O'Reilly jumped back off the stage.

Taliaferro waved at Miyuki's face with his hand. Her eyes
didn't open, but her pulse felt all right. There was a small
gash on her forehead, and he could feel a substantial bump
in back, too. He screamed at O'Reilly to hurry.

One B-girl had stayed on stage, and Taliaferro gestured for
her to hand him Miyuki's purse. He opened it up and yanked
out the passport—bright red, Japanese. He rifled through it.
The picture first. It was the same woman for sure, even if he
couldn't make out the Japanese characters that identified her.
Then he flipped through the other entries. A visa for entrance
to the United States—1937, Honolulu. But the name was
Serikawa. Miyuki Serikawa, married. He went on, pulling out
a very official-looking paper that was folded into the passport.
It was the *mikudarihan,* the divorce, but, of course, Taliaferro
couldn't make head nor tail out of the Japanese. But when he
turned the passport page, there it was: another entry in
English—a visa issued at the consulate of the United States of
America in Nagasaki, December 2, 1941, for Miyuki Drake,
married.

"Okay, she *is* Cotton's wife," Taliaferro said, and he went
back into the purse, fishing out the hotel key. He looked at it:
room 816. He slid it into his pocket and started to root back
into the small purse again, and there was Cotton's picture, of
him in his vestments, standing before a mission church. On
the back, in English, was written: "Tochigi, Easter, 1941."

"Here, sir," O'Reilly said, kneeling back down on the stage, holding two cups—one of ice, one of water.

"Napkins?" Taliaferro said. He slipped Cotton's photograph back in the purse.

"They're all out, sir."

"Shit," Taliaferro snapped, and he yanked up the bottom of his barong, dipped it into the cup of water, and started dabbing at the cut. The B-girl was leaning over, still topless, holding her clothes. "Gimme your shirt," the captain said impatiently. "Come on, gimme, gimme—if you're not going to wear it, let's put it to good use!" He yanked it from her, filled it with ice, turned Miyuki's head gently to the side, and dabbed at the big bump in the back. Then he drew the icy shirt softly across her forehead.

Her eyes flickered open, and what she made out was the one face, looking down on her. She blinked. "You Liz husband," Miyuki said right away.

"Yes, I am." He was amazed.

"Cotton get Christmas card."

Taliaferro didn't wait any longer. "Come on, O'Reilly, let's get her outta here," and he lifted her up, carefully. O'Reilly jumped down off the stage, and Taliaferro handed Miyuki to him, then jumped down himself. Her dress slipped off, and Taliaferro rushed to cover her chest again.

A young airman with a foolish smile on his face, his barong soaked through with beer and sweat, sidled up to O'Reilly. "Hey, Mikey, after you're through with that, save a piece for me."

In a flash, Taliaferro grabbed the man's shirt by the collar, twisting it hard. "What's your name, soldier?"

He gulped, recognizing an officer. "Taylor, sir."

"Well, Taylor, you get your ass outta this hotel this instant." Taylor gulped. "Where you based?"

"I'm at Clark, sir."

"You get there on the double, somehow—and you're confined to your quarters until further notice." He let go.

"Yes sir." Taylor turned away, but Taliaferro reached out

again, grabbing the young airman by the back of his collar this time. "You raised in a rabbit hutch, Taylor?"

"Sir?"

"Don't you apologize?"

Taylor saluted. "I'm sorry, sir."

"Not to me, you dumb dickhead."

"Sir?"

"To the lady."

Taylor nodded to her. "I'm sorry," he said.

"I'm sorry, ma'am," Taliaferro said.

"I'm sorry, ma'am."

Taliaferro waved his hand. "Go on, get your sorry ass back to Clark."

"Yes sir."

"Come on, O'Reilly." They cut through the crowd to the elevators, Miyuki hanging around Taliaferro's neck, and went up to her room. Softly, he lowered her down onto the bed and sat there next to her, holding her hand.

"Thank you, Liz husband."

Taliaferro smiled. "Captain," he said.

"Captain."

He leaned closer. "Now, tell Captain—where's Cotton?"

Miyuki blinked. "Japanese got Cotton. Nagasaki. Maybe kill Cotton. Maybe jail." Then, suddenly, frightening Taliaferro with such a quick, impetuous move, her one hand shot out, grabbing him by the arm, twisting it over so she could read his watch where he wore it, face on the underside of his wrist. It was a little past midnight, and Miyuki tried to calculate the time change with Hawaii. "Three hour," she said, pointing to the watch.

"Three hours?"

"Three hour, Japanese attack Hawaii." And this time, she made airplane swoops with her hand, and the accompanying noises as well.

"I heard you say something like that on stage."

"The—the—" Miyuki couldn't think of the word for "purse." Her eyes darted around the room before she spied it on the dresser across the way, where O'Reilly had placed it.

She pointed vigorously. "Prease . . . please." O'Reilly brought it to her and Miyuki tore into it. Her money was there. Her passport. Cotton's picture. But the paper wasn't there. Then she remembered. She'd taken it out on stage. It was gone. She had to speak the best she could. She paused. And: "Japanese war Hawaii."

"Yes, you said."

She tried to remember eight. She couldn't, though. She could only remember numbers in English if she counted up to them. So she started, on her fingers: "One, two, three, four, five, six, seven, eight—" Stop. Yes. Eight. "Eight hours."

"Hawaii?" Taliaferro asked.

Miyuki nodded. But even that little gesture hurt; she grimaced with the pain. "Eight."

"Eight o'clock there? Hawaii?"

"Yes." She grabbed his watch and pointed at it vigorously. "Three. Three."

"Three o'clock here in Manila?"

Miyuki shook her head. "Three more hour."

O'Reilly said: "Christ almighty."

Taliaferro tried to remain calm. "How do you know? . . . *Know?*"

"Cotton know. And Kiyoshi know."

"Kee-noshi? Who he?"

"Husband one." She held up a finger. "Kiyoshi die. Seppuku. Cotton husband two." Two fingers.

Taliaferro nodded. "You sure?" he asked. He wanted to add her name, for emphasis and familiarity, but he'd forgotten it. "Mrs. Drake," he said. "You're sure?"

"I Christian," Miyuki responded stoutly. "Promise to Jesus."

O'Reilly stepped closer. "Captain, we've got to tell General MacArthur."

Miyuki rose up a little off her pillow. Her head screamed. But: "No. I try General. 'Go way.'" She pantomimed the guard with his gun, driving her off.

"You've already tried to reach General MacArthur?"

Taliaferro shook his head in some wonder. "*God* wouldn't dare to do that."

"This is some dame," O'Reilly said.

"High house," Miyuki said, and she pointed up.

"Well, all right," Taliaferro said, reaching for the phone. "Let's talk to Baker, and he'll get us to Mac." He turned back to Miyuki. "General Baker's our commanding general." She nodded, ignorant, but out of courtesy. The hotel operator came on. "Operator, this is Captain Taliaferro of the Twenty-seventh Bombardment Group. Urgent—get me General Edmund Baker. . . . Taliaferro." He pronounced it "Tal-ee-ah-fer-roh," the way it was spelled, rather than "Tolliver." He'd given up trying to make people understand how "Taliaferro" could be "Tolliver"—especially army people and Philippine people.

The operator connected him with General Baker. "Sir, this is Captain Taliaferro of the Third Wing, and I must talk to you immediately. . . . Yes sir, I do not what hour it is. . . . Yes sir, but this is about war—with the Japanese. Imminently, sir. . . . Yes sir, right away. Room 629."

Taliaferro and O'Reilly stepped outside to let Miyuki get dressed. She found another bra, threw the blue dress back on, and slipped on her last pair of shoes, some flats. Her head throbbed, but she found some aspirin, and she also dabbed quickly at her cut and brushed back her hair. Then the three of them went down to the sixth floor and knocked on General Baker's door. He had pulled his trousers on, but no shirt, and he was surprised to see a woman. However dubiously, he ushered the three of them into his room, offering Miyuki the one easy chair. The general took the desk chair, while Taliaferro and O'Reilly stood.

Then, forbiddingly, General Baker crossed his arms, as, first, a signal for Taliaferro to begin and, second, an indication that this damn well better . . . be . . . good. And Taliaferro started:

"General, I appreciate that what I'm about to tell you is going to come as a shock, and the source of the information may be unusual, but this lady is the wife of an old friend of

mine." He explained briefly who Cotton Drake was, and then
he went over how they had come to find each other this evening. Baker remained without expression; his only response
was to pass a pack of Chesterfields around so he could have
one himself.

"And . . . ?" he said.

"Mrs. Drake has knowledge that the Japanese are about to
attack Pearl Harbor, sir. Very soon."

Miyuki nodded vigorously. "Eight hours morning."

"That's this morning, sir. Oh-eight-hundred Honolulu
time. That's oh-three-thirty here." He glanced at his watch.
"About three hours from now."

Baker digested this impassively behind the smoke he blew.

Taliaferro took a step closer. "I know this sounds incredible, General, but—"

"How did this Jap find out?"

"Since she doesn't speak much English, sir, I don't know
exactly, but through her husband—my American friend. I understand that much."

Timidly, O'Reilly said: "Sir, would you like me to try and
find an interpreter?"

Baker shook his head, waving the idea off with irritation;
instead, he started flipping through Miyuki's passport, which
Taliaferro had handed him. "What's her husband's name,
Captain?"

"Drake, sir. Cotton Drake. The Reverend Cotton Drake."

"Well, what is *this* bullshit?" Baker pointed to the old
United States visa for Hawaii. "This says she's Mrs. Miyuki
Serikawa. That's a Jap. Who the hell is that?"

Miyuki caught on. "Husband one. Dead." And she held up
a forefinger.

Taliaferro bent down and showed Baker the Nagasaki entry, which identified her as Mrs. Drake.

"When did she marry him?"

"I don't know, sir." He turned to Miyuki. "When did you
marry Cotton?"

"Yes. Cotton husband number two." Two fingers.

"No, no—*when?*" He leaned down and touched her wedding ring, pantomiming putting it on.

"No Cotton ring. Kiyoshi ring."

Baker rolled his eyes. "But when marry Cotton? When Miyuki marry Cotton?" Taliaferro touched his own ring, and O'Reilly's as well, and whistled "Here Comes the Bride."

"Jesus H. Christ, Captain!" Baker said.

But Miyuki caught the question. She was counting again, in English, in her mind: one, two, three, four, five, six. "Six," she said out loud.

"Six?"

She nodded proudly.

Taliaferro knew it wasn't six years. "Six months?" he asked.

"Six days," Miyuki declared firmly.

Baker shook his head. "Six days married, but we don't know where he is." General Baker was nobody's fool. That's how you get to be a general.

"Yes sir," Taliaferro said. This was not going well. O'Reilly wanted to just get the hell out of here and go back to the party.

Baker rose. He ignored Miyuki completely, talking to Taliaferro as if she were an inanimate object. "Now, Captain Taliaferro, let's forget for the moment that you woke me in the middle of the night."

"Yes sir."

"But correct me if I'm incorrect in any way, shape, or form."

"Yes sir."

"You go to a party and have a few drinks." Taliaferro lowered his head. O'Reilly swallowed; he had just made staff sergeant, and he could see the rocker flying off his uniform already. "You meet a Japanese woman at a party. She purports to have just arrived in the Philippines, having married an American missionary a few days ago, although already he may be dead. Conveniently. Have I got it so far?" The sarcasm didn't drip. It gushed.

"Yes sir."

"What do you think, Sergeant? Have I got it right?"

O'Reilly managed a foolish smile.

"Good. You've never set eyes on this dame before, never even heard of her, but you know the deceased husband—excuse me, the man she *claims* is her husband—and she tells you the Japs are about to bomb Hawaii, and you swallow it hook, line, and sinker."

"Yes sir, I know that's—"

"And I'm supposed to go wake up Douglas MacArthur with this information?"

"Sir," Taliaferro said, swallowing, "maybe it's sufficient just to alert Hawaii."

Miyuki looked back and forth between the two men. She had a hunch this was not going Captain Taliaferro's way.

"Thank you for that option, Captain. Now, now, let *me* make some assumptions." He chain-lit his cigarette, not bothering to offer the pack around this time. "It would occur to me, Taliaferro, that if, *if* I am to take any of this bullshit seriously, it would be that the Japs have planted this dame here, hoping some dumb sonofabitch like you would believe her cock-and-bull story, and the last—the very last—fucking place on the face of the earth that they're going to attack is Hawaii!" His voice rose until he was almost screaming at the end. Pause. Quiet. "There, that's my assumption. What do you think, Sergeant?"

"Sir?"

"Do you think that's a good assumption?"

"Yes sir, I do."

Taliaferro held up his hands, trying to remain properly deferential yet also trying not to give in. "Sir, General Baker," he began, "I will grant you this is farfetched, but she knew me. She knew me from a Christmas card that Cotton—"

"Oh, for chrissakes, Captain! Spare me the Christmas cards. Please. Of course she recognized you. You were the one who knew Drake. You were the one they set up."

"But sir—"

"She was on the stage when you *met*, right?" Taliaferro nodded. "She wasn't leaving anything to chance, was she?

Probably had her shirt off, showing those little yellow titties. Right?"

"Yes sir, but it wasn't—"

"Come on, Captain. She baited you. Don't you see? O'Reilly can see, can't you, O'Reilly?"

"Yes sir."

Taliaferro tried again. He knew the story sounded contrived, somehow sounded even worse every time he explained it, but he also was sure it was a coincidence that the woman had found him, was sure she was too real—too dumb?—to be some master spy. "But just suppose, sir. Just suppose." He looked at his watch for dramatic effect. "It's probably no more than two and a half hours now. I mean, if she's telling the truth, sir."

"All right, all right," Baker growled, and he sat back on the desk. "When's the attack?"

"Eight—" Taliaferro began.

"Let *her* say, let *her* say! When is it, Charley-mama?"

Miyuki paused, unsure. "When, when?" Taliaferro said, making his own airplane swoops with his hands.

"Eight hours, Hawaii morning."

"*This* morning?" She nodded.

Baker leaned in. "Where from? Where? Where?" His patience was deserting him.

"Sir, have you a map?" Taliaferro asked.

The general grumbled, but he pulled one out of his briefcase. Miyuki brightened. Without an invitation, she stood up immediately, even before he could lay it out on the bed. First she pointed to Kagoshima. Even Taliaferro had to say: "What's that?"

"Kagoshima," Miyuki said, and she took her hand and made like the Zeros swooping down. The men looked at her blankly. What the hell was here, in the south of Japan? She spied the bathroom, ran in, turned on the sink, and beckoned them in. Then she ran her hand just under the surface of the water, and when it hit the side of the sink, she cried out "Boom!"

"Torpedoes, sir," Taliaferro said.

Miyuki beamed. "Yes, yes—torpedoes, Zeros, Kagoshima."

"That's where they must have practiced. Kago—"

"Yes, yes. Kagoshima, plactice." And she ran back to the map on the bed, tracing a finger up the eastern coast of Japan, pausing just a moment when she got off Tokyo, lifting her finger and dropping it back on the map just above Tokyo. "Cotton—Tochigi." She held her hands in prayer. Baker looked at Taliaferro.

"Where was Drake?"

"I really don't know, sir. My wife would." As soon as he said that, he was sorry he had.

"Your wife? How would she know?"

"Uh . . . she, uh . . . she used to go out with Drake, sir."

"Well, isn't this cozy?"

Miyuki gurgled: "I Christian now. Cotton baptize me, Nagasaki."

Baker barked again. "Go back to the ships! Where? *Where?* Charley-mama?" And promptly Miyuki caught on and put her finger back on the coast, drawing it up to Hokkaido, leaving it on Hitokappu Bay.

"Ships go." And carefully then, in a bit of an arc, she took the fleet across the North Pacific until her finger came to rest just above Kauai. "Now," she said. She started to point to her wrist then, remembered again she'd lost her watch, and pointed to Taliaferro's. "Eight hours morning. Boom. Boom." And she resumed swooping her hands. She even darted back into the bathroom and played torpedo in the sink again. "Bombs," Miyuki said, holding her hands out to the general. "Much bombs. Pearl."

"Pearl Harbor?" Baker asked.

"Yes. Much bombs. Ships. Pearl. Ships!" And the booming noises—she made those again, louder! Taliaferro was transfixed. He felt chills. The whole performance seemed so patently authentic, so raggedly honest.

But Baker . . . Baker held up his hand. "All right. All right," he snapped. "Enough. Sergeant, you escort Charley-mama here outside while Captain Taliaferro and I discuss things." There was no give in his voice.

Taliaferro beckoned for Miyuki to go with the sergeant. He turned back when they had left. "You know what room she's in, right?" the general said.

"Yes sir. I have the key."

"Good. I want you to have someone watch that room. And if the Japs just happen to attack us here or the Panama Canal or Singapore or any other goddamn place besides Hawaii, then we will have her ass dead to rights."

"I think that's a wise precaution, General."

"Captain, that is not a precaution. That is an assessment that that fuckin' femme fatale is full of shit."

Taliaferro drew himself up tall, to attention. Whatever it cost him, he could not agree. Taliaferro spoke like a soldier. He spoke like a West Pointer. But he disputed his general. "I'm sorry, sir, but with all due respect, I believe her."

Baker shook his head mournfully. Further debate was pointless, he made it plain. "Yes, that's painfully obvious, Captain."

"Sir, I don't expect you to agree with me."

"That's awfully good of you."

"But sir, just suppose. Suppose"—he started to say "you're wrong," but he caught himself in time—"uh, it's a longshot, but just suppose she is what she says she is." He glanced at his watch again. "We could still get some patrol planes up. We could alert Pearl and Hickam, Schofield." Taliaferro stepped forward. His hands . . . his hands were hanging before him. He wanted to grab the general around the neck and shake him till he believed Miyuki. Instead, he made fists of them, pounding the air. "Sir, I have served on Hawaii. I know what it's like there Sunday mornings. It's the perfect time to attack. If the Japs studied it, they would attack Sunday morning."

"Just like the Charley cocksuckers."

"Yes sir."

Baker lit another cigarette, shaking his head as he shook the match out. "You know, Taliaferro, you've got a fine record—"

"Thank you, sir."

"—and I guess everybody has a right to get one wild hair up their ass once. Especially after they've had a few drinks and a couple nice little tits shook in their face." A pause. A smile. "I'll, uh, I'll advise CINCPAC—"

"Yes sir! Thank you, sir. Here's the summary"—and, hurriedly, Taliaferro began to write out some notes even as General Baker kept talking.

"I'll advise CINCPAC immediately that there is a rumor—a *rumor*, Captain—to the effect of your notes, and to be on alert. I suppose you can't be too careful these days. And what the hell, it's just Uncle Sam's money."

"Yes sir." Taliaferro handed the general the paper, and Baker read it:

Report of Japanese aerial attack. From carrier fleet based north. At Hawaii today 0800 your time, Sun. 7 Dec. Expect main attack Pearl—Zeros, torpedoes.

Baker chuckled, and, almost patronizing in his manner, he crossed out the word "report" and wrote in "rumor."

Taliaferro didn't argue. "Thank you, sir."

"Now, Captain, I'll send this right off, and you post the guard before the dame's room."

Taliaferro saluted. "With your permission, I'll handle that assignment myself, sir."

"Sure," Baker said, and he winked. "*Outside* the room, of course, Captain."

"Sir, she is my friend's wife."

"Oh yes," General Baker said. "Of course."

Outside, in the hall, Taliaferro dismissed O'Reilly and escorted Miyuki up to the eighth floor. He opened the door for her and stepped in, closing it gently behind. "Miyuki," he said. "General Baker is telegraphing Hawaii." She looked puzzled. Taliaferro pointed to the phone. "General Baker call—"

"Ahh," she said.

"—call Hawaii." He pantomimed putting a phone to his ear. "Say, look out, Japanese attack Hawaii eight hours morning."

Miyuki positively beamed. "Hawaii safe. No war." Taliaferro nodded. "Oh, thank you, Captain-san. Thank you." He bowed. She didn't. She thrust out her hand and grabbed his, pumping it hard. "Cotton learn Miyuki shake American."

It was as good a handshake as he'd ever had—from a woman, anyhow. "Yes," Taliaferro said. He went outside then, and, as soon as Miyuki closed the door, he plunked himself down on the floor across from her room and waited to hear that the Japanese fleet had been spotted, just as she had said.

At that same time, the Hour of the Hare off Hawaii, two hundred and twenty-five miles to the north of Pearl Harbor, the pilots of the Zeros began preparations to head toward their planes on the decks of the carriers. They were wearing headbands with the word *hissho*—Certain Victory—painted on them, and they moved confidently, imbued with destiny, as their ships and rolled on the sea. On the cruisers *Chikuma* and *Tone*, the first planes of the Second World War, two small reconnaissance craft, took off and headed south, the *asahi* over their wings.

General Baker kicked off his trousers and sat back at his desk in his skivvies. He stubbed out his cigarette, then picked up the phone to get a line to call U.S. headquarters a few blocks away at Military Plaza. It was past twelve-thirty now, and the hotel's one graveyard shift operator didn't come on right away. Baker waited, reading over the notes Taliaferro had handed him. Somehow, the story—rumor or report—seemed even more preposterous written out than coming from the lips of the alluring Japanese woman.

"Sorry, hello here," said the operator. Baker didn't reply. "Hello, yes."

"Never mind" was all General Baker said then, before he laid the phone back in its hook. Suppose they put the whole fleet on alert? Sunday morning. Scrambled a lot of planes? If he sent the message—he, a general—it might even be delivered personally to Admiral Kimmel or General Short. Themselves. Five-thirty Sunday morning. No, this was insane. Did you hear about Eddie Baker's wild-goose chase Sunday morning? The Charleys in Hawaii—really! The more General Baker thought about it, the more he decided he wasn't going to risk making a fool of himself, handing this strange woman's story any further up the line.

He crumbled up the paper and chucked it into the wastebasket, then turned out the light and fell back into bed. He slept well.

Miyuki herself fell asleep about that same moment, her head still throbbing, but her heart full that she had made the lives of her husbands honorable, and her own self worthy of them both, wherever they might be.

Commander Fuchida's lead Zero arrived over the northernmost jut of Oahu right on schedule, at twelve minutes before eight. The sky was sky blue, the rays from the *asahi* so symmetrical, so wonderfully duplicating the Japanese battle flag that Fuchida wanted to stand up and salute. Instead, in his little cockpit, he could only beam and scan the pristine heavens. There were no American patrol planes anywhere that he could see—just as Serikawa had promised him. The waters below were soft and glimmering, the cane fields as still and peaceful as Pearl itself should be.

And there it was below, the harbor. There, just as advertised, were the ships, all lined up at weekend anchor—just as the planes at the air bases stood, trapped by themselves, jammed wingtip to wingtip. There is nothing to stop us,

Fuchida thought, as elated—even incredulous—as he could be. He reached for his radio, to send the signal that complete surprise had been achieved, calling out the code word, for "tiger," three times. *"Tora! Tora! Tora!"* Fuchida cried.

He and his men flew on. And then they were dead over Pearl, the Zeros diving. *Oklahoma* was the first battleship they hit, and next, *West Virginia, California,* even the ancient old *Utah* (why not?), *Nevada, Maryland, Tennessee.* Bombs. Then torpedoes. The torpedoes skimmed the surface, holding their trajectory. The torpedoes worked.

The *Arizona* took a direct hit from above—an eighteen-hundred-pound armor-piercing bomb that came through the decks and into the forward magazine, firing almost two million pounds of explosives. The ship blew up with such force that some of Fuchida's pilots, watching in awe, swore to their commander that the whole great battleship rose out of the water before it fell apart and sank to the bottom of the harbor.

Still, though, most of the people on Hawaii thought these were only maneuvers, inconsiderately scheduled early on a Sunday morning. But then the second wave of fighters poured in, the second fleet of bombers. AIR RAID, PEARL HARBOR—THIS IS NO DRILL went out the message, to Washington and the world.

By ten o'clock, Fuchida and his colleagues had returned to *Kido Butai,* the first wave landing back on the carriers with reports that were almost too fantastic to believe: a score of ships smashed, almost two hundred planes destroyed. It was devastating. It was complete.

Yamamoto studied the reports as they came to him on the *Nagato.* "It is beyond my wildest dreams," he said. But even then he began to break the numbers down, analyze them. "When did the *Arizona* get hit?" he asked.

"Early on, sir," replied the intelligence officer. "Only ten, fifteen minutes after we struck."

"And a lot of the other battleships were hit before that?"

"Yes sir."

"How many of their planes did we take out of the air?"

"I don't know exactly how many, but all the reports were that most were on the ground."

"And how many planes did we lose?"

"Almost none till the end, Admiral."

"The second wave had to deal with antiaircraft fire, didn't it?"

"Yes sir."

"And the Americans finally got some of their planes up to go after us?"

"A number, yes sir, but I—"

"They made a fight of it at the end, though, didn't they?"

"I think the reports would suggest that, yes sir."

Yamamoto nodded and turned to Admiral Ugaki. "You see, Ugakikun, they'll never be easy. Never again." The dawn was breaking in Japan now, and he turned and stared out the pothole over the water, toward the first *asahi* light falling on the mainland. "No, there's no such thing as a free lunch," he chuckled to himself.

"What's that, Yamamoto Shirei Chokan?" Ugaki asked.

"Just an old American expression. But we ought to instruct our generals with that wisdom as much as with the details of our glorious victory today." Ugaki nodded. "Do you know what this tell us?"

"Sir?"

"Everything we did, everything we planned—so perfectly, so brilliantly—"

"Thank to you, sir."

"Thank you, but it only worked because of the surprise. The complete surprise, Matome. Just one leak, one wrong whisper." Yamamoto threw up his hands. "Just one hour's warning. Hell, if they'd only had a few minutes to know." And he shrugged.

"Yes sir."

"So, Ugaki-kun," Admiral Yamamoto said. "Now, where do we go from here?"

67

Just past dawn Miyuki woke up to Taliaferro banging on her door, calling her name. She slipped on her kimono and opened the door. "Come—come quickly," he said, and then, speaking slowly, forming his words: "The Japanese have attacked Pearl Harbor. We need you."

Miyuki frowned. "General never phone Hawaii," she snapped.

Taliaferro lowered his head, for that's what he believed too. "Please, Miyuki, come with me" was all he said. "Hurry."

At the same time, five hundred miles north of Manila, a couple hundred other Japanese pilots sat on the ground in Formosa, the fog thick around and above them. Now that Pearl had been hit and the world knew, they felt surely that an American attack would come up from the Philippines. The weather reports said it was clear down there. But the fog socked them in, and they had to stay on the ground, exposed, unable to take off.

When Miyuki came out of the room a few minutes later, she had on her other dress—that same white one, with red trim and flowers, that she had worn with Kiyoshi to Admiral Yamamoto's party last September. But as pretty as she looked, her face was set in anger, and she and Taliaferro took the elevator down to General Baker's room in stony silence. Taliaferro felt so out of place, for he was still in his fancy barong. He'd planned to go back to Clark after the party was over, so he'd brought no other clothes with him.

A little Asian in his Sunday best stood outside the general's room. Immediately, Miyuki recognized him as Japanese. *"Ohayo,"* she said. *"Ohayo,"* he replied, bowing.

The door was open. Taliaferro knocked on it, and Baker called for them to come in. He beckoned for the Japanese man, too. He was an interpreter. Then Baker stamped a very organized smile on his face and said to Miyuki: "Naturally, I apologize for having my doubts about your story last night, Mrs. Drake." Although, she couldn't understand, she nodded politely and he went on. "I'm afraid there was some difficulty in, uh, transmitting—"

Miyuki interrupted: "You call Hawaii Japanese attack?"

Taliaferro looked away uncomfortably. Baker fumbled with his cigarette pack; his ashtray was filled with butts. "Uh . . . trans-Pacific communication is not perfect yet . . . and, uh . . ." Louder, formal voice now: "That is all moot now, and we must get on with it. We have an interpreter."

Baker gestured to the man, who introduced himself to Miyuki. "Ask her if she knows if the Japs will hit anywhere else?"

The interpreter repeated the question in Japanese, and then he and Miyuki shared several exchanges.

"What'd she say?" Baker asked.

"She says, General, that the only specifics she was aware of concerned Hawaii, and she has already relayed that information to you."

"That's all she knows?"

"Well, it is her general understanding that the Japanese will also hit here—"

"The Philippines?"

"Yes."

"Well, when?"

The interpreter repeated the question to Miyuki, and she replied. "Any time, sir," the interpreter reported. "And surely mainland Southeast Asia, too. But she is not privy to those particulars."

"But the Charleys—the Japs—will definitely attack here? The Philippines?"

The interpreter repeated the question to Miyuki, and she

responded directly to Baker, shaking her head vigorously in the affirmative.

"Well, thank you very much," Baker said. He excused the interpreter and turned to Taliaferro: "And you will be personally responsible, Captain, for making sure that Mrs. Drake receives all of the courtesies of the United States Air Corps Command in the Philippines."

"Yes sir."

Baker turned to Miyuki then, but he avoided her eyes. Even as easy as it was speaking to her when he knew she didn't understand, he still couldn't look her in the face. It was all for Taliaferro's benefit; if there was ever an inquiry . . . "And Mrs. Drake, we thank you so much for coming forward as you did. I only regret there was a snafu that made it impossible for Hawaii to receive the information before the attack. But you can be assured that this command will respond here in the Philippines now with all proper vigor and diligence."

Taliaferro had never heard such crap in his life.

Even though Miyuki could hardly fathom a word Baker said, it occurred to her that she had never heard a man lie so poorly.

As they left, Baker said: "Oh, and Taliaferro—there may well be a promotion in this for you, you understand."

"Yes sir," he said, and even though none of it was his fault, he was ashamed. As soon as he was alone with Miyuki in the hall, Taliaferro turned to her. "I am very sorry, Mrs. Drake, and I apologize to you on behalf of the United States of America."

"Cotton thank you for try," she said.

"We thank Cotton for you," Captain Taliaferro answered her.

Not far away, at his headquarters, General MacArthur himself vacillated as much as Baker had. Even as the War Department in Washington sent him a telegram that the United States was at war with the Japanese Empire, he waited, curiously afraid of action, even of preparing any defense. He looked up from his desk to his aides. "Be patient, gentlemen," MacArthur said. "The Japanese will honor the neutrality of the Philippines."

On Formosa, the fog still lay on the ground, and with it the Zeros and the Mitsubishis and the nervous Japanese pilots. They didn't have radar yet, and naturally they assumed that the American planes had already taken off from Clark Field and must be circling somewhere overhead already, prepared to strike as soon as the cover lifted. The weather report indicated that the fog would be clearing soon, and all men were ordered to put on gas masks in preparation for the certain American assault from the sky.

But still MacArthur waited. Even now, a lot of the men in his command refused to believe that Pearl had actually been attacked, notwithstanding the official reports. And up at Clark, the American planes still sat bunched on the ground, waiting too.

In Miyuki's room, Taliaferro stuck out his hand to her. "I must go," he said.

"Go? You?"

"I must return to Clark, to my planes, to my men."

"So, Miyuki go with Captain."

"No, no, Miyuki. This is war. Clark is an air base."

"I go with Captain," Miyuki repeated.

Perhaps she didn't understand. He began, slower still, more gently: "I must go now—"

"Your wife love my husband past."

"Yes, I know."

"So, she want you care Miyuki now."

"Listen, Miyuki, I'd like—"

"I help soldiers. Cook." She didn't know the words for sewing or cleaning, so she pantomimed them.

Taliaferro had to smile. Besides, he knew she was right. "Yes, of course—okay," he said, and when he said that, Miyuki reached up and pecked him the best she could on his whiskery chin.

"Captain is Miyuki number-two American man."

He blushed and pointed to his watch, trying to tell her to meet him down in the lobby in ten minutes, but she grabbed hold of his barong and wouldn't let him go. Miyuki was not taking any more chances with the promises of United States military officers. She even made him stand in the room with her while she threw her few belongings in her bags, and although she had to go to the bathroom, she skipped that for now—she wasn't risking losing the captain. Not for a minute. Together, they rushed to the elevator and downstairs.

There was a major, Cress, standing in the middle of the lobby, restlessly smoking a Lucky Strike, playing with the green pack that wasn't long for this world. "Come on, Win—hurry up," Cress said.

Taliaferro merely yanked a thumb toward Miyuki. "Frankie, say hello to Mrs. Drake. She's coming with us."

"The hell you say. We're full up. This ain't no nookie wagon."

Taliaferro put on an indignant face, but he didn't stop walking. "Hey, Frankie, Mrs. Drake is married to an American missionary, and she's coming with us even if I have to ride the whole way to Clark on the running board."

"The colonel isn't going to like this shit," Cress said.

They came to the revolving door, and Taliaferro sent Miyuki through. "Frankie, I'm sorry. The colonel is going to have to go up to the sixth floor and argue with General Baker, 'cause it's his orders." Then he pushed through, outside. The sun was up, the day already warming.

But Major Cress was right. Colonel Fogarty was already waiting at the car, and he was not happy. "She's a Jap, for chrissake!" he said.

"Sir, she's married to an American," Taliaferro replied.

"You can't change a Jap just 'cause you fuck her."

"Well, sir, then go up to 629 and tell that to General Baker."

"I'll tell it to General MacArthur himself is who I'll tell it to," the colonel said, but the whole time he was carrying on, fussing, he was getting into the front seat. "Let's get our asses outta here," he said to Delgado, his driver, slamming the door. Taliaferro jammed into the back with Cress and Captain Poleski, then motioned to Miyuki to climb onto his lap.

"Mrs. Drake tried to alert us about Pearl Harbor," he said.

"I still think that's a bunch of shit," Cress said. "It's just some crap to get us all fired up."

Poleski seconded that motion. "I know a guy, Johnny Simpson, Second Wing, knows a major on Mac's staff, says the general guarantees we won't see a fuckin' thing from the Charleys till the spring, after the monsoons."

"You tell me how they'd get to Hawaii," the colonel said lighting up a good Philippine cigar. "Tell me that shit."

Miyuki waited a few moments to see if anybody was going to add anything else, and when no one continued the conversation, she thought carefully about what she was going to say and then she spoke up, loud and clear: Japanese bomb Hawaii, kill Americans." She paused. "War real."

The little voice came out of the blue, but with such authority that nobody responded, except with some coughs and shuffling, and when finally somebody spoke again, it was a long ways down the road and on a whole other, benign subject: "Can you believe it?" Cress said. "They're gonna raise beer a nickel a six-pack the first of January at the PX." And everybody agreed that was hard to believe.

Delgado made good time, there wasn't much traffic this Monday morning. Still, once they got out of Manila, all the roads on Luzon were narrow and rough, and the sixty-five miles stretched out. They stopped for cold drinks at a crossroads, and another time for everybody to take a pee. So it was noon before they turned off what had passed for a main road and onto the one that led to Clark.

It was lunchtime there, this warm, hazy blue midday, and

a lot of the men were out sunning on the grass. All the P-40s were still lined up, wingtip to wingtip, just the way it had been at Hickam and Wheeler fields, in Oahu, barely eight hours ago. Only one of Taliaferro's colleagues had his B-17 aloft on patrol, while all the others were grabbing a bite or a snooze.

As the staff car made the last turn on the dusty road toward headquarters, it was Colonel Fogarty, in the front seat, who happened to look up, dead ahead in the bright sky. Quizzically, he said: "What is that, a cloud?"

Delgado slowed the car, and they all peered out, except for Poleski, who'd dozed off. Cress said: "Where?"

Said Miyuki: "Is much Zeros."

"Aw, come on," Cress said. That was when they heard the siren go off, and Poleski woke up.

"Jesus, turn this sonofabitch around!" the colonel screamed at Delgado. "Get us outta here." The driver struggled with the wheel, but the road was narrow for such a big car, and there was a drainage ditch on one side, heavy foliage on the other. He was just backing it over that way when they could see—they could feel—the first bombs fishtailing onto the heart of Clark.

"Can't anybody fire back?" Poleski asked, almost plaintively. Everybody else screamed at Delgado to turn around. Hurry. Faster. Faster.

The bombs came closer. Suddenly, buildings were on fire everywhere, and a lot of the planes, too, lined up. The Mitsubishis came in, lower, and one dive bomber overshot the base, so that its payload looked like it was going to hit the car dead-on, but it soared just beyond and thundered into the road, leaving it one big hole, mostly. There was no escaping now. And their car was a juicy target.

Cress threw open his door, Poleski scrambling after him. Delgado wasn't far behind, tumbling out up front. Just then, barely a couple of hundred yards ahead, a hanger took a solid hit and blew to pieces. The parked P-40s were like a wildfire now, the flames leaping one plane to the other, one huge cauldron, the black smoke curling high up into the clear Pacific sky.

On the other side of the car, Colonel Fogarty jumped out while Miyuki reached for the door handle in back. "Go!" Taliaferro said, and he fell out right behind her, running around behind the car over to the ditch. Delgado, Cress, and Poleski were already there, diving in. It was so shallow, though, it was as if they were trying to burrow down.

The colonel lit out alone to the other side. But he couldn't find cover—not quickly enough. And he saw the Zeros bearing down, strafing. He threw himself flat, into what little underbrush was there, but the bullets hit him neat and ran down his body, ripping it dead. What hadn't been destroyed by the bombs, the Zeros took care of with their tracer bullets. Right after Colonel Fogarty was killed, another rash of bullets stung the staff car. Some of them found the gas tank, and it exploded. The four people in the ditch tried to bury themselves deeper as the shrapnel blew above them.

Taliaferro held Miyuki's head down. The planes were so low, when she peeked she could see some of the pilots' faces, and she wondered whether maybe these were the same ones she had seen that morning in Kagoshima. Or did they all go to Pearl? Or what did it matter? It was the same here, exactly what they'd practiced for Pearl—except for the torpedoes, all the same. The Zeros kept swooping down, right over Clark, over the burning planes and the burning buildings. Only four American P-40s managed to get aloft, and just the one B-17 that had already been up. It was carnage—American bodies everywhere. And every time it seemed that it was over, yet another wave of Zeros would swing back and come down.

At last, there was one brief lull between assaults.

"Come on!" Taliaferro yelled to the other men. "We gotta get some more planes up." He rose to dash for it, and maybe he would have made it too, but he remembered Miyuki was there, and he paused for just an instant, grabbing at her. "Run!" he cried. "You run out that way!"—and he pointed off to the jungle.

"Win—down!" Cress screamed, and Poleski reached up

and grabbed at him. Taliaferro glanced back. Here came two more Zeros—and he threw himself back down so furiously that he landed hard on top of Miyuki, all but pushing her head into the mud.

The two Zeros drew nearer, rushing in on them. One of them was a little higher, so that it wasn't able to point right at the heart of Clark Field. Instead, by the time the pilot got low enough, he was almost past the headquarters, and his tracers ran up the road, chasing after everything in their path, including the people he saw huddled helplessly in the ditch, just over from the fiery shell of a car, easy targets, all of them. The pilot was close enough to see they were all in civilian clothes, but they were on the base and he couldn't be choosy, and when he had them perfectly in his sights, he put his thumb down on the trigger. Just before he took the plane back up and off to Formosa, he could see the bullets tear into their bodies, raking them for the honor of Tenno Heika and for all the glory of His Majesty's precious Sun-Begot Land.

1945
KINO TO TORI
THE YEAR
of the
WOOD ROOSTER

68

Sometimes Liz Taliaferro would feel terribly guilty, because as the time passed and her child grew older, Liz only remembered Win occasionally and vaguely. She did not think about him the way she did about Cotton; she did not dream about Win. And Win, of course, was her child's father. She had loved two men in her life, and one was dead and one was lost. But she only dreamed about the one lost; she only dreamed about Cotton.

Cotton's mother wrote Liz back and reported that, still, no one had the foggiest idea what had happened to Cotton. The church had lost track of him just before Pearl Harbor—but at least he was healthy then, and strong, and probably he'd been sent to a prison camp and, God willing, would be home whenever the war ended.

So Liz tried to forget about Cotton. She even started to date again; and for a while, about a year ago, she had had a serious romance with a naval officer she met on his furlough. They made love on the beach at Cape May. But then, almost as soon as he shipped out, the passion faded, and she started dreaming about the Reverend Cotton Drake again. It certainly didn't ease her guilt any, either, that the baby looked so much like his father, and was a junior to boot—everybody called him Little Win.

Then Liz's father brought the letter with him when he came down over Labor Day to spend a week with his grandson and all the women at the beach house on the Jersey shore. Besides

Liz, there were her mother and her friend Emily, who was now Emily Wylie, the wife of Lieutenant Colonel Howard Wylie, and mother of their new daughter, Mimi.

It was still difficult for Emily to appreciate that Howard had actually survived the war. Even when they came down to Mantoloking at the start of August, the war was still on. There had been no bombing of Hiroshima yet, no Nagasaki, no V-J day. All of that took place after they got to the beach. On September 1, after the children went to bed, the three women sat in front of the radio with another bottle of champagne and heard the accounts of General MacArthur and the Japanese officials signing the surrender on the deck of the *Missouri.* The war had been over for two weeks now, but one more time Liz went to Emily and hugged her. "He made it," she said.

"He really did," Emily said, and they both cried. Until that moment, Emily was always sure someone in a uniform would come to the door and tell her that she too, like Liz, was a widow with a child. They finished the champagne, joyously, even raucously.

The next morning was when Liz's father came down from Philadelphia and brought the letter. Curious, Liz ripped it open right away. The handwriting was peculiar, and the postmark obscured, but as soon as she read the first line, Liz's face fell, and she hurried out of the house to read the rest of the letter by herself, sitting in the sand, poking with her toes.

Dear Mrs. Taliaferro please,
   My name is Mrs. Miyuki Drake because I marry to the rev. Mr. Drake on the 2nd December 1941.

That concluded the first line, the one Liz couldn't get past with the other people around her. Now, alone on the beach, she lit a cigarette and went on from there:

I not talking English much four years now, so letter is written here help by friend in Manila city. I sorry for mistakes. Forgive me much please.

I also want write you many years know it was with me your husband Lt. Taliaferro as he was kill 8 December 1941. If not for him I be dead to is possible. And my baby. My baby not born then 8 December 1941 but it was my baby coming with rev. Drake. Also I chrissten lady.

I alway want to tell you this. Your husband most brave man when die is as fallen on me. This may save my life I think, don't you mrs. Liz.

It is also I need your help. I have your street number from lieutenant wallet when die and I never rite then and so Japanese come in and cant anymore. Understand please do. I sorry take so long rite mrs. Liz. I do not learn where Cotton mother and father missionary Drake are. Please can you tell me their street in United states so I write them now war over about baby and maybe Cotton to. It is one big story.

Now I need help take baby and me back Japan. And rev. Mr. Drake there maybe. Also, he can be in heaven now as I don't tell you for sure. But I need go look for Cotton please.

Lt. Taliaferro tell me how much he love you plus baby. This make me think how much rev. Mr. Drake tell me how much he love very pretty Liz at least before Miyuki. I think seems like every man love Liz so maybe she so nice will help me find mother and father missionary Drake for me find Cotton maybe. Of course if he alive.

Thanking you much if I can now.

Sincerely for you.
Mrs. Miyuki

Liz walked down to the water's edge first, kicking at the waves where they lapped in, then went back to the cottage. She didn't say a single word to anyone, only took out another Pall Mall and passed the letter on. She sat there, crying and smoking, until they had all read the letter through. Then Liz hugged Little Win and began the task of getting a long distance operator, so she could get hold of the Drakes, which she finally managed an hour later.

It took barely a month, which was really quite fast, for Emily to be able to pass on the information to her husband in Okinawa, and then for Colonel Wylie to pull enough strings to get on a plane to Manila and locate Miyuki. Not only that, it took him only another two weeks to find her space on a C-47 to Tokyo. Miyuki assured Wylie that she'd sleep with the pilot if that would help. She certainly didn't want to, but she'd had to do so much of that for the past four years that one more man hardly made a whole lot of difference, considering the circumstances, trying to get back to Japan to look for her husband.

"I also maybe have be whore in Japan till find the Reverend Mr. Drake," she explained to Wylie.

He assured her, though, that it really wouldn't be necessary to give up her body to get space on the C-47 to Tokyo. In fact, it was a good fifth of Old Grand-dad bourbon Wylie handed over to the transport officer that took Miyuki back to Tokyo on Tuesday, October 16, 1945, which was the sixteenth day of the tenth month in the twentieth year of Showa, Enlightened Peace, being two thousand six hundred and five years from the accession of the Emperor Jimmu.

Already, incredibly, Tokyo was zooming back to life. Miyuki had been certain that when she saw the city again, saw her land, it would be so devastated that it would lay her own soul as bare and desolate, too. And indeed, the place was as awful as she had imagined it would be—even worse than she could remember when she was a little girl in '23 and the great earthquake hit. But, nevertheless, it was not the ruin that struck her nearly so much as the dauntless spirit and energy of her people. Already, barely two months after the surrender, only six weeks after the occupation had begun, the reconstruction—the recreation—of the Sun-Begot Land had started in earnest. Some of the streetcars were already running again; there was heat for a few buildings by the time the first breath of winter came; even some of the bombed-out blocks were coming back. The hub had been changed, but the spokes were the same, and the wheel was turning again.

The little family house in Asakusa was still standing—terribly damaged, but it seemed possible to build it back. And Miyuki was rich. Liz and her family had mailed five hundred dollars to Howard Wylie to give her, and the Drakes two thousand more. They had known Miyuki years ago, when she was a little girl, growing up near the old mission down in Gifu prefecture. They'd also known that she'd been working for Cotton at his church in Tochigi; but, of course, they didn't know anything else. They didn't know that she and Cotton had fallen in love and Kiyoshi had been killed and they had married and she had borne Cotton a child. But then, for that matter, through all her pregnancy Miyuki didn't know herself whose child she was carrying, Kiyoshi's or Cotton's. Not till she saw the baby's Western eyes did she know whose seed had taken root in her womb. It was funny, really. When the mid-wife brought out the baby, Miyuki was more interested in what it looked like than whether it was a boy or a girl. Whoever's child it was, though, she did want a boy, a son for the father; and she was happy she got all of what she wanted most: Cotton's boy.

Miyuki kept the letters from America, from Liz and from Cotton's parents, with her all the time. Those were her treasures, almost as much as the money. But two thousand five hundred U.S. dollars in Tokyo in the autumn of 1945 made her an absolute queen. She was able to hire any labor she needed, and soon her little house stood neat and bright, alone among so many other of the little houses in the neighborhood that were still only rubble and hope. Miyuki even found some new furniture. And soon after, she hired a baby-sitter, so she could begin her search.

Miyuki didn't know where her mother was; but if she was alive, Miyuki was sure, she would still be with her sister-in-law down in Aimoto, so she wrote her there. The trains were starting to come back, but they were deluged every day by great masses of travelers, so Miyuki put off going down to Aimoto herself for now. Besides, she wanted to be at home that day when Cotton came back. So in all her letters to Aimoto, she told her mother just to get on a train and come back to Asakusa.

At last, though, a letter came from Aimoto. Only it wasn't from her mother; it was from her aunt. Mrs. Serikawa had been injured in a bombing a year ago, and two weeks later she'd died.

Thus, Miyuki understood that there weren't any Serikawas left anymore. For now, the only family that Miyuki had was one named Drake, somewhere over the United States of America.

It made her even more anxious to find Cotton—or, anyway, find out about him. Every day Miyuki would leave the baby-sitter and begin making her rounds. Some days she would work the American side, going to the occupation offices or to St. Luke's Hospital or to the Episcopal mission headquarters out in Tsukiji. Other days she would knock on all the official Japanese doors. Were there any records of the Reverend Mr. Cotton Drake? Did anyone know where he had been held prisoner? Well, *if* he had been a prisoner. Did anyone remember him? Remember the name? Or, all right: is there any evidence he had been killed? Maybe he was killed right after they caught him in Nagasaki—and she understood there were no records left in Nagasaki. There was nothing left in Nagasaki. Sometimes Miyuki couldn't decide which would be worse, which would be more ironic: for Cotton to have been the first one killed in the war, that day she made the boat out, or the last one killed, with the A-bomb. Most times, she tried not to imagine that he had been killed, anywhere, ever. But with each day it became harder to believe that.

Cotton's mother and father wrote her often, from Virginia, where they lived. They assured Miyuki that they were searching for news of Cotton through the United States government. Now that gas rationing was over, they'd even traveled up to Washington several times. But there wasn't ever anything they could find about the Reverend Mr. Cotton Drake. Nothing. Cotton's parents said they were trying to get permission to come to Japan themselves, so they could bring Cotton's wife and his son back to America.

That made Miyuki very happy, but it also made her very nervous. She hadn't told the Drakes absolutely everything. They didn't know all there was to know about Miyuki Drake, and maybe that would cause problems.

She wrote the Drakes herself—and wrote Liz, too. She sent them all photographs, as the Drakes sent her old snapshots of Cotton, so that she could show them to Cotton's son. His name was Kiyokuni, which meant Pure Country. It all seemed pretty silly to Kiyokuni. He was three years old now, and he kept hearing about his father, but it wasn't like hearing about anything real, flesh and blood. It was more like hearing about Jesus, for example. Kiyokuni had been baptized in Manila by an army chaplain. It was almost the first thing Miyuki did after Major Tanaka and the other Japanese troops were finally driven off and she was liberated by the Yanks.

November 23 was Niiame-sai, the ancient harvest holiday, and most of the Japanese went to worship this day, the people praying harder than ever for food this first winter of peace. So that day Miyuki went back over to the American offices, going through the routine that had come to be second nature to her. Maybe some new lists of names had come in from somewhere; maybe something had been uncovered in Nagasaki. Maybe this, maybe that. But there was nothing new. There never was. And on Niiame-sai, she was discouraged all the more. She had to get on with things. She set December 14, Gishi-sai, the festival day of the forty-seven *ronin*, as the last day she would look for her husband.

First, though, she would go up to Tochigi. Her letters to the church there had all come back, because there was no one at the church anymore; but maybe if she went up there she could find some clue. The train tracks were still mangled in that direction, and it would be months before they would be fixed, she knew. So Miyuki went downtown, to the building known simply as Dai Ichi—Number One Building—MacArthur's headquarters, an old insurance office opposite the Imperial Palace that had somehow survived the bombing;

and soon enough, she found a jeep driver in the Seventh Cavalry who would happily take a hundred dollars U.S. to sneak his jeep out one day and drive her up to Tochigi and back.

Miyuki cried out happily when she saw the town. It was intact; it was still 1941. The Americans bombs hadn't bothered with it. By the time the Yanks could have come in and blown up the geta factory, there weren't any airplane parts for the making, so the bombers had passed on to more vital sites, and Tochigi was spared. "See—pretty," Miyuki told the driver, who was Corporal Randall T. Breckinridge from Owensboro, Kentucky. "Real Japanese town, no war." Breckinridge was impressed, too. He came from a river town himself.

Unfortunately, the mission was all boarded up. The one old man in the town office who seemed to be in charge said that he remembered Miyuki (and she said she remembered him, too, even if she didn't), and he certainly remembered Drake-san, but the missionary had simply vanished one afternoon just before the war with America, and since there was nobody to take his place at the mission, soon it all just sort of petered out. One day that next spring of '42, several of the parishioners came over and boarded it up, concluding the formal practice of Christianity in Tochigi, at least until now. Miyuki and Breckinridge went back over the bridge, and she peered into the windows and saw that the old man was right: the mission looked almost exactly the way it had been, the way she remembered it. In Tokyo, a hundred people would have crowded into the place to sleep.

She walked around the mission grounds for a while, then, and tried to explain to Breckinridge what it was like here when she fell in love with an American priest who coached the town baseball team, on the diamond right over there. Then she had Breckinridge drive her all through Tochigi in his jeep. Miyuki stopped to greet several people she knew, but none of them knew anything about Cotton. He had just disappeared that Saturday, and right after that there'd been Pearl Harbor and a war with America to worry about.

Miyuki did find Hanako, sitting by herself outside a little house on Rice Street. She was so skinny and ragged Miyuki hardly recognized her, but she brightened up right away. Hanako's parents had both died, within two weeks of each other, in the winter of '43-'44. "Starve?" Miyuki asked, and Hanako kind of shrugged.

"No. It was more like they just gave up," she said. So after that, Hanako said, she came into town and took up whoring again, bartering her body for whatever she could. It was a hard loaf, but better than trying to work the paddies—and business was actually picking up some since the war had ended and the men had started straggling home.

Miyuki took a long breath. "And Kensuke?" she asked. "Did he come back?"

"Just his bones and ashes," Hanako said. "Like so many of the boys. Just bones and ashes."

Miyuki shook her head from side to side. "Oh my. Poor Kensuke! I thought maybe since he was in the *kempeitai*—"

"Yeah, but when the bastards started to run short of infantry to get killed, they couldn't afford a strong boy like that just being a policeman."

"Oh yes. When—?"

"He almost made it," Hanako said. "Okinawa. They sent him down there. The final battle."

Miyuki bowed her head and said a little prayer, and then she told Hanako about the last time she saw Kensuke—and saw Cotton.

"There were so many of them—soldiers," she said. "I'm sure they were beating Cotton. And Kensuke ran to him, and jumped on them." She sighed. "I always believed that Kensuke saved Cotton's life. That day, anyway."

Hanako threw her arms around Miyuki and hugged her. "Honey, if I ever hear anything about Cotton up here, I'll let you know first thing," she said, and Miyuki stopped sniffling and fished out a twenty-dollar bill and gave it to her, which made Hanako blubber with thanks. It was enough to get her through the whole winter.

Then Miyuki went back to the jeep. She had planned to have Corporal Breckinridge take her up to the hill so she could pay her respects to Kiyoshi, but it was getting late. Besides, she just felt so sad now. She told herself that if Cotton ever did come back, they would return to Tochigi together, and then they would go up and find Kiyoshi's bones and bring them back down together and have him cremated properly, his ashes buried at the temple to which they had belonged.

Back in Tokyo, the next afternoon, Miyuki went down to the General Station and bought a ticket for Kobe for December 14, Gishi-sai. Her mother would find it most appropriate that Miyuki came to visit her and light incense for her memory on the festival day of the forty-seven *ronin*. Then, after she bought the ticket, Miyuki went up to Yasukuni, and even though she didn't worship Shinto anymore, she was sure that her father and her brother would appreciate it that she went there again to pay their spirits her respects, just as she had gone with Kiyoshi four years ago.

It was growing dark by the time she left Yasukuni, but somehow she found a taxicab. It was only the second cab she'd even *seen* since the war. The baby-sitter, Sachiko, was very excited when she saw Miyuki come in the cab; she had no idea Japanese were driving any sorts of cars again. In fact, she was so beside herself that she almost forgot to tell Miyuki about the man who had come to the house earlier.

"Well, what did he want?"

"I'm sorry, Mrs. Drake, but he said he could only talk to you," Sachiko said.

"Did he say what it was about? Was it about Mr. Drake?"

"He only said that it was important, that he'd been looking for you and this house. He was amazed that this house had already been built back. It looked exactly as he'd been told it looked before the war."

So Miyuki thought to herself: Well, at some point Cotton must have told this man about me. And so now the man had come, found my house, so he could tell me what had happened to Cotton. This is probably not good news, she allowed herself to admit. If Cotton were alive and well, nobody else would have to come to the house. Cotton would have come home to me himself.

"What did the man look like?" she asked Sachiko.

"He was very skinny, and his skin was gray, and his eyes were way back down inside his face."

Miyuki thought: That sounds like someone who's been in a prison camp. That figures. He must have known Cotton in a camp somewhere.

Sachiko went on: "He moved very slowly. It hurt him just to move, and when I asked him if he would like anything, he asked if we had any fruit. He said he needed fruit most of all."

"And did you give him any?"

"Yes, ma'am. We only had one orange, but I gave it to him."

"That was the right thing to do, Sachiko. But wasn't there anything else about this man? Didn't he give his name?"

"No, but he did wear a Christian cross around his neck."

So, Miyuki was even more certain that the man had known Cotton, probably had been imprisoned with him somewhere; and when she added it all up, she decided that the man must have come to tell her about how Cotton had died some time during the war.

That's why Miyuki was so completely surprised the very next morning when the man came back—only this time he was not alone. He was pushing an old cart. And in the cart was Cotton.

Miyuki happened to be outside, with Kiyokuni, hanging up the wash, and she was the one who saw them when they rounded the street corner. It was like the continuation of some circle: the last time she saw Cotton, it was when he'd been taken around a street corner, and now here he was, returning to her the same way.

She screamed his name, and she screamed Jesus' name, and she screamed the baby-sitter's name, and then she dashed down the street, throwing the clothes she was going to put on the line this way and that as she ran.

Cotton said: "I'm back."

Miyuki cried and laughed and hugged and kissed him. "I love you," she said in English. Not a day had gone by in four years that she had not practiced saying that so she could say it just right at this moment if this moment ever came.

"I love you too" was all that Cotton said back to her, and if he was so weak that there didn't seem to be much emotion, Miyuki could see enough just in his eyes.

She was kneeling on the ground, rubbing his head, and although she tried to mask her expression, she knew she couldn't help reflecting how terrible he looked. The scurvy had piled onto the starvation, and Cotton looked worse than most dead people do. He knew it, though, and he knew how it must have affected her, so he actually managed a smile. "You should have seen me a couple months ago when I really looked bad," he said. "Right, Haruki?"

The other man nodded. "He's very sick," he told Miyuki. "Very weak. But there's nothing crippled. He kept taking care of the Christians. And the guards kept beating Cotton, but they couldn't break him."

Cotton introduced his friend to Miyuki. He was the Reverend Mr. Fukabori, who had been locked up with him in the camp since late in '42. Miyuki bowed to him, but then she eased the poor fellow aside and began to push Cotton's cart herself toward the house. "Tomorrow you are going straight to St. Luke's," she declared. "But tonight you are staying at home."

Kiyokuni was standing outside the house watching his mother wheel this strange, emaciated, dirty man toward him. He was frightened, but he understood that this must be his father even if it certainly didn't look like that strong, handsome man he had seen in the photographs. But Kiyokuni did not run inside. He held his ground until his mother wheeled the cart right up before him.

"Bow to your father," Miyuki said, and the little boy instantly brought his head low, obeying her command.

"I have a boy?" Cotton gasped.

"Yes, he is our son."

"I have a boy, Haruki!" And when Kiyokuni raised his head back up, Cotton brought one hand up by the other and somehow managed to clap twice for the boy and for his very grown-up bow.

Then Miyuki prodded Kiyokuni. "And what do you say to your father?" The little boy pursed his lips and thought for a long time. "Go on, you know."

He did, but he was nervous. Miyuki had taught him this one thing in English, but he hadn't the foggiest idea what it meant, and he had it down only by rote. Finally, he took a deep breath, and here is what he said to Cotton: "Pop, I will be a third baseman."

And Cotton clapped again, the tears running down his cheeks. "No, a shortstop, I think. You'll have some of your mother's grace." He turned his head to Miyuki. "You've brought up a good boy. What's his name?"

"What is your name?" she asked her son.

"Kiyokuni."

"Ah, I like that. 'The 'Kiyo' will always help us remember Kiyoshi."

"I write Kiyokuni so that it means Pure Country," Miyuki said.

"And yes," Cotton said, "we shall have a pure country here now."

"Come on, Cotton," Mr. Fukabori said, "you're getting tired again. We must get you inside."

Miyuki beckoned to Kiyokuni. "Help us with your father now. He is coming into our house to live with us forever."

Miyuki leaned down to Cotton, lifting his arm over her shoulder. Mr. Fukabori moved to help. Cotton hadn't the strength to walk on his own. But at that moment the *amado* opened, and Sachiko appeared, holding a little girl. Cotton lifted his head. "And who is this?"

"Sachiko is living with us, helping out," Miyuki said. "And the little girl . . . Cotton, the little girl is mine."

"My, she's beautiful! What is her name?"

"Miwako."

"Oh, that's a lovely name." It meant Beautiful Peace.

"She is a year old," Miyuki said.

"Bring her to me, please," Cotton asked, and Miyuki withdrew her arm from around him and let him back down, gently into the cart. Then she took the baby from Sachiko and handed her to Cotton. "Well," he said, "where is her father?"

"He's dead. He was a major in the army, but he was killed in the Philippines after General MacArthur landed." Cotton took his finger and wiggled it over the little girl's lips, making her laugh. Miyuki kneeled back down to him. "Cotton, please understand, I didn't want—"

He turned to her. "Those were difficult times for us all." He looked into her eyes. "Weren't they, darling?"

"Yes," she said. "They were very difficult times."

"So," said Cotton, "it doesn't matter anymore. I am her father now." Cotton kissed the child. "You see, what is very good is that she looks so much like you. With my *gaijin* blood, we never would have gotten a girl as beautiful as her mother." He handed Miwako back to Miyuki. "Okay, we'll go inside now, if"—with a smile—"there's no more surprises."

"No," Miyuki said, and she passed Miwako to the babysitter and once again guided Cotton's arm around her shoulder, and this time, with great effort, he got to his feet. He paused there, catching his breath, and then he sort of snuggled his head into the crook of her neck. "I never once stopped loving you," Miyuki told him, and she pulled him tighter to her. "Remember you told me once what hell was?"

"Sure. It's where no one has any elbows."

"Now, we finally have our elbows. And we will have them for the rest of our lives."

"Yes, yes," Cotton said, and he leaned on her and beckoned to Kiyokuni, and the little boy edged closer. "Your father will walk into his house," he told him, and although Mr. Fukabori gasped, Cotton had one arm around his wife and his son's hand in his other, and he took his first step back that way.

Postscript

Especially since this work was something of a departure from my earlier novels, the encouragement that I received at the outset was particularly meaningful. Sterling Lord has been my agent for thirty years, but he has never been more enthusiastic or supporting than with this book. Christine Pevitt, the former publisher and editor-in-chief at Viking, believed fervently in the idea from the first discussion. I was also fortunate that when Christine left Viking, Pamela Dorman, an editor with great insight, took over the project and helped me improve it.

In Japan, Keiichi Sato was my right arm and my right eye—and both my ears. He was also wonderful company in shepherding me about his native land. Reiko Ueda and Mark Schreiber went over my manuscript with a diligence matched only by their gentle tolerance for the dense *gaijin*, making sure that all the mistakes I made could be set right. *Arigato gozaimashita.*

Many other people in both Japan and the United States were so helpful, but I would particularly thank Otis Cary, Henry von Kohorn (Sr.), Judith Ames, Michael Paxson, and Marty Kuehnert. I would also especially cite Marty's wife, Miyuki, for letting me appropriate her lovely name to put at the center of things.

As all these good people know, I am not a scholar, historical or otherwise, and coming, as I do, from another time and place, I'm sure that I have not always perfectly portrayed the subtleties and nuances of the people who lived in pre-war Japan. I have also, in a few instances, taken some dramatic license. There was, for example, neither an Episcopal mission nor a town baseball team in Tochigi in 1941. But there well could have been. Likewise, the few historical figures who find themselves dragged into the story—notably Admiral Yamamoto, Ambassador Grew, and Emperor Hirohito—have only been placed in scenes consistent with where history tells us that they might fairly have found themselves.

In all matters of consequence, in anything bearing on the war, though, I have been altogether faithful to history. Of course, so many fantastic things happened during this period that there really is no need to trick it up. This truly was one of those times when, looking back, no rational person could discern the difference between truth and fiction, let alone divine which was stranger.

Frank Deford
Westport, Connecticut
May 7, 1993